The
AMISH
GREENHOUSE
MYSTERIES

3 Amish Romances from a
New York Times Bestselling Author

The
AMISH
GREENHOUSE
MYSTERIES

WANDA &
BRUNSTETTER

BARBOUR
PUBLISHING

The Crow's Call © 2020 by Wanda E. Brunstetter
The Mockingbird's Song © 2020 by Wanda E. Brunstetter
The Robin's Greeting © 2021 by Wanda E. Brunstetter

ISBN 978-1-63609-284-3

eBook Edition:
Adobe Digital Edition (.epub) 978-1-63609-286-7

Scripture quotations are taken from the King James Version and the New International Version of the Bible.

All German-Dutch words are taken from the *Revised Pennsylvania German Dictionary* found in Lancaster County, Pennsylvania.

This book is a work of fiction. Names, characters, places, and incidents are either products of the author's imagination or used fictitiously. Any similarity to actual people, organizations, and/or events is purely coincidental.

This book contains some Amish home remedies that have not been evaluated by the FDA. They are not intended to diagnose, treat, cure, or prevent any disease or condition. If you have a health concern or condition, consult a physician.

For more information about Wanda E. Brunstetter, please access the author's web site at the following Internet address: www.wandabrunstetter.com

Cover Design: Buffy Cooper
Cover model photography: Richard Brunstetter III, RBIII Studios

Published by Barbour Publishing, Inc., 1810 Barbour Drive, Uhrichsville, OH 44683, www.barbourbooks.com

Our mission is to inspire the world with the life-changing message of the Bible.

Member of the
Evangelical Christian
Publishers Association

Printed in Colombia

Amish Greenhouse Mystery
Book 1

The
CROW'S
CALL

Dedication

To my Amish friend, Cindy, who suffered a great
loss but came through victoriously.

What time I am afraid, I will trust in thee.
PSALM 56:3 KJV

Chapter 1

Strasburg, Pennsylvania

An April wind's flurry sent swirls of dust into the air and across the yard. *This isn't a good day for a celebration.* Amy King shielded her eyes for a moment. The current of air rustled her dress as she cradled a basket of spring flowers from her parents' greenhouse up to their home. Amy's sister, Sylvia, and her family would be coming for supper soon to help them celebrate Mom's birthday, and she wanted everything to be perfect.

Amy's brothers Henry and Abe still lived at home, but their older brother, Ezekiel, and his family were now part of an Amish community in New York State. They had hired a driver and planned to join them this afternoon. Amy always looked forward to the times when their whole family could be together.

As the wind calmed down, Amy gazed at the basket of flowers and smiled. She would put the lovely blooms in a glass vase and set it in the center of their dining-room table. Mom had a love for flowers, which was why she'd worked faithfully in the greenhouse with Dad for so many years.

Amy liked flowers too, but there were other things she enjoyed more, such as spending time with her boyfriend, Jared. He'd begun courting her almost a year ago, and Amy figured most any time now Jared would ask for her hand in marriage. She was prepared to say yes, of course, for Jared was all she'd ever wanted in a husband. He was courteous, kind, strong, and gentle, and of course she thought he was the most handsome man she'd ever met.

Amy halted her footsteps when the eerie sound of a crow's call invaded her dreamy thoughts. She'd had an aversion to crows ever since she was a young girl and one had flown over the blanket she'd sat upon, dropping a corncob right on her foot. It had left a nasty bruise, and following the incident, the crow carried on like Amy had done something wrong. It was superstitious of her, but ever since that day, whenever she saw or heard a crow, Amy expected something bad might happen. Today was no exception. The crow, sitting on a fence post and making such a fuss, seemed to be taunting Amy as she stood with goosebumps on her arms and chills tingling her spine.

Refusing to give in to her anxiety, Amy hurried toward the house.

Caw! Caw! Caw! The crow's foreboding call continued.

Amy shuddered and moved on. It was childish to allow an irrational belief to take over her thoughts, but she couldn't help feeling that something bad was on the horizon. Maybe this time it would be worse than a simple corncob bruising her foot.

She brushed the notion aside and stepped into the house. Amy wanted everything to be special for Mom's birthday, and she wouldn't let a silly old crow and her unfounded trepidation put a damper on this evening's celebration.

"It's so good to see you again!" Amy gave Ezekiel and Michelle a hug and reached her hand out to stroke the top of their little girl's head. "Angela Mary has grown so much since we last saw her. It's hard to believe she's two years old already."

Michelle smiled and placed one hand against her stomach. "I wasn't going to share this till we were all sitting around the supper table tonight, but in about five months our daughter will have a little sister or brother."

Amy clapped her hands and gave Michelle another hug. "Oh, that's *wunderbaar!*"

"What about your big brother? Don't I get another hug?" Ezekiel nudged Amy's arm.

"*Jah*, of course." She gave Ezekiel a second hug.

When Amy stepped back, he looked around the yard. "Where is everyone? Figured when our driver's van pulled in, we'd be greeted by the whole family."

"Henry went out to buy a gift for Mom. Abe's still at work. Dad and Mom are in the greenhouse, getting ready to close up for the day. They might not have heard the van come into the yard."

At that moment, their parents stepped out of greenhouse and headed for Ezekiel and his family. Hugs started all over again.

"It's so good to see you." Mom teared up. "I wasn't sure you could come."

Ezekiel shook his head. "We wouldn't have missed your birthday for anything."

"That's right," Michelle agreed. "Happy birthday, Belinda."

"*Danki.*" Mom leaned down and swept Angela Mary into her arms. "How's my precious little granddaughter doing?"

The child giggled when her grandpa reached over and tickled her under the chin.

"She's doing well." Michelle looked over at Ezekiel. "Should we tell them our news now?"

He nodded. "May as well, since you already let Amy know."

"Let her know what?" Mom's eyelids fluttered. "Are you planning to move back to Strasburg?"

"No, it's nothing like that, although we do miss everyone here. My business is doing well, and we're all settled into the community at Clymer." He pointed to Michelle's stomach. "We have another little one on the way."

Dad thumped Ezekiel's back, while Mom handed Angela Mary

to Amy and then gave Michelle another hug. "That's great news. When is the *boppli* due?"

"In about five months." Michelle's blue-green eyes glistened. "Sometimes I have to stop and pinch myself to see if I'm dreaming. Becoming a Christian, joining the Amish church, and marrying Ezekiel were the best things that ever happened to me." She smiled up at him. "I feel like my life is complete."

Amy smiled too. It was a joy to see the radiance on her sister-in-law's face. It was hard in the past when Michelle used to be English and had deceived them into believing she was the Lapp's granddaughter, whom they'd known nothing about for too many years.

Thank the Lord that through the power of God's love and forgiveness, people can change and start fresh with a new life in Him. Amy held her little niece close and said a silent prayer. *Heavenly Father, may this child grow up to be a woman who seeks Your ways and walks the right path that will be pleasing unto You.*

"Well, let's get your suitcases out of the van, and we can all go up to the house." Dad's booming voice ended Amy's prayer.

"Good idea." Ezekiel's head moved quickly up and down. "I'll remind our driver what day to pick us up, and then after we get the luggage out, he can be on his way."

Amy waited beside the van until everything had been taken out. Then she handed Angela Mary to her mother, picked up one of the suitcases, and started for the house. As soon as Sylvia and her family got here, they would get things going for supper.

Everyone sat around the living room and visited until Sylvia and her husband, Toby, arrived with their two-year-old boy, Allen, and four-month-old baby girl, Rachel. Henry returned from shopping about the same time, and Abe, who worked for a local buggy maker, showed up a few minutes later. After greeting everyone, they grabbed some chairs and joined in on the conversation.

Amy smiled, seeing Henry sitting by his twenty-one-year-old brother. He appeared to be attentive as Abe told Dad about his day at work. Henry and Abe were close, despite their six-year age difference.

I wonder if Henry will become a buggy maker as well. Or will he end up helping us full-time in the greenhouse? Amy shifted on her chair.

It wasn't long before Ezekiel announced Michelle's pregnancy to the rest of the family, who were enthusiastic at the news.

Amy thought how much easier it would have been if they'd shared their good news once everyone had arrived. *I suppose it's more exciting to share the news more than once.* Amy rose from her chair. "I believe supper's about ready. If you all want to take seats at the dining-room table, I'll bring everything out."

"I'll help." Mom started to rise from the couch, but Amy shook her head. "Not tonight, Mom. Since it's your birthday, you're the guest of honor."

Mom's brows furrowed. "Now how can I be the guest of honor in my own home?"

"Because we say so." Dad grinned at her and then looked around the room. "Isn't that right, family?"

Everyone nodded.

"I'll help get supper on the table." Michelle gestured to her daughter. "Ezekiel, would you please keep an eye on Angela Mary?"

"Of course, but I doubt I will be the only person watching her." He glanced across the room at their mother and winked. "Right, Mom?"

"Absolutely."

Michelle left the room with Amy. "Your family is so special," she said when they entered the kitchen. "You are blessed to have such loving, caring parents."

"I think so too." Amy grabbed two potholders and opened the oven door. Warm steam escaped along with the tantalizing aroma of ham and baked potatoes. She placed the ham and potatoes on the kitchen table and asked Michelle to dish up the green beans on the stove, while she took sour cream, butter, and freshly cut chives from the refrigerator.

"When I was growing up, I would have given anything to have parents like yours." Michelle frowned as she placed the green beans in a serving bowl.

"I'm sorry you had such a difficult childhood."

Her sister-in-law shrugged. "It's in the past. I had to move on with my life."

Ezekiel had told Amy about the abuse Michelle and her two younger brothers, Ernie and Jack, had suffered at the hands of their parents. She couldn't imagine how hard it must have been for Michelle to endure such a thing, or to be taken from her parents and put in foster care with people she didn't even know. What made it worse was that Michelle and her brothers had all gone to different homes and never saw each other again until the day of Michelle and Ezekiel's wedding. What a wonderful surprise it was when Mary Ruth's granddaughter, Sara, located Ernie and Jack and brought them to meet her.

So many good things had happened in her family. Amy knew folks who had dealt with worry, fear, and even tragedy, but things had been going along quite well for her family. The greenhouse ran smoothly, providing for them financially, but since Sylvia was a full-time wife and mother and no longer worked for their folks, Amy had left her job at a dry goods store to help in the greenhouse full-time. Dad took care of advertising, billing, and making sure everything ran smoothly, while Amy and her mother were responsible for the plants and flowers they sold to the public, as well as providing a few florists in the area with flowers to make their floral arrangements. It was a good life, and Amy felt content. The only thing that would make it better would be if Jared proposed marriage to her soon.

Michelle tapped Amy's shoulder. "You look like you're a hundred miles from here. Didn't you hear what I said?"

Amy shook her head. "Sorry. I was deep in thought. What did you say to me?"

"I was wondering if you're ready to take the food items out to the dining room yet. I'm sure our hungry family is waiting eagerly."

She laughed. "Of course they are, and I'm eager to join them."

Amy picked up the platter of ham and was about to leave the kitchen when Abe stepped in.

"Hey, Sister, what's taking so long? Don't you know we're starvin' in there?"

She rolled her eyes. "Well, if you're starving, grab a couple of dishes and take them in."

Thank You, God, once again for my family. Amy glanced around the table at the smiling faces looking back at her as they all enjoyed the tasty meal.

Mom was in especially good spirits this evening, laughing and enjoying the antics of her three grandchildren. It wouldn't be long before she'd be blessed with four little ones to dote on.

Amy thought of Jared, wishing he could be here with them as part of the family. But since they were only courting and not an engaged couple, she felt it wouldn't have been right to ask him to join them. She would be seeing Jared tomorrow night anyway, when they went out for their evening meal at the Bird-in-Hand Family Restaurant.

"Let's not worry about doing the supper dishes right now," Sylvia said when the meal ended. "We can just put them in the sink till after Mom opens her presents and we've had cake and ice cream."

Amy thumped the side of her head. "Oh, no. When I went shopping yesterday, I forgot to get some ice cream."

"That's okay." Mom flapped her hand. "We can get by without it."

"No, we can't." Dad shook his head. "It wouldn't seem like a birthday celebration if there wasn't cake and ice cream."

"We could crank out some homemade if we had all the ingredients." Amy leaned her elbows on the table. "Trouble is, we don't have any heavy whipping cream and maybe not enough eggs. Even if we did, it would take too much time to mix it all, crank till it froze, and then let it set until we could eat it." She looked over at Mom. "So, I agree. . . . We should settle for just cake."

Dad shook his head again—this time with a determined set of

his jaw. "I'll hitch my horse to one of our carriages and head for the grocery store." He glanced around the table. "Anyone wanna come along for the ride and to keep me company?"

"I'll go." Toby pushed his chair away from the table.

"Me too." Abe also left his seat.

"Okay, guess I'll take the two-seater. Anybody else want to join us?" The others, including Amy, shook their heads.

"After that good meal, plus the long ride down here from New York, think I will try to catch a few winks while you're gone." Ezekiel yawned and stretched his arms over his head.

Mom rose to her feet. "Well, if we're going to wait on ice cream to have our dessert, we may as well do the dishes." She reached for her plate, but Michelle grabbed it out from under her.

"This celebration is in honor of you, so you ought to go relax in the living room. Amy, Sylvia, and I will take care of the dishes. Right, ladies?"

"Absolutely," Amy and Sylvia said in unison.

"All right." Mom heaved a sigh. "I can see I'm outnumbered."

Amy got up right away and started clearing dishes. Sylvia and Michelle did the same. Mom led Angela Mary and Allen to the living room, and when Amy glanced over her shoulder, she saw her mother peek at baby Rachel, where she lay sleeping in the playpen.

Dad, Toby, and Abe said their goodbyes, put on their straw hats, and went out the back door.

A short time later, as Amy began filling the sink with warm, soapy water, she saw her father's horse and buggy go down the driveway at a steady pace. She placed all the silverware into the sink and glanced out the window again in time to see Dad's rig ease out onto the road. The horse and carriage had gone only a short distance, when a semitruck came out of nowhere. Amy clutched her throat and screamed as the semi rammed the back of Dad's buggy. For a few seconds, her mind went blank, as if her brain had stopped working. Then, just as quickly, Amy screamed for the rest of the family to come, before she raced out the back door.

Chapter 2

Amy's chin trembled as a wave of grief threatened to consume her. *Lord, I don't understand at all. . . .* Through blurry eyes, she saw Henry sitting alone on the sofa. His collapsed body posture and distant, empty stare revealed that his heart was also breaking. Amy worried about him not having Abe and Dad around anymore.

She sniffed and blotted her tears. A funeral service for three family members on the same day was unimaginable. But that's exactly what would happen tomorrow. The caskets of her father, brother, and brother-in-law had been placed in this room for the viewing that had occurred a few hours ago.

Nothing about today seemed real, and tomorrow would be worse. Relatives and friends from their community as well as other areas would be here for the funeral service and to say their final goodbyes. People would speak kind words and offer comfort, but nothing in the King family would ever be the same. When that semitruck hit her father's buggy, three men's lives had been snuffed out. Dad's horse had also been killed, but the animal could be replaced. No one could replace Dad, Abe, or Toby. And nobody but God could heal the rest of the family's broken hearts as they continued living without their loved ones.

Amy swiped again at the tears rolling down her cheeks. *Poor Sylvia. She's taken her husband's death so hard, I don't know how she's ever going to cope. With two small children to raise and no financial support, she'll have no choice but to move in with us.*

During the last three days, Amy's older sister had spent most of her time tucked away in her room, hardly eating or talking to anyone. Sylvia's children were too young to grasp the reality of the tragedy, which in some ways made the situation that much more difficult.

Amy struggled to accept and deal with the tragedy that had befallen her family. She continued to stand in the living room, contemplating whether to go out to the mailbox. After what had happened, it was hard to go out there. The sight of a semitruck passing their place caused her to relive the accident, and she dreaded going anywhere in the buggy. Thankfully, their friends had offered meals as well as comforting words, so she could avoid making a trip to the store for now.

Caw! Caw! Caw! A crow calling from the yard sent chills up Amy's spine, and she glanced toward the window. She had never been one to believe in superstitions or omens but couldn't help thinking about the crow she'd spotted in the yard three days ago, before their company arrived for Mom's birthday party. Had the black bird with its raucous-sounding cry tried to warn them of impending doom?

Amy shivered and rubbed her arms. It wasn't cold in the house, yet she felt chilled to the bone.

Maybe it's warm, but I don't feel it because my body and soul have been numb ever since that horrible accident took away three important men from our family.

"It's hard to believe they're gone, isn't it?" Ezekiel's deep voice drove Amy's thoughts aside.

She blinked. "How long have you been standing here?"

"Just came into the room a moment ago." He glanced in Henry's direction. "Let's go sit with him."

Amy followed Ezekiel over to the sofa, but Henry remained quiet as he scooted over, barely glancing at them.

"I keep wishing I was caught in the middle of a nightmare and would wake tomorrow morning and find out Dad, Abe, and Toby are still here and everything's as it should be."

"I know." Ezekiel groaned. "If only Dad hadn't been so determined to go for ice cream. If the three of them had just stayed home...." His voice trailed off. "Guess there's no point in rehashing all of this. We can't bring 'em back by wishing."

"That's for sure." Henry's voice sounded strained.

"No, but if we could, I'd wish upon a star, toss a penny in a wishing well, and put candles in Mom's birthday cake that none of us ate, and then make a mighty big wish." Ezekiel slipped one arm around Amy's shoulder and the other around Henry's. It was a comfort to have her big brother here and know he would take care of them. She felt certain that under the circumstances, Ezekiel and Michelle would move back to Strasburg to help in the greenhouse and offer emotional support to her, Mom, Sylvia, and Henry during this most difficult time. *Of course, Ezekiel's grieving too,* she reminded herself. *He's bound to realize that his place is here with us now, not in Clymer, New York.*

Ezekiel turned toward Amy with glassy eyes. "We need to get the funeral behind us and let things settle down a bit before we talk about plans for the future and let you in on what Michelle and I have decided."

"What's that?"

"Jah, what's your idea?" Henry leaned forward.

"Okay, guess I'll tell you now rather than waiting. I'm going to give up my business and sell our home so we can move back here and help run the greenhouse." Ezekiel's hands and arms hung limp at his sides. "It's either that or Mom will have to sell this place and you'll all have to move to Clymer to be with us."

"I don't wanna move." Henry shook his head. "Let's not talk about this right now."

"I don't think Mom will go for that idea, Ezekiel. She was born and raised in Strasburg, and this is her home." Amy motioned toward the window, where the crow still carried on. "Besides, she enjoys working in the greenhouse and would not want to sit around while you try to support us all financially."

"I wouldn't be carrying the whole load. Mom would have money from the sale of this home and the greenhouse."

Amy rose from the couch and shook her head. "Your house isn't big enough for all of us. The best thing would be for you to sell your place and move back here."

"Nobody is selling or moving anywhere."

Amy whirled around when Mom stepped into the room. "You heard our conversation?"

Mom gave a quick nod. Her pained expression and unsteady voice said it all. "This is not the time to be discussing our future, but since the topic has been brought up, you may as well know that I am not going to sell my home or the greenhouse your *daed* and I worked so hard to establish and keep going." She pointed a trembling finger at Ezekiel. "As far as you and your family moving back here, that's not going to happen either."

He touched the base of his neck as deep wrinkles formed across his forehead. "Why not, Mom? You can't run the business by yourself, and it's only logical for me to. . ."

Tears sprang into Mom's eyes, and she dabbed at them with the handkerchief in her hand. "It's not logical at all, Son. You've made a new life for yourself there in New York, and you're happy making bee supplies." Mom kept her gaze fixed on Ezekiel as she spoke in short, strong sentences. "You were never happy working in the greenhouse. You found satisfaction in working with the bees and selling honey." She paused. "Amy, Sylvia, and Henry will be here to help, so let's not talk about this anymore."

When Mom moved to stand beside Dad's casket, Ezekiel shrugged his broad shoulders and shuffled out of the room.

Henry got up and joined Mom. He stayed there a few minutes then turned aside. "I'm goin' out to the barn and check on the horse. It's feeding time anyways. The mare seems to be missing Dad's horse that died."

"I'm sure she is lonely out there all by herself and also with none of us using her for several days. Your daed and I. . ." Mom choked up, looking back at Dad's coffin. "We bought those two horses at the same time. It's been almost ten years ago now." Using her handkerchief, she blew her nose.

"I'll go get on my shoes and take care of the horse now. Maybe I'll even do some brushing while she eats." Henry's bare feet padded across the floor to the hallway, where he disappeared.

Amy was tempted to try and talk some sense into her mother, but it would be better to wait a few days for that. She felt certain that Mom was riding an emotional roller coaster right now, which made sense under the circumstances. So instead of voicing her thoughts, Amy walked up to Mom and slipped an arm around her waist.

No words were spoken between them, but she could almost read her mother's thoughts. Mom was wishing that she could ask Dad what to do. As head of the house, he'd been the one to make final decisions. Now Mom felt that the burden of providing for the family fell on her slender shoulders. Well, that wouldn't be fair, and Amy was not going to let it happen. If she had any say in this at all, she'd do all she could to talk her determined mother into letting Ezekiel move back home. At a time like this, living close by the family was exactly where he belonged. If she could not get through to Mom, the burden of helping to run the greenhouse would fall on Amy. Mom had made many sacrifices for her children over the years, so taking charge of the greenhouse was the least Amy could do.

Belinda took little comfort in Amy's presence. Truth was, she preferred to be alone as she stared at her husband's lifeless form.

Oh Vernon, I miss you so much. How can I go on without you? If only you could tell me what to do about the greenhouse. She touched the side of the casket. *Ezekiel thinks I should either sell it and move to New York or allow him to move back here and run the business. I don't want to move, and I don't want him to give up what he has there. The question is: Do I have enough strength and wisdom to run the greenhouse without you?*

Will our children who live here be willing to help?

Her gaze came to rest on Toby's coffin. *Sylvia's in a bad way right now and probably won't be up to helping for some time, if at all. Even if she felt able, what about her* kinner? *Who's going to take care of them while their mother is busy working? It wouldn't be practical to bring them out to the greenhouse during business hours. It would be a distraction for Sylvia and most likely the customers too.*

She looked at the casket where her son lay and blinked back the stinging tears almost clouding her vision. Abe had a girlfriend, and they'd been talking about marriage. But now Sue Ellen had no future with him.

And I've lost one of my kinner so dear to me. Belinda pressed her lips tightly together. It was hard to accept that even one of these special men were gone, let alone all three. She lowered her head. *If only they had listened to me and not left the house for something as unimportant as ice cream.*

"Mom, we're going to make it through this; I promise you that." Amy's sweet voice broke through Belinda's troubling thoughts.

She swallowed hard, nearly choking on the sob in her throat. "Jah, we need to believe that God will be with us every step of the way."

🐦

Weeping continued as Sylvia spoke above a whisper. "How can I be of any help to myself or anyone else without Toby?" Nothing seemed right with her husband, father, and brother gone. Less than a week ago, everything was perfectly fine, but today, like yesterday and the day before, was too painful to bear.

Sylvia lay in a fetal position on her bed in the room that used to be hers before she married Toby and left home. Her two children lay next to her, oblivious to the fact that their father, uncle, and grandfather had died. All Sylvia had told Allen was that these three special men had gone to heaven to live with Jesus. At his young age, she wasn't sure how much he comprehended. Baby Rachel was too little to understand anything at all about this sad situation. Poor little girl would never have any recollections of her daddy. As time moved on, Allen quite likely would not remember Toby either.

Tears slipped from Sylvia's eyes and rolled down her hot cheeks. *Oh Lord, how could You have taken my dear husband from me? Don't You know or even care how very much I loved and needed Toby?*

Ever since they'd been given the grave news that Toby, Dad, and Abe had died in the accident, Sylvia had barely been able to function. She couldn't imagine trying to get through the funeral service tomorrow.

I didn't just lose my precious husband either. Sylvia moaned and covered her mouth with her hand when both little ones began to stir. *I lost my daed and oldest* brieder *all at the same time. Oh, how could God be so cruel?*

Sylvia's conscience pricked. She wasn't the only one hurting right now. Mom had lost a husband and a son. She couldn't imagine how hurt her mother must be from losing those who'd been so dear to her. She and Dad had been married a good many years. Sylvia hadn't been with Toby nearly as long, yet she felt broken to the core.

Sylvia looked at her sweet, sleeping children. *I don't know how anyone gets through losing their child. I can't imagine how I'd feel if one of my precious little ones were taken from me.* She rolled over onto her back and reached out to touch each of her children. *Lord, please protect them.*

Sylvia's mind wandered as she thought about her siblings. Amy, Ezekiel, and Henry had also lost three people they cared about. And of course Toby's parents had lost their only son. They, along with Toby's three sisters, had been devastated and were struggling to deal with their loss.

If only the men had listened to Mom and been satisfied with just cake for dessert, they'd be here with us right now, and none of us would be grieving. Mom would be enjoying her birthday presents—none of which she opened—and Ezekiel and Michelle would be on their way home after a satisfying, enjoyable visit with our family.

Sylvia sniffed and swiped at the fresh onset of tears that had escaped under her lashes. *I don't know how I'm going to provide for or do right by my children. Nothing in my life will ever be the same.*

Chapter 3

As Belinda stood at the kitchen window, her knuckles turned white while she held on to the rim of the sink, watching Amy and Henry's rigid forms in the yard. Their raised voices and body language alerted her to the fact that an argument had ensued. She couldn't imagine what their disagreement might be about.

My children should be getting along better than this especially now, when we ought to all be pulling together. Her eyes closed tight. *Oh Husband, how I am missing you. My heart feels as though it's been torn asunder.*

Things were different now, dealing with everyday life—even something simple like her kids not getting along. Belinda couldn't talk things over with Vernon anymore or be consoled by him when things went wrong. All she had now were friends and family to offer support. And the news that the investigation had found her loved ones had truly died in an accident—the semi driver had been blinded by the setting sun—hadn't provided any comfort.

Belinda wanted to be strong for her family, but it took a lot of energy to keep it going. She hadn't a clue how to work through losing three people so dear to her. She couldn't think of another person in their community who'd dealt with anything like this. It was true that some had lost a family member because of an accident, but not three—maybe in other Amish communities, but not here. Theirs was the first that she knew of.

Yesterday during the funeral, graveside service, and even the meal afterward, Henry had barely spoken to anyone. She understood his grief, but shutting oneself off and refusing to communicate with anyone would not help the grieving process. Belinda felt it best to talk about her feelings—reflect on the love she felt for all three men who'd been buried yesterday and let the tears flow.

With everything else on her mind, Belinda was most worried about her fifteen-year-old son. He hadn't been to school since the accident but would start back Monday morning. She hoped he could deal with things well enough to get through the next couple of weeks leading up to his graduation, after having completed his required eight grades.

Maybe I should go out there and find out what's going on between Henry and his sister. The last thing we need is for them to be at odds with one another.

Belinda moved away from the window and went out the back door. Stepping between her son and daughter, she placed a hand on each of their shoulders. "What's going on? From what I saw out the window, it appeared as if you two were quarreling."

With furrowed brows, Amy turned to look at her. "I just asked him a simple question, but he refused to answer. Then when I asked again, he snapped at me."

"Everyone's emotions are high right now." Belinda spoke softly. "We need to be patient with each other." She patted her son's shoulder. "This is a difficult time for all of us, but with God's help, we'll get through it."

Henry shrugged her hand away. "Where was God when he took Dad, Abe, and Toby from us? He could have prevented that accident." Before Belinda could form a response, Henry ran off toward the barn.

A lump formed in her throat, and she swallowed hard, trying not to break down. Tears were cleansing, but she wouldn't give in to them at the moment. Belinda had to be strong for the rest of the family. She felt sure that was what Vernon would want her to do.

Amy came alongside her mother and slipped an arm around her waist. "Ezekiel asked me to talk to you about him and Michelle moving back to Strasburg."

"Forever more! Why doesn't your *bruder* talk to me himself instead of sending you to speak on his behalf?" Mom cheeks darkened.

Amy cringed. She'd figured it wouldn't go over well if she tried to play go-between, but she hadn't wanted to deny his request. "I guess Ezekiel assumed since he'd already brought up the subject and his idea was rejected, you might change your mind if I mentioned it and—"

"And tried to talk some sense into me?" The ties on Mom's white, heart-shaped *kapp* swished back and forth as she shook her head forcefully. "When he brought up the subject to me again last night, I thought I'd made it perfectly clear that I don't want him making such a sacrifice—especially since he was recently chosen by lots to take the place of a deceased minister in their church district."

"What? This is the first I knew of this happening. How long ago did it occur, and why didn't he say something sooner?"

"I'm not certain, but I assume he didn't want us to know because it would be one more reason I would use to try to talk him out of moving back here to help in the greenhouse—which is exactly what I did last night."

"Did you get anywhere?"

Mom shook her head. "He said he was tired and headed for the guest room before I could say another word."

"Wow! I'm stunned by this news. I never imagined that my big brother would become a minister." Amy's thoughts swirled so quickly it was hard to follow them.

"It's an honor to be chosen, although it means a lot of responsibility in addition to Ezekiel's full-time job." Mom pursed her lips as she clasped Amy's arm. "I can't, and won't, ask him to leave his home in New York and move back here. Can you help me run the greenhouse until Sylvia's up to helping?"

"That could be awhile, and besides, with her two little ones to care for, I don't see how she could work in the greenhouse too."

"Maybe Henry could watch the kinner. He'll be out of school soon."

Amy lifted her gaze toward the sky. "I hardly think my teenage brother would make a good babysitter for any child, Mom. You know how impatient and sometimes forgetful he can be. Henry would probably become preoccupied with something and wander off, leaving little Allen and baby Rachel by themselves."

Mom's head moved slowly up and down. "Good point. There are many other chores for Henry to do around here, as well as helping us with some things in the greenhouse. I guess once Sylvia feels up to working, we'll have to hire someone responsible who can come to our house and take care of the kinner." As though the matter was settled, Mom turned and headed in the direction of the barn.

"Where are you going?" Amy called to her retreating form.

"To talk to Ezekiel. He went to the barn a while ago to let our horses into the corral. I need to make it clear to him once and for all that we can make it without his help, and he's staying put at his place in New York."

"Good luck with that," Amy whispered as she turned and headed for the house. Her padded steps moved through the grass until she halted in thought. *It would be nice if Henry could do more around here, despite his mood. Mom wants to show Ezekiel that he isn't needed, which I don't understand. I still feel like he should move back with the family to help out.*

Something hit her face, and Amy realized a honeybee had flown into her. It was on the ground now, buzzing and whirling around. "That was weird. I've never had that kind of thing happen before." She rubbed the spot where the flying insect had hit her. "Sure hope there's not a mark on my face."

Amy watched the bee right itself and disappear on the breeze, and then she headed inside and looked in the bathroom mirror. Leaning in close, Amy couldn't see anything but the small, nearly invisible mole on her right cheek. She felt thankful she hadn't been stung.

After Amy left the bathroom, she found Michelle in the living room, wearing a different dress than she'd seen her in earlier today. "Did you have to change your *frack*?" Her voice was nearly a whisper.

Michelle nodded as she sat in the rocking chair, holding her little girl, who'd obviously fallen asleep. "I did have to change my dress." She looked down at Angela Mary. "My messy little girl ate a brownie with chocolate frosting, and she managed to get some on me."

"Sorry about that." Amy took a seat on the couch.

"How are you doing?" Michelle turned her head to look at Amy.

"As well as can be expected, I suppose. But I'm kind of in shock right now."

"Because of the buggy accident, you mean?"

Amy shook her head. "I'm still sad about that, but the shock has worn off, replaced with deep sorrow and concern for all our family members."

"It's a rough time for everyone." Michelle stroked the top of her daughter's head. "Angela Mary has been kind of fussy today. I'm sure she senses my stress and maybe everyone else's around her as well."

"That could be." Amy sighed. "What shocked me is hearing that Ezekiel is now a minister in your church. Mom told me a few minutes ago that he'd given her the news. Now we are both wondering why he didn't speak up and say something about it sooner."

"We were going to tell everyone the night of your *mamm*'s birthday supper, but after the accident occurred, our thoughts were consumed by what had happened." Michelle heaved a sigh. "The lot falling on my husband doesn't seem so important anymore."

"It is important, Michelle." Amy crossed her legs. "It's one of the reasons Mom doesn't want you and Ezekiel to move back here. You've established a new life there, and things are going well. Mom knows how important Ezekiel's business is too." She glanced at one of the barn cats that had snuck into the house and sat on the other side of the room, licking its paws. Then she looked back at Michelle. "Can't you convince your husband to abide by Mom's wishes and stay put in Clymer?"

When Angela Mary stirred, Michelle got the rocking chair moving at a steady pace. "When we first moved to New York, I didn't like it at all. It was hard to make new friends, and I struggled with depression because I missed everyone here so much. But now, things are different. Ezekiel and I both have a bond of friendship with several other young couples in our community. It also brings me joy to see how happy he is with his beekeeping supply business."

"How do you feel about his new ministerial position?"

"At first I felt nervous, wondering what expectations there might be of me as his *fraa*. But after I prayed about it, God gave me a sense of peace." Michelle pushed her shoulders against the back of the chair as she continued to rock. "I miss everyone here, but whether Ezekiel decides our place is in Strasburg or Clymer, I will go along with his decision."

"I guess we'll know what he decides soon, because Mom is in the barn talking to him right now."

Ezekiel grabbed a curry comb and started working on Dad's buggy horse. His thoughts and emotions had been running amuck ever since the tragic accident. Through all the years of working in the greenhouse, all he'd been able to think about was his desire to do something else. When the opportunity to move to a fairly new Amish community in New York was offered to him, he'd jumped at the chance. He remembered when he told his folks about his plans, Dad had said that Ezekiel had a right to live where he wanted and work at the job of his choosing. He'd reminded Mom that they could not stand in the way of that.

Ezekiel never had been as happy as he had been the last two years, and the idea of leaving the new life they'd established and returning to Strasburg to run the greenhouse held no appeal. Now that he was a minister, he had a new obligation in Clymer, but he had one here too.

He paused from his chore to reflect further on the matter. *It would be selfish to stay in Clymer when my family here needs my help right now.*

Just dealing with the trauma of losing Dad, Abe, and Toby will be difficult enough for Mom and the rest of our family, not to mention trying to run the greenhouse by themselves.

Ezekiel thought about Sylvia and how he'd seen her last night, sitting in the rocking chair holding her baby girl. She hadn't said a word to anyone else in the room—just sat there, staring off into space. There was no way in her condition that she'd be able to help out in the greenhouse. He shook his head. *No way at all. It'll be all my sister can do to take care of her two kinner. And Mom, well, she's grieving deeply too, and so are Amy and Henry. They all need my support.*

Ezekiel also grieved for his father, brother, and brother-in-law. Who wouldn't be deeply saddened when they'd lost three family members?

After Ezekiel and Michelle had retired to the guest room last night, she'd mentioned that he should pray about the matter. He'd agreed, but as far as Ezekiel was concerned, there really wasn't much to pray about. His presence was needed here more than in Clymer; it was just that simple.

When Mom entered the barn and called out to him, Ezekiel pushed his thoughts aside.

"I'm back here in your horse's stall."

She walked toward him and leaned on the stall door, looking at him with her chin held high. "I am well aware that you are determined to move back here, but I have a proposition for you."

He set the curry comb aside. "What proposition did you have in mind?"

"How about giving me, along with your sisters and younger brother, a chance to prove ourselves?"

His brows furrowed. "What do you mean?"

"You and your family can return to Clymer to take care of your job and duties as the new minister."

"Huh-uh."

She held up her hand. "Please, hear me out."

Ezekiel remained silent.

"Give us, say, six months to see if we can make a go of things on our own, and if we succeed, you remain in New York." His mother stood tall with her shoulders back. "If we can't make it, you can choose to move back here if you want."

Ezekiel rolled his neck from side to side as he contemplated her suggestion. "How 'bout three months instead of six?"

"Let's make it four. How does that sound?"

The whole thing sounded impossible, and he felt sure they wouldn't succeed, but Ezekiel nodded slowly. "Agreed."

Chapter 4

For almost two weeks, the greenhouse had been closed for business, and Henry had finished his schooling. Ezekiel and his family had returned to Clymer a week ago. It was time to get things up and running again so they would have some money coming in. The one thing that hadn't been settled yet was which of them would be in charge of what tasks.

"If we're opening the greenhouse today, shouldn't we come up with a plan for who will be responsible for what?" Amy asked her mother as they prepared breakfast on Monday morning.

Mom continued stirring pancake batter, giving Amy a sidelong glance. "I suppose you're right. You and Henry will need to make sure that the plants are arranged properly and that the watering system is working as it should." She paused long enough to add a few sprinkles of cinnamon to the batter. "And of course we'll need to take turns waiting on customers."

"Who will be responsible for placing orders and tallying up the expenses as well as the items sold each day?" Amy placed silverware on the table. "Since Dad used to do that, and now he's not here. . ."

"I didn't need that reminder, Daughter." Mom's jaw clenched as she tapped her foot, the way she often did when she was annoyed.

"Sorry, Mom. I just meant. . ."

"I know what you meant, and I apologize for overreacting. The agony of losing three members of our family is still raw, and it's hard to control my emotions." Mom teared up. "We're taking on a daunting job, especially without Sylvia's help."

"Maybe you should have accepted Ezekiel's offer to move back here."

"No! I will not ask him to make that sacrifice."

Amy could see by the stubborn set of her mother's jaw that she was not going to change her mind, so she decided to drop the subject, at least for now. Perhaps once they got the greenhouse going and Mom saw what a chore it was, she would come to her senses and call for Ezekiel. In the meantime, Amy would do all she could to keep the greenhouse open for business, because they certainly needed some money coming in.

"Sylvia could do the books and place orders if she were feeling better," Mom said. "But right now, she's barely able to take care of herself and the kinner. Losing Toby has been the most difficult thing she's ever faced, not to mention losing her father and brother in the same accident." She moved over to the stove with the pancake batter. "Your sister has always been the sensitive type and doesn't adjust to change easily. And losing one's mate is a terrible thing for anyone. I had no idea how difficult it would be until it happened to me." Her voice faltered. "I am still struggling to comprehend how I could have lost my husband and son the same day. Abe was in the prime of his young adult life, and so was Sylvia's husband."

"It was a terrible tragedy, and I doubt any of us will ever fully recover." Amy's lips trembled, and she pressed them together.

Mom turned and placed one hand against her chest. "We will always miss them, but we must find the strength to go on. As our bishop said when he and his wife stopped by the other day: 'In time, the pain will lessen.'"

Amy wasn't sure that was true, but it was obvious that Mom was trying to set an example for the rest of the family. She would persevere despite her grief and their current situation.

Amy went to the cupboard and took out the glasses. *If only there was something I could do to lighten Mom's load.*

In frustration, Amy marched toward the outbuilding where her brother had gone. It was time to eat, and she'd been asked to go get him. She and Henry weren't getting along these days.

I sure miss the old Henry. Before the accident, her little brother had usually been in good spirits and often told goofy stories or jokes that made others laughed. Now all he did was sulk, complain, or say curt things that hurt Amy's feelings. She wished there was a way to reach him, but she had no idea what to do.

Amy opened the barn door and poked her head inside. Looking around the dimly lit area, she spotted Henry seated on a bale of straw with his head down. Amy understood they were all trying to get through their grief, but Henry dealt with it in such a negative way. At least Sylvia, who was almost drowning in sorrow, didn't say snappish things or gripe about every little thing.

How can I talk to my brother without him getting temperamental or defensive? Amy collected herself the best she could. *Okay, here goes.*

"Mom sent me out here to tell you that breakfast is ready." Amy moved closer to him. "I assume your chores in here are done, or you wouldn't be sitting there doing nothing."

"I ain't doin' nothin'." He lifted his head and crossed his arms.

"Looks like it to me."

Henry's eyes narrowed as he stared at her with a look of defiance. "I'm thinkin' on things—trying to figure out what all's expected of me now that Dad and Abe are gone."

"I thought Mom made it clear what chores she'd like you to do around here this summer."

"She did, but I'm wondering how I'm gonna get 'em all done with no help from anyone. Mom will probably come up with some other things she wants me to do—stuff in the greenhouse."

"We will need help in there because Mom and I can't do it alone."

"If Sylvia helped out, I'd be free to look for some other kind of work—something I'd like to do rather than a job that's expected of me." He looked at Amy with a glassy stare. "Ezekiel oughta be here doin' his fair share, even if he doesn't like working in the greenhouse. He may be livin' someplace else, but he's still part of this family, ya know."

Amy placed both hands behind her back, gripping one wrist with the other hand. "Our brother has responsibilities in his church district now that he's a minister. He also has a business to run."

"I don't care. If I have to do a bunch of things I'd rather not do, then he should too."

Amy realized she wasn't going to get through to Henry—at least not today. He needed time to mature and come to grips with the way things were. "Let's go inside. Breakfast is ready."

"You go ahead. I ain't hungry."

This isn't good. Now look what I've done. I don't want to be the reason my brother isn't cooperating again. Amy drew a quick breath and released it before speaking. "You'll have more energy to get your work done today if you eat, but it's your choice." She whirled around and tromped out the door. Things were bad enough with everyone attempting to deal with their loss. Did her little brother have to make it worse by being so uncooperative and martyring himself?

Sylvia sat at the breakfast table, forcing herself to eat one of her mother's banana-flavored pancakes. Allen sat in his highchair beside her, enjoying the breakfast treat with his sticky fingers full of maple syrup. *He's lucky to be young and carefree—barely noticing that his* daadi *is missing.*

Sylvia wondered what the future held for her and the children. It would be difficult for them to grow up without a father. Some widows her age might hope for remarriage but not Sylvia. She could never love another man the way she loved Toby. She would not get married again for the sake of providing Allen and Rachel with a father either. The children's uncles would have to be their father figures. Of course, with Ezekiel living several hundred miles away and Henry taking no interest in the children whatsoever, it wasn't likely they would have much "uncle time" either. They still had one grandfather left. It was too bad Toby's parents didn't live closer.

"Would you like a cup of tea, Sylvia?"

Mom's question pulled Sylvia out of her musings.

"Uh, no thanks. I'm fine with my glass of *millich*."

"Okay." Mom looked over at Amy. "I wish you could have talked your brother into eating breakfast. He's gonna turn into a twig if he doesn't eat more."

"His appetite will come back in time. And if I know Henry, he probably has a stash of candy bars to snack on."

"Puh!" Mom wrinkled her nose. "I taught all my kinner that too much *zucker* isn't good for them."

"Right now, I'm afraid my little brother doesn't know what is good for him."

Sylvia tuned out their conversation as she put all her energies into finishing the pancake that seemed to have no flavor at all. Nothing tasted good to her these days, but at least she was forcing herself to eat.

About the time they finished eating, Sylvia heard the baby crying. "I'd better feed Rachel and change her *windel*. I'll wash the dishes after I'm done."

"If you're not up to it, I can do them," Amy said.

"No, you and Mom need to get the greenhouse opened."

Sylvia pushed back her chair and was about to take Allen from the highchair when Mom said, "I'll take care of getting the boy cleaned up. You go ahead and tend to the baby's needs."

Sylvia gave a quick nod and hurried from the room. This was only the beginning of another long day—a day when she would only be going through the motions of trying to take care of her children's needs. Truthfully, she wished there was someone who could provide for her needs right now. She blinked back tears of frustration. *It would help if I had someone to watch Allen and Rachel for a while so I could lie on my bed and let the tears flow all day.*

When Belinda stepped into the greenhouse and saw all the plants waiting to be sold, a flood of emotions threatened to overpower her. *Oh Vernon, how can I do this without you by my side? If only you were still alive and could be here right now.* Nothing about the greenhouse held any appeal for Belinda anymore. Yet this was their livelihood and the only way she knew of to make a living for her family. Even if they closed the doors on the business permanently and she and Amy found other jobs, they would never make enough money between the two of them to equal what they could make here in the greenhouse. In addition to their returning customers, as well as new ones, they earned a decent amount selling flowers to some of the florists in the area. Those businesses counted on them.

The first thing Belinda did was put the OPEN sign in the window. Then she checked a row of plants to be sure they'd been getting enough water. Next, she got out a dust rag to clean off the counter where they waited on customers. She'd just finished cleaning it when Amy came in.

"I finished the dishes and checked on Sylvia and the kinner."

"Are they doing all right?"

Amy nodded. "Sylvia's in the rocking chair with the baby, and Allen's stacking wooden blocks on the living-room floor."

"Did you by any chance think about going out to the phone shed to check for messages?"

Amy shook her head. "No, but I can do that now since we have no customers yet. I'll see if the mail's come too."

"Danki." Belinda heaved a sigh. "If you see Henry, would you please tell him there are a few chores in here I'd like him to do?"

"Sure, Mom." Amy opened the door and stepped outside.

Belinda took a seat on the tall wooden stool behind the counter. *I probably should pick some dead blossoms off some of the flowers, but I honestly don't feel like it.* She really didn't feel like doing anything at all. Everything about the greenhouse seemed so overwhelming. Things she used to take for granted that had once seemed like simple chores now felt like heavy burdens she could hardly bear. As time passed, she hoped they would settle into a routine and things would become easier.

The bell attached to the main door at the front of the greenhouse jingled, and Belinda turned her head. She was surprised to see Mary Ruth Lapp enter the building, since she'd been under the weather recently with sinus issues. Mary Ruth was such a dear, sweet woman—always helpful and putting others needs ahead of her own.

"*Guder mariye.*" The elderly woman smiled as she approached the counter. "I came by to see if there was anything I could do to make your load a bit lighter."

Tears gathered in the corners of Belinda's eyes, and she was powerless to stop them from spilling over. "Bless you, Mary Ruth. I appreciate the offer so much, but I really don't know what you can do. Besides, from what I understand, you haven't been feeling well lately, so you should probably be home resting."

"I'm doing much better since the antibiotics the doctor gave me did their work on my sinus infection. It's not easy having such horrible face pain and pressure, but I was able to get through it."

Belinda patted her friend's arm. "Glad you're doing better."

"Danki. Now back to what I'm here for. . . . What can I help you with?" She set her purse on the counter. "If not out here in the greenhouse then how about inside the house? I'm sure there are plenty of things I can do there."

Belinda couldn't deny it as she slowly nodded. "Sylvia's in the house with her children, but I doubt she'll get any housework done. She's taken Toby's death really hard and can barely function."

"It's understandable. It was difficult for me when Willis passed, but keeping busy helped."

"Busyness is a good antidote for depression. However, Sylvia hasn't realized that yet."

Mary Ruth stepped around the counter, put her hands on Belinda's shoulders, and massaged them. "I don't have a lot to do these days except dote on my great-grandchildren, so feel free to let me know whenever you need anything done in the way of housecleaning, pulling weeds in the garden, cooking, or even babysitting the little ones."

"That is so kind of you, Mary Ruth."

"So, what should I start on today?"

"The kitchen may need some tidying. Amy did the dishes, but she probably didn't take time to do much else."

"I'll take care of it. Anything else?"

"Maybe sweeping the front and back porches."

"Consider it done." Mary Ruth stepped back around to the other side of the counter. "I'll check in with you after those chores are done and see what you all might like for lunch." She ambled out the door before Belinda could respond.

How nice it was to have friends willing to help in a time of need. Several other women from their Amish community had come by these past two weeks with food and offers of help. Belinda didn't know how anyone could get through something like this without family and friends.

A few minutes later, Amy came back in and handed her mother a stack of mail.

"Did you see Henry and give him my message?"

"No, Mom. I didn't see him."

Belinda lifted her gaze to the ceiling. *Oh, great! This is certainly not what I need today.*

Chapter 5

With her last bit of energy, Amy yanked on the green hose and turned on the water to reach some thirsty flowers on display. She gently sprayed them and rearranged the whole group after removing some of the empty trays the plants sat on and placing them on the concrete floor. They'd sold quite a few bedding flowers, and it seemed the bright yellow ones were the most popular.

When Amy finished her chore, she coiled the hose back in its spot. Then she picked up the wooden trays and stacked them near the rear of the greenhouse. Mom had said she would do it, but Amy was more than willing to take care of the task.

She wiped her forehead with the back of her hand and reached for a bottle of water she'd left sitting on a shelf. Taking a needed break felt good, and the cool drink relieved her parched throat.

It was almost time to close the greenhouse, and Amy's feet hurt so bad she couldn't wait to soak them. She'd been busy all day walking up and down the plant aisles either pruning, repotting, or repositioning to make some of them more noticeable. When she wasn't doing that, Amy answered customers' questions and directed them to various plants, seed packets, and other gardening items. Mom had spent the day behind the counter, waiting on a steady stream of customers.

Amy didn't know if the larger-than-usual number of people who came into the greenhouse today was because most folks in the area knew about their tragic loss and wanted to help out financially or if it was simply a matter of the greenhouse having been closed for two weeks and so many were in need of things for their garden. Either way, she felt thankful for the money that came in and also the offer by some to help out with chores or whatever Amy's family needed to have done.

Jared, who'd arrived a short time ago, was one of those people, and he stood beside Amy now. She couldn't help her attraction to him, and his tender smile made her heart melt. Jared had a sweet way about him, but Amy wouldn't allow her feelings to undo a thing. Her mind was centered around the work that needed to be done at the business and the support her family required at home. The combination was proving to be exhausting.

Jared shifted as he stood looking at Amy. *What a pretty color his brown eyes are. And that genuine smile nearly melts my heart. Oh, I wish things could be different, but they're not, and I must accept it.* Amy blinked away her thoughts.

"If your stables need cleaning, I can do that now for you," he said.

"The offer's appreciated, but Henry should have done it this morning."

"Are there any other chores I can do?" Jared's words were rushed as he rubbed his hands down the sides of his trousers.

"I can't think of anything, but you may want to check with my brother. Mom and I have been in here most of the day, so Henry would be the one to know if there were any chores left undone." Amy swiped a hand across her sweaty forehead as she offered him a tired smile.

"Okay, I'll do that in a few minutes, but first, I wanted to ask if you'd like to go out to supper with me this evening. It's been a while since we spent any time together, and I've missed you so much."

"I've missed you too, but I'm too tired to go anywhere this evening. We had a very full day here, with so many people coming in. We barely had time to eat the lunch Mary Ruth brought out to us."

"Glad to hear you had lots of customers, but sorry to hear you're too *mied* to go out for supper. I was looking forward to us being together for a few hours."

She drew in a weary breath. "Maybe some other time, Jared, when things slow down and Mom and I get more organized."

"How long do you think it'll be?"

She shrugged. "I have no idea. With only the two of us working here right now and Henry running a few errands for us, it could be some time before I'm free to go anywhere just for fun."

Jared's shoulders slumped, and he lowered his head. Just as quickly, he looked up at her, and his brown eyes softened. "I understand, and I want you to know that I'm not being selfish wanting to take you out." Jared gestured to the array of plants nearby. "Just figured it would be good for you to get away from all this for a while and do something fun and relaxing."

Amy didn't want to hurt Jared's feelings, but her grief over losing Dad and the others was still too raw to consider doing anything for fun, not to mention her lack of free time. It also wouldn't be right to take off for the evening and leave Mom, Sylvia, and Henry home alone. They might think she was insensitive to their needs, and indeed, she would be. At least that's how she felt about it.

Bumping Jared's arm lightly with her elbow, Amy looked up at him and offered another smile, more heartfelt than the last one. "Things will get better in time, and then we can begin courting again." *If only Jared could help my brother somehow. Or maybe he could fill in here at the greenhouse temporarily until Sylvia can help out.* Amy rubbed away the dirt smudges from her hand. *But I won't ask because he's too busy with his roofing business, and that's his livelihood, so it should come first.*

He shuffled his feet a few times and gave a quick nod. "I'll go see if I can find Henry now. If he has more chores to do, I'll help out before heading home."

"Okay, Jared. Danki."

"Sure, no problem. Take care, Amy, and I hope things go better for you soon." Jared gave her arm a gentle squeeze and hurried from the building.

Amy looked at her mother, still sitting behind the counter with a slumped posture and shear exhaustion clearly written on her face. *I could never have gone out with Jared this evening and left cooking supper up to Mom. She looks like she's almost ready to collapse. Her needs come before mine even if it means I have to sacrifice my relationship with Jared. The next time he comes around, I should tell him that he should look for someone else to court, because it doesn't look like I'll be free for that anytime soon. It wouldn't be fair to expect him to wait for something that may never occur. Mom will always need my help to keep the greenhouse running. And for sure, Sylvia—and even Henry—need me right now.*

As Jared headed for home that afternoon, all he could think about was Amy. If they couldn't spend time together, their relationship would suffer.

He had courted two other young women before he met Amy, but neither of them stole his heart the way she had. Thoughts of her were never far from his mind. It wasn't Amy's pretty face, shiny brown hair, or soft brown eyes that attracted him—it was her gentle, sweet spirit and concern for others.

Jared remembered the first day he'd met Amy and seen her consoling her little brother after his dog had run away. She'd not only given him a pep talk but had also combed the neighborhood, helping him search for the dog. There was no doubt about it: Amy would make a good wife and mother.

His thoughts went to Henry. Things weren't right with him. Henry had taken his father and brother's deaths really hard. Jared had a feeling the boy was full of pent-up anger that would not be resolved until he gave it over to God. During his visit at the Kings' today, Jared had found Amy's brother leaning against the corral gate. Henry's drooping shoulders and negative comments told Jared the trauma of losing three family members must be burning inside the young man. He'd asked Henry about helping in some way today, but his efforts had been squashed. Amy's kid brother was either too proud or too stubborn to accept Jared's help.

As Jared's horse and buggy rounded a bend in the road, he kept a firm grip on the reins. *Since Amy doesn't have time to go out anywhere with me, maybe I should go over to her place some evenings and we could play a few games. No doubt there would be other family members hanging around, but at least we could see each other and have a little fun. Think I'll drop by the greenhouse in a few days and mention the idea to her.*

Amy watched her sister out of the corner of her eye. Sylvia hadn't said a word during supper, and now, as she sat holding her baby in the living room, she remained quiet. Two weeks wasn't enough time to heal her broken heart, but holding everything inside and refusing to talk about it wasn't good for her either.

Henry had talked some while they ate, but it was mostly complaints. He'd gone outside as soon as they'd finished the meal. *If only there was someone he could talk to, he might feel better.* Henry looked up to Ezekiel, so he should be the one. But what were the chances of Henry going out to the phone shed and calling his big brother? Slim to none.

Amy rubbed her hands down the front of her apron as she continued to fret and seek answers. *Maybe I should give Ezekiel a call in the morning and ask him to phone here and leave a message for Henry, saying he'd like to talk to him and asking him to call. If anyone could get through to our younger brother, it would be Ezekiel.*

Amy remembered how when Henry was a boy, he used to follow Ezekiel around, asking all kinds of questions and seeking his attention.

She glanced over at Mom, seated in Dad's favorite chair with her eyes closed. Today had been exhausting for her mother, even though she had been sitting most of the time. The last thing she needed was to deal with Henry's complaints and angry attitude. All of them were sad about what had happened to Dad, Abe, and Toby, but getting mad and taking it out on the others didn't make things better.

Yes, she told herself, *I'm definitely going to call Ezekiel again in the morning. He has the right to know what's going on with Henry and be updated on how the rest of us are doing.*

Clymer, New York

"Have you heard anything from your mamm in the last few days?" Michelle asked as Ezekiel sat beside her on the sofa that evening.

"No, but Amy left a message this morning, saying they would be opening the greenhouse for the first time since the accident. She asked for our prayers that everything would go well and lots of customers would come in." With a grimace, he set the newspaper he held aside. "I can't help but worry about them. How are two grieving women and a troubled teenage boy supposed to take over a business that did so well with my daed in charge?" Ezekiel rushed on before Michelle could respond. "Dad knew everything about running the greenhouse, and he had a certain way of doing things. I don't think it'll be long before Mom comes to her senses and realizes they can't do it without my help."

"Your mother and Amy may be stronger than you think."

He shook his head. "This is not just about being strong or full of determination. Running a business is a lot of work, and it takes a person with a business head to make it succeed." Ezekiel touched his chest. "Just ask me. I had no idea when I took over my beekeeping supply business what all was involved."

"But you have done well and are making a decent living to provide for our little family."

"True, but it hasn't come easy. I'm still learning new ways of doing things almost every day. I can't help worrying about them."

Michelle placed her hand on his arm. "I'm gonna give you the same piece of advice that you offered during the message you gave to our church members last week on the topic of worry." Michelle stood and got the Bible from the side table nearest the couch. She opened it to the book of Matthew and read from chapter 6, verse 27: "'Which of you by taking thought can add one cubit unto his stature?' You explained that the verse means we can't add a single hour to our life by worrying. Remember?"

"Jah." Ezekiel took the Bible from Michelle and held it against his chest. "If I can't even practice what I preach, then how am I ever gonna be a good minister?"

"You'll get there, dear husband. Just remember to trust God in all things."

"You're right. That's what I promised myself I would do if the lot ever fell on me."

Ezekiel reflected on the recent event of choosing a new minister for their church district and how he'd received enough votes from the congregation to be nominated as a candidate for ministry. Ezekiel had broken out in a cold sweat as he and the other men who had also received more than three votes chose a hymnal. He, like the others, was well aware that one of the songbooks held a slip of paper with a scripture verse written on it. He couldn't help holding his breath as the bishop inspected each of the books to see which one the lot had fallen upon. When Ezekiel's hymnal was opened and the verse was found inside, he nearly collapsed from the emotion and realization of what it meant.

Becoming a minister in the Amish church was not viewed as an honor, as some might believe. Rather it was a serious, heavy responsibility. Ministers usually served in their position for life and received no salary. But that wasn't what bothered Ezekiel. His greatest concern was whether he was spiritually and emotionally up to the task. His duties as the new minister included studying the scriptures in preparation for preaching a sermon on Sundays and at other church-related functions; assisting the bishop in administering church discipline when necessary; baptizing; and helping to regulate any new changes within the church district. Each Saturday, Ezekiel would need to spend a good amount of time preparing for their biweekly Sunday services, where he could be expected to preach an hour-long sermon.

The worst part was that he was supposed to preach without any notes.

The first week Ezekiel had preached was the Sunday before he and his family had gone to Strasburg to celebrate his mother's birthday. Never in a million years had he expected such a tragedy would occur. It was proof that people should live each day as if it were their last for no one but God knew when a person's life would come to an end.

Ezekiel bowed his head and closed his eyes. *Heavenly Father, please guide and direct me in the days ahead. Give me the wisdom to make good decisions and deliver messages to the people in our congregation that we all need to hear. And please be with my mother, sisters, and brother. Let them feel Your presence, and help each of us as we deal with the grieving process. Amen.*

Chapter 6

Strasburg

Amy stepped into the phone shed and took a seat on the wooden stool. She dialed Ezekiel's number, hoping he or Michelle might be nearby and would hear the phone ring. No such luck; she had to leave a message. "Hi, it's me, Amy. Just wanted to give you an update on things. We opened the greenhouse yesterday and were busy the whole day. So many people came to buy plants and other things, and Mom feels hopeful that it'll be full of activity throughout the spring and summer months. Sylvia's not up to helping us yet, but Mom and I did okay by ourselves. Henry popped in a few times and did some things to help, but he mostly kept busy with other chores outside the greenhouse."

Amy paused when she heard that irritating crow creating a ruckus somewhere in the yard. Refocusing, she said, "Henry has an attitude problem, and I was wondering if you could call or write to him and say something that might help him deal with our family's loss. He won't talk about his feelings to anyone, and holding them in is not good. Danki, Ezekiel. I love you, Brother."

When Amy hung up the phone, she checked for messages and found one from Sara, asking if they had any carnations they could sell to her flower shop. With many English young people graduating from high school in June, Sara stated that she had several orders already for floral bouquets, corsages, and boutonnieres.

Figuring it would be best to return Sara's call right away, Amy picked up the phone again and dialed the number. She didn't want to miss this opportunity for more business.

After she made the call and wrote down the number of flowers Sara needed, Amy left the phone shed and went to the end of the driveway to check for mail.

Once Amy opened the mailbox and retrieved a stack of mail, she turned toward the road and was surprised to see two men standing in the yard across the street. The home there had recently come on the market and had a FOR SALE sign on the lawn near the edge of the property. One man, who appeared to be asking the other man questions, was quite tall and dressed in blue jeans and a beige jacket. The older man wore dark gray dress slacks and a white shirt. Could they be father and son? Or might one of them be a Realtor?

Amy didn't want to appear snoopy, so she started back up the driveway toward the house. An elderly English couple used to live in that home across from them, but they couldn't keep it up anymore and ended up moving in with their daughter, who lived in Lancaster. Amy missed seeing them sitting on their front porch, always offering a friendly wave. Mr. and Mrs. Benson had come over to the greenhouse a few times, and Mom offered them produce from her garden on several occasions. It was nice to have good neighbors, and Amy hoped whoever moved into the vacant house would be friendly too. It didn't matter whether they were Amish or English as long as they were good neighbors.

Sighing, Amy came up to the checkout counter where her mother stood. "Can I help in some way?"

"Jah, this customer is waiting for some assistance with a tree," Mom replied.

An elderly English woman stood at the register with her cane. She was the last patron for the day. "I would like to buy one of your small ornamental trees back there along the greenhouse wall." She pointed her walking stick in that direction.

"Did you have a particular one in mind?" Amy looked at the woman and smiled. "I can go get one for you."

"I know exactly which one. I'll come with you, dear." The woman pulled a tissue from her sleeve and blotted her damp forehead with it.

Amy felt tired and sleepy in the unrelenting heat. She walked ahead of the lady and visited with her until they stood next to the trees.

The older woman looked over the selection while Amy waited for her to pick out the one she wanted. However, all the woman did was look back and forth with furrowed brows. "Thought I knew what my choice would be, but now I can't decide. They're all so lovely."

Maybe I should give her some input about the trees and see if that would help. Amy touched the slender trunk of the closest tree. "This one is the smallest and will bloom white flowers in the spring. Those two next to it have pink blooms, but all of them will need pruning during their growing season."

"Good to know." The woman moved toward the pink variety. "I'd like this one—the largest tree."

"Okay, I'll get my brother's assistance to bring it up to the register and then take it out to your vehicle." Amy plucked the price tag off and handed it to the lady. "You can take this up to the checkout counter; I'll meet you there soon."

"Thank you." The woman turned and ambled along, using her cane.

Amy left the greenhouse and hurried outside, where she found her brother playing fetch with his dog. "Hey, Henry, I need your help inside."

With a shake of his head, Henry frowned and said, "I'm done for the day."

"I just need you to do one more thing. Our last customer wants an ornamental tree, and she is paying for it right now."

Henry's frown deepened. "If Dad was here, he'd be the one doin' it. Now I'm stuck doing everything."

Amy brought a hand to her waist. "Not everything, Henry. I just need your help for this last person, and then you can do whatever you want."

Groaning, he made his way to the greenhouse with Amy following. Her brother's attitude was getting old, and she bit her tongue to keep from saying anything more. If she said what was really on her mind, Henry would end up getting mad and might not help her at all.

When they got to the trees, Amy showed Henry which one they needed to lift and set in the wagon. His face reddened as he struggled to put the tree in the four-wheeled cart, but he wouldn't allow Amy to help. Then with an extra loud huff, Henry wheeled the plant up to the register, where Mom and the elderly lady waited. Soon, they headed out to the parking lot and loaded it into her small pickup truck.

"Thank you both for helping me with my purchase." She teared up. "My children are going to help me plant this tree in my yard in tribute to my late husband. He passed away a few months ago."

Henry remained silent while Amy felt led to say something. It was a bit awkward, but she went ahead and spoke up. "We understand your grief, for my brother and I lost our father, older brother, and a brother-in-law. They were killed in an accident."

"I'm so sorry to hear that."

"What you are planning to do with this tree is a wonderful thing in remembrance of him." Amy teared up too but somehow managed not to fall apart.

"Thank you both again." The woman turned away and got into her vehicle.

Henry was already on his way back to the yard when Amy caught up to him. "Henry, wait! I want to thank you for helping me back there."

"No problem," he mumbled with his head down. "When will the pain go away, Sister? Did you hear what that woman said? She's hurting too."

"Yes, losing a loved one is painful, and it takes some time to come to grips with it all."

"Yeah, well things keep reminding me of my hurt, and I don't need some stranger opening up my wounds again."

"Henry, she didn't mean to hurt us. Besides, she said she was sorry about our loss."

He leveled Amy with a frown that went even deeper this time. "You shouldn't have said anything about us losing Dad, Abe, and Toby. It was none of that woman's business."

Amy placed a hand on his arm. "There is no reason we shouldn't talk about it. Discussing the way we feel can actually help in the healing process."

He shrugged her hand aside. "Let's drop this topic. I've gotta finish something Mom asked me to do earlier." Henry sauntered off in the direction of the barn.

Amy lingered for a moment and then headed back to the greenhouse, where she found her mother counting out money from the cash register.

"How'd it go?" Mom asked.

Amy told her what the elderly woman had said and what had transpired between her and Henry.

Mom shook her head. "Your brother is a challenge, but we need to be patient and keep showing him love."

"You're right." Amy came around and gave her mother a hug. Then she helped her count out the rest of the money. Henry popped in to flip over the sign on the door so it read CLOSED. Then he left just as quickly without saying a word to either of them.

That evening, shortly after they'd closed the greenhouse for the day, Jared showed up. Before Amy had a chance to say anything, Mom invited him to stay for supper.

He gave her a bright-eyed smile. "Danki, Belinda, I'd be happy to join you. My folks are eating out this evening, so I would have been at home by myself with a boring sandwich."

"Well, you certainly won't have to do that tonight, so why don't you come on in with us?" Mom gestured to the house.

Jared nodded then turned to Amy with another pleasant smile. "Sure am glad for the opportunity to spend some time with you and your family."

You might not be when you hear what I have to say. Amy kept her thoughts to herself and forced herself to offer him a brief smile. She wouldn't say anything to Jared about her decision unless they had a few minutes alone. No point in telling anyone in her family right now that she planned to break things off with Jared. Mom liked Jared and would probably try to talk her out of it. She'd no doubt feel guilty for keeping Amy from marrying the man she loved all because of her duties at the greenhouse. One thing was certain: Mom couldn't run the business by herself, so Amy needed to give it her full attention. The only logical thing to do was release Jared of his obligation to court her. Of course, he may not see it as an obligation, but in the long run this was the best thing for both of them.

Jared's mouth watered as he smelled the enticing aroma from the meal being cooked in the next room. So far he hadn't had a chance to be alone with Amy, since she was in the kitchen with her mother and sister while he sat in the living room alone. Henry had come in briefly but barely mumbled a hello before heading down the hall to take a shower.

Jared shifted on the sofa and picked up a copy of *The Budget* from the coffee table. He browsed a few pages then set the newspaper aside. *Sure wish Amy would come out here and talk to me. Maybe I should go into the kitchen and see if there's anything I can do to help.* Jared massaged the bridge of his nose. *That may not be a good idea. The women might think I'm impatient about waiting for supper.*

Jared got up and went to look out the window. The wind had picked up, and he noticed several blossoms had blown off some of the trees and were scattered about the yard. Wind and rain were typical weather for spring, and he'd be glad when the warmer days of summer swept in. Of course, summer heat usually brought humidity, which made roofing or any other kind of strenuous outdoor work a challenge.

Jared heard footsteps, and he turned around. Seeing Henry had returned to the room, he smiled and said, "How'd things go in the *griehaus* today?"

Henry shrugged and flopped into an overstuffed chair. "Don't really know. I didn't work in the greenhouse that much."

"Really? I thought—"

"I've been stuck doin' a bunch of outside chores this week, and I also have to make deliveries when one of the flower shops in our area places an order." Henry's facial features sagged, and he dropped his gaze to the floor. "Ezekiel used to do most of that stuff before he moved away, and then Abe took some of it over when he wasn't helpin' out at the buggy shop."

"Do you have to hire a driver to take you around for the deliveries?"

"Only when there are more plants and flowers than will fit in the back of our market buggy. Otherwise, I deliver 'em myself. That ain't all I have to do either. Now that Abe's gone, I'm stuck takin' care of the bees and trying to sell off the honey."

Jared was about to comment when Amy entered and announced that supper was on the dining-room table. Henry and Jared got up at the same time and headed in that direction.

After everyone was seated, all heads bowed for silent prayer. When Jared heard the rustle of napkins, he opened his eyes and looked up.

Belinda ladled some stew into a bowl and handed it to Jared.

"Danki." He smiled and sniffed deeply of the savory aroma. Then Amy passed him a basket full of fluffy biscuits. He took two and passed it to Henry.

As they began eating the meal, Jared noticed that Sylvia, whose face looked pasty white, said very little and ate even less. Dark circles rimmed the poor woman's puffy eyes. No doubt she hadn't been getting enough sleep.

None of the others were saying much either, so Jared decided to break the silence. "I was talking to the people I was working for today, and the husband mentioned that he heard a new greenhouse is going to be built on a stretch of land between Strasburg and Paradise." He looked at Belinda. "So, it looks like you may have some competition."

Amy's forehead wrinkled as she glanced at her mother. "If that's the case, we're gonna have to work even harder to encourage customers to come here for their gardening needs."

"You're right. This news worries me a bit." Belinda pinched the skin on her throat.

"I wouldn't worry too much about it." Jared reached for another biscuit. "It'll probably be a while before the other greenhouse is up and running. Besides, your business is already established, and you have a lot of repeat and steady customers." He hoped his confident tone would put their minds at ease.

Everyone fell silent again. Jared saw the women's tight facial muscles and the scowl on Henry's face. Now he wished he'd never brought up the topic of the new greenhouse.

After supper, Jared decided it was time to go home. He'd resigned himself to the fact that he and Amy would not get any time alone. Truth was he still felt bad about blurting the news concerning another greenhouse and thought it best if he took his leave now, before he said something else that might upset this nice family.

He grabbed his straw hat and was almost to the door when Amy called, "I'll walk you out to your buggy."

"Sure. . .okay." *Maybe Amy's not put out with me after all. She must want us to spend a few minutes in private conversation.*

As they approached his horse and buggy at the hitching rail, Amy offered Jared a flash of a smile, but it disappeared quickly. "Umm. . ." She twisted the ties on her head covering around her fingers. "There's something I need to tell you."

"Oh?" He leaned in closer and felt disappointed when she took a step back.

"Is there something wrong, Amy?"

She moved her head slowly up and down. "I'm sorry, Jared, but we can no longer court."

"Huh?" Jared reached under his hat and scratched his head. "Why would you say something like that?"

"Because I don't have time for courting anymore. I have too many responsibilities at home and in the greenhouse."

"I understand that, and I'm willing to wait until things slow down and level out for you and your family."

Amy shook her head vigorously. "It's over between us, Jared. It has to be. Mom needs me now, and she may need me indefinitely. You and I have no future together."

"You can't mean that, Amy. I love you, and I want to make you my—"

She held up her hand. "Please don't say anything more. I'm sorry, but I've made up my mind. I care about you too much to have you waiting around for something that may never happen. You need to find someone else—someone who can make you happy."

"No one can make me as happy as you do, Amy."

Tears welled in her pretty brown eyes, but she said not a word. Instead, Amy whirled around and bounded off toward the house.

Jared stood with his mouth slightly open and both arms hanging loosely at his sides. He felt like someone had punched him in the stomach and taken away his ability to breathe. He'd been on the verge of asking Amy to marry him, but she didn't want to hear it. Now it looked like that may never happen.

What should I do? Jared asked himself as he undid his horse and climbed in the buggy. *Should I accept her decision or try to make Amy change her mind?* Jared would never be happy without her, so he'd make every effort to say and do the right things. Maybe he would enlist the help of Amy's best friend, Lydia Petersheim. If she couldn't get through to his girlfriend, no one could.

Chapter 7

Clymer

Before Ezekiel headed out to work, he went to the phone shed to check for messages and make a few calls. One of them was to leave a message, asking Henry to give him a call.

Ezekiel had thought about writing Henry a letter but decided it would be best if he could talk to his brother man to man. A letter would be too impersonal, and he might not put down the right words or say something that could be taken wrong.

Ezekiel punched in his mother's number, and when the voice mail came on, he spoke the words he'd wanted to say. He ended his message by reminding Mom that if she needed him, he'd come home.

Ezekiel left the phone shed and headed off toward his shop. He enjoyed his work here so much, and it would be hard to go back to working in the greenhouse and making honey to sell, but he'd do it if it came to that.

Strasburg

Belinda entered their phone shed, and seeing a green light blinking, she clicked the button on their answering machine. She was pleased that the first message was from Ezekiel. She settled herself on the stool to listen.

"Hi, Mom. I'm calling to see how you're all doing, and also I'd like to talk to Henry. Would you please ask him to call me at noon today? I'll be sitting by the phone at that time, waiting to hear from him."

Belinda smiled. It was nice that Ezekiel was taking an interest in his younger brother. Henry needed to know that his brother cared about him, not to mention be exposed to Ezekiel's positive influence, which Henry was lacking right now. Belinda had little influence on her teenage son these days. She could also see that Amy spent more time butting heads with Henry than getting along. Belinda kept praying for her family because each of their lives needed the Lord's mending.

Soon, she found herself staring out the open door of the little shed toward a tree line on the property next door. Somehow the swaying of their branches on the breeze made her feel at ease. A few minutes passed, as she felt herself melt and relax in the quiet solitude, but just as suddenly, it was over when the telephone rang.

"*Ach!*" Belinda jumped. She drew in a deep breath to calm herself and picked up the receiver. A man who was obviously hard of hearing asked for the address of their business. It became a bit frustrating when she had to keep repeating herself. Belinda tried to be patient with him and felt relief when the conversation ended. She could only imagine what his family must go through each day, probably repeating a good deal of their dialog. Did he have hearing aids, or was he like Belinda's father, who had refused to admit his hearing was diminished or to have his hearing tested?

Belinda drew a sharp intake of breath. *Well, if the man does show up at the greenhouse, I shouldn't have a hard time picking him out.*

Most of the rest of the messages were from other prospective customers, asking questions about what was available in the greenhouse right now. A few of their family's friends had called to check on them, which was most appreciated. Dear Mary Ruth had been back a few times to offer her help wherever it was needed.

Belinda wrote down all the messages and stepped out of the small wooden building, already stuffy from the sun beating down with not much ventilation inside.

A crow cawed repeatedly from a tree in their yard as Belinda headed for the greenhouse.

She found Henry outside the building wearing his beekeeping gear. It hadn't been long since his brother had been the one out collecting honey. *Oh, how Henry reminds me of Abe in that getup.*

"Came to tell ya that I'm goin' out to check for honey," Henry mumbled. "Sure hope I don't cook in this outfit, since it's already heating up outside."

"You'll be okay. Your brother did all right wearing that gear, and you'll do the same. Oh, and before you go, I need to tell you something."

Henry stood with his legs slightly apart and one hand against his hip. "What do ya need me to do now?"

"Nothing at the moment, but there was a message from Ezekiel. He wants you to call him at noon."

"How come?"

"He'd like to talk to you."

"About what?"

"Your brother did not give any specifics—just asked you to call and said he'd be waiting in his phone shed at twelve o'clock."

"Okay, whatever." Henry turned and sauntered off in the direction of the beehives.

Belinda grasped the doorknob and stepped into the greenhouse. If things weren't too busy close to noon, she'd remind Henry to make the call.

Amy smiled when Mary Ruth came into the greenhouse with her granddaughter, Lenore. Lenore carried her two-month old son, Noah, in her arms, while Mary Ruth held the hand of Lenore's three-year-old stepdaughter, Cindy. Both children were adorable, and Amy felt a pang of regret. With all her responsibilities here, it was doubtful that she'd ever get married and have a family of her own.

"What can I do for you ladies?" she asked, trying not to stare at the dark-haired baby, sleeping contentedly in his mother's arms.

"We came by to see if you have any radish seeds," Lenore replied. "I planted some last month but would like to plant more."

"We'd also like some plants for ground cover if you have them." Mary Ruth smiled. "Lenore's husband, Jesse, created a few more flowerbeds in our yard the later part of March, so now they need to be filled with color."

"I'm sure we have some flowers and plants to your liking." Amy thought it was nice that Lenore's husband had been willing to move into Mary Ruth's house after he and Lenore got married. It gave them a place to call home that was big enough to raise a family, and it allowed Mary Ruth to remain in her home. Otherwise, she'd have felt the need to sell and move to Paradise to live with her son and his wife.

Amy led the way to the aisle where several multicolored ground covers sat in pots.

"These are so *schee*." Lenore pointed to a vivid pink plant.

"Jah." Mary Ruth gave a nod. "They are all quite pretty."

"I'll let you two do your choosing." Amy pulled a metal wagon over beside the women. "You can put whatever you decide on in here and pull it around until you're ready to check out at the counter."

"Danki." Mary Ruth placed a hand on Amy's shoulder. "When I was here the other day, I didn't get to talk to you much. Just wondering how you're holding up with all your responsibilities."

Amy couldn't hold back a sigh. "I have a lot more responsibility now, but so far, I'm managing."

"Your mamm really appreciates the way you've pitched in. She told me that when I was here."

"She's a good *mudder*, and there isn't anything I wouldn't do for her." *Including setting aside my plans for marriage.* Amy didn't voice her thoughts.

"I've known Belinda a good many years, and she's made plenty of sacrifices for her family. Guess it's her turn to be on the receiving end and accept help from you and your sister and brother."

Amy nodded. No way would she admit to Mary Ruth that Sylvia

could barely help herself, much less anyone else, or that Henry was being so difficult and hard to live with since the accident.

"We'll see you in a bit," the dear woman said.

Lenore laughed. "I'm sure by the time we're ready to check out, we'll have a whole wagon full of plants."

Amy smiled. As she moved back up the aisle, she overheard Marilyn Yoder, who was married to one of their ministers, talking to Mom at the counter.

"Say, I heard from Monroe Esh's sister the other day. She said he's bought a business in the area and plans to move back here soon. He's been away a long time, so it'll be kind of strange having him living here again."

"That's interesting." Mom continued to ring up Marilyn's purchases. "I'm sure his family is happy about that."

"I would think so." Marilyn spoke quietly but not so much that Amy couldn't hear what she said. "As I recall, Monroe left Lancaster County soon after you broke up with him."

Broke up with him? Amy had never heard her mother mention a man named Monroe Esh. She assumed Mom must have been courted by him before she met Dad.

She reached behind her back and tightened her apron ties. *Maybe someday when I'm Mom's age, I'll look back and think about Jared and how it was when we courted and had to break up. Only I may not be married to anyone by then. I may still be an old maid.*

Sometime later, when it was close to noon, Amy heard her mother remind Henry that he needed to go out to the phone shed and call Ezekiel.

"Jah, okay." With his shoulders curled forward, he slumped out the door.

Mom looked over at Amy and shook her head. "You'd think he'd be eager to talk to his bruder."

Amy swatted at an irksome fly. "My brother's not eager about anything these days."

Ezekiel stepped into the phone shed and took a seat. Hopefully, Henry had gotten his message and would call him on time. With all the work that needed to be done in his shop, he couldn't afford to sit here all day waiting. *Sure hope I can reason with my brother enough for him to change his negative attitude. This has to be wearing on my mother's and sisters' nerves.*

Since he'd been asked to speak to his brother, Ezekiel wanted to help fix this problem. He pulled his fingers through the back of his thick hair. *Henry is a lot like our daed—not too good with change.* Ezekiel's father was the last one to agree to the idea of replacing their old horse and letting the old gelding live out his days in the pasture. He wouldn't throw away his old straw hat either, no matter how much Mom had pestered him about it. She'd bought Dad a new one, but he still wore the old hat most of the time when around home or if he went fishing.

I sure miss you, Dad. Ezekiel let his head fall forward into his outstretched hands. *It's strange to be seeing so much of you in my little brother.*

There were moments, like now, when Ezekiel still wondered if he should pack up his family and go back to help Mom and the rest of the family. It was overwhelming to feel helpless and unsure of what to say to his brother. *Dad, if you were still alive, I wouldn't be faced with this matter right now. But you, Toby, and Abe were called home. Guess it was your time to leave us and join others who died in the faith.*

Ezekiel remained in thought for a while then closed his eyes and prayed for his family. He asked the Lord to give him the right words to say to Henry and that whatever was said on the phone today would help somehow. Even if it didn't go the way he hoped, Ezekiel would put his trust in the Lord. He had a lot on his mind and much to learn as a new minister. Ezekiel remembered how Mom had often stressed the importance of being patient and showing love to those who were hurting.

A few minutes later, the telephone rang. Ezekiel opened his eyes and picked up the receiver. "Hello."

"It's me, Henry."

"Hi, buddy. It's good to hear from you. How are you doing?" Ezekiel kept his tone on the cheerful side, although it was hard to be upbeat these days.

"My name ain't Buddy."

Ezekiel frowned. "Don't get *umgerennt*. It was only a figure of speech."

"Who says I'm upset, and why'd ya want me to call ya?"

"I wanted to see how things are going."

"You coulda called Mom and asked her that."

Ezekiel shifted the receiver to his other ear. "I wanted to talk to you and find out how you are getting along."

"How do ya think? Dad's gone; Abe's gone; and I'm stuck doin' all their chores." Henry's voice cracked. "I—I wouldn't mind doin' any amount of chores if they were here with me right now."

At least he is venting on me instead of Mom or one of our sisters. I'm certain that my brother needs to say it again and again, but how many more times will it be needed? This is agonizing for all of us. Ezekiel's eyes stung as he listened to the raw pain in his brother's voice. "I miss them too, Henry."

"Then you oughta be here with us to help us get through."

A deep sense of remorse settled over Ezekiel like a heavy blanket of fog. "I told Mom I'd move back to help out, but she wouldn't hear of it."

"Since when did you ever do what our mamm said? You ran around with Michelle when she was English, even though Mom didn't approve."

"That was different. I was in love with Michelle. And eventually, Mom and Dad came to love and accept her." Ezekiel didn't know why he felt the need to defend himself. This phone call wasn't about him—it was about Henry and his attitude.

"If things don't go well and Mom needs me, I won't hesitate to come back to Strasburg, even if it's not a permanent move."

"So, you'd just come for a visit and then go back to New York?"

"Jah, unless Mom decided she needed us there permanently."

Henry grunted. "Like that's ever gonna happen. She's got it in her head that she can make it without your help, which means I'll never have a life of my own."

"Sure you will, Henry. Someday Mom might get married again, and then. . ."

"She'd never do that. Mom loved Dad too much, and nobody could ever replace him." Ezekiel held the phone away from his ear. His brother was practically shouting.

"I don't believe you have to worry about anything like that happening anytime soon, if ever. The main thing is, you need to be supportive of her and help out wherever you can." When Henry didn't comment, Ezekiel added, "I'll be in touch again soon, and we can talk some more."

"Okay, sure, whatever. I've gotta go now, big brother. Mom's probably got lunch on the table." Before Ezekiel could say goodbye, Henry hung up.

Ezekiel rubbed his forehead and moaned. *Sure hope something I said got through to him. It's hard enough for Mom to deal with Dad and Abe's death without having to put up with my little brother's negative attitude and self-centeredness. It's not like he's the only one struggling with grief and unpredictable emotions right now. We all need to lean on God so we can get through this with a stronger faith and greater reliance on Him.*

Chapter 8

Strasburg

Jared had been so busy with roofing jobs, he hadn't found the time to visit Amy's friend and try to enlist her help. Since today was Saturday and his work week had come to an end, he was heading to see Lydia now.

"Sure hope she's willing to help me with this." Jared held tight to the reins as his horse picked up speed. "I can't let Amy go. I'll do whatever it takes to change her mind about breaking up with me."

When Jared turned up the driveway leading to the home of Lydia's parents, he spotted her sitting on the front porch with her mother. *Not good. I can't talk to Lydia about Amy in front of her mother. Darlene is a gossip. She's sure to repeat whatever is said to Amy or someone else.*

It was too late to turn his horse and buggy around; the women had seen him, and both had waved. He guided his horse to the hitching rail and climbed out of his rig. After securing the horse, Jared headed to the house and joined the women on the porch.

"Hello, Jared. It's nice to see you. Are you heading over to see Amy, or have you already been there?" Lydia tipped her head, and in doing so, a wisp of blond hair escaped her kapp.

"No, I...uh...haven't been over there for a few days." Jared shifted his weight and leaned against the porch railing.

"I'm surprised to hear that," Darlene spoke up. "Since you and Lydia's friend are courting, I figured you'd be over there every day. I'm sure with the recent death of her father and brother, Amy needs your support and probably some help with chores around the place."

Jared moistened his parched lips and moved away from the railing. "I have offered my help, and I was going over there often until Amy broke up with me." His teeth clenched so hard his jaw ached. *Now why'd I go and blurt that out in front of Lydia's mamm? By Monday, if not sooner, our whole community will know about the breakup.*

Lydia's eyes widened, and her lips parted slightly, but before she could comment, her mother spoke again. "Oh, my. . .I had no idea. What happened?"

Jared's fingers curled into the palms of his hands. He'd already said more than he should have. *How do I get out of this? Is it too late to ask if I can speak to Lydia alone?*

He cleared his throat a couple of times, and without answering Darlene's question, Jared looked at Lydia. "Could I speak to you alone for a few minutes?"

"Of course you may." Darlene jumped up. "I'll go in the house, and you can have my seat." She smiled at Jared. "It will give you two some time to talk, and then I'll bring out some millich and *kichlin.*"

"I appreciate the offer, but I won't be here long enough for milk and cookies. I have something I need to ask your daughter, and then I need to be on my way."

Darlene's shoulders slumped a bit, but her countenance brightened as a smile took over. "Maybe the next time you come calling you can stay long enough for a treat. For now though, I'll leave you two alone to talk."

Jared wasn't sure what the woman meant about the next time he came calling, but he simply nodded and sat in the chair beside Lydia.

She looked over at him with wrinkled brows. "Did Amy really break things off with you, or was it the other way around?"

"She broke up with me." He heaved a heavy sigh. "With all her responsibilities at the greenhouse, plus trying to cope with her father, brother, and brother-in-law's deaths, while offering support to her mother and siblings, Amy said she has no time for courting."

"But she will someday, right?" Lydia looked steadily at Jared.

He shrugged. "I don't know. She wants me to move on without her."

"I'm so sorry, Jared." Lydia placed her hand on his arm and gave it a few gentle pats. Her sympathy made him choke up.

"I came over here to see if you'd be willing to have a talk with Amy—try to make her see that she doesn't need to end our relationship. I realize she won't have time for social events and long buggy rides, but I'm more than willing to court her by simply going over to the house and helping out wherever I'm needed. Eventually things should get better for Amy and her family, and then we can start doing some fun things together again."

"But your job keeps you so busy. Would you have time to do extra chores over there?"

"I'll make the time." He leaned over slightly with both hands on his knees. "I would do most anything for the woman I love."

"Jah, I'm sure of that."

"So would you speak to Amy on my behalf—make her see that, despite the trial she and her family are facing right now, we can have a future together?"

Lydia slowly nodded. "I can't promise how Amy will respond, but I'll do my best to get through to her. In fact, I'll go over there on Monday."

"Danki." He rose from his chair. "I'll come by again sometime next week and see how things went."

"Keep the faith, Jared. Keep the faith," Lydia called as he stepped off the porch.

"I will." Jared turned and looked over his shoulder as a sense of hope welled in his soul. Amy and Lydia had been close friends since they were children. Surely Amy would listen to her.

"Hey, Daughter, could you please give me a hand? I'm losing my grip here." Mom nearly dropped the load in her hands.

Amy intercepted her mother carrying two large flowering plants. Then she set them down on a table that was nearby.

"Danki. Guess I shouldn't have tried to carry both plants at once, but I was too impatient and didn't want to make two trips." Mom massaged one arm and then the other before pointing to a large sealed cardboard box setting on the floor.

"What's in there?" Amy asked.

"You remember I ordered those shallow hanging pots awhile back. Well, they finally showed up, and we're going to arrange each one with starter plants to sell."

"Okay, but I'm not the best at arranging different flowers that are intended to go into baskets that hang."

"I'll see if I can talk Sylvia into coming out to the greenhouse for a little while and putting some together for us. Of course, it means I will need to go in and watch the kinner while she's in here."

"Do you think my sister will be up for it?"

"I'm hoping she might like to get out of the house and do something creative with these baskets." Mom gestured to the box again.

"Hanging baskets are a nice and easy way to spruce up a spot around the outside of one's house—maybe hanging from a porch or on a shepherd's hook in the yard."

"Jah, and the fuchsia starts are also ready to plant, so those will make a nice addition. We have a few different color variances, and of course some other flowers that can be included in the baskets." Mom smiled. "You know, Sylvia enjoyed doing this kind of work in the past. I'm hoping this idea might draw her out. It's not good to stay in the house so much of the time."

Amy touched one of the lovely plants. "I've always thought fuchsias look so pretty in full bloom—especially the red ones."

"They seem to be a favorite with folks to dress up a front porch or deck. A lot of customers like to give hanging baskets as gifts for different occasions."

"I agree. As summer continues, we'll probably sell out our supply like we did last year."

Mom nodded and stood there quietly for a moment as though in thought. "You know what I'd like to make for supper soon?"

"What?"

"Stuffed cabbage rolls."

"Those do sound good. We haven't had them in a while."

"They were one of your daed's favorite meals, and he liked creamy mashed potatoes to go with them." Mom rubbed a spot on her apron where a blob of dirt had attached itself. "Maybe we could invite our bishop and his wife for supper one night."

"That would be nice but also a lot of work. I'm not sure either of us would have time for that, and it's doubtful Sylvia would feel up to having company for a meal." Amy leaned against the stacked bags full of potting soil.

"You're probably right." Mom touched Amy's arm. "You could invite Jared, though. That would be only one extra person at our table."

Amy remained silent. *I was hoping this topic wouldn't come up so soon. Guess it was only a matter of time until Mom mentioned him.*

"It's strange, you know, but Jared hasn't been around lately." Mom reached under her head covering and pushed an errant piece of her mostly brown hair back in place. "I wonder if his workload has him tied down."

Mom gave Amy's arm a little nudge. "Daughter, did you hear what I said?"

"Jah." Amy tilted her head from side to side, weighing her choices. She could either go along with what Mom said about Jared working long hours or tell her the truth. She opted for the latter, figuring she may as well get it over with before someone else came into the greenhouse and blurted it out. No doubt Jared had at least told his parents by now.

"Jared won't be coming over to see me any longer." Amy lowered her gaze.

"How come?"

"When he was here for supper the last time, I told him we wouldn't be courting anymore." She lifted her head to see Mom's reaction.

Her mother's dark brows shot up. "For goodness' sakes, Amy, why would you do that?"

"Because with all my responsibilities here, I don't have time to be courted by anyone now."

"That's nonsense. You should make time for something as important as spending time with the man you love."

Amy shook her head determinedly. "Our days are long here in the greenhouse, not to mention all my other chores in the house. If Sylvia was up to helping more it might be different, but under the circumstances. . . Well, it's just better this way."

"Better for who?"

"For Jared. He deserves the chance to be happy. He's a wonderful man, and I'm sure it won't take him long to find a more suitable wife."

"But Jared loves you. I've seen his expression when the two of you are together, and I've heard the tender words he's spoken to you." Mom clasped Amy's arm. "Don't throw your chance at happiness away because of your duties here. Things won't always be so hectic, and there has to be a way for you and Jared to work things out."

"There isn't, and my mind's made up." Amy pushed up her dress sleeves. "Now, please, let's not talk about this anymore. There's work to be done."

Sylvia's head throbbed as she struggled to diaper the baby. Allen sat on the floor not far away, beating on a kettle he'd found in one of the kitchen's lower cupboards and dragged into the living room, where a portable crib had been set up.

The baby howled and kicked her chubby feet, making Sylvia's chore even more difficult while increasing the pain in her head. Every chore, no matter how simple, seemed insurmountable. She couldn't fathom how Mom and Amy managed to work in the greenhouse six days a week, dealing with customers and making sure everything from the watering system to proper ventilation worked as it should.

Don't think I could last even an hour out there, she told herself. *I'd cave in if one person even looked at me and asked how I was doing.*

Sylvia set the baby lotion back on the stand with the diaper wipes. She wanted to lie down on the bed and close her eyes. *If I could only get in a nap somehow, maybe that would lessen the pain in my head.*

Now that the diapering was done, Sylvia picked her daughter up and carried her to the rocking chair. She paused and looked back at her bedroom door. *Why does my head have to hurt like this? I've got household chores as well as my kinner to take care of, and I'm barely able to cope.*

Taking a seat, she got it moving at a steady pace. The only time she felt a moment's peace was when she sat here with her eyes closed, holding her precious child. Rachel burrowed her head against Sylvia's shoulder, as if trying to get comfortable. Sylvia patted the baby's back. *Too bad your daadi will never hold you again.*

Thoughts of Toby were never far from Sylvia's mind, which only added to her depression. She had a recurring dream about him that happened again last night. Toby was home with her and the children like he'd never left. It had seemed so real until she'd awakened to Rachel's crying. Sylvia wished she could simply will herself to stop hurting, but it was impossible.

She'd gone back to her own home only once since Toby's death to get more clothes for her and the children as well as some of Allen's favorite toys. When she'd entered the bedroom she used to share with her husband, Sylvia had thrown herself on the bed and sobbed for hours. She didn't think she'd ever be able to move back there, but she didn't have the energy to begin thinking about all that was necessary to sell the house. How thankful she was that Mom didn't mind having her and the little ones living here. At this point, Sylvia didn't think she'd ever be able to leave.

She opened her eyes and glanced across the room. Her gaze came to rest on the coffee table, where her father's Bible lay. *Dad was a good Christian man, and so were Toby and Abe. Why would God take them from us when we needed them so?*

Allen began pounding on the kettle even harder, until she thought she would scream. How was she supposed to be a kind, patient mother when she needed mothering of her own? Sylvia wished she was a little girl again, cradled in the safety of her mother's arms.

Rachel squirmed as the noise continued. *I can't let Allen keep making that racket. His sister will never be able to sleep, and my nerves need a break.*

Sylvia rose with the baby and placed her in the crib, and then she sauntered into the kitchen to get her son something to drink. She returned shortly and removed the noisemakers, replacing them with a sippy cup full of diluted grape juice. The room fell silent while Allen sipped his beverage and his baby sister's eyelids closed in slumber.

Sylvia felt like she'd won this battle as she took a seat in the chair again. Releasing a lingering breath, she felt the same awful feeling creep back into her soul. *Toby. . .Toby. . .I miss you more than I ever thought possible. It grieves me to know that our sweet children will grow up without you.*

She swallowed hard, trying to push down the lump that had formed in her throat. *It's best that none of us can look into the future and see what's coming. If I'd known that after only a few years of marriage, I would lose my husband, I'd never have gotten married at all.*

Chapter 9

Monday morning, Belinda had begun drying the breakfast dishes when she saw Amy sprinting across the yard. A few minutes later, she dashed into the kitchen with a reddened face and eyes wide. "What's wrong, Daughter? You look umgerennt."

"I am quite upset, and you will be too when you hear what I found."

"What was it?" Belinda placed the dish towel on the counter.

"I went out to the barn to remind Henry about the deliveries he has to make to Sara's flower shop today." Amy paused and wiped a trickle of sweat off her forehead. "On my way back to the house, I noticed water seeping out of the potting shed. So, I went inside to see where it was coming from and discovered a broken pipe. Water was leaking out everywhere."

Belinda put a hand to her mouth. "Oh dear. Were you able to get the valve turned off that supplies water to the shed and greenhouse?"

Amy shook her head. "Not by myself. I ran back to the barn to get Henry. He's out there now, looking for one of Dad's wrenches."

"They're in the toolshed." Belinda frowned. "He ought to know that."

"I'll run out and tell him." Amy turned and rushed out the door.

Belinda stood at the window, watching her daughter enter the barn. A few minutes later, Amy and Henry emerged and headed for the toolshed.

Belinda drew a deep breath to calm herself. They couldn't be without water in either the greenhouse or the potting shed, and she didn't like the idea of spending money to have the pipe repaired or replaced, but there was no other choice. They had to take care of the problem, no matter what it cost.

Belinda put her head down. "I'm trying the best I can to hold things together, but it's ever so hard."

"What was that, Mom?" Sylvia spoke quietly as she came into the room.

"Oh, I'm just fretting out loud. We have a water leak in the potting shed that needs to be dealt with right away. Your brother went out to the toolshed for a wrench so he can shut off the water. Amy is with him."

"That's sure not what we need." Sylvia sucked in her bottom lip. "I don't know how you three manage to endure all of this."

"When problems arise it's not fun, but we have to expect that things don't always go as we would like them to." Belinda looked toward the doorway. "I assume my sweet grandchildren are resting?"

"Jah." Sylvia yawned. "Is there anything you need me to do right now?"

"I'll need the phone book to find a number to call a plumber."

"No problem. I'll get the spare one sitting on Dad's desk." Sylvia left the kitchen and returned almost immediately with the phone book.

"Danki." Belinda began turning the pages. "Here we go. I've found the page I need, and it looks like your daed circled the one he liked to use. What a blessing this is. I wouldn't have known who to call."

"Sure hope you can get someone out here soon. You need water for all the plants that are for sale in the greenhouse."

"How well I know. We sure don't want to lose any of our flowers and other items in stock." Belinda reached for a pen and paper then jotted down the phone number. She hoped they would get prompt service so things could move forward.

"I'll be back soon." Setting the pen down and getting up from the kitchen chair, she went outside and began the trek to the phone shed.

Plodding along, her mind drifted to her dear husband. *Oh Vernon, I never had to worry about such things when you were here. You always kept our business running so smoothly. I'm juggling what I used to do with all of the new responsibilities you cared for in the past.* Her vision blurred. *If you were here right now, you'd tell me: "Belinda, I've got this covered. I'll have it fixed in no time at all."* She wiped at the tears dribbling down her cheeks.

When Belinda reached the phone shed, she opened the door and stepped inside. The blinking light on the answering machine flashed, but she had something more important to do before she would check messages. Belinda wiped her eyes and tried to calm down. She grabbed the slip of paper with the number on it and dialed the plumber. The phone rang a few times until a man answered: "Hello. Bailey's Plumbing. How can I help you?"

Once Belinda explained what had happened, the man said he could be out in an hour or so. She hung up, relieved that they'd soon have the problem fixed.

Belinda listened to the messages then. The first one turned out to be from Jared. "Hi, Amy, it's me." His voice sounded strained. "I wanted to let you know that I'd still like to remain friends. And if there's anything I can do for you or your family, don't hesitate to let me know." There was a pause, and then he hung up. By the tone of his voice, Belinda knew the man had been terribly hurt by Amy's rejection. She rubbed her temples. "Oh Amy, I wish you'd reconsider your decision to cut Jared out of your life. You're being so foolish, Daughter. Can't you see that?" She closed her eyes as more tears came. *Heavenly Father, my family is in need of Your help. I'm struggling to hold things together, and I need Your wisdom and guidance with everything.*

"You do realize this is only the beginning of our problems, don't ya?" From his kneeling position in the potting shed, Henry looked up at Amy and scowled.

"You're being negative, little brother. Something like this may never happen again."

"Yeah, right." He cranked on the wrench until the water shut off. "These old buildings have been around for a while, and there's no telling what else might go wrong."

"Well, if it does, we'll take care of it. Also, with your negative attitude, you're not helping things around here. Our mamm doesn't need this extra stress right now."

Henry stood. "Well, I've got the perfect solution to that."

"Oh? And what would that be?"

"Mom oughta close the greenhouse, and we can all get other jobs doing something we like."

"Mom enjoys working here, and so do I."

"Are you sure about that, Sister?"

She nodded.

"Yeah, well, Sylvia doesn't want to work here, and neither do I."

Her brother's caustic tone caused Amy to bristle. "You know perfectly well why Sylvia isn't helping in the greenhouse right now, and it has nothing to do with whether she likes it or not."

"I bet she feels guilty 'cause the three of us are doin' all the work."

"I can't say for sure if she does or not, but emotionally and physically, our sister is not up to helping, so we need to do the best that we can."

Henry glared at Amy as he stood with folded arms. "I hate working here—hate everything about my life right now."

The anger he obviously felt lingered in his eyes as he stared hard at her. That look frightened Amy, and she clenched her fingers. It was all she could do to keep from giving her brother a strong lecture. But what good would it do? She'd already tried to talk to him about his attitude, and according to Mom, so had Ezekiel. If Henry wouldn't listen to their big brother, he sure wouldn't listen to her. Even so, she felt compelled to say one more thing.

Her brother crouched again, putting a hand at the area where the pipe leaked. With his less defensive form, it gave Amy the opportunity she needed to say what else was on her mind.

"Hate is a strong word, Henry, and whether you like working here or not, you are able-bodied and part of this family." She pointed at him. "Your duty is to help out, so please, stop complaining." Amy swung her body around and tromped out of the potting shed. *Doesn't my brother realize his uncooperative, angry attitude is only making things worse?*

A plumber came shortly after noon and replaced the broken pipe. The man showed Henry another pipe that could likely give them issues in the future and said they should keep an eye on it.

Amy's brother seemed disinterested in what the repairman had to say, which to Amy was not a surprise. She watched in irritation as Henry rolled his eyes after the plumber turned his back and picked up his tools. *My brother sure is disapproving. Why can't he snap out of this?*

Amy chose to step outside for some cooler air, putting some space between herself and Henry. *If Dad could see this side of Henry, he'd give him a stern lecture.* She picked at a hangnail on her thumb. *Henry is so off-putting these days. If he doesn't shape up, he will never find a girlfriend when he reaches courting age. Of course, like me, he probably won't have time for courting.*

Amy looked up when the potting shed door opened. "I'll send you a bill," the plumber said before getting into his work van.

He'd just pulled out when Amy's friend Lydia showed up. The cheerful smile on her pretty face as she came toward Amy was a welcome contrast to Henry's unpleasant frown. *I wish it were possible to trade Henry for Lydia right now.*

"Do you have some time to talk?" her friend asked, stepping up to Amy.

"Maybe a few minutes. Mom's at the house checking on Sylvia and the kinner, so I'm by myself until she comes back—which won't be till she's fixed herself a bite to eat."

"There's only one person browsing around right now, and I doubt she's here to buy anything. I think I saw her walking along the road toward town about a week ago." Lydia gestured to the stringy-haired elderly English woman wearing a tattered dress and a faded pair of sneakers that looked like they should have been thrown away months ago. "I believe she resides in that abandoned old shack about a mile from here."

"It's so sad. That poor woman comes in here at least once a week," Amy whispered. "She never buys anything—just looks at all the pretty flowers and sometimes comments on how nice they smell." Her voice lowered even more. "I think she might not have a real home of her own and maybe no family either."

"That's a shame." Lydia turned her head as though unable to look at the woman anymore. "I can't imagine how it must be for people who have no place to go or money to buy things."

Amy nodded. She too felt sorry for the woman who had never given them her last name. Just said one time when they'd asked that her name was Maude. "Mom sometimes brings out a sandwich or some apple slices and cheese to share with the poor lady."

"That's very kind of her; it's the charitable thing to do. I have a few extra dollars on me. Maybe I'll buy a couple of those flowers from the table she's looking at and give them to her."

"Are you sure you want to do that?"

"Your mamm has been nice to her, and I'd like to do the same." Lydia handed Amy the money and headed over to the table where the woman looked intently at the petunias.

Amy watched as the bedraggled lady brushed aside a strand of gray hair and then touching the red flower, she glanced at Lydia.

"These are sure pretty, aren't they?"

"Yeah." The old woman moved on but didn't look at the plants anymore before she ambled toward the exit.

Amy saw Lydia pick out two of the red petunias and walk up behind the elderly woman. "Ma'am, I want you to have these."

The woman's brows furrowed. "Are. . .are you sure?"

"Yes. I've already paid for them."

A faint smile formed on the woman's face. "Thank you."

"You're welcome. Have a good day," Lydia called as the lady ambled out the door with the flowers.

"She looked happy. That was a nice act of kindness." Amy moved to the other side of the counter and motioned for Lydia to join her. "Did you come by for anything specific or just to chat?"

"I came here to see how you all are doing, and—"

"It's difficult, but we're getting by and keeping plenty busy."

"Is Sylvia doing any better?"

Amy shook her head. "She's still too distraught to work in the greenhouse. It's all she can do to take care of Allen and the boppli."

"That's too bad. If she could help out here, it might take her mind off her situation and help relieve some of the depression she feels."

Amy nodded. "Keeping busy has helped my mamm and me from falling apart. By the time we're done for the day, we are both so tired, we just fall into bed at night in dire need of sleep." Amy's forehead wrinkled as she slumped on the stool. "Of course, we still have plenty of moments when we give in to our tears."

Lydia gave Amy's shoulder a comforting squeeze. "I heard about you breaking up with Jared."

Wouldn't you know it? Amy's muscles tightened as she sat up straight on the stool. "Who told you?"

"He did. Came by my house the other day and asked if I would talk to you."

"Really?"

"Jah. He wanted me to speak on his behalf and try to convince you to let him continue courting you."

Amy's jaw clenched as she picked up a pencil and tapped it against the counter. "He had no right to do that."

"Jared loves you, Amy."

"I care about him too, but it's not going to work out for us." She made a sweeping gesture with her hand. "I am responsible for a good many things here and will be for a very long time."

"Is there any reason Jared can't share in your responsibilities?"

"Jah, he has his own business to run, and I could never ask him to give up what he enjoys doing to help run the greenhouse." Amy shook her head. "I don't have time for courting anymore. So, when you see Jared again, please tell him for me that he may as well accept the fact that our relationship is over."

Lydia looked at Amy with a pinched, tension-filled expression. "I'll give him your message, but I think you'll end up regretting that decision."

"I probably will, but I have no choice in the matter." Amy turned her attention to the door when a group of English people entered the greenhouse. "Please excuse me, Lydia, but I need to see if my customers need any assistance."

"Of course. Take care, my dear friend. I hope to see you again soon." Lydia hurried out of the building, and Amy set her mind on business and hopefully making at least one sale.

Chapter 10

Two more weeks went by, and soon it was the last Monday of June. Every day seemed to blend into the next. Amy had gotten into the routine and did her best to keep things running smoothly. She'd been happy a week ago when Mom talked Sylvia into helping them out. Amy had hoped her sister would come to the greenhouse to fill the hanging baskets, but Sylvia had been adamant about not having to speak to the public or be around too many people at once. Mom had been considerate and asked Henry and Amy to bring the baskets and needed supplies over to the house, where Sylvia could arrange them.

With Michelle's baby due in three weeks, Amy hoped Sylvia would be up to helping in the greenhouse so Mom could go to Ezekiel and Michelle's home in New York to help for a few weeks. Ezekiel had been so busy, and Michelle's back bothered her, so they hadn't made a trip to Strasburg since their stay after the funerals. They both called often though to see how everyone was doing. Mom always returned their calls, and Amy was sure nothing was ever said to give Ezekiel the impression that things weren't going well. She knew without question that her mother wanted to be independent and did not want Ezekiel to give up his new life and ministry in Clymer.

As Amy headed down the driveway to get the mail Monday morning, she saw a moving van parked in the driveway at the home across the road. Apparently, someone had bought the house. It would be nice to have new neighbors. The home had been sitting empty too long.

She kept watching as a middle-aged English couple got out of the older-model car parked behind the moving van. Amy was pretty sure the tall man was the same person she'd seen with the Realtor a few weeks ago. The woman appeared to be at least a foot shorter than he was. Her red hair was styled in a short cut, and she walked with a slight limp. They stood on the overgrown lawn, talking with the two men who'd gotten out of the van, and then they all went inside the house.

Amy glanced at the area out front, where the FOR SALE sign used to be, and noticed that it had been taken down. *I wonder if it's just the two of them moving into the house, or if there are other family members joining them.* They looked too old to have young children, but she supposed they could still have teenagers or college-age children who might live at home.

Well, it's none of my business, and I need to get back to the greenhouse before customers start coming in.

Remembering the reason she'd walked down the driveway, Amy opened the mailbox and removed a stack of envelopes. Thumbing through them quickly, she saw that most were advertisements, with just a few bills.

"That's good," Amy said aloud as she headed back up the driveway. The bill from the plumber they'd hired to fix the broken pipe had been high enough, and they didn't need any other large bills to pay right now.

"Are you sure you can handle things while I'm gone?" Belinda asked Amy at two o'clock. "My dental appointment is in half an hour, and afterward I want to go to the bank and stop by the grocery store. My driver should be here soon, but I wanted to make sure you're okay with me being gone that long."

"It's fine, Mom." Amy, although she looked tired, offered Belinda a smile. "I've already alerted Henry to the fact that I'll most likely need his help in here."

Belinda gave her daughter's arm a tender squeeze. Henry had become so moody, and Sylvia was still despondent. It was a comfort to be able to count on Amy.

The crunch of gravel could be heard outside the greenhouse, followed by the tooting of a horn.

"That must be my driver, Sandy." Belinda gave Amy a hug. "I'll see you in a few hours and will be praying that all goes well here for the remaining hours you are open."

"Danki, Mom. I'm sure everything will go fine, and I hope things go well at your dental appointment."

Belinda gave a nod, grabbed her purse from behind the counter, and hurried out the door.

Things became busy that afternoon, and Amy felt thankful for Henry's help, even though he walked around with a scowl on his face. Hopefully, none of their customers had noticed.

Amy looked toward the door when some English people came in and headed over to the area where a few gift items were located. It wasn't uncommon for tourists to check out the items for sale in the Amish-run greenhouse. Before Amy's father died, her parents had decided to carry some lawn decor, such as solar-lighted animal figurines, garden signs, wind chimes, and a few small fountains and birdbaths. All those things helped bring in more income.

While the place became busier, Amy found herself needing to leave the register more often to assist a couple patrons, but she didn't feel right doing that. A gray-haired man approached her and reached into his pocket to retrieve a slip of paper. Then he asked Amy for some help finding a certain plant. Amy assumed he must be hard of hearing because she had to repeat herself a lot. She glanced back at the checkout counter and saw a line of people beginning to form. Seeing her brother on one side of the greenhouse, she called: "Henry, could you please come over here?"

He took his sweet time and sauntered up to her with a disgruntled expression. "What do ya need?"

"This gentleman here needs some help, and as you can see, I should be up at the register where customers are waiting for assistance."

Henry looked around. "Where's Mom? Why isn't she helping people up there?"

"She went to the dentist, remember?"

"Oh, yeah, that's right." Henry motioned for the man to follow him down the aisle, while Amy made her way back to the counter. She hoped her brother wouldn't be too upset with her when he discovered that the man she'd asked him to wait on had trouble hearing.

Pulling her attention back to the immediate need, Amy smiled at the woman who'd picked out two sets of wind chimes. She wrapped each one in bubble wrap and placed them in a box. Amy hadn't expected things to be so busy while Mom was away, but at least with Henry's help, they'd managed so far.

She'd finished waiting on the woman when a tall, beardless Amish man entered the greenhouse and approached the counter. She didn't recognize him and figured he must be from a neighboring community.

He smiled and removed his straw hat, revealing a thick crop of brown hair with a few touches of gray here and there. "Hello." He extended his hand. "My name is Monroe Esh, and I was told that Belinda King owns this greenhouse."

Amy reached out a hand tentatively and shook his large hand. "Jah, Belinda is my mamm." She hoped he wasn't here to try and sell them something.

"Is she here?" Monroe glanced around as though expecting Amy to point out her mother among some of the Amish women looking at the plants.

"No, she's in town right now."

"Aw, I see. Do you know what time she'll be back? I'd like to talk to her."

"No, I don't. She probably won't return for a while yet."

"I see." His lips pressed tight into a grimace.

"Can I give my mother a message, or is there something I can help you with?"

"No message." He looked at Amy with a strange expression. "You remind me of Belinda when she was about your age—same color hair, same pretty face."

Amy's cheeks warmed as she looked up at him. "Did you know my mamm when she was my age?"

He gave a quick nod. "I not only knew her, but we were a courting couple. At least we were up until Vernon King came along and stole her from me." His brown eyes darkened further, and a muscle on the side of his neck quivered. "She ended up marrying him, and when that happened, I quit my job and left the area."

Unsure of what to say and unable to hold the man's steady gaze, Amy lowered her head to look at the floor.

"I heard about Vernon's passing, and I'd like to offer my condolences. Would you please tell Belinda I came by and that I'll return in a few days to see how she's doing?"

Amy lifted her head. "I will give her your message."

"Danki." He plopped his hat back on his head and strolled out the door.

Amy sank to the stool as an uncomfortable feeling settled over her. The fact that Monroe was clean-shaven meant he was obviously not married. She hoped he didn't have any ideas about getting back with her mother. It was way too soon for Mom to even be thinking of remarriage, and for that matter, Amy felt sure her mother would never get married again. The love she had for Amy's father went deep, and Amy felt certain that Mom would never love another man the way she had Dad.

Jared had only been home from work a short time when a horse and open buggy pulled into the yard. He walked out to the hitching rail as Lydia pulled up to it, and then he secured her chestnut-colored horse.

"I spoke to Amy on your behalf, and I'm sorry for not coming by sooner, but my parents and I had to go out of town due to a death in my dad's family."

"Sorry to hear that. Was it someone you were close to?" Jared asked.

"It was my great-aunt Matilda. She lived in Tennessee, but I didn't know her well. Even so, I wanted to attend the funeral in support of my daed."

"I understand." Jared waited until Lydia stepped down from the buggy. "So, what did Amy have to say when you spoke to her?"

Lydia slowly shook her head. "I'm sorry, Jared, but she wouldn't change her mind about the two of you courting."

He bent his head forward, releasing a heavy sigh. This was not the news he had hoped for. If Lydia couldn't get through to Amy, then what chance did he have?

"Danki for trying," Jared mumbled. "Guess I'll have to accept Amy's decision—at least for now."

Lydia patted his arm. "Maybe in a few months she will change her mind."

Jared wanted to believe Amy's friend, but he had a sick feeling in the pit of his stomach. As much as he hated to admit it, no matter how many times he went over and tried to talk Amy into letting him court her, her answer might always be no.

That evening, while Amy and Belinda fixed supper, Amy brought up a subject that sent a ripple of shock through Belinda.

"A man named Monroe Esh came by to see you this afternoon, Mom. He seemed disappointed that you weren't here and said he'd be back in a few days to talk to you."

A flush of heat erupted on Belinda's cheeks as she touched her parted lips. "I. . .I heard he was moving back here, but I had no idea he'd come to our place to see me. Did he say what he wanted to talk to me about?"

"Said he'd heard about Dad's passing and wanted to offer his condolences." Amy reached into the refrigerator for a slab of bacon. Tonight they'd decided to keep supper simple by fixing BLTs. "Monroe seemed eager to see you, and he looked disappointed when I told him you weren't here."

"I see."

"Monroe also mentioned that he used to court you. Is that true, Mom?"

Belinda nodded slowly, and her thoughts wandered as she leaned against the counter. She hadn't thought about it for a long time, but hearing that Monroe had been here took her mind back to the day she'd broken things off with him. She could still visualize his look of rejection when she'd informed him that she thought of him only as a friend and had agreed to be courted by Vernon. Monroe's eyes had appeared so dark and serious, and there'd been a grim twist to his mouth. "If you felt no love for me, Belinda, it was wrong to lead me on," he'd muttered.

Did I lead Monroe on? Belinda asked herself now. *During the brief time he'd courted me, did I give the impression that I'd fallen in love with him? If so, I hadn't meant to. I just assumed Monroe knew I wasn't serious about him.*

Pushing her memories aside, Belinda took out a loaf of bread and removed the plastic wrapping around it. *What will I say to Monroe if he does come back to the greenhouse to speak to me? I hope he's not harboring ill feelings.*

Chapter 11

When Virginia Martin woke up the following day, her whole body ached. She wished she knew of a good massage therapist in the area and could get in with them today. Virginia had overdone it by trying to move some of the boxes the movers had set in the wrong spots. Earl had caught her trying to move one of them and took it to the place she wanted in the dining room. With the exception of a quick trip to the grocery store yesterday before the movers arrived, she and Earl had spent most of the day unpacking boxes and putting things away. By the time they were ready for bed last night, she'd barely had the strength to put sheets on the bed. Fortunately, her husband didn't have to start his new job until tomorrow, which gave them today to do more unpacking. Virginia couldn't wait to be settled in—it sure was a draining process. She wanted to have everything where it needed to be.

Right now though, as Virginia sat on the front porch with a cup of coffee in her hand, all she wanted to do was relax. Her gaze trailed to the overgrown yard of their new residence, desperately in need of being cut. She could see that the previous owners had fallen behind on a good many things around the place. Either that or the place had sat empty too long.

Virginia sipped on her steaming beverage. *Too bad I couldn't get all the work done by simply snapping my fingers.*

One idea she'd been kicking around in her head since they'd

moved here was having a garden. With the amount of property they now owned, it was a no-brainer. Virginia had only grown a few tomato plants in a pot and some herbs in smaller containers when she and Earl had lived in the city. The idea of a full-blown plot of land growing an edible array of food seemed inviting. Maybe Earl could rent a tiller, and they could purchase some seeds or plants to get started.

It was so quiet here in the country. Virginia was used to city sights, noises, and odors. Birds chirping, cows mooing, and the smell of new-mown hay would take some getting used to.

Maybe it's a good thing, she mused. *I could use some relaxing days and quiet times in my life.* Being married to Earl for the last three years had brought many changes for Virginia, and this move was yet another one. Her husband had given hints of discontent about living in the big city, sometimes mentioning the growing traffic and the huge number of people in Chicago.

Virginia could see Earl gravitating to the country life. He'd even mentioned wanting to take up fishing. She figured he'd put a lot of thought into what he wanted to get out of this move. He said the change of pace and country living might do them both some good and could even add a few more years to their lives.

Virginia wrinkled her nose. *Now that I doubt.*

At the sound of a steady *clippity-clop, clippity-clop,* she glanced up the road. Here came not one but two horses and buggies. They slowed down and turned up the driveway leading to the house across from them. Or maybe it was the building on the left side of their property where those people were headed.

She craned her neck a bit and continued to watch. Sure enough, the rigs headed to the parking lot where the greenhouse stood.

"I hope there's not a steady traffic of buggies or cars all day," Virginia muttered.

"Were you speaking to me?" Earl asked, joining her on the porch.

"No, I was talking to myself." Virginia pointed across the road. "It's only 9 a.m. and there's buggy traffic." She looked up at him and scowled. "You never told me we'd be living in Amish country."

Earl lowered himself into the chair beside her. "Didn't think I had to say anything. Figured you knew there were Amish communities in Lancaster County."

She folded her arms and grunted. "Now how would I know that? I'm no expert on the Amish or where they live."

"For crying out loud, Virginia, information about the Amish is everywhere these days—in the paper, on TV, and even bookshelves in places like Walmart and Sam's Club."

"Doesn't mean I knew they'd be here where you bought this house without me even seeing it."

"Let's not go down that road again. You were sick with the flu when I came to Lancaster to interview for the job at the car dealership, and after I called and told you I'd gotten the position and wanted to look at some houses in the country, you said you would trust my judgment."

"You're right. Just didn't realize you'd end up picking a home way out in the boonies or that there'd be a place of business so close to us." Virginia pulled her fingers through the strands of her slightly damp hair. She'd been so tired when they went to bed last night that she hadn't bothered taking a shower until this morning.

"Now don't forget, I took plenty of pictures of this house." He reached into his pants pocket and pulled out his cell phone.

"Yeah, but those were of the inside of the house, not what we would see from our yard."

He shrugged. "Didn't think it was that important."

"It is to me." She gestured to another Amish buggy approaching. "I don't care for the road this house is on. With that greenhouse across from us, there's bound to be steady traffic most of the day."

"So what? You're used to all that traffic we had in Chicago."

"Yeah, but this is different. Instead of horns honking and exhaust fumes from cars, trucks, and buses, we now have to put up with smelly horses and the irritating sound of their feet clomping along the pavement." She stood up and pointed to the road. "And just look at all those ruts out there—no doubt from the buggy wheels."

"You'll get used to it, just like you did when we first moved to Chicago."

"I doubt it." She lifted her gaze toward the sky. "If I'd come here and seen the place before you signed your name on the dotted line, I would have told you I'm not a country kind of gal."

Earl said nothing. All Virginia heard was the slamming of the screen door.

She flopped back into her chair. *Earl doesn't understand my needs any more than my first husband did.* She sat for a while, watching the goings-on at her Amish neighbors' property.

Yesterday, after she and Earl had gone to buy a used pickup at the place where he'd be working, Virginia had planted herself at the living-room window and observed the quaint way those Amish people dressed—so old-fashioned. She hadn't seen any men around though—just a lanky-looking teenage boy and two women. She'd noticed one of them watering some flowerbeds in the yard. *Surely there's a man about the place, especially with a business on that property to run and all the outbuildings to keep up.*

She stood for another moment and then retreated inside to put her empty cup in the sink. *I'm not sure about those Amish across the street. They seem so odd and unconventional.*

🐦

"Would you like a second cup of *kaffi*, Son?" Jared's mother moved toward him with the coffeepot in her hand.

He shook his head and grabbed his lunch pail from the counter. "I don't have time for more coffee, Mom. I'm already running behind this morning and need to get out the door and head to my first job. By the time I get there, my newest employee, Sam, will probably be up on the roof of the grocery store that hired us, tearing off the old shingles."

"Can't you spare a few minutes to talk to your mamm? There's something I want to discuss with you."

"Can't it wait till this evening?"

"It could, but if your daed's around, which I'm sure he will be, he'll probably accuse me of *neimische*."

Then maybe you shouldn't say it, because if Dad thinks you're meddling, no doubt I will too. Jared didn't voice his thoughts. Instead, he turned to face her and said, "What is it you want to say, Mom?"

"It's about you and Amy."

Jared clenched his lunchbox handle. "She broke up with me. I told you about it and explained her reason right after it happened."

She gave a nod. "You've been upset about the breakup, jah?"

"Of course I'm upset. I love Amy and was hoping she'd be willing to marry me."

Mom took a few steps closer to Jared. "I've been thinking things over since this all happened."

"Oh?"

"It came to me last night that maybe her breaking things off was for the best."

Jared poked his tongue into the side of his cheek and inhaled a long breath. "How can it be for the best?"

"Amy's an independent, stubborn woman, so maybe she wouldn't make you a good fraa."

Jared tensed as heat coursed through his body. "Amy may be independent and perhaps even a bit stubborn, but I love her with all my heart. She's everything I've ever wanted in a wife."

"But if she doesn't want you to court her anymore, maybe it's time to move on."

Jared had heard more than he wanted to, and if he didn't leave now, he was likely to say some hurtful things to his mother. "I've gotta go, Mom. I'm even later now than before." Before she could utter another word, he headed out the back door. This was not a good way to start the day. He wished his father hadn't already left for his booth at the farmers' market, because he would have been an ally. For sure, Dad would have put Mom in her place. *My mamm has no idea how deep my feelings for Amy go.* He shook his head. *I'm not ready to give up on our relationship yet. I just need to be patient.*

"When I went up to the house to eat my lunch, I discovered that Sylvia had set out a container of vanishing oatmeal raisin cookies for us," Amy announced when she returned to the greenhouse. "She was also in the process of preparing to make some double-fudge brownies." Amy set the plastic container on the counter in front of her mother.

Mom smiled. "That's *wunderbaar*. If your sister has been in the kitchen baking, it must mean she is coping a bit better now."

"That's what I thought too until Allen said the word *Daadi* and Sylvia burst into tears."

Mom rested her elbows on the counter and folded her hands as though praying. "It's understandable. I have to blink back tears every time I hear someone mention your daed's name."

"Me too, and the same goes for whenever anyone talks about Abe." Amy swallowed hard. "I miss them both so much as well as Toby. He was a good brother-in-law—always so kind and helpful."

"Jah, but they will all live in our minds and hearts." Mom touched her forehead and then her chest.

"You're so right. We will never forget any of them and the good times we used to have."

Mom tapped the top of the cookie container. "I hope you didn't bring all these kichlin out here for us to eat."

Amy laughed. "Not hardly. Thought I'd take 'em across the road as a welcome gift to our new neighbors."

"That's a good idea. We need to introduce ourselves and let them know we're glad they have chosen to live in this area." Mom pointed to the closest aisle where a variety of potted plants had been displayed. "Why don't you take them something nice from our greenhouse as well?"

"Okay." Amy headed down the aisle and returned to the counter a short time later with a pot of miniature roses. She noticed that the lid on the cookie container was off. She assumed her mother had opened it and eaten a few, until she glanced to her left and saw the elderly homeless woman with a cookie in each hand. Mom was in the next aisle over, talking to an Amish couple from their church district.

Amy was on the verge of saying something to Maude about helping herself to the cookies but changed her mind. The poor woman was probably hungry. Maybe she even believed that the cookies had been placed on the counter for the customers to help themselves.

Amy set the roses down and closed the lid on the cookies before the rest of them vanished. As soon as Mom came back, she picked them both up. "If you think you can manage things on your own for a short time, I'll go over to the neighbors' right now. Otherwise, I could wait until we close the greenhouse for the day."

Mom shook her head. "No, you go ahead. There are only three customers right now, so I'm sure I can manage. And if it gets busy while you're gone, I'll call for Henry to come help. Oh, and please let the neighbors know that I'll come by to welcome them myself as soon as I can."

"Okay." Amy chose not to mention that the elderly woman had taken two cookies, although she felt sure Mom would have understood.

Amy left the greenhouse and started down the driveway. The place across the road still looked the same, except for the two vehicles parked in the driveway. The moving crew that had worked steadily was gone. It was sad that the older couple who'd lived there so many years had moved away. But Amy could see the house and yard were in need of new people who could handle the amount of care it required. *I wonder what these folks will do with this place.*

She crossed the road and walked up their driveway. While eager to meet the new neighbors, she felt a bit nervous as well. What if the man and woman she'd seen previously didn't welcome strangers or weren't friendly people? They might not answer the door or could even slam it in her face.

I'm worried for nothing, she reprimanded herself. *Hopefully, once they see that I come bearing gifts, they'll welcome me into their home.*

Chapter 12

Amy looked both ways before crossing the road. After the accident that had taken three of her precious family members, she'd been watchful and more cautious, whether on foot or with the horse and buggy.

Stepping onto the neighbors' porch, Amy set the miniature roses on a small table positioned between two chairs and rapped on the door. After waiting for a couple of minutes, she knocked again. Since two vehicles were parked in the driveway, someone had to be home.

A few seconds later, the door swung open. "Whatever you're selling, I'm not interested." The woman with short red hair scowled at Amy.

"I'm not here to sell you anything. My name is Amy King. My family and I live across the street." Amy paused and drew a quick breath. "I brought some oatmeal-raisin cookies and a plant from our greenhouse to welcome you into our neighborhood." Her lips formed into what she hoped was a pleasant smile.

The woman stepped back, eyeing the offerings. "Oh, I see."

"Who is it, Virginia?" A tall man wearing shorts and a cotton T-shirt came to the door.

"My name is Amy King and—"

"She lives over there." The woman pointed across the road. "Said she came over to welcome us into the neighborhood with a plant and some cookies."

"Well, that's sure a nice gesture." The man extended his hand. "I'm

Earl Martin, and this is my wife, Virginia."

Amy shook his hand and then Virginia's. "It's nice to meet you both." She handed the cookies to his wife, and then picked up the plant and gave it to him. "My mother is busy in our greenhouse right now, or she would have come over to meet you too. One of these days soon, while I'm keeping an eye on things there, I'm sure she'll be over to say hello and get acquainted."

A sheen of perspiration erupted on Virginia's forehead. "That place keeps you pretty busy, I'll bet."

"It can at certain times of the year. We close up a few weeks before Christmas, after many of our poinsettias and Christmas cactus plants have sold. Then we open up again in early spring."

Virginia's lips parted, like she was on the verge of saying something, but Earl spoke first. "I imagine running a greenhouse is a lot of work. Are both of your parents involved in the business?"

"My father died several weeks ago, so it's just me and Mom in the greenhouse full-time. My younger brother, Henry, helps some there too."

"Sorry for your loss," Earl said. As he spoke, his wife gave a brief nod.

Amy didn't feel led to explain the details of her father's death or to mention that her brother and brother-in-law had also died the same day as Dad. She also said nothing about Sylvia. As they became more acquainted with the neighbors, more details about her family would likely come out. Perhaps Mom would tell them when she came over for a visit.

Fiddling with the ties on her covering, Amy said, "Well, I'd better let you two get back to whatever you were doing when I showed up on your doorstep. I'm sure you still have unpacking to do, and I really should get back to the greenhouse."

"Thank you for coming over, Amy." Earl's smile stretched wide. "The cookies and plant you brought us are appreciated." He bumped his wife's arm with his elbow. "Isn't that right, Virginia?"

With lips pressed together, she nodded slowly.

"All right then, I hope you both have a good day."

When Amy turned and started down the stairs, Earl called, "After the cookies are gone, we'll bring the empty container back to you."

She lifted a hand in a backward wave. "No hurry."

As Amy made her way back across the street, she thought about the reception she'd received. While Earl had appeared friendly enough, his wife seemed kind of aloof and distant.

Amy gave a quick shake of her head. *They didn't even invite me inside or engage in much conversation. I wonder if Virginia is just an unfriendly person, or is there something about me she didn't like?*

Pushing her troubling thoughts to the back of her mind, Amy went to the mailbox. When she'd checked earlier this morning, it had been empty, but now when she pulled the flap open, several envelopes waited for her. Amy took them all out and walked on, stopping at the phone shed. *I may as well check for messages while I'm out here.*

She stepped inside, placed the mail on the wooden counter, and listened to the first message. There were several others, and while she was listening to them and writing things down, she heard the awful racket of a crow in the yard. *I wonder if it's the same one that's been in our yard before.*

A few seconds later, Amy saw and heard a horse and buggy come up the driveway. No doubt it was another customer coming to the greenhouse.

After Earl closed the door, he smiled at Virginia. "Wasn't that a nice surprise, receiving the plant and cookies from our neighbors?" He gestured to the container Virginia still held in her hand.

She passed it to him. "Those people aren't right. They live in the past." Virginia gave her earlobe a tug. "What was that gal's name again?"

"Amy King, and before you go ranting, would you like a cookie?" Earl opened the container.

"No thanks, and I'm not ranting."

He popped a cookie into his mouth. "Mmm. . . this is sure good. You should try one, honey."

"Enough about the cookies. Did you hear what Amy said about her mother planning to come over to meet us?"

"Yeah, but if it bothers you, then don't answer the door. You don't have to get to know her or become friends. It's all up to you."

"That'll work out fine, unless you're the one who answers the door."

"What's that supposed to mean?"

"You'd probably end up flapping your lips, and soon the woman would know our whole life's story."

Earl shook his head, "Oh, come on. I'm not like that, and you know it." He grabbed another cookie and bit into it. "I do admit though certain people can engage me in conversation."

Virginia rolled her eyes. "And when have you ever needed encouragement?" She rescued the container and snapped the lid on. "I'd better take these to kitchen and put them away before you end up eating all of them."

Her husband mumbled something as she left the room. Virginia sometimes felt like she was living with a child. She placed the container on a shelf in the pantry and took out her grocery list. She needed to come up with something for lunch this afternoon but wasn't in the mood to make anything. *Maybe we'll go out to one of the restaurants in town. That way, if the neighbor lady stops by to meet us, we won't be home.*

The bell on the door jingled, and Belinda turned in time to see a tall, cleanly shaven Amish man enter the greenhouse. His dark brown hair had a bit of gray in it, and a few wrinkles showed on his face. Even after all these years, she knew he was Monroe Esh. At the same moment she spoke his name, he said hers.

"Belinda, you've hardly changed a bit." Monroe removed his straw hat and stood looking at her from his side of the counter with a wide smile.

Her cheeks warmed, and she reached up to touch them with her suddenly cold hands. Monroe was every bit as good looking as she remembered him. Only now, much older and hopefully wiser, he was no longer a young man full of adventure and flirtation; Monroe was a mature-looking man in his midfifties. It was surprising that he sported no beard—a sign that he was not married. Either that or he'd been unable, like a few other men she'd met, to grow any substantial hair on his face.

"Did your daughter tell you I was here the other day?" he asked, leaning on the counter.

"Jah, she did."

"I wanted to let you know I was sorry to hear about Vernon."

"Danki. It's been most difficult to accept that he's gone." Belinda's throat felt swollen, and her eyes burned with unshed tears.

"My folks told me all about the tragic accident that took three of your family's lives."

Monroe's sympathetic expression was almost Belinda's undoing. Talking or even thinking about the accident was still very raw. The last thing she wanted to do was break down here in front of Monroe or any of the other customers in the greenhouse.

"I understand you're running the place by yourself." Monroe's tone was soothing.

"Amy and Henry—he's my youngest son—help out here, and we're managing."

"Do you have other children?"

"Jah. Sylvia, my oldest daughter, has been living with us, along with her two small children, ever since her husband was killed in the accident." Belinda shifted on the stool she sat upon. "I also have a son who lives in a small Amish community in New York."

"I'm sure it's a comfort for you to have family during this time of grief."

She gave a nod. "Do you have your own family, Monroe?"

"Just my folks and siblings." He reached up with one hand and rubbed the back of his neck. "I've never married, so. . . ." Monroe's words trailed off when Amy entered the store and stepped behind the counter next to Belinda.

"I see you came back empty-handed. Guess that means the neighbors must have been home?" Belinda tipped her head in Amy's direction.

"Yes, they were. The man thanked us, and I told them you'd be over to meet them soon." Amy glanced at Monroe then looked away. Belinda couldn't read her daughter's thoughts.

"Well, I should get going." Monroe placed his hat back on his head. "I'll drop by again sometime to see how you're doing. No doubt you could use an extra pair of hands around here from time to time."

Belinda could barely find her voice as she said quietly, "It's kind of you to offer, but we're getting along okay."

"Even so, it's not good for you to be here without a man." Monroe's forehead wrinkled. "You never know what might happen." He tipped his hat, said it was nice seeing her again, and went out the door.

Amy looked at Belinda with furrowed brows. "I hope that man doesn't have any ideas about courting you again, Mom."

Belinda lifted her gaze toward the ceiling. "Of course he doesn't. I chose your daed over Monroe, remember?"

"Jah, but. . ."

Belinda put a finger against her lips. "Let's not talk about this right now. There are other people here in the building."

"Sorry, you're right." Amy stepped out from behind the counter. "I'll go see if I can help any of them find what they need."

As her daughter walked away, Belinda's thoughts returned to her conversation with Monroe. *I surely hope he doesn't have any idea about us getting together again, because that's never going to happen. I loved Vernon with all my heart, and no one will ever replace him.*

Amy needed to talk to someone about Monroe Esh. She was concerned about the way he'd looked at her mother this afternoon. Didn't the man have work of his own to do or something else to keep him busy? Why would he want to come here and help out?

Who could I discuss this with? Amy asked herself as she closed things up in the greenhouse. Mom had already gone up to the house to rest awhile before it was time to start supper. Poor thing looked exhausted at the end of their workday, and she hadn't said much after Monroe left the greenhouse.

I wonder if seeing her old boyfriend upset my mamm. It sure upset me. It's way too soon for my mother to even be thinking about a suitor, and I have a feeling that's what Monroe has in mind.

Amy walked up and down the aisles, making sure everything was in place and all the hoses for watering were turned off. *I could call Ezekiel and leave a message, letting him know what happened here today. But if I do that, my brother will make a call to Mom right away, and then she'll be upset with me for alarming Ezekiel for what she would refer to as "nothing to worry about."*

But Amy was worried. She flexed her fingers, and then pulled them into the palms of her hands. *Oh Dad, if you hadn't been so determined to get ice cream, none of this would be a problem. Mom and I wouldn't be working so hard in the greenhouse; Henry would be in better spirits; and Sylvia could be at her own home with her children, living happily as Toby's wife.*

Amy had gone over all of this so many times, and the same words would pop into her mind. Of course, it did no good to rehash the past that couldn't be altered, but it helped to release some of her tension and the emotions she kept bottled up most of the time. She would like to talk to Sylvia about her concerns, but that would upset her sister even more. For now, at least, Amy would keep her thoughts and concerns to herself. She would, however, keep a close watch on things, and if Monroe kept coming around, acting all friendly and nice toward Mom, she might have to put the man in his place.

When Belinda opened the front door and screen door to the greenhouse the following morning, a swarm of honeybees headed right for her. She ducked, nearly hitting her head on a shelf full of vegetable plants. Looking up, she watched as the flying insects made a hasty exit out the open door and into the yard. She hadn't yet opened the door at the other end of the building, which they usually kept open during business hours for cross-ventilation.

Oh, dear. . . That was too close for my comfort. It's a good thing I'm not allergic to bees. Belinda's skin prickled as she straightened to her full height. "Henry King, where are you, young man?" she shouted as she hurried out the door.

"What are ya yelling about, Mom?" Henry stepped out of the barn, his straw hat askew.

Belinda pointed in the direction of the bees circling the yard. "How did those *ieme* get into the greenhouse?"

With open palms, Henry gave a brief shrug.

"Did you go back in after Amy locked up last evening?"

"Nope." He rubbed at the red blotch on his left cheek. "Well, come to think of it, guess I did."

"How come?"

"I remembered that I'd left my can of soda pop in the greenhouse, so I went back to fetch it." He dropped his gaze. "When I couldn't find the can, I stepped outside and looked around, thinking I might have gotten it earlier and forgot where I set it."

"Did you find it?"

Henry shook his head. "I left the door open a ways, and the screen door may have blown open in the wind when I went lookin' for it, but I wasn't gone long and I did eventually close and lock both doors."

"Apparently, while you were out looking for the soda can, a swarm of the honeybees got into the greenhouse. They almost hit me in the face when I opened the door a short time ago. What if it had happened when we had customers? Someone could have gotten stung. And no doubt it would have frightened them to see all those bees flying around." She tapped her foot, trying not to give in to the anger she felt.

"Sorry, Mom."

"Jah, well, the next time you come into the greenhouse for anything, be sure you shut all the doors, even if you're planning to come right back."

Henry dug the toe of his boot into the ground. "Ya know, if we didn't have those stupid bees, they wouldn't be flyin' all over the place. When Ezekiel moved, he shoulda sold the bees to someone else in Lancaster County who raises them for *hunnich*."

"He could have done that all right, but Abe agreed to take care of them."

Henry scrunched up his face. "Jah, Abe—not me. I hate takin' care of those ieme."

"They don't demand much of your time, Son. And the extra money we earn from the honey sales helps out."

Henry's arms hung at his sides as he stared at the ground. "Jah, okay. . .whatever. Nobody in this family cares about me and my needs anyway." He tromped off before Belinda could respond.

She gave a frustrated shake of her head. *Henry should set his own needs aside and realize that we all need to pull together right now.* Belinda understood that her son was still young and often acted impulsively. But he had to grow up sometime and learn to be more responsible. She couldn't think of a better time for that to happen than now.

"I'll join you in the greenhouse as soon as I get the mail," Amy called to Mom when she stepped out the front door. She'd left Sylvia in the kitchen to do the dishes by herself, since she and Mom were running behind and needed to get the business opened before any customers showed up.

Sylvia had said she didn't mind. With the exception of going to church every other Sunday, Amy's dear sister hardly went anywhere these days. Amy didn't think it was good for Sylvia to stay cooped up in the house so much, but she tried not to be pushy or pressure her about it. It was best to let Sylvia deal with things in her own way. Amy hoped that eventually her sister would come through this crisis stronger and better able to serve the Lord.

Amy hadn't admitted it to Mom or anyone else, but she too was having a difficult time coping. The loss of Dad, Abe, and Toby was never far from her mind or the fact that she'd also lost Jared by breaking up with him. The thing that helped her the most, however, was staying busy and concentrating on her duties in the greenhouse rather than focusing on all that she'd lost or given up. Amy felt thankful for every day she worked there and had the chance to talk to their customers about flowers and plants and answer all kinds of gardening questions. In addition to taking her mind off the grief she felt each and every day, Amy enjoyed being able to share her knowledge of gardening with others. She knew without reservation that Mom did too. It gave Amy a sense of satisfaction to be able to work alongside her mother to keep their business running and money coming in.

She'd heard a little more the other day about the new greenhouse that was in the process of being built. She'd read about it in the local paper, and it stated there would be three large buildings that would house nearly everything related to gardening. Amy hoped it wouldn't hurt their business, because it was a much smaller operation.

We might need to think of adding on and for sure offering more items for people to buy that would be related to gardening. It's important that we stay up with things so we don't lose customers to the new greenhouse when it opens.

As Amy drew close to the end of their driveway, her mouth gaped open when the mailbox came in sight. The sides and top of it had been smashed in so badly, Amy wasn't sure she could even get the flap open in order to retrieve the mail.

Her forehead creased. *Who would do such a thing?*

Amy looked at the mailbox next to theirs. It belonged to the neighbors across the street, but it had not been vandalized, nor had the ones up the road. For some reason only theirs had been singled out. Why? Could someone be angry or unhappy with them? Amy wondered what Mom would have to say about this. No doubt she'd be upset.

Amy grabbed the handle on the mailbox and gave it a tug, but it had been so badly bent, it wouldn't budge. She gave it another hard yank, but it still didn't move. She'd have to go get Henry and see if he could get the mailbox unbent enough to at least open the flap.

Amy ran back toward the greenhouse, but spotted her brother coming out of the barn. "Henry, I need to talk to you," she called.

He put both hands on his hips. "What do ya want now?"

"Our mailbox has been vandalized."

"Are you kidding?" He scratched under his straw hat.

She shook her head. "It's all bent up, and the door won't open. I tried to wrench on it, but with no luck."

Henry groaned. "I'd better go take a look. But first, I'll see what I can find in the toolshed to pop the lid free."

"Okay. I'd better get to the greenhouse now and tell Mom what happened."

"I'm so tired of bein' stuck here at this stupid greenhouse all the time." Henry turned and headed for the shed.

Amy chose to let his comment go. She was about to enter the greenhouse when their first customer arrived by horse and buggy. It was their bishop and his wife. She waved at them and stepped inside, where she found Mom sweeping around the checkout counter.

"What took you so long getting the mail?" Mom paused from her work.

Amy was about to respond when the bishop and his wife entered the building. Everyone exchanged greetings, and as Mom continued talking to the elderly couple, Amy picked up the broom and finished cleaning the floor. While their customers began browsing through the plants, Mom returned to Amy and asked a second time about the mail.

In a hushed tone, Amy explained about the mailbox.

Mom's eyes widened. "I can't believe anyone would do such a thing."

"It seems we were singled out for some reason, but I don't understand why someone would do this to us." Amy gave her mother a hug. "I told Henry about it, and he's going out to see if he can get the mail out of the box."

Mom leaned against the register. "This was not a good way to start our morning. We'll need to get the mailbox replaced."

Amy figured one of them, probably Henry, would have to go to the hardware store in town and buy a new mailbox. Perhaps it would be good to get a larger, stronger one this time—maybe the kind that locked. If someone was mean enough to ruin their mailbox, she wouldn't put it past them to steal the mail inside the box either.

That evening, after the little ones had been put to bed, Amy sat in the living room with her mother and Sylvia. After only a few minutes of idle conversation, Mom mentioned the vandalized mailbox as well as all the bees that had gotten into the greenhouse.

She stopped rocking in her chair and looked at Amy and Sylvia, sitting beside each other on the couch. "I waited until Henry went out to the barn to check on the animals before I brought this topic up, because I didn't want him to know what I've been thinking." She paused and pushed her reading glasses firmly on the bridge of her nose. "I'm deeply concerned about what happened today."

"Henry knows about the mailbox." Amy's lips pressed together in a slight grimace. "After all, he's the one who got the mail out of the box, and he also went to the hardware store to get a new mailbox. So why would you want to keep him in the dark about our conversation?"

"I am well aware of what your bruder knows." Mom leaned forward in her chair. "He also knows about the honeybees that got into the greenhouse, but I am equally sure he has no idea that I suspect he's the one who did both of those things."

Sylvia's eyes widened, and Amy shook her head in denial. Although Henry had a bad attitude these days, she felt sure he would not be capable of doing either one of those things.

"You're both aware that your brother is full of anger, and on top of that, he does not want to take care of the bees or help in the greenhouse. He may be looking for ways to vent that aggravation."

Amy sighed. "If it actually was our own brother who bashed in the mailbox, he may have gotten up early this morning and done it or even snuck out of the house sometime during the night. But do you really think our little brother would go to such lengths as to release the bees into the greenhouse and damage our mailbox?"

"I hope not, but it is a possibility that we can't ignore." Mom pinched the skin at her throat, as she often did when she was worried.

"Maybe Henry needs another phone call from Ezekiel," Sylvia suggested.

Mom shook her head vigorously. "If Ezekiel even thinks things are not going well for us, he might change his mind and decide to move back here." Her gaze traveled from Sylvia to Amy. "I don't want him to know anything about this."

"We could ask one of our ministers to talk with Henry." Amy pointed to the Bible on the end table closest to Mom's chair. "They're full of wisdom and know the Bible so well. Maybe it would help."

"Just having a little talk with him about facing his responsibilities without grumbling might improve things," Sylvia added.

"That's a good idea. I'll speak with one of the preachers sometime tomorrow. I'm sure he'll be willing to come over and talk to Henry." Mom gave a nod. "I'll go as soon as the greenhouse closes for the day."

Chapter 14

"Hang on!" Breaking hard, Amy's driver, Pauline, gripped the steering wheel so tightly that the veins on her hands protruded.

The van stopped and things were quiet, except for the steady idle of the engine.

Amy slowly opened her eyes. Even though a dog had run out in front of them, they'd avoided a bad outcome. "That was close." She drew in a shaky breath as she watched the pooch wander off the street and into a nearby yard.

Pauline drummed the steering wheel. "I wish owners would keep a better watch on their pets."

"Henry has a dog, but he keeps the mutt penned up when he's not able to keep an eye on him." Amy pulled on the seatbelt to get some slack again, as it felt like it was cutting into her neck. She hoped the flowers in the back of the vehicle weren't disturbed from the force it took to stop. She looked straight ahead while her driver resumed the proper speed.

It wasn't long before they pulled into a space in front of Sara's flower shop. Amy got out of the van and went inside.

"It's good to see you. How have you and your family been?" Sara asked when Amy stepped up to the counter.

"Not the best, but we're getting by." Amy was tempted to mention what had happened with their mailbox, but since it had been replaced with a larger, stronger one that locked, she saw no reason to bring the topic up. Lenore's husband, Jesse, had come over to help Henry erect the new mailbox, so everything was as it should be, at least for the time being.

Amy had suggested to her mother that they call the sheriff's office to report the incident, but Mom said it wasn't necessary since they had no evidence or even a clue as to who had done it. Amy figured if her brother was guilty of the vandalism, Mom wouldn't want the law involved.

Amy gestured toward the window, where her driver's van sat in front of the building. "I came with the cut flowers you ordered yesterday. I wanted to get them to you early in case you needed them for any orders you might have for today."

"I appreciate it because we got several new orders yesterday before closing time." Sara glanced out the window. "If you'll ask your driver to pull around to the back of the store, we can get them unloaded."

"Sure, no problem." Amy went out the door and gave directions to Pauline. This was the first time Amy had been the one to deliver flowers to Sara's shop and the first time she'd called upon their new driver.

While the van pulled around back, Amy returned to the flower shop. "Pauline should be at the back door soon," she announced to Sara.

"Okay, I'll let my designer, Misty, know. She and my new assistant, Stephanie, will unload the flowers and bring them into the back room." Sara disappeared into the other room and returned a few minutes later. "I spoke to your driver. She said she'd pick you up out front."

"Okay."

Sara moved over to front counter. "While they're unloading, I'll write you a check for the flowers."

"Thank you."

While Sara took care of that, Amy meandered around the floral shop, observing the lovely way Sara had decorated the place. She paused to admire a glass cross and several other pretty trinkets that adorned the table. She moved around the store, soaking it all in. The window display and every table and shelf in this room had something unique and attractive to look at in addition to some of the bouquets and houseplants Sara offered her customers.

Amy's excitement overflowed as an idea popped into her head. "If you have some free time some evening, Sara, if you wouldn't mind, maybe you could come by the greenhouse and offer us some suggestions as to how we might display the items we have for sale in a more appealing way. Once that new greenhouse we've heard about opens for business, we're going to have some competition, so we need to make an effort to keep up with them."

"One thing you must keep in mind, Amy, is that tourists seem to be attracted to the Amish way of life. And since your place is owned and run by Plain People, it is, and will continue to be, a tourist attraction. That is one key thing the new business probably won't have." Sara handed Amy a check. "Now, as for me coming over and giving you some suggestions, I'd be happy to drop by. If Brad isn't busy, maybe he'd like to come with me."

Amy smiled. "That would be nice. Maybe he'd be willing to have a talk with my brother. He needs cheering up and some guidance these days." She hoped she hadn't said too much or that her mother wouldn't get upset about it. Sara wasn't a family member or the first person Mom would turn to for advice about personal matters.

"I've suspected as much. Henry's the one who has been making deliveries since the deaths of your family members, and I've noticed a deep sadness in his eyes."

"It's not just his sadness, for we all have that. It's his angry, defiant attitude I'm most worried about." Amy's facial muscles tightened. "Mom's going to ask one of our preachers to speak with Henry, but it wouldn't hurt if Brad spoke to him too."

"When I go home this evening, I'll bring up the topic." Sara touched Amy's arm. "I'll also be praying for Henry as well as you and the rest of your family."

"Thank you." Amy caught sight of her driver's van out front, so she turned toward the door. "Guess I'd better go. Henry didn't want to make the deliveries this morning, and he's supposed to be in the store helping Mom. I need to get back there in case he's not cooperating."

"Okay, I'll see you some evening later this week."

Amy opened the door, but before she could exit the store, Sara's father, Herschel Fisher, stepped in. His towering form was unmistakable. He offered her a warm smile. "It's nice to see you, Amy. How are things going for you and your family?"

"We're getting by."

"I wish I lived closer and didn't have my store to run, or I'd come by and help out with some chores."

"It's okay, Herschel. We're managing." Amy started out the door, calling over her shoulder, "If you think about it, please let your mamm know that we're having a sale at the greenhouse next week."

"I surely will."

Amy waved and hurried to get into her driver's van. She didn't know Herschel all that well but remembered him coming to the greenhouse a few times with his mother. Amy thought he was a nice man, and it was refreshing to see how kind he was to his mother. Even though Herschel was in his early sixties, he seemed attentive to his mom's needs.

Not like Henry, she thought with regret. *He's too caught up in his own little world of grief and anger to care about how Mom feels these days.*

Rolling her shoulders to loosen the tension she felt, Belinda glanced at the battery-operated clock sitting on the counter. Just another hour and it would be time to close the greenhouse for the day; then she could hitch her horse to the buggy and pay a visit to Preacher Thomas Raber and his wife. Thomas was one of the older ministers in their church, and he'd had plenty of experience in the thirty-some years since he'd acquired the position through the drawing of lots. She felt confident that he'd be willing to speak with Henry. She just hoped her son would listen to the minister's words and heed his counsel, because she really didn't want to trouble Ezekiel again. Besides, it hadn't worked last time, so he probably wouldn't succeed with Henry anyhow.

"Oh, I forgot to tell you something." Amy interrupted Belinda's thoughts. "Sara and her husband might come by some evening soon. I asked her to take a look at how things are arranged here in the greenhouse and give me some ideas on how to feature our plants and flowers in a way that will draw the customers' attention."

Belinda tapped a pen against the tablet in front of her. "I suppose it couldn't hurt, but I don't see what's wrong with the way we're displaying things now."

"It couldn't hurt to get Sara's professional opinion."

"I guess you're right."

"She's going to ask her husband to come along, and I suggested that he might want to have a talk with Henry."

Belinda's toes curled inside her shoes. "Why would you do that, Amy? Didn't I tell you that I was planning to speak with one of our ministers about Henry's attitude?"

Amy's cheeks flushed. "Well, jah, but Brad's also a minister so I just thought—"

"You shouldn't have been talking to Sara about our problems."

"Why not?"

"Because they aren't a part of our family."

"Neither is Preacher Raber."

"No, but he is an important part of our Amish church—not to mention that he knows us quite well." Belinda rubbed her chin, mulling things over. "Since there are only a few people here at the moment and it's almost time to close up the greenhouse, I'm going to head over to the Rabers' right now. Will you please lock up after the last customer leaves, and then go help Sylvia get supper started?"

"Of course." Amy touched Belinda's shoulder. "I hope you're not umgerennt because I talked with Sara about Henry. She already suspected he was having a hard time because of how he's acted when he's made deliveries to her flower shop."

"Sorry, I probably overreacted. If Preacher Raber doesn't get through to Henry, then I have no problem with Sara's husband talking to your bruder." Belinda gave a deep sigh. "I just hope that someone will be able to get through to that boy. It's difficult enough to face all the negative things life can dish out. I can't stand the thought of losing Henry because he's chosen to pull away from us all."

As Amy stood in the kitchen next to her sister, each working on a different dish for supper, she couldn't help noticing the dark circles beneath Sylvia's eyes. With Amy's bedroom being across the hall from the room Sylvia shared with her children, she could often hear heart-wrenching sobs. Amy shed tears some nights too, but it was quiet crying, and at least she was able to sleep.

"Did you get a nap today?" Amy's question broke through the silence.

Sylvia shook her head. "I tidied up in the bedroom and bathroom, but afterward I felt drained." She gave the salad a quick toss. "A little later, I lay on the bed with the kinner, but I was unable to sleep—could not turn off the thoughts."

"I'm sorry." *Maybe Preacher Raber should talk to my sister too,* Amy thought. *She may not be grumbling all the time and saying hurtful things, but she hasn't even begun to let go of her grief and could certainly use some spiritual guidance.* When the minister came by to talk to Henry, Amy hoped he would see how badly Sylvia was hurting and spend some time counseling her as well. With the way things were now, it didn't look like Sylvia would ever be able to function as she once had. And if things didn't change, Henry might spend the rest of his life mad at God and taking out his frustrations on the rest of the world.

Chapter 15

The next day, shortly after the greenhouse opened, Preacher Raber and his wife, Rebekah, came by.

"Is your brother around?" the minister asked when Amy greeted them near the door.

Amy shrugged. "I think he's in the barn, but I'm not sure. Knowing Henry, he could be most anywhere." *Trying to get out of work*, she mentally added.

"I'll look there first, while my fraa does some shopping for gardening things." The preacher grinned at his wife and gave her a thumbs-up before heading out the door.

Amy smiled. *I hope if I ever get married, my husband is as generous as Thomas Raber.* Her smile faded. *But it doesn't look like I'll ever become a married woman. My responsibility is here helping Mom. That's just how it is.*

She had to admit though, seeing Jared at the biweekly services was a challenge. She would look anywhere but in his direction. She'd made up her mind about not seeing him anymore and wouldn't budge from her resolve. Sylvia had asked about Jared, but she didn't push at all or try to sway Amy's decision. Amy also had to admit, her life had become pretty boring staying home so much and not going to young people's gatherings with Jared. She kept so busy at the greenhouse, there wasn't time to even get together with Lydia anymore.

Maybe it's for the best, Amy told herself. *Lydia might try and talk me into seeing Jared again. She did go to bat for him when he asked for her help.*

While Amy sauntered through the greenhouse, absorbed in thought, her foot caught hold of a watering hose that had been left on the concrete floor. She nearly fell but caught herself in time. Amy looked around and brushed some dirt off the bottom of her dress. Mom's back was turned, so she apparently hadn't noticed Amy's near spill.

Since her mother was busy putting new seed packets on a shelf, Amy took a seat behind the counter. There were no customers other than the preacher's wife at the moment, which gave Amy more time to let her mind wander. *I wonder what Jared is doing today. Has he had many roofing jobs this week?* She leaned forward, resting her elbows on the counter. Amy pictured herself and Jared as a married couple, out running errands together.

She shook those unrealistic thoughts away and chided herself. *I have to stop thinking about him.*

Sitting up tall and looking around the greenhouse, Amy remembered her walk out to the mailbox this morning. She'd been relieved when she found the new box intact. Amy figured the attack on their old mailbox had most likely been done by some rowdy kids looking for something to do that they could brag about to all their friends. She didn't want to believe her brother could have done something like that, for if Henry was the guilty one, then his anger had gotten the best of him and needed to be brought under control.

Amy hoped Preacher Raber had been able to locate her brother and that Henry would listen to and heed everything being said.

Mom finished watering the closest plants and then coiled the hose and hung it on the hooks above the shelf. "I'd better get this up and out of the way before someone trips over it."

Too late, Mom. I already did. Amy snickered at her failure to watch where she stepped. It was a good thing it had happened to her though, and not one of their customers.

"How'd things go with the preacher and Henry?" Amy asked her mother after Thomas and Rebekah Raber left with a few bedding plants. "I assume the minister told you how his conversation went?"

"Jah, he did." Mom bobbed her head. "Apparently, Henry seemed to be listening, but that doesn't mean he will heed the preacher's words and change his attitude."

Amy nodded along as her mother spoke. "I guess we'll have to wait and see how it goes."

Her stomach growled, and she strolled over to the snack bag and took out an orange, which she peeled. "Mom, would you like half of my *aarensch*?"

"An orange sounds good. I could use a little pick-me-up."

They'd finished the treat, when Henry entered the building. His face was red, and a sheen of sweat glistened on his forehead. "Did you *hetze* the preacher on me?" He moved close to their mother.

"I did not sic Thomas Raber on you, Henry. I just told him you were having a hard time dealing with the death of our family members and asked if he would talk to you—offer some words of encouragement."

Henry's features tightened as he crossed his arms. "Sounds like siccing to me." He looked over at Amy and squinted. "You don't need to stand there lookin' so perfect, either. You miss Dad and Abe too, and truth be told, you don't like workin' here anymore than I do. You're just too nicey-nice to say so."

Amy drew a deep breath and held it as she counted to ten. *How could Henry speak that way to Mom? If Dad were here, he'd have something to say about this. Furthermore, I don't appreciate Henry's tone and what he's been saying to me either.* She had half a mind to put her brother in his place once and for all.

Mom stood up straight and looked at Henry. "I'll have you know, young man, that your sister hurts just as much as you do over the loss of your daed and bruder. I'm sure she misses Toby too. But Amy cares enough about this family to work in the greenhouse without complaint, and she doesn't take her frustrations out on others."

Mom's voice had grown louder. It was a good thing there were no customers at the moment. "She sacrificed being courted by Jared in order to give all her time and attention to helping me keep this business running and bringing in the money we need to survive." She pointed at Henry. "What sacrifices have you made, Son?"

"I guess none. At least that's the way you two see it." Henry whirled around and dashed out the door.

Amy lifted her gaze to the ceiling. "That didn't go over so well, did it?"

Mom shook head. "No, I should say not. We need to keep praying for your brother and not let up until we see a change."

"Jah, and the same goes for Sylvia. I think it would help if she kept busy with something other than household chores. And for sure, she needs to be around people and socialize more." *Just like Mom, I'll be praying too. I hope there will be a change for someone in our family soon.*

Sylvia was resting on the couch while the children napped, when she heard the back door open and slam shut. Henry stomped into the room.

"You'd best be ready, Sister, 'cause you'll probably be next."

"Next for what?" she asked, sitting up. "And please lower your voice. Your niece and nephew are asleep."

"Sorry." He sank into their father's favorite chair. "As I was saying. . . You'll probably be next to get chewed out by Mom. Maybe Amy will put in her two cents' worth too."

"Why would they do that?"

" 'Cause they did it to me—at least Mom did. Our sister just stood there listening and bobbing her head." Henry groaned as he leaned back in the chair. "Mom asked Preacher Raber to have a little talk with me, and later she got all over my case. It really irked me when she started comparing me to her sweet little Amy." With a stony face, he stared at Sylvia. "Mom favors Amy over us, ya know."

Sylvia shook her head. "No, she doesn't. I'm sure that's not true."

"Jah, she does. Started singin' Amy's praises because she works hard in the greenhouse without complaint, and she even brought up the fact that Amy broke things off with Jared so she could help Mom all the time."

Sylvia tugged at her sleeve. "Did she say anything negative about me?"

"No, but I'm sure Mom and Amy have talked about you—how you stay cooped up here in the house most of the time." Henry stomped his foot. "If I have to take care of the livestock, tend to those stupid bees, work in the greenhouse, and do a bunch of other chores, then I think you oughta find someone to watch the kinner so you can do some work out there too."

Her brother's harsh words stabbed Sylvia to the core. He didn't understand how exhausted she felt. Just taking care of the children and keeping the house running as smoothly as she could wore her out. Every single thing she did took all her energy and willpower, and as the days went on, it didn't get any better. The agony Sylvia felt over the loss of her husband, father, and brother felt so heavy that at times she almost couldn't breathe. If she even tried to go out to the greenhouse to work, she feared she might collapse. The idea of talking to people and answering questions all day was unfathomable. It was all she could do to face people when they went to church, which was why she sometimes looked for reasons to stay home.

Sylvia didn't mention it to Henry, but the preacher had stopped at the house to speak with her too. She hadn't felt up to talking to him and made the excuse that the children were sleeping, so it wasn't a good time to talk. He'd left, saying he would drop by some other time.

Sylvia lay back down and closed her eyes. *If Mom and Amy have been talking about me behind my back, so be it. The only thing I'm capable of doing right now is taking care of my kinner's needs. Don't know if I'll ever feel up to working in the greenhouse again.* Sylvia's heart clenched. *Could what Henry said about Amy be true? Does Mom care more about her than me and Henry?*

Jared was on his way to the Kings' place to try once more to get Amy to change her mind about seeing him when Dandy began limping.

Jared slowed the horse and found a suitable spot along the shoulder of the road to pull off. "This is not good." He shook his head. "Not good at all. He probably threw a shoe."

He set the brake, climbed down from buggy, and took a look at the horse's hooves. "It's okay, boy," he soothed. "I just need to see your shoes." After patting the horse's neck, Jared lifted the animal's right front leg. Sure enough, the shoe was missing.

Letting go of the gelding's limb, he stepped back. "Well fella, it's back to the barn for you this evening." Hopefully, he'd be able to get a farrier to come out in the morning. Otherwise, he'd have to borrow one of his parents' horses or call a driver.

"Maybe it's for the best," Jared muttered as he took his seat in the buggy again. "Amy would probably tell me the same thing as before, and then I'd be hurt all over again."

Jared thought about the last few Sundays when he'd seen her at church. He had tried to make eye contact with Amy a couple of times, but she never looked his way. After the noon meal, when he tried to seek Amy out, he discovered that she and her family had left for home.

He clenched his jaw. *If only Amy could give me a shred of hope, I'd hang on and wait for her.*

Jared wasn't sure what to do anymore. His heart told him to keep pursuing Amy, but his head told him otherwise. *If she loved me the way I love her, she'd let me help out whenever I could. And she wouldn't shut me out but would accept my love with open arms. Maybe Mom's right. Maybe Amy's not the woman God meant for me.*

Jared felt like a young boy who couldn't make up his mind about what flavor of ice cream to choose. *First vanilla and then chocolate. No, maybe strawberry would be better instead.* One thing Jared was certain of: if he prodded Amy too much, trying to get her to change her mind, he would likely push her farther away. *So maybe it was a good thing Dandy lost his shoe. It probably kept me from making a mistake this evening. If Amy wants a relationship with me, she needs to make the first move. It won't be easy, but I'll try to sit back and wait till she realizes how much she needs me.*

Chapter 16

"Ouch!"

"What happened?" Virginia turned from rinsing out a cup at the sink.

"I touched the cast-iron skillet on the stove, and it was still hot." Earl held up his index finger.

"Come on over here and run your finger under the cool water."

He shook his head. "It'll be okay. I'll just have a seat at the table, since you have our breakfast ready."

She gave a brief shrug and dished up some scrambled eggs on both of their plates.

"What are your plans for the day?" Earl asked.

She offered him some toast and butter. "Nothing yet. I need to take a shower first." Virginia pointed to the cardboard boxes on the other side of the room. "And I still have some things to put away in the kitchen cupboards."

"Yep. You better get busy then."

Virginia's brows furrowed as a fly buzzed her head. "Do you know what happened to our flyswatter? I've looked everywhere for it."

"We had one at the other house, and I thought we packed it." He scratched at his thinning hair. "Guess we may need to buy a new one."

She swatted at the fly hovering near her plate. "I don't remember having so many pesky flies at our place in Chicago."

Earl rubbed the spot on the finger he'd burned. "You have a point, Virginia."

Slapping at the table and missing the insect, she scowled. "I'm sure it's because of all the dirty critters living around us out here in the boonies. It's the perfect breeding ground for filthy flies."

"It might help if we get some fly tape and hung it here in the kitchen. That stuff works pretty good."

Virginia pulled her fingers through the ends of her short hair. "Looks like I oughta drive into town and do some shopping today."

"Good idea."

They ate in silence for a while, until Virginia looked at the open window. The subtle breeze moved the checkered curtains a bit, and she caught sight of something. "The screen in our kitchen window has a couple of holes in it. I bet that's how all the flies are getting in."

He glanced that way. "I can tape up those holes in a jiffy."

"That's just a temporary fix, Earl. We need a new screen."

"I'll tape it for now and will get a new screen as soon as I can."

She smiled. "Sooner, the better."

"What about that?" Earl gestured to the plastic container on the counter. "It's been empty for a couple of days. Don't ya think you should return it to the young neighbor woman who brought those tasty cookies to us?"

"I'll be too busy today. Besides, the little gal knows where it is. If she wants the container, she can come over and get it." Virginia blew on her coffee and drank some.

Earl's eyes narrowed as he stared at her from across the table. "You're kidding, right?"

"Not really. I have no desire to hightail it over there to meet that girl's family." She reached for a piece of toast and slathered it with butter. "Those people are strange. Not only do they dress in plain clothes like the pioneers, but they use those smelly horses that draw flies to pull their old-fashioned gray buggies." Virginia rolled her eyes. "There are no electric wires running to their house, so I can only imagine how they must live in that place."

He dipped his toast in the runny egg yolks. "Did you ever think that their plain ways may be better than ours?"

"Nope. I'd never want to live the way those folks do. I like having our modern conveniences. And what would I do without cable TV?"

"Maybe you'd get more unpacking done if you left the television alone for a while."

"I don't know what you're talking about, Earl. You act like I'm addicted to the thing."

"All I can say is, whenever you're watching some show and I try to ask you a question, you don't even hear me."

"You're exaggerating." She folded her arms. "Now, back to the topic of those Plain People living across the road—there is nothing on this green earth that would make me want to live the way they do."

"As long as we pay our electric bill, you'll never have to." Earl finished his breakfast and pushed away from the table. "And speaking of bills. . .I need to head for work or we won't have money to pay any of the bills that come in."

"I suppose you'd like me to look for a job so I can pay my share?"

Earl shook his head. "With that bum leg of yours, I don't expect you to do anything more than you're capable of." He picked up the container the cookies had come in and handed it to her. "But I do expect you to find some time today to return this. It's the polite thing to do."

"Okay, okay. I'll head over there as soon as I clear the table and put the dishes in the dishwasher."

Earl smiled and kissed her cheek. "Good girl."

It had been two days since Thomas Raber spoke to Henry, but the boy's attitude hadn't changed. In Belinda's opinion, her son had gotten worse. As she headed down the driveway to retrieve the mail, her thoughts took her back to the night before. Henry had been fairly quiet most of that day, until shortly before nine o'clock, when he'd said he wanted to go out for a buggy ride. When Belinda asked where he planned on going at such a late hour, Henry said nowhere in particular; he just wanted to be by himself for a while and enjoy some fresh air. Belinda was tempted to tell Henry he couldn't go anywhere but kept silent. After the discussion they'd had two days ago, she was fully aware of Henry's feelings and thought the buggy ride might do him some good. With a clearer head, he might have a new perspective on things. This morning, however, Henry had been just as sullen as ever.

Last night, Belinda had listened to a message from Sara, saying that she and her husband would be coming over sometime tomorrow evening. *Maybe if Brad talks to Henry, he will be able to get through to him. I can at least hope and pray for that.*

Belinda couldn't give up hope that things would change. She longed to have Henry back and reacting to things the way he used to when his father and brother were alive. "Oh Vernon," she whispered. "I wish you were still here."

That must be our new neighbor. Here's my chance to make her acquaintance. Belinda reached the mailbox about the same time as the red-haired woman across the road left her yard. Holding a plastic container in one hand while walking with a bit of a limp, she came up to Belinda.

"You must be Virginia." Belinda smiled at the woman.

"Yeah." Virginia rolled her blue eyes from side to side, pausing briefly to glance at Belinda. "Came on over here to return this." She held out the container. "The young woman—I guess she's your daughter—brought us some cookies in the container."

"Yes, that was my daughter Amy." Belinda took the container with one hand and reached to shake Virginia's hand with the other. "My name is Belinda King. It's nice to finally meet you, Virginia."

"Umm. . .yeah. Same here." Virginia glanced back toward her place.

"Where are you from?"

"Chicago." She looked toward Belinda's home. "It's taking a bit of getting used to, living around here."

"I see. Well, I've been meaning to come over and welcome you properly, but things have been so busy at the greenhouse, I kept putting it off."

"No problem." Virginia dropped her gaze. "I'm still unpacking boxes and arranging furniture, so I don't have much time for standing around yakking."

"I understand. Moving into a new home can be quite daunting." Belinda smiled, but when Virginia did not reciprocate, she figured it was time to wrap up their conversation. "When you're not so busy, why don't you come over sometime? I'd be happy to show you around the greenhouse, and if we're not too busy, maybe we can sit and visit over a glass of cold meadow-mint tea."

Virginia's nose wrinkled. "Never heard of it, but then I'm not much of a tea drinker. I prefer coffee."

"My other daughter, Sylvia, usually has a pot of coffee on the stove, so if that's what you'd prefer, we can drink coffee instead."

Virginia gave a brief shrug. "Maybe. I'll have to wait and see how it goes." With a mumbled goodbye, she turned and walked back across the road.

Belinda went to the mailbox, unlocked it, and took out the mail. It hadn't taken her long to realize that their new neighbor was certainly not the friendly type. She hoped after Virginia had been here awhile, she'd be a bit friendlier.

Belinda was about to start back up the driveway, when she caught sight of their sign at the left end of the driveway, advertising the greenhouse. Instead of hanging from the heavy wire where it had been attached to a metal frame, the sign now lay off to one side among some tall weeds. Leaning down for a closer look, Belinda realized the wire had been cut. *What is going on here?* Someone had obviously done it on purpose and tossed the sign in the weeds.

Who could have done this and why? Belinda rubbed her forehead. *Oh, I hope it wasn't Henry.*

"You're awfully quiet this morning." Lydia's mother tapped her shoulder. "Didn't you sleep well last night?"

Lydia turned from the stove, where she'd been stirring a kettle of oatmeal. "It wasn't the best sleep. I'm worried about Jared."

"Is he *grank*?"

"He's not physically ill, Mama, but Jared's heartsick because Amy broke up with him."

"Has he actually said that to you?"

"Well, no. It's just the way he's been acting. I can see the pain in his eyes."

"I'm sure he will get past it and move on to someone else who won't break his heart."

Mama lifted Lydia's chin so she was looking directly into her eyes. "Maybe that someone will be you."

Lydia's lips pressed together as she tugged on her apron. "Even if Jared seemed interested in me, I could never come between him and my best friend."

"You can't come between two people who aren't together anymore. Amy obviously doesn't want to be with Jared now, or she wouldn't have ended their courtship."

"She only did it because she has so many responsibilities now. I'm sure Amy still loves Jared. Maybe once things slow down for her, they'll get back together."

Mama got a faraway look in her eyes. "Jared's a nice young man. He'd make a good husband."

"Jah, he would, but not for me. He's in love with Amy."

"But if he took an interest in you, would you be willing to let him court you?"

"No. Amy is my friend, and I'm sure she still has feelings for him." Lydia turned back to the stove and continued stirring the oatmeal. *There is no way Jared will ever be interested in me, so this conversation is just plain silly.*

Sylvia had finished drying the breakfast dishes when Mom entered the kitchen. "Here's the mail." She placed it on the table and handed

Sylvia a plastic container she held in her other hand. "Our new neighbor lady across the road returned this to me, but it doesn't look like it's been washed." She shook the container. "See, there are still some cookie crumbs inside."

Sylvia opened the lid and dumped the crumbs into the garbage can under the sink. Then she placed it in the sink and ran warm water and liquid detergent into it. "Wouldn't you think she would have washed the container before bringing it back?"

Mom nodded. "I'll admit that was my first thought, but I'm sure Virginia's been busy what with unpacking and trying to get settled in her new home."

"What's she like? Do you think she'll be a good neighbor?" Sylvia sloshed around the dishrag inside the container.

"I can't say for sure, since we only spoke with each other for a few minutes." Mom paused and cleared her throat. "She did seem a bit standoffish though. Makes me wonder if people from the big cities are different than small-town people."

Maybe she's like me, Sylvia thought. *Could be that she doesn't feel comfortable around people.*

"Well, I just came in to deliver the mail and drop off the container, but now I'd better get out to the greenhouse so Amy's not there by herself when customers begin showing up. Oh, and then I'll need to seek out your brother. Someone cut the wire that holds up our sign at the end of the driveway, so I'll need him to get it hung back up right away. We don't want to lose any customers because they can't find us."

Sylvia whirled around. "You think it was cut down on purpose?"

Mom nodded. "I found it lying in the weeds, and the wire had definitely been cut."

Sylvia's hand went to her mouth. "Oh my. First the mailbox and now this? Who do you think is responsible, Mom?"

"I—I don't know for sure, but I still think it may be your brother. He could have bashed in our mailbox and let the bees in the greenhouse too."

Sylvia's mouth opened slightly. "But I still don't understand why

Henry would do something like that."

"He's angry and could be acting out."

"Have you asked him right out if he's the one responsible for knocking down the sign?"

"Not yet. You're the first person I've told about it."

"If he did do any of those things, he needs to be called out."

"Agreed." Mom emitted a noisy huff. "Henry's attitude seems to worsen every day, even though Amy, Ezekiel, Preacher Raber, and I have tried talking to him." She blotted at the tears that had fallen onto her cheeks. "I'm concerned that your bruder may never come to grips with the death of our dear family members."

Sylvia nodded. That much she understood, for she wasn't sure she would ever be free of the agony she'd felt every day since Toby, Dad, and Abe had died.

Chapter 17

"I can't believe someone would deliberately take down our sign," Amy said after listening to her mother explain what she had found. "Do you still think Henry could be behind all these incidents?"

"Yes, although he denied it when I asked him a few minutes ago." Mom kept her voice low as she took her seat on the stool behind the checkout counter in the greenhouse.

"Where is Henry now? Maybe I should go talk to him."

"He's outside rehanging the sign." Mom fiddled with the paperwork lying on the counter. "I don't think it would do a bit of good for you to talk to him, Amy. If Henry is acting out and releasing his emotions by doing destructive things, I doubt anything you or I can say will get through to him."

Amy leaned in closer to her mother. "What are we going to do? There has to be someone who can get through to my little brother."

"I ain't little, and I wish you two would quit talkin' about me behind my back."

Amy whirled around at the sound of her brother's angry voice. She'd been so engrossed in the conversation that she hadn't heard him come in.

"If you'd quit doing bizarre things, we wouldn't need to talk about you." Amy's fingers clenched as she tapped them along the counter. "How do you think Dad would feel if he knew you'd done things to destroy our property?"

He sauntered up to her and stood so close she could smell his minty breath. "I haven't destroyed anything. In fact, I came in here to tell Mom I fixed the sign—it's back in place." He glanced at their mother then back at Amy. "And if I'd bashed in the mailbox, do ya think I woulda gone to town for a new one and then helped put it in?"

"You did it because I asked you to," Mom interjected. "And it's certainly no proof that you're not the person responsible for the pranks."

"Mom, they were more than pranks." Amy flexed her fingers to keep from grabbing hold of her brother and giving him a good shake. "What was done to the mailbox and our sign out front was vandalism."

Henry held firm in his stance. "Jah, well you can believe what you want, but I'm not the person who did those things." He whirled around and stomped out the door.

Mom lowered her head, making little circles with her fingers across her forehead. "I hope and pray that if Henry is the guilty person, he'll realize he's done wrong and won't do anything like that again."

"I hope not either, but I wouldn't hold my breath." She pursed her lips. "I hope neither Dad nor Abe can look down from heaven and see the way Henry's been acting. If they could, they'd be very disappointed."

Mom gave no reply as she continued to rub her forehead.

"We'd better pull ourselves together," Amy announced. "I heard a horse and carriage coming up the driveway, so we need to put smiles on our faces and welcome our first customers of the day."

By late afternoon, Belinda had lost track of how many customers had come to the greenhouse in response to the ad about this week's sale that they'd run in their local paper. In the past, Vernon had been in charge of all the advertising for their business.

Recently, Belinda had gone through some old ads and gotten ideas from her husband's way of doing things. She'd also asked Henry to go into town and hang some flyers on bulletin boards. Belinda wanted to make the public aware of their business with minimal effort and little expense. Having a sale today made her think of how it was when Vernon had still been with them and the anticipation they'd felt getting everything ready for the event. Like she had in the past, Belinda hoped everything would go according to plan.

Pauline, their driver, entered the greenhouse and came over to the counter where Belinda stood. "Amy invited me to come by and have a look around."

"I'm glad she did." Belinda glanced at a large area where several customers mingled. "I believe my daughter is here somewhere."

As if on cue, Amy came up and greeted Pauline. "I'm glad you could come by for the sale. Let me show you around." The two of them headed off and disappeared among the other shoppers.

Belinda smiled. It was good to see more new customers venture into the greenhouse. Having a sale this week had been an excellent idea.

The best part of the day was when an English couple came in a few minutes later and bought over five hundred dollars' worth of plants and shrubs. Soon after they left, an elderly man showed up who was obviously hard of hearing. Amy pointed him out, saying he'd been here before, when Belinda was gone. The gray-haired man asked a lot of questions, and Belinda had to repeat herself several times. Remembering the phone call she'd had not long ago from a man who struggled to hear what she said, Belinda figured he might be the same person she'd spoken to on the phone. The gentleman ended up buying some pots of petunias and a bag of grass seed. He seemed nice enough. It was a shame he couldn't hear well. Belinda wondered why he didn't wear any hearing aids. Perhaps he was either embarrassed or too stubborn to wear them. Or else he wouldn't acknowledge that he was hard of hearing.

I wonder if Henry will be stubborn when he gets old. I love my son, but he certainly can be hardheaded.

Belinda smiled when another customer stepped up to the counter pulling a wagonload of plants and several gardening supplies. She couldn't let her negative thinking get the best of her, or she might appear unfriendly.

"Mom, you look like you could use a break." Amy slipped in behind the counter. "Why don't you let me take over here so you can go up to the house and rest for a bit? Henry's supposed to come into the greenhouse in a few minutes, and I'm sure the two of us can manage on our own for a while."

Belinda pushed some unruly hairs back under her head covering. "I could use a break—but only a short one. If things get busy again, you'll need my help out here."

"No problem. If too many customers show up, I'll send Henry up to the house to get you."

"Okay, you talked me into it." Belinda slid off the stool. "Is there anything I can get you when I come back out?"

"Maybe a glass of meadow-mint tea."

"Consider it done."

Virginia paced the length of her kitchen, gritting her teeth and slamming cupboard doors. She marched into the living room and looked out the window at the cars pulling onto the driveway across the road. She continued to watch as a horse and buggy came down the road and pulled onto the Kings' driveway.

"Just look at the mess that horse left on the pavement." She shook her head. "I wonder who is gonna clean up that nasty debris."

This morning, Virginia had been too tired to get much done, and by the time she'd felt like doing anything, the steady roar of vehicles, mingled with the irritation of the *clippity-clop* of horses' hooves on the road out front nearly drove her batty.

"And it's all the fault of that stupid greenhouse across the way." She paused and kicked one of the lower cupboard drawers but winced and had to sit down when a searing pain shot through her bad leg.

I've told Earl those Amish are strange, and now we're stuck dealing with their conservative lifestyle across the street.

Virginia shifted, trying to find a comfortable position, and reached down to rub her knee. *The pain from that fall I took down the stairs twelve years ago is always here to remind me of how stupid I used to be. Guess I got what I deserved.*

Another influx of customers arrived, and Amy was tempted to send for Mom. But before she could make the effort to call upon Henry, the man who used to court her mother showed up.

"Is Belinda around?" His eyes seemed to glow as he spoke her mother's name.

"She's up at the house, taking a break."

"Oh, okay. Guess I'll go knock on the door."

Amy was prepared to ask him not to bother Mom, when another customer stepped up to the counter, asking a question about the tomato plants that were being sold for 25 percent off. Amy didn't want to lose a sale, so she told Monroe she'd be right back and went off with the woman who'd asked the question to show her which plants were on special.

I hope Sylvia answers the door and tells Monroe that Mom is resting and can't be disturbed. There's something about Mr. Esh that doesn't set well with me. Don't know why, but I get the feeling he's not as nice as he appears to be. Maybe there's a reason Mom broke things off with him when they were courting.

It wasn't fair to judge the man when she didn't really know him, but Amy had always been able to read people well, and she'd rarely been wrong. Of course, there was a first time for everything, so in all fairness, she needed to give Monroe Esh the benefit of the doubt.

She pushed her nagging doubts aside and led the customer over to the vegetable plants. It wouldn't do Amy or anyone else one bit of good if she couldn't keep her focus on work.

When Belinda glanced out the kitchen window and spotted Monroe heading for the house, she quickly set her empty glass in the sink and hurried out the front door to meet him. *I wonder what he wants. Is he here to buy something this time, or is it a friendly visit?*

"When I heard you weren't in the greenhouse and had come over here, I decided to head on over and see how you are doing." Monroe offered Belinda a most charming smile. Back when they were young people, he would often smile at her that way.

"I'm doing as well as can be expected," she replied. "It's nice of you to ask."

He leaned on the porch railing but pointed to the front door, which hung slightly open. "Mind if I come in?"

"Actually, my grandchildren and oldest daughter are sleeping right now, so our voices might disturb them."

"Oh, okay." Monroe inched a bit closer to Belinda then gestured to the wicker chairs on the porch. "Is it all right if I sit down out here?"

"Help yourself." Belinda stepped back, out of his way.

"Aren't you going to take a seat? It'll be easier for us to talk that way."

Oh, bother. Belinda felt trapped. It would be rude to say no, but at the same time, she'd come to the house to spend some quiet time alone and wasn't in the mood for company right now. Reluctantly, she forced a smile and seated herself in the chair beside him.

Monroe took off his hat, and holding it by the brim, he fanned his face. "Sure turned out hot today, jah?"

Glancing toward the greenhouse, she gave a nod. Now that Belinda was outside, her focus returned to how things were going out there.

"Say, I was wondering if there's anything you'd like me to do around here—in the house, barn, or even the greenhouse."

"It's kind of you to offer, but we're managing okay with things."

"Your furrowed brows make me wonder if you're feeling stressed about something. Is everything okay with you, Belinda?"

"I'm fine." No way would Belinda make mention of the things she suspected her son of doing. Henry was her business not Monroe's, and if she brought him into it, things would get worse where Henry was concerned. If her son wouldn't listen to anything family members and close friends had to say, he sure wouldn't appreciate a stranger's two cents' worth.

From where she sat, Belinda saw people coming and going from the greenhouse. It wasn't easy to listen to Monroe talk about the custom-built furniture shop he'd purchased after moving back to Strasburg and how he had several employees and didn't need to be in the shop all the time.

"Just have to be there enough to make sure things are going as they should," he said with a nod.

Truth was, Belinda had other, more important things on her mind. *I hope Amy is managing okay.* She adjusted the pillow behind her back. *I wish Monroe would quit staring at me. It makes me feel uncomfortable.*

They talked for a few minutes more about the struggle to keep cool in the warm weather, and then Belinda stood. "I'm sorry to have to cut this visit short, but I need to get back to the greenhouse. I only came over here for a short break, and from the looks of all the buggies and cars parked outside the building, I'm quite sure my help is needed there right now."

Monroe's shoulders drooped a bit as his lips pressed together. "Are you sure there isn't something I can do out there to help you?"

She shook her head. "Unless you've ever run a greenhouse, I doubt you would know what to do."

"I doubt it can be that hard."

"People ask a lot of questions about gardening."

He rubbed his beardless chin. "Guess I'd be stuck either asking you or makin' something up."

She offered him another forced smile. "Have a good rest of your day, and danki for dropping by."

"You're welcome." Monroe plopped his hat back on his head and headed off toward the hitching rail.

Belinda hurried to the greenhouse, and without a glance in his direction, she stepped inside.

"You didn't take a very long break, Mom." Amy tilted her head to one side. "Monroe Esh was here. Did he come up to the house to talk to you?"

"Jah. We sat out on the porch for a few minutes and talked. Then I said I needed to get back here to help out."

"I see."

"Oh, and I'm sorry, but I forgot to bring you some meadow-mint tea."

"No problem, Mom. I still have plenty of *wasser*." Amy lifted her water bottle. "I'm just glad you cut your visit with Monroe short and came back here to help."

Is that a look of relief I see on my daughter's face? Belinda studied Amy for a few minutes. *I have a hunch she doesn't care much for Monroe. Well, that's fine with me, because he's just an old acquaintance and will never be anything more than that.*

Chapter 18

The next day seemed to drag on and on. It wasn't that they weren't busy; there had been plenty of people coming to the greenhouse. Amy was so tired, and she figured her mother was as well. She'd be glad when their workday ended and they could be back in the house where there wouldn't be a group of people posing questions and asking for assistance.

"I'm going to the house to take my lunch break." Mom tapped Amy's shoulder. "Is that okay with you?"

"Sure, Mom. Enjoy your hot meal." Drumming her fingers on the counter, Amy noticed that the bags of hummingbird food had gone down. She wasn't surprised to see the powdered nectar selling so well. She had observed the feeders at their house going empty with the steady flow of hungry hummers and figured many of their customers were also feeding the tiny birds.

Amy rose from the stool and strode toward the storage room. The bags that were ready to be put out sat off to one side. She grabbed all she could and toted them to the display area then put each bag in its place and straightened the rows. Afterward, Amy went to the seed display, where she discovered that certain packets were either low or out of stock.

She went back to the storage room to see if she had replacements to fill the rack that had been depleted. Amy took a notepad and pencil to jot down each item. She would need to get more green bean, radish, and carrot seeds.

"Amy, I'm gonna go eat since we're not busy," Henry hollered.

"Just give me a second with this list, and allow me enough time to get the packets of seeds before you leave."

Frowning, he stepped over to the rack. "What have you written down so far?"

She showed him the list. "I'm about done."

"I'm *hungerich*, Sister. I'll get the items you have listed, but only because I wanna eat." He snatched the piece of paper out of her grasp.

Amy's mouth dropped open. "Don't be so impatient."

Henry took off, and it wasn't long before he emerged with a brown bag full of seed packets. "Here ya go. Now, I'm outta here."

Watching him leave, Amy picked up the sack. She pulled out a few pieces at a time and began her work. When the rack was half done, she realized that the bag was empty. *Why am I not surprised that my brother didn't get all that I needed?*

Amy grabbed the paper sack and went to the back room to get the rest of the needed inventory. She peeked out twice to make sure there were no customers waiting at the checkout. Seeing no one, she went to the seed rack and finished her work.

A short time later, Mom returned with a box full of canned pickles. "I got to thinking about these *bickels* we canned from the garden last year." She gestured toward the storage room. "There's an empty wooden shelf in there that could be brought out and used to display these. We can also sell some extra jars of honey."

"That's a good idea. With all the tourists we get coming in, they don't often buy live plants. But they do seem to be interested in our jellies, jams, and honey, so why not try to sell some bickels too?"

Mom rested a hand on her hip. "The strawberries in the garden are coming along well, and it'll soon be time to make strawberry jam, and we can sell some of that as well. Sylvia agreed to make it, so that's one less thing for us to worry about."

"I like the idea." Amy nodded. "I'm sure the tourists will too."

"We have to come up with some ways that will set us apart from the new greenhouse." Mom slid the box aside. "Right now, however, I need to check on your brother and ask him to move some plants around for me."

"Okay, I'll stay close by." Amy yawned. *Maybe I'm just overly tired from rushing about for the last few days, helping people choose items that are on sale and answering far too many questions.*

She heard the door open and turned to see the homeless lady enter the greenhouse. *If she lives in that old shack quite a ways down the road, guess she's not exactly homeless,* Amy reasoned. *It's certainly not much of a home though. I bet she doesn't have hot and cold running water or indoor plumbing like we are fortunate to have.*

Amy glanced at the poor woman, wishing there was more they could do to help other than offering her free baked goods and garden produce from time to time. She remembered the day Lydia bought a plant for the elderly woman. If Maude had any money, it wasn't much, for she never bought anything from the greenhouse, just came in and looked around. Maude's clothing was worn and faded, and her hair never appeared to be combed. Amy wondered how the woman came to be in this predicament. Could something tragic have occurred that changed things for Maude?

Amy tried not to stare as the elderly woman ambled down one aisle and then another, looking at the various plants and flowers. Every so often, Maude stopped and glanced Amy's way then just as quickly averted her gaze.

When Amy's mother came in with a plate of chocolate chip cookies, which she placed on the counter, Maude ambled up and helped herself to six of the treats. She paused briefly and glanced at Amy then just as quickly looked away. It was almost as though the woman felt guilty about something. Without a word, she slipped out the door with her slender shoulders drawn up and her arms tucked against her sides.

Amy wondered if Maude had stolen some small gift item from the greenhouse and hidden it in the pocket of her baggy dress. *Guess I won't worry about it,* she told herself. *Even if she did take something,*

Mom would probably look at Maude in a kindly manner and say, "It's wrong to take things without asking. Next time you want something from the greenhouse, please come to me and ask."

Amy sighed. Sometimes her mother could be a little too nice.

Toward the end of the day, Herschel Fisher and his mother came into the greenhouse. They were all smiles as they made their way over to greet Belinda. It had been awhile since they'd dropped by, and she was pleased to see them. Vera seemed to be doing well, despite having to use a cane, and it was nice to see Herschel again. He always seemed so pleasant and sincere. The widower was quite attractive for a man his age. Belinda was surprised he'd never gotten married again. *But then,* she reasoned, *Herschel probably still loves his wife, just as I will always love Vernon.*

"Our sale is winding down," she said, after shaking both of their hands, "but there are still several nice plants and other things to choose from." She gestured to the items on sale. "You're welcome to look around, and feel free to ask either me or Amy any questions you may have."

"*Danki,* we will." Vera hobbled over to the hanging baskets, but Herschel held back. "How are things going for you, Belinda?" he asked.

"With the exception of a few minor mishaps, things are well enough, I suppose." She couldn't help noticing the kindness in his eyes. Although Belinda didn't know Vera's son very well, she'd heard from Sara what a kind, gentle person he was. He'd certainly taken an active interest in his daughter since learning that he was her biological father.

"What kind of mishaps?" Herschel's brows drew together.

Belinda mentioned the situation with the broken pipe in the garden shed, the bees that had found their way into the greenhouse, the vandalized mailbox, and the greenhouse sign that had been cut down and tossed in the weeds.

Deep wrinkles formed across his forehead. "Do you think all those things were done intentionally?"

Belinda shrugged. "The mailbox and our business sign for sure, and maybe even the ieme, but I believe the pipe that broke was ready to go because it was so old and rusty."

"Have you notified the authorities about the vandalism out front by the road?"

She shook her head. "Didn't see any reason to since we have no idea who did those things. I figure they could have been done by rowdy teenagers sowing their wild oats. You know how some of them can be when they're going through *rumschpringe*." She made no mention of Henry as a suspect since she had no proof it was her son who'd done those things. Even if he was the one responsible, it wasn't something she wanted anyone outside the immediate family to know.

Herschel gave a nod. "I can't speak on this firsthand, since I never knew I had a *dochder* until she was in her twenties. But from what other parents have told me, those growing-up days can be difficult to deal with, never knowing what your children might do during that time."

"And always wondering if they will ever settle down and join the Amish church," Belinda put in.

"Exactly."

"My son Henry isn't actually running around, but he's been a problem for me ever since his father and brother were killed." Belinda didn't know why she felt led to share this with a man she barely knew, but it felt good to get it out.

"I'm sorry to hear that. Would it help if I had a talk with Henry?"

"I don't think so. Others have tried, and it's made no difference at all." Belinda shifted her weight, leaning against the front side of the checkout counter. "Henry might resent hearing it from a near stranger even more."

"I understand, so don't worry. I won't bring up the topic should I see him. However, if he brings it up, would it be okay if I said something?"

Belinda nodded. "I think it's rather doubtful though. Henry keeps to himself as much as he can, and he's been bottling up a lot of anger and resentment."

"I know all about that." Herschel's eyes darkened. "I spent a good many years angry at God after my fraa died. Learning about Sara and being able to spend time with her has helped me so much. There's a purpose to my life, and she's given me a reason to live and love again."

"I still have my children and grandchildren, which I'm thankful for." Belinda's eyes misted. "I love them all dearly, and they are my reason to keep on living and doing the best I can."

Since the Fishers were the only customers in the greenhouse and it was almost closing time, Amy left them in Mom's capable hands and went up to the house to see about helping Sylvia with preparations for supper. She assumed she'd find her sister already in the kitchen.

When Amy entered the room, it was quiet and there was no sign of Sylvia. She and Mom had discussed this morning what they would eat for supper. *I suppose it won't be any trouble for me to get the bacon frying for the turkey-bacon club sandwiches.*

She washed her hands at the kitchen sink and got to work heating the pan after getting out the bacon to fry. Once the meat was done and she'd placed the pieces on paper towels to soak up the oil, Amy left the kitchen. She found Sylvia lying on the living-room couch with her eyes closed. *Is she really that tired, or is sleeping the way my sister copes with her sorrow—trying to shut it out?*

Amy glanced across the room, where Rachel sat in her playpen, holding a rattle in her chubby little hands. Allen knelt on the floor nearby, piling up wooden blocks and then knocking them over. It was a wonder the noise didn't wake his mother.

Amy was tempted to wake Sylvia herself but decided to let her sleep. Maybe once she got the rest of their supper going, her sister would smell the food and wake up. Or Allen might become louder and that would do the trick.

Amy returned to the kitchen and took a loaf of bread out, along with some lettuce and tomatoes. Some evenings when she felt extra tired, like now, Amy wished they could all go out for an evening meal. But in addition to going through the trouble of getting everyone ready, there was the cost of a restaurant meal to consider. Another reason the family hadn't gone out to eat was because of Sylvia. She still could hardly stand to be around people.

Amy took a knife from the drawer and grabbed the cutting board. The tomatoes and lettuce came from their garden, which she had picked yesterday. Mom possessed a green thumb for growing produce. Sylvia enjoyed it too, and she'd seemed to be following in their mother's footsteps until the accident happened.

I wonder how long it will take my sister to overcome her depression and realize she can't dwell on the past. For the sake of her children, she must eventually move forward with her life. Sylvia needs to find some joy in life and share it with them.

Amy gave a slow shake of her head. *Who am I to judge my sister for a lack of joy? All I've done since our dear family members' deaths is try to keep things running smoothly in the greenhouse and here at the house. I rarely feel any real joy these days, yet I force myself to smile so I appear cheerful—especially while at the greenhouse.*

Sometimes Amy felt as though she had the weight of the world on her shoulders, even though it was only five family members who shared this home with her.

"It's okay though," she whispered. "I love them all dearly and would make any sacrifice on their behalf."

"Who ya talkin' to in here, Amy?"

She turned at the sound of Henry's voice. "Myself," she admitted.

His brows lifted. "If you're that desperate to talk to someone, why don't ya go outside and visit with Sara and Brad? They just showed up, and wouldn't ya know it—Mom invited them to stay for supper."

Amy was glad they had plenty of sandwich makings to share, and she would also put together a fruit salad and open a bag of chips.

Henry gave an exaggerated roll of his eyes. "I'll bet that preacher husband of Sara's will end up givin' us all a sermon while we eat."

"That wouldn't be such a bad thing, would it?"

"Guess it all depends on what he decides to preach about."

Amy bit back a chuckle. It would do her brother some good to listen to another sermon. For that matter, it might be just what the rest of the family needed too.

Chapter 19

The following day, Amy hurried to the greenhouse, carrying a couple of hanging baskets her sister had made. Once inside, she found some empty hangers to put them on. At least her sister was willing to help, even though it was a nuisance to haul them from the house.

Amy picked up two more baskets from the porch then glanced over at their hitching rail where her buggy and horse waited. She would be going into town soon to grocery shop. That meant Mom and Henry would be working alone in the greenhouse until she returned. Amy hoped Henry would cooperate with their mother while she was gone for a few hours today.

Sylvia came out the door and stepped onto the porch. Allen was with her. "I hope those will sell." She gestured to the hanging baskets. "The plants I used this time were smaller than the last bunch, so the pots aren't quite as full."

"Don't worry. Lots of people have been buying lately, so I'm sure these won't last long."

Allen toddled over and tugged on the edge of Amy's apron. She reached down and tousled the little guy's hair. Her nephew was such a sweet child. Amy wished she could have a little boy like him someday. But she had to accept the fact that it might never happen. She could be an old maid all her life, helping to keep the greenhouse running.

"Guess I'd better get the rest of these baskets over to the greenhouse." Amy bent to pick them up when Allen squealed and pointed at a squirrel running through the yard.

Sylvia frowned. "Those rascals are sure pesky. Just what we don't need getting into the bird feeders."

"I know, but most of our feeders have been squirrel-proofed, thanks to Dad."

"Jah, he did a good job taking care of problems around here—big and small."

Amy nodded. Gripping the flower basket handles, she headed toward the greenhouse. "I'll see you both later," she called over her shoulder.

"Are you sure you wouldn't rather go grocery shopping and leave me here to run the greenhouse?" Amy asked her mother when she entered the greenhouse.

Mom shook her head. "Henry will be here with me, and I feel certain we can manage. If I go for groceries, I'll no doubt see people I know and end up talking too long." She smiled at Amy. "You, on the other hand, will hurry through the store, get what we need, and come right back home."

Amy couldn't argue with that. She was less likely to visit with people when she was on a mission to shop for food. "Okay, I'd better get going so I can get back here before noon. I just hope you don't get a swarm of customers while I'm gone."

Mom gave Amy's shoulder a squeeze. "Don't worry. We'll be fine."

Amy set the hanging baskets down, gave her mother a hug, and opened the door, nearly colliding with Henry.

He glared at her. "You oughta watch where you're going."

"I could say the same for you," she countered. Before her brother could think of another comeback, Amy clasped his arm. "I'm going shopping for groceries, so please make sure you stay in the greenhouse with Mom and don't go outside or wander off."

Refusing to look at her, he muttered, "You ain't my boss, so quit tellin' me what to do."

Amy opened her mouth to say something more, but thinking better of it, she hurried across the yard to where her horse and buggy waited. It seemed that no one could get through to her brother, regardless of how hard they tried, so what was the use? Last evening, when Sara and Brad joined them for supper, Brad had tried to engage Henry in conversation several times, but Henry gave little response. While it wasn't a reflection on their mother, Amy could tell how uncomfortable Mom had felt when Henry acted so disinterested in everything Brad or the rest of them said to him.

"Well girl, it's just you and me from here to the store and back again." Amy patted her horse's neck before untying the chestnut mare from the rail. "At least you're more cooperative than that stubborn brother of mine. And you don't talk back either."

Amy had only been gone a short time, when something unexpected occurred in the greenhouse.

"Look—there's a hummingbird in here!" One of their English customers pointed at it.

Ten other shoppers were in the building, and Belinda stood behind the counter, watching as people either ducked or began chasing after the poor bird.

"Be careful!" she hollered above all the noise. "Hummingbirds are delicate, and we don't want to hurt it."

"Here's the reason it got in." Frowning, Henry pointed to the screen door that someone had left open. "Maybe I need to stand guard and make sure it gets closed after every customer comes in."

"That won't work, Henry. Don't forget the back entrance is open during business hours for ventilation. The hummer could have flown in through there also."

Belinda rubbed her forehead. "It doesn't matter how the little bird got into the building. We need to help him find his way out." Looking upward, she observed the hummer trying to get through the top of the roof. It was hard to watch, because there were two exits, but the poor little thing was in such a frenzy, it couldn't find its way out either of the now open doors. The hummingbird soon became the focal point of everyone in the greenhouse. Belinda could only imagine how distraught the poor creature was.

"Well, chasin' after it sure isn't the answer." Henry cupped his hands around his mouth. "Everyone, please stop chasing the hummer and let me handle this situation."

As soon as the commotion died down and all the people stopped running around, Henry looked at Belinda and said, "I'll be right back." He made a hasty exit and came back a few minutes later with a hummingbird feeder in his hand.

"This oughta do the trick." Henry stood by the open front door-way, holding the feeder up high. "Come on, little guy. You're all confused, aren't ya? It's okay. Don't worry. Everything's gonna be all right."

Several minutes passed, and Belinda watched, along with the rest of the people, as the hummingbird made its way over to the feeder. Once it began eating, Henry backed slowly away until he and the tiny bird went out the door along with the feeder.

Everyone cheered as Belinda shut the screen door. It pleased her to see the softer side of her son, even if only for a few minutes. If Henry could show this much concern for one of God's wee creatures, she couldn't help but hope that the kind, gentle young man she and Vernon had raised would eventually resurface. It might take time and lots of love and encouragement, but she would never give up believing in any of her children.

Jared had come out of the bank, where he'd gone to make a deposit, when he saw Amy's friend Lydia walking down the sidewalk in his direction. She smiled and waved, so he waited for her to catch up.

"It's nice to see you." Lydia smiled when she joined him in front of the bank. "How are things going, Jared?"

I'd like to say I'm miserable, but I won't. "Everything's okay as far as work goes, at least."

"Have you been by to see Amy lately?"

He shook his head. "I want to, but I'm afraid she'll reject me again, and then I'd feel worse than I already do."

Lydia placed her hand on his arm. "I'm sorry, Jared. Amy's making a huge mistake, but she's so caught up in her work and trying to help her family get through their grief, it seems to be all she can think about or deal with right now."

"I get that, but she could deal with it better if she'd let me help."

"I agree." Lydia glanced at the restaurant across the street. "I came to town to buy some things for my mamm, and since it's almost noon, I'm going to have some lunch. Would you care to join me?"

Jared hesitated at first, but he hadn't eaten much for breakfast, and after finishing up a roofing job a short time ago, the thought of a good meal appealed. "Jah, okay, some pizza or a sub sandwich sounds real good."

"The pizza is sure *gut* here." Lydia smiled at Jared from across the table.

He nodded and swiped a napkin across his lips. "Messy but good."

"How's your summer going? Are you keeping busy with the quilts you and your mamm make?" Jared asked. It was an unexpected question; he hadn't said much since they'd ordered their lunch.

"Jah," she responded. "We keep plenty busy quilting and also working in the garden. Whenever I have some free time, I like to read."

"Do you enjoy quilting?"

"I do, but someday I hope to get married and start a family, so my life would then be going in another direction."

Jared picked up his glass of lemonade and took a drink. "If things would have worked out between me and Amy, we'd be planning our wedding right now."

"It's too bad I couldn't get through to her." Lydia studied Jared's handsome face. In addition to being so good-looking, he was such a nice man. She couldn't imagine Amy being foolish enough to let him go no matter what the circumstances.

After Amy left the grocery store, she stopped at Sara's flower shop to say a quick hello only to discover that Sara wasn't there.

"She had a doctor's appointment," Misty said. "I'm not sure what time she'll be back, but you're welcome to wait if you want."

"I'd better not. I have groceries in the buggy that need to be refrigerated, so I need to get them home." Amy smiled. "Please tell Sara I said hello and that we enjoyed our visit with her and Brad last evening."

"I'll give her the message." Misty came around from behind the counter and gave Amy a hug. "I haven't had a chance to tell you this, but I was sorry to hear about the horrible accident that took three of your family members."

Amy's chin trembled at the mention of their loss. It was easier not to think about it if people didn't bring up the topic. "Thank you," she murmured. Keeping her gaze fixed on a bouquet of pink carnations inside the standup cooler on the other side of the room, she said, "I'd better get going. It was nice seeing you, Misty."

"Same here. Take care."

When Amy exited the shop, she paused for a few minutes to gain control of her emotions. No matter how much time passed or how busy they kept, she was certain there would always be a huge void in her family's lives.

Amy heard laughter, and for a split second she felt as if her breathing had been suspended. There stood Jared in front of the pizza place. Lydia stood beside him with her hand on his arm.

Amy ducked under the canopy above the flower shop door and angled her body so that her face could not be seen. *Is my good friend being courted by Jared now? Could he have forgotten about me so quickly and moved on?* A surge of jealousy coursed through her body.

Amy glanced over her shoulder and watched as Jared and Lydia headed down the sidewalk together. When they were far enough away, she hurried to the area where her horse and buggy waited. She'd told Jared he should move on, but did it have to be with someone she knew—her best friend, of all people?

Chapter 20

"Would you mind watching the kinner for me?" Sylvia asked her mother after the supper dishes had been done one Friday evening. "I need to take a walk outside and get some fresh air."

"I don't mind at all." Mom smiled as she wrung out the wet sponge. "It's not good to be cooped up in the stuffy house with the little ones all day. I'm sure you could use a break, and the blueberry cobbler I made can wait. We'll enjoy the dessert with vanilla ice cream when we're all ready for it."

If only a walk would help me feel better or the fruit crisp, for that matter. Sylvia's jaw and facial muscles tightened. She hoped she wouldn't be subjected to another of Mom's lectures on the importance of getting back into life and a normal routine. Sylvia's routine had been derailed the minute her husband, father, and brother had been killed. While it may have been true that the glare of the sun had been in the driver's eyes, he should have been going slower.

Instead of responding to her mother's comment, Sylvia merely smiled and said, "Danki, Mom. I won't be outside very long."

"Take all the time you need," Mom was quick to say. "Amy will be upstairs from the basement soon, so if I need any help with the children, I'll call on her for assistance."

"Okay." Sylvia removed her work apron and was about to head out the back door, when she paused. "Can I ask you a question, Mom?"

"Of course."

"Is Amy your favorite over me and Henry?"

Mom blinked a couple of times. "Of course not, Sylvia. Why would you even ask such a question?"

"Because she willingly helps out in the greenhouse, and you can count on her for support."

Mom slipped her arm around Sylvia's waist. "Amy has been a big help to me in the greenhouse, but each one of my kinner is special to me, and I love you all the same."

"I'm happy to hear that, because sometimes I feel like I'm letting you down by staying here with my little ones and—"

Mom held up one hand. "You're where you need to be right now, and I'm grateful for all the chores you do in the house, not to mention so many meals you have prepared for us at the end of a long day. Danki for that."

"You're welcome." Feeling a little better about things, Sylvia stepped out the back door.

From where she stood by the railing, Sylvia saw their new neighbor man out by the road, closest to his side. He held a shovel and appeared to be scooping up something.

I wonder if he's getting some of the horse droppings left behind from all the buggies that travel this road. Sure hope he's not planning to spread the fresh manure on any of his plants in the flowerbeds, or worse yet, in a vegetable garden. Sylvia had a lot of knowledge when it came to what could or couldn't be mixed into the soil. She was fully aware that fresh horse manure could damage young plants. It also attracted flies and had a strong odor. Hopefully, the man across the road knew this too and would add the manure to a compost pile. It would take four to six weeks to turn from stable waste to being ready to put around the plants or in a garden. Sylvia wondered if either the man or his wife knew anything about composting.

After some time, the neighbor man went up the driveway and into his yard with the shovel. Sylvia thought it was a bit odd that he would be so eager to go out and collect horse droppings from the road. She had seen the wife a time or two, when she came out to her front porch. The new neighbors kept pretty much to themselves—nothing like Mom and Dad's previous, friendly neighbors.

Those nice people are surely missed. Sylvia wiped the perspiration from her forehead. "Typical weather for the second week of July," she muttered, stepping off the porch. The grass felt soft and cool under her bare feet. Sylvia paused to admire the newest flowerbed Mom had created. It was filled with summer colors.

Sylvia's first inclination was to lie in the free-standing hammock awhile, but that would only remind her of Abe. When they were teenagers, on hot summer nights he often slept out here under the stars. Whenever Sylvia and Amy slept outdoors, Dad set up cots for them on the porch. Ezekiel had never cared much for sleeping outside, but occasionally Sylvia and the rest of his siblings would convince him to join them. Even though Henry was several years younger than the rest of them, Mom and Dad sometimes agreed to let him take part in the sleep-outs.

Tightening the black scarf wrapped around her head, Sylvia remembered one time when Ezekiel and Henry lay on the grass in sleeping bags with a canvas tarp beneath them. Abe, like most big brothers, decided it would be fun to tease Henry by telling him made-up scary stories. One story in particular had made Henry cry and run for the house. It was about a wild animal that would sneak into the yard under a full moon and steal small children.

A few minutes after Henry ran screaming into the house, Mom came out, shook her finger at Abe, and said, "If you keep tormenting your little brother, you'll be sleeping in the barn by yourself, and Henry can have the comfortable hammock."

Sylvia's eyes filled with tears as she recalled more childhood memories. *I would give almost anything to have those carefree days back again.*

She smoothed the black fabric of her dress. Amy, Mom, and Sylvia all wore the drab color every day in remembrance of their loss. Wearing black during the mourning process was part of their Amish way. After a year of grieving, they would put away the dresses and wear regular colored frocks again. In the meantime, they all said that they hoped it would be a very long while before any of them would have to wear mourning garb again.

Sylvia's thoughts went to Toby's parents and siblings, who lived in Mifflin County. She'd received a letter from Toby's mother, Selma, the other day, asking how Sylvia and the kinner were getting along and stating that she and the rest of the family were still missing Toby and spoke of him often.

Feeling restless and struggling to keep her raging emotions under control, Sylvia made her way down the driveway until she came to the phone shed. Stepping inside, she took a seat, leaving the door hanging open. Despite the sting of losing loved ones, life continued to move on. It hadn't stopped or changed because of what had happened to Toby, Dad, and Abe.

The message light blinked, so she clicked the button then picked up the pen to write down any information they would need. The first one was from a man wanting to sell them something she was sure they didn't need. Sylvia deleted the message and listened to the next. This was from Ezekiel, letting them know that Michelle had delivered a nine-pound, twenty-one-inch baby boy at two o'clock this afternoon. They'd decided to call him Vernon Lee.

Sylvia felt a tightness in her chest that would not loosen. *Oh Dad, I wish there was a way you could know that you have a namesake. If only you could be here to hold the new boppli.*

She wrote down the details of the baby's birth, tore off the paper from the tablet, and stepped out of the phone shed. Sylvia couldn't help the envy circulating within her. *Michelle has a husband to share in the joy of raising their children. I, on the other hand, am without my mate and need extra support from my mamm and sister.* Sylvia hoped that in time things would get better—not just for her but for the others in her family, who'd also suffered a great loss.

As she started back toward the house, a crow flew over her head, screeching out its shrill call. It landed on a nearby treetop and let out several more aggravating calls. *I hope that silly thing doesn't have a nest somewhere in our yard.*

Ignoring the black bird, Sylvia hurried up the back steps and into the house. "Mom, there was a message from Ezekiel on our answering machine!" She rushed into the living room, where her mother and sister sat on the sofa. Mom held Rachel, and Allen sat on Amy's knee.

"What did your brother have to say?" Mom patted the baby's back.

"Michelle had her boppli this afternoon, and they named him Vernon."

Mom squealed so loud, Rachel began to howl. "Oh, sorry, sweet baby." She continued to pat the little girl's back as she looked over at Sylvia. "That is such good news. Are Michelle and the boppli doing okay?"

"They're both fine." Sylvia gave them all the details then leaned down and scooped her baby daughter into her arms.

"Dad would be so pleased to know they named their son after him." Tears welled in Amy's eyes as she looked at their mother. "Michelle's going to have her hands full now, with two little ones to look after."

Tearfully, Mom bobbed her head.

"She's no doubt going to need some help." Amy reached over and touched Mom's hand. "You should go there for at least two weeks to lend a hand." She looked at Sylvia. "Don't you agree, Sister?"

Sylvia shrugged. "I suppose so, but it would be a lot for you to handle the greenhouse by yourself. Every time I've looked out the window the past few weeks, there have been a good many cars and horse and buggies in the parking area. Busy is good, but not when you are working in the greenhouse pretty much by yourself."

"I'll have Henry's help."

"Jah, when he feels like helping," Mom put in. "Sylvia's right, Amy. I can't leave you here to run the place by yourself."

Amy set Allen on the floor, jumped up, and faced Sylvia. Planting her feet in a wide stance, she spoke with assurance. "We'll get someone to come here to watch the kinner, and then you can help me in the greenhouse."

Sylvia's forehead wrinkled as she gave a determined shake of her head. "No, Amy. . .I can't."

"Can't or won't?" Amy pointed at Sylvia with her index finger. "If you care about Ezekiel and Michelle, you'll step out of your comfort zone to help out so Mom can go there to help."

Sylvia took a deep, pained breath and closed her eyes. She disliked being made to feel guilty. Didn't her sister realize how hard it would be for her to leave the children with someone else and spend a good portion of her days in the greenhouse? *I can't do it,* she told herself. *It would be too difficult to deal with people asking me questions all day and giving me looks of pity. Hiring someone to help out in the greenhouse would be better.*

Sylvia bit down on her lower lip. *But honestly, it would take some time to train a new person, and I already know what to do.*

"Don't feel like you have to say yes, Daughter." Mom looked at Sylvia with a tender expression. "But it would be ever so nice if I could go to Clymer to see my newest grandchild and stay a few weeks to help out."

No pressure. I really do need to deal with my stress and anxiety, so I'll force myself to do it. Either I'll be able to work through the two weeks Mom's gone, or I'll be very desperate for her return.

Sylvia stroked the sides of her little girl's silky head while clearing her throat a couple of times. "All right, I'll do it. I will help in the greenhouse, but only till Mom gets back. After that, I'll be right here with my precious kinner again."

"You've been actin' like a bumble grumble all evening. What's the problem?" Earl moved closer to Virginia on the couch and bumped her shoulder.

"You'd be a bumble grumble too if you had to be stuck in this house all day listening to all the traffic coming down the road in front of our place." Virginia wrinkled her nose. "I tried sitting on the front porch for a while, but the nasty stench from all those horses was unbearable."

"That's good ole' country air." He nudged her again. "You'll get used to it in time."

She folded her arms. "I doubt that. Also, Earl, I'll have you know that my car has horse stuff on most of its wheels. That sort of thing would never have happened in good old Chicago."

"Well, dear, you'll just have to try harder to dodge all the road apples when you're out driving." Earl chuckled. "Actually, I went out earlier and collected some of that stuff. A guy from work told me that it's good for fertilizing around the shrubs in the flowerbeds."

Virginia merely glanced at him and gave a look of disapproval.

"Did you get started on the garden yet?"

"Nope."

"How come? I got the plot all ready for you."

"I'm still unpacking boxes. Besides, I don't have any vegetable seeds."

Earl gave a disgusting snort. "Really, Virginia, there's a greenhouse right across the street. I bet ya anything they sell packets of seeds. Probably have some vegetable plants already started too, which would be your best bet since it's already the middle of summer." He pointed toward the front window. "You oughta go over there tomorrow morning and check it out."

She groaned. "Do I have to? Can't we buy the seeds at a hardware store or anyplace else that might sell them?"

Earl shook his head. "Don't be ridiculous. There's a place right across the road, so why make a special trip into town to get what you need?"

With my luck, that Mrs. King will try to arrange a tea party with me. I feel stuck in the middle with Earl making me go over there and me trying to avoid any contact with those Amish people.

Virginia sighed. "Okay, okay. Sometime tomorrow I'll head over there and see what they have." *Maybe I'll tell 'em what I think of the stench their place causes too.*

Amy stood in front of her bedroom window, staring out at the night sky. Only a sliver of the moon shown tonight, and a light wind blew in through the partially open window. Tomorrow morning Mom's driver would be by early to pick her up for the roughly six-hour journey to Clymer.

Amy figured her mother must be pretty excited about seeing Ezekiel and Michelle's new baby. It would be good for her to get away for a few weeks to help out and enjoy two of her grandchildren.

Amy moved away from the window and picked up her hairbrush. As she pulled the bristles through her long hair, she thought about Sylvia agreeing to help in the greenhouse. *It will be nice to have my sister working in there with me again.*

Amy clicked her tongue. She hoped Sylvia's little ones would adjust to having an unfamiliar person taking care of them. Mom had been in touch with Mary Ruth, and she'd agreed to come over each workday to watch Sylvia's children while Mom was away.

Amy wished she could go with their mother to see Michelle and Ezekiel's new baby. How exciting it must be to have a new addition to their growing family. Once more, Amy thought about how her plans for marriage and children had been changed.

She continued to run the brush through her smooth waves. *I hope it all goes well tomorrow and that it's not too much for Sylvia to work with me in the greenhouse.*

Amy's thoughts turn to Jared and the jealousy she'd felt seeing him with Lydia. *But can I really blame him? I did tell Jared he was free to court someone else. And who better than my dear sweet friend?*

She set the hairbrush down and sank to the edge of her bed. *If Jared decides to marry Lydia or someone else, I'll have to accept it and try to be happy for them. In the meantime, I need to keep my focus on running the greenhouse and helping everyone in the family overcome their depression.*

Chapter 21

Sylvia swallowed multiple times as she hugged her mother and told her goodbye the following morning. Mom would be gone for at least two weeks, and during that time Sylvia was expected to help in the greenhouse. She could hardly believe she had agreed to do it.

Sylvia gripped her hands together behind her back as she watched Henry put Mom's suitcase in her driver's van. Sylvia's apprehension increased when Henry and Amy hugged their mother and then Mom got into the van.

How am I going to be able to cope? Sylvia asked herself. *What if I can't carry through with my promise?* Mary Ruth would be here soon to look after the children, so that problem had been taken care of. Sylvia felt sure Allen and Rachel would be in good hands, but that didn't make her job of waiting on customers and being available to answer questions at the greenhouse any easier. There was no turning back now. The vehicle had pulled out of the yard and turned onto the road.

As if she were able to read Sylvia's thoughts, Amy joined her on the porch and slipped her arm around Sylvia's waist. "I have every confidence that you'll be able to do this, dear sister." She glanced toward the greenhouse, where Henry had already gone. "It will be time to open soon, so I'm going to head out there now. You can join us as soon as Mary Ruth shows up."

"Okay." Sylvia's single word came out in a squeak. It was selfish to think such thoughts, but she wished Mom hadn't agreed to help at Michelle and Ezekiel's. *But she came over to my house to help when both of my bopplin were born,* Sylvia reminded herself. *It's only fair that she would do the same for my brother and his wife.*

"I'll be there as soon as I can," Sylvia said, turning toward the front door of the house. She glanced over her shoulder and saw Amy sprinting across the yard toward the greenhouse.

For the umpteenth time, Sylvia wished she could turn back the hands of time and be living at her own home again with Toby and the children.

Clymer

Ezekiel sat beside Michelle on the couch while she fed their precious son. He held Angela Mary on his lap, stroking her soft cheek.

"Your little brother is Vernon Lee and is named after your grandfather," he said in Pennsylvania Dutch.

"Bruder?" The little girl tipped her head back and looked up at him with wide eyes.

Ezekiel nodded. "Jah. Someday when he's a little bigger, the two of you can play together."

Angela Mary reached over and touched Vernon's arm. "*Mei boppli.*"

"He is your baby, but he's also your mama's and my baby."

Angela Mary nodded as though she understood and then leaned her head against Ezekiel's chest and closed her eyes. It was a special moment, the four of them here in the living room, waiting for Ezekiel's mother to arrive. "It'll sure be good to see Mom again and introduce her to Dad's namesake."

"Yes, it will be very nice."

When Michelle finished nursing the baby, she put him over her shoulder and patted his back. It wasn't long before a good burp came forth.

Angela Mary sat up straight and pointed at her brother. "*Der boppli waar am uffschtoose.*"

Michelle chuckled, and so did Ezekiel. "Jah." With a gentle touch, he rubbed his daughter's back. "The baby was belching." He looked over at Michelle and grinned. "Our daughter is pretty *schmaert*."

"Jah, she's a very smart little girl."

Ezekiel's head turned toward the door when he heard a vehicle pull into the yard. "I bet that's my mamm and her driver right now."

Belinda had no more than stepped out of the van, when she saw Ezekiel come out of the house and sprint toward the vehicle. She greeted him with open arms. "*Ach*, it's so good to see you again."

"Likewise, Mom." Ezekiel hugged her tightly. "Michelle's in the house with Angela Mary and the boppli. They'll be excited to see you too."

While Ezekiel opened the back door to retrieve Belinda's suitcase and tote bag, she paid the driver and reminded her of what day and time she would need to be picked up for the return trip to Strasburg. With Ezekiel carrying the suitcase and Belinda the tote, they hurried toward the house.

Excitement welled in Belinda's chest when they entered the house. "Go on into the living room," Ezekiel said. "I'll put your things in the guest room while you visit with Michelle and the kinner."

"Okay."

Belinda found Michelle sitting on the couch holding the baby, and Angela Mary sat beside her.

Seeing her granddaughter's eyes light up when she saw her, Belinda bent down, swooped the little girl into her arms, and gave her a kiss.

Angela Mary giggled and touched Belinda's cheeks. She turned her head and pointed at her baby brother, snuggled in his mama's arms. "Mei bruder."

Belinda placed the child on the couch and took a seat between her and Michelle. "Jah, sweet Angela Mary, you have a little brother now." A lump formed in Belinda's throat as she gazed for the first time on her newest grandchild. *"Er hot en lieblich boppli."*

"We think he's an adorable baby too." Michelle reached around Belinda's shoulders and hugged her. "Danki for coming. It's so nice to see you again."

"I am glad Sylvia agreed to help out in the greenhouse, or it would have been hard for me to get away." Belinda stroked the baby's soft cheek.

"Would you like to hold little Vernon?"

"I surely would."

When Michelle placed the baby in her arms, Belinda choked up. "If only his grandpa could be here to see him right now. He would feel honored that you named the boppli after him."

Ezekiel stepped into the room. "It was my fraa's idea, Mom, but I was in total agreement."

Belinda smiled and touched her daughter-in-law's arm. "It was a sweet thing to do."

"If our little Vernon turns out to be even half as kind and loving as your husband was, Ezekiel and I will be happy parents."

"Those are my thoughts too." Ezekiel took a seat on the other side of Belinda and pulled Angela Mary onto his lap.

"How are you and the rest of the family doing?" he asked, reaching over to stroke his son's forehead.

If only I could be forthright, but. . . "We're getting along okay." No way would Belinda say anything to the contrary. The last thing she wanted was for Ezekiel to worry about them or believe things were not going well in the greenhouse or even within their home.

"How's Henry's attitude? Has his temperament improved any since I last talked to him?"

"Some. One of our ministers spoke to him, and so did Sara's husband, Brad."

"That's good. The more people who take an interest in him, the better it will be."

"Jah." Belinda changed the subject by asking how Michelle was feeling since the birth of her second child.

"I'm doing okay physically but not well enough to be on my own yet, so I'm ever so thankful you'll be here for a couple of weeks." Michelle's eyes glistened with tears. "I have no mother to help out, but I feel blessed to have you."

Belinda teared up too. Although Michelle wasn't the woman she would have originally chosen for her son, she'd come to care deeply for her. Michelle had proven her loyalty and love many times since she joined the Amish church and married Ezekiel. Belinda felt bad for the cool way she'd treated her daughter-in-law in the past but was thankful for the opportunity to make it up to her now.

Strasburg

Amy felt concern when she saw her sister's rigid posture as she clutched a pot of petunias close to her chest as though it were a shield. Sylvia was undeniably filled with unease. She'd made it through the morning but avoided speaking to anyone unless they spoke to her first. When Sylvia had come back to the greenhouse after taking her lunch break, Amy noticed her sister's glassy stare and trembling hands.

Less than an hour later, Sylvia announced that she wanted to go check on the children. Amy didn't argue. They didn't have any customers at the moment.

After Sylvia left, Amy stepped outside in search of Henry. If they did end up with any customers while Sylvia was in the house, she would need her brother's help.

"Henry! Where are you, Henry?" Amy called.

"I'm right here."

She glanced toward the barn and spotted him sitting in the wide opening of the hayloft, crossed-legged and looking out as if he didn't have a care in the world.

"What are you doing up there? Don't you know there's work to be done?"

"I like to be up high so I can watch the birds," he hollered. "I've seen a cardinal, a few robins, and look. . .there's a big black crow over there."

Amy turned to look at the roof of the greenhouse where Henry pointed. *Caw! Caw! Caw!* The bird flapped its wings and swooped to the ground, continuing to make a racket. Amy shuddered. It seemed like every time that annoying bird came around, something bad happened.

Amy's slender covering ties swished across her face as she shook her head. *I need to stop such superstitious thoughts.*

She looked up at Henry, sitting in the same spot, and pointed her finger. "You'd better come down here right now, because I need your help in the greenhouse."

Henry cupped his hands around his mouth. "I thought Sylvia was helpin' you today."

"She went in the house a few minutes ago to check on the kinner."

"Well, you'd better get back to the greenhouse then 'cause I see that new English neighbor lady from across the road walking up our driveway. I forgot her name, but I bet she's needin' some kind of plants or gardening supplies."

"Her name is Virginia."

It wouldn't be good to have customers walking around the greenhouse without anyone to wait on them, so Amy turned and ran back inside.

I wonder how this is going to play out while Mom's away. Since she left us, Sylvia's apprehensive about helping me, and Henry thinks he can sit in the barn during business hours and bird-watch. Amy moaned in despair. *I hope these two don't leave me on my own out here to manage things, because if they do, I'm going to be real upset and disappointed. Why don't they understand that I am struggling to function too?*

A few minutes later, Virginia came in, dressed in a floral print, citron shirt and tight-fitting lime green pants that matched the color of her sandals. The woman's flashy attire caught Amy off guard, and it was hard not to stare.

Without saying a word, the neighbor headed over to the racks where the seed packets were located. She picked out a few before meandering down the row of vegetable plants.

Thinking she might need some assistance, Amy hurried over to her. Virginia's bangle bracelets rattled together on her wrist as she withdrew a small vegetable plant and looked it over. Amy greeted the woman and asked if she needed help with anything.

Virginia placed the tomato plant down. "Wouldn't be here if I didn't need somethin'." A sheen of sweat covered the woman's cheeks, nose, and forehead. She took out a handkerchief from her bright yellow cross-body bag and dabbed at the sweat. "Sure is warm in here. If you had electricity, you could cool the place down."

Amy smiled. "What are you in need of?"

"I'm lookin' to buy some tomato plants that already have fruit on them and will ripen soon." Virginia avoided eye contact with Amy. "What other varieties do you have?" She gestured to the smaller tomato plant. "I put that one back since it only has flowers on it."

"Since it's the middle of July, most of our vegetable plants are pretty picked over, but I'm sure I can find you a few good ones." Amy stepped over to another spot and picked up a cherry tomato plant. She also grabbed one of the larger types of tomatoes that would make good slicers. "Will these do?"

"Yeah, sure." Virginia's eyelids twitched. "I read in the paper that there will be another greenhouse going in not far from here. Sounds like it'll be a pretty good size."

"Yes, I've heard about it."

"Aren't you worried that it'll take a lot of your customers away?"

"I'm not bothered." Amy spoke with assurance, although she did have some concerns. But as a Christian, she needed to have the faith to believe that things would work out according to the Lord's plan, and she reminded herself that worrying over things wouldn't help. She figured Virginia wouldn't be interested in her way of dealing with the knowledge that they would soon have competition.

Amy placed the plants in a wagon. "Is there anything else you would like?"

"Well, I'm not sure. Let me think about it for a sec." With her backside to the shelf where the vegetable plants sat, Virginia folded her arms and leaned back. She stood that way several seconds, and then, slapping her hands against her reddened cheeks, she jumped away from the shelf as if she'd been stung by a bee. "For goodness' sakes!"

"What's wrong?" Amy felt concern, seeing Virginia's curling lip and wrinkled nose. "The back of my pants is all wet. Someone in here obviously doesn't know what they're doing with a hose."

Before Amy could respond, Sylvia, who only moments ago had returned to the greenhouse, stepped up to Virginia and apologized. "I'm so sorry. I–I must have watered a little too much this morning."

"Yeah, well, it's just a good thing it's only water I backed into and not somethin' I can't get out of my pants." With a huff, Virginia grabbed the wagon's handle and pulled it up to the front counter.

Amy followed.

After the woman paid for her purchases, Amy put them in a cardboard box. "Would you like me to ask my brother to carry the tomato plants over to your house so you can walk with your hands free?"

Virginia shook her head. "No thanks. I'll haul it over there myself." She paid for her items, and carrying the box, she limped out the door.

"I wish she would have let me ask Henry to help her," Amy said when Sylvia joined her a few minutes later.

Sylvia looked down at the floor. "I can't deal with this right now, Amy. I wish I'd never agreed to help you in the greenhouse while Mom is gone." Without waiting for a response, Sylvia flung the door open and dashed out.

Amy sank onto the stool behind the counter with a groan. *What if Sylvia won't come back to help tomorrow? How am I going to manage things for the next two weeks with only a little help from Henry?*

Chapter 22

Clymer

A multitude of thoughts swirled in Belinda's head while she stood at the kitchen window and watched her son head to the barn to do his chores. Ezekiel's mannerisms and the way he carried himself reminded her of Vernon. After not seeing Ezekiel for a while, it caught Belinda off guard when she witnessed her son's comforting traits.

Through the open window, she heard him whistling a cheery tune; again, something her husband had done now and then. Belinda also noticed the way Ezekiel's arms swung as he strolled across the grass.

Aside from her own pain of missing Vernon and seeing him in a way through her eldest son, she ached to be close to all four of her children. *I won't be selfish. The Lord has given Ezekiel a new path to follow. I can't stand in the way and cause him to deviate from it.*

Belinda lowered her head. Staring at the floor, she pondered the happenings of the day before. *He's happy here,* she noted. She'd heard it in his voice and seen the sparkle in his eyes last evening during supper when he talked about his role as a minister. Ezekiel read his Bible in the evenings and said he wanted to walk close to the Lord. He'd also mentioned the satisfaction of owning his own business, saying he was glad he had the chance to do something for a living that he truly enjoyed. He downplayed his disinterest in the work he used to do back home but said if the need arose, he would go back to it. Although it was kind of Ezekiel to offer, Belinda wouldn't hear of her son leaving his new life here in Clymer.

She filled the coffeepot with water and put the right amount of coffee in the filter then set it on the stove and turned on the gas burner. Her thoughts went back home for a spell. *I wish Henry took some pleasure in helping us in the greenhouse and taking care of the bees.*

Belinda watched the bluish flame heating the pot. *My youngest son needs support, and I pray he'll wake up and feel the love and encouragement from his family as well as those in our church district.*

Belinda was well aware of Henry's frustration and dissatisfaction with his new tasks, but she saw no alternative to his situation—at least not until he was a few years older and she felt sure they could run the greenhouse without him.

I wonder what kind of work Henry would like to do. He's never really said. It might be good for me to ask and let him know that eventually he will be able to branch out on his own if he still wants to by then. Belinda moved away from the stove and opened the refrigerator to take out a carton of eggs. *At least it would give Henry a ray of hope, which might help to improve his negative attitude.*

Their lives had changed so much after the accident. The light at the end of the tunnel wasn't there yet. They all seemed caught in a perpetual unrest, trying to balance their everyday tasks around home and keeping the business running.

Belinda realized that most of Henry's problem was due to the anguish of missing his father and brother. She wished there was some way to help him rise above it and see that his life must go on. *Maybe if Henry found some things to do that he enjoyed, it would give him something positive to focus on. Perhaps a new hobby or time spent with his friends would be helpful. I dare say he could probably use a good role model in his life. But it won't be with a stepfather.* Belinda shuddered. *I can't see anyone in the future for me. Oh Lord, I miss my Vernon so very much.*

She drew in her bottom lip. *I might be expecting too much of Henry. He's not a man yet—still a teenage boy. It could help if I give him a bit more freedom to do some things on his own—things that don't involve working all the time.*

Belinda resolved that when she returned home, she would have a talk with Henry and express some of the things she'd been mulling over this morning. *Perhaps this time away from me telling him what to do will help too,* she reasoned.

Belinda glanced at the battery-operated clock above the refrigerator and noted the time. It was 6:30 a.m. No doubt her daughters would be up by now, preparing breakfast, and would soon be getting ready for another day in the greenhouse. *Should I call and leave a message for them today? I really need to check and see how things are going. I hope everything is fine and that Sylvia doesn't feel too overwhelmed working in the greenhouse while I'm gone.*

Belinda sniffed the air. The brewing coffee filled the kitchen with a wonderful rich aroma. Thoughts of home still drifted into her mind though, and it was difficult not to rethink things. Belinda needed to know she'd made the right choice in coming here and wasn't being selfish somehow. *Sylvia might have only been trying to please me by agreeing to help while I'm gone even if she didn't feel ready. I certainly hope that's not the case.*

Belinda's eldest daughter had begun working in the greenhouse as soon as she graduated from the eighth grade, so she knew what needed to be done. Hopefully, her nerves had calmed down and her reluctance to talk to customers was a thing of the past.

A shrill baby's cry halted Belinda's thoughts. She needed to get breakfast made so that all Michelle had to do was take care of little Vernon. Belinda couldn't wait to see the grandkids this morning. Their pure hearts and sweet faces were a joyful tonic. She'd brought along her journal to write down all the things that were taking place. Belinda wanted to remember as much as she could about this special visit. It would be fun someday to read to her grandchildren what she'd written about them. She could also share the notes with her family back home. Every person in Belinda's family was special, and she felt blessed to have each of them in her life.

Belinda heard the patter of little feet and looked toward the doorway of the kitchen. She smiled when she saw Angela Mary enter the room holding the baby doll Belinda had given her yesterday. The child padded up to her wearing a tender smile.

"Are you hungry, sweet girl?" Belinda asked in Pennsylvania Dutch.

Angela Mary nodded and rubbed her tummy.

"What would you like for breakfast?"

"*Pannekuche.*"

Belinda grinned. "Are you sure?"

"Jah, *Grossmudder.*" Angela Mary gave a little hop.

Belinda hadn't planned on making pancakes today, but she didn't want to disappoint her granddaughter. "All right, Angela Mary—pannekuche it is." She set the eggs on the counter, picked the little girl up, and gave her a kiss. Spending time with her grandchildren and doing things to make them smile—that's what would keep Belinda going and looking to the future with hope.

Strasburg

The sunlight pouring into his room caused Jared to wake up with a start. When he checked his alarm clock, he realized it had never gone off.

"Maybe I forgot to set it last night." He picked it up. Sure enough, the button on top had not been pulled out. He'd been forgetting a lot of things lately—phone calls he hadn't returned; notes he'd made about jobs; and errands he should have run. Jared's only excuse was that his mind seemed to be elsewhere most of the time. No matter how hard he tried, Jared couldn't get Amy out of his thoughts. Common sense told him to move on with his life and find someone else, because it didn't look like she would change her mind. When he'd talked to Lydia the other day, she had commented that Amy kept really busy with her responsibilities at home and in the greenhouse. Lydia also stated that her friend didn't have time anymore to go out to lunch or take a few minutes to talk.

Jared grunted as he rolled out of bed. He wanted so badly to drop by the greenhouse to check on her but figured Amy would be too busy. More than likely she'd think he only came over to pressure her into letting him court her again. He saw Amy every other Sunday, but her body language remained the same. Amy kept her distance, but at least he could see that she was okay. The only news Jared had about Amy and her family these days was through the Amish grapevine. His mom had talked to someone who'd stopped at the greenhouse for something the other day, and whoever it was (Mom wouldn't say) had informed her that Amy's demeanor was always so serious, and the dark circles beneath her eyes revealed extreme fatigue.

Jared pinched the skin at his throat. *Even though she doesn't want to see me, I think I'll come up with an excuse to visit the greenhouse sometime this week.*

🐦

When Amy approached the greenhouse early the following morning, she was surprised to see the front door standing open; although the screen door was shut. She poked her tongue against the inside of her cheek and inhaled a long breath. *Henry King, didn't you close and lock the door like I told you to yesterday evening?*

After she'd closed the greenhouse for the day, Amy remembered later that she'd left some money in the till and had asked Henry to fetch it. He'd returned to the house with the cash, so she assumed he would have locked both the front and back doors, since that was the standing rule.

Cautiously, she stepped inside. All was quiet, and there was no sign of anyone, but when Amy walked down one of the aisles, she was stunned to see several of the potted plants had been dumped onto the floor. *Oh, no—the flowers!* She looked around again in desperation.

"How in the world did this happen?" Amy drew a shaky breath, walking backward toward the entrance to the building. Whoever had done this might still be inside, hiding somewhere. She wasn't about to turn her back on them.

"How did what happen?"

Amy gasped and whirled around. "Henry, you about scared me to death. I thought you were still in the barn feeding the livestock."

"I'm done with that." He tipped his head to one side. "You never answered my question? What happened in here?"

She explained about the plants and led the way so he could see the evidence.

"Oh, great." He thumped the side of his head.

"When you came out to get the money last night, did you make sure to shut and lock both doors?"

He shifted his weight from one foot to the other. "I remember shutting them, all right, and I—I think I locked the doors too."

"Do you actually remember doing it, Henry?"

"Umm. . .let me think." Henry rubbed the bridge of his nose.

"Well, did you or not?"

"I don't actually remember doing it, but I'm pretty sure I did." He glanced at the ruined plants then back at Amy. "Are you gonna let Mom know about this?"

"No, I am not." She placed her hand on his shoulder. "And I don't want you to mention it either."

"How come? Don't ya think she has a right to know about the vandalism that's struck us again?"

Amy was on the verge of offering a response when Henry spoke once more.

"And don't try to put the blame on me for what happened either." Henry's eyes narrowed as he pointed at the plants. "What reason would I have for ruining all these?"

"Well, umm. . ."

He held up his hand. "You think I did it, don't ya?"

Amy shrugged her shoulders. "Truthfully, the thought had crossed my mind."

"Why?"

"You've made it more than clear that you don't like working here. And last night, when you didn't know I was within earshot, I heard you mumble that you were sick and tired of the greenhouse as well as caring for the bees."

"Jah, well, I don't like either of those jobs, but I wouldn't be dumb enough to wreck plants or do anything else destructive in the greenhouse. After all, the money we earn here is what pays the bills and keeps food in our bellies." Henry thumped his stomach.

"Okay, okay, calm down, little brother."

He raised his eyebrows and gave Amy a glassy stare. "I ain't little, so quit callin' me that."

"Sorry, it was just a figure of speech. Don't forget, you are my youngest bruder, Henry."

"Yeah, with Ezekiel living far from us now and God taking Abe away, I feel like I've become your *only* brother."

The look of hurt Amy saw in Henry's eyes let her know that she'd said enough. She moved closer and hugged his shoulders. Relieved that he didn't pull away, she said, "Let's try to work together from now on, okay?"

Henry gave a slow nod. "Sure. Whatever you say." He moved away and set to work cleaning up the mess that had been made. "I have to wonder if some animal got into the greenhouse and pawed through these plants, which knocked 'em to the floor."

She shook her head. "It looks more intentional to me, but I could be wrong."

"This is a waste, though it won't take long to clean up." Henry picked up all the ruined plants and hauled them away.

Amy watched as her brother grabbed a broom and swept up the remaining soil. Nearby sat a bucket he dumped all the dirt into. Then Henry carried off the emptied containers toward the storage room.

Amy sighed. She'd helped Mom months ago get those plants started from seeds. *I agree with Henry—it is a waste.*

She groaned inwardly. Their mother had only been gone two days, and already unpleasant things had happened. She hated to think of what else might occur during Mom's two-week absence.

Try not to borrow trouble, she told herself as the distinctive sound of the crow's call filtered in through the open door. *Caw. . .Caw. . .Caw. . .*

Chapter 23

"I hear a steady *clip-clop* of horses' hooves this morning. I bet that greenhouse across the road is getting business already this morning." Virginia's fingers tightened as she handed her husband a piece of toast.

"Yep. You're probably right." Earl kept his focus on the sports section of the newspaper lying next to his plate.

"I am still a bit irritated about getting my lime green pants wet when I went to the greenhouse yesterday."

He chuckled. "You should be more careful where you're leaning your backside."

She lifted her gaze to the ceiling. "You would say something like that."

"I have to say, that greenhouse of theirs was plenty warm inside. It made me sweat like a pig. If they had electricity at their place, they could have several fans running to circulate the air."

"Well, dear, they are Amish, and who knows what else they don't do." Earl pushed the paper aside and drank some coffee. "Did you get the tomato plants you bought put in the ground?"

Virginia shook her head and buttered the toast on her plate. "Not yet." She took a bite of it and tried to relax.

"When ya do, don't forget to add some of that horse manure into the soil."

"Earl, I'm eating. Can't you see that?" She wrinkled her nose. "I'm not about to touch any of that yucky stuff, and I sure don't wanna talk about it at the breakfast table."

Earl set his coffee mug down and gave an impatient huff. "I'm not suggesting you handle the manure with your bare hands, Virginia. Dig a hole in the area where you want the tomato plants to go, and then shovel some of the manure in and spread it around. After that, put the plants in the hole and cover the rest of it with dirt. The last step will be to give the tomato plants plenty of water."

She flapped her hand. "That sounds like a lot of hard work. Anyway, is that how you think those Amish folks do their gardening—by mixing all their horse droppings into the soil?"

"I suppose." He finished his toast. "Why don't you ask 'em?"

"No way!"

"I did notice at the Kings' place that their plot of vegetables looked healthy, and all the flowers they grow to sell are gorgeous."

"What else would they use, Virginia? They've got an endless supply of horse manure."

"All I know is they run around barefoot a lot over there. Don't they worry about stepping in some of it?"

Earl laughed. "Good question. Why don't you run on over there and ask that question too?"

"Very cute, Earl. I was just pointing out what I've noticed is all."

"Have you been using my binoculars to spy on them?"

"No, of course not. But I have good vision and can see details that are pretty far away."

Virginia drank the rest of her apple juice, pushed her chair aside, and stood. "As soon as I put our dishes in the dishwasher, I'll get started on the garden plot. I can't wait to see how well our plants grow."

"Sounds good." He stood and kissed her cheek. "I'd better get to work. I hope you have a nice day."

"You too, dear."

After her husband went out the door, Virginia watched out the front window as he got into his truck. Since their place had only a one-car garage, Earl let Virginia park her car inside, and he left the truck in the driveway.

She walked out onto the porch and waved to Earl as he backed his rig out of the driveway and headed down the road in the direction of Lancaster. When he was out of sight, she glanced across the road and noticed a lot of cars in the greenhouse parking lot. *They're sure busy over there again. No doubt there'll be more noise for me to put up with today.*

Virginia moved away from the porch railing and went back inside the house. *One good thing. . . At least Earl and I will have a nice crop of tomatoes to enjoy in the days ahead. Maybe country living won't be so bad after all—at least in that regard.*

When Virginia returned to the kitchen, she cleared the table. After placing the dishes in the dishwasher, she found her gardening gloves and went out the back door. *Even though it was my idea to grow some fresh produce, I hope this project isn't more than I can handle.*

Jared had quit working a little early today so he could go home and take a shower before heading to the greenhouse. He didn't want to show up at the Kings' smelling like a hog or with clothes covered in dirt and sweat.

Jared snapped the reins to get Dandy moving along. "If Amy saw me like that, she might never change her mind about us."

The gelding's ears twitched, and he bobbed his head. It seemed as if Dandy agreed with Jared. He couldn't control the nervousness he felt as he drew closer to the Kings' place. But, oh, how he looked forward to seeing Amy, even if the reception awaiting him would be less friendly than he'd like.

When Jared guided Reckless up the Kings' driveway, he was pleased to see four cars in the graveled parking lot as well as two horse and buggies at the hitching rail. *Their business must be doing well, and that's a good thing. I wonder how Amy and her family are doing emotionally though.*

Jared directed Dandy to the rail and set the brake. Then he

climbed down and secured the horse. Jared paused to brush away a few smudges on his trousers from the carriage wheel he'd come in contact with, although he was sure his efforts in looking nice wouldn't do anything to help him win Amy at this point. Jared still loved her, and his heartbeat quickened, thinking about being close to her.

As he walked toward the entrance of the building, an English man he'd done business with came out carrying a hanging basket in one hand. He smiled at Jared as he approached. "It's nice to see you."

"Nice to see you too, Mr. Chandler."

"You and your crew sure did a good job on my roof. In fact, I've handed out several of your business cards to others who have complimented the job you did." The man shook Jared's hand. "Would you have any more of those cards on you? I'll give some of them out to the fellows I work with in case they might be thinking of having a new roof put on their home, shop, or garage."

"Sure. That'd be great." Jared pulled his wallet from the pocket in his trousers and withdrew ten of his cards. "Is that enough?"

"I believe so. At least for now." Mr. Chandler clasped Jared's shoulder. "I've had other work done by Amish men and have always been satisfied, so keep up the good work."

"Thanks, I will. And I appreciate you spreading the word about my business."

"Not a problem. When I know a good thing, I always like to tell others." He tapped Jared's arm. "Have a good evening."

"Same to you, sir."

When Jared entered the greenhouse, he saw Amy standing behind the checkout counter with three people lined up on the other side, waiting to check out.

Jared didn't want to interrupt, so he headed down one of the aisles in search of the right birthday gift for his mother. About halfway down, he spotted Henry moving some plants from one wooden shelf to another. "How's it going?" Jared asked when he approached the boy.

With tight lips, Henry merely gave a shrug.

"It looks like you're keeping busy."

"Yeah, too busy," the boy mumbled. "Amy's always tellin' me what to do, especially now that Mom's not here."

Jared glanced over his shoulder and saw Amy still waiting on customers, then he turned back to face her brother. "How long till your mamm returns?"

"She'll be gone at least two weeks. I'm guessin' maybe longer if they need more help."

Jared didn't want to appear nosey, but he was curious as to where Belinda had gone and who needed her help. Under the circumstances, it seemed unlikely that she'd leave her home, greenhouse, and family that long. "If you don't mind my asking. . .where'd your mother go?"

"Up to Clymer, New York, where Michelle and Ezekiel live. Michelle had a baby boy recently, and Mom went there to help out."

"I see. Makes sense that she'd want to be there."

When Henry gave no response, Jared posed another question. "So, is it just you and Amy working in the greenhouse while your mamm is gone?"

Henry shook his head. "Sylvia's helpin' out too, and Mary Ruth is taking care of her kinner while she's out here." He pulled his suspenders out with his thumbs and gave them a snap. "I don't like working here and having someone always tellin' me what to do. You're lucky to be your own boss."

"Running my own business has its good points, but there are some negative things about it too."

Henry folded his arms. "Like what?"

"Well, being my own boss means I have to be responsible for hiring a good crew of roofers. There is also lots paperwork to do when you run a business."

"I'm well aware. Amy does that kind of stuff for the greenhouse. She's always busy with something or other, even when the greenhouse is closed." Henry's brows furrowed. "Whenever she's not workin', she's reminding me about chores and saying something I've done is wrong."

"Anything specific?" Jared asked.

Henry's voice lowered. "Well, someone got into the greenhouse last night and dumped over some of our potted plants. Amy accused me of not locking the doors." His face colored as he reached up to rub the back of his neck. "I'm sure she thinks I'm responsible for all the vandalism that's happened here since my daed, brother, and brother-in-law died."

Jared's eyes widened. "What are you talking about, Henry? What kind of vandalism?"

He listened with concern as Henry told him about the mailbox, greenhouse sign, and a few other things that could have been done on purpose. "Does Amy believe those things were done intentionally?"

"Jah, and as I said before, she thinks they were done by me."

"Did you do any of them, Henry?" Jared felt led to ask.

He shook his head vigorously. "Wanna know what I think?"

"Of course."

"I think some of my friends might have done all those things."

Jared tipped his head. "Why would they do that?"

"'Cause they're mad about me not bein' able to do anything fun with them this summer, thanks to all the work I have to do here." Henry groaned. "Me and my buddies had planned all sorts of fun things to do after we got out of school. Now I can't do nothin' because of all the work that's been forced on me." There was a hard edge to the young man's words, and Jared saw a look of bitterness on Henry's face.

Jared searched for the right words to offer comfort or advice, but before he could form another sentence, Henry turned away and tromped off.

Jared rubbed his jaw in contemplation. *I believe that young fellow needs someone to talk to. I may not be the one he'll open up to, but I can sure be praying for his situation.*

Jared picked up a hanging basket filled with pink and white petunias and started down the aisle toward the checkout counter. As he approached, he couldn't help but notice the look of exhaustion on

Amy's face. There was no doubt about it—she'd been working too hard. "Hi, Amy. It's nice to see you."

"Hello, Jared." Amy drew in some air, trying to slow her breathing. Even though they couldn't be together, her feelings for him hadn't changed. "That's a lovely basket you've chosen." *I wonder if it's for Lydia. I'm sure they must be courting.*

He gave a nod. "It's for my mamm. Today's her birthday."

"Oh. I'm sure she will like it. Please tell her I said happy birthday."

"I will." Jared's eyes darkened. "How have you been, Amy?"

"Okay." She kept her gaze fixed on the basket.

"You look mied."

"I am tired, but it's nothing I can't handle."

"Are you sure about that?" He sounded concerned.

Her head came up. "Of course, I'm sure."

"I was talking to Henry earlier, and he mentioned that your mamm's in New York, helping out since your sister-in-law had her baby."

"That's correct."

"Henry also said he and Sylvia are helping you here."

"Jah."

"I'm glad your sister is able to work again."

"I am too." Amy didn't mention how hard it was for Sylvia to be around people or that she went into the house several times a day to check on the children, as she had done a while ago. Since they weren't a courting couple anymore, she saw no need to fill him in on any of their personal business.

"Henry also said you've had some problems with vandalism."

Amy shifted as she gave her apron a tug. "It's nothing serious, and we're all okay, so please don't mention it to anyone."

"Why not? If somebody has singled you out for some reason then—"

Amy shook her head. "Jared, I'd rather not discuss this right now."

"Okay, but please be careful, and if any more damage to your property occurs, you should call the sheriff's office right away."

"We'll deal with it in whatever way we feel is best." Amy made sure to keep her voice down during this conversation. "Did you need anything else?"

He shook his head. "No, but I was wondering if you've talked to Lydia lately." He leaned against his side of the counter.

"I just spoke a few words to her at the last church meeting." Amy gave a sidelong glance when another customer came into the store. Truth was, she'd been avoiding her friend. It would be too painful for Amy if Lydia were to admit that she'd been seeing Jared socially.

Amy rang up Jared's purchase, and he gave her the money. "I hope your mother likes what you got her."

"I'm sure she will." Jared picked up the hanging basket. "Tell your family I said hello." He started toward the door but turned around. "If you need anything while your mom is gone, please let me know."

All Amy could manage was a slow nod. Her throat felt so thick, she couldn't utter another word. She watched Jared as he walked out of the building. It had been difficult to chat with him and maintain an indifferent attitude.

After Jared left the greenhouse, she turned her attention toward the young English woman who had come in. "May I help you with anything?"

At that moment, Sylvia arrived with two bottles of water, which she placed under the counter before stepping behind it while Amy dealt with the customer.

The English woman moved closer to her. "My grandmother is in the hospital, and I'm looking for a pretty plant to give her."

"Right this way. I'll show you what we have available." As Amy headed down the aisle where the houseplants were displayed, one more thought about Jared popped into her head. *If we were still a couple, I would have talked more with him about the troubles we've had here lately. But I'm sure I did right by not discussing it further. But really, what would be the point? There's nothing Jared can do for us.*

Chapter 24

Virginia moaned and rolled over in bed. Her throat hurt something awful. She'd coughed and sneezed so much last night that Earl had slept in their guest room. Virginia hadn't been out of the house for two days and had spent most of her time in bed or on the couch. She eyed the throat discs lying on her nightstand, grabbed one, and popped it into her mouth. They helped a little with her pain when she needed to swallow.

"I see you're awake." Earl stepped into the room and handed her a glass of water. "Maybe you ought to see a doctor."

Virginia grabbed a tissue from the nightstand and blew her nose. "I might do that if we had a doctor. Since we're new to the area, I wouldn't have any idea who to call. Besides, it's rare when a person can get in to see a doctor the same day they call."

"You have a point. Might be best for you to go to the hospital emergency room."

She shook her head. "Think I'll go to the pharmacy in town and see what they have to offer."

"Suit yourself." Earl stepped away from the bed. "I've gotta go. I'll see you this evening when I get home from work. Hopefully, by then you'll feel somewhat better."

After Earl left the room, Virginia lay in bed for a while. Finally, mustering up her strength, she pulled herself out of bed. "If Earl cared anything about me, he would have taken time off work to look after me," she grumbled.

Virginia threw on a pair of jeans and a button-down blouse before stumbling into the kitchen. With a diminished appetite, nothing appealed to her, so she fixed herself a cup of tea. Even though she didn't care much for the taste, the warm liquid felt good on her scratchy throat. When the cup was empty, she placed it in the sink, which was devoid of any breakfast dishes. Apparently, Earl had put his dishes in the dishwasher. She felt thankful for his consideration in doing that much at least.

Guess I can't blame him for not taking the day off to be with me. He's a new employee at the car dealership, and it probably wouldn't go over well with his boss. Besides, we're not rich, and we need a steady income to stay up with the bills coming in, not to mention food, clothes, and other essential items.

Virginia grabbed the car keys and her handbag then opened the back door. She wanted to check on the tomato plants she'd put in the ground two days ago, before getting her vehicle out of the garage.

Walking toward her small garden patch, she was shocked to see that her tomato plants had both died. They looked like someone had struck a match and lit them on fire. It made no sense. The last two evenings it had rained, so the plants had to have gotten enough water.

"I don't understand this. All my plants seemed healthy the day I brought them home. I bet that young Amish woman sold me some diseased plants." She broke off a piece from one of the plants. "I don't think those people across the road can be trusted." Virginia continued to bluster out loud as she tossed the plant debris away. "My poor garden looks terrible. Maybe if I go back there and complain, she'll give me all new plants." She paused from her ranting and rubbed her sore throat. *I need to quit talking to myself.*

Virginia kicked at a clump of dirt with the toe of her sneaker. *I wonder what went wrong with those tomato plants.*

Sylvia yawned as she sat at the kitchen table, trying to eat her breakfast while feeding Allen from his highchair. The baby had been fed and gone back to sleep, so she only had one child to worry about before Mary Ruth showed up.

"Would you like me to take over helping Allen eat his breakfast?" Amy asked. "That way you can eat yours in peace."

Peace? Sylvia's jaw clenched. She hadn't felt a moment of peace since her husband, father, and brother had died. Now with their mother away in New York and Amy counting on Sylvia to work in the greenhouse, she felt more stressed than ever.

"Sister, did you hear what I said?" Amy reached over and touched Sylvia's arm.

"Jah, I heard. If you're willing to oversee Allen trying to feed himself, that's fine with me."

"Course I'm willing."

"And are you also willing to clean up the mess he makes?"

Amy nodded. "If it takes too long, our brother can open the greenhouse today."

From his seat across the table, Henry gave no response.

When Amy took over with Allen, Sylvia picked up the newspaper lying on the corner of the table. "There's an article in here about the new greenhouse. Seems they're having a big grand opening sale this weekend—including Sunday." She looked over at Amy. "With them being English, they're bound to be open on days we are closed."

"We can't worry about it." Amy spoke softly, although wrinkles had formed across her forehead. "We just need to be confident that God will take care of our needs."

Sylvia pursed her lips. "If He was really taking care of our needs, Toby, Dad, and Abe would still be here. A lot of good it's done us to try and live a good Christian life." Her feelings were out, and Sylvia was glad she'd voiced her thoughts. As far as she was concerned, God had abandoned them, and they now had to fend for themselves.

"Remember, Matthew 5:45 says that the rain falls on the just as well as the unjust," Amy said.

"You sure know how to quote scriptures." It was the first thing

Henry had said since they'd sat down to eat breakfast.

"I've learned by reading the Bible every day and also from listening to our ministers' sermons during worship services." Amy looked over at Sylvia. "You know God's Word as well as I do. Your faith should be as strong as mine."

"Well it's not." Sylvia leaped out of her chair, nearly knocking it over. "I'm going to check on Rachel before the babysitter arrives."

As she fled the room, a strangled cry of frustration burst from her throat. *Will I ever feel whole again?*

Amy's gaze settled on her nephew as she took a couple of deep breaths. "Your mamma feels cheated from the loss of our family members. But as a Christian, she needs to let go of her anger and bitterness because it's not doing any good."

Allen looked up at Amy with a curious expression. She realized the little guy had no idea what she was talking about.

After Allen finished eating and she cleaned him up, Amy took her nephew to the living room to play. Then she returned to the kitchen, where Henry still sat at the table, looking at his pocketknife.

Amy picked up the small container of raspberries sitting on the counter, poured them into a colander, and turned on the water to wash them. "I was surprised to see these had already turned red, so I collected all that there was."

Henry only grunted.

"Would you please go out and open the greenhouse now?"

He squinted at Amy from across the table. "Why don't you do it, like you usually do?"

"I still have a few chores to do here, but I should be out there before any customers show up. Sylvia will come out with me as soon as Mary Ruth arrives."

"Okay, but can I borrow your *schlissel*?"

Her brows furrowed. "Why do you need my key when you have your own?"

"I—I can't find it. Must have lost it somewhere," he stammered.

"When was the last time you saw the schlissel?"

With palms up, Henry shrugged his shoulders. "Guess it's been a few weeks—maybe longer, since I wasn't asked to unlock the doors for some time."

"Did you have your key when you were asked to lock the doors at the end of the workday?"

"Don't know, but I never locked 'em with a key anyways. Always just turned the lock on the door knob before pulling it shut."

Amy stiffened. "Maybe the person who knocked over the potted plants found your key and picked it up. That could be how they got into the greenhouse."

"Yeah, maybe, but I'm gonna start lookin' for the key." Henry jumped up from his seat and made a mad dash for the back door.

Amy leaned forward with her hands resting on her forehead. *Heavenly Father, if Henry's key is still around, please, help us find it.*

Clymer

Warm water churned the soap into frothy suds as Belinda filled the kitchen sink and added liquid detergent. With breakfast over and the dishes soaking, she was ready to take care of another task she had wanted to do this morning. "Before I start washing the breakfast dishes, I'd like to walk out to the phone shed and make a call to the family at home. I want to let them know how things are going here and see how they're all doing," Belinda announced.

"That's a good idea, Mom." Ezekiel poured himself a second cup of coffee and added a spoonful of sugar. "Feel free to check the answering machine. There could be a message from Amy, Sylvia, or even Henry."

"I will. If there are other messages, I'll make sure they don't get erased, and you can check them when you have time."

"Sounds good." He smiled, dropping his spoon into the sink. "It sure is nice having you here—and not just to help out. We enjoy your company."

Belinda returned his smile. "And I enjoy yours." She looked at Angela Mary, sitting on a wooden booster seat Ezekiel had made to heighten the chair the little girl occupied. Although it saddened Belinda to miss out on so much that would go on in her son and his wife's family here, she wouldn't say a word about it. She wanted Ezekiel to feel good about remaining in Clymer.

Michelle entered the kitchen and took a seat at the table. "I finally got little Vernon settled. He did a lot of fussing throughout the night and even when he woke up this morning." She shook her head. "Angela Mary wasn't like that at all when she was a boppli. In fact, the only time she cried was when she was hungerich or her windel needed to be changed."

"All babies are different. I'm sure once you've established a routine, things will improve."

Michelle massaged her forehead. "I sure hope so, and I hope it happens before you have to return to Strasburg. I don't know what I'd do without you right now."

"Well, not to worry; I'll stay as long as you need me." Belinda hoped it wouldn't be more than two or three weeks at the most. As much as she enjoyed being here, she had responsibilities at home.

"I'm going to head out to the phone shed now." Belinda tightened the dark scarf on her head and went out the back door.

When she got to the phone shed, she stepped inside and took a seat. The green button on the answering machine blinked, so there were definitely some messages.

She clicked the button and listened to each one. Most were from customers interested in purchasing supplies for their bee business, but the last one was from her youngest daughter.

"Hi, it's me, Amy. I'm calling to see how things are going there and to tell Mom not to worry about us or the business. We're getting along fine here and keeping plenty busy."

Belinda decided to return the call right away and respond to

Amy's message. She dialed the number and was surprised when Henry picked it up after the second ring.

"Hello. If you're calling about the greenhouse, we're not open yet. If you have a message for someone in the family, I'll be glad to take it."

"Henry, it's your mamm."

"Oh, hey. How are ya, Mom?"

"I'm fine. We're all fine here. How are things going there?"

When Henry gave no response, she phrased the question again.

"Umm. . .well. . ."

"Is there a problem, Henry?"

"I lost my key to the greenhouse. I've been lookin' everywhere I can think of, but it hasn't turned up."

"It's nothing to worry about, Son. Amy and Sylvia both have a key."

"I know, but. . ." Henry's voice trailed off.

"But what? Is there something going on I should know about?"

"Jah, but Amy told me not to say anything to you about it."

"About what?" Belinda pressed her trembling fingers against her chin. "I need to know what's going on, Henry."

"Okay, I'll tell ya. A couple days ago, someone got into the greenhouse during the night—or maybe it happened in the wee hours of the morning."

"Who was it? Did they take anything?"

"We don't know who it was, and nothing seemed to be missing. Amy told me that as soon as she has the time, she'll go to the hardware store and get another lock and all new keys made just in case we don't find mine. We'll ask Jesse Smucker if he has time to put it on." There was a slight pause before Henry continued. "We found a bunch of potted plants dumped over onto the floor."

"Maybe your *hund* or one of the *katze* got in and knocked over the plants."

"I don't think so, Mom. Blackie slept in my room that night, and I don't think any of our cats would be strong enough to knock over the pots. They were some of the heavier ones. Besides, how would a dog or one of the cats get the door to the greenhouse open?"

Belinda blinked rapidly as she clutched the folds in her dress. "I don't like the sound of this, Henry. I'm needed here, but I might be needed there more."

"It's okay, Mom. We're all fine, and there's no need for you to come home right now. If it'll make ya feel any better, I'll ask one of the men in our community to come over and take a look around."

"Jah, that would put my mind at ease. Oh, and Henry. . . I want you to let me know right away if anything else out of the ordinary happens at our place. Understood?"

"Jah, Mom."

"All right, Son. Give your sisters my love, and let them know that I'm praying for all of you."

"Okay. Bye, Mom."

"Goodbye, Henry."

When Belinda hung up the phone, she remained in the shed for several minutes, mulling things over. She felt sure that the vandalism that had been done to their mailbox, the sign out front, and now this happened for a reason. Someone either didn't like them or wanted their business to fail. The question was who and why?

Chapter 25

Virginia lay on the couch, reading a magazine she'd picked up at the pharmacy. She had slipped back into her comfy pajamas as soon as she got home. Swallowing still hurt, and the cherry-flavored lozenges weren't helping anymore. Virginia wanted so badly to feel better.

Thinking a cup of herbal tea might help, she pulled herself up and plodded into the kitchen. After filling a cup with water and putting it in the microwave, Virginia took a seat at the table. Once it was hot enough, she added a teabag along with a heaping spoonful of honey.

Once the tea had steeped, Virginia took the cup and went back to the living room. Sitting on the couch, she sipped the warm brew gratefully. Even though she wasn't much of a tea drinker, the soothing lemon herb tea went down easy, and it tasted pretty good with the addition of the honey.

Virginia hadn't started anything for supper and didn't plan to. Earl would have to either get them takeout or barbecue something on the grill. Of course, there wasn't much Virginia was in the mood to eat. She'd picked up a few things to help her cold and sore throat, but so far, it hadn't helped much. She'd gargled with salt water and nearly gagged. *There oughta be something that'll make me feel better. Maybe I should have gone to the ER.*

Virginia reclined on the couch again and had rolled onto her side when Earl came in through the front door. "How'd your day go?" he asked. "Do you feel any better?"

"Not really. I got some things at the pharmacy, but I still feel lousy." She pulled herself to a sitting position. "By the way. . .those tomato plants I got from the greenhouse across the street are dead. I think that young Amish woman sold me some defective plants."

He took a seat at the end of the couch, picked up her feet, and put them in his lap. "Oh, oh. I'm afraid it might be my fault they died."

Virginia coughed and massaged her throat. "How was it your fault?"

"The fellow at work who told me about putting horse manure on plants brought up the topic again today." Earl cleared his throat a couple of times, and spots of color erupted on his cheeks. "Said he forgot to mention that fresh manure was too strong to put on the plants. It needs to age, and mixing it with compost then letting it set a few months would be the best way."

"Oh boy. No wonder those plants keeled over."

"I'll go over to the greenhouse and get you two new plants, and then we can start over."

"I wanted to have a small garden, but with me not feeling well, I've lost my desire. So, don't worry about getting any new plants. I'll forget about gardening this year and buy our tomatoes at the grocery store or one of the local farmers' markets."

"Suit yourself, but I wouldn't mind going to the greenhouse and buying some new plants."

Virginia shook her head forcibly. "I don't want anything more to do with those people. The way they live is strange to me—sort of like the Quakers and pioneers did many years ago." She waited to see if Earl would comment, but when he remained silent, she added something else. "While I was at the pharmacy today, I saw a couple of Amish women there. They were speaking to each other in a strange, foreign-sounding language."

"It's Dutch, Virginia—or more to the point, Pennsylvania Dutch."

"Well, whatever it's called, it seems odd-sounding to me." She pulled her fingers through the ends of her tangled hair. "Anyway, back to my dilemma. They should have given me instructions on how to plant the items I bought. I hope that new greenhouse runs the King family right out of business."

Earl's eyes widened as his mouth fell open. "That's a hateful thing to say, Virginia. What have you got against those people?"

"I keep telling ya, but you're not listening—they're strange, and all the traffic on this road, mostly brought on by their business, gets on my nerves. I thought by moving to the country everything would be quiet and peaceful."

"I do listen to you, by the way, but I don't know what you think can be done about our neighbors. It's a new place, and we haven't even finished unpacking." He gave her feet a little squeeze. "Trust me, Virginia, you'll get used to it in time."

"No, I won't. I don't like livin' here, and I never will."

By the time Jared finished bidding a new job, it was almost noon, so he decided to stop at Isaac's Famous Grilled Sandwiches for lunch. He'd always enjoyed coming here to eat, since it was near the Choo Choo Barn model train layout and the Strasburg Train Shop.

Jared's fascination with trains began when he was a boy and he and his folks had traveled by train to see relatives in South Bend, Indiana. Someday he hoped to make a trip by train all the way out to the West Coast. He'd heard others who had gone there talk about the Rocky and Cascade Mountains, as well as the Pacific Ocean. One of Jared's friends who'd made such a trip came back with all kinds of interesting stories.

Jared had thought if he and Amy ever got married, he would take her on a trip to see some of the western states. Maybe they would be able to see the Grand Canyon or Yellowstone National Park.

But if I can't convince Amy to let me court her again, there will be no marriage or train ride out West. Jared gripped the reins as he guided Dandy to the hitching rail. *It wouldn't be any fun to take a trip like that by myself.*

When Jared entered the restaurant a short time later, he spotted

Lydia sitting at a table by herself. He placed his order then walked over to her table. "Mind if I join you?" he asked.

A deep dimple formed in her right cheek as she smiled up at him. "You're more than welcome to eat here at my table."

Jared pulled out a chair and sat down. "What's new with you these days, Lydia?"

"Nothing exciting. I'm still helping my mamm make quilted items. In fact, before I came here, I was out delivering some finished quilts to a couple of shops in the area that sell on consignment."

"Sounds like you're keeping busy then."

"Jah. How about you? Have you been doing a lot of roofing jobs this summer?"

"Sure have. I'm keeping my crew plenty busy, and I always make sure to have plenty of water on hand for my guys so they don't get overheated up there on the rooftops."

"I'm sure they appreciate it."

They visited more about the warm weather, and then Lydia posed another question. "Have you seen Amy lately?"

He gave a brief nod. "I stopped by the greenhouse the other day and bought a plant to give my mamm for her birthday."

"How's she doing?"

"You mean my mother?"

"No, I meant Amy."

"Oh. Well, it was great to see her and talk a short while. But I must tell you, I do have concerns about her."

"Anything specific?"

"She looked awful tired, and when we spoke, her voice sounded strained." Jared wasn't sure if he should tell Lydia what Henry had told him, but he decided to bring up the topic and see if she already knew about the vandalism that had taken place. "Did you know that there's been some damage done to the Kings' property?"

Her eyebrows rose as she gave a little gasp. "I had no idea anything like that was going on. Did Amy give you any details?"

"Not much, but Henry's actually the one who told me about the things that have been done." Jared spoke in Pennsylvania Dutch so none of the English people who might be nearby would understand what he said.

"What exactly was done?"

After Jared told Lydia all that he'd learned, he thought about Amy and hoped she wouldn't mind that he'd discussed this with Lydia. She had asked him not to say anything, and he didn't want to do anything that might push away any hopes of them getting back together. Even so, Lydia and Amy had always been close. Surely she wouldn't care if her best friend knew about the vandalism.

"Oh, my! Do you think somebody is out to destroy their business, or could someone in the King family have an enemy they don't know about?"

Jared shrugged. "It could be either one, I suppose, or maybe it's just some teenage kids sowing their wild oats. Henry mentioned that his friends might be upset because all of his chores have kept him from spending time with them."

"Have they called the sheriff or told anyone else about it?"

"Amy said they haven't notified the sheriff, but I don't know about friends. I doubt it though, since she asked me not to say anything." Jared paused for a quick breath. "I wish there was an adult male present on the property. I mean, Amy's brother is fine and all, but I really think if whoever is doing this had to deal with a man living there, it could deter the problem."

"I agree." Lydia picked up her glass and drank some water. "I'll have to stop by the greenhouse soon and talk to Amy."

"That's fine, but it would probably be best if you didn't tell her that I told you."

"Okay, I'll just drop by to see how things are going. Hopefully, since we've been friends a long time, Amy will open up to me."

Jared hoped that would be the case, but he had his doubts. He and Amy had been friends for some time too, but she hadn't opened up to him. If not for Henry blabbing, Jared wouldn't know a thing.

'I'm going up to the house to get my sack lunch and check on our sister," Amy called to Henry from her place behind the counter. Since there were no customers at the moment, she figured it would be okay to leave him alone in the greenhouse for the short time she'd be gone.

"Yeah, okay," Henry hollered from the other end of the building. "Would ya bring my lunch out too?"

"Of course, but you'd better come up here and keep an eye on things while I'm gone. If someone shows up, it wouldn't be good to leave the cash register unattended."

"No problem. I'm coming."

Amy left the greenhouse and hurried toward the house. Sylvia had developed a bad headache and gone up an hour ago to take something for the pain.

When Amy entered the house, she found Mary Ruth in the kitchen fixing lunch for the little ones.

"Where's Sylvia?" Amy asked.

"She's in there." Mary Ruth nodded with her head in the direction of the living room.

"I'd better check on her." Amy made her way to the living room, where she found her sister lying on the couch with a washcloth over her forehead.

"Has your *koppweh* gotten worse?" Amy rushed across the room.

Sylvia moaned. "Jah. I feel like a stampede of horses is inside my head. Sorry, Amy, but I don't think I can work in the greenhouse anymore today."

"Well, as long as we don't get too busy, I guess Henry and I will be fine on our own."

Amy leaned down and patted her sister's hand. "Is there anything I can get for you before I head back outside?"

"No, but would you please let Mary Ruth know I'll be staying inside? I hope she's willing to stay and watch the kinner until you close the greenhouse and come in for the day. With the way my head is pounding, I don't think I could manage to take care of

Allen and Rachel right now."

"I'll let her know. And don't worry about anything, Sylvia. Just get some rest."

"Danki." Sylvia's voice, filled with emotion, told Amy that her sister was close to tears.

Amy returned to the kitchen and took her lunch sack as well as Henry's from the refrigerator. Then she grabbed two bottles of water. "Sylvia's not feeling well enough to return to the greenhouse today, so she's going to stay here and rest." She looked at Mary Ruth. "Are you willing to stay until I close the greenhouse late this afternoon?"

"Most certainly." Mary Ruth smiled. "I'll try to keep the kinner quiet so your sister can sleep."

"You might suggest that she go to her room. If she remains in the living room, she'll never get any rest."

"I will." Mary Ruth moved closer to Amy. "Do you think you and your brother can manage things in the greenhouse without your sister's help?"

"We don't have much choice, but I believe we should be okay. Business has been kind of slow—probably because of the extreme heat, so I doubt we'll have too many customers this afternoon." Amy said goodbye and scooted out the door.

As she approached the greenhouse, she saw a horse and buggy at the rail. She hurried into the greenhouse and placed the water and lunch sacks on the counter.

Mom's old boyfriend stood nearby. "Good afternoon, Amy. I came to talk to your mother. Is she here?" Monroe asked.

"No, she's at my brother's place in New York, helping out with their new boppli."

"How long will she be gone?" He looked at Amy intently as though he didn't quite believe her.

"She should be back the week after next. Would you like to leave her a message?"

He moved his head from side to side but then changed it to a nod.

"Just tell her I came by to see her and that I'll come back when she gets home."

"Okay, I'll let her know." Amy was glad she could tell Monroe that her mother wasn't there. She still couldn't put her finger on it, but there was something about the man that made her nervous.

Monroe looked around as though he was inspecting the building. "So, there's no man here to protect you?"

Amy stood tall with her head erect. "My brother's here and we're getting along fine."

Monroe snorted as he looked at Henry, who stood a few feet from them sweeping some dirt off the floor. "That brother?"

"Jah."

"Why, he's hardly a man. He's not much more than a boy."

Amy's fingers curled into her palms. "Henry is old enough to do most chores a fully grown man can do."

"If you say so. Maybe I misjudged him."

Maybe you did. Amy bit back the words on her tongue. "Is there anything else I can help you with, Mr. Esh?"

He shook his head. "Nope. Just remember to tell your mamm I was here." He turned and went out the door.

Amy looked at Henry to see if he would comment, but he merely kept sweeping the floor.

She picked up one of the water bottles and took a drink, allowing the liquid to cool her mouth. *I hope that man doesn't keep coming around, and I especially hope he has no designs on our mother.*

Chapter 26

The following Monday as Amy finished watering the two hanging baskets on their front porch, she thought about her mother and how much she missed her.

I am glad Mom will be home soon. Even though they'd been managing the greenhouse okay, Amy felt as though she carried most of the burden. She'd handled all the customer relations so far, and Henry usually needed prompting to get things done each day.

Amy turned off the spigot and put away the hose then headed for the greenhouse to get things in order for the day.

The first thing she did after entering the building was to put the OPEN sign in the front window. Following that, Amy went to open the back door and check the plants, making sure everything looked in order. Ever since the incident with the potted plants, Amy couldn't help being a bit skittish when first coming in to open things up. She liked it better when she and Henry went in together. But not every day played out the way she wanted. This morning, Henry had been delayed for a bit while helping Sylvia take down some clocks to change the batteries.

After Amy gave a thorough look around and felt satisfied with things, she headed up front to check the shelves that displayed her mother's jellies, jams, and honey. She tidied up the pieces and moved back to the register. They'd been selling a lot of her mother's canned goods, which Amy knew would make Mom happy to hear when she returned.

A few minutes later, the front door opened. Amy was surprised when Lydia came in. It had been awhile since she'd been by, and the only time Amy had seen her friend recently was at church yesterday.

"How are you?" Lydia stepped up to the counter.

"Doing okay." Amy hoped her tone sounded sincere. "How are you?"

"I'm keeping busy helping my mamm but otherwise good." Lydia's voice lowered, although Amy didn't know why. She was the only customer in the building at the moment. "Is anything wrong, Amy? You would tell me if there was, wouldn't you?"

"Everything's fine. Why do you ask?"

"Because you're picking at your cuticles like you've always done whenever you're stressed about something."

Amy glanced down and pulled her hands apart. "It's just a bad *aagewehnet*."

"Jah, a habit you've had since we were girls, but you only did it when you were stressed or worried about something." Lydia tapped her fingers against the countertop as if to drive the point home.

"Guess I am a little bit stressed," Amy conceded.

"About what?"

"My mamm's in New York right now, helping Michelle with her new baby."

"I didn't realize she'd given birth. What did she have?"

"A little boy. They named him after my daed."

Lydia smiled. "How nice. I bet that made your mom happy."

"It did."

"So, who's helping you run the greenhouse while she's gone?"

"Sylvia and Henry, although they're still at the house right now." Amy touched her temples while closing her eyes briefly. "Things have been really busy here, and there are times when it's hard to keep up even with my siblings' help."

"That would explain why you're tired, but what I see in your expression and tense posture is more than fatigue."

Amy sighed. "Well, we have had a few things go wrong since Mom's been gone."

"Such as?" Lydia leaned forward.

"Just a little episode with some pots of plants getting tipped over."

"Who tipped them over?"

"We don't know." Amy felt relieved when another customer came in. She didn't want to talk about their problems. And why bother? It wouldn't change a thing or keep more vandalism from happening.

"Did you come here to purchase anything?" she asked.

Lydia shook her head. "I just wanted to see you and find out how things are going because that's what best friends do."

"Danki for thinking of us." Amy stepped out from behind the counter and gave Lydia a hug. "Wish I could talk with you longer, but I have to see what the woman who just came in needs."

"I understand. I'll see you at church for our next gathering. In the meantime, if you need anything, please don't hesitate to ask."

"Thank you." Amy glanced toward the door and was glad to see her brother step in as Lydia left. "Will you please stay at the checkout counter until Sylvia comes out?" Amy asked when Henry approached.

"Okay, since you asked so nice." Henry moved away before Amy could comment. She didn't appreciate his sarcastic tone, but at least he hadn't refused to do as she asked.

Sylvia had spent more time in the house than she planned to, but after she and Henry had hung up the clocks, the baby needed to be fed. Afterward, even though Allen had been playing happily with his toys, he started crying and clinging to Sylvia. Mary Ruth had quite a time getting him calmed down so Sylvia could slip out the door. It tore at Sylvia's heartstrings to leave her children so she could work in the greenhouse, but until Mom returned, she had no other choice. She hoped at the end of Mom's two-week stay at Ezekiel's that she wouldn't decide to extend her trip. Sylvia was anxious to resume caring for her children full-time and letting Mom and Amy run the greenhouse with whatever help they could get from Henry. Each day of helping in the greenhouse became a little harder for Sylvia. Some days she wasn't sure she could force herself to go there at all.

As she stepped into the yard and headed for the building, a tour bus pulled in. The next thing Sylvia knew, about forty people got out, all talking at once as they headed for the greenhouse.

Sylvia drew in several quick, shallow breaths. She saw spots in front of her eyes and feared she might faint. No way could she handle being around so many strangers crowded into the greenhouse. She wanted to turn around and run back to the house, but that would leave her sister and brother to deal with the people on their own.

Sylvia rushed in ahead of the tourists. She found Henry sitting behind the counter doodling on a piece of paper. "What are you doing? Where's Amy?"

"I'm doing what she told me while she waits on a customer." Henry pointed to the nearest aisle. "But since you're here now, you can take my place. I've got some things I need to do outside of the greenhouse."

"No, please don't leave me." Sylvia looked toward the open door as people from the bus began filing in. "With all these folks here, I might need you."

Henry stepped off the stool. "You'll be fine. As I said, there's something I need to do." Before Sylvia could protest, he made a dash for the door.

"Oh, this is so exciting." One of the tourists smiled at Sylvia. "It's my first time in Amish country, and I'm having so much fun."

Sylvia forced her lips to form a smile. *Amy. Hurry up, Amy. You're better at talking to people than I am.*

Wiping her damp hands along the front of her black apron, Sylvia went behind the counter and took a seat. Her rigid form relaxed a bit when the noisy group of people dispersed down all five aisles.

"You look a bit overwhelmed," the man who had been driving the bus said. "I take it you're not used to having a bunch of eager tourists roaming around your greenhouse."

"There have been a few tour groups stop by but not since I've been working here." Sylvia took in a few more deep breaths.

"Well, this could be your lucky day." The man grinned at Sylvia. "This group of people has been buying stuff from every store we've stopped at so far. You may make a nice profit today."

Sylvia wasn't sure how best to respond, so she forced herself to offer the man another smile.

"From here we'll be stopping at the Strasburg Railroad so that those who want to can take the short train ride." He reached into his pocket and pulled out a package of gum. "Then our last stop of the day will be at an Amish farmhouse in Paradise for a homemade sit-down supper. I'm sure everyone on the bus will enjoy that."

She nodded. *I wish this man would stop talking to me. I need some time by myself before anyone comes up to the counter with a purchase.*

Sylvia craned her neck to see where Amy had gone. *Sister, why aren't you coming to rescue me?* She glanced toward the door. *Henry, where did you run off to? Mom wouldn't like it if she knew you weren't here helping like you're supposed to be.*

The more Sylvia thought about her situation, the more panicked she became. Sweat beaded on her forehead and trickled down her cheeks. Was it the heat and humidity inside the building or just her nerves?

Sylvia heaved a sigh of relief when she saw Amy heading down aisle 2 with four women following her. Each carried some item—a plant stake, a jar of honey, a candle made of beeswax, and a brass wind chime. Hopefully, once they paid for their purchases, they'd leave the greenhouse and get back on the bus.

As if she sensed Sylvia's distress, Amy joined her behind the counter. "I'll do the talking, and you can take the money and make change if needed," Amy whispered as she bent close to Sylvia's ear.

"Okay." Sylvia pressed a palm to her chest. Now that her sister was here, she felt a little better.

"Where's Henry?" Amy asked after all the customers had left.

Sylvia shrugged. "I don't know. He said he had something to do outside."

Amy frowned. "Well, he'd better get back in here soon. One of those tourists opened a bag of potting soil, and then someone else came along and knocked it over." She puffed out her cheeks. "So now there's a mess to clean up and no Henry."

"Should I go outside and look for him?" Sylvia offered.

"Jah, if you don't mind."

"Don't mind at all. In fact, I could use a bit of fresh air."

When Sylvia left the greenhouse, she headed to the barn, figuring her brother may have gone in there. Although she saw no sign of him, Sylvia detected the unmistakable odor of cigarette smoke. *Now who would have been in here smoking? Could one of those tourists have wandered into the barn to look around and lit a cigarette?*

She cupped her hands around her mouth. "Henry! Are you in here, Brother?"

Except for the gentle nicker of one of their horses, all was quiet within the wooden structure.

"Henry," she called again. Still no response.

Sylvia left the barn and was about to go up to the house to see if Henry had gone there, when he stepped into the yard.

"Where have you been all this time?" Sylvia slapped both hands against her hips. "Amy needs you, and. ..."

"Oh, she always needs me for somethin'. What's she want this time?"

"Someone spilled a bag of potting soil, so. . ."

"And I'm supposed to clean it up?"

"Jah."

Henry's eyes narrowed as he clenched his jaw. "I always have to do the dirty work, and I never get to have any fun." His voice rose. "I'm gettin' sick and tired of it."

"Henry, you're just as much a part of this family as the rest of us, and we all need to pull together."

"Well, I didn't see you doin' much to help out till Mom left, but then you didn't have much choice."

Sylvia recoiled. Her brother's sharp words stung like fire. "You have no right to speak to me like that," she shot back. "You don't know what it's like for me to be faced with two kinner to raise and no husband."

Henry glared at her. "Well, you don't know what it's like to have your dad and older brother killed and be stuck with all the chores they used to do. And besides that, I miss the fun stuff Dad, Abe, and I used to do."

Before Sylvia could think of a response, Henry tromped off to the greenhouse.

Tears sprang to her eyes. *None of us has been the same since the accident that took three precious lives, and I'm not sure we'll ever be again.*

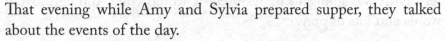

That evening while Amy and Sylvia prepared supper, they talked about the events of the day.

Amy went to the refrigerator and took out a package of ground beef. "Thanks to all those tourists who came in, we sold more today than I expected."

Sylvia bobbed her head. "I would have been even more nervous than I was if you hadn't been up at the counter with me."

Amy joined her sister by the cupboard, where she was busy slicing fresh tomatoes to go on the burgers they'd soon be grilling. "You haven't always been uncomfortable around people. Is there any specific reason they bother you so now?"

Sylvia's features tensed up. "My nerves have been on edge ever since Toby, Dad, and Abe died. And now, with the vandalism that has occurred here, I wake up every morning wondering if something else unpleasant has happened."

"We can't live in fear, and worrying doesn't add even one more minute to our lives." Amy set the ground beef on the counter and placed her hand on Sylvia's shoulder. "Besides, the vandalism that's been done is minor. No one's been hurt or even threatened."

Sylvia lowered her head. "But they could be, and I can't help but be afraid. The fact that some stranger is trespassing on our property, doing damage to things, is creeping me out."

"It's best not to worry—especially about things that are beyond our control. We need to pray every day and put our faith in God. And it wouldn't hurt to ask Him to put a hedge of protection around us."

When Sylvia gave no response, Amy added, "I'm praying for you too, dear sister."

Sylvia's chin lowered, almost to her chest. "You can pray all you want, but I doubt it'll do any good."

Amy felt helpless at that moment. All she could do was lean on her heavenly Father. She closed her eyes. *Lord, we need Your strength to get through this time of trial. Please help me to be a reflection of You to my family.*

Amy wouldn't say anything more to Sylvia right now. If her sister's faith was going to be restored, it would come through loving words and lots of prayer.

Chapter 27

"I can't believe Mom will finally be coming home tomorrow." Sylvia wiped her hands on a paper towel after she finished clearing their messy supper dishes. They'd had baked spareribs with barbecue sauce, and as good as the meal had been, their plates showed the telltale sign of sticky sauce.

Amy smiled as she took out the dishtowel in readiness to dry the dishes her sister would soon wash. "I wonder if she's as excited to see us as we are to see her."

"No doubt she is, but it will be hard for her to leave Ezekiel and his family. I'm sure Mom enjoyed getting to know her new grand son and spending time with sweet little Angela Mary." Sylvia rinsed off their dishes and put them in the warm, soapy water that awaited them.

"Jah, but she'll be equally happy to be here with us and your adorable kinner."

"You're right, I'm sure." Sylvia sloshed the sudsy dishrag over a plate, rinsed it well, and placed it in the dish drainer. "If Ezekiel and his family moved back here, it wouldn't be a problem for Mom at all. We'd all be together in the same town and could be there for each other when there was a need."

Amy nodded. "I agree, but Mom's dead set against them leaving Clymer. They're settled there, and our brother's happy with his business and new role as minister. Mom thinks it wouldn't be fair to ask him to give that all up."

"Nothing's fair. Not in this life anyway." Sylvia slapped the dishrag against the next plate so hard, some water splashed up, almost hitting her in the face.

Amy didn't respond. It was difficult to see her sister in this state. Although Sylvia needed to come to terms with her bitterness and anger toward God in her own way and time, Amy hung to the hope that things would eventually get better.

She heard a knock on the front door and voices in the living room. It sounded like Henry was talking to someone. Amy tried to listen while drying another dish, hoping to hear who the other person might be. *I hope it's not Monroe. He's been wanting to see our mamm. Is he interested in her the way he was when they were young adults?* Something about the man still didn't set well with Amy.

A few minutes later, Henry entered the room. "My friend Seth is here. He wants me to sleep over at his place tonight and then go fishin' with him tomorrow morning."

Amy felt relieved that at least it wasn't Monroe. "Tomorrow's Saturday, Henry, and as you know, that's always a big day at the greenhouse. Sorry, but you'll need to be here to help out."

"Not only that," Sylvia spoke up, "but Mom's coming home tomorrow, and she'd be disappointed if you weren't here."

"Great! You're both ganging up on me now." Henry's brows drew together. "If Mom leaves there in the morning, she won't be here till late afternoon. I'll be home by then."

"Sorry, Brother, but the answer is no." Amy spoke with authority.

Henry looked back toward the other room, where Seth obviously waited. "I think I've been more than helpful since Mom left for Clymer. I've put up with bein' told what to do the whole time, and I'm sick and tired of it. You two ain't my mamm," Henry mumbled as he tromped out of the room.

A moment later, Amy heard the front door open and slam shut.

Sylvia looked at Amy. "That didn't go too well, did it?"

"It never does unless Henry gets his way. One minute he promises to cooperate, and the next minute he gets belligerent and shows us his temper." Amy sighed. "I'll be glad when Mom is here so she can deal with our brother, and I won't have to be the voice of authority."

Once the dishes were done, and the little ones had been put to bed, Amy and Sylvia retired to the living room to do some mending and enjoy a glass of cold root beer Mary Ruth had brought them this morning. She said Lenore's husband had made it with a recipe that had been handed down in his family.

"This root beer is sure good, isn't it?" Amy licked off some of the cool liquid that had stuck to her upper lip.

Sylvia nodded. "Are you sure you don't want some, Henry?"

Henry looked up from the newspaper he'd been reading. "No thanks. In fact, I'm headin' upstairs to bed."

"So early?" Amy glanced at the clock on the far wall that played music on the hour. "It's not like you to be tired at eight o'clock in the evening."

"Who says I'm tired? I just wanna be alone." Henry tossed the paper on the coffee table and stood. Without telling them good night, he ambled out of the room and clomped up the stairs.

"Maybe he's punishing himself for his harsh words earlier by not having any root beer and going to bed before he normally would," Sylvia commented.

Amy set her empty glass on the side table by her chair. "I think it's just his way of trying to show us that he can make some decisions for himself."

"Well, whatever the case, I'm kind of glad Henry went to bed early. He's beginning to get on my nerves." Sylvia leaned back in her chair. "Truth be told, nearly everything bothers me these days, and I'll be glad when I don't have to work in the greenhouse anymore."

Amy's chin tilted down as she frowned. "I was rather hoping you'd continue to work there with me and Mom. It would be like old times, before you got married."

Sylvia's mouth twisted grimly. "Being around so many people is too stressful for me, Amy. My place is with the kinner. They need their mamm not a babysitter who isn't part of our family."

"Hasn't Mary Ruth done a good job taking care of Rachel and Allen?"

Sylvia nodded. "But she's not family, and even if she was, I don't want to work in the greenhouse once Mom returns home. It's just that simple." Sylvia rose from her chair. "I am going to check on the kinner, and then I think I'll also go to bed."

"Oh, okay. I'm going to stay up for a while and do a bit more mending."

"All right then. Good night, Amy."

"Night. I hope you sleep well."

Sylvia mumbled something Amy couldn't quite understand and quickly left the room.

Amy set her mending aside and picked up her Bible to read a few verses from Psalms. She couldn't let her discouragement tear down her faith. The best remedy was reading God's Holy Word.

"Giddyap, Dandy. Don't be such a slowpoke." Jared snapped the reins. He'd left Lydia's house a short time ago and was eager to get home. He'd gone there to give them a bid on a new roof for their house, and Lydia's mother had invited him to stay for supper. Jared didn't want to be impolite, so he had accepted the invitation. He'd hoped it would give him a chance to talk more to Lydia about Amy, but that never happened. Lydia's mother had monopolized the conversation. Jared wondered if she'd been trying to impress him. Darlene kept trying to get Jared to eat more and then almost insisted that he have seconds on dessert. When it was time for him to leave, she seemed intent on keeping him there by bringing up even more topics. Lydia's poor dad barely got a word in during supper because his wife monopolized the conversation.

Maybe it's just as well that I left when I did, Jared thought. *Lydia's mamm is a bit of a gossip, and I wouldn't want her listening to or commenting on anything either Lydia or I might have said concerning my broken relationship with Amy.*

As Jared's horse and buggy approached the Kings' place that evening, he saw a car pull up along the road about six feet from the Kings' driveway. A few seconds later, Amy's teenage brother ran out from behind some bushes and got in the passenger's side of the vehicle. It was well after nine o'clock and almost dark. *I wonder where Henry could be going at this hour. I doubt that Amy or Sylvia would allow him to go anyplace at this time of the night.*

Jared was tempted to stop at the house and say something to Amy or her sister but swiftly concluded that it was none of his concern. *If they knew Henry was out and about, they might not appreciate me butting into their business.*

Clymer

The following morning, Belinda said a tearful goodbye to Ezekiel, Michelle, and the little ones. It had been a joy to spend the last two weeks with them, but Michelle insisted she was doing well enough to be on her own now, and it was time for Belinda to go home.

"We promise to come for a visit as soon as the baby is a little older and Michelle gets all of her strength back." Ezekiel gave Belinda another hug.

She sniffed. "That would nice. We'll look forward to it."

"Danki for all you did to help out." Michelle, holding the baby, hugged Belinda with her other arm. "I couldn't have managed without you."

Belinda leaned down and kissed Angela Mary's soft cheek. She tried to capture in her mind the softness she'd felt. "Be good for your mamm and help her out when you can, okay my sweet girl?" As usual, Belinda spoke to her granddaughter in Pennsylvania Dutch since the child spoke no English yet.

The little girl nodded soberly, then her face broke into a wide smile.

It melted Belinda's heart, seeing the special look on her granddaughter's face. *Oh, how selfish I feel right now. If only it were possible, I'd bring all of them home with me to Strasburg.*

Belinda kissed baby Vernon's forehead. "I hope he doesn't grow too much before I see him again."

"Maybe by the first week of September we can come for a visit." Ezekiel put Belinda's bags in her driver's vehicle. "Tell everyone hello and please give them our love. We pray for each of you every day."

"Prayers are always appreciated, and we'll pray for you too."

Belinda gave them all one last hug before climbing into the passenger's seat. With a lump in her throat, she waved goodbye as the van backed out of the driveway. Even though Belinda felt sad about leaving her family here, she had something to look forward to at home. Later today, Belinda would be hugging Sylvia, Amy, Henry, and her other two grandchildren. She could hardly wait to see everyone and find out how each of them was doing.

Strasburg

For a second time, Amy stood by the kitchen doorway and called Henry to come eat breakfast. "He should have been down here an hour ago to do his outside chores," she told Sylvia.

Her sister nodded. "Maybe he forgot to set his alarm clock."

After a few more times of calling him, Amy went upstairs. She knocked on his door, and when there was no answer, she opened it. Henry was not in his room, but the bed had been made. She lifted her gaze to the ceiling. *If Henry made his bed without a reminder, that's a first. I wonder what came over that boy.*

Amy went back to the kitchen and let Sylvia know that their brother was not in his room. "But the strange thing is, his bed was made, and neatly at that," she added.

"Since he knows Mom's coming home later today, maybe he wants to make a good impression," her sister replied as she set the table.

"Or maybe," Amy said, "our brother was trying to impress us by making his bed so we won't mention anything to Mom about him being uncooperative most of the time while she was gone." Amy moved toward the back door. "Guess I'll go outside and tell him breakfast is ready. He probably got up earlier than usual and is still out in the barn taking care of the livestock."

"When you see Henry, tell him to hurry because the quiche is getting cold."

"Will do." Amy stepped into the yard but saw no sign of Henry. All seemed quiet as though her sibling was nowhere around. She went to the barn but didn't see or hear any sign of her brother there, even though she called his name several times.

Amy was about to leave the barn when she spotted an empty cigarette pack on the floor. *I wonder where that came from.* She picked it up and tossed it into the trash can near the barn entrance.

Back outside, Amy checked inside the greenhouse, pump house, potting shed, and even in the phone shack, but her brother wasn't in any of those places.

She tapped her chin. *This is so odd. What's going on here this morning? I'll look one more place before I begin to panic.*

In desperation, she walked down the driveway to see if he might have gone to the mailbox to mail a letter or get the mail. She and Sylvia had been so busy yesterday that neither of them had taken time to get the mail.

Amy went to the box and put the key in the lock. Sure enough, there was mail inside. *At least I know my brother didn't take care of this.* Holding onto the stack of letters, she looked up and down the road. No sign of Henry, but Amy noticed the neighbor man leaving for work and his wife waving to him from their front porch. Amy gave a wave too before heading back to the house.

"Did you find Henry?" Sylvia asked when Amy entered the kitchen.

She placed the envelopes on the counter near the door. Full of frustration, Amy shook her head. "The only thing I found was this morning's mail. There was no sign of our brother in the yard or any of our buildings. She made no mention of the cigarette pack she'd seen in the barn. No point in upsetting Sylvia further. "I'm worried. I think I should hitch my horse to the buggy and go looking for him."

"That's a good idea." Sylvia's gaze flitted around the room, never settling on any one thing. When she looked at Amy again, tears welled in her eyes. "If we haven't found Henry by the time Mom gets home, I don't know what we're going to tell her."

Chapter 28

"I bet our bruder never slept in his bed at all. I believe he may have snuck out of the house after you and I were in bed and gone over to Seth's." Amy looked at Sylvia with a firm resolve. "I can't believe it. Neither of us ever did anything like that during our *yuchend*. Yet our kid brother did even though he knew it was wrong." She drummed her fingers on the counter. "Henry's not going to get away with it, and he can't use the excuse of being young, either. If he's not here by the time Mom arrives, she's going to be very umgerennt."

"It sounds to me like you're a little upset yourself." Sylvia gestured to the kitchen table. "Why don't we take a seat? We can talk about the situation while we eat our sausage and vegetable quiche. It'll give us a chance to decide what we should say when Henry's confronted."

"Okay." Amy moved over to her chair but didn't sit down. In addition to the egg dish, there was fresh fruit and moist banana bread. It was a shame to have all this nice food and their brother wasn't here to eat it with them.

Normally, Amy's mouth would water in anticipation but not today. The concern she felt about Henry had diminished her appetite.

"We'll have plenty of leftovers for Mom to have tomorrow morning." Sylvia poured herself a glass of orange juice and gave one to Amy. "When we're finished eating breakfast, you can go over to Seth's place and see if Henry's there."

"I suppose it could wait till after we eat, but while I'm over there, you'll be stuck opening the greenhouse and working by yourself until I get back."

Sylvia stood next to the table with one hand clasping the other at the elbow. "I—I hadn't thought about that. I'm not sure I can handle being by myself in the greenhouse with customers." Perspiration beaded on her forehead.

Amy had hoped by the end of these two weeks, her sister's apprehension would have lessened some and she'd be more at ease around other people. Amy certainly felt her sister's stress. *I think it's necessary to give Sylvia some relief right now. If I were my sister, what would I need to hear?*

She slipped her arm around Sylvia's waist. "Maybe you'd rather go after Henry once Mary Ruth gets here."

Sylvia shook her head. "I can't drive the horse and buggy yet. It would make me too nervous."

"Then I'll go—either now or after we eat our breakfast."

Sylvia pulled out a chair and sat down. "I am really not that hungry, but let's eat now. Once Mary Ruth shows up, you can go over to Seth's place and I'll open the greenhouse."

"Danki, Sister." Amy sat too.

"After we've finished eating, I'll check on the kinner and see if either of them is awake. They were both sleeping soundly when I left the room, so I decided it would be best not to disturb them."

"I agree. Now shall we bow for prayer?"

Sylvia bowed her head, though Amy suspected her sister wasn't praying.

Heavenly Father, Amy silently prayed, *if I don't get to Seth's house before Henry leaves there, please bring him home safe.*

When Amy's prayer ended, she opened her eyes. About to reach for the salt and pepper, she lowered her hand when she heard the back door open and shut. A few seconds later, Henry stepped into the kitchen. His hair looked disheveled, and his clothes were a rumpled mess like he'd slept in them. *Thank You, Lord, for bringing my brother home safe and sound.*

Amy left her chair and marched up to her brother. "Where have you been, young man?" She stood with both hands firmly against her hips. "You were gone all night, weren't you?"

He gave a slow nod.

"That wasn't a schmaert thing to do, sneaking out at night and without our permission."

"Where did you go? Were you at Seth's?" This question came from Sylvia, who had also left her seat and turned to face their brother.

Silence filled the room as they stood waiting for Henry's response.

"Jah, I went over to Seth's, and I spent the night." Henry lowered his head. "Figured I'd be back early this morning before you missed me, but we overslept."

Amy was so angry, her hands shook. She was about to give Henry a piece of her mind, but Sylvia spoke again. "You'd better get cleaned up, Brother, and then eat some breakfast. You have chores yet to do, and we expect you to be in the greenhouse on time for opening."

Henry stared at his feet and then shuffled out of the room.

Amy looked at Sylvia and heaved a sigh. "Wait till Mom hears about this."

"Maybe we shouldn't say anything to her," Sylvia responded.

"How come?"

"It might take the joy out of her trip and make her wish she hadn't gone at all. Besides, our brother seemed quite desperate to have some sort of fun yesterday."

"Yes," Amy said, "and then he went ahead and got his way without our consent."

Sylvia frowned deeply. "He sure did, but honestly, did he look happy this morning?"

"It didn't appear so to me."

"So how about if we keep quiet about Henry's escapade?" Sylvia suggested again. "We don't want to stir things up when our mamm gets home."

"I see your point. And with Mom here to take control of things, it's not likely that Henry will pull another stunt like that."

Soon, the soft patter of little feet came into the kitchen. Amy bent down and scooped her nephew into her arms. "Guder mariye, sweet boy."

Allen grinned at her.

Sylvia stepped over and tickled her son's chin. "Are you hungerich?"

He bobbed his head.

"I'll take Allen back and get him dressed while you fix his cereal. We won't be long." Amy left with the giggling boy in her arms.

"Where'd you go last night?" Jared's mother asked as he sat at the table with his folks, eating breakfast. "I heard you come in, but your daed and I had already gone up to our room and were in bed."

"Figured as much." Jared drank the rest of his apple juice. "I had supper at Lydia's house."

"Is that so?" Mom leaned slightly forward. "Does that mean the two of you are courting?"

Jared shook his head. "I went over to her folks' to give them a bid on a new roof, and Lydia's mamm asked me to stay for supper. I didn't want to be rude, so I accepted."

In order to take the pressure off himself, Jared turned the conversation in a different direction. "On the way home, I saw something that has me kind of worried."

Jared's dad tipped his head. "What was that, Son?"

"As I was going past the Kings' place, I saw Henry run out of the bushes and jump in a car that had stopped along the side of the road." Jared squeezed the bridge of his nose. "It was after nine o'clock, which seemed a bit too late for Amy's brother to be out with a friend."

"How do you know it was a friend?" Mom asked.

He shrugged. "I don't for sure, but I suspect it was. I almost stopped to talk to Amy about it but decided it was none of my business, so I kept going in the direction of home."

"You did the right thing, Son." Dad thumped Jared's arm. "A person who goes around stickin' their nose in other people's business is likely to get it chopped off."

Mom squinted her eyes at Dad. "That's an awful thing to say, Emmanuel. Besides, I wouldn't be one bit surprised if Amy's brother was up to no good. He has a sneaky look about him."

Dad shook his head. "Now how in the world can you tell if someone's sneaky by lookin' at them?"

"I just can. In my younger days, I was a schoolteacher, don't ya know?" Mom added a spoonful of sugar to her coffee cup and stirred it around. "None of the scholars in my school could pull the wool over my eyes because I could tell by their expressions whether they were telling the truth or trying to pull a fast one."

"Well, Ava dear, even if you're right about Belinda King's boy, it's none of our business." Dad gave Jared's arm another thump. "Right, Son?"

Jared managed a smile, but he couldn't help feeling concerned about Henry. He hoped the boy wasn't hanging around with a rough crowd, which could eventually get him into trouble.

Virginia woke up in a stupor and crawled out of bed. *I need to get some coffee into me to clear my head.*

As she stood at the window, after opening the shade, Virginia thought about how yesterday she'd seen a beautiful cardinal in their yard. *Maybe I could ask Earl to get me a nice birdfeeder to hang in that tree where the cardinal sat. It would be nice to see birds in the yard more regularly.*

Virginia yawned. She didn't feel like she'd gotten a good night's sleep and could barely keep her eyes open, yet she didn't want to go back to bed. She'd probably feel worse when she woke up again. At least she'd finally gotten over her cold and sore throat. That was something positive to think about.

When she reached the kitchen and saw the clock, Virginia realized that her husband had already left for work. *It was nice of Earl to let me sleep in. I sure must have needed it, because I slept right through him getting ready for work.*

The coffeemaker was turned off, but if Earl had used it this morning, the coffee might still be warm. Curious, she touched the carafe, but it felt cold. Virginia poured some into a mug and heated it in the microwave.

Think I'll go out on the front porch and see what's happening across the road. She stepped out the door and took a seat on one of the chairs.

Last evening, Virginia had seen the neighbors' teenage boy getting into a car that had pulled onto the shoulder of the road. She could only imagine what a teenager would be doing out at that time of the night with his friends. Why hadn't the vehicle pulled into the Kings' driveway by the house to pick him up? In Virginia's suspicious mind, it didn't add up.

She squinted against the glare of the sun and spotted Amy outside on the lawn with a toddler. They seemed to be looking at something in the grass, but Virginia had no idea what it was. It was endearing to see them together. Virginia wished her kids were still little and she could be with them right now. She'd sure do things different if she could raise her children again.

When Amy was about to bring Allen inside, she spotted Henry standing by the fence dropping birdseed on the ground.

"What are you doing?" she asked.

"I'm feeding the pretty crow that likes to hang around here all the time. I've discovered, in addition to eatin' lots of bugs, he likes birdseed."

Amy frowned as she gazed at the black bird. It did have a blue tinge to its tail feathers, although it was not what she would call *pretty*.

"That noisy crow is nothing but a nuisance, and if you feed it, it'll just keep hanging around."

"I thought you liked birds."

"Not *grappe*."

"What have you got against crows?"

"This one in particular makes too much of a racket." Amy didn't mention that the crow always seemed to make an appearance right before or after something bad happened. Henry would probably laugh and say she was superstitious.

"Just don't keep feeding it," she warned. "There are enough birds around here already."

Henry said nothing, but the crow responded. *Caw. . .Caw. . . Caw. . .*

Amy had a hard time concentrating on her work that afternoon. She kept watching for her mother's arrival. Every time a vehicle pulled onto the gravel parking lot, she had to open the screen door and look out.

At four o'clock, when there were no customers in the building, Amy heard another vehicle pull in. She hurried to open the door and was pleased to see their driver's van pulling in.

"Mom's here," Amy hollered to Sylvia and Henry. They joined her as she stepped outside.

"It's so good to see all of you!" Mom stepped down from the van and rushed forward.

"It's good to see you too. Welcome home!" Sylvia hugged Mom first, followed by Amy and Henry.

They all tried to talk at once, and after Mom got her luggage and paid the driver, she suggested they go into the greenhouse.

"Everything looks good." She smiled. "I appreciate how you all handled things so well while I was gone."

Amy wanted to tell Mom that things hadn't gone well all the time, but she kept quiet, not wanting to ruin their mother's happy homecoming.

"Tell us all about the new boppli," Sylvia said after they'd entered the building.

"He's a sweet baby." Mom gave them an update on Ezekiel and his family. "He said they would try to come see us in early September."

"Oh, that'd be so nice." Amy smiled and gave Mom another hug.

"Now I'd like to go to the house and see my other two precious grandchildren." Mom looked at Sylvia. "Since there's no activity in the greenhouse right now, why don't you go with me?"

"That's a fine idea."

Mom and Sylvia locked arms and headed out the door. "Amy, as soon as you close the greenhouse for the day, please come right up to the house so we can visit more while we fix our evening meal," Mom called over her shoulder.

"Okay, Mom. Henry and I will both be there."

When the door shut behind Mom and Sylvia, Amy turned to face her brother. "Please make sure that all the plants are watered well. We can't afford to have any of them die from lack of water on these hot days like we've been having."

"Jah, okay." He scuffed the toe of his boot on the concrete floor. "Will ya do me a favor, Amy, and not say anything to Mom about me bein' gone last night?"

"I won't say anything this time, but if you ever pull another stunt like that, Mom will be the first to know." She shook her finger in Henry's face. "And I guarantee you, she won't like it one bit."

Chapter 29

"Guder mariye," Amy said when she entered the kitchen Sunday morning and found her mother at the table going through a stack of mail Amy had set aside for her.

Mom looked up and smiled. "Good morning."

"Did you sleep well?"

"Jah. It felt good to be back in my own bed." Mom gestured to the mail. "I surely appreciate all that you, Sylvia, and Henry did while I was gone. Just keeping up with sorting the mail and paying bills must have kept you busy, not to mention running the greenhouse, plus cooking and cleaning here in our home."

"We were glad to do it so you could be a help to Ezekiel's family." Amy poured them each a cup of coffee and took a seat at the table.

"It was my privilege to help, and I enjoyed my time with Ezekiel, Michelle, and the little ones. But I have to admit, it's real nice to be home. I thought about all of you a lot and always wondered how things were going."

"We managed okay, Mom."

"How did Henry do while I was gone?"

"We had a few problems but nothing I couldn't handle."

"What kind of problems?" Mom tipped her head.

"He complained about some of the chores I asked him to do." Amy drank some of her coffee before she proceeded. "Henry was also a bit careless. Somehow he managed to lose his key to the greenhouse doors, but Lenore's husband came over and put new locks on both doors, so now we have new keys for everyone but Henry. I don't trust him with it. He's so careless, he might lose a new key too."

Mom rubbed her forehead. "So, he never found the old one?"

Amy shook her head. "Henry looked everywhere for it, and so did I."

"That's not good. What if someone else found it and. . ." Mom's voice trailed off as she looked at Amy with a serious expression. "Henry told me about plants that had been dumped over. Why didn't you call Ezekiel's and tell me what happened? Didn't you think I had the right to know?"

"I didn't want you to worry about something that was out of your control." Amy patted her mother's arm. "And you needn't look so concerned now, because not all the plants in the greenhouse were ruined, and none of us were harmed."

Mom sat staring at the table. Amy could almost read her thoughts. Between hearing about the missing key and the overturned pots, her dear mother was undoubtedly worried.

And with good reason. Amy chose not to mention that Henry had snuck out of the house last night, since she'd promised she wouldn't say anything unless he did something like that again. *So, I'll keep quiet for now, but if he messes up again, I won't hesitate to tell Mom.*

Monday morning, Sylvia sat beside Allen on the couch, tying his shoe. In a few years, her precious boy would be old enough to tie it himself.

He looked up at Sylvia with such a tender expression it brought tears to her eyes. Allen reminded her so much of his father—not just his curly black hair. It was mostly the determined set of his jaw when he wanted something. Sylvia could still see Toby's unwavering expression the day he proposed marriage. He'd proclaimed his love to her and said he'd do everything in his power to be a good husband and provider. And he had been, right up until his untimely death.

Sylvia forced her musings aside and finished tying her son's shoes.

Then she lifted him onto her lap and stroked his cheek. "You're such a *gut bu.*"

"Good boy," he repeated in Pennsylvania Dutch.

"Jah, a very good boy."

When Allen began to squirm, she allowed him to get down from the couch. He turned, grinned at her, and then darted across the room for his toy box.

Sylvia leaned against the cushion behind her back and sighed. It was a relief not to work in the greenhouse today. She hoped Mom and Amy wouldn't expect her to work there anymore, because being here with her children was where she belonged, not dealing with anxious or curious customers.

Hearing Rachel's cry from the bedroom, where she'd been sleeping, Sylvia rose from the couch. Today would be a better day for her than the last two weeks.

The greenhouse had been open only a few minutes when Monroe showed up. He seemed to be dressed in nicer clothes today and smelled of some kind of men's cologne—or maybe it was his aftershave. Belinda thought it looked strange to see an Amish man Monroe's age clean-shaven, but since he'd never married, it made sense. *I hope he didn't get all fancied up on my account. Maybe Monroe has some appointment to go to later.*

She smiled and tried to be polite, but the strange way he looked at her made Belinda apprehensive.

"You look real nice today, Belinda." Monroe moved close to the counter where she sat. "It's good to see that you're back home where you belong." His brows wrinkled as the aroma of his cologne grew stronger. "You know, it's not safe for you and your kinner to be alone without a man in the house."

"My children are all grown, and they did fine while I was gone. In fact, we're all getting along well on our own."

"Are you sure about that?" He leaned on the counter so close that

Belinda could feel and smell his minty breath.

Fussing with her apron ties, she moved slightly away. "I am quite sure. Now if you don't mind, Monroe, I have work to do here."

He glanced around. "Doesn't look like you're all that busy. In fact, at the moment, I'm the only customer in the building."

"If you're a customer then I assume you came to buy something?"

"Well, I. . ."

"If so, either my daughter or son can help you." She gestured toward the other end of the greenhouse and the row in front of the checkout counter.

"I really don't need anything right now, but I'll wander around a bit and see what all you have." He grinned at her and headed down the aisle she had gestured to. As Monroe meandered, he seemed to be inspecting things as he went along.

About the time several customers showed up, Monroe came back up the aisle and said goodbye to Belinda. "I'll be back soon to see how you are doing."

When he went out the door, Belinda felt her rigid body begin to relax. Although at one point in her young adult life she'd thought she might care for Monroe, she had no romantic feelings for him now. Belinda was still in love with Vernon and figured she always would be.

When she felt sure Mom could handle things in the greenhouse with only Henry's help, Amy slipped out to get the mail. She took a quick side tour and looked at the garden to see if anything would need picking later. The tomatoes looked like they were doing well, and so did the radishes. *Sometime later I'll come out with a container and collect what is ready.* Amy turned and headed down the driveway.

When she reached their box, she met Virginia, who was also getting her mail.

Amy said hello and tried to make conversation, but Virginia wasn't sociable.

"How are those tomato plants I sold you?"

Virginia wrinkled her nose. "They both died a few days after I put 'em in the ground."

"I'm so sorry. You should have come over right away and told us about it. If you'd like to bring them back, we'll gladly refund your money or give you some new plants."

Virginia shook her head. "The plants weren't bad. It was the fresh horse manure I put in the dirt when I planted them. It wasn't my idea, you understand. I was only doin' what my husband told me to do. He said horse manure would make the plants grow." Deep wrinkles formed across her forehead. "We found out, a little too late, I might add, that it's best to use manure that's been aged awhile."

"That's correct. I should have given you planting instructions when you bought the plants that day."

Virginia shrugged. "What's done is done. I just won't have a garden this year."

"We always grow a big garden, so I'm sure we'll have more than enough produce to share some with you."

Virginia lifted her hand and waved it about. "No need for that. Me and Earl will get by just fine."

"Oh, but we'd like to help out."

"We ain't rich, but we're not poor neither. We'll buy whatever produce we need at the grocery store or one of the farmers' markets in the area."

Amy didn't want to press the issue, so she smiled and said, "Whatever you wish, but please let us know if you change your mind."

"It's doubtful." Virginia grabbed her mail from the box and limped back across the street.

Amy watched until she got safely to the other side. *I wonder if that poor woman has a bad knee and is in need of a knee replacement. She seems able-bodied enough except for that terrible limp. I suppose it would be impolite to ask her about it.*

When Amy turned and headed back up the driveway, she was greeted with the raucous cry of the pesky crow that kept hanging around. *I hope Henry's not feeding the bird again. It's ridiculous that my brother thinks he can make a pet out of the crow. If I had my say, we would figure out some way to get rid of that irritating bird. For me, it's nothing but a reminder of everything that's gone wrong around here since our dear family members perished.*

Virginia came to the front door with her mail and turned the knob. It wouldn't open. "What on earth? Did I lock myself out of the house?" Gritting her teeth with determination, she gave another try. The knob still didn't budge.

Virginia felt in her pockets. *I don't believe this! My key's in the house, and I can't even call for help because my phone's in there too.*

Virginia set the mail on the wicker table that had been placed between two matching chairs and clenched her teeth. If she had her phone, she could call Earl and ask him to come home and let her in. *Of course, he might not take too kindly to me interrupting his workday.*

She eyed the phone shed across the road. *Should I go over there and ask one of those Amish people if I can use their phone?* Virginia shook her head. *That's not a good idea. They don't need to know I was stupid enough to lock the door and go outside without my key or cell phone. I'll deal with this issue on my own. After all, I've been through worse situations and come through them okay.*

Virginia stepped off the porch and limped around back. She tried that door but found it was also locked. Next, she checked every window and discovered that only the kitchen window had been left partway open. "Oh, good. Sure hope I can wiggle my way through the opening, because I'm not sixteen anymore."

Virginia stepped over to it and surveyed the size. She put her hands to her hips, and, keeping the same measurement, put her hands in front of the window. *I think I can fit through there, but I'll need to take the screen off first.*

She noticed how it was fastened and gave it a pull. The screen snapped off, but it had broken apart. "Oops! Earl sure won't like what I did there," she mumbled. "Of course, that screen does have some holes in it that he still hasn't fixed. It's way past time for a new one anyway."

Virginia set the unusable piece aside. She was glad their kitchen window faced the backyard, because she wouldn't want anyone to see her trying to crawl through it. She eased the bottom frame upward, but it stopped and wouldn't go all the way.

Desperate to get inside, Virginia hoped she could squeeze through. She started going feet first, but found out quickly that her bum leg didn't like that one bit. Then she changed her idea to lying on her stomach and wiggling in that way.

Virginia stuck her head through and slowly worked her way in but got hung up. She saw her phone where she'd left it and tried to reach over, but the device wasn't close enough. The sink was right under her, and she could now use the faucet to tug on in order to get herself farther in. Virginia pulled on it hard and screamed when the faucet broke, spraying water everywhere.

"Oh, no!" She worked to get back out of the open window. It took some time, but she finally made it. Now, drenched from the waist up, there was a fountain of water running in her kitchen that she had no idea how to deal with.

Virginia moved from the window to the back door, which had a small window in the upper part of it. As far as she could tell, there was only one recourse. *I'll need to break in; that's all there is to it. I have to shut off the water before the whole kitchen is flooded.*

She looked around for something to use. "Hey, that might work." Virginia grabbed a hand shovel that she'd left in one of the flower-beds and used it to break the window glass. Then she carefully eased her hand inside and released the lock.

Whew! That's a relief.

Once in the kitchen, she waded through the water and opened the cupboard door under the sink. Virginia reached the shutoff valve and somehow managed to close it tight. She stood up and looked at her kitchen in dismay. "Oh, boy. . . I've got some work to do here."

Her first chore was getting the water soaked up, and the second was to clean up the broken glass on the floor by the back door.

Virginia grabbed a mop and began using it but decided old towels might be easier and faster. She got some from the utility room closet and tossed them on the water. Then she wrung out the waterlogged towels in the sink. It took a while to get the floor dried, but the chore was finally done. She then moved on to sweep up the shards of glass. This day had turned into quite a workout.

Virginia would still have to explain to Earl and show him what she'd done to the kitchen faucet. *I'll just call him at work when I'm done and tell him what happened to me. That way it will soften the blow and he'll have a chance to cool off before he gets home.*

She picked up her phone and pressed his number. When her husband answered and asked what was up, she began telling him the story until he interrupted. "Virginia, need I remind you that I'm at work? Can't you wait to tell me what happened after I get home later today?"

"No, it can't wait. I broke the screen on the kitchen window trying to go through in order to get into the house."

"Why didn't you just open the door and walk in?" he asked.

"Because the door was locked, and I didn't think I could get in any other way."

"How come you didn't call me?"

"I couldn't; my phone was in the house."

"You could have asked the neighbors across the road to use their phone."

"I didn't want to go over there. Those people are strange."

"If all you ruined was the screen, that's not so bad. I can replace it with a new one. I'll stop at the hardware store on the way home."

"No, Earl, you don't understand. There's more."

"More what?"

"More that went wrong." She drew a quick breath. "I also ruined the kitchen faucet."

"What?" Earl's voice grew louder. "How'd you do that, Virginia?"

"I used the faucet to pull myself through the window, but I couldn't fit and it broke from all the tugging. I think it must have already been loose and ready to go."

To Virginia's surprise, her husband chuckled. "Your backside got you hung up, did it?"

"It figures you'd say something like that. And quit laughing. It wasn't funny."

"Wish I'd been there to see it. Course, if I had been, it wouldn't have happened because I had my house key with me."

Virginia said nothing in response.

"So, is that it then? You finally got in through the window?"

She groaned. "Not exactly."

"What's that mean? Did you get in or not?"

"I was able to back out of the window and eventually got in through the kitchen door."

"But you said you got locked out, right?"

"Yes."

"So how did you get in?"

"I used the shovel and broke the glass out."

"Are you kidding?"

"Wish I was, but I needed to get in and turn off the water. It was shooting up like a geyser."

He groaned. "Are you okay otherwise?"

"My knee hurts, but other than that I'm fine—just pretty wet, and I'm tired from cleaning up the mess."

"Sorry you had to go through all of that. I'll take care of putting in a new faucet and screen when I get home, but I need to get back to work now. I'll see you later, Virginia."

"Okay, bye, Earl." Virginia pressed the END button. *Whew! I'm glad that's over. Sure hope he doesn't think it over and come home angry at me.* She leaned down and rubbed her throbbing knee. *Who knows what could happen?*

Chapter 30

Belinda couldn't believe she'd been home two weeks already. It seemed like just yesterday that she'd been holding baby Vernon and reading stories to Angela Mary.

Where has the time gone? Belinda wondered as she went outside to see if Henry had gotten her horse out for a trip to the store. *And now here we are, halfway into August.*

Seeing him standing beside her horse at the hitching rail, Belinda realized they had been so busy in the greenhouse lately, she'd forgotten about the talk she wanted to have with her son.

Smiling, she stepped up to him. "There's something I've been meaning to ask you, Henry."

He tipped his head. "Something I need to do in the greenhouse while you're in town?"

"No, it's about your future."

Crossing his arms, he stared at her. "I suppose you want me to take over the greenhouse someday when I'm older."

She placed her hand on his shoulder and gave it a gentle pat. "I would never expect you to take full control of the business unless it was something you wanted to do."

Henry shook his head. "I'd rather do somethin' else, Mom."

"Like what?"

"I'm not sure. Just know it's not in a humid greenhouse with a bunch of flowers, trees, and plants."

"I understand. Ezekiel didn't care for that kind of work either."

Henry dug the toe of his boot in the dirt. "I might wanna learn the woodworking trade or become a roofer like Jared."

"Whatever job you choose will be your decision. However, for the next few years, I'm going to need your help here, just as I need Amy and Sylvia's."

"Jah, right. Sylvia hasn't done anything in the greenhouse since you got home from Ezekiel's. All she does is stay in the house and take care of her kinner."

There was a hard edge to Henry's voice, and the tightness around his eyes reminded Belinda once again that her son still harbored bitterness in his heart. Although she too hurt deeply from the death of their loved ones, Belinda realized she must press on and try to find some joy in life. Spending time with her children and grandchildren had given her a sense of purpose and something to smile about.

"Son, you need to understand that your sister's children are small, and they need their mother's full attention."

"They did all right with Mary Ruth takin' care of them."

"That may be, but friends can't give a child what their mother can. The fact that Sylvia is taking care of her kinner the way she feels best is a good thing." Belinda paused to choose her next words. "Also, Sylvia's still struggling with her loss and doesn't do well in situations where she must converse with a lot of people—most of whom she doesn't know."

"Puh!" Henry pulled off his straw hat and fanned his face with it. "I don't like talkin' to strangers neither, but I put up with it."

Since Belinda was having no success getting Henry to understand his eldest sister's situation, she gave her horse a pat then climbed into the driver's seat. "I won't be gone long, and since it's near the end of our workday, there shouldn't be too many customers. Is there anything you would like me to get you while I'm in town?"

Henry shook his head, but then, as she backed the horse and buggy slowly away, he hollered, "Wait! I'd like some chocolate milk. And Mom, could you stop at the hardware store to get some suet for my pet crow? I think he'd like that better than seeds."

Belinda didn't mind picking up a few things for her son. "You got it, Son!" she shouted.

Amy had decided to wear her new sandals to work today. They felt comfortable as she sat on the stool behind the cash register, watching a young Amish couple who'd come into the greenhouse a short time ago.

Amy reached for her can of tropical punch, but in so doing, she lost her grip. The sticky liquid spilled onto the front of her apron and dripped all the way down to the floor, just missing her sandals. She hopped off the stool and snatched a roll of paper towels and cleaning spray from under the counter. Amy worked quickly to clean the mess off the floor, and then she moved on to her apron. She did her best to clean it off, but it was too wet to wear any longer, so she took off the apron and hung it from a peg on the wall behind her. She would put it in the laundry room when she went up to the house.

After putting the cleaning items away, Amy glanced at the Amish couple again, observing their happy expressions. Caleb and Susan were newlyweds from their church district. Their wedding had taken place two weeks ago, while Mom was gone. Amy had been invited to the event, but with so much to do at the greenhouse, she'd decided not to go. She felt it was more important to keep their business open and money coming in than to attend the ceremony for a couple she didn't know that well. Susan and Caleb seemed happy as they walked down the first aisle, talking about all the plans they had for their new home and yard. Susan mentioned planting flowers this fall that would bloom in the spring, and Caleb said he'd like to have a few fruit trees.

Amy thought about Jared and how well their relationship had been going before the horrible accident. *I can't help thinking about what we'd be doing these days if things would have remained unchanged.* Amy was almost certain that he'd been about to ask her to marry him, and she'd felt ready to accept his proposal.

She struggled to hold back tears. *I have to keep reminding myself not to give in to self-pity. My first obligation is to Mom and keeping the greenhouse running. Maybe someday, when Henry is old enough to take over the greenhouse, I'll be free to begin a relationship again. Only it won't be with Jared because I can't expect him to wait for me that long. Maybe I'll be so old by the time I'm free to marry that no man will want me.*

Amy's self pity was getting her nowhere, so she shook herself mentally and walked down a row of indoor plants to make sure they'd been getting enough water. They appeared to be fine, so at least it was one less thing to worry about. Now on to the next row.

Virginia had finished her breakfast when the cell phone rang. She left the table and limped over to pick it up. "Hello."

"Virginia, is that you?"

"Yep. Who's calling?"

"It's Stella. I haven't heard from you since that first call you made right after your move to Pennsylvania, and I've been wondering how things are going."

"Not the best. Livin' here with all the country odors has been hard for me to adjust to." Virginia took the phone over to the table and sat in her chair. It had been awhile since she'd talked to her friend from Chicago, and it might take some time to get caught up, so she may as well be comfortable.

"Have you made any new friends in the area?" Stella asked.

"No, not really. Earl's made a few at work, but because of my bum knee flarin' up so often, I hang around the house most of the time."

"That's too bad. You should get out more and maybe attend some community functions. Those kinds of events are good places to seek out new friends."

"Didn't ya hear what I said, Stella? My knee hurts—especially when I walk a lot."

"I assume you're still too stubborn to use a cane?"

"No, I don't use a walking stick. I'm only forty-six years old, and using a support would make me look and feel old." Virginia drank the last bit of water in her glass. Truthfully, she wasn't interested in making new friends, but there was no point in telling Stella that.

"Are you completely unpacked?"

"Pretty much. There are still some boxes in the garage, but I've put all my dishes and other kitchen items away. It's looking pretty good in here." Virginia glanced at her new faucet above the sink, remembering how calm Earl had been over her damaging the old one when she'd tried crawling through the kitchen window. He'd replaced the window in the back door without a complaint too. She had half-expected him to blow up when he saw the mess she'd created.

"Are you still there, Virginia?"

"Yeah."

"I was wondering if you heard my last question."

"Sorry, Stella. What was it you said?"

"I asked if you planted a garden this summer. As I recall, you mentioned wanting to do that when you moved to the country."

"I tried to but didn't have much luck." Virginia went into detail about the tomato plants that had died.

"That's a shame. Guess we have to learn some lessons the hard way."

"You got that right. I've learned a good many lessons over the years." Virginia released a lingering sigh. *Too bad I can't undo the past and start fresh again.*

"Do you think you might try a garden again next year?" Stella asked.

"Maybe." Virginia fingered the edge of her empty plate. "There's a greenhouse across the road where I can buy seeds and plants, but I'd rather not go there again."

"How come?"

"The people who own it are Amish."

"Is that a problem?"

"It is to me. They're so old-fashioned."

"But if they have the items you need for gardening, why worry about the way they live?"

Virginia's toes curled inside her sneakers. "I'm not worried about it. I just don't care to be around them that much."

"Each to his—or in this case *her*—own, I guess."

Virginia determined it was time to hang up before her friend asked a bunch more questions she'd rather not answer. "I should go, Stella. I just finished eating and still have dishes to do."

"All right, but let's keep in better touch."

"Okay. Talk to you later then."

When Virginia ended the phone call, she leaned back in her chair and let out a puff of air. *Stella has no idea how hard it is for me to live here in the middle of nothing but horse sounds and smelly manure.*

Jared felt pleased with how well things were going as he and his crew worked on the roof at the home of Lydia's parents. Even though the place had been added onto through the years and there were different pitches to work with, the challenge was kind of fun. This type of encounter was usually common on Amish farmhouses due to the addition of more children and the attached *daadihaus* for grandparents who either needed or chose to live with their adult children.

It was a hot and sultry day, but Lydia's mother kept them well supplied in snacks and cold drinks. Sometimes Lydia brought the refreshments out. Other times her mother delivered them to the men, like now.

"Our new roof is certainly going to look nice." Darlene directed her comment to Jared. "We should have done this long ago, but I couldn't talk Lydia's daed into putting out the money until now."

Jared smiled and drank a glass of the lemonade she'd brought out. "I'm glad we were able to fit you in, because your old shingles were pretty worn and many were missing. Probably wouldn't have been long before you had a leak in the roof during a bad storm."

"My thoughts exactly." Darlene glanced at the wicker lounge chair on the lawn, where Lydia sat reading a book. "My daughter's birthday is coming up in a week, and we're going to have a little gathering for her. Would you like to come, Jared? I'm sure Lydia would enjoy having you there."

Jared couldn't control the apprehension he felt from his head down to his toes. *Should I do this? What would Amy think if she heard about it?* He reached for one of the peanut-butter cookies Darlene held out to him. *Maybe I'll see Amy at the party.* "What night will it be?" Jared asked.

"Saturday. Will you be free to join us?"

Jared figured that Amy, being Lydia's best friend, would also be invited. So, if he came, it would give him a chance to talk with her for a bit. At the very least, he could find out how she was doing and ask if things were going okay at their place. He swallowed the last bite of his cookie. *I sure do miss my* aldi. *If only there was a way to win my girlfriend back.*

Jared looked at Lydia's mother and nodded. "Sure, I'll be there. What time will the party start?"

"Six o'clock. We're planning to have a barbecue supper and then play a few games. Of course, there will also be ice cream and chocolate cake for dessert, since those are Lydia's favorites."

"Mine too." Jared finished his lemonade and gave the glass to Darlene. "Danki for the refreshments, and if I don't talk to you before, I'll see you Saturday night."

"Jah, we'll see you then, Jared." Darlene spoke in a bubbly tone. "I have a few things to do inside now, so if you need anything, just let Lydia know." She walked away humming a cheerful melody.

After Darlene returned to the house, Jared glanced into the yard at Lydia. *I wonder if her mother is hoping Lydia and I will start courting. Could that be the reason she invited me to the birthday gathering?*

Belinda's first stop in town was the hardware store, where she purchased two packages of suet. She still couldn't get over her son's attention to the silly crow hanging around their place and his wanting to feed it. Belinda understood that Henry needed a few distractions these days, which might make him happier. But a crow?

After Belinda left the hardware store, she went to Sara's flower shop to see if she might need any more summer flowers.

When Belinda entered the shop, she spotted Jared's mother talking with Sara. She held back until they concluded their business, looking casually at the various things Sara had for sale in her store in addition to floral arrangements.

Maybe we should try selling more things in the greenhouse that might attract people's attention. Although some local people, as well as tourists, bought the jams, jellies, and honey she sold, there might be other items of interest that could bring people into the greenhouse. This was something Belinda would ponder and talk to Amy and Sylvia about.

"Well, hello there." Ava Riehl smiled as she approached Belinda. "I didn't realize you were back from your visit to New York."

"I've actually been home two weeks and was at church last Sunday. I'm surprised you didn't see me there."

Ava rubbed her chin. "Now that you mention it, I do recall you sitting on a bench by your daughters. How have you been, Belinda?"

"Doing fine. And you?"

"Things are going well at our place too." Ava's voice lowered to a whisper. "My son told me what happened with Henry." She clicked her tongue. "It's such a shame when young people think they have to ride around with their friends in cars, especially when they go sneaking around in order to do it."

Belinda's brows furrowed. "I'm not sure what you're talking about."

"One night while you were gone, Henry was seen coming out of the bushes and getting in a car that sped off. Jared was going by at the time and saw it. The next day, he mentioned it to me."

Belinda's facial muscles went slack. She glanced around to see if Sara might be listening, but she'd slipped out from behind the counter and had gone to her desk for something.

"This is the first I've heard of this incident. I'll have to ask Henry about it."

"I hope I didn't speak out of turn. Jared didn't say I shouldn't mention it."

"It's all right. Don't worry about it." Belinda's fingers trembled as she touched Ava's arm. "It was nice seeing you."

"Jah, you too." Jared's mother blinked rapidly. "Since my son and your daughter are no longer courting, we don't get to see Amy or any of your family that much anymore."

Belinda gave a slow nod. "I'm sorry about their breakup. I tried to tell Amy that it wasn't necessary for her to make such a sacrifice, but she wouldn't listen." She sighed. "I wish there was something I could do to get those two back together."

"It might have been for the best. Did you ever think maybe they weren't meant to be together?"

Belinda's thoughts swirled so quickly, it was hard to follow them. Surely Ava didn't mean what she'd said.

"Well, I'd better go. I still have several errands to run." Ava said goodbye and hurried out the door.

Belinda remained in place, trying to let everything Jared's mother had said sink in. *I don't want my son to become the topic of other people's conversations. I hope Ava doesn't mention it to anyone else.*

"It's nice to see you, Belinda. Did you come in to see about my next order from your greenhouse?" Sara stepped up to Belinda, scattering her contemplations.

She cleared her throat and tried to collect herself. "Umm. . .yes, that is why I came by."

"I have a list on my desk of things I need to order. Funny thing, I called and left a message on your answering machine a short time ago." Sara smiled. "If I'd known you'd be dropping by, I would have waited to let you know in person about the flowers I need."

"I came to town to do some shopping," Belinda explained. "So, I figured while I was here, I'd stop in and see if you needed anything from the greenhouse."

"Well, it was perfect timing. Let's go over to my desk and I'll give you the list."

If not for Sara's request, Belinda would have already left the store. She was anxious to get home and speak to Henry.

Chapter 31

"I wonder how things are going for Mom as she runs her errands," Amy commented to Henry while he restocked the shelf full of honey jars.

He shrugged. "Beats me. I hope she gets back soon though. I'm eager to hang out the *fett* she promised to buy for me."

"I'm sure all the birds that come into our yard will appreciate having suet to eat in addition to the seeds we put in their feeders."

"The fett is for my pet crow not all the other birds that hang around."

Amy looked upward and shook her head. "I've told you before—the crow is not a pet. Furthermore, if you hang out the suet, you can't keep other birds from eating it." *I don't even like crows, and this one in particular whenever it caws. I'd be happy if that pesky fowl doesn't get any of the suet and the other yard birds hog it all. Maybe he'd find someplace else to make a home.*

Amy's paranoia over the crow hadn't lessened, but she wished it would. Allowing superstitious thoughts to overshadow her faith was not a good thing. She needed to pray harder and put her trust in the Lord.

Henry set the last jar of honey on the shelf and picked up the empty cardboard box. "I'm gonna put this away in the barn, okay?"

Amy handled the jars on the shelf with care, turning each of them with the label-side forward. "Sure, go ahead. But don't take too long because when more customers show up, I'll probably need your help."

Henry just ambled out the door with the box.

Amy pinched her lips together as she continued the task. *He'd better not fool around. He needs to get back here to help. Mom won't appreciate it if I tell her Henry's not working like she asked.*

Amy thought about the night her brother had snuck out to be with Seth. It was burdensome to be holding the goods on Henry and keeping his misdeed from their mother. How long would it be before Henry did something else wrong? If and when he did, Amy wouldn't hesitate to tell Mom.

Amy finished with the display shelf and moved away. It was quiet in the greenhouse for the moment, which gave her time to ponder. She visualized Jared's face for a few seconds, remembering when he'd been in here last. *He's a handsome guy, and I'm sure in a matter of time he'll be courting someone new—probably Lydia, if my suspicions are correct.* Thinking about this bothered Amy. *I've got to get Jared out of my thoughts. If only there was a better distraction.*

Since there were no customers at the moment, Amy made a trip up and down all four aisles. Everything looked good, so she paused to observe a pretty yellow butterfly flitting from flower to flower. She pursed her lips. *Here I work in the greenhouse nearly every day, yet I rarely take time to enjoy the beauty found in this building.* She drew in a breath, inhaling the lovely fragrance of all the colorful flowers that adorned this row. *Only God could have created such beauty.*

Amy lingered a few more moments before returning to the checkout counter and taking a seat. While sitting there, she reflected on the message from Lydia that had been waiting for her on their answering machine this morning. Amy's good friend would be having a birthday supper this Saturday, and she wanted Amy to come.

Of course I'll go. Amy smiled. *Lydia's been my best friend for a good many years, so I wouldn't miss helping her celebrate a special birthday. It'll be fun for the two of us to spend some quality time together. We haven't done that in a long while.*

A short time later, Maude entered the greenhouse. She hadn't been in for some time, and Amy had begun to wonder if the elderly woman had left the area and moved on.

Amy watched in shock as Maude shuffled down aisle 1, pinching one or two leaves from every plant on the wooden shelves. *Oh dear, she's going to ruin them all if I don't stop her.*

Amy rushed after Maude, calling, "Please don't do that to the plants."

The old woman stopped and turned to look at Amy. With her head tilted to one side, she asked, "Is something wrong?"

"Yes. I—I mean, why are you pulling leaves off the plants and throwing them on the floor?"

"I'm pruning 'em. All plants need to be pruned." The wrinkles in Maude's forehead deepened. "Since you work here, ya oughta know that."

Exasperated, Amy stepped between the woman and the next plant in line. "I do know when a plant or bush needs to be pruned, but the ones you plucked leaves off of are just fine and don't need any kind of pruning at all right now."

"Humph!" Maude folded her arms and stamped one foot. "Shows ya what you know. If this place was mine, I'd sure do things different."

I can only imagine. Amy clenched her teeth. She didn't want to appear rude, but she wished there was a nice way of asking the elderly lady to leave. Then an idea popped into her head. Remembering the apples and grapes she'd brought out for a snack this morning, Amy offered them to Maude.

The old woman's eyes held a hint of a sparkle. "Yeah, sure, I'd be happy to take 'em."

Amy led the way up to the counter, reached underneath, and withdrew a plastic container. "Here you go. Feel free to take the fruit home in the container. You can bring it back the next time you come here."

Maude gave a toothless grin, took the offered gift, and ambled out of the building. Amy heard her mumble something, but it didn't make much sense. The container was an old one, so even if Maude never came back with it, there wouldn't be a problem.

Amy called Henry to sweep up the scattered leaves then returned to the checkout counter. She was about to take a seat on the wooden stool, when a tall English man came in. "Hello. My name is Clarence Perdue. Are you the owner of this greenhouse?" he asked.

She shook her head. "My mother is, but she's not here at the moment."

"I see. Well, I just came in to look around. Wanted to check out the competition."

"Competition?" Amy repeated, pulling back slightly so as not to inhale the lingering cigarette smoke on his clothes.

"Yes. My wife, Patricia, and I own the new greenhouse on the other side of town, and we've been curious about your place and what all is being sold here." He gave her a pointed stare. "Mind if I have a look around?"

Amy wasn't sure how to respond. She wanted to tell the man no, but that would be impolite. "I guess it would be okay." Her voice cracked. Not once since the new greenhouse opened had she thought to visit there in order to see what they sold. *But maybe I should have.*

Amy watched helplessly as Mr. Perdue headed off down aisle 1, where Henry was busy cleaning up the mess Maude had left. *I bet the man thinks our place of business is pathetic compared to his. After a trip through the building, he will probably realize we are no competition to him at all.*

"Where's Henry?" Belinda asked when she entered the greenhouse a little after noon. She was glad no customers were at the front counter, because what she had to say to Amy was not for other people's ears.

"He was supposed to have gone up to the house to get the lunch sacks Sylvia said she would prepare for us," Amy responded. "Oh, and Mom, there's something you might want to know."

"I already know more than I want to." Belinda bent close to her daughter's ear. "Why didn't you tell me your bruder snuck out one night while I was gone?"

Amy blinked rapidly. "I—I promised him I wouldn't say anything unless he messed up again. I didn't want to worry you about something I hoped was a one-time occurrence." She glanced to her right. "Can we talk about this later, Mom? Someone's coming up with their purchases."

"No problem. It's Henry I need to talk to right now." Belinda turned and rushed out the door.

When she entered the house, she found Sylvia in the kitchen feeding Allen his lunch.

"Hi, Mom, I'm glad you're back." Sylvia smiled. "There's a tossed green salad in the refrigerator. Would you like some for lunch?"

"Not right now. I'm looking for Henry. Is he here in the house?"

Sylvia shook her head. "I haven't seen him since this morning."

"Oh, really? Amy said he was supposed to come here to get their sack lunches." With forced restraint, Belinda spoke through her clenched teeth.

"Their sandwiches are still in the refrigerator. Maybe he's out in the greenhouse."

"No, I just came from there, and Amy said. . ." Belinda ended her sentence and tousled Allen's hair when he stopped eating and looked up at her with innocent eyes. *I must not let this little fellow see my irritation.*

She moved across the room and motioned for Sylvia to join her. "I found out from Jared's mamm this morning that Henry was seen getting into a car one evening while I was gone." She was careful to keep her voice down and spoke in English so Allen wouldn't understand any of their conversation. "Amy admitted that she knew about it, so I assume you were also aware."

"Jah. He said he wouldn't do it again, and we wanted to give him the benefit of the doubt. What I don't understand though is how Jared's mother knew about the incident."

"Ava said Jared was going past our place the evening it happened, and he saw Henry come out of the bushes and get in a car." Belinda looked directly at Sylvia. "Do you know where he went?"

"He spent the night at Seth's even though earlier, Amy told him he couldn't go."

"So, he decided he could do whatever he pleased?"

"I guess so."

Belinda's face heated as her muscles tensed. "I'd better go find him and deal with this matter."

She stepped out the back door and stood on the porch, scanning the yard. Then after several seconds, she stepped down into the yard. *Where is that boy of mine?*

She heard a whistle and looked up, surprised to see Henry sitting inside the opening at the top of the barn with his legs crossed.

Belinda cupped her hands around her mouth. "What in the world are you doing up there?"

"I'm talkin' to the birds!"

"Well, come down here right now. I want to talk to *you.*"

Henry disappeared, and a few minutes later, he came out of the barn. "What's up, Mom? Did ya get the fett for my crow?"

Belinda took hold of her son's arm and led him back to the barn so they could talk without being heard by any potential greenhouse customers. "I did get the suet but not the chocolate milk you asked for. However, that's not what I want to talk to you about."

"If it's about me not bein' in the greenhouse, Amy sent me in to get our lunches."

"So I heard, but you obviously did not do as you were told."

"I was planning to, but then I spotted the crow." Henry grinned. "I'm gonna make a pet out of him, Mom."

She shook her head. "It's my understanding that you cannot tame a crow. They aren't trainable like a parrot or some other indoor bird."

"Maybe not, but there's always an exception, so I was thinking—"

Belinda held up her hand. "Enough about the crow, Henry. We came in here to talk about you and why you snuck out of the house and spent the night with Seth while I was at Ezekiel's place."

Henry let out a forceful breath and stomped his foot. "I can't believe Amy blabbed—or was it Sylvia who told ya?"

"It was neither of your sisters who did the telling. I heard it from someone I saw at Sara's flower shop this morning."

Henry gave his earlobe a tug. "How'd Sara know about me spending the night with Seth?"

"It wasn't Sara who mentioned it."

"Who then?"

"That doesn't really matter, Son. The point is, you did something you should not have done and then kept the truth from me." Belinda gave a frustrated shake of her head. "I'm disappointed in you, Henry. I thought I could trust you to do what's right while I was away."

He dropped his gaze to the floor and shuffled his boots in the straw beneath them. "Sorry, Mom. I promise, it'll never happen again."

"I should hope not. If your daed was here, he would also be very disappointed."

"I know." Henry looked up. "Guess you're not gonna give me any suet for the crow now, huh?"

"I will give it to you, Henry. There's no reason the bird should suffer because you snuck out of the house and worried your sisters."

"Danki, Mamm."

"But that doesn't mean you shouldn't be punished for your misdeed."

"I figured as much. What's my punishment besides no chocolate milk?"

"You'll have extra chores to do for the next two weeks, and you're not to go anywhere with your friends, or even by yourself, until I say so. Is that understood?"

"Jah."

"All right then, please go into the house and get yours and Amy's lunches like you were supposed to do."

"Okay, I'm on it."

They left the barn, and while Henry sprinted for the house, Belinda made her way to the greenhouse.

Clymer

Ezekiel sat across from Michelle at their kitchen table, eating lunch. "You look tired. Have you been doing too much?"

Michelle shrugged. "Maybe a little. I'm managing on my own, but I sure miss your mamm. She was such a big help to me."

"Jah, she was. I miss her too and so does Angela Mary." He reached over to where their daughter sat in her booster seat and tweaked her petite nose. "I think even the boppli misses his grandma because she held him so much."

"Do you still think it's possible for us to visit there in September?"

"I believe so." Ezekiel took a drink of iced tea. "It'll be good to see everyone."

She smiled and handed him another egg salad sandwich. "Have I told you lately how much I love you?"

He grinned back at her. "Every day, and I tell you the same."

"That's true." Michelle sighed. "The best thing I ever did was to join the Amish church and marry you."

"So I've heard." Ezekiel winked at her. "But I never get tired of hearing it."

"Sometimes, like when I'm in church surrounded by all the others in our district and listening to you preach, I have to pinch myself to make sure I'm not dreaming."

Ezekiel leaned forward in his chair. "How do you think I'm doing with that, Michelle? Do I stumble too much over my words?"

"Certainly not. It's plain to see that God has called you to be a preacher. Your messages are uplifting and encouraging. My only advice is to keep doing what you're doing and stay as humble as you are now."

"No worries about that." Ezekiel thumped his chest. "I have asked God to give me a kick in the pants if I ever become full of *hochmut*. All I want to do is be a good husband, father, and preacher and allow God to work through me so I can minister to those who are in need."

Michelle placed her hand on his arm. "You've always been there to minister to me—even before I invited Christ into my life."

"Well, I wasn't perfect by any means, and I knew in my heart that you and I had a lot to learn during our courting days, and even before when we were full of rebellion. It just goes to show that God can use any person who is willing to repent and turn their life around."

Chapter 32

Strasburg

Saturday evening, as Amy's horse and buggy approached her friend's house, she had mixed feelings. As much as she looked forward to spending the evening with Lydia and helping her celebrate a birthday, Amy worried that Jared might be there. With rumors going around and the fact that she'd seen them together a few times, Amy felt sure they must be courting.

"Well, it's too late now to change my mind," she murmured as her horse picked up speed and turned, of his own accord, into the driveway. Buster had been here numerous times and was probably eager to visit with the Petersheims' horses.

"I'm so glad you could be here." Lydia greeted Amy at the hitching rail. "Tonight wouldn't be the same without you."

Amy smiled, and when she stepped down from the buggy, she gave Lydia a hug. "Happy birthday."

"Thank you. Let's get your *gaul* put in the corral, and we can join the others who have come this evening."

"Okay. Oh, and by the way. . .you smell nice. Are you wearing perfume?"

"No, it's the new hand-and-body lotion my mamm got for my birthday." Lydia walked over, opened the paddock, and waited for Amy's gelding to enter.

Amy unhitched her horse and led him to the corral. His ears perked up, and he whinnied when she put him inside.

Lydia laughed while she closed the gate. "Looks like Buster's happy to be here."

"Jah, I believe he is." Amy stepped along with Lydia and could smell the odor of wood smoke. It smelled good floating through the air, but Amy wasn't very hungry, so she probably wouldn't eat much. Truth was, since breakfast, she'd felt a sense of apprehension about the possibility of seeing Jared this evening.

As they drew closer to the bonfire, Amy heard the voices of her friend's guests. She wondered how this evening would play out with Lydia and Jared.

"Let's head over to the tables my folks have set up in our yard. Several of our friends are here, and I'm sure they'll be glad to see you."

As Lydia led the way, Amy reached up and checked her hair to make sure none of it had come out from under her kapp. The colorful paper plates and napkins looked festive. Amy figured Lydia's mother wanted to make everything just right for her daughter's special gathering.

As they approached the tables that had been set up on the lawn, Amy's heart pounded when she saw Jared sitting on a bench. She wished she could turn around and run back to get her horse and buggy, but Lydia would be disappointed if Amy left now.

Plastering a smile on her face, Amy made the rounds greeting everyone present including Jared.

"It's nice to see you, Amy." Jared smiled. "How have you been?"

"I'm fine. How are you?"

Before he could respond, Lydia's mother came out of the house with a tray full of hot dogs and buns. "Come on, everyone—grab a hot dog and a roasting stick. Lydia's daed has the fire going, so anyone who wants to can roast theirs as soon as we have prayed. He also has some ground beef patties cooking on the grill."

All heads bowed for silent prayer. When it ended, Jared stood and asked Amy if she would like him to roast her a hot dog.

"No, that's okay," she said with a shake of her head. "I can do my own when I'm ready. I may start with a burger."

"Okay." Was that a look of disappointment she saw on his face? Or maybe it was a look of relief. No doubt he'd been trying to be polite.

"You can roast a hot dog for Lydia," Darlene spoke up. "Since she's the birthday girl, she deserves to sit and be waited on this evening."

Lydia's cheeks turned crimson. "Mama, I'm not an invalid or a young child. I can most certainly wait on myself." She grabbed a hot dog and followed the others to the bonfire.

It was indeed awkward for Amy being here this evening. Not to mention having many of hers and Amy's peers who had been invited. She could only imagine what some of them must be thinking about her. *I'm sure they'd like to ask why I broke things off with Jared, but I hope no one does.* Having to respond to a question like that would only make Amy feel worse.

For the rest of the evening, Amy tried to avoid Jared as much as possible and kept her responses short whenever he spoke to her. She visited with some of the other guests during the party, but her heart wasn't in any of it. Fortunately, no one asked about her and Jared's breakup.

Amy couldn't help noticing the care Lydia's mother gave to Jared. It seemed as if Darlene might be paving the way for him to give her daughter some extra attention. Seeing the way Lydia talked so much to Jared made Amy think that her good friend had feelings for him. It hurt, but at the same time, Amy couldn't fault Lydia if she was attracted to Jared. He would make any woman a good husband. The question was, did he return those feelings?

"What a busy day we had. I'm ever so glad it's over." Belinda joined Sylvia in the kitchen to finish cooking their supper.

"I assumed that's how it went since I heard cars and buggies coming and going most of the day when I wasn't busy taking care of the kinner."

Belinda rinsed a couple of tomatoes to slice. "It was nonstop at times. I'm a little surprised with that new place open on the other side of town that things haven't slowed down here."

"I think we get more tourists than the other greenhouse does. I saw a couple of vans loaded with people pull in at different times today." Sylvia rolled her eyes. "Some began taking pictures of our flowerbeds as soon as their feet hit the ground."

"Perhaps there's an appreciation on how well we did when a perfect stranger has to take home a picture. Of course, I'll not allow myself to get prideful regarding our gardening abilities."

Sylvia moved over and patted Belinda's arm. "You don't have to worry about that, Mom. You're not full of hochmut at all."

Belinda grabbed the potholders and drained the hot water from the potatoes. As she worked, thoughts about the conversation she'd had with Amy a few days ago floated through her head. Amy had mentioned that the owner of the new greenhouse in the area had come by, wanting to check out the competition. Belinda couldn't figure out why he would even care, because, from what she'd heard, his place of business was much bigger than hers. She wished she'd been there when he came by, so she could ask him a few questions, such as why did he feel the need to check out the competition.

Oh well, I suppose it really doesn't matter. He will go about his business, and we'll go about ours. We'll probably never see or hear from Mr. Perdue again.

Belinda had finished mashing the potatoes to go with the pot roast Sylvia had put in the oven for supper, when a knock sounded on the front door. "Would you please see who that is?" she asked her daughter.

"Sure, Mom."

A few minutes later, Sylvia returned to the kitchen with Monroe trailing behind her.

Belinda tried to conceal the shock she felt at that moment. Being tired from the hectic day she'd had, she wasn't running at full speed this evening. But she'd be pleasant to their guest, nonetheless, and she put a smile on her face for him.

"Good evening, Belinda. I hope I'm not interrupting." He glanced at the table, set for three people, and then his gaze landed on Allen's highchair. "I had hoped to catch you before you'd prepared your meal for this evening. Sorry for disturbing you."

"Today was quite busy in the greenhouse, and I thought that we'd get a later start fixing our meal. But this is our usual time for supper."

"I see." Monroe shifted from one foot to the other. "Well, I guess I'll just state what I came for and be on my way."

"What is the reason for your visit?" Sylvia asked before Belinda had a chance to say anything.

Monroe turned to face her. "I was heading to a restaurant in town for supper and thought I'd drop by and see if your mamm was free to join me."

A warm flush swept across Belinda's cheeks. "It's kind of you to think of me, but as you can see—"

"Jah, I can see and smell the wonderful aroma from the meal you've prepared." He tipped his head back and sniffed the air. "I'm betting you have a roast in the oven."

"You have a good sniffer." Belinda smiled despite her anxiety at him showing up this evening. Had Monroe really expected she would accept his invitation to go out with him for supper and with a last-minute invitation, no less? *Even if I did want to go, which I don't, I would have said no. If someone I know saw me out having a meal with Monroe, I can only imagine all the gossip that would run wild.*

Since Monroe seemed in no hurry to leave and because their meal was ready to eat, Belinda did the only thing she felt was polite. "Monroe, would you care to join us for supper?"

"Of course. Danki for asking."

Belinda looked at Sylvia and noticed her raised brows. Was she also questioning this man's motives?

"We'll all be seated as soon as my son comes inside." Belinda gestured to the table. "After you've washed up at the sink, you may as well take a seat."

Monroe nodded briefly. While he washed his hands, Belinda

opened the back door to call Henry.

"What do you want, Mom?" he shouted in return.

"Supper's ready and we have a guest. Please come inside now."

"Okay, I'll be there in a minute."

Sylvia set another place at the table. "I'll go see how the baby is doing and put Allen in his highchair."

Even though Belinda couldn't see where Henry was, she felt certain he was someplace in the yard trying to coax that noisy crow to eat from his hand. She'd caught him doing it this morning before breakfast.

She shook her head. *Silly boy. I doubt he will ever succeed in training that crow or making it a pet. But I guess if it makes him happy to try, it shouldn't be an issue.*

Belinda returned to the kitchen. As she dished up the potatoes, Henry came in. He stopped short when he saw Monroe sitting at the head of the table. Looking at Belinda, Henry pursed his lips. She could almost hear what her son was thinking. *Why is this man here?* Of course, even though Monroe had explained his reason, Belinda wondered that herself. *He has to realize I'm still in mourning. My black dress ought to be proof enough.*

Belinda instructed Henry to wash up, and once he'd finished, everyone took a seat. Silent prayer was said, and then the food got passed around.

During supper, Monroe seemed to be pleased with the meal, as he polished off his first helping of mashed potatoes and a slice of meat. "This is a very tender roast."

Belinda set her fork aside. "Thank you. Would you like some more?"

He smiled at her. "Jah, sure, I'd be delighted to have seconds." Monroe held out his plate as he waited to be served. After a few bites, he mentioned his concern for Belinda and her family. "You know, it's really not a good idea for you all to be alone without a man in the house."

Belinda merely shrugged and said, "We're getting along fine."

And they were—for the most part. At least they were still getting enough customers to keep sales going, and as far as she knew, no more vandalism had been done. With fall just a month away, many people, as they had in the past, would come into the greenhouse to buy fall flowers and plants. So for now, at least, Belinda wasn't worried about their safety or financial situation. As she'd reminded herself many times since the three men in their family died, *God will take care of us.* To which she added, *And we don't need any help from Monroe Esh.*

Jared felt slighted that Amy hadn't said much to him all evening. Truth was, it seemed as if she tried to avoid him. When Lydia's mother had called everyone to the tables, she'd indicated that Jared should sit beside her daughter. Once more, he'd been disappointed. If he could have been seated beside or even across from Amy, it would have given him a better chance to speak to her.

Throughout the meal, Darlene kept talking to Jared, asking him countless questions and complimenting him on how well their new roof had turned out. No one else, even Lydia, who sat beside Jared could get a word in. Jared was beginning to wish he had declined the invitation.

At eight thirty, Amy said she needed to leave the party, using the excuse that she had several things to do before going to bed. "Besides, tomorrow is church day, so I need to get to bed a little earlier than usual."

Jared jumped up and offered to get Amy's horse, but she declined. "Thanks anyway, but I can manage."

"No, I insist." He waited until she'd said goodbye to everyone then walked with her to the corral. After he took Buster out and hitched him to the buggy, Jared helped Amy into the driver's seat. "It was good seeing you. I only wish we'd had more time to talk."

Amy swallowed hard and fought against the tears pushing the

back of her eyes. "You'd best get back to the party. Lydia's there waiting." She gathered up the reins and backed up her horse. "Good night, Jared."

"Good night, Amy." She watched him walk back to the tables then guided Buster down the driveway and out onto the road.

"I should not have come to Lydia's party tonight." She spoke out loud, glad that no one was in the buggy with her and could see her tears. Amy was convinced that she'd lost Jared, which she'd known could happen when she broke things off with him. Nonetheless, it still hurt more than she would ever admit.

But taking care of Mom is my responsibility now, she reminded herself. *I have no free time for courting, and becoming someone's wife is out of the question because I wouldn't have enough time to put into a marriage relationship anyway. So, I must come to grips with the choice I made concerning Jared. It's for the best, all the way around.*

Amy tightened her grips on the reins. *How much longer do I have to keep reminding myself?*

Chapter 33

Clymer

Ezekiel woke up in a cold sweat. He felt relieved to be awake and out of the dream he'd been trapped in. Something terrible had happened at his mom's house, but now he couldn't remember what it was. Lying there in the dark room, he pulled the sheet to one side. *That feels better. Now if there was just some fresh air blowing through the open window.*

He rolled over and sat on the edge of the bed, hoping he wouldn't disturb Michelle. *What happened in the dream that was so stressful it woke me up? Could the nightmare have been a warning or some impending doom? Are Mom and my siblings in some kind of trouble?*

Ezekiel pushed the button on top of his illuminated battery-operated alarm clock. It was 2:00 a.m.—too early for anyone at home to be up. He sat there a moment and reached for his glass of water, but it was empty.

Grabbing his flashlight in the other hand, Ezekiel headed to the kitchen for a refill. Once there, he checked the back door to be sure it was locked then got his water.

Heading to the living room, Ezekiel checked the front door too. *Guess after that dream, I'm feeling a bit paranoid. Everything's fine here. I need to get back to sleep because there's plenty of work waiting for me in my shop.*

After returning to the bedroom, Ezekiel set his glass on the nightstand and sat on the edge of the bed, not sure he if could get back to sleep. *Maybe I should have stayed in the kitchen and done some reading to make myself sleepy.*

There weren't many options for him at this hour, and it would be pointless to go out to the phone shed now. When he got up to get ready for work, he'd go out and leave a message saying he was just checking on them and asking Mom to give him a call. Ezekiel would also let her know that he and his family would definitely be coming there the first Saturday of September. Both he and Michelle looked forward to the trip, and so did Angela Mary. Someday when Vernon was older, he'd also be eager to see his relatives in Strasburg.

"Is everything all right? Why are you sitting on the edge of the bed?" Michelle's groggy-sounding voice caused Ezekiel to jump when she touched his arm.

He lay back down and pulled her close to his side. "It's nothing to worry about. I had an unpleasant dream and couldn't get back to sleep."

"What was it about?"

"I'm not sure. It was enough to wake me though, but I can't remember any of the details." Ezekiel didn't mention that he thought the dream was about his family in Strasburg or that he was concerned for their welfare. No point in giving his wife cause to worry. Besides, he was probably being paranoid. Mom and the rest of his family were no doubt sleeping comfortably in their beds.

Strasburg

That nasty wind is making a ruckus out there, and it's not helping me relax. Belinda tossed and turned, fluffing up her pillow and pushing it down. She'd gone to bed shortly before midnight and had lain awake ever since. So many thoughts swirled in her head. Even though some things had improved in her life, she had many problems to deal with yet—at the greenhouse as well as in her home.

Several orders had come in for chrysanthemums and other fall foliage. It was easy to get the areas needed in the greenhouse ready for the new stock because the more they sold, the more they had available.

They still had some varieties of summer flowers that hadn't yet sold. Belinda had already discounted many different types of plants, and they were fast disappearing. Whenever possible, she liked giving her customers a bargain.

Belinda would need her son's help moving heavier things and had the weekend for another sale circled on the calendar that hung in the greenhouse. A lot of what needed to be done from season to season was written on that date-keeper Vernon always kept.

Belinda shifted for more comfort and lay there, continuing to think about things. *I sure hope my youngest son will never again pull anything like what he did while I was away.*

Henry's punishment had ended, and since it had been the last Friday of August and summer would soon be over, she'd given him permission to go fishing with Seth at a nearby pond after they closed the greenhouse in the afternoon. Belinda liked fish and had hoped Henry would catch some they could have for supper.

I remember when my Vernon caught and brought home fish to fry. Belinda pictured her husband, all smiles, when he'd have a successful day at the pond. Sometimes he would go with Ezekiel, Abe, and Henry, and they'd have a nice time enjoying the peace and quiet near the water's edge. *If only I could go back and relive the good times, but unfortunately, that's not possible.*

When Henry had come back in time for supper, something about his demeanor hadn't seemed right to her. She'd also noticed a faint smell of what she thought was cigarette smoke on his clothes. When Belinda had asked Henry about it, he'd shrugged and said, "I don't smell anything."

Then Belinda had asked if he'd caught any fish, and her son's reply was, "A few, but they weren't very big, so I tossed 'em back in the water."

Maybe I'm overly suspicious, Belinda thought as she rolled onto her other side. *But I have a hunch my son may have been fibbing to me and didn't catch any fish at all. Why would he lie about that though?*

Belinda sat up in bed as another thought came to mind. *What if Henry didn't go fishing at all? Could he and Seth have gone somewhere that he doesn't want me to know about? How can I find out? Should I speak to Seth's mother and ask if she knows for sure where her son was today?* She shook her head. *Maybe it's best not to bring up the topic. Unless he does something out of the ordinary, I need to have a little faith in my boy.*

Belinda turned on the battery-operated light on her nightstand and picked up Vernon's Bible. Somehow it made her feel closer to him when she held it.

Opening the book to a place her husband had placed a marker, she saw that he'd underlined a few verses. One of them jumped right out at her. It was just the reminder she needed in this wee hour of the morning. *"The LORD is my strength and my shield; my heart trusted in him, and I am helped: therefore my heart greatly rejoiceth; and with my song will I praise him"* Psalm 28:7.

Tears clouded Belinda's vision. "Oh Vernon, how I still miss you. Thank you for being a godly man and a fine example to me, our family, and the entire community."

When Jared left the phone shack early Saturday morning and returned to the house, his mind replayed the message he'd received from a man who'd said his name was Earl Martin. Earl wanted to put a new roof on his detached garage. Jared noticed right away that the address the man gave was almost the same as the Kings' place—just a few numbers were different. He figured the Martins had to live across the road from Amy's family.

Jared's workload had lightened a bit, but with the weather changing, it would no doubt get busier. He'd returned Mr. Martin's call and set up a time to meet.

Jared entered the kitchen, where Mom was clearing the breakfast dishes. "How'd it go in the phone shed?" she asked. "Were there any messages?"

"Nothing on yours and Dad's line, but I had a few. One is a potential job near the Kings' place."

Her face seemed to tighten. "You're always so busy. Do you have time to work for a new customer?"

"I believe I can squeeze it in."

Mom offered him a brief smile. "I'm glad you had a good time at Lydia's the other night. When I saw Darlene a few days before the party, she seemed excited about throwing her daughter a nice birthday celebration."

"It turned out well, and there was plenty to eat."

"Lydia's a nice girl."

Jared nodded and grabbed his lunchbox. "I'd best get moving."

"All right, Son. I'll see you sometime this evening."

"Sure thing." *The only girl for me is Amy,* Jared thought as he walked out the door. *Why can't she see how much I want to be with her? Doesn't she realize a relationship with me is not impossible? If only there was something I could say or do to win her back.* Jared had revisited those thoughts many times since Amy broke up with him. Try as he may, he couldn't get Amy King out of his mind.

As Amy worked with her mother in the garden during the early morning hours, she noticed something and pointed. "What happened to that pumpkin plant? Looks like it's wilted, but I know it's been getting plenty of water."

"I bet we've got a beetle problem." Mom moved from what produce she'd already gathered and examined the base of the plant. "Jah, it's from beetles, all right. I'll need some straw to put around the plants." She discarded the bugs into the weed bucket.

Amy and her mother continued picking. They'd decided to get the chore done before it was time to open the greenhouse. And because the weather was cooler at this hour of the day, the work was easier.

Amy liked cucumbers, and there were plenty to pick from the rows. She wouldn't mind having some of them to eat with lunch or dinner. Their tomatoes were ripening nicely, and Amy thought about the neighbor across the road. She'd offered to let Virginia have more tomato plants when hers had died soon after planting them. Amy felt sorry for their new neighbor lady because she didn't know much about fertilizing properly.

"It's too bad I didn't give her some basic instructions on how to care for the new plants," Amy said as she pulled more weeds in the radish rows.

"What do you mean? Who are you talking about?" Mom asked.

"Guess I was speaking my thoughts out loud." Amy gave a self-conscious laugh. "I forgot to tell you about the neighbor's tomato plants. I talked to Virginia at the mailbox the other day, and she said they'd all died."

Mom swatted at a pesky gnat. "Does she know why?"

"Jah." Amy explained what had happened.

"That's too bad." Mom gestured to the nearest tomato plant that had already turned a nice red color. "It would be good to give her some fresh tomatoes, and we have plenty to share."

"I agree, but Virginia said she didn't want any—that she'll get what she needs at the grocery store or farmers' market." Amy moved away from the cucumber and cleaned the weeds crowding the tomato plants.

"She's a different person—not very friendly, that's for sure. But maybe there's a reason for it. We need to pray for her, Daughter."

"You're right, Mom." Amy glanced up from the weeds she'd been pulling and cleared her throat. "Would you look at that? Henry's got the crazy crow practically eating out of his hand. Now the noisy thing will probably never leave our yard."

Mom glanced in the direction Amy pointed and shook her head. "That bird may not be a pet, but Henry's succeeded in being able to get close to him. Sure didn't expect to see anything like that."

"I'd never have believed it if I hadn't witnessed it myself."

Amy returned to her chore until Henry's deep laughter rang out. It was good to hear this positive side of him. She looked up again to see what he found so humorous.

"Amy. . .Mom. . .look over there!" Henry pointed at Rachel's crib sheet hanging from a branch in a nearby tree. Sylvia stood below it, looking up and shaking her head.

Amy figured the breeze that had begun blowing a few minutes ago must have caught hold of the sheet while her sister had been trying to pin it to the line.

"Is that a new way to hang the laundry?" Henry laughed harder than Amy had heard him in a long time, but Sylvia wore a frown.

"It's not funny, little bruder. Now how am I going to get that down?"

"I'll get it for you, Sylvia. Just give me a few minutes." Henry jumped up, and the crow flew off as he darted for the barn.

Amy had to admit, seeing the small sheet dangling helplessly from the tree was quite funny. Mom must have thought so too, for her laughter brought forth an unladylike snort.

Amy giggled, and soon even Sylvia was laughing. It felt good to share in a little merriment—something they'd done so little of since their loved ones had been killed.

Henry came out of the barn carrying a ladder. He set it against the tree and began the upward climb.

"Be careful, Son," Mom called up to him. Her expression had suddenly turned sober.

Amy held her breath as Henry climbed higher. She released her breath when he had hold of the sheet and began his descent. His feet had no more than touched the ground when the crow flew into the same tree and let out several obnoxious screeches.

Amy covered her ears. She wished the crazy bird would fly far away from here and never come back.

Almost out of nowhere, a car sped up the driveway, turned into the greenhouse parking lot, and slammed into one corner of the building.

Amy and Mom jumped up at the same time, and they, as well as

Henry and Sylvia, dashed toward the vehicle. When they arrived, a middle-aged man with a nearly bald head got out and surveyed the damage.

"I'm so sorry, folks." His face was covered in perspiration. "A cat ran out in front of me, and I lost control trying to avoid hitting the critter."

Amy looked around but saw no sign of a cat. Of course, that didn't mean one hadn't been there. The poor animal had most likely been scared and run off.

The man stepped up to Mom. "I'll call my insurance agent right away, and in the meantime, I will go to the hardware store and get some heavy plastic to staple over the damaged area. That should help till it can be permanently fixed."

He and Mom talked for a few more minutes before he got into his car and drove off.

"He's going to the hardware store," Mom explained. Her voice quavered.

Amy felt shaky too. This event had been an accident, while the other things that had happened on their property seemed to have been done on purpose.

"You don't think that man hit the greenhouse intentionally, do you?" Sylvia asked their mother.

Mom shook her head. "No, of course not. Why would anyone do something like that on purpose?"

Caw! Caw! Caw! Caw! What a horrible screech.

Amy looked toward the tree where the crow had flown. Was that bird trying to tell them something?

Chapter 34

"See you both later. Have a good day." Sylvia watched her sister and their mother head for the greenhouse. She had a few things to finish before Ezekiel and his family arrived.

Sylvia closed the front door. The children had been fed and were settled in the living room. Allen pulled out a few toys from the box, and Rachel made baby sounds from her playpen. Sylvia looked at the bedding that needed to go on the guest bed upstairs. "I suppose there's no time like the present. Allen, please come with Mommy."

The little guy grabbed some toy figures and went with her. Sylvia had him sit in a chair in the room where she needed to work. Her pace quickened as she put the fresh sheets on the bed and placed a lightweight coverlet at the foot. She looked around the room to be sure everything was in order. Mom and Amy had cleaned in here yesterday evening, so Sylvia insisted that she make up the bed this morning. The space looked good and ready for Ezekiel and Michelle. Since it was the largest of the guest rooms, there was space for the cot Angela Mary would sleep on as well as a cradle for baby Vernon.

Sylvia tapped her son's shoulder. "I'm done now, so let's go back downstairs and check on your sister." As always, she spoke to the boy in the Pennsylvania Dutch language of her people. Although Allen knew a few English words, he wouldn't learn to speak it fluently until he started school.

When they entered the living room, the baby began to fuss, so Sylvia picked her up. Looking out the front window, Sylvia thought she saw someone out by the road. She watched longer, and sure enough, there was a person off by the shrubs. It was kind of weird and happened so fast, she wasn't sure if the person was a male or female.

She took a seat to tend to her little girl's needs. After Sylvia began nursing the baby, she kept watching out the window. Shortly thereafter, the person she'd seen moments ago came into full view. It was the poor lady who lived in the shanty not far from them. The woman walked up the driveway, while a horse and buggy approached the business ahead of her. Not long after, one of their ministers and his wife got out of the buggy and headed for the greenhouse.

Sylvia rocked and kept watching outside. *I see Maude is wearing a jacket this morning. Maybe it's a little chilly for her.*

Although Sylvia was absorbed with watching, she wondered where Henry might be. She hadn't seen him since breakfast and assumed he may have gone to the greenhouse to help Mom and Amy. At least she hoped he had and was not shirking his duties. *Of course, he might be checking on the bees,* she thought. *I believe during breakfast he said something about doing that this morning.*

Sylvia kept her eye on the gray-haired woman. She thought Maude would go into the greenhouse, but instead she veered off and headed toward the garden in their yard. *That's odd. I wonder what she's doing there.*

Soon, the bedraggled woman picked a couple of ripe tomatoes and popped them into her pockets. She moved over and picked a cucumber then hurried out of the yard and down the driveway.

Sylvia slowed the rocking chair, stroking the top of Rachel's head. *I think Mom and Amy will be interested in hearing about this. I feel sorry for Maude. She must really need food to be taking from us in broad daylight. Or maybe she can't stop herself from stealing.*

Ezekiel sat in the front of the van with their driver, while Michelle and the children were in the back. The day had finally come. Ezekiel looked over his shoulder. "I bet Mom will be surprised to see how much Vernon has grown." He couldn't help feeling pleased with his family, because after God, they were his world.

Michelle smiled and stroked the baby's head in the car seat where he sat strapped in beside her. In his sleep, the little guy seemed to be smiling at the attention his mom gave him.

"*Grossmammi!* Grossmammi!" Angela Mary kicked her small feet and shouted from the seat behind them.

"Shh. . .Jah, soon we'll see your grandma as well as your aunts and uncle." Michelle spoke quietly in Pennsylvania Dutch with her finger against her lips. "I know you're excited, but we don't want to wake your little brother."

"Okay." Angela Mary began to hum softly.

Ezekiel looked at their driver, Hank, and smiled. "In case you couldn't guess, we are all looking forward to seeing my family today."

Hank grinned. "That's how it should be, and you won't have to wait long because, as you can see, we are approaching Strasburg."

Soon, they turned onto a back-country road. A short time later, shouts of glee went up as the van drove up the Kings' driveway. Fond memories mixed with the sadness of his father, brother, and brother-in-law dying caused Ezekiel's throat to clog.

The vehicle stopped, and he jumped out and opened the door behind him. After helping his wife and children out of the van, Ezekiel paused to look around. Seeing no one in the yard, he figured they were either still in the greenhouse or in their home. They'd left Clymer a little over seven hours ago, which allowed for a few stops along the way. From his calculations, it would get them here by five o'clock, which was when the greenhouse closed each day.

Ezekiel was about to get their luggage from the back, when Mom and Amy came out of the greenhouse and rushed toward them with open arms.

"It's so good to see you." Mom hugged Ezekiel and Michelle then bent down and scooped Angela Mary into her arms. "How's my sweet *maedel* doing these days?"

"Gut, Grossmammi."

"I'm happy to hear you are good."

After Amy greeted everyone with a hug, she gazed with a longing expression at the baby in Michelle's arms. "And this must be my newest nephew. What a cutie he is." She leaned in and kissed little Vernon's forehead. "He's adorable. Ezekiel and Michelle, you must be so pleased."

"We are," they said in unison.

"Oh, my. . ." Mom stroked the infant's cheek. "I can hardly believe how much he's filled out since I was at your home."

"Bopplin grow so quickly. I bet you can still remember when I was a baby." Ezekiel winked at Mom.

With a chuckle, she poked his arm. "Of course I remember. You were such a character, I could never forget."

Everyone laughed. Then Ezekiel, with the help of his driver, removed their luggage.

"Where's the rest of your family?" Michelle asked.

"Sylvia's in the house with the kinner," Mom replied. "And I'm not sure where Henry is. He left the greenhouse the minute we put the CLOSED sign in the window, but I don't know where he went."

"He's probably somewhere with that irritating grapp." Amy wrinkled her nose.

"What crow?" Ezekiel raised his eyebrows and blinked a couple of times. "Why would my bruder be with a grapp?"

"Let's all go up to the house, and I'll fill you in." Amy picked up one of the suitcases and headed toward the front porch. Everyone but Ezekiel grabbed something and followed. He first had to pay their driver and set up a time for them to be picked up in five days. That was as long as Ezekiel felt he could be away from his job. Hopefully, it would be enough time to get caught up on how things had been going here with his family.

Amy sat quietly on the couch, holding baby Vernon, while Michelle visited with Mom and Sylvia. Angela Mary and Allen played happily together. After Ezekiel had come into the house and greeted Sylvia, he'd gone outside to look for Henry. Before he left, Amy had told him all about their brother's so-called pet crow. Ezekiel had laughed and said, "Now, this I've gotta see."

Amy smiled. She could only imagine what her older brother would think when he saw the crow and heard Henry carrying on about how he'd been trying to train the bird. *He will probably think our bruder is either quite strange or desperate for something to do besides work.*

Amy turned her full attention on Dad's little namesake. She hoped this child would grow up to be as kind and loving as her father had been. With Ezekiel and Michelle as parents, she didn't see how Vernon could grow up to be anything but well-behaved, loving, and kind toward others.

Holding the child and snuggling him close brought tears to Amy's eyes. *Will I ever experience the joy of becoming a mother, or will I spend the rest of my life unmarried and childless?*

Be careful, Amy, she told herself. *You are giving in to self-pity again, and that doesn't benefit anyone.*

"I hate to break up this wonderful time of visiting," Mom said, rising from her chair, "but we need to get supper made."

"That's not a problem," Sylvia spoke up. "I put a ham in the oven over an hour ago and cut up some vegetables from the garden to steam." She got up too. "I'll go to the kitchen now and check on things."

"And I'll join you," Michelle said. "After our long drive, I need to move around for a bit. And what better way than to set the table?" She smiled at Amy. "Feel free to stay here with the baby. He likes to be held and will probably fall asleep in your arms."

"Okay."

After the three women left the room, Amy moved over to the rocking chair with the baby. It was a treat to hold a younger baby. He smelled so nice of lotion and soap. The warmth he unknowingly provided Amy as she held him seemed to relax her. It wasn't long after she got it moving that little Vernon's eyelids closed. *I hope I don't fall asleep too.* Watching his slow, even breathing made her feel sleepy, but she kept her eyes open and focused on her niece and nephew playing with a set of building blocks across the room. They were so cute and got along well with each other. It was fun to observe them interact and sometimes entertaining to see the way they communicated despite their limited vocabulary.

Oh, to be young again, when life was so simple. Those two adorable children have no idea how easy they have it.

Ezekiel walked around the yard for a while, looking for Henry. *This is so weird. Where is that kid brother of mine? I hope he hasn't been pulling this trick on our mom very long.*

When he didn't find Henry in the yard, Ezekiel decided to check in the barn. Upon entering the building, he smelled the aroma of cigarette smoke. His fingers curled into the palms of his hands. *That boy had better not have taken up smoking.*

Ezekiel stood there a few minutes, looking around. He saw no sign of Henry and was about to call his name, when Henry came down the ladder that led to the hayloft.

"Oh, hey, Ezekiel. I'm glad you and your family made it okay. How was the trip?"

"It went well. We've been here awhile, and I've been looking for you."

"Well, ya didn't have to look far. I've been looking out the window of the loft, watchin' all the birds in our yard." He shook Ezekiel's hand as though they'd met for the first time. "It's good to see you. How ya doin'?"

"I'm fine, but I am not so sure about you."

Henry took a step back. "What do you mean?"

Ezekiel tipped his head back slightly and sniffed. "I smell cigarette *schmoke*. Have you been smoking, Brother?"

Henry shook his head vigorously. "Course not. I noticed the odor too when I came into the barn."

Ezekiel eyed his brother curiously. "If you're not the one who created the stink, then who?"

"Beats me. Maybe one of the people who came to the greenhouse today wandered in here and lit up a cigarette. I've smelled it in the barn before, so that's what I think must've happened."

Ezekiel reached up and rubbed the back of his neck. He had no proof that Henry had been smoking, but the kid kept shifting from one foot to another as though he might feel guilty about something. *Just to ease my own curiosity, I'd like to have a look up there in the hayloft later on.*

"I'm not saying I don't believe you, but if you have been smoking, you need to quit." Ezekiel looked into his young brother's eyes. "It's bad for your health, not to mention how Mom would react if she ever found you with a cigarette."

"She ain't gonna find me with no cigarette 'cause it's not true." Henry stuffed his hands in his pockets. "Now can we talk about something else?"

"Sure thing." Ezekiel pulled his brother into his arms and gave him a bear hug. "We can talk about why you gave me a handshake instead of a hug."

Henry wiped a trickle of sweat off his forehead. "Cause that's what men do when greeting each other—they shake hands."

Ezekiel was tempted to remind Henry that he wasn't a man yet but chose not to say anything that might rile the boy. Instead, he smiled and said, "I hear you've made a pet out of a crow. Why don't you tell me about it?"

Henry's eyes brightened as he stood to his full height. "Charlie's a beautiful crow, and he's gettin' more used to me all the time, and I've even gotten him to eat outta my hand for a while."

Ezekiel had to hold back a chortle. "So, you've even given the *voggel* a name, huh?"

"Jah. Not every bird deserves a people name, but my crow sure does." Henry's lips parted slightly as he looked right at Ezekiel.

"Wanna know something I've never told anyone else?"

"Sure, I'm all ears." Ezekiel leaned a little closer to his brother.

"I've decided to take up a new hobby."

"Oh, and what would that be?"

"Birding."

"You mean, as in watching for birds and writing things down about them in some sort of a journal?"

Henry gave a nod. "Exactly."

"Sounds like it could be a fun hobby."

"And I'll learn a lot too."

Ezekiel gave his brother's shoulder a squeeze. "Good for you, Henry. I like your idea."

"I haven't said anything about it to Mom, Amy, or Sylvia yet, so I'd appreciate it if you kept quiet and let me do the telling when I feel ready."

"No problem at all. I won't say a word."

"Do you wanna go outside with me now and see if Charlie's up in one of the trees or hanging out on a fence post?"

"We can do that, Henry, but it won't be long till we're called in for supper, so if the bird's not around, we can't linger. We'll need to go inside."

"No problem."

Ezekiel lifted a silent prayer to God. *Thank You for helping my brother find something to get excited about. And please, if Henry has been smoking, make him fall under conviction and admit what he's been doing.*

Chapter 35

Belinda had showered and picked out a clean dress. They'd all been invited to have supper tonight at Mary Ruth's house, where Lenore and her husband and children also lived. It felt good to do something fun for a change. *I need to make more of an attempt to move on with my life.*

Belinda got out her head covering and retrieved some white hairpins to pin it in place. *Ezekiel seems to be moving on with his life, and I couldn't be happier for him.*

This was Ezekiel and his family's second day in Strasburg, and the time was already going too fast. She appreciated the fact that Ezekiel had helped in the greenhouse part of the day while Michelle stayed in the house with Sylvia and their children. With her eldest son visiting, she found herself missing the days gone by, when he still lived at home. The extra pair of hands from the start of work today was a reminder of that, and it made things easier on her—especially given how busy it had been.

Ezekiel had pointed out the jars of honey that were being sold, along with jams, jellies, and other canned goods. He seemed impressed and stated his approval on it being a nice touch in the greenhouse. Belinda liked to hear the positive feedback, and in her heart she hoped Ezekiel would see that they were getting by okay. Of course, she had reminded him of the agreement they'd made back in April—that if she could prove they were doing fine on their own within four months' time, he would stay put at his place in Clymer.

It gave Belinda a feeling of security having Ezekiel and his family here, but she'd accepted the fact that in three days they would return to their own home. Having a taste of them here and enjoying their company made it tempting to ask Ezekiel to move back to Strasburg. But Belinda, still determined to make a go of things, had made up her mind months ago to do it all without her eldest son's help.

Belinda placed her head covering on and made an adjustment so it was squarely in place. Then she reached for a white hairpin to secure the kapp to her hair. *I'd better do a good job since we'll most likely eat outside. Don't want the wind taking my head covering off.*

Looking at herself in the mirror, Belinda gave a nod of approval. *Think I'm done getting ready. I just need to grab my comfy pair of shoes and then it's out the door for me.*

A knock sounded, and Belinda turned her head toward the bedroom door. "Come in."

"Are you about ready, Mom?" Amy asked as she stepped into the room. "Our driver showed up with the largest of his vans, and everyone's in the living room, all set to go."

"I'm ready, and I'm glad our driver came in the van I requested yesterday." Belinda picked up her black purse and slipped the straps over her shoulder. "We don't want to be late for supper, and I'm sure Mary Ruth is eager to see Ezekiel and his family. She's missed them too—same as we have."

Amy nodded. "It's hard not to have all our family members living close by. We miss out on so much by not seeing them often—especially watching the kinner grow."

Belinda couldn't miss her daughter's wistful expression. *Did I make a mistake insisting that Ezekiel remain in New York when he offered to move back home?* She had asked herself this question many times since her husband and son's deaths. But each time, Belinda reminded herself that Ezekiel had his own life to live and that she wouldn't ask him to sacrifice the new life he'd made for himself and his family.

During supper last night, Ezekiel had sounded so enthusiastic as he talked about his work. And Michelle shared fondly what the family had been up to. Later, Ezekiel mentioned that he'd noticed the corner of the greenhouse near the parking lot and wondered why it looked new. Belinda filled him in on what had happened. He'd appeared surprised and then commented on how relieved he was that no one had been hurt and only a small portion of the building had suffered some damage. Ezekiel didn't know about all the other things that had gone wrong, and Belinda intended to keep it that way. After all, they were all fine and still managing to stay afloat financially despite the setbacks.

As she and Amy left her bedroom and headed down the hall, the sounds of cheerful voices emerged. *Now this is the pleasant noise I miss around here. I hope there will be lots more visits from Ezekiel and his family in the coming years.*

Belinda shook her thoughts aside and followed Amy into the living room, where the others waited. She was eager to go and have some fun. Sharing time with her loved ones meant a lot, and the memories made tonight would not soon be forgotten.

Belinda smiled as she turned to face her family. "All right, everyone, let's all pile into the van and be ready to spend the evening with some very dear friends."

When they arrived at Mary Ruth's house, Amy noticed a car parked in the driveway and a horse and buggy at the hitching rail, so she knew they had other company.

"Looks like it's gonna be a full house this evening," Ezekiel commented.

"That shouldn't be a problem," Michelle interjected. "There's plenty of room in Mary Ruth's house, and from the looks of it, I'd say we'll be eating outdoors." She pointed at the folding tables and chairs set out on the lawn.

With Michelle holding baby Vernon and Sylvia holding Rachel, everyone headed for the house. Mom held Allen's hand, and Amy guided Angela Mary up the front porch stairs, while Ezekiel and Henry brought up the rear.

When they entered the house, Mary Ruth gave them a warm greeting. "It's ever so good to see you." She slipped her arm around Michelle's waist while leaning down to kiss the baby's head. "And look at you, little miss." Mary Ruth lifted Angela Mary into her arms and gave her a kiss. The child giggled and squirmed a bit, but she didn't ask to get down.

Amy thought it was touching that Ezekiel and Michelle had chosen Angela Mary's middle name in honor of their friendship with Mary Ruth. Since Michelle had lived with Mary Ruth and her husband for several months before she joined the Amish church, she'd gotten to know them well. It was no wonder that Michelle wore a big smile this evening, as she answered the older woman's questions about the children, their new community, and how she liked being a minister's wife.

When they made it into the living room, Amy spotted Sara and Brad, along with Sara's father, Herschel. The three of them stepped forward, and the joyful greetings began all over again. Although Sara and Michelle had not always been friends, once they'd set their differences aside, a close friendship had ensued.

A few minutes later, Lenore and her husband, Jesse, entered the room with their daughter, Cindy, and baby boy, Noah. This brought another round of greeting and excited chatter.

After all the chaos subsided, Mary Ruth announced that it was time to eat. They all gathered in the kitchen for silent prayer, and then everyone who could grabbed a container with food in it and took it out to the tables.

The three babies, now asleep, were placed in a playpen Jesse had brought out and set in the shade of a leafy maple tree.

Amy thought it felt wonderful to spend an evening with the two families. *What a shame Dad, Abe, and Toby can't be here with us*, she thought as the food got passed around. *Maybe there's a window in heaven, where they can look down and see us all together. Even though we* miss our loved ones very much, I'm sure it would please them to know we are carrying on with our lives the best we can.

"Sara, have you told these good people your exciting news?" Herschel spoke up.

"Not yet, but I guess this is as good a time as any." Sara looked over at Brad. "Would you like to make the announcement?"

"Sure." He pushed back his chair and stood. "My dear wife and I would like you all to know that in about six months, we'll become parents."

A round of cheers went up, and everyone clapped.

Although Amy was happy for the couple, she felt a twinge of jealousy like she always did whenever she saw someone with a baby or heard that they were in a family way. *Will this great desire I have to be a wife and mother stay with me if I never get married?* she wondered. *Is my sister affected by this news too?* Sylvia had loved Toby so much and would probably never remarry and have more children.

"Will you continue working after the baby is born?" Sylvia's question cut into Amy's thoughts.

Sara shook her head. "I want to be at home with our child as a full-time mother."

"What about the flower shop?" This question came from Amy's mother.

"I'll either sell the place or hire someone who has a good business head to run the store."

"We're praying about the matter." Brad returned to his seat and reached for his glass of lemonade. "Prayer is essential in a Christian's life, and we feel sure that God will reveal His will for us about Sara's business."

Amy glanced at Sylvia, sitting beside her, and noticed her downturned eyes. She reached for her sister's hand under the table and gave her fingers a gentle squeeze. *I know our situations are different and we are hurting in separate ways, but I want to offer you comfort because that's what sisters should do for each other.*

Amy got a quick smile from Sylvia as she returned a soft clasp of her hand. Even so, Amy couldn't shake the helpless feeling in her heart. It wasn't easy to think about how broken her family still was. *I shouldn't be so impatient for us to rebound from something like what we've been through.*

She watched little Allen come to his mom and give a big hug. What a blessing that the Lord had given Sylvia two beautiful and healthy children to care for. *How can she not see the handiwork of our Maker who created them? Does she ever pray anymore and ask for God's direction in her life?* Even if her sister had given up praying, Amy was determined not to let her own prayer life slip. Not only did she need God's guidance, but the rest of her family did as well.

Sylvia felt uncomfortable listening to Brad talk about prayer and God revealing His will. Where had prayer gotten her, anyhow? Ever since she was a teenager and had joined the Amish church, Sylvia had prayed and read her Bible faithfully. But that all stopped the day Toby, Dad, and Abe were killed.

She pulled her hands into tight fists and placed them in her lap, where no one could see them. Sylvia wasn't sure she could ever let go of her bitterness and be able to trust God again.

She glanced across the table at Henry. As far as she could tell, he didn't put much stock in prayer anymore either. Like her, he was probably angry at God for taking three people he loved. So far, Henry didn't talk about the Bible, as he had done in the past. Sylvia remembered how Dad and Henry would chat about messages from the sermons given at church on Sundays. Other times, Henry would get into deep conversations with Abe about Revelations and what some of the things written in the last book of the Bible meant. She had to admit that listening in on some of those conversations had been interesting and sometimes funny with her brother's interpretation of things.

It was difficult for a young teenager to be without a father, and with Abe gone and Ezekiel living over six hours away, Henry had no male guidance—and it showed. An uncooperative son with a rebellious spirit was not what their father would have wanted. *If the accident hadn't happened and our daed was still alive, Henry's actions would be a disappointment. Of course, if Dad were still here, Henry probably wouldn't be acting so rebellious.*

Sylvia felt helpless when it came to dealing with her young brother. He didn't listen to anything she or Amy said. Most of the time, Henry carried on as if he had a chip on his shoulder. That certainly did nothing to help the situation. Even around Mom, Henry often acted like a spoiled boy. Yet Sylvia felt sure he wanted to be treated like an adult. Henry needed the right help to get his act together before something else went wrong.

But what would help? she asked herself. *If Mom got married again, would that make a difference in Henry's life? He'd have a stepfather, but he might resent someone other than a family member telling him what to do.*

Sylvia bit her lip so hard she tasted blood. *If Mom should ever marry again, I'd accept it if I thought it would make her happy. But for me, I'll never allow myself to fall in love or get remarried. Toby was the love of my life and always will be. There isn't a man in this world who could ever take his place.*

Chapter 36

Ezekiel couldn't believe how quickly their five days had gone, but tomorrow they would be making the journey back home. It felt bittersweet. Although he was eager to get back to Clymer and his growing business, he felt bad about leaving Mom and his siblings. *Sure wish I could talk my mamm into selling the greenhouse and moving close to us. But I guess she'll never consider that as long as her business is doing well and my siblings are willing to keep working there—at least until one of them gets married.* Ezekiel shook his head. *It seems like my mamm is becoming stronger and more confident. I'd say the Lord is at work in her life.*

He tugged his beard. *I wonder if Sylvia will ever remarry. Her children do need a father.*

Ezekiel got up from the couch, where he'd been reading his Bible, and looked out the front window. So many memories had been made here while he was growing up. Most were good, but he also remembered some bad.

"Course most of the bad things that happened were my fault," he said under his breath. *I was a stubborn, rebellious teenager who thought he wanted something other than what he already had.* Looking back on it, Ezekiel was glad he'd sold his truck and settled down to join the Amish church. That and marrying Michelle were the best decisions he'd ever made.

"What are you doing in here by yourself? I thought you'd be

outside with the rest of the family, watching the sun go down."

Ezekiel turned at the sound of his mother's voice. "Just wanted to sit awhile and do some thinking."

"Mind if I ask what you've been thinking about?" She joined him at the window.

He slipped his arm around her waist. "You and my brothers and sisters, mostly."

"You're not still worried about us, I hope."

"Concerned might be a better word for it."

"There's nothing to be concerned about."

"That's not what Henry told me this morning."

His mother's posture stiffened, and she let out a forceful breath. "What exactly did he tell you?"

"Said an old boyfriend of yours has been hanging around and that he even asked you to go out for supper with him."

She took a step back. "Well I didn't go, and if Monroe asks again, my answer will still be no."

Ezekiel closed his eyes briefly, releasing a quiet exhale. "Good to hear. It's too soon for you to be thinking about getting married again."

Her forehead wrinkled. "Now who said anything about getting remarried? Monroe Esh is just a friend from the past, nothing more."

Ezekiel didn't say anything further on the subject, but he felt a sense of relief knowing his mother had taken a stand. He'd never met this old beau of Mom's, but if and when he did, he'd make it clear to the man that Mom was still in love with Dad and hadn't gotten past the pain of losing him in such an unexpected way.

"I think Sylvia and the little ones have the right idea. I'm a little tuckered out, so I'll head off to bed too." Belinda rose from her chair.

"Good night," everyone else said.

"See you all in the morning." Belinda left the living room and went to the kitchen to fetch something to drink. After filling her glass with water, she made sure the back door was locked. The odd things that had occurred on their property made the uncertainty resurface more at night. Belinda tried to shrug it off, but since there'd been no identification of who had done those things yet, the unresolved situation was frightening to her. It was a comfort to have her eldest son here to give that sense of security.

It's funny how when my children were small, I protected them. Now there are times when it feels as though our roles have changed.

Belinda left the kitchen and walked down the hall to her bedroom. Upon entering the darkened room, she felt around and clicked on the battery-powered light by her bed. She took a drink of water and set the glass on the nightstand.

Tomorrow would be a day of goodbyes before Ezekiel and his family headed back to Clymer. She hoped anything Ezekiel had said to Henry while he was here had left an impression and would help in some way. Belinda wanted her youngest boy to have the right priorities.

She removed her head covering and placed it on the dresser before changing into her nightclothes. Next, she took out her hairpins from her bun, reached for her hairbrush, and brushed out the long, coiled strand. Once that was done, it felt good to climb under the cool sheets after an eventful day. Belinda then clicked off the light and closed her eyes.

As Belinda lay in bed, she reflected on the conversation she'd had with Ezekiel earlier this evening. It had been hard not to tell her eldest son about the problems they'd had over the last few months. If she'd said anything about the vandalism though, he would surely have decided to make the sacrifice and move back to Strasburg.

Belinda felt relieved that neither Henry nor his sisters had said anything to Ezekiel either. It was bad enough that her youngest son had told him about Monroe.

Belinda bunched the pillow in an attempt to find a more comfortable position for her head and neck. *Now my son has one more thing to worry about. Hopefully, I put his mind at ease concerning Monroe and his possible intentions toward me.*

Belinda stared into the darkened room and sighed. The house would sure seem quiet after Ezekiel and his family left in the morning. She dreaded saying goodbye but clung to the hope that they would return to Strasburg for Thanksgiving, which was only two and a half months from now. Last year they had stayed in Clymer and entertained Michelle's brothers, as they had done two years previous to that. Maybe this year Ernie and Jack would have other plans. If that were the case, then Belinda saw no reason Ezekiel, Michelle, and the children could not join them for the holiday meal.

Would it be selfish to pray for that? Belinda readjusted her pillow. *Guess I'd better try and get some sleep. Before I know it, the sun will rise and it'll be time to start breakfast.*

"Oh, look at the time." Mom turned away from the clock and frowned.

Amy could tell her mother felt overwhelmed, what with her brother and his family so close to leaving. Breakfast had been good, and visiting with one another had used up a lot of time.

Ezekiel sipped on his cup of coffee. "We tried to make sure everything we came here with is going back home with us."

"You could leave my grandchildren here, and I wouldn't mind." Mom chuckled.

Ezekiel winked. "One of these days, you'll get your wish."

"You movin' back?" Henry asked.

"No, little brother. I meant when the kinner are older and want to spend a week or so here without their parents." He poked Henry's arm. "You can put 'em to work helping you with chores."

Everyone laughed.

A few minutes later, Ezekiel's driver pulled in and honked his horn.

"Hank's here," Michelle announced from where she stood in front of the kitchen window, drying the last of the breakfast dishes.

"Why don't you invite him for a cup of kaffi?" Mom suggested.

"That's right," Amy agreed. "It'll be a few minutes before you're all ready to go."

Ezekiel shook his head. "I can offer, but if I know Hank, he will say that he'd rather wait in the van till we come out."

Amy looked at her mother, raising her eyebrows in question.

Mom merely shrugged and said, "We can send a thermos of coffee with you."

"That's really not necessary. We'll be stopping along the way, and Hank no doubt had breakfast and coffee before coming here this morning." Ezekiel stepped over to Michelle. "If you're fully packed, I'll start hauling suitcases out to the van."

Michelle nodded, and Amy saw tears in her sister-in-law's eyes. "All I need to do is change the baby's windel and we'll be ready to go."

A short time later, they were all on the front porch saying tearful goodbyes. Amy especially felt choked up at the moment, as she held little Vernon one last time and kissed his soft cheek. What an adorable baby he was, and the fact that he had been given such a special name made her feel even more emotional.

"Guess we'd better not keep Hank waiting. If we don't go out to the van soon, he'll be honking again."

Final hugs were given, and as the van drove out of the yard, Amy, Mom, and Sylvia waved goodbye.

When Rachel began to cry, Sylvia went into the house with Allen and the baby. Amy and Mom remained on the porch, waving until the van was clear out of sight.

Tears spilled out of Amy's eyes and rolled onto her cheeks.

"It's okay, Daughter." Mom patted Amy's back. "We'll see them again soon. If not for Thanksgiving then maybe Christmas."

Amy sniffed. "I will miss them terribly, but something else is bothering me."

Mom motioned to the porch swing. "Why don't we have a seat over there? You can tell me about it."

"Okay."

Mom seated herself on the swing, and Amy sat beside her.

"Whenever I have an opportunity to spend time with a boppli, I'm reminded that I'll probably never have any of my own."

"Why not, Amy? You're bound to get married someday."

Amy shook her head and wiped her eyes. "I'm still in love with Jared, and he is the only man I'll ever want to marry, but it's not meant for us to be together."

"Why would you say that?"

"If it was, that horrible accident would never have occurred."

Mom took hold of Amy's hand and gave it a squeeze. "I've told you this before, but you haven't been listening. Just because you're helping me in the greenhouse doesn't mean you can't have a relationship with Jared."

"But Mom, courting couples go places together, and I have no time for courting."

"You can make the time. I've never expected you to be chained to me, the greenhouse, or household chores. Sylvia does most things in the house, and Henry does chores around here too."

"I realize that, but—"

"There are no buts about it, Daughter. Instead of trying to do multiple chores every evening, sometimes you need to go and have a little fun with other unmarried young people—Jared included. Your life should not be only about working, and neither should Jared's."

Amy sighed, leaning her head against the back of the swing. "But it may be too late for us."

"Why's that?"

"I think he and Lydia might be courting, and if they're not, they probably will be soon. They sat with each other at Lydia's party and had their heads together most of the evening, talking whenever they could. Besides, I've seen them together and heard rumors that. . ."

"You won't know if he cares for Lydia unless you ask. If you find out that they're not courting, you need to speak up and tell Jared you still care for him and would like to resume your relationship." Mom spoke in strong sentences.

Amy's chin dipped slightly. "I'll give it some serious thought."

Virginia had said goodbye to Earl before he'd left for work but not before she'd complained about their yard again. Although he mowed the lawn once a week, she thought the place needed some sprucing up.

She'd been sitting out on the front porch looking at all the work that needed to be done. She certainly wasn't up to it, that was for sure. And with Earl so busy at his job, he'd probably never do much more than mow the lawn. All the bushes needed trimming, the grass should have been edged weeks ago, and a tangle of weeds had taken over most of the flowerbeds. Virginia had pulled some of the weeds, until her lower back began to hurt. Some days she felt worthless, especially when it came to doing strenuous tasks. Virginia's past mistakes had taken a physical toll on her.

Her thoughts changed course as she watched a passenger van pull out of the driveway across the street and onto the road. She'd seen from a distance a couple of new people she hadn't noticed before milling around the Kings' yard for the last few days and wondered if they had company. Maybe some relatives or close friends had come to visit.

Virginia leaned back in her chair and brushed her long bangs aside. She'd colored her hair yesterday with an auburn shade of henna, but her bangs still needed to be cut. The salon she'd gone to when they lived in Chicago had done a decent job with her hair, but she hadn't looked for anyplace here yet and wasn't sure which salon might be best.

Maybe I can cut my own bangs. Virginia got up and ambled into the house. She stood in front of the hall mirror and made pretend cuts on her bangs with two fingers. *Nope, it shouldn't be too hard at all.*

In the bathroom, Virginia located the pair of scissors Earl used to trim his moustache. Then, picking up her comb, she dampened it under the faucet, pulled the comb through the ends of her bangs, and cut. Virginia liked the bangs shorter and out of her eyes, but now they were crooked. *That shouldn't be a problem. I'll just trim away till they're straight.*

A few minutes ticked by along with more attempts at trying to make them look even. Her bangs were nearly dry, but they'd shrunk too. Virginia was in a panic. "I haven't had bangs this short since kindergarten! What am I going to do?"

She put the scissors and comb away and stood staring at herself in the mirror. "Wish I could glue the hair back on, but now, because of my stupidity, I'm stuck with how ridiculous I look. I will never cut my own hair again."

Virginia headed to the kitchen and poured herself some coffee. *I wonder what Earl will say when he sees my trim job. Sure hope he doesn't get mad.*

Chapter 37

After some serious prayer and Bible reading, Amy decided to approach Jared and see if he might be interested in courting her again. She wasn't sure yet when she might get the opportunity, but she thought perhaps after they had supper this evening, she might take a ride over to his place.

In need of some reassurance, Amy went to her sister to share the news. She found Sylvia in her bedroom changing the baby. "I know you're busy, but I wanted to talk to you about something."

Sylvia turned her head in Amy's direction. "Sure, come on in."

Amy entered the bedroom and took a seat on the edge of her sister's bed. "I've decided to talk to Jared and see if there's a possibility of us getting back together."

"Really? I thought you believed that you didn't have time for courting."

"It's true, but after Mom and I talked, she convinced me otherwise." Amy shifted her position on the bed. "I'm mostly concerned about whether Jared will want to start over, because I believe he and Lydia have been courting."

Sylvia slipped Rachel's little dress over her curly head. "It hasn't even been six months since you broke up with Jared. I can't imagine that he'd move on so quickly or forget about what the two of you had together. And if he were going to court someone else, I doubt it would be your best friend."

"So, you think I should go ahead and talk to him about it?"

"Jah."

"Okay, then it's settled. I'll talk to him soon." Feeling a bit more confident, Amy rose from the bed. "Right now though Mom asked me to go out before the greenhouse opens and check for phone messages, so I'd best get to it."

As Amy approached the phone shed, she glanced across the street and saw Jared in their neighbor's yard talking with Virginia's husband. His horse and buggy was in the driveway, and she noticed that Dandy had been secured to a fencepost. Seeing Jared made her heartbeat quicken. She remembered when the two of them had been seeing each other regularly and how she'd felt every time they were together. Amy had felt a connection with Jared and wanted to have that same bond again.

I wonder if he went over to the neighbors' to bid on a roofing job. I suppose he could have stopped by for some other reason.

Amy was tempted to walk over and talk to Jared but didn't want to interrupt their conversation. If he was in the middle of conducting business, which she suspected, an interruption would be rude, and he might not appreciate it.

So instead, Amy tried a different approach. She walked close to one of the shrubs and plucked some dead leaves off then waited a few minutes, hoping Jared might look her way. But he kept his attention focused on the English man.

This is so frustrating. If he would just glance over here, I could at least offer a friendly wave. Maybe then, once Jared's business was done, he'd come over and say hello.

Amy looked up at the crow flying overhead, emitting its irritating cry as it swooped through the air. "Probably after some poor bug," she mumbled. "Go away."

Amy stepped away from the shrub and brushed off her apron where some debris had stuck. She looked across the road again and realized that Jared and Virginia's husband had disappeared. They'd either gone into the house or around to the back of the home.

Amy figured it would be best if she went to the phone shed now, before any customers showed up at the greenhouse. It was disappointing not to have at least made eye contact with Jared. Perhaps by the time she came out, he would be finished with his business across the road and there might be another chance to get his attention.

As Amy approached the shed, she spotted Henry in the yard throwing a stick for his dog. *I do hope Henry will eventually get over his anger toward God and become a pleasant young man again.*

She entered the phone shed, and a short time later, holding a slip of paper with a list of messages, Amy stepped out of the building. Much to her dismay, Jared's horse and buggy were gone.

I suppose I should stick to my original plan and go over to his place this evening.

"Are you sure we can afford to get the garage roof redone?" Virginia asked after Earl came inside. "It seems like a waste of money to me."

His face tensed. "We can't afford not to reroof the garage, Virginia. It's in bad shape, and if we let it go, we'll probably have more than one leak to deal with." He pointed a finger at her. "Do you want that?"

"Of course not. I just thought. . ." She moved over to stand in front of the hallway mirror.

"You need to relax and let me do the thinking." He grabbed the lunch she'd prepared for him that morning. "I've got to go now or I'll be late for work." Earl paused and kissed her cheek. "I'll bring a pizza when I come home this evening. How's that sound?"

She smiled up at him and played with her tiny bangs. "That'd be nice. It'll save me from wracking my brain to come up with something to fix for tonight's supper."

"Exactly. And your hair looks fine, dear, so quit worrying so much. Those bangs look kinda cute so short in the front." Earl gave Virginia a thumbs-up and went out the door.

"Yeah, right." She left the mirror, picked up her cup of lukewarm coffee, and poured what was left of it in the sink. *That husband of mine always seems to know the right thing to say. And I'm thankful he's considerate of my needs. Even when I mess up on things here in the house or with myself, he's kind. Sure hope he stays that way.*

Amy was surprised when Lydia's mother came into the greenhouse that afternoon. She hadn't seen Darlene since Lydia's birthday party, and because she rarely came here for anything, Amy had to wonder what her reason was now.

Mom had gone into the house to get them more water and a snack, and Henry was busy loading plants into the back of a customer's van. That left Amy alone for a short while to wait on customers, so she smiled at Darlene and said, "May I help you with something?"

"I came for a few jars of honey," the woman replied. "I know where they're located, and I'll be back soon to pay for them."

Amy waited behind the counter until Darlene came up with the items she wanted. "How's your quilting business going?" she asked, wanting to be polite.

"It's doing well. We've had a lot of orders lately." Darlene fingered the jars of honey, sliding her thumb around the rim as though inspecting them. "Lydia's a big help to me. I'm hoping she'll keep quilting after she and Jared are married."

Amy's whole body felt numb. She breathed deeply through her nose, hoping she wouldn't faint. "I—I had no idea Jared had asked Lydia to marry him. She's made no mention of it to me."

"No, she wouldn't have. I only heard my daughter talking about it yesterday when her friend Nadine dropped by to pick up a quilted table runner for her mother."

Amy hardly knew what to say. She was aware that Lydia and Jared had been seen together, and the rumors going around all pointed to the fact that they might be courting. But Amy had no idea their relationship had progressed that quickly to a marriage proposal.

Her jaw clenched, despite her best efforts to appear relaxed. *For goodness' sakes. . .it hasn't even been six months since I broke things off with Jared. He sure managed to forget about me quickly. I should never have believed him when he said he loved me. No man who supposedly loves a woman should move on to another so quickly. Guess it's a good thing I found out what he's really like now.*

"Ah-hem!" Darlene cleared her throat. "Did you hear my question?"

Amy blinked a couple of times as her mind came back into focus. "Sorry. What was it you asked me about?"

"I wanted to know if you'll be closing the greenhouse for the season early this year."

"No, we'll be open through the week after Thanksgiving, as usual. We'll want to make our poinsettias available to customers who like to buy them before Christmas."

"I see. Well, I may come back sometime between now and then. I might buy some more honey or a plant to give my sister as a Christmas present this year."

Amy nodded, still reeling from the news that the man she loved would be marrying her best friend. She was tempted to ask if the wedding date had been set, but in all honesty, she didn't want to know.

🐦

"I saw your friend Amy today," Lydia's mother said as they stood in the kitchen, preparing supper.

"Oh? Did you visit the greenhouse or see her someplace in town?"

"At the greenhouse. I went there to get some hunnich."

Lydia smacked her lips. "Yum. I love their all-natural raw honey. It's super good on pancakes, and it goes well with peanut butter on toast or in a sandwich."

Mama nodded as she grabbed a potato peeler from the utensil drawer. "I've been meaning to say something to you all afternoon, but with customers coming and going to pick up quilted items, I never got a chance."

"What did you want to say?" Lydia asked as she chopped cabbage for a coleslaw.

"I just want you to know how pleased I am about you and Jared courting and even more so now that I know he's proposed marriage to you."

Lydia's brows shot up. "Where in the world did you get such an idea? Jared and I aren't courting much less planning to be married."

"Really? But I thought—"

"Where did you get such an idea, Mama?"

"I heard you talking to your friend Nadine. I couldn't be sure of everything you said, but I got some of the conversation—the important part that is."

"What did you think you heard me tell her?"

"That you and Jared are courting and that he proposed marriage."

Lydia's mouth gaped open. It seemed she'd been caught between a stone and a brick wall. It was time to tell her mother the truth.

"I have something to confess, Mama."

"Oh, and what is it?"

"I've been secretly seeing Rudy Zook."

"Did you say Rudy Zook, or are my *ohre* playing tricks on me right now?"

"No, your ears are not playing tricks. Rudy's a kind and gentle man, and I love him very much."

"You can't be *anscht*, Lydia."

"I am as serious as anyone can be." Lydia was aware that her parents, especially Mama, had never approved of Rudy because he worked in a general store and didn't make much money since he was not the owner. Mama had pointed out once that a man like that would be unable to support a wife and children properly, so the poor fellow would probably never find a woman willing to let him court her. In addition to that, Rudy stuttered, and Mama thought his speech impediment and crooked nose made him a less than desirable boyfriend. For these reasons, Lydia had kept her relationship with Rudy a secret, and whenever they'd gone anywhere together, it was someplace out of the area. If her parents had gotten wind of her feelings for Rudy, they'd do everything in their power to turn Lydia against the idea.

"But you've been seeing a lot of Jared since Amy broke up with him." Mama broke into Lydia's thoughts. "I was so sure. . ."

Lydia held up her hand. "Jared and I are just friends. The reason you've seen me with him so much is because we were talking about Amy—trying to figure out some way to get them back together. It also bought me some time to pray and decide how and when I should let you know the truth about Rudy and me."

Lydia's mother set the potato peeler aside and collapsed into a chair at the table. "Oh, dear. I'm afraid I've made a terrible mistake."

"You've changed your mind about Rudy?"

"No, not really, but if he's the man you love then I guess I have no choice but to give you my blessing. But I'll need time to prepare your daed for this news."

Lydia leaned down and gave her mother a hug. "Danki, Mama. I appreciate you paving the way with Dad. I can hardly wait to tell Rudy."

"Life can sure throw us a curve ball sometimes, and I've managed to swing and miss this time." Lydia's mother placed her elbows on the table and leaned forward, pressing her fingertips against her forehead. "The mistake I made was in telling Amy what I thought I heard you telling Nadine."

"About me and Rudy?"

"No, Daughter. I told Amy that I heard you telling Nadine that you and Jared were planning to get married."

"Oh, dear. Oh, dear." Lydia rocked back and forth with her arms crossed over her chest. "Amy must be so upset with me—and angry with Jared too. She no doubt feels that we've betrayed her." She moved quickly toward the back door.

"Where are you going, Lydia?"

"I need to go over to the Kings' house right away and talk to Amy. She needs to know the truth."

"I understand, but it will have to wait until tomorrow morning."

"How come?"

"The bishop and his wife are coming here for supper this evening. I can't believe you could have forgotten that."

"I remembered earlier, but the shock of what you said to Amy must have caused me to forget." Lydia placed a hand on her mother's shoulder. "Can I go as soon as we've finished eating supper?"

With a determined expression, Mama shook her head. "That would be impolite. You can go over to see Amy first thing in the morning."

"Okay." Lydia didn't feel that she had much choice in the matter. It was bad enough that she'd been deceiving her folks for the last several months by seeing Rudy on the sly. She didn't want to rile Mama any more by leaving the house this evening while their company was there.

Amy might not sleep very well tonight, but tomorrow when I go over to see her, she'll feel a lot better. Lydia rubbed her chin. *But then maybe hearing that Jared and I were planning to be married didn't upset my friend at all. She did, after all, break up with Jared, so perhaps she doesn't care about him anymore.*

Later that evening, Mom, Sylvia, and the children were settled in the living room after their meal. Henry said he was going outside to the barn.

Amy put away the last of their clean supper dishes and stepped outside to enjoy the setting sun. She stood on the porch, looking toward the west as the sky turned brilliant colors. The sight helped alleviate some of her depression after hearing about Jared and Lydia. *The Lord sure knows how to dress up the sky.*

She continued watching a little longer then headed to the barn. *Maybe Henry would enjoy seeing the gorgeous sunset too.*

Once inside the darkened building, instead of calling out to her brother, Amy used her flashlight to climb the ladder to the loft. She found him there, looking at a car magazine, with a battery-operated light, like they used for campouts.

"Hello."

Henry quickly laid the magazine aside. "What's up?"

"I came to find out if you'd like to see the sunset. It's really beautiful."

"Sure, let's go take a look." He followed her down the ladder.

When they stepped outside and looked toward the sky, it had turned an incredible pink.

Henry whistled. "Wow, that's gorgeous!"

Amy waited a minute, and then she spoke. "I noticed the magazine you were looking at."

"What about it?" His tone had become defensive.

"When did you get it?"

"Not long ago."

"You're not thinking about getting a car, are you?"

Henry stared straight ahead. "I'm only looking at it. The magazine belongs to Seth."

"Oh, that's good."

"I best go check on the horses' water before I get ready to go in the house. Thanks for showin' me the sunset." Her brother turned back toward the barn.

"You're welcome." Amy had misgivings about how honest her brother had been with her. *What if Seth has put some silly notion into Henry's head about getting a car when he's old enough to drive? It happened to Ezekiel when he went through his running-around years.*

Amy paused and looked up at the sky and the diminishing sunset. *Should I say something to Mom or let it go?*

Chapter 38

The next morning, when Amy entered the greenhouse still feeling depressed, she discovered that all their pots of fall flowers had died. She felt stunned. "How could something like this have happened?"

Amy raced out of the building and back to the house. "Where's Mom?" she asked Sylvia, who sat feeding the baby.

"I think she's still in the kitchen. She said she had a few things to do there before she joined you in the greenhouse."

"Something terrible has happened!"

Sylvia's eyes widened. "What is it? Has Henry been hurt?"

Amy shook her head. "I didn't see our bruder outside anywhere. So as far as I know, he's fine."

"What is it then?" Sylvia's chin quivered as she placed Rachel against her shoulder and began patting the baby's back.

"All the mums and other fall flowers are dead." Amy's body trembled with the pent-up anger she felt.

"Hasn't Henry been watering them?"

"I check every day to be sure, and none of them have appeared to be dried out. I just don't understand what happened." Amy tapped her chin. "I wonder if. . ." Her voice trailed off. "I'd better go tell Mom."

Belinda was removing a jug of cold tea from the refrigerator to take to the greenhouse when Amy burst into the room.

"I'm sorry to have to tell you this, Mom, but all our mums and other fall *blumme* are dead."

"What?" Belinda put down the jug. "But how can that be?"

Amy shrugged. "I—I don't know. I'm sure they've been getting enough water and fertilizer."

"Come on, Amy, we'd better go see if we can figure out what happened to those plants." Belinda tied a black scarf on her head and hurried out the back door.

When they entered the greenhouse and Belinda's eyes beheld the disaster, she brought a shaky hand up to her forehead. "This is worse than I imagined." She looked at Amy. "We have no more fall *blanse* left to sell."

Amy joined Belinda as they walked up and down the rows. "Do you think this could have been done on purpose?"

"Who would do such a thing, and how would they gain access to the greenhouse when we're not here?" Belinda pulled a tissue out from under her dress sleeve and blew her nose. "Where's your bruder?"

"I don't know. I haven't seen him since breakfast." Amy moved closer to Belinda. "You don't think Henry would do something so horrible, do you? I mean, he has to know that we were counting on the money we earned from the sale of these plants."

The tissue slipped from Belinda's hand, and she bent down to pick it up. In so doing, she noticed a bottle of weed killer under one of the wooden counters where this section of plants sat. "Oh, my!"

"What is it, Mom?"

When Amy leaned over, Belinda pointed.

"That's really odd. We never keep weed killer near the flowers, shrubs, or anything else it could damage or kill. I wonder how this got moved from the storage area where it's kept."

Belinda picked up the container and realized very quickly that it was almost empty. All of the weed killers they sold were completely full. "I am convinced that whoever did this used weed killer to destroy the plants, and then they set the near-empty bottle underneath this counter." She clasped her daughter's hand. "Oh Amy, what are we going to do?"

"The first thing I plan on doing is finding Henry and questioning him about this. He may be smiling more these days, thanks to that stupid crow he messes with, but I can tell by some of the things he says and does that his heart is still bitter."

Belinda stood up tall and pulled her shoulders back. If her boy was responsible for this, she would deal harshly with him. But if there was even a possibility of his innocence, she couldn't punish him. What they needed more than anything right now was something else they could sell that would bring in some money. "I'll handle Henry. Please go find your brother and let him know I need to see him."

Amy found Henry in the barn and said, "Mom needs you in the greenhouse."

"Tell her I'll be there in a few minutes. I still have a couple of chores to do."

"Please, Henry." Amy pointed in the direction of the greenhouse. "Mom needs to see you right now."

"Okay, okay." Henry ambled toward the greenhouse and Amy followed. Mom might need her help getting the truth out of him.

When they entered the building, Mom stood near the door with her hands on her hips and a stony expression. It was a good thing no customers had shown up yet, because it wouldn't be nice for anyone to hear this conversation or see all the dead plants. They would need to get them cleared out quickly before anyone arrived.

Amy waited quietly while Mom told Henry what had happened to the plants and about the weed killer she'd found. "Do you know anything about this, Son?"

A flush appeared on Henry's face and neck as he broke eye contact with Mom. "I hope ya don't think I would do such a terrible thing." He shuffled his feet. "I work here too, ya know, and I count on the money you pay me."

"Of course, but you've also complained about working here, and since you have access to the greenhouse with the new key Amy had made for you and eventually entrusted you with, I felt the need to question you."

His eyes narrowed. "Well, you can question me all ya want, and my answer will still be the same—I am not the one who destroyed the fall plants."

Amy wanted to believe her brother, but he'd lied to them before and snuck out of the house when he was supposed to be in bed. *He could be holding back the truth so he doesn't get in trouble.* Amy tapped her foot. *But if Henry is telling the truth, then someone has access to our greenhouse and must have come in during the night. That means they either had a copy of our key somehow or picked the lock on the door. Was it the same person who did the other things to our property? Does someone really dislike us that much, or could they be trying to make things difficult so we'll give up and close the greenhouse for good?*

"Standing here debating this matter is not accomplishing a thing." Mom broke into Amy's contemplations. "The three of us need to get busy hauling all the dead plants out behind the barn, where no one will see them."

"Who cares if anyone sees them or not?" Henry's voice grew louder with each word he said. "When people show up here today, they're gonna see that we have no fall flowers or plants to sell."

"We still have a few hanging baskets that Sylvia put together," Amy chimed in.

"But they're not specifically fall colors," Mom replied. "Also, what are we going to do about the orders Sara placed recently? She's expecting one of us to deliver them sometime this week."

"As soon as we finish hauling the dead plants out, I'll go to the phone shed and give her a call." Amy's heart thudded dully in her chest. "She'll probably end up ordering from the new greenhouse."

Mom gave a nod. "Be that as it may, we can't promise something we are unable to make good on."

Henry pulled his hat off and fingered the brim. "Here's somethin' else to think about. Once Sara sells her flower shop, the new owner might decide to buy from the other greenhouse. He or she could be more interested in dealin' with a place that's closer to town and is run by the English."

When Amy saw her mother's eyebrows draw together, she could have kicked her brother for saying that. Mom didn't need one more thing to worry about.

"It's just a shame we had to lose all those beautiful mums and other fall foliage." Amy stood near her mother next to one of the wagons filled with dead plants.

"Jah, but there's not much we can do about it now."

"I keep wondering who could have done this and why we're their target."

Mom looked at Amy and slowly shook her head. "This is really going to set us back."

Amy heaved a frustrated sigh. They'd hauled out about half of the ruined plants when a horse and buggy pulled into the parking lot. Amy stood in the doorway watching as Mary Ruth climbed down from her buggy and went to the hitching rail to secure her horse.

Amy waved as Mary Ruth headed their way. "Our first customer of the day is here," she called to Mom.

"What? Oh, no." Mom's facial features slackened. "I had hoped we could finish this job before anyone showed up. Is it someone we know?"

"Jah, it's Mary Ruth, and she's coming this way."

Wearing a cheerful smile and holding a toy wooden horse, Mary Ruth entered the greenhouse. "Guder mariye."

"Morning." Amy managed to smile in return.

"I believe this belongs to your nephew." Mary Ruth handed the toy to Amy. "I found it the day after you and your family came for supper at my place, but I kept forgetting to bring it over until now."

"No problem. Allen hasn't asked for it, so most likely he hasn't even missed the toy."

Mom came up to them, pulling a wagonload full of dead plants. "Good morning, Mary Ruth. I hope you're not here to buy any of our *harebscht* blanse, because we don't have any now."

Mary Ruth touched her parted lips as she looked at the pathetic plants with an incredulous stare. "What in the world happened to those?"

Mom explained, while Amy grabbed another wagon and piled on more dead plants.

"I'm sorry to hear about your autumn plants." Mary Ruth gestured to the two wagonloads waiting to be taken out. "I don't need any myself, but I'm sure you'll get lots of customers coming in for fall foliage."

"You're right, and we may as well put up a sign here at the front of store so people will know when they first come in that we have none to sell." Mom's shoulders slumped as she heaved a heavy sigh. "This is certainly not what we needed right now."

Amy hadn't seen her mother look this despondent since she'd returned from her visit to Ezekiel and Michelle's place. She wished she could say something to cheer Mom up, but she too felt the pain of this latest act of vandalism. It was a mystery to her that anyone would want to do this to them.

"I may be able to help with your problem," Mary Ruth spoke up. "Lenore and I planted more mums and dahlias than we know what to do with, so I'd be happy to let you have most of them to offer your customers."

Mom's eyes brightened a little. "That is a very generous offer, but don't you usually sell them at the farmers' market or set up a roadside stand in front of your place?"

"We've tried that a few times, but it's a lot of work. And with Lenore being so busy with two little ones, it's more than I can keep up with by myself." She touched Mom's arm. "Please, Belinda, I want you to have them. I'll just keep a few out for ourselves is all."

Mom nodded and gave Mary Ruth a hug. "All right then, but I insist on paying you. I'll send Henry over with our market wagon to get them as soon as he finishes disposing of the rest of the lifeless plants."

"If you sell a lot, you can give me a small payment, but I want you to be able to make a profit." Mary Ruth's big smile and light, bubbly voice indicated that she was more than willing to share from her abundance. It was kind and generous people like her who made the world a better place. It appeared that things might be looking up for them again.

Chapter 39

Later that morning, Lydia got out her scooter and headed to the greenhouse to talk to Amy. She needed to set her straight on how things were between her and Jared. She could only imagine what her friend must have thought when Mom told her that Lydia and Jared were talking about getting married. *Amy probably thinks I betrayed her. If I don't set things straight right away, it could be the end of our friendship.*

Lydia thought about Rudy and how she'd kept her relationship with him a secret even from her best friend. "I should have at least told Amy," she mumbled as she neared the Kings' place. "I'm sure she would have kept my secret, and she wouldn't have gotten the wrong idea about me and Jared."

When Lydia arrived outside the greenhouse, she parked her scooter near the building and went inside. She found Belinda sitting on a stool behind the counter, sorting through some papers.

"Guder mariye, Belinda." Lydia smiled. "Is Amy here? I need to speak with her about something important."

Amy's mother shook her head. "My daughter had a dental appointment. She hired a driver to take her there. I believe she may have had a few errands to run too, so she probably won't be back for several hours."

"Oh, I see." Lydia was tempted to tell Amy's mother the reason she had come over and ask her to give Amy the message, but she decided against that idea. It would be better if she talked to Amy herself. Perhaps she could put in a good word for Jared too, like she'd tried to do in the past. Only this time, maybe she could talk some sense into her friend.

Lydia pulled her shoulders back. *If Amy could take time out to attend my birthday gathering, she could certainly find the time for Jared to court her. I just need to make her see that and then act upon it.*

"Now that was sure strange." Belinda stroked her chin, watching as Lydia rode out of the parking lot on her scooter. *I wonder why she wouldn't give me a message for Amy. She didn't even ask me to let my daughter know she had stopped by here looking for her. Oh well, I guess she'll come back if it was anything important.*

Remembering the new watering cans she'd purchased to sell in the greenhouse and left outside the door, Belinda stepped out. Her forehead creased as she looked down at the spot where she'd placed them. There had been four cans earlier, but now there were only three.

I wonder if Henry thought they were for our personal needs and hauled one off to use somewhere.

She looked up toward their garden but saw no sign of her son. *Maybe he took it up to the house for Sylvia to use in the flowerbeds near the back door.* Belinda was tempted to walk up there and see but didn't want to leave the greenhouse unattended. *Guess it'll have to wait until Henry shows up.* She picked up two of the watering cans and brought them into the building then went back and got the third one.

Twenty minutes passed, and two customers had come in, but still Belinda saw no sign of Henry. *What could that boy be doing all this time? He was supposed to join me here as soon as Amy left for her dental appointment.*

Another ten minutes went by before Henry finally made an appearance. "Where have you been?" she asked. "There are people here who might need some assistance, and I can't do that and be up here at the checkout counter too." Belinda kept her voice down, hoping none of the patrons could hear her conversation with Henry.

This business of him showing up late for work and disappearing all the time was getting old. She'd need to have a talk with him about this, but it would have to wait until a more opportune time.

"I was lookin' for my crow. Haven't seen him in the yard for a few days, and I'm worried about him."

Belinda rolled her eyes. *Is that crow really so important?*

He shrugged and started walking toward the customers, but Belinda stopped him with one more question. "There were four brand-new watering cans outside the door, but now there are only three. Did you take one of them?"

He shook his head. "I never saw four cans, only three, and that was when I went lookin' for Charlie."

Belinda waved her hand. "All right then, go ahead and see if any of the customers have questions or need help with anything."

As her son headed down aisle 1, Belinda leaned forward with her elbows on the counter. *Am I losing my mind? Could I have purchased only three watering cans to sell and thought it was four?*

Clymer

"I wonder how things have been going for your mom and siblings," Michelle commented when Ezekiel came into the house to get his lunch. "Have you talked to any of them lately?"

He shook his head. "Guess it's been close to a week. I've been meaning to phone them and ask, but I've had so many orders to complete in my shop, I keep putting off making the call."

He combed his fingers through the ends of his beard. "Guess my priorities are mixed up right now. I'll stop at the phone shed and call before returning to my shop."

"Would you rather I do it for you?" Michelle offered. "I could do it right now while you're in the house or wait till the baby and Angela Mary are down for their naps."

Ezekiel shook his head. "No, that's okay, it's my responsibility to check on my family back home." He pulled Michelle into his arms and gave her a kiss. "You have enough to do taking care of the kinner as well as the house."

"I don't mind, really."

He kissed her again. "I know you don't. You're such a sweet and caring person. I feel *seelich* that you agreed to marry me."

She stroked his face. "I'm the one who is blessed."

He grinned at her and grabbed his lunchbox. "I'll see you later this afternoon."

"I look forward to it." Michelle's dimpled smile almost made Ezekiel change his mind about going back to work, but his responsibility to the customers who'd placed orders won out.

As he headed to the phone shed, Ezekiel thought about Henry and how he had suspected the boy might be smoking. He'd made good on his decision to climb into the hayloft while he and his family were there visiting and had been relieved when he didn't find anything except a pair of binoculars by the open window. Maybe Henry wasn't lying when he said he hadn't been smoking. Ezekiel hoped it was true.

Strasburg

Amy came away from her dental appointment feeling more depressed than ever. It turned out that the sensitive tooth she'd been dealing with for the last week—and hadn't told anyone about—was abscessed. The dentist had prescribed an antibiotic to deal with the infection and offered her two choices: a root canal, followed by a porcelain crown, or pulling the tooth. Due to the expense of the first procedure he'd offered, Amy had gone with the second option and scheduled an appointment for next week. The tooth in question was near the back of her mouth, so at least having it gone wouldn't be noticeable.

"Seems like there is always some kind of trouble," Amy mumbled as she approached the pharmacy, which was a block down the street from the dentist's office.

When she entered the building, she checked at the counter for her medicine, and they told her it wasn't quite ready, but Amy went ahead and paid for it. While she waited, she milled around the aisles, looking at things.

Amy looked up and saw their neighbor come in and walk up to the prescription counter. "I'm Virginia Martin, and I'm here to pick up a prescription for my hormones."

"All right, let me go check." The man stepped away.

"Amy King!" the other clerk called.

"Yes." She stepped up to the counter.

"Here's your antibiotic, and the receipt is in the bag."

"Thank you." Amy turned to her neighbor. "Hello, Virginia."

"Oh hi. So, you had to come in here too, huh?"

"Yes. I have a tooth that's giving me some trouble."

"That's too bad." Virginia looked at the pharmacist who had returned with her prescription.

"Here you go. Do you need anything else today?"

"Nope. That's all." She pulled out her checkbook.

"Well, have a good day, Virginia." Amy left the counter.

"You too." Virginia barely glanced her way.

Mom's right. She is a person of few words.

When Amy came out of the pharmacy with her prescription, Helen, one of their new drivers, was just pulling into the parking lot. After Amy approached the van, Helen rolled down her window and stuck her head out. "I'm sorry to have to tell you this, Amy, but I just got a frantic call from my mother. She said my dad was in a car accident and is being rushed to the hospital in Lancaster. She wants me to meet her there right away."

"I'm so sorry to hear about your father. I hope he'll be okay."

"So do I. Listen, would it be all right if I call a friend of mine and ask her to come and take you home?"

"That's okay. I'll walk."

"Are you sure? Your place is a good two miles from here."

"It'll be fine. I've walked that road before, and it wasn't too bad. Besides, the fresh air and exercise will do me some good."

"All right then. Thanks, Amy."

"Please give us a call later and let us know how your father is doing."

"I will."

Amy watched as Helen's van pulled out of the parking lot and onto the street. She knew all too well the agony of losing her father. Right then, Amy said a prayer that Helen's dad would be okay.

Before Amy started her trek toward home, she stopped at Strasburg Country Store on Main Street for a bottle of water. Despite the cooler weather they'd been having, the warmth of the sun beating down on her head caused Amy to wonder if she'd made a mistake telling her driver not to call someone else to take her home.

Well, it's too late to change my mind now. Amy trudged along and soon headed out of town and down the country road in the direction of home.

She'd gone a short way when a horse pulling a market buggy came up beside her. "Where ya headed?"

Amy turned and was surprised to see Jared in the driver's seat. "I'm going home." Her heartbeat picked up speed as he gave her a friendly smile. "Hop in. I'll give you a ride."

Common sense told Amy she should say no, but her heart won out. As much as it hurt, the only right thing to do was tell Jared that she wished him and Lydia all the best. She truly did want the best for her friends, but it would be impossible to say she was happy for them. Just a sincere "Well wishes to you both" would have to suffice.

Amy climbed into the passenger side of the buggy. "I appreciate the ride. I thought I was up to the two-mile walk, but I'm not feeling my best today."

Jared turned in his seat to face her. "I'm sorry to hear that. What's wrong?"

Amy explained about her tooth and what the dentist had said. "Guess it could have been worse." She touched her jaw. "The prescription I got should relieve the ache until the problem can be fixed." *If only there was something that could take away the pain I feel in my heart.*

"Are you going to get a root canal?" he asked, guiding his horse back onto the road.

She shook her head. "It would be too expensive, so I made an appointment to let the dentist pull my abscessed tooth."

"If it's about the money, I'd be happy to pay for it, Amy."

She shook her head so vigorously the ties on her kapp swished across her face. "Since there are marriage plans in your future, you'll need all the money you earn."

"Marriage plans?" Jared glanced at her and tipped his head.

"To Lydia."

His head flinched back slightly. "Where in the world did you get that idea?"

"Lydia's mamm told me that you and Lydia were courting and also talking of marriage."

"I have no idea where Darlene would have gotten that idea. Lydia and I aren't courting, much less planning to get married."

"You're not?" Jared's denial didn't make sense. Amy saw no reason that Lydia's mother would make up such a thing."

"Lydia has secretly been seeing Rudy because she knew her parents did not approve of him."

"Rudy Zook?"

"That's right."

"But. . .but you and Lydia have been seen together several times, and at her birthday party, you were with her most of the evening."

"Jah, thanks to her mamm. She kept pushing us together." Jared reached over and lightly touched Amy's arm. "The only reason Lydia and I have been together is because we were talking about you. She was trying to help me figure out some way to—"

A car with a couple of teenage boys inside came roaring up beside them. Amy recognized the blond-haired fellow sitting in the passenger's seat. She didn't know the boy's name, but he and his family lived down the road from them. Sometimes she had seen him mowing lawns or doing yard work for other people along their road.

Amy was preparing to wave, but before she could lift her hand, the young driver honked the horn and sped on by. She could hear the boys' laughter through their open windows.

All the noise must have spooked the horse, because Dandy took off like a shot as they neared a Y in the road. Amy wasn't sure they'd even be able to make the turn that veered to the right.

Her heart pounded erratically as she clung to the edge of her seat, and Jared's knuckles turned white as he clutched the reins and hollered, "Whoa, Dandy! Whoa!"

As if in a frenzy, the horse's hooves kept pummeling the road. Several times the gelding crossed over the white line, and then he would jerk back again.

Amy's mouth went dry when she saw a car coming from the opposite direction. All she could think about was that she'd lost her father, brother, and Sylvia's husband in a tragic accident less than six months ago. *Please, Lord, don't let anything happen to Jared or me. Our families would be devastated.*

Chapter 40

Amy hung on for dear life and kept praying as the vehicle approached. Jared pulled sharply on the reins, forcing Dandy to the lane they should be in. When the car passed, the driver shook his fist and blew the horn, which only riled the horse more. Amy was so scared, she couldn't speak. Didn't the man behind the wheel of that vehicle realize Jared had not directed his horse into the other lane on purpose?

It seemed that the more Jared hollered for his horse to stop, the faster Dandy galloped down the road. Amy feared if he didn't get the horse under control soon, they could end up in a ditch with the buggy toppling over. And if the horse kept moving into the opposite lane, they would most surely be involved in a head-on accident.

Sweat poured off Jared's forehead and ran down his face as he continued the struggle with his horse. Finally, when Amy felt sure the buggy would tip over, Dandy quit running and slowed to a trot.

"Whew, that's a relief. Are you okay, Amy?" Jared reached across the seat and touched her arm.

"I'm fine," she said, barely able to catch her breath. "That ordeal really shook me up."

"Same here." Jared guided Dandy to a wide stretch of the road where there was plenty of room to stop. "I think we need a little time to catch our breath and quit shaking."

Amy nodded her agreement.

Still holding tightly to the reins, Jared looked over at Amy with such a tender expression, tears flooded her eyes. He let go with one hand and reached over to wipe them away with his thumb. "I love you, Amy, and I always will. Please say that I can begin courting you again. I would do just about anything to get you back."

"What about Lydia? Did you come to care for her during the time you and I were apart?"

Jared pointed his finger at her. "Didn't you hear a word I said before Dandy started acting up?"

"Well, I wasn't sure. . ."

"It's you I love, Amy, not Lydia. Like I said, she's secretly been seeing Rudy, and the only reason Lydia and I have gotten together is to talk about what I could do to get you back." A muscle in Jared's right cheek twitched. "I think if you'll just listen to me, we can work things out."

Amy pressed a trembling hand to her chest. "Oh Jared, I've missed you so much, and I have been praying about our situation."

"Did you receive an answer?"

"I thought I had until I ran into Lydia's mamm and she mentioned that you and Lydia were talking about marriage."

He chuckled. "Oh, Lydia's talked about it all right, but it's not me she's eager to marry. Your good friend is eager to become Rudy's fraa." Jared lifted Amy's chin so she had no choice but to look right in his eyes, and then he leaned forward and gave her lips a sweet, gentle kiss. "And I'm eager for you to become my wife. After we have courted a respectable time, will you agree to become Mrs. Jared Riehl?"

Amy nodded slowly as a renewed sense of hope welled in her chest. They had a lot to talk about the rest of the way home.

When Belinda heard a horse and buggy pull into the parking lot, she opened the greenhouse door and looked out. *Are my eyes playing tricks on me?* Her mouth nearly fell open when she saw Jared helping Amy out of his market buggy at the hitching rail.

"What's going on? Where's Helen?" Belinda asked as Amy and

Jared approached the greenhouse. "I thought she was supposed to pick you up after your dental appointment."

"She met me outside the pharmacy where I went to get an antibiotic for my abscessed tooth."

"Your tooth is that bad?"

"Jah, but we can talk about it later."

Belinda listened with puckered brows as Amy told her about Helen's father.

"I'm so sorry to hear that. I'm sure she must be quite worried about him."

"Jah. I asked her to call and let us know how he's doing."

"So how is it that you ended up bringing my daughter home from town?" Belinda looked at Jared.

"When I saw her walking along the shoulder of the road, I stopped and asked if she'd like a ride." The grin on Jared's face looked like it might never come off.

"And what a ride it turned out to be." Amy glanced at Jared then back at Belinda.

"What do you mean? What kind of ride?" Belinda questioned.

"I'll let Jared explain."

As Jared told Belinda what had happened with the car that passed and his horse getting spooked when the driver of the vehicle blew the horn, Belinda stood speechless.

"But I finally got Dandy under control, and your daughter and I are both okay."

Belinda's tense muscles began to relax. "I'm ever so glad."

"So are we. It could have ended in disaster."

"Do you think that young fellow tooted the horn on purpose to see if he could scare the horse?"

Jared shrugged. "I don't know, but it's a definite possibility. Some teenagers, even those who are Amish, think it is fun to fool around and do mean or destructive things. Like the vandalism that's been done to you good folks."

Belinda met Amy's gaze. "You told him about it?"

"Jah, Mom, but he already knows some of the things because Henry blabbed it some time ago. I also explained how Henry's been acting and that we are concerned about him. I figured if Jared and I are going to begin courting again, there should be no secrets between us."

Belinda's eyes opened wide. "You're back together?"

"Yes, we are, and if you would kindly give us your blessing, Amy and I would like to be married next fall."

Belinda placed one hand on Jared's arm and the other one on Amy's. "You most assuredly have my blessing. Oh, how I wish Vernon, Abe, and Toby could've lived to hear this wunderbaar news." Her eyes misted.

Jared felt such relief when Belinda gave her approval, although to him next fall seemed like a long time to wait. But they would need about a year to plan for a proper wedding.

"There are still a lot of things that need to be worked out," Jared said in a confident tone. "But together, and with the Lord's help, we'll figure it all out."

Amy leaned heavily against him and sighed. "As our bishop said during the last church meeting, 'With God, all things are possible.'"

"That's for certain," Jared agreed. He wasn't 100 percent sure what all had caused Amy to change her mind about them being together, but he was ever so pleased that she had. With them courting, Jared would be coming around more, which would give him an opportunity to check on things and make sure the women and Henry were safe. *I hope I can help Henry in some way to have a better attitude and be there for support in case any more weird things should happen around their place.*

That evening, Amy sat at the kitchen table going over the books to see where they stood financially with the greenhouse. Thanks to the fall plants Mary Ruth had given them, they had remained in the black.

It was hard for Amy to concentrate with Jared on her mind. All she could think about right now was her future with him. Although the future of their family business might be uncertain and even though they still did not know who had vandalized their property, Amy felt confident that things would go better for them now. If Henry was the one behind the damage done to their property, she hoped he would stop doing it and own up to his misdeeds.

All she and the rest of her family needed to do was to put their faith and trust in God, asking Him with prayerful and humble requests to protect and provide for them.

Caw! Caw! Caw!

Amy tipped her head toward the kitchen window. This time the annoying crow's call didn't bother her at all. As long as Henry kept feeding the bird, it was bound to keep coming around, so she would have to get used to its noisy ruckus. Perhaps in some strange way, God had sent the crow to warn them of things to come. Or maybe it was just a coincidence that Charlie the Crow had appeared when he did.

In an hour or so, Jared would be here for supper and their courting days would resume.

Amy sighed and repeated Psalm 56:3, a verse she'd read in her Bible last night. "What time I am afraid, I will trust in thee."

Recipe for Amy's Vanishing Oatmeal Raisin Cookies

1 cup butter or margarine, softened

1 cup packed brown sugar

½ cup sugar

2 eggs

1 teaspoon vanilla

1½ cups flour

1 teaspoon baking soda

1 teaspoon cinnamon

½ teaspoon salt

3 cups quick-cooking oatmeal

1 cup raisins

Preheat oven to 350 degrees. Cream butter and both sugars in large bowl. Add eggs and vanilla. Beat well. Combine flour, baking soda, cinnamon, and salt in separate bowl. Add to butter mixture and mix well. Stir in oats and raisins. Drop by rounded tablespoons onto greased cookie sheet. Bake for 10 to 20 minutes or until golden brown. Cool for 1 minute on cookie sheet before removing to wire rack. Yields about 4 dozen cookies.

Discussion Questions

1. Have you ever suffered a catastrophic loss like the King family did? How did each of the main characters in this story cope with their loss? Which character do you think handled it the way you would?

2. Do you think Amy's refusing to continue a courtship with Jared was a reasonable way to handle things? Could she have continued the courtship and still worked at the greenhouse and helped at home?

3. Was there anything Jared could have done to win Amy back? Did it appear that he gave up too quickly?

4. Sylvia went into deep depression after her loss. Have you ever suffered from depression? What did you do to get better?

5. Henry became rebellious and uncooperative after his father and older brother died. Were you a disobedient teen? Do you have a rebellious teen at home? How can you help a defiant teen?

6. Why do you think the Kings' new neighbor, Virginia, was so unaccepting of the Amish way of life? Have you or someone you know dealt with people who are prejudiced?

7. Belinda was unsure of who was vandalizing them and wondered if it could be her own son acting out his frustrations. Do you trust your children? Can doubting them with no solid proof damage your relationship with them?

8. Ezekiel struggled with whether he should move back to Strasburg to help his family or remain in New York, where his home and growing business were located. What would you do if you were in a similar situation?

9. What would you do if a homeless person like Maude came and took vegetables out of your garden without asking? Would you be angry or offer to help them?

10. If someone caused vandalism on your property, what would you do? Would you get a watch dog, an alarm system, or call the sheriff? Do you think Belinda did right by not notifying law officials and not wanting anyone outside their immediate family to know about it?

11. Amy's friend Lydia kept a secret from her parents. Is there ever a time when keeping secrets is okay?

12. Did you learn anything new about the Amish way of life by reading this story? If so, what did it teach you? Were there any particular scriptures that spoke to your heart or helped with something you might be going through?

Amish Greenhouse Mystery
Book 2

The
MOCKINGBIRD'S
SONG

Dedication

To prayer warriors and encouragers Andy and Linda Barthol.
Many thanks for all that you do!

Weeping may endure for a night,
but joy cometh in the morning.
Psalm 30:5

Chapter 1

Strasburg, Pennsylvania

With her nose pressed against the cold glass, Sylvia Beiler gazed out the window at the fresh-fallen snow in her mother's backyard. The back of her eyes stung as they followed the outline of objects the light of day cast into the yard.

Sylvia's breathing deepened, and she began to relax as she remembered a previous holiday. She smiled for a moment, thinking about her deceased husband on a night such as this. How wonderful it had been to be with him and the children, sharing the joy the holiday brought them.

And such special times I had here growing up, before starting my new life with the man I loved. How would things be right now if nothing had happened to our precious loved ones?

Sylvia shifted her weight when she heard a familiar sound that echoed of bygone days. Laughter and excited conversation drifted from the living room into the kitchen where she stood, but she felt no merriment on this holiday. This was Sylvia's first Christmas without the three men who'd been so special in her life—her beloved husband, devoted father, and caring brother.

It was hard to understand how the rest of her family could be so cheerful today. Didn't they miss Dad, Toby, and Abe? Didn't they care how much Sylvia still grieved? Why weren't they grieving too?

With a weary sigh, Sylvia turned away from the window and sank into a chair at the table. She had offered to get the coffee going and cut the pies for dessert, but all she really wanted to do was go to her bedroom and have a good cry.

Closing her eyes, Sylvia let her mind drift back to that horrible day eight months ago when Dad, Toby, and Abe had decided to go after ice cream to have with Mom's birthday cake. Dad's horse and buggy had barely left the driveway to pull onto the main road when a truck hit them from behind. All occupants in the buggy, along with the horse, had died, leaving Sylvia without a husband and the job of raising two small children on her own.

She'd been depressed for so long she hardly remembered what it felt like to feel normal and happy. Unable to live in the home she and Toby had shared, Sylvia had moved in with her mother, where her sister, Amy, and brother, Henry, also lived. Each of them had faced challenges since that fateful day, but Amy seemed to be coping better than any of them.

Probably because she and Jared are back together, Sylvia told herself. *She's excited about her wedding next year and seems to enjoy helping Mom in the greenhouse. I can't blame her for that, but today, of all days, my sister should be missing our departed love ones.*

Sylvia's youngest brother still had a chip on his shoulder and had done some rebellious things since the accident. He'd been doing a little better lately, but Henry's rebellious nature and negative attitude had not fully dissipated.

Another thing that bothered Sylvia was Mom's old boyfriend Monroe, and how he'd made a habit of coming by to check on them and asking if there was anything he could do to help out. Monroe had reminded Mom several times that it wasn't good for her and the family to be alone without a man to watch out for them. Monroe always seemed to know when to drop by and would often stay, at Mom's invitation, to eat a meal with the family.

Those times when he waited for Mom to come in from the greenhouse were awkward too. Sylvia always tried to come up with topics of conversation, which had made her feel more uneasy as she wasn't comfortable around people she didn't know well. Each time Mom would come in from work, Monroe seemed eager to please. In Sylvia's opinion, the man was trying to worm his way into their lives. Something about the fellow wasn't right, but she couldn't put her finger on it. As far as she could tell, Monroe seemed to avoid the greenhouse. If anything was to be fixed, it usually pertained to the house or barn. It was obvious to her that Henry wasn't thrilled with the fellow either. He seemed even more irritable and standoffish whenever Monroe came calling. With more time on her hands during the winter months, Mom's routine was random, and she could come and go freely. Sylvia felt sure that was why they'd seen less of Mom's male friend lately. For now, things were nicer around the Kings' place.

Sylvia felt thankful her mother's greenhouse was closed for the winter and wouldn't reopen until early spring. She'd only worked there for the two weeks Mom had been in Clymer, New York, helping their brother, Ezekiel, and his wife, Michelle, when she'd given birth to a son in July. Those days had been difficult for Sylvia, and it was all she could do to conduct business or talk to customers who'd visited the greenhouse. Leaving her children to be cared for by their friend Mary Ruth had also been hard, even though Sylvia felt they were in capable hands. For now, she'd be able to breathe easy and forget about the greenhouse until spring.

Keeping her eyes closed, Sylvia massaged her forehead and then her cheekbones. *My place is here with Allen and Rachel.* Rachel had turned one last week, and Allen would be three in January. They needed a full-time mother, not a babysitter.

Sylvia's mother seemed okay with the arrangement, but things might be different once Amy and Jared were married. After the newlyweds moved into a place of their own, Amy might not work in the greenhouse anymore—especially when children came along.

Henry also helped in the greenhouse, but not in the same capacity as Amy, who waited on customers, kept things well-stocked, and did the books to make sure they remained in the black. Between their place being vandalized, as well as a new greenhouse springing up in the area, there had been some concern about whether they could survive financially. So far, they were making it, but if more destruction to the greenhouse or other areas on their property occurred, it might set them back too far to recover their losses. Since the greenhouse had closed for the winter, there had been no attacks of vandalism. Sylvia could only hope it would stay that way once the business reopened in early spring.

I've got to stop thinking about all of this, she reprimanded herself. *Worrying has never gotten me anywhere.*

"Sylvia, are you all right?"

The soft touch on her shoulder and Mom's gentle voice drew Sylvia's thoughts aside. "*Jah*, I'm fine. Just thinking is all."

"About Toby?"

Sylvia's head moved slowly up and down. "This is our first Christmas without him, Dad, and Abe. I miss them all so much."

Mom pulled out the chair beside Sylvia and sat. "I miss them too, and the rest of our family does as well."

"With all the merriment going on out there in the other room, it doesn't sound like anyone else is missing our loved ones as much as I am today."

Mom gave Sylvia's shoulder a light pat. "That is certainly not true. Everyone deals with their grief in different ways. Also, with this being Christmas, which should be a most joyous occasion, it's a day to be thankful and celebrate."

Sylvia's throat felt so swollen, it nearly closed up. She couldn't say the words out loud, but truth was she was still angry that God had taken her husband, father, and brother. If their heavenly Father loved the world so much that He sent His only Son to earth to die for everyone's sins, couldn't He have prevented the accident that took their loved ones' lives?

"Don't you think your *kinner*, as well as Ezekiel and Michelle's children, deserve a happy Christmas?" Mom spoke quietly, with her mouth close to Sylvia's ear.

All Sylvia could manage was another slow nod.

"All right then, let's get out the pies and try to be happy for the rest of the day. Everyone has moved into the dining room, and they're waiting for dessert."

Mom rose from her chair, and Sylvia followed suit. For her children's sake, she would put a smile on her face and try to enjoy the rest of the day, even if her heart was not in it.

"Who made the pumpkin pies?" Amy's boyfriend, Jared, asked as they all sat around the dining-room table.

"She did." Amy pointed at Mom, and then she gestured to Sylvia.

"My sister and I are responsible for the apple and chocolate cream pies."

Jared smacked his lips. "Since I had a small slice of each one, I can honestly say they're all delicious. Truthfully, though, pumpkin's my favorite."

Amy looked over at him and smiled. "Guess after we're married I'll be making lots of pumpkin pies."

"I look forward to that." Jared grinned back at her, before lifting his coffee mug to his lips.

A stab of envy pierced Sylvia's heart, seeing the happiness on her sister's glowing face. She remembered the joy bubbling in her soul when she'd first realized she had fallen in love with Toby. Their courting days were such happy ones, and being married to him made Sylvia feel complete in every way. She'd been convinced that they were meant to be together and felt sure they would have many years of marital bliss. Sylvia had looked forward to raising a family with Toby and growing old together. How could God have taken her hopes and dreams away?

She looked down at the napkin in her lap and blinked against the tears threatening to spill over. *I've got to quit feeling sorry for myself. It's not doing me or the rest of my family any good. For the sake of everyone at this table, I will try to act cheerful during the remainder of this day.*

Sylvia lifted her head, put a slice of apple pie on her plate, and then passed the chocolate cream pie to Ezekiel. "Here you go, Brother. I know this is one of your favorites."

He gave her a wide grin and nodded. "You bet. Whenever my *fraa* asks what kind of pie I would like, I always pick chocolate cream." Ezekiel's smile grew wider as he looked at his wife.

A tinge of pink spread across Michelle's cheeks. "I do try to keep my husband happy." She poked Ezekiel's stomach. "Especially when it comes to his requests for certain foods."

Ezekiel chuckled. "I'll admit it—I'm spoiled."

Sylvia forced herself to laugh along with most of the people at the table. Her children, as well as Ezekiel and Michelle's daughter, Angela Mary, were focused on eating their pie and wouldn't have understood what was so funny anyhow.

Sylvia glanced at her nephew, Vernon, asleep in the playpen that had been set up across the room. It was hard to believe he was five months old already. The little guy was such a good baby—hardly fussed at all unless his diapers were wet or he'd become hungry.

I wonder if Michelle knows how lucky she is to be married to my brother and able to have more children. Sylvia blotted her lips with the napkin. *Guess I should be grateful for the two kinner I have, because they will never have any more siblings.* The idea of getting married again was so foreign to her that she couldn't wrap her mind around it. No man could ever replace Toby.

Needing to focus on something else, Sylvia's ears perked up when Ezekiel began a conversation with her brother who had recently turned sixteen.

"Say, Henry, I haven't had a chance to ask—how are things going with you these days?"

"Okay, I guess," Henry mumbled around a slice of pumpkin pie.

"Is that crow you showed me when we visited this fall still hanging around the place?"

Henry shook his head. "Haven't seen Charlie since the weather turned cold. Guess he left the area for someplace warmer—probably flew off with a flock of other crows." He tapped his chin. "I have heard of some crows that don't migrate in the winter. Guess my crow wasn't one of 'em though."

Maybe the bird is dead. Someone could have shot him, or he might have died of old age. Sylvia didn't voice her thoughts. No point in upsetting her temperamental brother. Although Henry seemed a bit more subdued now that the greenhouse was closed for the winter, leaving him with fewer chores to do, the chip on his shoulder had not fallen off.

"That's too bad," Ezekiel said. "I was hoping for another look at that noisy bird."

Henry shrugged his shoulders. "It don't matter; I've been watchin' other *veggel* that come into our yard, and I look for them whenever I go for long walks."

"Are you birding?" The question came from Michelle.

"Jah. Watching for different birds and writing down what I notice about them has become a new hobby for me."

Mom's brows lifted high. "Really, Son? Why haven't you mentioned this before?"

"I did. Guess you weren't listening."

"Bird-watching is a great hobby," Jared interjected. "I'd do it myself if I wasn't so busy with my roofing business and some other projects I've been helping my *daed* with."

Henry didn't respond as he poured himself another glass of milk. Sylvia figured he was probably upset because Mom hadn't listened when he'd talked to her about bird-watching before. Sylvia did recall him having mentioned it, and it really was no surprise, what with the interest he'd taken in the crow.

It's good that my brother has found something positive to keep him occupied and out of trouble, she thought. *Being on the lookout for certain birds, and jotting down information about them is a lot better than Henry hanging out with his friend Seth. From what I can tell, that young man has been a bad influence on my impressionable brother. Henry was not like that when Dad and Abe were alive.*

A knock on the front door pulled Sylvia's thoughts aside once more. "Would you like me to see who it is?" Ezekiel looked at Mom.

She gave a quick nod.

Ezekiel rose from his seat and left the room. When he returned a few minutes later, blinking rapidly, he looked at Mom and said, "There's a clean shaven Amish man in the living room who says he came to see you. He even has a gift."

Sylvia clutched her napkin with such force that it tore. *I bet it's Monroe Esh. I wonder what he's doing here. I hope Mom doesn't invite him to join us at the table.*

Chapter 2

Sylvia watched as Mom left the table and headed for the living room. In an effort to be positive, she thought that maybe their visitor wasn't Monroe.

Michelle gave Sylvia's arm a light bump. "When you get the chance, I'd like to have your chocolate cream pie recipe. I believe it might be better than the one I've made before."

"No problem. I'll make sure to do that before you and your family head back to Clymer in a few days."

A few minutes went by, and then Mom returned to the dining room with her old boyfriend at her side.

All smiles, Monroe held a basket of fruit in his hands. "Merry Christmas everyone. I brought a gift that the whole family could enjoy."

Sylvia forced herself to smile and say, "*Danki*, that was kind of you." While the fruit basket was nice, she'd hoped they could slide by this holiday without him coming by.

Amy also greeted him, but Henry merely sat there, fiddling with his fork. He clearly did not care for Monroe and had told Sylvia so several times. She couldn't blame her brother; Mr. Esh had some rather strange ways and was quite opinionated. He was also overbearing and obviously pursuing their mother.

Mom gestured to Ezekiel and Michelle. "Monroe, I'd like you to meet my son Ezekiel and his wife, Michelle. They live in Clymer, New York, but came down to celebrate the holiday with us."

Monroe set the basket of fruit on the floor and extended his hand. "I should have introduced myself when you answered the door, instead of just asking to speak to your *mudder*."

"It's nice to meet you." Ezekiel rose from his seat and clasped Monroe's hand. Michelle did the same.

"Your *mamm* and I were friends during our youth. In fact, I courted her before your daed came into the picture and stole her away." He took a few steps closer to Mom. "Isn't that right, Belinda?"

Her cheeks turned crimson as she nodded. "That was a long time ago, Monroe."

"Seems like yesterday to me." He cleared his throat a couple of times. "'Course, that might be because I never got married or raised a *familye* of my own, the way you did." His gaze traveled around the table. "And what a fine family I see here right now."

I wonder if Monroe's trying to impress us or Mom by his compliment. Sylvia clutched both halves of her napkin. *Well, I, for one, am not impressed. Monroe owns his own furniture store, but maybe he's trying to acquire Mom's business too. He could be what some folks call "an Amish entrepreneur." Who knows? Since Monroe has no wife or family, he might be quite wealthy and could be looking to make even more money. Surely his interest in Mom goes deeper than just reminiscing about how they'd once courted. Monroe knows how much Mom loved Dad, so I wouldn't be surprised if he wasn't looking to marry our mother so he could get his hands on the greenhouse.*

Mom pulled out an empty chair and said, "Monroe, would you like to join us for *pei* and *kaffi*?"

His sappy grin stretched wide. "Why, jah, I surely would. Danki, Belinda."

Sylvia rubbed her forehead. *Oh great. This man's presence at our table is not what we need today—or any other time, for that matter.* She looked over at Amy, who had set her cup down and crossed her arms. *No doubt my sister isn't happy about Monroe being here either.*

Sylvia's gaze went to Ezekiel and then Henry. Neither of them looked the least bit pleased when Monroe took a seat.

"Looks like you have a variety of pies on the table," the man said. "But I don't see any *minsfleesch*. Weren't those included in your Christmas desserts?"

Mom shook her head as she poured coffee into a clean mug and handed it to Monroe. "To be honest, none of my family cares much for mincemeat."

His mouth opened slightly. "Not even you, Belinda?"

"I don't mind it, myself, but it's not one of my favorites." She pointed to the pies on the table. "As you can see, we have apple, pumpkin, and chocolate-cream. Would you care for one of those?"

Monroe hesitated a moment, before pointing at the pumpkin pie sitting closest to him. "Guess I'll have a slice of that."

Mom cut a piece, placed it on a clean plate, and handed it to him. "Enjoy."

Sylvia watched in disgust as he dug into it with an eager expression. She hoped he would leave as soon as he was done eating. The family had plans to play a few games after dessert, and it wouldn't be nearly as much fun if Monroe hung around.

She got up and went over to check on Rachel, who had begun to fuss. After changing the baby's diaper, she went to the bathroom to wash her hands, before returning to the table.

"What do you do for a living, young man?" Monroe's question was directed at Ezekiel.

"I have my own business in New York, making and selling various products for people who raise bees for their honey," Ezekiel replied. "I also have hives and sell my local honey to many people who live in our area. I used to raise bees and sell honey here before my wife and I left Strasburg." He gestured to Henry. "My young brother has taken over that business now."

Henry offered Ezekiel a smile that was obviously forced. "Oh, jah, and it's my favorite thing to do."

Sylvia felt the tension between her brothers as they stared across the table at each other. No doubt Ezekiel heard the sarcasm in Henry's voice. The last thing they needed were harsh words being spoken, especially with Monroe here taking it all in.

In an effort to put a lid on things, Sylvia stood. "How about if those of us who have finished eating take our dishes into the kitchen to be washed?"

"Well, I'm definitely not done eating," Monroe announced. "If no one has any objection, I'd like to try some of that apple pie now."

"We've all had seconds, so I'm sure there would be no objections." Mom reached for the pie pan right away and cut him another piece.

Sylvia groaned inwardly. Was her mother trying to be a polite hostess, or did she fancy Monroe's company? Sylvia hoped that wasn't the case. She couldn't even imagine having Monroe as her stepfather.

"Now don't look so worried." Amy patted Sylvia's arm as they stood in the kitchen getting ready to wash their dessert dishes. She kept her voice lowered and turned to check the doorway. "Mom was only being polite when she invited Monroe to join us for pie and coffee. She has no interest in him whatsoever."

"How can you be so sure?" Sylvia filled the sink with warm soapy water.

"Because she's told me so."

"She has said that to me too, yet whenever the man comes around, she always welcomes him."

"Our mamm welcomes everyone who comes to our door. She's kind and polite, even to people like the homeless woman, Maude, who last summer took things without asking from our garden and helped herself to cookies that had been set out in the greenhouse." Amy nodded. "I've let poor Maude get away with a few things too."

"I wonder how that elderly woman is faring inside that old rundown shack during this cold, snowy weather." Sylvia reached for a sponge and began washing the dessert plates.

"I don't think she's there anymore. Jared and I stopped by the shack last week with some groceries Mom wanted to give Maude, but there was no sign of her—just an empty cot and old table in the middle of the otherwise barren room."

"Maybe she moved out of the area. Or perhaps, if she has any family, she went to spend the winter with them."

Amy picked up the first plate to dry. "I asked her once if she had any family, and she said no."

"I can't imagine how it would be not to have any family at all."

"Me neither," agreed Amy.

"Do you two need some help with the dishes?" Michelle asked, joining them in the kitchen.

"If you don't mind, you can put the dishes away once they've been dried," Amy responded.

"I don't mind at all." Michelle moved closer to the counter near the sink. "Your mamm is keeping an eye on the kinner in the other room, while Monroe plies Ezekiel with more questions about his bee-supply business."

"What are Jared and Henry doing?" Sylvia asked.

"Jared made a few comments here and there, but Henry left the room. Said he was going upstairs to read a magazine."

Amy chuckled. "Leave it up to our teenage brother to make a quick escape. He probably would have done that anyway, even if Monroe hadn't showed up."

"I have a hunch Mr. Esh has taken an interest in your mamm." Michelle put a stack of dry plates into the cupboard.

"Jah," Amy said with regret in her tone. "But I am certain that Mom doesn't want anything but a casual friendship with him. Besides, Dad hasn't even been gone a year, so in my opinion, Monroe shouldn't be trying to worm his way into our mother's life."

Sylvia gave a decisive nod. "Agreed."

When the last dish was done, Sylvia felt the need for some fresh air. "Think I'll slip into my boots and outer apparel and take a little walk outside in the snow. Do either of you care to join me?"

"I'll pass on that idea. I'd like to spend some time with Jared, and by now Mom may have set some games out for us all to play," Amy replied.

"It's too cold outside for me." Michelle rubbed her arms briskly. "Just thinking about going out in the snow makes me feel chilly."

"Okay then, I'll join you in the dining room after I come back inside."

Sylvia went out to the utility room, where everyone in the family kept their boots, along with jackets, sweaters, and shawls. After taking a seat on a folding chair to slip into her boots, she wrapped a heavy shawl around her shoulders, put on a pair of woolen gloves, and went out the back door.

Although it wasn't snowing at the moment, the air was colder than Sylvia expected. Unfazed by it, however, she tromped through the snow, reliving the days when she and her siblings had been children. They'd spent many happy days in this yard, frolicking in the winter snow; jumping through piles of leaves in the fall; flying kites in the field behind their house on windy spring days; and chasing after fireflies on hot, humid summer evenings. Oh, how Sylvia missed those carefree days, when her biggest worry was who would be the first one up to bat whenever they got a game of baseball going.

Will my children have fond childhood memories when they grow up? Sylvia wondered. *When Rachel and Allen are both old enough to be given the freedom to roam around the yard by themselves, will they find things to do that'll leave them with good memories?*

Sylvia worried that not having a father around to help in their upbringing and take them on fun outings might hamper what she'd hoped would be a normal childhood for them. Even if she didn't feel like doing anything just for fun, Sylvia promised herself that she would make every effort to spend quality time with Allen and Rachel in hopes of giving them some joyful memories.

Sylvia continued her trek through the backyard and made her way around to the front of the house. She looked in the window and saw Monroe sitting in Dad's old chair as he chatted with Ezekiel. It was difficult seeing this fellow trying to move in on her family.

I wish Monroe would leave soon. Doesn't he realize he's cutting into our family time? Sylvia tightened her scarf with her gloved hands. *Ezekiel seems to be conducting himself in a pleasant manner with Monroe. But he's a minister now, so I guess he has to be nice and do the right thing with everyone he meets. I hope my sister is right about Mom only wanting to be friends with Monroe and nothing more. I couldn't stand the idea of him moving in and trying to take Dad's place.*

Not quite ready to go back inside yet, she walked down the driveway to check for any messages they may have waiting in the phone shed.

After stepping into the small, cold wooden building, she saw the green light flashing on their answering machine. She took a seat on the icy metal chair and clicked the button.

"Hello, Sylvia, it's Selma. I'm calling to see how you and the children are doing and to wish you a Merry Christmas."

Tears sprang to Sylvia's eyes at the sound of Toby's mother's voice. She hadn't heard from her in-laws in nearly a month and had wondered how they were doing. She'd been meaning to call them, but the busyness of getting ready for Ezekiel and his family's arrival and helping Mom and Amy with holiday baking had taken up much of Sylvia's time. Of course, that was no excuse. Wayne and Selma were Allen and Rachel's paternal grandparents, and they had a right to know how their grandchildren were doing.

After Sylvia listened to the rest of her mother-in-law's message, she dialed the number and left a response, suggesting that they come down from their home in Mifflin County sometime this spring to see the children. Sylvia also mentioned how much Rachel and Allen had grown.

When Sylvia left the phone shed, she glanced across the road and stood staring at the twinkling colored lights draped around their neighbors' front window. They also had a colorful wreath on the front door.

I wonder why so many English folks feel the need to decorate their homes at Christmas. Is it their way of celebrating the birth of Christ, or do they do it because they enjoy looking at the colored lights?

Sylvia hadn't seen much of Virginia and Earl Martin since the weather had turned cold. During the summer, and into the fall, she'd seen Virginia out on her front porch many times. Earl's truck sat parked in the driveway out front, but no other vehicles were in sight. Apparently, the Martins had no company today, or perhaps they had gone somewhere to celebrate Christmas. Since their detached garage was around back, Sylvia had no way of knowing if Virginia's car was there or not.

Sylvia turned back toward the house. *I would have been happier if Mom had asked the Martins to join us for dessert, or even Christmas dinner, then inviting Monroe to sit at our table. If he doesn't leave soon, I may do like Henry and retreat to my room with Allen and Rachel.*

Chapter 3

Virginia's gaze went from her husband, sleeping in his recliner, to the small Christmas tree Earl had bought from a local tree farm three days ago. They'd decided to go smaller than the past years when they had picked out a much larger tree together. For some reason, Earl didn't want a big tree this year. Except for the lights he'd put in the front window at her suggestion, he didn't seem to be in a festive mood.

She flipped her fingers through the ends of her bangs. *But that's okay, since I'm not excited about the holiday this year either. In fact, I feel kinda empty inside.*

A loud snore from Earl brought Virginia out of her thoughts. From where she sat on the couch, her eyes began to water and burn from allergies. She'd dealt with this sometimes when they'd brought a live tree into the house.

She leaned forward and yanked a tissue from the box sitting on the coffee table. *I'm pretty sure that silly little fir is the problem.* It sat on a small table across the room with pretty red-and-green fabric draped around its base. She had decorated the tree with colored lights and hung a few small ornaments from the boughs.

Virginia yawned and massaged her leg where it had started to throb. She shifted on the couch, trying to find a more comfortable position, while Earl continued to sleep like a baby.

In truth, for Virginia, Christmas was nothing special—just another boring holiday, since it was just her and Earl. She bit her bottom lip to keep from crying. *Family. I wish we had some family to share the holiday with and buy gifts for.* She pressed her palms against her cheeks. *Maybe I deserve the empty feeling I have inside. Could be that a woman like me isn't worthy of being happy and fulfilled. No man but Earl has ever really cared about me, and sometimes I'm not even sure how he really feels.*

Virginia closed her eyes, trying to remember if there had been any good Christmases when she was a girl. Maybe a few when her dad was sober. She'd had some fairly decent holidays when her first husband was alive too, but they'd been few and far between. For the most part, Virginia's life had been full of challenges and lots of mistakes.

Pushing her negative thoughts away, Virginia glanced out the front window at her Amish neighbors' house. No colored lights there, that was for sure. It hadn't taken her long to learn that the Plain people didn't celebrate Christmas with flashy decorations on the outside of their homes.

She poked her tongue against the inside of her cheek. *Probably no trees or ornaments of any kind inside the house either.*

Two days ago, Virginia had seen a van pull into the Kings' yard. She'd been curious to see how many people had come to visit, but with the snow blowing she couldn't see well enough to make out much at all. The van had left a short time later, and Virginia didn't know if the people it had brought to the Kings' were still at the house. For all she knew, they'd come and gone already. It wasn't snowing at the moment, though, so she left her seat on the couch and went to peer out the front window.

Earl would call me snoopy if he caught me doing this, Virginia thought as she picked up the pair of binoculars she'd bought him for Christmas. Truth was, the gift was more for her than Earl, since she was home most of the time while he was in Lancaster selling cars at the dealership where he'd been hired earlier this year.

Moving closer to the window, and holding the binoculars up to her face, she saw two Amish buggies parked near the house. *They have company, of course. I think those people get more company than I've had in my entire forty-seven years.*

Virginia spotted an Amish woman step out of the phone shed and walk up to the house. *No doubt one of those King women, either making a phone call or checking for messages.*

She set the field glasses down and went out on the front porch for a breath of fresh air and a better look at the weather. Winter was not her favorite time of the year, but the one good thing about it was that the greenhouse across the road was closed, bringing less traffic noise and smelly horse manure. The sign out by the Kings' driveway even said: CLOSED FOR THE WINTER.

Of course, she reminded herself, *it'll open up again in the spring, and everything that irritates me about living here will start all over.* One thing for sure—Virginia wasn't about to go over there in the spring and buy anymore plants. The tomato plants she'd put in last year had both died; although that wasn't the Kings' fault. If she did decide to grow a garden next year, however, she would get everything she needed from the new greenhouse on the other side of town. At least she could relate to those folks a little better, since they weren't Amish. Virginia had absolutely nothing in common with their neighbors across the road.

A frigid breeze blew under the porch roof, causing Virginia to shiver and rub her arms. *I was stupid for comin' out here without a coat. I need to get back inside where it's warm.*

When Virginia entered the house, she found Earl still asleep, only now his snoring had increased. In fact, the whole room seemed to vibrate with the aggravating rumble.

Irritated, Virginia marched across the room and picked up the remote. When a channel came on to a game show, she cranked up the volume.

A split second later, Earl came awake. "Hey, what's going on? Why's the TV blaring like that, Virginia?"

"Nothing's going on. I figured it was time for you to wake up. Thought I'd slice that pumpkin pie I bought at the local bakery the other day. Would you like a piece, Earl?"

He yawned and stretched his arms over his head. "Yeah, I guess so." He got up and snatched the remote from her hands. "I'll find us something decent to watch while you get the dessert ready."

"Okay, sure. . .since you asked so nice." Virginia limped out of the room. That cold air she'd subjected herself to had not done her bum leg any good. No doubt some arthritis had set in to the area where her old injury had been.

Virginia entered the kitchen and took out the pie, when she heard some Christmas music coming from the living room. She figured Earl must have found some sentimental holiday movie to watch on TV, where everything would come out perfectly in the end. *If only real life was like that.*

"Earl might be satisfied with watching some make-believe story, but not me," she mumbled. *I'm lonely and bored out of my mind living here in the middle of Amish country. Sure wish there was some way I could talk Earl into moving back to Chicago. At least there I had a few friends who seemed to actually care about me.*

Virginia cut the pie and placed two pieces on plates. *Maybe one of these days I'll get a bus ticket and go back to Chicago for a visit with my friend Stella. It would sure beat stickin' around here all the time.*

By eight o'clock, both babies had been fed and put in their cribs, and even Allen and Angela Mary were winding down.

Henry hadn't come down from his room to join the board games being played in the dining room, and Sylvia couldn't blame him. Regrettably, Monroe was still here, sitting beside Mom at the table as they played a game of Uno with Jared, Amy, Ezekiel, and Michelle. Sylvia had played a few hands with them, but as fatigue set in, she'd moved into the living room to read to her son and niece, choosing a storybook written for young children. The pictures with the story helped to hold the youngsters' interest.

By the time she'd reached the last page of the book, Allen had dozed off and Angela Mary's eyes appeared droopy. Sylvia was tempted to let Michelle know that her daughter looked ready for bed, but she didn't want to interrupt the game everyone else seemed to be enjoying. Apparently, they had all accepted Monroe's presence and perhaps even appreciated his company. Either that or they were too caught up in the game to be irritated with the sappy expression on his face whenever he looked at Mom.

I need to quit fretting about this, Sylvia told herself as she picked Allen up and rose from the couch. She would put him to bed and then come back down to say goodnight to the others and let Michelle know that Angela Mary was now lying on the couch.

After Sylvia got Allen tucked into bed, and she'd checked on Rachel, she went across the hall and tapped on Henry's door. Since she saw a shadow of light coming from under the door, she figured her brother probably wasn't asleep.

"Who's there?" Henry called.

"It's me, Sylvia. Is it okay if I come in?"

"Jah, sure."

Sylvia opened the door. When she stepped inside, she found Henry on the bed, propped up with two pillows behind his back. "What are you up to?" she questioned.

"Just doin' some reading." He lifted the magazine in his hands.

"What's it about?" Sylvia hoped it wasn't the car magazine Amy had told her she'd caught him reading a few months ago.

"It's a bird magazine, and there's an article about our area, with a list of interesting facts concernin' the birds we could likely find here."

Even though Henry's room was dimly lit, Sylvia saw excitement on his face. "You're pretty enthused about bird-watching, huh?"

"For sure, and not just the ones that come into our yard. I plan to go into some of the areas mentioned in the magazine and look for certain birds." He set the magazine down and moved over to the side of the bed. "You should come with me sometime, Sylvia. Ya might wanna take up birding too."

Sylvia tugged on one of her apron straps. "It sounds like it could be interesting, and maybe even fun, but not in this cold weather. Just the short walk I took outside a few hours ago nearly chilled me to the bones."

"You could either bundle up with extra clothes or wait till the weather warms up. In the spring there'll be lots more birds to look at anyway."

"I might consider that, but it'll have to be when I can get someone to watch the kinner. Tromping through the woods or some meadow is no place for two little ones, who would no doubt get fussy and scare away the birds."

Henry nodded. "Well, let me know when you're ready to try it, and then we can plan which day we want to go out."

"All right, I will." Sylvia started for the door, but turned back to face him. "You coming back down to join the others?"

He shook his head vigorously. "Nope. Not unless Monroe is gone."

"Sorry, but he's still here, playing Uno with the rest of our family."

"Figures!" Henry crossed his arms and gave a huff. "That man irritates me more than the bees I'm stuck takin' care of."

Sylvia waited to see if Henry would say more, but he only sat with a grim expression, staring straight ahead.

"Monroe's not one of my favorite people, either, but he is a friend of Mom's, so I think we should at least be *manierlich*."

"I was as polite as I could be while we ate our dessert, but watchin' the puppy-dog looks he kept giving our mamm made me feel like I was gonna *kotze*."

Sylvia lifted her gaze to the ceiling. "I think you're exaggerating a bit, Brother. I doubt that you felt like you were going to vomit."

"Did so. My stomach started to curdle, the minute that man came into the dining room. He's after our mamm. Can't ya see that, Sister?"

Sylvia gave a slow nod.

"So what are we gonna do about it?"

"I'm not sure there's anything we can do other than hope Mom doesn't get sucked in by all the compliments and offers of help Monroe shoots her way."

"How about this—I'll ask Ezekiel to put the man in his place, and you can have a little talk with Mom. In case she's not seeing it, she needs to be made aware that Mr. Esh is trying to worm his way into her life."

"I suppose I could bring up the topic to her, but I'll have to do it with care. I don't want Mom to think I'm meddling or trying to control her life."

"Makes sense." Henry rubbed his chin. "Maybe if Ezekiel sets the man straight, that'll be the end of it, and we can go back to the way it was before Monroe started hangin' around."

Sylvia hoped Henry was right, but she had a feeling it might take more than Ezekiel talking to Monroe to get him to back off. What really needed to happen was for Mom to tell the man she wasn't interested in a relationship with him. She'd done it once before, during their youth, and he'd accepted it and left Strasburg. Perhaps if she told him that again, he'd leave the area for good and move on with his life.

Chapter 4

The following morning while Ezekiel helped Henry do chores in the barn, he decided to pose a question that had been on his mind since yesterday. "So Henry, I've been wondering. . .what do you think of Monroe Esh?"

Henry's brows furrowed. "Let's see now. . . Where do I begin? Mr. Esh started comin' by during the latter part of summer, and then it became more often and he stayed longer. He'd wait around to see our mother after she closed up the greenhouse, and poor Sylvia would have to make conversation with him till Mom came up to the house. Sylvia mentioned once that Monroe often commented how there should be a man around here to keep an eye on things." Henry's forehead wrinkled. "He'd chat with Mom and bring up about doin' some work in the barn or around the house."

"Did she let him do either?"

"Nope." Henry leaned forward with one hand on his knee. "I've always thought the fellow seemed pushy, and I don't like the way he looks at Mom with this phony lookin' grin." He paused a few seconds. "I personally think Monroe's a bit odd, not to mention that I'm almost sure he's waitin' for the right opportunity to ask our mamm to marry him." Henry reached down to pet one of the cats that had been rubbing his leg. "I'm glad you brought up the topic, because I was plannin' to talk to you about Monroe this morning."

Ezekiel forked some hay into Mom's horse's stall and leaned on the handle of the pitchfork. "And so you have. Is there anything else you wanted to say?"

"Yeah. I was hopin' you might have a talk with Monroe and let him know that Mom has no interest in getting married again, so he should quit comin' around."

Ezekiel chuckled. "That'd be pretty direct, wouldn't you say?"

Henry's head moved up and down. "That's what Monroe needs, 'cause I don't think he's good at takin' hints."

"Have you talked to Mom about this—asked if she has any feelings for Mr. Esh?"

Henry shook his head. "Sylvia's gonna talk to her though. She doesn't care much for Monroe either, and from what Amy has said to me in the past, she also doesn't appreciate him coming around all the time."

"Neither do I." Ezekiel tossed another clump of hay into the stall. "But I don't feel right about *neimische* either."

"You have every right to meddle. You're the oldest brother, and it's your responsibility to look out for our mamm. It's the least you can do since you're not here anymore to help out with other things."

Oh boy. . .Henry's still upset with me for not moving back here. Ezekiel was taken aback by his brother's harsh tone and pointed stare. He'd thought by now that Henry would have accepted how Mom had said many times that she wanted Ezekiel and his family to remain in New York. In fact, she'd insisted upon it, stating that she could manage the greenhouse with the help of Amy, Henry, and Sylvia—although from what Ezekiel understood, Sylvia helped more with household chores than anything related to the greenhouse.

Ezekiel didn't want to return home without trying to do something helpful, though. He thought it would be good to mention the things Henry had told him about Monroe and get Mom's input as to how he might bridge the gap between him and Henry. *If only my brother would try to understand why my family and I have remained in New York.*

"Listen, Henry, if I thought it was the right thing to do, I'd borrow your horse and buggy right now and head over to Monroe's furniture store for a little chat." Ezekiel paused to sort out his thoughts. "And I'm not saying I won't talk to Monroe, but I think I should speak to Mom about it first, and see how she's feeling in regards to Monroe hanging around. If she's not happy about it, and wants me to intercede, then I'll seek the man out. Otherwise. . ."

Henry shook his head. "Our mamm's too nice to say anything negative about Monroe. Even if she felt the way I do, I doubt she'd ever say it to his face. Someone in our family needs to take the horse by the reins and put Mr. Esh in his place. And if you're not gonna do it, then I will."

Oh boy, I hope Henry isn't serious about confronting Mom's friend. It would only make matters worse and add more stress to the situation.

Ezekiel held up his hand. "Whoa now, Brother, just calm down. Let me have a talk with Mom, and then I'll decide what to do. In the meantime, you need to focus on the chores you're supposed to do out here."

Henry stomped off to the other side of the barn in a huff.

I'd like to approach this situation with wisdom and understanding. Ezekiel closed his eyes and paused to offer up a prayer. *Heavenly Father, please give me the right words when I talk to Mom about Monroe. I don't want to say anything that might upset her.*

🐦

Sylvia had gotten the children up and seen to their needs, although things had been a bit hectic this morning with her littlest one being so fussy. Another tooth was trying to come in, and Sylvia massaged the area, hoping to help it break through. When she'd finally gotten Rachel settled down, she headed for the kitchen but paused outside the door. Taking in some deep calming breaths, she did her best to collect herself. *I hope I don't lose my nerve.*

Sylvia opened the door and stepped into the room. "Mom, if you have a minute, can I talk to you about something?" She wiped her sweaty hands on her apron before crossing the room to her mother, who stood at the counter, cracking eggs into a bowl.

"As you can see, I've already started fixing breakfast, but we can talk while I mix up the *oier*."

"Okay. I'll help with whatever else needs to be done as soon as we have our talk." Sylvia moved closer to her mother and made sure to keep her voice down so no one else in the house would hear. "What I have to say is about Monroe."

"What about him?" Mom began beating the eggs.

"It was a little disconcerting to have him join us yesterday."

"How so?" She kept whisking. "It's not like it's the first time Monroe's dropped by."

"You're right, but he's not part of our family, and in my opinion, he should have spent Christmas Day with his parents and siblings, not with us till way after dark."

When Mom offered no reply, Sylvia continued. "I, along with Henry and Amy, think Monroe is trying to worm his way into your life."

"That makes four of us," Ezekiel announced as he entered the kitchen.

Mom turned with a frown to face him. "Well, you and the rest of your siblings can quit worrying, because there is nothing going on between me and Monroe. He's just an old friend, not a single thing more."

"So you have no interest in him at all?" Ezekiel tipped his head.

"Not romantically." Mom placed her hand against her heart. "The only man I'll ever love is your daed. Plain and simple."

"I'm glad to hear it." Ezekiel flopped into a chair at the table.

"But Monroe is interested in you in a way that goes beyond friendship, Mom," Sylvia interjected. "We all know it. I'm sure you must realize it too."

Her mother nodded. "Jah, it's obvious to me as well."

"Want me to talk to him about it?" Ezekiel asked. "I can do it today or tomorrow, before we head back to New York."

Mom shook her head. "No, I'll take care of the situation. It's my place to let Monroe know that I am still in mourning and have no interest in a personal relationship with him or any other man at this time. If he doesn't back away, I'll let you know, and then you can have a talk with him, via a phone call if necessary."

"Okay." Ezekiel gave a nod. "I won't step in unless you say so."

"Danki." Mom turned back to her job of stirring the eggs.

Sylvia figured it wouldn't be long before her mother had the chance to speak to Monroe. After the warm welcome he'd received yesterday, he would no doubt be dropping by regularly again. She hoped the next time would be the last time he would come by to pay a social call. The fact that he didn't seem to understand, or even care, that Mom was still in mourning, was enough to turn Sylvia off toward Monroe, not to mention his strange behavior at times.

I can't worry about this right now. I need to help Mom get food on the table before the rest of the family comes in for breakfast.

🐦

Amy nearly jumped out of bed when she looked at the clock on her nightstand and realized she'd overslept.

And no wonder, she thought as she pulled the covers aside. *I was dreaming about Jared, and it was our wedding day. We looked so happy, as we stood before the bishop, answering his questions. If only it had been real and not a dream.* Amy wasn't good at waiting for things—especially something she wanted so badly.

Amy stood and plodded across the room. The fall of next year seemed like such a long ways off. She wished she could marry Jared tomorrow, but they needed enough time to plan all of the details that would need to be done for the wedding.

Amy had already chosen the material for her wedding dress. It was a dark burgundy fabric. She hadn't cut out the pattern yet but planned to do so after Ezekiel and his family returned to their home. Since the greenhouse would be closed until sometime in March, Amy had all winter to make the dress. Her excitement about the wedding would probably drive her to get it done as soon as possible, though. Just looking at it hanging inside her closet would give Amy a sense of joy. She loved Jared so much and couldn't wait to become his wife.

Amy reflected on the day she'd broken up with Jared, soon after her father, brother, and brother-in-law had been killed. She'd convinced herself that due to her added responsibilities, there would be no time for courting. Amy had always been one to make sacrifices for others, and this unexpected, tragic situation had been no exception. She'd firmly believed that her responsibility was to help Mom run the greenhouse, which meant giving up her desire to continue a courtship with Jared and eventually agreeing to marry him. It had taken Amy some time to realize she could make the time to spend with Jared, despite her busy work schedule.

Amy hurried to get dressed and put her hair up in a bun. She needed to get downstairs to help with breakfast. She was surprised someone hadn't already rapped on her door to remind her what time it was.

She opened her door a crack and looked up and down the hallway. Although no one was in sight, the wonderful odor of coffee brewing on the stove, mingled with the mouth-watering aroma of sweet sticky buns indicated that their morning meal was in the works. One more reason to hurry downstairs to the kitchen.

Belinda kept her thoughts to herself, but she was a bit miffed that Ezekiel felt the need to intervene on her behalf where Monroe was concerned.

Doesn't my son realize I can speak for myself? Belinda fretted as she heated up the frying pan to cook the scrambled eggs. *Did my oldest son and daughter really think I would be flattered enough to even consider a relationship that went beyond friendship with Monroe or any other man?*

Belinda and her husband Vernon had enjoyed a strong and sure marriage. She'd never loved anyone the way she had him. Her beloved husband was not a man who could easily be replaced, and truthfully, Belinda didn't see herself ever getting married again. Even though Vernon had died, her love for him would always remain strong.

Monroe needs to know that, she told herself. *The next time he comes over here, or if I should see him someplace in town, I'm going to let Monroe know how I feel, so he can clearly comprehend exactly where he stands. I'm sure once he realizes there is no chance for a romantic relationship with me, he will stop coming around. Then my life will go on as it was before he moved back to Strasburg.*

Belinda glanced at Amy and Sylvia, who were now working together to set the table. *My concentration needs to be on my children—helping Amy plan for her wedding; supporting Sylvia in every way I can; and guiding and directing Henry's life so he grows up to be a responsible, Christian man. I also have an obligation to be a good grandmother to my four precious grandchildren.*

Belinda prayed daily for her children and the little ones. Although she fell short at times, she always tried to set a good example. Even Ezekiel, who'd become a minister in his church district, needed her prayers.

Last night before going to bed, Ezekiel had spoken to Belinda about Henry, and the fact that he still harbored bitterness because Ezekiel hadn't moved back to Strasburg.

She closed her eyes briefly and offered a quick prayer. *Lord, help me to keep my focus on You first and then on my dear family. Please guide and direct my life in the days ahead, and give me the wisdom to provide for my children and grandchildren whatever they require—whether it be physical, emotional, or spiritual needs.*

Chapter 5

It had been two days since Ezekiel and his family left Strasburg, and Belinda felt the emptiness in her house, all the way to her bones. When there weren't chores to do, Henry had his nose in some book or magazine about birds. Amy spent every free moment working on her wedding dress and making lists that pertained to her and Jared's special day. Belinda helped with some of those lists, but when it came to her wedding dress, Amy wanted to do it by herself. Allen had come down with a bad cold yesterday, so Sylvia kept busy taking care of him and trying to keep her active little girl out of things.

Belinda felt at loose ends and found herself wishing she could move time forward to spring. She needed to be busy and missed working in the greenhouse. It had kept her mind from dwelling on the huge void in her life since Vernon and Abe had died. Work also helped Belinda not to dwell on the fact that Ezekiel and his family lived so far away and she didn't get to see them often enough.

"I have myself to blame for that, because I insisted that he remain in Clymer, even when he offered to move back here to help out," Belinda whispered as she finished putting their clean dishes from lunch in the cupboard.

She closed the cabinet door, and was about to leave the kitchen, when she heard a horse's whinny outside.

Belinda went to the window and looked out. A horse and buggy she recognized as belonging to Monroe pulled up to the hitching rail. She saw the horse's breath as it stomped at the rail, sending a few hunks of snow into the air.

Henry wandered into the kitchen and opened up one of the cupboard doors. "I heard a horse and carriage come up the driveway. Who's here?"

"Monroe pulled in, and he's getting out of his buggy." Belinda turned away from the window and glanced at her son.

Henry grimaced, while he got out a box of crackers. "Oh great. Not my favorite person," he mumbled. "Why is he here?"

"Probably came to visit." *Or try to sway me into letting him do some work, and then I'll feel obligated to feed Monroe and let him stay around the rest of the evening.*

Henry stepped up next to her and looked out the window. "He's tromping the snow down by his rig, and now he's moving gingerly in this direction. If you need me, I'll be in my room—so you and Mr. Esh can chat with each other without me here to listen and get sickened."

"Henry, I can't believe you said that. I do appreciate you letting me speak to Monroe alone, however." She gave his shoulder a tap. "What I have to say to Mr. Esh is a private matter."

He nodded and hurried from the room.

She moved away from the window and waited for Monroe by the back door. It would be weird for her to tell this man twice in his lifetime that she didn't share the same feelings for him as he did her. Belinda almost felt sorry for putting Monroe through it again, now, years later. But the fact of the matter was she wasn't ready to move on, especially under a timetable of less than a year. *And my children are not ready for that either.*

Having Monroe show up now was the opportunity Belinda had been waiting for, so she would gather up her courage and deal with the uncomfortable situation. Even though she'd been in black dresses since the accident, apparently it hadn't seemed to affect Monroe's way of thinking, because he seemed not to waver at coming by and visiting as usual.

Belinda stood off to one side of the door and listened as heavy footsteps clomped up the stairs and onto the porch. She waited for the knock before opening the door.

"Good afternoon, Belinda. How's your day been going so far?" Monroe greeted her with a cheerful smile and a slight tip of his head.

"So far so good." Belinda opened the door wider and stepped aside. "Won't you come in out of the cold?"

"Of course." He glanced toward the kitchen doorway. "I hope I'm not interrupting your *middaagesse*."

She shook her head. "We ate lunch an hour ago, and I just put away the last of our clean dishes."

Monroe's shoulder drooped a bit, and he made a strange noise in his throat. "Oh, I see."

Belinda figured he'd probably hoped for an invitation to join them for the noon meal. "I'm surprised you're not at work." She pulled out a chair at the table and gestured for him to take a seat.

He removed his hat and jacket before responding. Once seated, Monroe looked up at Belinda and said, "I checked in at the shop to make sure things were running smoothly this morning, and everything was going fine."

"So what brings you by here this afternoon?" she asked.

"Came to see you and make sure you and your family are doing all right." He glanced at the kitchen door, as though expecting someone to walk through it. "Did your oldest son and his family go home?"

"Jah, they left two days ago."

"That's good. I—I meant to say it's good that they could spend *Grischdaag* with you."

She gave a nod. "Our Christmas wouldn't have been the same without them."

"Makes sense. If I had a family like yours, I'd want to spend time with them too." Monroe blinked rapidly as he stared at Belinda. "You're still just as pretty as the day we first met."

She flapped her hand in his direction. "Need I remind you that we knew each other when we were children attending school together?"

"I know very well when we met and need no reminder." His brown eyes seemed to grow even darker as he continued to gaze at her. "You were a pretty girl then, and grew more beautiful when you became a young woman. I envied Vernon when you chose him over me."

Belinda felt the heat of a flush creep across her cheeks and radiate down to her neck. She was not used to receiving such compliments and didn't know quite how to respond.

"Sorry for making you blush. I just wanted you to know how I felt back then. . .and even now. I'd like to think I might have a chance for a future with you, Belinda, and—"

Belinda held up her trembling hand. "Please don't say anything more, Monroe. You must realize that I'm still in mourning." She pointed to her black dress.

"I am well aware, but in four more months, it'll be a year since Vernon's death, and—"

Belinda shook her head determinedly. "While that is true, it won't change the way I feel about my late husband, or about you."

Laying a hand against his chest, Monroe drew a noisy breath. "I understand, and if my coming around so often is a problem, then I'll back off." A slight smile formed on his lips. "I'm a patient man, so I will wait till you're not wearing mourning clothes and feel ready to begin a new relationship."

Belinda pressed her lips together tightly. *Doesn't this man understand? Why is he not getting it?*

She cleared her throat and looked directly at him. "I may never be ready to begin a new relationship, Monroe."

"Then again, after some time's passed, you might change your mind."

This man is relentless. I hope I don't weaken and give in to his influence. "Although anything is possible, it's doubtful that I will ever change my mind, Monroe. I loved my husband very much and still do." She paused to collect her thoughts and make sure her words were spoken correctly. "I hope you understand, but it would be in everyone's best interest if you didn't come around asking about us."

He winced, as though he'd been slapped. "I've only asked about you because I care and am worried about your welfare. And I thought maybe now that Vernon is gone, I might have a chance with you."

"I appreciate your concern, but as I said before—"

"There's no need to say another word. I understand completely." Monroe pushed back his chair and stood. "I won't come around anymore unless I need to buy something from the greenhouse." He hurried from the room so quickly Belinda didn't have a chance to say anything else.

When she heard the back door open and click shut, she lowered her head and closed her eyes. She'd hurt Monroe's feelings and felt bad about that, but it was necessary to let him know where he stood. Unless sometime in the future Belinda changed her mind, she would never have a relationship with Monroe Esh. From some of the things he had said, it almost seemed as if he'd been waiting for Vernon to die.

She pulled her fingers into her palms. *Oh, surely that couldn't be possible. No decent man would wait for a woman in hopes that her husband would pass away.*

"Did we have company?" Sylvia asked when she entered the kitchen a few minutes later. "I heard a horse and buggy pull into the yard, and then you speaking to Henry briefly. After that, I thought I heard you talking to someone else in here."

Belinda turned to face her daughter. "It was Monroe."

Sylvia frowned. "What did he want this time?"

"Said he came by to see how we were doing, and he seemed disappointed that we'd already eaten lunch."

Sylvia's gaze lifted upward. "That's not such a surprise. Whenever he comes around it's usually close to mealtime."

"Well, he won't be coming here again unless it's to buy something from the greenhouse."

"Oh?"

Belinda pointed to a chair at the table. "Have a seat and I'll tell you about it."

Sylvia did as asked, and Belinda sat in the chair beside her. She quickly went over everything that had transpired while Monroe was there. "I think I hurt his feelings, though."

Sylvia leaned close and gave Belinda a hug. "You did the right thing, Mom. I'm glad he took it so well and agreed to back off."

"I'm not really sure that he did take it well, but at least I finally got up the courage to speak my mind. By inviting Monroe to join us for meals and such, it probably seemed to him that I was interested in a personal relationship that could eventually lead to marriage." Belinda sighed. "There's a fine line between being courteous to people, and showing them so much kindness that they take advantage or expect something of you in return. I think that's what happened where Monroe was concerned. My being friendly and nice made him believe that he might have a future with me. And the fact that he'd mentioned that in four more months it'll be a year since your daed's death made me even more eager to put a stop to his pursuing me."

"I can't imagine you being married to someone other than Dad. It wouldn't seem right for another man to move in here and take over the role of your husband."

Belinda gave a nod. "I love your daed very much, and always will."

"I understand, because that's the way I feel about Toby. No one could ever take his place in my heart."

"I understand, Daughter. I wholeheartedly understand."

"What a lousy day I've had," Virginia mumbled. She'd decided to make something new for supper, and it was taking longer than she'd anticipated. *Earl won't be happy if he comes home and there's nothing ready to eat.*

The lamb roast she'd bought yesterday wasn't a tender cut, so she'd chopped it into smaller chunks to hurry it up. The microwave had been acting funny, so Virginia had put the baking potatoes in the oven, but they still weren't ready to serve.

Virginia walked from the kitchen out to the living room. Looking at the front door, she stepped out onto the porch for some fresh air. She saw Amy come out of the house and get into an Amish buggy. The man with her looked familiar. *Hey, isn't that the fellow who reroofed our garage?* Virginia stared intently. *Yep, I think it is him.*

Virginia had met Jared when he'd come over to give them an estimate and had spoken to him again during the roofing process. He seemed like a nice young man, although she still wasn't too sure about the Amish people in general. In fact, when she had first seen Jared's horse and buggy parked in her and Earl's driveway, she'd nearly freaked, hoping the beast didn't do his business right there on the concrete. Virginia had felt sorry for the horse in a way. The poor animal having to work like it did, hauling people and work supplies around every day, seemed like animal abuse.

But then what do I really know about horses? she mused. Virginia had heard it said that horses, like mules, were beasts of burden and didn't mind the hard work of pulling a wagon or carriage.

I just don't get the whole Plain life those Amish people live. Yet they seem content with it. Shaking her head, Virginia moved away from the porch railing and went back into the house. After checking the potatoes and seeing that they still weren't done, she picked up her cell phone and called Earl. She wanted to catch him before he headed home from work.

Virginia punched in her husband's number and a few seconds later, he answered. "What's up, Virginia?"

"Well, the meal I thought would be good tonight isn't cooking so well, and it's taking longer than I expected."

"Don't worry about it. I'll pick up some take-out when I'm done here, which should be soon."

"Oh, that would be nice, because the oven isn't heating up well, and I'm sure that our microwave is completely shot."

"That's a bummer. Appliances don't last like they used to, and it may mean we'll have to buy a new microwave, or even another oven. I'll take a look at both when I get home. Gotta go for now, though. See you soon, Virginia."

"Okay, bye." She clicked off the phone and took a seat at the table. It didn't seem like Earl was upset, and for that, she was relieved. It never ceased to amaze Virginia how calm and understanding her husband could be.

Since Earl would be bringing take-out home, there was no point in having the oven on. She turned it off, took the still-undercooked potatoes out of the oven and threw them in the garbage. By tomorrow evening, she'd hopefully have a new microwave, and then she could at least heat up something for them to eat.

Chapter 6

Sylvia stood in the barn beside her horse, Sugar, wondering if she would ever work up the courage to take the mare out by herself. After Toby's death, Sylvia had sold his horse to her neighbors, Enos and Sharon Zook, who also kept an eye on her place. Henry had brought her horse over to Mom's place, where she'd been put in the barn. In the nine months Toby had been gone, Sylvia hadn't taken the horse out even once. Henry kept Sugar exercised and often took her on the road to run errands or make deliveries. Since he had no horse of his own and complained about Mom's horse being too slow, the arrangement for him to use Sylvia's mare had worked out well so far.

The thought of taking her horse and buggy out on the road by herself sent shivers of apprehension up Sylvia's spine. Although their family members' deaths hadn't been the fault of her father's horse, the reality was that a horse and buggy couldn't compete with the power of a truck or any other motorized vehicle. One never knew what a vehicle on the road might do. Sylvia's sister could attest to that. While riding in Jared's carriage this past fall, a car driven by a teenage boy had spooked the horse, which could have ended in disaster. Fortunately, Jared had managed to get his horse under control before an accident occurred.

Sylvia gave Sugar's flanks a gentle pat. "I'm sorry if it seems like I've abandoned you."

The horse's ears flicked as if she was listening.

"Maybe someday, if I ever get over my fear of a potential accident, I'll take you for a ride somewhere."

"Let's do it now."

Sylvia whirled around at the sound of her sister's voice. "*Ach*, you startled me."

"Sorry, I wasn't trying to sneak up on you. I figured you would hear the barn door open and close."

Sylvia shook her head. "I didn't hear you come in at all."

Amy put her hand against the small of Sylvia's back. "If you want to go somewhere with the horse and buggy, I'll ride along to help bolster your confidence."

Sylvia clutched her woolen shawl tightly around her neck. "I'd like to go over to my house and check on things, but I don't have the nerve to be the one in control of my *gaul*. When I first came out here to the barn, I thought maybe I could do it, but I didn't get Sugar any farther than taking her out of the stall and putting on her bridles before I realized that I'm definitely not ready." She paused to draw in a quick breath. "Even though Mom said she would watch the kinner while I was gone, I think I'll wait till Henry gets back from Seth's and see if he's willing to go over to the house with me. Of course, he will have to drive my horse."

"I can be in the driver's seat, and I'm more than willing to go over to the house with you."

"But I thought you were working on wedding plans this morning."

"I was, but I didn't plan to work on my lists all day." Amy glanced toward the front windows of the barn. "Since the snow we had at Christmas is almost gone, now's the perfect time to make the two-mile trip to your place. With this being the third week in January, you never know what kind of weather awaits us, so we need to take advantage of the nice day we're having."

"You're right, and we're likely to get a lot more snow before winter is over."

"That's true, so I'll hitch Sugar to your buggy, and you can go up to the house and let Mom know we'll be gone for a couple of hours."

"Okay, I'll grab some cardboard boxes from the utility room, in case there are some things I want to bring back with me."

"Sounds good. See you in a bit."

As Sylvia headed back to the house, a sense of thankfulness filled her soul. Amy had been supportive of her since Toby, Dad, and Abe had died. She was definitely a lot stronger emotionally than Sylvia. Her sister hadn't lost faith in God either.

What will I do without my dear sister after she gets married? Sylvia's throat constricted. *Amy might not have much time for me once she and Jared are married, and she may not even be able to work in the greenhouse anymore.*

Clymer, New York

"Have you talked to your mamm or any of your siblings lately?" Michelle asked when Ezekiel came into the house to get the lunchbox he'd left on the counter after heading out to his shop earlier that morning.

"Just a short message from Mom, which I found on the answering machine last evening. Sorry, I forget to mention it."

"That's okay. You were busy with paperwork for your business, and that was important."

"I was kinda busy, but I should have thought to tell you about her message."

"Did she say how things have been going for them lately?"

"Just said everyone was fine, and that most of their snow had melted." Ezekiel poured himself a cup of coffee, blew on it, and took a cautious drink. "She also mentioned that a group of young people would be coming to their house this Friday evening to roast hot dogs and marshmallows around the fire-pit."

"That sounds like fun. I wish we could join them."

Ezekiel couldn't miss the wistful expression on his wife's face as she stood near the kitchen sink, with her back facing the window. Was it the idea of sitting around a bonfire she longed for, or the pleasure of spending time with his family in Strasburg? He was about to ask, when Michelle posed another question.

"Did your mamm say anything about Monroe? Has he been back to see her after she made it clear that she has no interest in him romantically?"

Ezekiel shook his head. "She didn't mention Monroe at all, but if he had been coming around, I'm sure she would have mentioned it. I was pleased when Mom called us the day after she'd let him know where he stood." Ezekiel took another drink from his mug. "That gave me one less thing to worry about."

"Jah, me too. I hate to say this, but I have to wonder if Mr. Esh has more on his mind than a romantic interest in your mother."

Ezekiel tipped his head to one side. "What other kind of interest?"

"A financial one. He might want the greenhouse for himself."

"You could be right, I suppose, but if I have anything to say about it, that's never going to happen."

Michelle pushed a wisp of auburn hair back under her heart-shaped head covering. "Since your mother put Monroe in his place, I don't think we have to worry about him anymore."

"I hope not." Ezekiel pursed his lips. "From the moment I met that man, I had an uneasy feeling about him."

Michelle came over and kissed his cheek. "You're such a *schmaert* man."

He pulled Michelle into his arms and held her close. "I don't know how smart I am about other things, but I was schmaert enough to talk you into marrying me."

She tipped her head back and looked up at him. "You didn't have to talk me into anything. Besides, I was the schmaert one for saying yes to becoming your fraa."

Strasburg

When Sylvia opened the front door to her house and stepped inside, she dropped the cardboard boxes on the floor in the hallway. As she entered the living room, memories overwhelmed her like water from a broken dam. In spite of her efforts to stay calm, tears started flowing. "Oh Sister. . ." She gulped on a sob. "It's so hard for me to be here anymore."

"It's okay. Let the cleansing tears fall." Amy led Sylvia over to the couch, and they both took a seat.

"I. . .I'm sorry for being such a big bawling baby." Sylvia took a tissue from the end table beside the couch and wiped her nose. "It's just so hard being here in the home I shared with Toby and knowing I'll never have that kind of happiness again."

Amy clasped Sylvia's hand. "I understand how coming here must make you feel sad. Have you considered selling the place and staying with Mom permanently?"

Sylvia scooted back against the couch and rested her head. "I have given it some consideration, but the idea of letting the house go to strangers doesn't sit well with me."

"Maybe you could find a suitable renter. Have you thought of that as an option?"

"No, not really, but it might be a possibility." Sylvia blotted the tears from her cheeks with another tissue. "My biggest concern with renting the house would be who might want to rent it. I've heard terrible stories about people renting homes and leaving the owner with a big mess when they moved out. Some folks don't pay their rent on time or at all. So it might be a bigger challenge to become a landlord than to just sell the house and be done with it."

"I understand. My advice is to pray about the situation and ask God to help you decide what the best course of action would be."

Sylvia gave no response as she massaged the bridge of her nose. The truth was, she saw little help in praying. Even after so many months had passed since the accident that took their loved ones, her faith in God had not been restored, and she doubted it ever would be strong again. There was a time when she did have faith, and believed in miracles, but it seemed so long ago.

She glanced around the room at all the familiar furniture. "What would I do with all these things if I did sell the house?"

"You might be able to take a few things over to Mom's, and maybe Jared and I could buy some pieces of your furniture and other items to put in our new home."

Sylvia blinked rapidly. "Now there's a thought."

"You mean about us buying some of your things?"

"No, I mean what if you and Jared bought my house, or even rented it from me? Nothing's been decided about where you will live yet, right?"

"Well, no, but. . ." Amy's voice trailed off, and then she picked up her sentence again. "Wouldn't it be difficult for you to come over here and visit? You said a few minutes ago that it was hard for you to be here anymore. I would feel bad if you didn't want to come over to my place to see me, and if we had a family function here you would not be left out."

Sylvia leaned forward with her arms against her knees. "I—I hadn't considered any of that. You're right, Amy, it would be most difficult for me to come to the home that had been mine and Toby's and see you and Jared living here happily together. It would be a reminder of how much I have lost." Sylvia rubbed her forehead. "Am I being *eegesinnisch* to think this way?"

Amy gave Sylvia's back several light pats and made slow circles with her fingers in a gentle rub. "You're not being selfish at all. Only you know what you can and cannot deal with. Besides, since Jared and I will be just starting out, we can't really afford to buy a home yet. We'll most likely look for something inexpensive to rent."

"Which could be my place, if I wasn't so emotional about being in this house."

"Don't worry about it, Sister. Even if you were willing to rent your home to us, our wedding's over seven months from now, and you'd have to continue to leave the house unattended all that time." Amy continued to rub Sylvia's back until she sat up.

"I'll give this some more thought. Maybe I'll end up selling the place and be free of all the memories that haunt me. Right now, let's get busy and gather up all of the things I want to take back with me today. I don't want to be here any longer than necessary."

🐦

"Let's go outside and get some fresh air." Belinda bundled her grandkids, as well as herself, in warm attire. Allen and Rachel seemed eager to head out with Grandma as their voices raised a couple of octaves.

Once outdoors, the sun provided some warmth. They walked around the yard where snow had concentrated in more of the shaded areas. Allen's boots crunched in the snow as he made his way over to the frozen birdbath. He touched the solid water and slid his gloved fingers across the surface. "Look, *Grossmammi*—I'm skating."

"You sure are." Belinda smiled as she pulled Rachel across the yard on the wooden sled Sylvia had used as a child. *I wonder how my daughter is doing right now. She gets so emotional whenever she returns to the home she and Toby shared.*

Belinda was well aware that Sylvia still struggled with the past, but she tried her best to raise the children with love and tender care.

She stopped pulling the sled and bowed her head. *Lord, please keep mending Sylvia's heart and allow her to find peace and joy in her life again.*

Belinda's eyes opened and she looked at her precious grandchildren, so innocent, and with no knowledge of the inner struggles their mother faced on a daily basis. *I must keep hoping and praying that each member of my family will heal a little, day by day. The Lord has provided for our needs, despite each one of the setbacks and the vandalism on our property. Even so, I will continue to trust Him in the days ahead and not give in to despair.*

Chapter 7

"Being here this evening and sitting around the bonfire talking and singing is so much fun. Danki for inviting me and Rudy to join you." Amy's friend Lydia spoke with excitement as the two of them carried hot dogs and buns from the house to the area where the fire had been started by Jared and the other young men present.

Amy smiled. "I'm glad you could both come. It wouldn't have been the same without you." She leaned closer to Lydia. "I'm real happy that you agreed to be one of my witnesses at Jared's and my wedding."

"I'm looking forward to it. Now I have a question. Will you be one of my witnesses?"

Amy's fingers touched her parted lips. "Are you and Rudy planning to be married?"

"Jah, but not till November."

Amy clasped her friend's hand. "That's *wunderbaar*, Lydia. Congratulations, and jah, I would be honored to be one of your witnesses."

"Thank you. We're very excited about it, and even more so since both sets of our parents have given us their blessing."

"When your folks approve of the man you want to marry, that does make it much easier for everyone."

"For sure." Lydia placed the packages of buns on the picnic table near the fire. "I bet your mamm approved of Jared from the beginning of your courtship."

"Jah and so did my daed." Amy drew a breath and released it slowly. "It makes me sad when I think about not having him at our wedding."

"It is a shame, but if he was here, I'm sure he'd approve and be happy for you."

"I agree." Amy placed the hot dogs next to the ketchup and mustard that had already been brought out. "I invited Sylvia to join us this evening, but she seemed hesitant and made up some excuse about not wanting to leave the kinner."

"Wouldn't your mamm watch Allen and Rachel?"

"Of course she would, and Sylvia knows it, but I believe she's unwilling to allow herself the freedom to have a little fun."

"How come?"

"Because she hasn't let go of the anger and emotional pain she's felt since Toby, Dad, and Abe died. Sometimes I think my sister wallows in her self-pity, hoping to somehow drown out the pain."

"That's too bad. I'll remember to pray more often for her."

"Danki. Sylvia, like the rest of us, needs a lot of prayer."

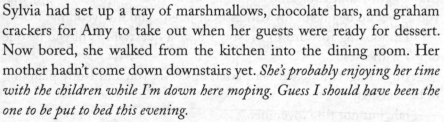

Sylvia had set up a tray of marshmallows, chocolate bars, and graham crackers for Amy to take out when her guests were ready for dessert. Now bored, she walked from the kitchen into the dining room. Her mother hadn't come down downstairs yet. *She's probably enjoying her time with the children while I'm down here moping. Guess I should have been the one to be put to bed this evening.*

Muffled sounds of conversation and laughter could be heard from the goings-on outside, while Sylvia remained alone with her thoughts. *It seems like only days ago when that was me outside with all my friends. Toby and I were courting and so happy together. I remember the bonfire and how the glow from it made my beloved's eyes sparkle.*

Sylvia placed both hands against her chest. *Toby captured my heart from the first moment we met, and the more time I spent with him, the more I knew he was the only one for me.* She expelled a lingering sigh. *We made so many good memories at gatherings like the one going on outside. Those were precious times of bonding with our friends and each other.*

Sylvia's eyes watered, obscuring her vision for a moment. Knowing what she did now, Sylvia wouldn't have changed a thing. She felt blessed to have had those special times with Toby during their courting days and after they were married. The sweet children upstairs were also a blessing to her. Sylvia had no regrets about becoming a mother. Her only regret was that Allen and Rachel had no father to help nurture and guide them into adulthood.

She continued to wander around the room barefooted, until boisterous laughter caught her attention. Sylvia paused at the dining-room window, watching the glow of the bonfire outside. Amy and her friends seemed to be having so much fun. She felt a stab of envy. Her carefree, fun-loving days were behind her. Other than spending time with her children and sometimes laughing at their cute antics, Sylvia had little to feel joyous about. In a few months, it would be time to put her black mourning clothes aside, but her heart would still long for what she had lost.

Sylvia's mother came into the room and joined her at the window. "Looks like they're having a good time out there."

"Jah. It would seem so."

"The kinner are in bed, sleeping soundly now, so why don't you join your sister and her friends?"

Sylvia shook her head. "Henry was invited and he declined."

"That's only because he was invited to spend the night at his friend Seth's place tonight."

"Well, I'm not going out there. I wouldn't fit in."

"Of course you would. You're not that much older than those who have come here tonight."

"I'm a widow, and those four couples are all courting, Mom. Surely you must understand how displaced I would feel, sitting among them and trying to join their conversation."

"No more than I would, but Amy invited me to join their gathering also."

"Then by all means, you should put on some warm clothes and go outside. I need to stay here where I can hear Allen and Rachel if they should wake up and need me." Sylvia turned away from the window. "Think I'll go back to the living room and look at the book Henry loaned me on bird-watching. I might learn something new about the birds found in this area."

Mom's eyes widened. "I didn't realize you were interested in birding."

"I'm not really, but Henry's so fascinated with it, and he seemed to want to share his interest with me, so I thought I'd at least look at the book. Maybe when the weather warms up a bit, I might sit outside more and study the birds that come into our yard. Henry sure enjoys doing that. I've seen him sitting in the loft of the barn, looking out the open doors, usually with a pair of binoculars in his hands."

Mom shook her head. "I don't like him sitting up there. If he gets too close to the edge, it could be dangerous for him."

Sylvia figured it was time for a change of topic. Lately Mom had been a bit overprotective, and not just of Henry. She worried more and voiced her opinion about things Amy, Sylvia, and the children did too. Hopefully when Mom got busy in the greenhouse again, things would go back to the way they were and her concentration would revert to other things.

Virginia hurried to get the wonderful cut of meat she'd cooked on the table. She'd followed the instructions to the letter and felt sure it would be nice and tender. She placed their dishes on the table and poured brewed tea over ice in the glasses.

When Virginia carried the carved meat to the table and brought out the vegetables cooked in beef broth, her mouth watered. The rolls came last, steaming underneath the foil covering them.

Once everything was on the table, she stepped into the hallway and stopped at the mirror to fluff up her hair. Then she checked the new lipstick she'd put on earlier. "Earl, it's time eat."

"I'm coming, dear. The meal smells tasty, and you look nice too." He chuckled. "I saw you primping in the mirror."

Virginia grinned as she followed her husband to the table. As soon as they took their seats, she passed him the roast. Her mouth watered once again as she dished up her food.

Earl smiled as he loaded his plate and took a first bite. "This is a pretty good pot roast you fixed this evening." He smiled at Virginia from across the table. "You did a good job with supper."

She grinned right back at him. "I'm glad you like it, but I can't take all the credit. If you hadn't bought a new oven and microwave, nothing but the stovetop would cook well in this kitchen."

"I really had no choice, since I didn't want to get take-out every night." He wiggled his dark brows at her.

She rolled her eyes. "It figures all you'd be thinkin' about is satisfying your stomach."

"I think of lots of other things too."

"Like what?"

"My job and making my quota of cars sold every month."

"That's important all right; or else we wouldn't have money to buy food and pay the bills." She ate some of her microwave-baked potatoes and blotted her lips with a napkin. "Do you want me to look for a job so there's not so much pressure on you to provide for us? I could see if one of the stores in the area might be hiring."

Earl shook his head. "With the trouble you have with your leg, you'd never last eight, six, or even four hours of having to stand on your feet."

"I could look for a sit-down job, although I don't know what it could be."

"There's no need for that. I've been providing for us since we got married, and I will continue to do so."

"You're such a nice man—always thinking of me."

"That's 'cause I love you, Ginny."

"I love you too, but please don't call me Ginny. My first husband used to call me that, but I've always preferred to be called Virginia."

"Okay, got it."

Virginia didn't want any reminders of her past or the man she had come to despise. She'd never admitted it to anyone or even said it out loud, but she'd been relieved when her first husband died.

"Sure is a nice evening for a bonfire." Earl's comment pulled Virginia's thoughts aside.

"Huh? What does a bonfire have to do with anything?"

"When I arrived home from work and got out of my truck, I noticed there was a bonfire going across the street. Figured it must be some kind of a young people's gathering at the Kings' place."

She wrinkled her nose. "More horse droppings in the road, no doubt."

"That could be a good thing. If I go out there and shovel it up, we'll have more manure for our compost pile."

She pressed her hands against her ears. "This is not good table talk."

"You brought it up, not me."

Virginia shrugged and let her hands fall into her lap. "Guess I did. From now on, I'll have to be more careful how I choose my words."

Gratz, Pennsylvania

Dennis Weaver sat in the barn, with a gas lantern above him, staring at his father's empty horse stall. It was unbelievable to think that the horse had died the same day as his dad.

Dennis, now thirty-one, had loved being around horses since he was a young boy. He had a special way with them too. With a little patience and time well spent, he could get most horses to do pretty much anything he wanted. While Dennis wasn't what some would call a "horse whisperer," he had an understanding of them, which led to respect and obedience on the horses' part.

In time, when many of the Plain people in his community saw what he could do with his own family's horses, they began to offer him payment to train their horses to pull their buggies. By the age of sixteen, after Dennis finished his eighth-grade education, he trained horses part-time when he wasn't helping his dad on the farm. As more people moved into the area, his business picked up. Unfortunately, there weren't enough Amish in the area to provide Dennis with a fulltime income. Even after his dad passed away and his brother, Gerald, took over the farm, Dennis helped out.

His greatest wish was to not only train horses fulltime, but raise them as well. Dennis was convinced, however, that he'd have to move to an area where there were more people in need of his type of services if he wanted his business to succeed. So he'd asked around and decided that Lancaster County would be a good place to move. There was really nothing keeping him here. He had no wife or children—just his mother and four siblings, who were all married and had families of their own.

Dennis felt secure in the knowledge that if he moved away, Mom would be cared for. She'd have his brother and three sisters, as well as ten grandchildren to fuss over and spend time with. Soon after Dad died, Gerald had built a *daadihaus* for Mom, and then he and his family moved into the larger home that used to be their parents'.

Dennis moved from the empty stall over to where his own horse was kept. "How's it goin' today, Midnight? Are ya ready for me to extinguish the lantern?"

Midnight whinnied as if in response, and then the gentle gelding nuzzled Dennis's hand with his nose.

He grinned and rubbed the horse behind his ears.

Dennis stood by the stall door for a few minutes, contemplating his future. He'd grown up in Dauphin County but was more than ready for a change. *Maybe the Lancaster area would be a good place for me to relocate.*

Dennis knew only a few people in Lancaster County. He had a friend he'd gone to school with who lived in Ronks now.

Maybe I'll contact James and see if I can stay with him for a few weeks, until I find a place of my own or a house I can rent. It would need to have enough property where I could train horses and hopefully raise a few of my own.

Although Dennis had saved up some money over the years, he didn't have enough to pay cash for a home and didn't want to go into debt. Renting a place would be a better choice for now.

Think I'll give James a call in the morning and see what he says about my idea to relocate to Lancaster County. If he thinks it would be a good move for me and offers to let me stay there for a while, I'll pack up my things and make the move by early spring.

Dennis turned off the lamp overhead and strolled out of the barn, letting the flashlight he now held be his guide back to the house. He paused and stared up at the twinkling stars overhead. *I have no idea what the future holds for me, but anything would be better than staying here with all the haunting memories from the past that are never far from my mind.*

Chapter 8

Strasburg

This is one of my favorite recipes. Sylvia spread the crust batter for Cherry Melt Away Bars into a 9" x 13" inch pan. Picking up a quart of cherry pie filling Mom had bought at the store recently, she poured it on top. Normally, when the pie cherries in Mom's yard ripened, Sylvia and Amy helped to make the filling and processed it all in canning jars. But due to losing their loved ones in the spring and the busyness that followed, they hadn't done anything with the fruit. So the whole tree had been a happy place for the robins that came into their yard. Hopefully, this year things would go better in that regard and they'd have plenty of home-canned cherry pie filling to use in special desserts.

As Sylvia beat the eggs whites with cream of tartar, she glanced at her children sitting on a throw rug across the room playing with some pots and pans as though they were drums. In times past, this kind of noise would have given Sylvia a headache, but today she wasn't bothered by the pounding. It was nice to see Allen and Rachel, who were only two and a half years apart, getting along well with each other.

Once the egg whites were stiff enough, she gradually beat in some sugar and vanilla, then spread it over the filling she'd previously put on top of the crust. Before sprinkling chopped walnuts over the top, Sylvia paused to look out the kitchen window. One of her guilty pleasures was walnuts, of which she grabbed a handful to munch on. While pausing to enjoy the crunchy texture and hearty flavor, she saw Mom heading in the direction of the greenhouse and Amy going down the driveway toward the phone shed. They both walked with a spring in their step, with arms swinging at their sides. No doubt they felt the exhilaration of the lovely weather that had greeted them on this twenty-first day of March. From the way Mom and Amy had talked during breakfast, they looked forward to opening the greenhouse today.

Better them than me, Sylvia thought as she sprinkled the nuts and opened the oven door. *If I had to work in the greenhouse today, I'd be on edge and thinking the whole time about how my precious little ones were getting along with whomever I had hired to watch them.*

Sylvia closed up the bag of walnuts and put it away. Then she tossed the empty cherry pie can in the garbage and began cleaning up the mess she'd made on the counter. When she glanced out the window again, she saw what looked like a mockingbird sitting on a branch in the maple tree. Its feathers appeared to be gray.

Curious, she left the kitchen and found the bird book on the coffee table in the living room. Sylvia thumbed through the index for mockingbirds, eager to know whether the bird she'd seen was what she believed it to be.

She found the correct page and noticed some different colored pictures of mockingbirds. One in particular caught her attention. It looked similar to what she'd seen in the tree, although she couldn't be sure and would wait to talk to Henry about it.

When Mom and Amy get done for the day, maybe I'll ask one of them if they'd be willing to keep an eye on the kinner while I take a walk to look for birds. Sylvia placed the book back on the coffee table. *If Henry's not busy this afternoon, maybe he'll want to get out his binoculars and join me. That would be better, especially since he knows more about birding than I do right now.*

Excitement bubbled in Belinda's soul as she placed the Open sign on the front door of the greenhouse. *I hope we have another good year.*

She hardly got much sleep last night, with her mind busy thinking about everything that needed to be done. She always had a nervous stomach on opening day. It reminded her in some ways of the first day of school. Belinda knew the feeling would wear off soon enough, and she'd be as good as rain again. What a relief to have winter behind them and be able to do the work she enjoyed so much.

Of course, she had spent some time out here during the colder months, tending to seedlings in pots and making sure the heat in the building remained at an even temperature. Plants and trees also needed watering, but not as often as they did during the warmer months.

Belinda looked forward to their first customers of the day, and she hoped they would stay busy until closing time.

She glanced at the small clock sitting on a shelf under the checkout counter, wondering what was taking Amy so long. She'd gone to the phone shed to check for messages and said she'd come to the greenhouse as soon as she was done. Either there had been a lot of messages that needed to be responded to, or Amy had taken the time to see if their mail might have come early.

It didn't really matter if Amy wasn't here at the moment, since there weren't any customers yet. Henry was still in the barn feeding the animals, but he should be here soon too, and then Belinda would have plenty of help.

While she waited, Belinda walked up and down the aisles, making sure everything was placed appropriately so customers would have no problem finding whatever they'd come in to buy. The shelves full of seed packets had been fully stocked; jars of honey and jam sat ready for purchase; bulbs that needed to be planted in the spring had a place of their own; and all the solar lights, fountains, and outdoor items were positioned so people would see them as soon as they walked through the door. When the weather got warmer, they would move the outdoor items, now in the greenhouse, to a special area outside.

When Jared had no roofing jobs to do this winter, he'd made a small shed with double doors that housed many gift items Sylvia and Amy had made. Even Henry had gotten into the act by painting some horseshoes for people to hang up as decorations. It amazed Belinda what things the tourists would buy because they'd been made by the Amish. At least, that's what she'd heard many people say.

An image of Monroe popped into her head. She wondered if he would come by to purchase something and ask how they were doing. Belinda wasn't ready to deal with him. Monroe could be so pushy, and he didn't take hints too well. Regardless, she'd have to walk that path when and if it happened. For now, she needed to concentrate on running the greenhouse in an orderly fashion.

Once Belinda was certain that everything was ready for customers, she returned to the checkout counter and took a seat on the wooden stool. While she waited for Henry and Amy to show up, she would make a list of some things she hoped to get done in the greenhouse this week, in addition to getting caught up on some chores in her home.

Ronks, Pennsylvania

Dennis grinned at his friend James from across the table. "Your fraa sure makes some tasty *pannekuche*."

James nodded as he forked a piece into his mouth. "You're right about that. Alice's pancakes are the best. You can tell her how much you liked them when she comes back to the kitchen after feeding the *boppli*."

"I will." Dennis gestured to the newspaper beside his plate. He'd been looking through the ad section to see if there were any homes in the Strasburg area that he could rent. He'd found a few, but none of them had the large property he needed. He could probably move into a smaller house for now and then offer horse training to people in the area, but he'd have to go to their property to do it. If he went that route, the idea of raising his own horses would have to be put on hold.

"Would it be okay if I used one of your horse and buggies for a while today, since mine haven't arrived yet?"

"Sure, no problem. I'll be working in my shop all day. I have lots of orders for windows and doors, so I won't need my gaul or the *waegli*."

"Danki, I appreciate that." Dennis picked up the newspaper. "Think I'll take this with me today so I can drive by some of the places listed. Afterward, I may do a bit of bird-watching. It'll be interesting to see which birds are common here compared to what I've seen up in Dauphin County."

"Maybe they're pretty much the same," James responded. "Strasburg is only a few hours from Gratz, you know."

"True, but the lay of the land is different. Some of the birds I saw up there may be scarce down here, and visa-versa."

"Well, you know more than I do about it." James pushed his chair away from the table. "I'd best be getting out to work in my shop. If I don't see you till suppertime, I hope you have a successful day."

"I hope your day goes well too." Dennis smiled up at his friend. "Once again, I appreciate you letting me stay here temporarily. With any luck, it won't be much longer and I'll be out on my own."

Strasburg

After checking for mail, and finding none, Amy went to the phone shed and took a seat. *What was that I saw moving there in the shadow near my feet? I hope it isn't a* maus.

Amy froze inside the small cubical, until her eyes honed in on what she'd seen. *It's not a mouse—only a toad. I can deal with that.* She chuckled and shooed the little fellow out the door.

The green button on the answering machine blinked rapidly, letting her know there were messages. The first one was from Brad Fuller, sharing good news. Sara had given birth to a nine pound baby boy yesterday morning. The infant had been over a week late, and mother and son were both doing well. They'd named their child, Herschel Clarence, after Sara and Brad's fathers.

Amy smiled. She was happy for the Fullers and looked forward to having children of her own someday. She would call and leave a message of congratulations, and maybe some evening in the next week or so, they could hire a driver to take them to Lancaster so they could see the new baby.

Amy listened to a few more messages from people checking to see what day and time the greenhouse would be opening. She was pleased that folks seemed eager to have the greenhouse up and running for business again.

The last message, although a bit garbled, caused Amy to take a sharp intake of breath. "You need to sell out and move, before it's too late."

Amy replayed it several more times to be sure she'd heard the words correctly. Each time she listened, it became clearer that someone wanted them gone.

She sat several moments, feeling rooted to her chair. *Who is this person who wants to shut our business down, even to the point of saying we should move?*

Once Amy gained control of her emotions well enough to stand on her shaky legs, she flung the door open and ran all the way to the greenhouse. She found Mom inside, sitting behind the counter, but there was no sign of Henry.

"Daughter, your face is whiter than snow." Mom's brows drew together. "Is something wrong?"

Amy hesitated. *I don't want to add more worry to Mom's already full plate. There's been enough to deal with so far, but she has a right to know.*

Making no mention of the message from Brad, Amy told her mother about the threatening call.

Mom gasped and covered her mouth with both hands.

"Don't you think we ought to let the sheriff know about this?" Up to this point, Mom had refused to divulge the previous incidents to anyone but their immediate family—excluding Ezekiel. She'd remained insistent that he should know nothing about the vandalism, for if he knew, he'd insist on moving back to Strasburg.

Mom removed her hands and spoke to Amy in a strained voice. "Tell them what? We have no idea who left that message, so there's no evidence for anyone at the sheriff's office to go on."

Amy shifted her weight from one foot to the other. "Even so. . ."

Mom leaned forward, lowered her head into the palms of her hands, and massaged her forehead. "When the vandalism stopped last fall, I thought it was all behind us. Now with the phone threat we received, I fear more destruction to our property will follow, and I—I don't know what we should do."

"Pray. We need to do a lot of praying," Amy responded.

"Jah, for sure." Mom clasped Amy's arm. "Let's not say anything to Henry or Sylvia about the threatening message you discovered."

"How come?"

"You know your *bruder*—he tends to blab things when he should keep quiet." Mom shifted on her stool. "And Sylvia would be troubled if she knew about the message. There's no point in telling either of them because they—especially Sylvia—would only worry." She rubbed her arms briskly, as though she'd been hit by a sudden chill. "And for sure, we don't want Ezekiel to know about the phone call we received. You know how he'd respond to that."

"He'd be ready to sell out and move back to Strasburg."

"Exactly. So, unless I change my mind about telling anyone, mum's the word. Understood?"

Amy gave a slow nod. "I understand."

Chapter 9

Tossing another old T-shirt into the bag she held, Virginia scratched her head. Ever since she and Earl had moved here, she'd wanted to go through the closet and discard some of her older clothes but hadn't taken the time.

She slid a few tops off their hangers. *I'd like to go out and do some shopping. Even living in this small community, a gal needs to look presentable.*

Virginia continued to fill the sack and stopped when a dress from the past came into view. "Oh, now, this needs to go. I can't believe it's even still in the mix." She held up the dowdy, navy-blue dress. She'd worn it during her first marriage, and seeing it now was a negative reminder of the past.

"Goodbye." She stuffed the dress deeply into the bag. "Think I'll quit with this one." All the clothes needed to go to the local thrift shop, but Virginia would wait until she'd gone through everything first.

Growing hungry, she stowed the bag in a corner of the closet, closed the door, and made her way to the kitchen. She'd been on her feet too long and should have sat on the bed to do her sorting.

In the kitchen, Virginia opened the refrigerator to see what she might fix for supper this evening, when her cell phone rang. She closed the door and limped across the room to pick up the phone.

Virginia recognized the number and quickly answered. "Hey, Stella. How's it going?"

"Everything's fine here. How about you?"

"Same as usual. Nothing exciting, that's for sure." Virginia reached down to rub her throbbing knee. "Unless you call listening to the steady *clippity-clop* of horses' hooves exciting."

"Still getting lots of horse-and-buggy traffic on your road, huh?"

"Yeah, and now that the greenhouse across the road is open for business again, the noise will only increase. There have been cars, trucks, and of course, smelly horses pulling Amish buggies going past our house today."

"Guess there's never a dull moment."

"Yeah, and sometimes I think I'm goin' out of my mind."

"Say, I've been thinking it's about time that I come to Pennsylvania and pay you a visit. Would it work out for you, or are you too busy with other things?"

Virginia snorted. "Not hardly. Most of my days are spent watching game shows on TV and working crossword puzzles, although yesterday I washed all the windows, inside and out. And today I started sorting through old clothes." She groaned "Big mistake, and I'm paying for it now."

"Your bum leg?"

"Yep." Virginia pulled out a chair at the table and sat. "Most evenings are just as boring. After supper, it's watching television or working crossword puzzles again, while I listen to Earl snoring up a storm from his easy chair. So feel free to come anytime. It'll be a welcome change for me."

"How about a week from next Monday? Since your hubby will be at work during the days, maybe he won't mind an extra person in the house."

Virginia perked right up. "Sounds great, Stella. How long can you stay?"

"Maybe three days, if that's okay. Sure don't want to wear out my welcome."

"Not a chance. I'll look forward to seeing you."

"As you know, there's a meadow on the other side of our neighbor's property, and it's a good place to spot birds," Henry said as he and Sylvia walked along the shoulder of the road. "So let's head over that way first."

"Okay, but I don't want to go too far or be gone too long, because I need to be back in time to help fix supper," Sylvia replied.

"Didn't ya hear what Mom said before we left? She and Amy are gonna take care of fixin' supper this evening, and we'll eat a little later than usual."

"I did hear that, but I would feel guilty if I wasn't there to help."

"You oughta get over that, Sister, because you have the right to have a little fun once in a while."

Sylvia wasn't sure how much fun this little trek would be, but she offered no response to her brother's comment.

As they neared the clearing, Henry pointed to an Amish man holding a pair of binoculars up to his face. "Looks like someone else had the same idea as us, and I'm pretty sure he must've spotted some kind of interesting bird on the branch of that bush over there." He lifted his own binoculars and took a look. "Yep, I was right. There's an eastern kingbird." He handed the field glasses to Sylvia and pointed. "Here, take a look. It's a gray-black bird with a white belly and chin."

She looked in the direction he'd pointed, but all she saw in her vision was the Amish man's straw hat, sitting atop a full head of dark hair.

Sylvia lowered her hands and handed the binoculars back to Henry. "I didn't see any sign of the bird." She made no mention of the Amish man's head.

"It's right there." Henry stood next to her and held the lenses in front of her eyes. "Do ya see it now?"

She shook her head.

"Oh, for goodness' sakes. Are ya lookin' where I pointed?"

"I thought I was."

"Then ya must be completely blind." He puffed out his cheeks and groaned.

"Don't speak to me like that," she snapped. "I am not blind, and I'm not stupid."

"Never said you were."

"The way you spoke to me, in that disgusted tone of voice, made it seem like you thought I was *dumm*."

"Well, I don't think you're dumb. I just can't understand why you're not able to see the kingbird."

"I'll try again." Sylvia held the binoculars close to her face.

"Don't bother. The bird's gone now anyways. Let's walk into the meadow a ways farther and see what other birds we can find."

"Okay." Sylvia was glad she'd worn a pair of sturdy shoes and her long black stockings.

As they approached the middle of the open field, the Amish man turned in their direction. "I thought I was alone till I heard voices." He glanced at Henry's binoculars. "Are you two bird-watchers, like me?"

Henry bobbed his head. "Don't recall seeing you around here before. Are you new to the area?"

"Jah. I've only been here a few days." He held out his hand. "My name's Dennis Weaver. I moved down a few days ago from Gratz." The man glanced at Sylvia, then back at Henry.

Henry clasped the man's hand. "Nice to meet you. My name is Henry King, and this is my sister Sylvia."

Dennis shook Sylvia's hand too. "Do you two come here often?"

Sylvia was about to respond, but Henry cut her off. "I've been here looking for birds, but this is my sister's first time. She's new to birding."

"I see." Dennis looked at Sylvia again, and this time he smiled.

Her cheeks warmed as she lowered her head a bit.

"So where are you staying?" Henry asked. "Do you own a place here in Strasburg? Did you bring your family here?"

"Henry, don't be so nosey." Sylvia bumped her brother's arm.

"It's okay. I don't mind." Dennis kept his attention on Henry now. "My mother and siblings live in Dauphin County, and I'm single, so I moved down here by myself. I'm currently staying with a friend in Ronks, but I have been looking for a place to rent that has some acreage with it."

"I own a home you might be interested in," Sylvia blurted out. "Maybe you'd like to look at it sometime." Her face grew warm. *Now what made me say that?*

With an eager expression, Dennis nodded. "That'd be great. How about tomorrow morning? Would that be too soon?"

"Umm. . .well. . ." Sylvia realized that she'd have to drive her horse and buggy over to her house if she agreed to meet him there in the morning, and she'd need someone to watch the children while she was gone or bring them along, which would make it difficult to show the house.

"If it's going to be a problem, I understand."

"No, it's not a problem. Tomorrow morning won't work for me, but I could meet you at the house around five-thirty tomorrow evening."

"That'll be fine."

"If you have a pen and something for me to write on, I'll give you the address and also the phone number where I can be reached, in case you have to cancel for some reason."

"I have something to write with, but no paper." Dennis pulled a pen from the pocket of his dark-colored trousers. "I'll just write it here on my arm."

Sylvia bit back a chuckle. She'd never seen anyone use their arm instead of paper. When she could speak without laughing, she gave him the information, and he wrote it down on the inside of his left arm.

"We really should get going now." Sylvia looked at Henry.

"Jah, okay. Guess we'll have to do more bird-watching another day." He looked at Dennis. "It was nice meeting you, Mr. Weaver."

"Nice meeting you too." Dennis returned his gaze to Sylvia. "I'll look forward to seeing you tomorrow."

All Sylvia could manage was a quick nod. She had no idea why she'd offered to let a total stranger look at her house with the idea of possibly renting it. *I don't know what came over me. I must be daft in the head.*

On the way home, Henry remained quiet for a while, before slowing his pace and clasping Sylvia's arm. "What were you thinking, agreeing to show that man your house? He's a complete stranger, and we know nothin' about him except where he's from."

"He seemed nice enough. I saw a kindness in his eyes. If he likes the place, I'm going to rent it to him."

"Why?"

"Because I can't keep expecting my neighbors to watch the place, and I'm never moving back there, so it doesn't make sense to let it sit empty any longer. Next month it'll be a year since the accident, Henry."

"I don't need that reminder."

"Sorry, but it's a fact, and I need to find some closure."

Henry kicked at a stone with his boot. "Don't see how rentin' your house is gonna give you any closure."

"For one thing, I won't have to go over there anymore or worry about whether someone might break in and take things."

"I get that part, but havin' someone living in your house is not gonna bring an end to your grief."

"I realize that, but having someone living in the house will give me a sense of peace."

"So you're set on doin' this, assuming Mr. Weaver likes the place and wants to rent it?"

"Jah."

Henry shook his head. "Oh boy. Our mamm's not gonna like it when she hears what your plans are."

"Please don't say anything to her, Henry. I'm the one who should tell her, since I'll need to ask if she or Amy can watch the kinner for me tomorrow." She stopped walking and reached over to touch his arm. "I do have one favor to ask."

"What's that?"

"Would you mind taking me over to my house tomorrow to meet Mr. Weaver? I wouldn't feel right about meeting him there alone. Besides, as you know I'm not comfortable taking the horse and buggy out by myself."

He lifted his shoulders in a brief shrug. "Sure, why not? If Mom knows I'll be goin' along, she's less likely to make a big deal of it."

"My thoughts exactly." Sylvia tapped his shoulder. "Oh, and Henry, before I forget... danki for going with me today to look for birds. It was an interesting adventure."

"Well, we only found one specific bird, but sure, no problem. Besides, the other day you told me about the gray bird you'd seen. I'd hoped we'd both get to see it today, and I could be sure it was a mockingbird. So anytime you wanna go birding again, just let me know."

She gave a nod. "I definitely will, and hopefully there's another pair of field glasses around the house for me to use when we do go out again."

As Dennis traveled back to his friend's place in Ronks, he tried to figure out if the young woman he'd met was married or single. There'd been no mention of a husband, but it seemed odd that she would own a place to rent out. Maybe some relative, like a grandparent, had died and left Sylvia their home and land, and rather than selling it or moving there herself, she'd chosen to rent it out.

There were so many questions Dennis wished he had asked, and maybe he would when he met up with Sylvia at her house tomorrow.

While Henry ran out to the barn to make sure his dog was fed, Sylvia hurried into the house. She found her mother and sister in the kitchen scurrying about, and the table had already been set.

"You're back sooner than we expected," Mom said. "Didn't you and Henry find any interesting birds?"

"Just one that's worth mentioning. Although I never actually saw it. Henry spotted the bird through the binoculars, but for some reason, I could not locate it. All I saw through the field glasses was an Amish man's straw hat."

Amy stopped what she was doing and turned to look at Sylvia. "Was the hat on the ground?"

"No, the man was wearing it." Sylvia glanced around the room, and when she didn't see Rachel or Allen, she said, "Where are the kinner? I figured with supper being made, they'd both be in the kitchen wanting to play with pots and pans."

"They're in the living room, playing quite nicely," Mom replied. "Now what were you saying about an Amish man's hat?"

Sylvia explained about meeting Dennis Weaver, and how she'd offered to let him look at her house as a possible renter.

Mom's eyes widened as she folded her arms across her chest. "You did what?"

"I said he could look at the house, and I was hoping to do it tomorrow after the greenhouse closes for the day, because I need one of you, if you're willing, to watch the kinner for me again."

"I'm always willing to spend time with my grandchildren, but don't you think you're rushing things a bit? I mean, what do you really know about this man?"

"Well, nothing, but he had kind eyes and was very polite, so. . ."

"It's not like you to be so trusting of a stranger," Amy cut in. "And how are you planning to get over to your house? Are you going to walk, or ride your scooter?"

Sylvia shook her head. "Henry said he'd take me with the horse and carriage, so since he'll be there when I show Mr. Weaver the house, that should give you both one less thing to worry about."

Chapter 10

I wonder what's up with Sylvia. Why would she jump right into something without giving it a good amount of thought? Belinda fidgeted with her apron straps. *Her father and I didn't raise our children to make such rash decisions. Oh Vernon, if only you were here to offer your opinion on this.*

She rested a hand on her waist as she studied Sylvia's body language. "Are you certain you're doing the right thing by showing your home to the stranger you met yesterday?" Belinda asked when Sylvia got ready to head out with Henry that evening.

"I am quite certain, Mom. I have to rent out the house, and Mr. Weaver needs a place to stay."

I'll do a little more pressing to make sure she's thinking this through. "But you don't know much about him," Belinda argued. "And you haven't even run an ad or notified others that your place is available to rent."

"I don't need to now, since I've already found someone." Sylvia grabbed her handbag and opened the back door. "Henry's waiting outside with the horse and buggy, so I'd better go. I hope the kinner are good for you and Amy while I'm gone."

"I'm sure they will be fine. Oh, and don't forget. . ." Belinda's words were cut off when her daughter went out the door. "Well, thanks for listening," she mumbled with a huff. "I think my daughter is acting headstrong and foolish."

Belinda moved to the kitchen window and watched as Sylvia got into the buggy. A few seconds later, she heard footsteps coming up the porch steps and figured it must be Amy.

"I don't know what's come over your sister lately," Belinda said when

Amy entered the room. "She seems to have lost all sense of good reason."

"Because she's thinking of renting her house to a man none of us knows?"

"Jah. I definitely dislike the way that sounds. It's not like Sylvia to speak to strangers, much less make such an unexpected offer." Belinda released a heavy sigh. "I wish your sister hadn't run into that fellow when she and Henry were out bird-watching."

"Perhaps we are worrying too much about nothing." Amy spoke in a soft tone. "Maybe when she meets the man at her house, he will have changed his mind. Or he might not show up at all."

"Guess I can hope for that." Belinda tapped her chin. "Having a renter you don't know at all could mean nothing but *druwwel*. And believe me, we've got enough troubles already to keep us busy and on our toes."

Amy nodded. "Speaking of trouble. . . Have you told Sylvia or Henry about the threatening message I heard on our answering machine yesterday?"

"No, and I'm not planning to." Belinda looked directly at Amy. "I hope you erased that horrible message."

"I did, Mom, but by erasing it, the evidence that it happened is now gone."

Belinda tapped her foot. "And that's how it should be—gone and forgotten."

"Forgotten? How can we forget something like that? It was the creepiest message ever left on our machine. Gives me the shivers just thinking about it."

"I have to agree with you, Amy. Whoever it was needs help." Belinda paused. "You and I need to get past this though, and we can if we try not to think about it."

"What if it happens again?"

"Then we'll pray a little harder and ask God to convict the person responsible for the call." Belinda slipped her arm around Amy's shoulders. "That's all we really can do, Daughter."

I hope Mom can understand me better and see how much this means, even if I have acted spontaneously. I'm trying to heal, and so far, the decision I

made is making me feel like I've taken control of something that needs to be done. Sylvia watched her brother, who seemed so comfortable driving the horse and buggy. *At least he appears to be in my corner, and that'll help me be able to see this through.*

When Henry guided Sylvia's horse and buggy into her yard a short time later, she saw another horse and carriage waiting at the hitching rail. Dennis Weaver sat on a wooden bench on her front porch.

She grabbed her purse. Mr. Weaver being here already waiting for them was a good sign that he truly was interested in seeing the place.

As soon as Henry pulled up to the rail, Sylvia got out of the buggy and headed for the house. "Have you been waiting long, Mr. Weaver—I mean, Dennis?"

"Nope. Got here about five minutes ago." He stood and gave her hand a warm, firm handshake. "From what I've seen outside so far, it looks like you have a nice place here."

"Danki." Sylvia put her key in the door and opened it. "Let's go inside, and I'll show you around."

Shortly after Sylvia and Dennis entered the living room, Henry came into the house. "What do you think so far, Dennis?" he asked. "It's a nice place, jah?"

Sylvia wished she could give her brother's arm a poke, but he wasn't standing close enough to do so. "Let's allow him to make his own decision, okay, Brother?"

"Jah, sure." Henry pulled off his straw hat and tossed it by the door.

"I'm liking what I see so far." Dennis lifted his own hat, revealing a good amount of thick brown hair. "This room has a comfortable appeal. Looks like a nice place for relaxing at the end of the day."

Sylvia's mind flashed back to some of the evenings she and Toby had spent in their living room. She'd always felt comfortable when they relaxed here together, but now, being anywhere in this house made her scalp prickle.

"It's an older home, with creaky floorboards and drafty rooms, but it could be quite nice if some of the rooms, like the kitchen, were updated a bit."

"Looks okay to me just the way it is." Dennis leaned against the back of the sofa. "Will any of the *hausrod* be left in the home, or would I need to provide my own furniture?"

"I'm planning to remove all my personal items, but most of the furniture will stay here."

"I see."

"Would you like to look at the rest of the house now?"

"Sure thing."

"All right then, please follow me." Sylvia looked at Henry to see if he wanted to join them, but he waved her on and flopped onto the couch.

After Sylvia gave Dennis the complete tour, including the four bedrooms, attic, and basement, they went outside to look at the barn and all the property that went with the house.

"The *scheier* is plenty adequate for horses," Dennis commented.

"Jah, there are four stalls in the barn, which was more than I needed."

When they left the building Sylvia showed him the pasture. "Ten acres comes with this house."

"Sounds good. Have you decided how much you'll be asking for the rent?"

She stated the amount, and he nodded. "Sounds reasonable."

"When my husband was alive, he fenced in the pasture, but we only had two horses, so they had all the room they needed to roam around."

Dennis's head jerked back slightly. "Oh, I didn't realize you were a widow, but then I should have guessed, since you're wearing all black. I'm sorry for your loss, Sylvia."

Before she could form a response, Henry spoke up. "Sylvia's husband, along with our dad and brother, were killed in an accident last spring." He dropped his gaze to the ground. "It was a tragedy that none of us was prepared for."

Dennis's brows pulled down. "That's sad. I extend my condolences to both of you."

Sylvia swallowed hard, hoping she wouldn't break down in front of this near stranger. "I've been living with my mother and two siblings since the accident, and it's been a difficult transition."

"I can imagine how it must have affected your whole family, because. . ." Dennis paused and pulled his fingers down the sides of his cheeks. "Umm. . . This is not something I normally talk about—especially with people I barely know, but I think I should share it with you."

Sylvia tipped her head. Dennis looked so serious. "What is it you wish to say?"

"I lost my daed in a hunting accident. We'd gone deer hunting with my uncle, and it ended in tragedy when Uncle Ben accidently shot Dad. I saw the whole thing happen, and I couldn't do a thing about it."

Sylvia gasped, and Henry stood with his mouth gaping open.

"I'm so sorry for your loss." Those were the only words she could think to offer.

"Life is hard, and there are usually no explanations that make us feel better about the hardships we must face on this earth. We just have to figure out the best way to get through them." Dennis looked at Henry, then back at Sylvia. "Were your family members riding in a carriage when their accident happened?"

Sylvia nodded.

Henry explained the details of the accident, while Sylvia tried to keep her composure. It was always hard to talk about the sorrowful event, and the look of sympathy on Dennis's face didn't make it any easier. One thing was certain: he understood the way she felt.

Will the pain of losing our precious family members ever end? Sylvia asked herself. *Will I always carry a deep ache in my heart?*

Dennis leaned on a fence post as he stared out at the pasture. "Yep, the more I look at this area the more I feel that it would work out well for training horses."

"That's good to hear."

"How soon would it be before I could move in?"

"Probably by the beginning of next week. I'll need some time to clear out all my personal items, along with any furnishings I don't want to part with that will fit in my mamm's house. Would that be soon enough, Mr. Weaver?"

"That should work out fine. And please, call me Dennis."

"Right. I'll try to remember." Sylvia reached up to make sure her head covering had not become crooked from the wind that recently picked up. "One more thing. How many beds will you need?"

"Three would be nice. One would be for me, of course, and the others for any of my family who might come down from Dauphin County to visit."

"That should work out fine then, since I'm staying at my mamm's place, where there are enough beds."

Henry interrupted their conversation when he pointed to a tree on the right side of the pasture. "Look. . .there's a male cowbird! See its glossy black feathers and chocolate-brown head? If there were feeders out in your yard, Sylvia, I bet he'd come right to them."

Sylvia and Dennis both looked in the direction Henry pointed. At least she was able to see the bird without the aid of binoculars.

"It's a member of the blackbird family," Dennis commented. "It reminds me of a female red-winged blackbird." He looked at Henry. "Did you know at one time cowbirds followed bison to feed on insects that were attracted to those immense animals?"

"Didn't know that. How interesting." Henry leaned forward with one hand on his knee. "I like finding out new information about the *veggel* here in this state."

Dennis gave him a thumbs-up.

Sylvia couldn't help but notice the enthusiasm in her brother's voice. Bird-watching, which began for Henry last year when he started feeding the crow in their yard, was definitely a good hobby for him.

When the bird flew out of the tree and across the road, Dennis turned to face Sylvia. "May I go ahead and write a check for the first month's rent now?"

"It would be better if you wait until I get everything out of the house that I want, and I will also need to clean the place real good."

He flapped his hand. "Don't worry about that. I can clean it myself before I move in."

Sylvia shook her head vigorously. No way would she allow him to move into the house without her cleaning it first. "If you will give me a phone number where you can be reached, I'll call as soon as the place is ready. Then I'll schedule a time to meet you over here with a key and you can pay for the first month's rent at that time."

Dennis smiled and held out his hand to shake hers. "Agreed."

When Sylvia and Henry arrived home, Mom met them at the door. "I'm glad you're back. Supper's ready and we need to hurry and eat, because our driver will be here at seven-thirty."

Sylvia touched the base of her neck. "Why do we have a driver coming? Did something happen that I should know about? Has someone been hurt?"

"Yeah, Mom," Henry questioned. "What's going on?"

"We're going over to the Fullers to see their new boppli. Don't you remember that I mentioned it this morning?"

Sylvia shook her head. "I was aware that Sara had had her baby, but I didn't realize any plans had been made for us to go visit them this evening."

Mom looked at Henry. "Do you remember me mentioning it, Son?"

"Yeah, but I thought it was tomorrow night that we'd be going."

Their mother sighed. "I'm beginning to think no one listens to me anymore. I got better response from my kinner when they were growing up than I do now."

Sylvia looked at Henry and shrugged her shoulders, then followed Mom into the kitchen where Amy waited near the stove. Allen was seated at the table on his booster seat, and Rachel sat in her wooden high chair.

"Mammi," Allen said.

"Mammi," Rachel repeated, clapping her chubby hands.

Sylvia bent to kiss the tops of their heads. "I hope you were both good for Grossmammi and *Aendi* Amy while I was gone."

"They were sweet as cotton candy." Amy smiled and came over to tweak Allen's nose.

He giggled. Rachel did too, even though her nose hadn't been tweaked.

"How did it go over at your house with Mr. Weaver?" Mom asked after she put a loaf of bread on the table.

Sylvia figured they were having sandwiches for supper, because a tray had been piled high with lunch meat and three kinds of cheeses. "It went fine," she replied. "He liked the house, barn, and the amount of land that comes with it. As soon as I get the rest of my personal things out and have cleaned the house from top to bottom, he'll move in."

Mom pursed her lips, but she didn't say a word. Sylvia hoped she'd thought it over and had come around to accept her hasty decision. But even if her mother didn't approve of the idea, Sylvia wouldn't change her mind. She'd made an agreement with Dennis, and she would not go back on her word. Despite what Mom, or anyone else thought, in Sylvia's heart, she felt that she'd made the right decision.

Chapter 11

Ronks

"I have some *gut nei-ichkeede* to share with you," Dennis said when he arrived back at his friend's house and found James in the barn, cleaning his horse's hooves.

"What's the good news?" James looked up at Dennis with a curious expression.

"I'm gonna be renting the place I told you about."

"From the woman you met when you were out birding?"

"Jah." Dennis leaned against the horse's stall. "I should be out of your hair in about a week."

"No problem. Is the place furnished?"

"Yeah, but Sylvia said she might take a few pieces of furniture. There will still be enough stuff for me to use without having to buy anything, though."

"That's good. How about the property? Is there enough land for you to train horses?"

"Yep. Ten acres comes with the place. I could raise horses there if I decide to go in that direction."

"Sounds like things are working out for you then."

"It would seem so, but only time will tell." Dennis lifted his shoulders briefly, and then let them fall. "Also found out she's a widow, and she doesn't want to sell the house."

James set the tool he'd been using aside and straightened. "Is she planning to move back there sometime in the future?"

"Not from the sound of it, but then, one never knows. Hopefully if she does, she'll give me plenty of advance notice. Sure wouldn't want to buy any horses and then find out I was gonna have to find someplace else to relocate them."

"Well, you know the old saying: Take one day at a time."

Dennis gave a nod. He knew that saying all too well, because ever since his dad passed away, the only way he could survive emotionally was to take one day at a time.

Lancaster, Pennsylvania

Sylvia was surprised to see their driver Polly pull up in a smaller van than she usually drove. She got out, went around, and opened up the sliding door in the back. "Hello, Sylvia," Polly said in her usual robust voice. "It's nice to see you and the children, but where's the rest of your family?

Sylvia smiled as she walked to the van with Rachel and Allen. "They should be out soon. How's it going?"

"Pretty well. My mother is at one of her bingo games, and Dad's out fishing." Polly gestured to the van. "My larger rig is in the shop getting work done, but this one is big enough to haul your family this evening."

"You're right. There should be plenty of room."

"Your children are sure cute. Seems like they've grown since the last time I saw them."

"Yes, and the proof is that I had to let the hem down on two pairs of Allen's trousers the other day."

Mom, Amy, and Henry came out of the house, while Sylvia put the children in the back of the van and fastened them into their safety seats.

"Hello, Polly." Mom and Amy greeted her with a smile, but Henry said nothing. It appeared that he wasn't too thrilled about going on this trip to Lancaster. No doubt he'd rather spend the evening with Seth or one of his other friends.

Mom chose to sit in the back with Allen and Rachel, while Amy sat in the seat in front of them, next to Sylvia.

"Now where are we headed?" Polly asked as she climbed into the driver's seat.

"Hang on a minute. This doesn't want to clip in." Mom struggled with her seatbelt until it finally fastened. "We'll be heading over to Brad and Sara Fuller's place. Sylvia has the address."

Sylvia reached into her purse and handed the slip of paper to Polly, as Henry, still quiet, got in and took the passenger's seat up front.

"Thanks," Polly said. "I have to take care of a few errands for myself and my mom. How long do you think you'll be there visiting?"

"I'm not sure," Mom replied, "but I'll call your cell number when we're ready to be picked up."

"Okay, sounds good."

As they headed in the direction of Lancaster, Sylvia eyed the farms along the way while listening to Mom chatting to the children. The closer they got to their destination, the farther away Sylvia wanted to be. It would be difficult seeing how happy Sara and Brad were with their new baby. *Just one more reminder that my husband is gone and we'll have no more children together.*

Rachel began to kick the back of Sylvia's seat as she fussed and carried on. Sylvia reached into her tote bag and pulled out a toy, which she handed back to Mom. She hoped it would suffice and felt relieved when her daughter quieted.

Sylvia fidgeted with her purse straps, wishing she had come up with a good reason to stay home this evening. She'd been taught from an early age that it was wrong to allow jealousy to take over when someone had something you wanted. While she had no logical reason to be jealous of Sara, Sylvia's envy came from the fact that the Fullers' child would have two parents to love and nurture him, while her children only had a mother. *I'm not sure how good of a parent I am,* she thought. Without Toby's assistance, raising Allen and Rachel was proving to be a challenge.

In the last week or so, Allen had begun throwing temper tantrums whenever he didn't get his way. Sylvia struggled to deal with them and often felt like giving in and allowing him to have his own way. But that would not be good parenting. It probably wouldn't be long before Rachel began to imitate her brother's actions, and then Sylvia would have more trouble on her hands.

Maybe Sylvia wouldn't have such a difficult time making decisions on how to handle her children if she felt content and her soul was at peace. But even the few moments when she did feel a bit of happiness, like when she went birding with Henry, something usually happened to snatch it away. Sylvia wondered if she would ever really know what true contentment and tranquility felt like.

"We're here." Their driver's announcement halted Sylvia's introspections. It was time to put on a pleasant face.

When they entered the parsonage, which had been built on the lot next to the church where Sara's husband preached every Sunday, Brad greeted them at the door.

"Come in. Come in. It's so good to see all of you." He shook everyone's hand and gave Sylvia's children a pat on the head. "Sara and I have been looking forward to your visit and introducing you to the newest member of our family."

Brad led the way to the living room, where Sara sat in a rocking chair, holding the infant. Everyone gathered around—even Henry—to get a look at the bundle of joy.

"He's a beautiful baby." A sense of joy mixed with anticipation filled Amy's soul. Oh, how she looked forward to marrying Jared and hopefully becoming a mother someday.

After everyone pummeled Sara and Brad with questions about how she and the baby were doing and how much the child weighed, Sara asked if anyone would like to hold the baby.

"I would." Amy was the first to speak up.

Sara stood and let Amy take her seat, then handed the precious bundle over to her. Following that, she took a seat on the couch between Mom and Sylvia.

"We have a little something for the baby." Mom reached into her tote bag and removed a package wrapped in blue tissue paper. She handed it to Sara.

While Sara opened the gift, Amy watched Sylvia's expression. Her pinched expression and flushed cheeks made Amy believe that her sister struggled with envy.

Does Sylvia wish she could have another boppli, or is my sister thinking about Toby right now and feeling envious because Sara has a husband and she doesn't? Amy put the baby against her shoulder and gently patted his back. *How will Sylvia deal with it when Jared and I get married? Will it pull us apart when I move out of Mom's house and set up housekeeping in the home Jared and I choose to live in?*

Amy glanced in the direction of her sister again. *Perhaps my being gone will strengthen Sylvia and Mom's relationship. It has seemed a bit strained lately, especially since Sylvia announced her intentions to rent her house to a man she barely knows.*

Like their mother, Amy didn't approve of her sister's decision, but it was Sylvia's life, and she had a right to do as she pleased. Amy hoped everything would work out okay, and that Mr. Weaver would prove to be a good renter and not take advantage of Sylvia's willingness to offer him a place to stay.

Refocusing, Amy watched as Sara held up the pair of light-weight blankets Mom had taken the time to make. In addition to those, they'd all chipped in and put seventy-five dollars in the card that went with the gift.

"We thought you could use some money to buy whatever you still need for the baby," Mom explained when Sara removed the bills from the envelope.

"Thank you all so much. This money will surely be put to good use."

Amy looked over at Henry. He and Brad sat in chairs next to each other, but she couldn't tell if they were actually talking to one another, because their heads were turned away from her.

Sara got up and went over to stand beside Brad. "Look at the nice blankets Belinda made for the baby." She handed the card to him. "And the Kings gave us money to get the baby something he needs."

"That was a thoughtful gift. Thank you." Brad smiled up at Mom and thanked Amy, Sylvia, and Henry as well.

"Have you had many visitors since you brought your little one home from the hospital?" Amy asked.

Sara nodded. "A lot of the church people have come by with gifts and food, so I wouldn't have to worry about cooking."

"Mary Ruth along with Lenore and her family were here last night," Brad interjected. "We enjoyed having them, and it was good to see how

Lenore and Jesse's children are growing." He looked at Rachel and Allen, playing on the floor with some toys Sylvia had brought along. "It's also nice to see your little ones, Sylvia. They've both grown since the last time we saw them."

"They don't stay little long enough to suit me," Sylvia commented. There was that wistful expression again. Amy hoped her sister could hold it together and wouldn't start crying, like she often did at home.

"How does it feel to be a daddy?" Mom asked. "Have you gotten used to the idea yet, Brad?"

He shook his head. "It's sort of surreal. The first night Sara and the baby came home from the hospital, I hardly slept a wink."

Sara chuckled. "It was the baby's crying that kept us both awake."

Everyone laughed, including Sylvia, but her expression continued to appear strained. Amy was almost positive her sister was merely going through the motions of being polite and trying to do the right thing. It had probably taken all of Sylvia's willpower to come here tonight.

Poor Sylvia, she thought. *I hope someday she finds the kind of happiness I've found with Jared.*

Strasburg

"How'd your day go at work?" Virginia asked as she took a seat on the couch beside her husband.

"Okay." Earl's gaze remained fixed on the newspaper he held.

Virginia grimaced. *Sometimes I wonder how he can be so engrossed in that stupid paper.* She looked down at her clenched fingers. *It's either the dumb news blaring on the television, or him staring at the newspaper in front of his nose.*

"Did you sell many cars?" she asked.

No response.

Virginia waited a few seconds then she bumped his arm. "Did ya hear what I said?"

"Uh-huh."

Virginia grew weary of her husband's lack of attention. *I'd like to wad up that newspaper and toss it in the trash.*

"Then why didn't you answer my question?" she asked through clenched teeth.

He looked away from the newspaper and blinked. "What question was that?"

She lifted her gaze to the ceiling. "I asked if you sold many cars today."

"A few."

"Guess a few is better than none."

"Right."

"Don't you wanna know how my day went?"

"Sure."

"It wasn't the best. I started to clean and organize the guest room but discovered the sheets for that bed are worn out and need to be replaced. The curtains also need to go, because they're faded."

"Okay, sure. Do whatever you think needs to be done."

"Something else bothered me too."

"What was that?"

"There was more traffic than usual going down the road."

"Is that so?"

"Yes, and as I have pointed out before, it's because of that stupid greenhouse." Virginia groaned. "I didn't have a moment's peace."

Earl dropped the paper into his lap and turned to look at her with furrowed brows. "Will you please keep your mouth shut long enough for me to read the paper? All you ever do is flap your gums about things you can't control." His eyes narrowed as he breathed audibly through his nose. "It's no wonder your first husband left you."

Virginia pounded a fist against her right thigh. "He did not leave me. I've told ya before—he died. Did ya hear me, Earl? My first husband died!" *Wow, how hard can it be for my man to remember something like that? Furthermore, doesn't he realize how much it hurts for me to talk about my first husband?*

Earl let the paper fall to the floor as he held up his hands. "For heaven's sake, woman, calm down. You're makin' a big deal out of this."

Virginia sucked in some air and tried to relax. Just talking about her first husband made her edgy. Why did Earl have to bring up this topic, anyhow?

He reached over and clasped her hand. "Sorry, if I upset you. I just wanted a little peace and quiet tonight and a chance to read the paper without interruption."

"No problem, Earl. You can have the rest of the evening to yourself. I'm going to bed." Virginia stood up and limped out of the room. She still hadn't told Earl about Stella coming, but tonight was not the time to do it. Hopefully, tomorrow he'd be in a better mood and then she would let him in on the plans. In the meantime, Virginia needed to spruce up the guest room a bit, to make sure it was ready for her friend.

As she entered their bedroom, a horrible thought came over Virginia. *Earl got really upset when I tried to talk to him about how I feel. His angry expression made me think he might want to hit me.*

She flopped down on the bed and let her head fall into her hands. *Would he ever go that far? If so, what would I do about it?*

Chapter 12

"I didn't realize this house was so dirty," Sylvia said as she swept the area in her bedroom closet where all her and Toby's clothes had once been. His, she'd donated to a local thrift shop, and hers had been taken to Mom's and hung in the closet of the bedroom where she'd been sleeping since Toby's death.

"Places we don't see have a way of accumulating dust bunnies." Amy laughed. "Like under a bed. When no one is in a home for a while, the dust can truly settle on things."

"Jah." Sylvia stepped into the middle of the room and looked around. "Everything in here looks pretty good now, don't you think?"

Amy nodded.

"We have more to do upstairs, in the other rooms—also the closets and bathroom need to be cleaned."

"I have a feeling we'll be here for a while, Sister."

"Probably so."

"Too bad Mom didn't have the energy to come with us. You could have let the kinner fall asleep here while we all pitched in and cleaned."

"If they would have cooperated, that is. More than likely we'd have spent most of the time getting my two active little ones out of things."

Amy chuckled. "You could be right about that."

"I know I am."

"So which room do you want to tackle next?"

"Let's head upstairs and work on the bathroom." Sylvia held onto the mop and bucket.

Amy carried the broom with the dustpan and headed for the stairs.

"I'll be right up," Sylvia called. "I'd better grab some disinfectant wipes from the downstairs bathroom."

"Okay. I'll see you upstairs."

After entering the bathroom at the end of the downstairs hall, Sylvia picked up the box of wipes. *My sister looks tired this evening. I hope I'm not pushing too hard to get this work done. She should have said no if she wasn't up to helping.*

Sylvia left the bathroom and started down the hall. *I'm looking forward to renting this house out and earning some money. Now I'll be able to help Mom with some bills, or at least pay for groceries so I won't feel like I'm taking advantage of her hospitality.*

At the bottom of the stairs, Sylvia paused, recalling how sounds of her own little family used to be heard in this home. She wasn't ready to let go of this house permanently, but maybe someday she would feel strong enough emotionally to make that big decision.

She climbed up to the second floor and entered the bathroom, where her sister stood in front of the counter, cleaning the mirror.

"Mind if I ask you something?" Amy questioned.

Sylvia set the wipes on the counter. "Of course not. Ask me whatever you want."

"Is there a specific reason you decided to rent this place, rather than sell?"

Sylvia winced. This topic was difficult to talk about without crying, and she'd done way too much of that since Toby, Dad, and Abe died.

"I'm trying to understand your reasons," Amy persisted, "but if it was my house, and I had no plans to move back, then I'd sell and use the money to buy something else."

"You and I handle things differently. Also you're not married yet and don't have children. The bond between Toby and me was strong. We enjoyed our life together until the accident." Sylvia stared toward the window. "Why would I need to buy another home? The kinner seem content to live at our folks' place. They like being close to their grossmammi, and she enjoys them."

"What about you, Sylvia? Are you content to live there indefinitely?"

Sylvia lifted her shoulders in a brief shrug. "I'm okay with it, at least for now."

"If you're content to stay with Mom, then why not sell your house?" Amy slipped an arm around Sylvia's waist.

She swallowed hard, trying to push down the lump that had formed in her throat. "If I sell my house, it'll be like parting with the last shred of evidence that I was married to Toby."

"That's not true. You have Rachel and Allen. There's a part of their *daadi* in each of them, just like there's a part of you."

Sylvia dabbed at the tears that had escaped her lashes and rolled onto her cheeks. "This is the place where Toby and I set up housekeeping together. We made so many wonderful memories."

"Being here makes you sad, though, right?"

"Jah." Sylvia could barely get the word out.

Amy's hand went from Sylvia's waist to the middle of her back, and she gave it a few gentle pats. "I'm sorry that I don't fully understand the way you feel, because I've never lost a husband. Even so, if it were me, I'd sell the house."

"Maybe someday I will. Just not now." Sylvia picked up the box of wipes and pulled a few out. "We'd better get this room done so we can work on the others and make sure they look presentable. Now that the furniture I decided to keep has been taken to Mom's, I plan to let Dennis Weaver know he can move in. Who knows—maybe someday I'll sell the house and property to him."

Belinda leaned back in her easy chair and closed her eyes. *This feels good, and the smell of the lavender lotion I rubbed on my hands is soothing. If I could, I'd take a warm bath and soak for a while. But since my daughters are still gone, that wouldn't be a good idea in case one of the children needed me.*

Today had been busy at the greenhouse from the moment they'd opened until Henry put the Closed sign in the window on the front door. It had been nice to see so many regular customers as well as a few tourists come in. Two women who'd come together bought some of Belinda's canned goods and several potholders Sylvia had made to sell. Belinda remembered the comments they'd made while she rang up their purchases at the checkout. The first woman mentioned stopping by the bigger greenhouse on the other side of town, but said she enjoyed the Kings' greenhouse more. The second woman added, "My sister and I traveled all the way from California because we wanted to see Amish country and learn more about Plain living. We've enjoyed chatting with you because there are no Amish people where we are from."

Belinda had to admit she felt better hearing those women talk positively about her business. She needed to let go of the worry she'd been carrying about the future of the greenhouse.

She stretched out more fully and wiggled her bare toes. *I need to pray more and keep trusting God to provide for our needs.*

Belinda didn't know how Amy had found the strength to go with Sylvia to her house for cleaning after such a long day of waiting on customers. But the two of them had headed out as soon as they'd finished supper, after Belinda offered to wash and dry the dishes.

Although tired herself, Belinda would have gone with them if they'd had someone to watch the children. Taking them along would have been a mistake. Henry had gone over to see his friend Seth again, but even if he'd been here, he wasn't responsible enough to keep an eye on Rachel and Allen. It seemed like he always had his nose in a magazine or some book about birds these days. She'd hoped he would take more interest in the honey bees, but that didn't seem to be the case. At least he complained about the job less, so that was a good thing.

Since the children were tuckered out from playing so hard, Belinda had been able to put them to bed sooner than their normal bedtime. It wasn't that she didn't want to spend time with her grandchildren. She just felt too exhausted tonight.

The house seemed peaceful as evening crept along. Belinda hoped her son and daughters would arrive home soon. Another day of work was around the corner, and she needed to get her rest. *Even if I went to bed, the fact is, I'd just lay there worrying until they all arrived home.*

Belinda yawned. *Think I'm going to check on Allen and Rachel.* She rose from her chair, then headed upstairs. When she peeked in on the children and heard their soft, steady breathing, she smiled. Since all was well, she headed back to the main floor and went to her room.

After slipping into her nightgown, robe, and slippers, she couldn't help but smile. Vernon had given them to her for Christmas two years ago. He'd been such a thoughtful husband. Oh, how she missed him.

Back in the living room, she took a seat in the recliner again. She sat with her eyes closed, thinking about Vernon and how, when their children were young, they used to enjoy spending a few hours alone each evening after their sons and daughters went to bed.

Switching her train of thought back to the greenhouse, lest she give in to depression, Belinda reflected on how Maude, the near-homeless woman, had come by looking for a handout today. Belinda had never said no to someone in need and ended up giving Maude a jar of honey, a loaf of bread, and several other food items that didn't need refrigeration. Even though the bedraggled woman hadn't said thank you, Belinda felt good about helping her.

Thankfully Monroe hadn't come by since their conversation after Christmas. Apparently he respected her wishes and realized she was not ready for a relationship that went deeper than friendship. She was certain there was no way she could ever get married again. She'd done the right thing by letting Monroe know where he stood.

She glanced at the clock across the room and frowned. It was almost ten-thirty. *Henry should have been home by now. I told him no later than ten.*

As worry took over, Belinda got up and went to the window, looking out into the darkened yard. A chill of apprehension shot through her as she thought about Amy, Sylvia, and Henry, who could all be out on the road at this very moment, heading for home. She knew all too well how suddenly an accident could occur, and hoped no one in her family would ever experience such a tragedy again.

Leaning against the windowsill, Belinda closed her eyes. *Dear Lord, Please keep my children safe and bring them home soon.*

A horse whinnied, and when Belinda opened her eyes, she saw the lights on the open buggy Henry had used this evening. She sighed with relief. At least one of her children had made it home safely. Now if Amy and Sylvia would only get here.

Belinda moved away from the window and went back to her chair. A short time later, Henry came in.

Belinda got up and went over to give him a hug.

"What was that for, Mom?" He looked at her with a curious expression.

"I missed you, and I'm glad you're home, even if you are late."

"Sorry, there was more traffic on the road than usual."

Belinda tilted her head toward him and sniffed. "Is that cigarette smoke I smell on your *hemm*?"

Henry's posture went rigid as he took a whiff of his shirt. "Umm. . . yeah. . .guess so."

"Henry King, have you been smoking?" Her body tensed as she waited for his response.

"No, Mom."

"Then why do your clothes smell like *schmoke*?"

He blinked rapidly while rubbing the back of his neck.

She tapped her foot. "I expect an honest answer, Son."

"Seth's the one who smokes cigarettes." Henry shifted from one foot to the other. "I'll admit, I did give smoking a try once, but I hated the way it smelled and tasted."

"So the smoke your sisters and I have smelled in the barn a few times was from Seth?"

Henry shrugged. "I've never seen him light up a cigarette in our barn, but I suppose he could have come in there sometime when I wasn't looking."

Belinda's fingers clenched into her palms. "Seth is a bad influence on you, Henry. I don't think you should hang around with him so much anymore."

The door opened and Belinda's daughters stepped in.

"I'm so glad you're home." She gave them both the same kind of hug she'd given her son. "It's late, and I was getting worried."

"We had more cleaning to do than I realized," Sylvia explained. "Were the kinner good for you? I assume they're in bed?"

Belinda nodded. "They were tuckered out, so I put them to bed a little earlier than they usually go down."

"That's good. A little extra sleep won't hurt them." Sylvia yawned noisily. "And speaking of sleep. . . I'm really tired, so I'm going up to bed." She kissed Belinda's cheek. "Night, Mom."

"Good night."

"Think I'll head for bed too." Amy gave Belinda another hug. "See you in the morning."

When her daughters left the room, Belinda turned to speak more with Henry, but he was gone. No doubt he'd quietly left the room while she'd been talking to his sisters.

He was probably trying to avoid more lecturing from me. Belinda sighed. She hoped Henry was telling the truth when he'd said he had only tried smoking but quit. The last thing she needed was one more thing to stress about.

Chapter 13

Ronks

"Alice wrote down a message for you, Dennis," James said, stepping out onto the porch. "It's from that Amish woman you told me about who wants to rent you her house."

Dennis got up from the rocking chair, where he'd been reading the latest edition of *The Connection* magazine, and took the piece of paper his friend handed him. The corners of his lips twitched as he read Sylvia's message. "Her house is ready for me now." He grinned at James. "She wants me to meet her there at seven o'clock this evening to give me the keys. That's when I'll pay her for the first month's rent."

James thumped Dennis's back. "I can tell you're pretty excited about this."

"Jah. I needed this change in my life, and Sylvia's house and property is the perfect place for me to live at this time."

"I wonder why she wants to meet you so late in the day." James leaned against the porch railing.

Dennis pulled his fingers through the back of his hair as his shoulders lifted. "Maybe she's not quite finished clearing things out of the house. Or it could be because she's working in the greenhouse."

James's brows lifted on his forehead. "What greenhouse?"

"The one her mamm owns. She mentioned it the other day while she was showing me through her house. Sylvia said it's on the same property as her mother's house."

"What about her daed and other family members. Do any of them work at the greenhouse?"

"I'm not sure about other family members, but Sylvia's husband, father, and brother were all killed in a tragic accident when a truck hit their buggy. Remember, I told you she was a widow."

"Yeah, that's right. Just didn't know the cause of her husband's death or that others from her family had also died." James shook his head slowly. "Sounds like she's been through a lot."

"Jah. I could see the sadness in her eyes. It's the same look my mamm has whenever she talks about my daed."

"Certain circumstances in our lives can sure be hard."

Dennis gave a nod. "Unfortunately, some are more difficult than others." *And some people, like me, experience tragedies that are too difficult to talk about, so we try to hide them from others who wouldn't understand.*

Strasburg

"While I open the greenhouse, would you mind going out to check the mail and see if we have any phone messages?" Mom asked Amy after the breakfast dishes were taken care of.

"Sure, I can do that. I'll head out there right now and meet you in the greenhouse shortly."

"Sounds good. See you there."

Amy went out the back door and headed down the driveway. Her first stop was the mailbox, which she found empty. Apparently it hadn't come yet.

She glanced across the road and saw Virginia's husband come out of the house and head for his truck. Before she had a chance to wave, he cupped his hands around his mouth and hollered, "Morning. How are ya?"

"I'm well. How about you and your wife?"

"We're doin' good." He gave another wave, got into his vehicle, and drove off.

Amy smiled. Earl was a lot friendlier than his wife. Whenever Virginia saw Amy, she either looked the other way or sometimes mumbled a brief *hello*. Amy didn't understand what the problem could be, but then she guessed some folks just weren't the friendly type. Earl's wife might be one of those people who preferred to keep to herself.

Amy turned and headed back up the driveway. When she reached the small wooden shed where their phone was housed, she opened the door and stepped inside. There was no blinking light on the answering machine, and when she picked up the phone to make a call, there was no dial tone either.

I wonder what's going on. Amy stepped out of the phone shed and looked up at the place where the wire was connected. A cold chill ran through her body when she realized it had been cut. *Oh, no. . .not another act of vandalism.*

🐦

Belinda had barely taken a seat behind the checkout counter when Amy rushed in, wide-eyed and face ashen.

Belinda felt immediate concern. "What's wrong, Daughter? You look *umgerrent.*"

"I am very upset." Amy's hand shook as she brushed at a piece of lint on her dress.

"The line going into the phone shed has been cut. There's no electric power in the building at all."

"Are you sure it was cut and didn't blow down from the wind or something?"

Amy shook her head. "No, Mom, the line was definitely cut."

Holding onto the edge of the counter, Belinda sucked in her breath. "Oh my. I bet whoever left that muffled message on our answering machine was the one responsible for cutting the wire." She clasped Amy's arm. "What are we going to do about this?"

"The first thing we should do is call the sheriff. Then we need to let the phone company know our line needs to be replaced."

Belinda shook her head determinedly. "No one's been hurt, and I am not going to bring the law into this. We will, however, need to ask the neighbors across the road if we can use their phone to call the phone company."

"I'll walk over there and see about it right now." Amy leaned down and gave Belinda a hug. "If Henry's still in the barn, I'll ask him to come here so you're not in the greenhouse by yourself. I don't think any of us should be alone anymore."

✦

"Now how did I forget to buy dishwashing detergent? I'm sure I wrote it down on my list when I went grocery shopping." Grumbling with each step, Virginia went to her purse and drew out the paper. Tracing her finger along each crossed off word, she found there were a couple of unmarked places.

She thumped her head. "I can't believe this. Besides the detergent, I forgot to pick up the deodorant Earl asked me to get."

Virginia put the list aside and walked down the hall toward the bathroom. Entering the room, she opened Earl's drawer and rummaged through his toiletries. "There's his deodorant." When she lifted the container, it felt light. A feeling of regret came over her as she pulled off the lid to reveal an empty cartridge. Although he hadn't mentioned it, her husband had been a little out-of-sorts and short with her this morning. Discovering that she hadn't bought the deodorant he'd asked for, in addition to her burning his toast could have been the reason for his sullen mood.

Virginia replaced the lid and tossed the empty deodorant in the garbage can. She would go to the store before he got home and get him a new one.

Standing in front of their bathroom mirror, she fiddled with her short hair. Virginia pursed her lips. *It needs something fresh done to it. My friend will be visiting from Chicago soon, and I don't want to look like a drab country bumpkin.*

She grabbed a tube of styling gel, squeezed some into the palm of her hand, and rubbed it into her hair. Virginia smiled as the gel began to give her hair some lift. *I do believe that style looks kind of good on me.*

Leaving the bathroom, Virginia stopped to look in at the guest room. She felt happy with the new curtains she'd purchased for a reasonable price. She'd also found a set of sheets with a nice thread count for the bed.

Leaning against the dresser, Virginia thought about how good it would be to see Stella again. *I wonder what we can do for fun while she's here. Guess I could get some ideas from the internet.*

She stepped out of the room and closed the door behind her, then headed for the kitchen. *Sure hope my friend doesn't want to check out the Amish while she's here. As far as I know, Stella hasn't shown any interest in them or mentioned to me that she might want to meet any of the Plain people who live in Lancaster County.*

Virginia was about to start up the dishwasher, using what was left of the detergent, when a knock sounded on the front door. "Now who in the world could that be? I hope it's not someone selling something I don't need."

She dried her hands and made her way to the front door. When Virginia opened it, she was surprised to see Amy King standing on the porch. *Well, wouldn't you know. . .speaking of the Plain people, here's one now.*

"I'm sorry to bother you, Virginia, but could I borrow your phone?"

"I thought you Amish folks had a phone in that little wooden building near the end of your driveway." Virginia leaned against the door frame, trying not to stare at the young woman's plain but pretty face and her quaint-styled dress. *I don't understand why they don't see the need to wear makeup, nail polish, or stylish clothes.*

"Yes, we do keep our phone in a shed, but someone cut the wire that leads to the shed, so the phone is not working" Amy's statement pulled Virginia's musings aside.

"Is that so?" Virginia gave her earlobe a tug. "I wonder who would do such a thing."

"We don't know, but I need to call the phone company to let them know what happened and see how soon they can come out and replace the line."

"Oh, okay. I'll go get my cell phone and look up the number for you."

"Thanks so much. I really appreciate it, Virginia."

"No problem." Virginia limped her way to the kitchen and got out the phone book. Even though she didn't care much for her Amish neighbors, she couldn't very well refuse to let Amy use the phone. How would that make her look?

After Virginia brought her phone and the number out to Amy, she went to the kitchen for a cup of coffee. As she stood sipping the enticing beverage, while giving the young woman some needed time to make the call, Virginia tried not to listen in on the conversation.

When Virginia returned to the living room a few minutes later, Amy was off the phone.

"Did you get a hold of someone to fix your phone line?" Virginia asked.

Amy nodded. "I was told they would be out sometime today to take care of it for us." She handed Virginia the cell phone. "Thank you for letting me use this."

"Sure, no problem." Virginia opened the door to let her neighbor out, in time to see a horse and buggy turn up the driveway to the greenhouse. She was tempted to make some comment about it, but what was the use? Short of lighting a fire to the place, Virginia figured there wasn't much she could do about the greenhouse.

Clymer, New York

Ezekiel yawned and drank the rest of his coffee. He'd had some difficulty sleeping lately, because his family in Pennsylvania had been on his mind. Were they doing all right? Mom said so the last time they'd talked, but he could never be sure without going there himself to check on things.

He closed his eyes. *I need to give my worries to You, Lord. I can't add one more minute to my life by fretting about things that are out of my control.*

Ezekiel set his empty mug aside. It was hard not to worry about his family back home and the burdens they'd carried since the accident. Even though he no longer lived there, Ezekiel knew how much effort it was to keep the greenhouse running.

Scratching his head, Ezekiel's focus changed. Recently, he'd gone with Samuel Stoltzfus, another Amish minister in his church district, to talk with someone getting ready for surgery to remove a cancerous tumor. At first, Ezekiel felt overwhelmed, but as he listened to the church leader give needed comfort to the ill person, he got a better understanding of the importance of this part of his ministry. Samuel had spoken calmly, as he gave reassurance and hope, which made the tension in the room ease. Ezekiel was inspired by the other minister's way of handling this person's situation. He knew it would be good to read his Bible daily.

Following the good advice from the bishop, as well as the other minister and a deacon who'd been called to this type of work several years ago, Ezekiel would do his best and try to keep his focus on the Lord.

As Ezekiel took a seat at the workbench in his shop, he glanced at the calendar hanging on the nearest wall. In a few weeks it would be his mother's birthday, as well as the one year anniversary of his father, brother, and brother-in-law's deaths. It would be a difficult day for him, as well as the rest of his family. He wished he could simply blot the day off the calendar and out of his mind, but it was not possible.

Ezekiel still missed the special men in his life, and could only imagine how difficult it would be for his mother, sisters, and younger brother to celebrate her birthday this year and not think about the accident that had occurred the evening of her party last year.

He left his chair and paced the room as an idea began to form. *Think I'll take my fraa and kinner there for a visit that day. It might help Mom to have her whole family around on her birthday. I won't tell her we're coming. We'll just show up and give her a birthday surprise.*

Chapter 14

Strasburg

"Morning, Belinda. How are things going here?" Monroe asked when he entered the greenhouse at two o'clock that afternoon. He smelled of men's aftershave, as he often did, and his pale blue shirt looked new. This was Monroe's first visit since Belinda talked with him after Christmas. She hoped he wasn't here to pester her about seeing him socially again. She'd set him straight once and didn't want to have to do it again.

Belinda felt her stress level rising as Monroe stood with a wide grin, looking at her and no one else. *Why do I feel like a weak kitten when I'm in his presence? I have to give Monroe credit, though—he's sure insistent.*

Belinda shifted uneasily on the stool she sat upon behind the counter. "We're doing all right. How are you, Monroe?"

"My business is going well, but I miss seeing you."

Looking away from his gaze, she bit the inside of her cheek. "May I help you with something, Monroe?"

He placed his hands on the surface of the counter and leaned forward, until she felt his warm, minty breath on her face. "Just dropped by to see how you're doing now that you're open for business again."

She pulled back slightly. "We're all fine."

"As I was coming down the driveway I saw a man from the phone company outside your phone shed. Looked like they were putting up a new line."

Belinda nodded. "Amy discovered that the old line had been cut this morning."

His brows furrowed. "That's not good, Belinda. Sounds to me like someone is trying to antagonize you and your family. Has there been any other vandalism done besides the phone line?"

She shook her head, choosing not to mention the garbled phone message they'd received. It wasn't actually vandalism anyway, and there was no need to tell him about it.

Monroe glanced around and pulled off his straw hat, revealing his thick head of hair. He fanned himself with the brim a few times, which filled the air with more of that heavy aftershave. "Where's the rest of your family? You're not out here alone, I hope."

"Henry and Amy are helping me today," Belinda replied stiffly.

"Really? I don't see them anywhere."

"Henry's outside putting a customer's purchase into her car, and Amy's in the storage room right now." Belinda didn't appreciate being treated like a child. As she listened to him go on about what he deemed important, she wanted to say what was really on her mind. *Monroe, never you mind. There's no need to worry about me. I'm fine and so is my family.*

"Well, if you ask me, someone should be up front here with you at all times," Monroe continued. "You never know when a person could come in and try to rob you of all the money."

Belinda bristled. Why was this man being so persistent and overbearing? Was he really that concerned about their well-being, or did Monroe enjoy being so controlling?

Monroe placed his hat back on his head and looked past Belinda when Amy approached. He fiddled with his suspenders a few seconds and gave them a tug. "It's good to see you finally have some help here again."

Belinda felt relieved when Amy joined her behind the counter.

"Hello, Mr. Esh." Amy offered him a smile, even though Belinda knew her daughter didn't care much for Monroe. "Are you here to buy some outdoor plants or maybe seeds for a vegetable garden?"

He gave a quick shake of his head. "Just dropped by to see how everyone was doing." He still looked only at Belinda.

She was reminded again of their courting days, and how Monroe could make her feel uneasy with his controlling mannerisms. *This may be far-fetched and wrong of me to think, but what if Monroe is the one behind the vandalism?* Belinda didn't know where that thought had come from.

It was unlike her to think that way. She glanced at Monroe, with guilt mounting inside her head. *How ridiculous of me to think such a thought. What reason would Monroe have for vandalizing our place or trying to hurt my business? I'll need to pray about my unkind feelings toward him.*

"We're all fine, Monroe," Amy responded. "We are keeping plenty busy since the greenhouse reopened."

"That's good." He shifted nervously. "I just want to be sure your family stays safe."

"We'll be fine and appreciate your interest in our welfare." Belinda managed a smile.

About that time, Henry came through the doorway and walked past Monroe without saying a word. Right behind him, two couples entered the building, so Belinda held her tongue. Later, when she could speak to her son alone, she would reprimand him for being impolite.

"Guess I'd best be on my way. I have a few other stops to make yet today." Monroe tipped his straw hat in Belinda's direction. "It was good seeing you. Please let me know if you need anything."

"Danki for stopping by." Belinda got off the stool and approached one of the couples who'd come in. "May I help you with anything?"

She glanced over her shoulder and saw Monroe head out the door. Hopefully he wouldn't be back anytime soon, unless it was to buy something. It wasn't in her nature to feel this way about someone, but Monroe's behavior got on her nerves.

Since Virginia's friend would be arriving today, she had spent the morning making sure the house was picked up and the guest room looked presentable. She figured Stella most likely wouldn't be here until close to suppertime, so there was time for her to rest awhile.

She took a seat in her recliner, hit the lever, and lay back with her feet elevated. This position felt good and always made the pain in her leg subside.

Virginia picked up the remote and turned on the TV. Her favorite game show came on, and it didn't take long to become absorbed in the questions being asked of the contestants. Of course, Virginia tried to guess the answers along with them.

Fifteen minutes into the show, her eyes became heavy and her eyelids closed. A little power nap would feel good, and she'd be refreshed by the time Stella got here.

Virginia was on the verge of nodding off, when a knock sounded on the door.

I hope it's not Amy needing to use my phone again.

Virginia pulled the lever on her chair and when the footrest came down she got up and made her way to the door. When she opened it, she was surprised to see Stella on the front porch.

"Well, for goodness' sakes. I didn't expect you this soon." Virginia gave her friend a hug and invited her in.

"I got an earlier start yesterday than I'd planned, stopped early for the night, and left the hotel as soon as I woke up." Stella pulled her fingers through the ends of her short blond hair and yawned. "I'm pretty tired, but it's good to be here."

"I'm glad you made it okay." Virginia gestured to the sofa. "Should we sit awhile and visit, or did you want to get your luggage out of the car?"

"Let's sit first." Stella took a seat on one end of the couch.

"I'll go get us a cup of coffee. Unless you'd rather have something else."

"Coffee's fine. It'll keep me from falling asleep."

"Maybe you'd like to take a nap."

"No, I didn't come all this way to sleep in the middle of the day. I'd much rather get caught up with you."

Virginia smiled. "Same here. Make yourself comfortable. I'll be right back."

When Virginia returned to living room, she found her friend standing in front of the window facing the street.

"Here's your coffee." Virginia placed two mugs on the low table in front of the couch.

Stella turned to face her. "I was watching a horse and buggy coming down the street. It turned up the driveway by the sign for the greenhouse."

Virginia grunted. "Yeah, that's what I have to put up with all day." She wrinkled her nose. "*Clip-clop. Clip-clop.* The noise is so distracting."

"You think so?" Stella tipped her head. "I kinda like the sound. It's relaxing."

"You wouldn't say that if you had to hear it all day. When I sit out on the porch, it's even louder, not to mention the putrid smell of the droppings those horses leave in the middle of the road."

"You'll get used to it in time." Stella took a seat, picked up her mug, and took a drink. "Nice... This hits the spot."

Virginia joined her. "I have some store-bought cookies, if you'd like some."

"No thanks. I don't want to spoil my appetite for whatever you're planning for supper."

"I have a chicken cooking in the crockpot."

"Yum." Stella glanced toward the window. "I'd sure like to have a look at that greenhouse while I'm here. Could we take a walk over there?"

"You mean now?"

"Sure, why not?"

"Those people who run it are different. I'm sure you wouldn't like them."

"I'm not prejudiced, Virginia."

"Maybe we can go over there tomorrow. My leg's been acting up today, and I don't feel like goin' anywhere right now."

"I guess tomorrow might be better." Stella drank more coffee. "We'll both be rested up in the morning."

Virginia nodded. By tomorrow, she would make up some other excuse. The last thing she wanted to do was to take her friend over to that greenhouse and expose her to those strange people.

When Henry guided the horse and buggy up to the rail, Sylvia saw Dennis waiting on the porch for them in the same place he'd been when they'd met him here last week.

She stepped out of the carriage, and held her horse until Henry got down. Once he took over, she headed for the house and joined Dennis on the porch.

"Good evening, Sylvia. It's nice to see you again." Dennis's smile seemed so genuine—nothing like the fake-looking ones Monroe offered Mom and the rest of the family.

"Good evening." Sylvia took the key from her handbag and opened the front door. "The house has been thoroughly cleaned and everything is out of it that I won't need. If you'd like to walk around and inspect each of the rooms before you sign the rental contract, it's fine with me."

He shook his head. "No need for me to look around. I'm sure the rooms are okay."

Sylvia went in first, and Dennis followed. She led the way to the kitchen, and placed the written agreement on the table, along with a pen. "There's a carbon paper under the first page," she explained. "That way, we'll both have a copy."

"Makes sense to me." Dennis took a seat at the table and read the agreement. "Everything looks good. I have no problem with any of it and will gladly sign the papers." He reached for his wallet and handed her the first month's rent. "Since your address is on the invoice I'll know where to send the check each month. And if it's okay, I may drop by some time to check out the greenhouse."

"I may not be there when you come over, but either my mother or sister can show you around and offer any help you may need if you decide to purchase anything."

He gave a nod. "Do you and your brother have plans to do more birding anytime soon?"

Sylvia shrugged. "I don't know. We haven't talked about it."

"Let me know if you do. If it works into my schedule, maybe I can join you."

"Umm. . .maybe. We'll have to see how it goes."

Although the idea appealed to Sylvia, she wasn't sure going bird-watching with Dennis was a good idea. She didn't want to start any gossip or speculation going around that either of them might have some interest in each other, for that was certainly not the case—at least not on her part. Furthermore, Dennis had given no indication that he might be interested in her. With him being new to the area, he was probably looking for companionship and someone to share his interest in birds.

Since Dennis was older and more mature than Henry, he could also be a good role model for her brother. If Sylvia went along, it would only be if Henry wanted her to join them. It would also depend on whether either Mom or Amy was free to watch Rachel and Allen.

After Dennis signed the rental agreement, he asked a few questions, and she agreed to his requests regarding the use of the property. When he handed Sylvia the papers, she put her copy in her purse, along with Dennis's check and left his copy on the table. "My brother and I should get going, but don't hesitate to call if you have any questions about anything here in the house or other parts of the property."

"I appreciate that." Dennis shook her hand. "Danki for your willingness to rent this place to me. I'll do my best to keep everything nice and in good working order."

Sylvia said goodbye and returned to her horse and buggy, where Henry waited.

When they pulled out of the yard, a strange feeling came over her. Getting the first month's rent and giving Dennis a key to the home she used to share with Toby made his death seem so final—like coming to the end of a novel. Only, Sylvia didn't feel the satisfaction that came from reaching the end of a book. Her heart ached more than ever.

Chapter 15

Dennis awakened the following morning, feeling a bit disoriented. The mattress he'd slept upon was not the unyielding cot he'd used at James's place. This bed was comfortable, making it hard to come fully awake.

He rubbed his eyes and sat up. Looking around the cozy room, Dennis appreciated that, unlike the drab accommodations he'd had before, this room looked freshly painted in a warm tan. It also came furnished with an oak dresser, bedframe, coat rack, and cedar-lined storage chest at the foot of the bed. The room, along with the others in the house, had oak-trimmed mopboards and window and door frames. Even the floors were finished in oak throughout most of the rooms, except the bathroom and kitchen. Dennis liked the place so far. It was more than adequate for his needs and quite comfortable.

He sat up and put his feet on the soft area rug next to the bed. *This is what I envisioned for myself—a nice house with homey comforts.* Dennis smiled. *I wonder if Sylvia would mind if I got a* hund *and brought it into the house at night.*

He shook his head. *Guess that's not the best idea, since I'll be working most days and don't really have time to care for a dog. She may be opposed to having an animal in the house too.*

As Dennis made his way to the window and lifted the shade, he felt a sense of exhilaration. Last evening, after he'd signed the rental agreement, Sylvia had given him permission to mow down the field and create a track where he could train horses to pull a carriage. He would get started on that as soon as he'd eaten breakfast.

His stomach growled at the thought of food, but then he remembered there was nothing in the refrigerator yet. He would need to eat breakfast at one of the local restaurants and do some grocery shopping this morning.

Dennis looked for his wallet on the dresser but realized it wasn't there. *I seem to have misplaced it. I'd better keep looking.*

Dennis hurried to get dressed and went out to the kitchen for a glass of water. As he sipped it, he noticed his wallet sitting near the coffee pot on the counter. He groaned. *I remember now—I set it there last night to remind myself to buy some coffee.* He grabbed the wallet and put it in his pocket. It was nice that Sylvia had left plenty of dishes, as well as pots and pans in the cupboards for his use. He sure hadn't expected her to leave him coffee or other food staples.

Dennis had thought he would make out a grocery list but figured there was no use in doing that. He needed pretty much everything to start out with, so he'd just wander through the store and put whatever items he wanted into the cart as he went along.

Guess I'd better comb my hair and brush my teeth before hitching my horse to the buggy and heading for town. He pushed his chair back and stood. *Think I might pick up some birdseed today too. May as well see if I can lure some interesting birds into the yard. Then I can record them in my birding journal, along with the others I've seen while out bird-watching.*

Dennis hoped Sylvia had no regrets about renting her place to him, because he had a good feeling about living here. Sylvia had said she had no plans of moving back here, so someday, if things worked out, maybe she would agree to sell him the house and property. In the meantime, Dennis would make the most out of living here.

For the first time since moving to Lancaster County, Virginia found herself feeling less anxious and able to relax. She figured it was because Stella was here and her loneliness, if only for a short time, had gone away. Virginia wished her friend could live in Pennsylvania too. They could do many things together, like they did when she and Earl lived in Chicago. Now she and Stella only had a short time to squeeze in some fun and make a few memories.

Sure wish I could convince her to move here, but since Stella's husband has a good job in Chicago, it probably won't happen.

"Would you like more toast or another boiled egg?" Virginia offered as she and Stella lingered at the table over a cup of coffee. Earl had left for work half an hour ago. She reached for the creamer, added some to her coffee, and gave it a gentle stir. *My husband has been getting along well with our guest. He seemed to enjoy chatting with Stella last evening.*

"No more toast for me. I'm plenty full from what I already ate." Stella lifted her mug and took a drink. "As soon as we finish our coffee, let's put our dishes in the dishwasher and head across the street to your neighbor's greenhouse."

Virginia groaned inwardly. She'd hoped her friend would have forgotten about the silly notion of seeing the greenhouse and meeting the Amish family who ran it. *Stella acts like a full-blown tourist, wanting to see the Plain people. I hope she doesn't expect me to drive her all over the place in order to see more of them.*

"Virginia, did you hear what I said?"

Virginia blinked. "Umm...yeah, I heard you. Just not sure going over there's a good idea."

"Why not?"

"I told you yesterday—those people are strange. I have nothing in common with them, and neither will you."

"You never know. We might hit it off famously and discover we have some things in common." Stella winked.

Virginia lifted her gaze to the ceiling. "Right."

"So can we go?"

"Why don't you head over there while I take care of the dishes? The place is open now. I can tell by all the horse and buggy traffic."

Stella shook her head. "No way. I want you to introduce me to your neighbors."

"Can't you make your own introductions? I mean, you're not a shy person."

"True, but I'd rather you went along."

Virginia wasn't sure what else she could say to dissuade her friend from going over there. *If I said I have a headache, would that help? No, Stella would probably see right through the fib. I could tell her my leg hurts this morning and I don't want to do much walking. Yeah, that's the best approach.*

Virginia finished the last of her coffee and reached down to rub her knee. "I'm in quite a bit of pain this morning. Don't think my leg can handle walking that far."

"Not a problem. We can drive over there in my car." Stella finished her coffee and pushed back her chair. "You sit there and relax while I put the dishes in the dishwasher. Then we'll be on our way."

This is getting me nowhere. Stella is determined to follow through on this silly endeavor, and now I feel like I have no choice. Virginia's shoulders curled forward as she cringed internally. She figured short of passing out cold, there was no way she could get out of going.

When Virginia entered the greenhouse with Stella, her palms became sweaty. Several Amish people wandered up and down the aisles, and she caught sight of Belinda talking to one of them. This was definitely not Virginia's favorite place to be.

"Aren't you gonna introduce me to the young lady behind the counter?" Stella whispered close to Virginia's ear.

"Uh. . .yeah. . .sure." Virginia approached the counter, with Stella at her side. "This is my friend, Stella," she said, barely looking at Amy.

Amy stretched out her arm to shake hands with Stella. "It's nice to meet you. I'm Amy."

Stella smiled. "This is a really nice place you have here. I've always been fascinated with greenhouses."

Seriously? Virginia pursed her lips in an attempt to maintain a neutral expression. This was news to her. In all the time she'd known Stella, she'd never once heard her mention going to a greenhouse, much less having a fascination with them.

"I'm glad you like it." Amy smiled. "But the greenhouse isn't mine. It belongs to my mother. I just work here, along with my younger brother. Sometimes, in a pinch, our older sister helps out too."

"So it's a family affair?"

Amy nodded just before a customer approached the counter with a wagonload of plants.

"We'd better get going." Virginia nudged her friend's arm. "Things are getting busy here, and we don't want to get in the way."

Stella's gaze flicked upward. "I'm not ready to go yet. We just got here. I'd like to have a look around." She touched Virginia's arm. "If your leg's bothering you too much to walk with me, why don't you go out and wait in the car?"

Virginia's toes curled inside her sneakers. If she sat in the car, Stella would probably take longer to look around. But if she walked with her, Stella might hurry things along. "I'll be fine. I'm not waiting in the car," she responded.

"Okay then, we can walk slowly, so it doesn't put so much pressure on your leg," Stella slowed her pace.

Oh great. At this rate we'll be here all day.

By the time they'd made their rounds and seen all of the greenhouse, Stella had picked out several packets of seeds, plus some gardening utensils. She mentioned the idea of buying a few plants but decided not to since she wouldn't be going back to Chicago for a few more days, and was worried that they might not survive the trip home.

When they went to the counter to check out, Amy and Belinda were both there. Amy introduced Stella to her mother, and the two women shook hands.

"It's nice to see you again, Virginia." Belinda offered her a pleasant smile.

Virginia managed to smile in return, while mumbling, "Uh, same here."

Several more minutes went by as Stella conversed with the Amish women. Virginia was relieved when her friend gathered up her purchases and moved toward the door with a cheerful, "Goodbye." Of course, Virginia felt forced to say goodbye to Amy and Belinda, before following Stella out the door.

Virginia wasn't sure what hurt the most—her pounding head or the throbbing in her leg.

As they drove the short distance back to her house, Stella chattered on about the lovely greenhouse.

When Stella pulled her vehicle onto the driveway and set the brake, she turned to face Virginia. "I can't understand why you don't like those people. Both women seemed very nice to me."

"Yeah, well, that's easy enough for you to say. You don't live across from them, and you're not being forced to hear the traffic noise brought on by all those people visiting that greenhouse nearly every day." Virginia got out of the car and limped her way onto the porch.

"I'm glad we went there," Stella said, upon entering the house.

"How's your family doing?" Virginia asked, needing to change the subject.

"Everyone's fine. Jim's wife got a new job last month, but I must have already told you about it."

Virginia shook her head. "I'm sure I'd remember if you did. What about your daughter? How's she getting along since her divorce?"

"It's been difficult, but she's adjusting to the change. Judy comes by and visits us quite often."

Lucky you. Virginia took a seat on the couch and motioned for Stella to do the same. *How nice it would be to have a family who would come and visit me and Earl.*

After Sylvia put the children down for their afternoon naps, she went outside to check the clothes on the line. With the gentle warm breeze that had been blowing for the last few hours, all or most of the clothes were bound to be dry by now.

When Sylvia stepped outside, the sight of clean sheets flapping in the breeze brought back childhood memories. Ever since she was a girl, Sylvia had enjoyed helping her mother hang the laundry. The fresh scent that followed her into the house when the clothes were dry was something she'd always looked forward to. It was strange how she viewed as special what some would see as a mundane chore.

Two sparrows splashing in the birdbath nearby caught Sylvia's attention. She paused from her job of removing the sheets to watch as the birds took drinks then flew in and out of their nests in the trees.

No wonder Henry enjoys watching the birds so much. If I had more time I'd take a seat on the porch and just watch and listen.

A bird on a branch overhead let loose with its mesmerizing song as it imitated other birds in the yard.

"That mockingbird is really something, isn't it?" Henry asked as he joined Sylvia by the clothesline.

She nodded. "I can't tell if it's trying to entertain or mock us."

"It's hard to say." Henry stared into the tree. "Did you know that young males often sing at night?"

Sylvia shook her head. "I don't know much about any kind of bird, but I'd like to learn."

"I bet Dennis could tell us more than I know. He seems to have a lot of knowledge about birds found here in this state."

"You could be right, Henry, but if you keep studying birds and learning all you can about them, it won't be long before you'll know as much as Dennis."

Henry's eyes brightened. "You think so?"

"I do." Sylvia took a sheet down from the line and placed it in her wicker basket. "You know, when Dennis met us at the house to get the key, he said that if either of us would like to go bird-watching again, to let him know, and he'd be glad to go along."

"I'd like that. Do you have his phone number? Can we give him a call?"

"He gave me his cell number, but I think it might be too soon to pester him about going bird-watching with us. He just moved into my house last night and will need time to get settled in. He'll also have to advertise and get his business of horse training going. If you want to go birding again soon, you can either go by yourself when you're not working, or wait till I'm free to go with you."

"I'd rather wait for you. Bird-watching is more fun when you do it with someone else."

Sylvia smiled. She was pleased that her brother had not only found a new hobby to enjoy but also wanted to include her. Hopefully, they'd be able to take some time to go birding soon.

Chapter 16

Belinda stood in front of the bathroom mirror, staring at her reflection. She still needed to put on her headscarf before leaving for work. She turned her head from side to side, checking to be sure no hairs had come loose from her bun. After fixing a few stray ones, she tied the black scarf in place.

Belinda sighed. Today was her fifty-first birthday and the depression she felt made her feel like she was a hundred years old. But it wasn't turning a year older that put a lump in her throat. Today was the anniversary of her husband, son, and son-in-law's deaths. Just when she thought she was doing a little better, she was hit once again with the reality that the three of them were gone and wouldn't be coming back.

Poor Sylvia. I'm sure she must be hurting real bad too. This day must also be hard for my other children as they think about the family members they lost.

Tears welled in Belinda's eyes. *I hope the children haven't planned anything special for my birthday this evening. I need to keep my mind off what day it is, so I'll focus on my work in the greenhouse. This evening, it'll be a quiet meal with the family, and then off to bed. No fuss—no bother—just another regular day.*

Belinda dried her eyes and blew her nose on a tissue. Then she splashed cold water on her face. *I'll feel better once today is over.*

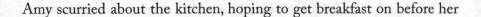

Amy scurried about the kitchen, hoping to get breakfast on before her mother got up. It was bad enough that Mom had to work on her birthday. She shouldn't have to cook for everyone too.

The children padded into the kitchen in their bare feet, and Allen asked his auntie what was for breakfast.

"I'm fixing pancakes," Amy replied. "If you and your sister will go out to the living room and play, I'll call you when breakfast is ready."

Allen grinned, grabbed Rachel's hand, and trotted out of the kitchen.

Amy smiled as she went back to preparing the meal. She hoped the day would go well for her mother and that she would have a pleasant birthday.

As a surprise, Amy and Sylvia had made plans to hire a driver and take their mother out for supper at Shady Maple this evening. They hadn't told Henry yet, but Amy felt sure he'd enjoy going to the big buffet restaurant in East Earl. With so many options to choose from, diners found it nearly impossible not to find something they wanted to eat. Because today was also the one-year anniversary of their loved ones' deaths, it would be better to go out to celebrate Mom's birthday than to celebrate at home where the memory of that fateful day still lingered in each of their minds. She hoped by being in a public place with lots of food and action, Mom, as well as the rest of the family, would have an easier time. *Who knows*, she thought. *We might all relax and enjoy ourselves, even though we'll wish Dad, Abe, and Toby could be with us.*

Amy thought about Jared and how brokenhearted she'd be if something happened to him. Just pondering the idea was enough to put a lump in her throat. She couldn't fathom how Mom and Sylvia must feel, having lost their husbands.

When Sylvia entered the kitchen, she saw that Amy had already set the table and was now busy mixing pancake batter. Three banana peels lay next to the bowl, signaling that Amy was stirring together Mom's favorite—banana pancakes.

"I'm sorry for leaving you with all the work," Sylvia apologized. "When I woke up this morning and the reality of what day it was set in,

I had to remain in my room awhile to get control of my emotions."

"It's fine. I understand."

Do you really? Sylvia wanted to ask, but she kept it to herself. There was no way Amy could understand, so nothing would be gained by posing such a question.

"Is Mom up yet?" Sylvia questioned instead.

Amy shrugged her slender shoulders. "She hasn't come in here, but she might be in her bedroom or the bathroom, getting ready to face the day."

"When should we tell her about our plans for this evening?"

"Not till the greenhouse closes for the day and we come up to the house. She'll no doubt say something about needing to get supper started, and that's when we can tell her our plans."

"So it'll be a surprise until then." Sylvia got out a cube of butter and the maple syrup bottle, along with a jar of honey, which she actually preferred on her pancakes.

Amy nodded. "I think eating supper at Shady Maple will be good for all of us."

"I hope so." Sylvia released a heavy sigh, looking toward the doorway. "Do you think it'll be a mistake to take Allen and Rachel along?" she whispered. "We could drop them off at Mary Ruth's. I'm sure she and Lenore wouldn't mind watching them while we're gone. I could go out to the phone shed and leave a message for them right now, which should give plenty of time for their response."

"It's up to you, Sister, but I'm fairly certain that Mom will want the whole family at her birthday supper."

"True, but our whole family won't be there. Ezekiel, Michelle, and their kinner will not be with us."

Amy turned to face Sylvia, with her chin tilted down. "I still wish our bruder would have moved back to Strasburg after Dad, Abe, and Toby died. We could certainly use his help in the greenhouse, not to mention the emotional support and spiritual guidance he would offer."

Sylvia didn't care about receiving spiritual guidance from her brother or anyone else, but it would have been nice if he'd decided to move back here and help in the greenhouse. It would take some of the load off Mom, Amy, and even Henry. It would also mean Sylvia would never have to work in the greenhouse again. She couldn't help thinking that things might be better for all of them if Ezekiel and Michelle lived closer.

🐦

By the time their mother entered the kitchen, breakfast was done and ready to be put on the table. Coming into the room, she sniffed. "Something smells wunderbaar in here."

"Happy birthday, Mom," Amy and Sylvia said in unison.

"Danki." Mom's gaze went to the table. "For goodness' sake, you girls have outdone yourself this morning." She put both hands against her cheeks as she looked at the stack of pancakes piled high on a plate in the center of the table. "And it appears that you've fixed my favorite banana pannekuche."

"We sure did." Amy's lips pressed together. "Now if Henry would just get here, we could all eat."

"Where is our bruder?" Sylvia asked. "Shouldn't he be in from choring by now?"

Mom bobbed her head. "You're right, he should. Would one of you mind going out to the barn to see if he's still in there?"

"I'll go," Sylvia volunteered. "The kinner are still playing in the living room and will come to breakfast when you call them." She pointed to the table. "There's no point in letting those delicious-looking pancakes get cold, so Mom and Amy, why don't you go ahead and start eating? I'll be back soon with Henry."

Mom called out to the children and tilted her head, as if weighing her choices. "Okay, if you insist, but when you see your brother, please ask him to hurry. If he's late eating breakfast, he'll be late coming to the greenhouse today."

"I'll give him your message." Sylvia seated the kids before she left the kitchen and then went out the back door. It didn't take long to see why Henry hadn't come into the house. She spotted him on the far side of the yard, looking up at a tree with his binoculars.

She hurried over to stand beside him. "What are you doing, Brother? Mom, Amy, and my kinner have already started eating breakfast, and

Mom said you need to hurry so you're not late to work."

"I'm lookin' at a red-winged blackbird." He pointed, and then handed Sylvia the binoculars. "See it up there?"

She held them up and peered through the lenses. Sure enough, there sat the pretty bird that had begun warbling a pretty song. Sylvia watched it several seconds, then handed the binoculars back to Henry. "As nice as it is to watch the *voggel*, today is Mom's birthday, and the least we can do is sit with her at the table and enjoy the nice breakfast Amy made."

Henry continued to watch the bird. "I realize it's Mom's *gebottsdaag*, but I can't forget that it's also been a year since Dad, Abe, and Toby were killed in that horrible accident in front of our house." He sniffed a couple of times then cleared his throat. "I don't feel much like celebrating today, and I bet Mom doesn't either."

"None of us do, Henry, but sitting around all day feeling sorry for ourselves won't change our circumstances, will it?"

He gave a slow shake of his head.

"Mom doesn't know it yet, but we're all going out for supper this evening at the Shady Maple buffet." She touched his arm. "So please be careful you don't let it slip."

"I won't say a word, but I bet goin' out to supper won't keep Mom from thinkin' about what happened to our family members."

"Probably not, but it might cheer her up a bit."

"What about you, Sylvia?" Henry looked at her pointedly. "Will a trip to Shady Maple take the pain of losing your husband, father, and brother away?"

"No," she admitted, "but after a year of mourning, I've come to the conclusion that it's time to put my black clothes away and at least try to start living again and looking for things to smile about. My kinner deserve a mudder who isn't always sad and moody."

"Guess you're right." Henry took hold of Sylvia's arm and started walking toward the house. "You wanna know something?"

"What's that?"

"I'm still mad at God for takin' three important men in my life away."

Me too, Henry, and I'm not sure my faith will ever be restored again. Sylvia gave her brother's arm a little squeeze, but she kept her thoughts to herself.

"Are you all packed, Michelle?" Ezekiel called when he entered the house at nine-thirty that morning. He'd returned from his shop where he'd made sure he had plenty of work laid out for his employees, Joseph and Andy, to do during the four days he and his family would be in Strasburg. There was no point in traveling such a distance unless they could stay at least that long.

With their nine-month-old son in her arms, Michelle stepped into the living room, where Ezekiel waited. "Almost ready. Angela Mary's looking for one of her shoes, and I was trying to help her find it when you called out to me."

"Here, let me have this little guy while you assist our daughter." Ezekiel held out his arms and smiled when Vernon went to him willingly.

"You're looking forward to going to see your family as much as I am, aren't you?"

He nodded. "I'm glad we decided not to tell them we're coming. It'll be a fun surprise birthday gift from us when we show up unexpectedly."

"I hope they're home when we get there. But in case they're out somewhere, you might want to take your key to their house."

"I doubt they'll be gone, but don't worry. I have a spare on my key ring."

"Good. I'd like to be prepared in the event that they may have made plans to go out somewhere for supper to celebrate your mamm's birthday."

Ezekiel shook his head. "I can't remember a time in the past when we celebrated her or my daed's birthday anyplace but at home. They always said home was the happiest place they could be with their family."

Michelle leaned forward and encompassed Ezekiel and the baby in a hug. "I feel that way about my little family too. I have to admit, though, it is nice to eat out at a restaurant once in a while."

"Same here, but I assure you, when we get to Strasburg around five this evening, everyone will be home, and soon after we get there it'll be time for supper." Ezekiel gave a wide grin. "I can hardly wait to see the look on Mom's face when we show up."

Chapter 17

Strasburg

Virginia set her crossword puzzle aside and made her way to the kitchen for a cup of coffee. It would be several hours yet before Earl came home from work, and she would need to come up with something for supper.

She scratched her head. *I'm drawing a blank on what to fix. Something different would be nice for a change.*

Her gaze came to rest on the new cookbook sitting there, full of Amish recipes. Unbeknownst to her, Stella had bought them both a copy, and she'd surprised Virginia with it on the last day of her visit.

She exhaled noisily. *Stella's my only true friend, and I miss her company.* Virginia lifted the cookbook and thumbed through the pages. *I wonder if she's tried any of these recipes.*

If Virginia had her way, she and Earl would go out to eat every night, but that was unrealistic. He made enough selling cars to pay for their basic expenses, but he'd been trying to put some money into their savings account and had stated several times that there should be no unnecessary spending. He'd made it clear to Virginia that going out to a restaurant once or twice a month was all they could afford. Even then, he almost always chose less expensive restaurants.

At least my husband isn't a cheapskate when it comes to buying new appliances when they quit working and cost too much to be repaired, Virginia reminded herself. *Guess I should be grateful for that. And, he's never insisted that I get a job to help with our expenses.*

She filled her mug with coffee and took a seat at the table. *Stella and I had some good chats while she was here a few weeks ago. Sure wish I had a friend like her who lived close by.*

Virginia blew on her coffee. *I can't make friends with any of the Amish women who live nearby. We have nothing in common.* She tapped her fingers on the table. *What would we have to talk about—how many bales of hay they need to feed their horses? Or maybe we could discuss how to wash dishes by hand or sew a plain dress.* She wrinkled her nose. *I don't think so. If I'm going to find a new friend, I'll have to look elsewhere, because sitting home by myself five days a week has left me in a depressed state.*

Belinda felt thankful that they'd been busy in the greenhouse all day, because it had kept her mind occupied and free of negative thoughts. Amy tried to be cheerful too, which helped a lot. Henry, on the other hand, hadn't said much to either of them, other than his quick, "Happy birthday," to Belinda this morning before they opened for business.

She still looked forward to a quiet supper with her family this evening and figured if it didn't rain, as predicted, they might get out the barbecue and grill some burgers. She hoped her daughters hadn't made any plans to fix an elaborate meal, because all she wanted was something simple. After supper and the dishes had been done, Belinda planned to sit in one of the recliners with her feet up and listen to the chatter of her grandchildren as they played with their toys.

The greenhouse door opened, and she shifted on her stool to see who'd come in. She was surprised to see Monroe enter the building, carrying a yellow gift bag.

"Happy birthday, Belinda." He handed her the gift. "I hope you like what I got for you."

Belinda wasn't sure how to respond. His appearance with a gift had taken her by surprise. She'd never expected Monroe to remember that today was her birthday, even though he'd attended a few of her birthday gatherings when they were teenagers.

"Umm. . .well, danki, Monroe. It was thoughtful of you to remember me today," she said earnestly.

"I think of you most every day, Belinda." He leaned close to the counter. "Go ahead—open it."

Belinda pulled the card from the bag first and read it silently. "*To someone special, on her birthday. Your good friend, Monroe.*"

She smiled and gave him a nod, then reached into the bag and took out a box of pretty stationary with yellow daisies and a matching kitchen towel. "These are lovely. Thank you, Monroe."

"Glad you like 'em." A relaxed smile crossed his face as he puffed out his chest a bit. "So are you doing anything special this evening to celebrate your birthday?"

"No, not really. It'll be a nice quiet evening at home with my family."

"I see."

Belinda held her breath, wondering if Monroe would drop any hints about joining them for supper, but to her relief he said nothing in that regard.

"Well, that's all I came here for—to give you the gift and wish you a happy birthday. So I guess I'll be on my way." Monroe started for the door.

"Thank you for coming," Belinda called to his retreating form. When the door clicked shut behind him, she breathed a sigh of relief. With Monroe being so nice and giving her a gift, it was difficult not to give in and invite him to join them for supper. But she'd made the decision not to encourage him in any way, and she needed to stick with it.

⸻

"You'd better hurry and change your clothes," Amy instructed her mother. "Our driver will be here soon to pick us all up."

Mom crooked an eyebrow. "What driver? Where are we going?"

"It's a surprise." Amy grinned. "Come on now, you need to get changed. Sylvia's getting the kinner ready, and as far as I know, Henry's dressed in clean clothes and ready to go too."

"Is Jared coming with us?" Mom asked.

"Jah, he should be here any minute." While Jared wasn't a family member, he would be soon, and as far as Amy was concerned, he should be at all family functions.

It's too bad Ezekiel and his family can't join us tonight, she thought with regret. He'd sent a birthday card for Mom, which had been in yesterday's mail, but there was no phone message from him today, which Amy thought was a bit strange. *If my brother was too busy, I would think Michelle would have reminded him to call our mother on her special day.*

Amy wondered if Mom's birthday and the anniversary of Dad, Abe, and Toby's death could have slipped her brother's mind. If so, then he had too many other, less important things, to think about.

Amy turned to her mother and said one final time, "Please, Mom, hurry now and change into a different dress."

"All right, I'm going." Mom glanced around, as if looking for some answers before hurrying from the room.

East Earl, Pennsylvania

"I wish you'd tell me where we are going," Mom said from the back seat of their driver Helen's van. "And I don't see why I have to wear a scarf over my eyes."

Sylvia tapped her mother's shoulder. "You'll know soon enough."

"We're covering your eyes so you don't guess where we're going," Amy added from the front seat.

"I bet she knows anyhow, even with the blindfold," Henry chimed in. He sat beside Mom on the first seat in the back, with Sylvia and the children behind them.

"No, I don't." Mom shook her head. "But it's taking us a while to get there, so I'm sure it's not some restaurant close to home."

"You are right, Belinda," Helen interjected. "And we're almost there."

When they pulled into the parking lot in front of Shady Maple, Sylvia leaned forward and untied the scarf around her mother's eyes. "We're here—at your favorite place to eat."

"Mine too—especially when I'm really *hungerich*," Henry put in.

Mom looked around and giggled like a schoolgirl. "Oh my—it's Shady Maple!"

Sylvia smiled. She hadn't seen her mother this happy since the last time Ezekiel and his family came to visit.

After Helen parked the van, they all got out and headed for the restaurant. Although Sylvia's mood wasn't the best it could be, it was good to see Mom so happy. And she certainly deserved to be.

Strasburg

"We're here!" Michelle exclaimed when their driver pulled into her mother-in-law's home. "After a seven-hour drive, it's nice that we can finally relax and stretch our legs."

Ezekiel gave a nod. "Why don't you take the kinner on up to the house, while I get our luggage out of the van and talk to our driver about the day and time we'll need to return home? Tell Mom and the rest of the family that I'll be in soon."

Michelle got out, helped Angela Mary down, and took Vernon out of his car seat. Then she told her daughter to walk beside her as they made their way onto the front porch.

"Knock on the door, Angela Mary," Michelle instructed.

The little girl did as she was told, but when no one answered, she turned and looked up at Michelle with a frown. "How come nobody's lettin' us in?"

"Maybe you didn't knock loud enough. Try it again, a little harder this time."

Angela clenched her small fist and pounded on the door.

Michelle bit back a chuckle. If someone inside didn't hear that and answer the door, they must need a hearing aide.

Michelle was about to try the door, when Ezekiel stepped onto the porch with two of their suitcases. "What's going on?" he asked. "Didn't you knock?"

"Our daughter did—the second time really hard—but nobody answered." She looked at her husband, then back at the door. "Do you think it's possible that no one's home?"

"Anything's possible, but it's doubtful. I can't remember Mom ever being anywhere but home on her birthday." Ezekiel rapped on the door. When there was no answer, he turned the knob, but the door didn't open. "Oh boy—it's locked. Now what are we gonna do?"

"Don't you have a key?"

"Oh, yeah, that's right, I do." Ezekiel fumbled in his pocket and withdrew a key. He put it in the lock, turned the key, and the door opened. "Anybody here?" he called.

There was no response, and the house was dark. His family had obviously gone somewhere.

"Let's turn on one of the overhead gas lamps and look around to see if they left us a note," Michelle suggested.

"There'd be no reason for them to have left a note, because they didn't know we were coming, remember? Our being here for Mom's birthday was supposed to be a surprise."

"I guess we're the ones who are surprised." Michelle placed the baby in his carrier on the living room floor. "What are we going to do now, Ezekiel? We're all hungry."

"I suppose we could make some sandwiches. I'll go to the kitchen and see what's in the refrigerator while you take the kids' outer garments off." Ezekiel walked away before Michelle could respond. A few minutes later he was back with a desktop calendar. "I know where they've gone. It's written right here. Good thing I thought to open the roll-top desk and look around." He grinned at Michelle. "I really wasn't sure what to look for, but something told me to open the desk before checking for food in the refrigerator."

"So where'd they go?" Michelle asked. "I'm anxious to know."

"Shady Maple—Mom's favorite place to eat." He did an about-face. "I haven't taken all our things from the van yet, which means we still have a driver. Get the kinner ready, Michelle. We're goin' to Shady Maple!"

East Earl

Belinda looked at her plate full of food and shook her head. This was more than she ate during an entire day, and she'd no doubt pay the price for it tonight when she tried to sleep. But it was ever so kind of her children to plan this surprise for her birthday, and she planned to enjoy every bite of the delicious food.

Belinda watched Amy and Jared from across the table. The love they felt for each other caused their eyes to glow and faces to smile whenever they looked at each other.

My dear Vernon used to look at me like that, Belinda mused. *And I hung on his every word.*

But those days were long past, and now she had to look to the future and be open to whatever plans God had for her. She felt sure, however, that they didn't include remarriage, and most assuredly not to Monroe.

"Well, well. . . So this is where you've chosen to spend your evening, is it?"

Belinda's head came up at the sound of a familiar voice. Her eyes widened as Ezekiel and Michelle stood beside their table, each holding one of their children. "What are you doing here, and how'd you know where we would be?"

"We decided a few weeks ago to come down from New York to surprise you on your birthday, but we're the ones who got the big surprise when we arrived at your house and discovered you weren't at home." Ezekiel shook his finger at Amy and then Sylvia. "Why didn't one of you tell me you had plans to bring our mamm here?"

"We didn't tell you because we had no idea you were coming to see us." Amy shook a finger right back at him. "You should have called and let us know about your plans."

"And take the chance that Mom might find out? Never!"

"How'd ya know we were here?" The question came from Henry.

"When we discovered nobody was home, I used my key to open the door. Then, while Michelle and the kinner waited in the living room, I went to the kitchen to see if there was anything we could use for sandwiches. It was while I was there that I happened to look in the desk." Ezekiel paused a few seconds before he continued. "The words, "Shady Maple," were written on the calendar inside the desk, so I figured that must be where you'd all gone."

Tears welled in Belinda's eyes, nearly obstructing her vision. She left her seat and gave her New York family a hug, with extra kisses for the children. "If you and Michelle would like to go fill your plates and Angela Mary's, we'll keep an eye on the children here at the table. Then when you get back, we can finish our meal and catch up with each other's lives."

"Good idea." Ezekiel situated Angela Mary on a chair, and placed little Vernon on Amy's lap. "We'll be back soon."

Belinda closed her eyes. *Thank You, Lord, for giving me such a loving family.* Although her birthday was somewhat bittersweet, because she missed their departed loved ones and wished they could be here to celebrate with them, Belinda was aware of God's many blessings.

Chapter 18

Strasburg

After Virginia saw Earl off to work the following day, she sat on the front porch with a cup of coffee and her crossword puzzle book. It was a beautiful spring morning, with birds chirping from every tree in the yard, as well as those across the road. Her Amish neighbors across the street had a feeder hanging off a branch of a maple tree. It was nice entertainment to use her binoculars and watch the feeding frenzy going on. Sometimes the teenage boy in his straw hat would stand off gazing at the winged action. It seemed intriguing that Amy's young brother was interested in birds. Virginia figured he'd be off running around with other teenagers.

Virginia could see herself bird-watching as a hobby. It would be fun to be able to identify the species of birds in the area. *Maybe I'll buy a bird identification book the next time I'm out shopping.*

She blew on her hot coffee and tried to relax. Her leg had been hurting this morning, so she wouldn't do too much today. Instead, Virginia would sit here awhile, but once the horse-and-buggy traffic started, she'd have to go back inside if she wanted any peace and quiet.

She noticed Belinda King's teenage boy outside. She couldn't tell for sure from this distance, but it looked like he held a pair of binoculars in his hands. When he tipped his head back, as though looking into one of the trees in the yard, a bearded man came out of the house and joined Henry on the lawn. No doubt, the King family had overnight guests. What other reason would they be coming out of the house so early in the morning?

A short time later, a little Amish girl came out of the house, and the bearded man picked her up, then pointed to the tree.

Virginia left her chair and stood at the porch railing, hoping for a better look. *Maybe I should go inside and get my binoculars. I might be able to see what they're looking at.*

Virginia stepped inside, but by the time she came back out, Henry and the visitors were no longer in her line of vision. They'd either gone back to the house or moved somewhere else in the yard.

She thought of Stella and how she'd enjoyed sitting out here, soaking up the country air. One morning, they'd sat on the lounge chairs for over an hour, drinking coffee and chatting. Every now and then, her friend would jump up to watch an Amish carriage go up the road or turn onto the Kings' driveway. Stella had commented, "Don't you just love the quaintness of those Plain people and their old-fashioned mode of transportation?" Virginia would smile, not wanting to ruin Stella's enthusiasm over the very thing that left unsightly messes and brought in more flies.

She snapped her fingers. "Guess I may as well go back inside. So much for spying on the neighbors. Maybe I'll see more the next time."

❧

When a horse and buggy pulled into the yard, Sylvia looked up from her job of pulling weeds in the flowerbed by the house. She was surprised to see Dennis get out of the carriage.

"*Guder mariye,*" he called after he secured his horse to the rail.

"Good morning." Sylvia rose to her feet and headed in his direction.

He met her halfway and offered a pleasant smile. "I'm sorry for the interruption, but I came by to ask a few questions I forgot when we met at your place and you gave me the key."

Sylvia wondered why Dennis hadn't called and left a message with his questions, but she supposed he preferred to ask in person. "What did you need to know?"

"There are some tools in the shed, and I wondered if you plan to take them, or would it be possible for me to buy them from you?"

Sylvia removed her gardening gloves and swiped one hand across her sweaty forehead. The tools had belonged to Toby, and she'd almost forgotten they were in the shed. "I'm not sure I want to sell them at this time, but you're welcome to use any of the tools while you are renting my house."

His chin tilted down as he broke eye contact with her for a few seconds, but then he smiled and said, "Okay, that's fine. I just didn't want to touch 'em till I'd spoken to you."

"I appreciate your consideration."

"I have another question."

"Oh? What's that?"

"I'm interested in getting a dog. Would you have a problem with that, if I kept it outside during the day and only brought it into the house in the evenings?"

Sylvia fingered her apron band as she mulled over his request. Her husband hadn't been a dog person. He'd said having a dog would be one more thing to worry about when they were away from home.

"Would you be leaving it inside when you're not at home?"

Dennis shook his head. "He'd be an outside dog during the day, and I'll even build him a pen to stay in when I'm away from the house." He offered Sylvia a boyish grin. "I've been thinking it would be nice to have a companion around to keep me company—especially in the evenings. Besides, it never hurts to have an extra pair of eyes and ears to let me know when a visitor comes by."

Sylvia smiled. How could she say no to his honest request? "Jah, it's fine. I don't see a problem with you getting a dog."

"Danki." He lifted his straw hat and pulled his fingers through the back of his thick hair. "Thought I'd take a ride Sunday afternoon to enjoy the nice weather and look for some unusual birds. Would you and your brother want to join me?"

A part of her wanted to instantly agree to his offer, but another part of Sylvia—the sensible one—remembered they had company.

"It would be fun to join you, and I'm sure Henry would enjoy it too, but my older brother and his family are here from New York right now. They came to help us celebrate my mamm's birthday, which was yesterday."

"Oh, I see. And I guess they'll still be with you on Sunday?"

"Jah. In fact, my brother Ezekiel, who is a minister, will most likely preach one of the sermons."

"So you'll be expected to spend the day with your family?"

"Not expected," she corrected. "We don't get to see Ezekiel and his family very often, so I want to be with them."

Dennis gave a nod. "I understand. Some families are very tightknit."

Sylvia was on the verge of asking if he and his family were close, when Ezekiel came out of the barn with Henry.

"That's my older brother." She gestured to them, then invited Ezekiel and Henry to come over.

"Hey, Mr. Weaver, it's good to see you." Henry gave Dennis an eager grin when he and Ezekiel joined them.

Sylvia made the introductions, and while Dennis and Ezekiel shook hands, she told Henry why Dennis had dropped by.

"It wasn't just about the tools either," Dennis said. "I wanted to invite you and your sister to go for a ride with me tomorrow afternoon to look for birds."

"Oh, jah, that'd be great. Count me in." Henry gave a wide grin.

Sylvia placed her hand on his arm. "Henry, I told Mr. Weaver we couldn't go because we have company and will be spending the day with them."

"No problem," Ezekiel was quick to say. "I doubt you'll be gone more than a few hours, and you'll be with us the rest of the day."

Henry's head moved up and down. "See Sylvia. . . Ezekiel said it's okay."

Sylvia felt like she was a fly caught in a sticky trap. If she agreed to go birding with Dennis, what would the rest of her family say? Could they be as agreeable as Ezekiel, or might they think she ought to be with them the whole day?

Dennis waited for Sylvia's response, wondering if he'd made a mistake by asking her to join him Sunday afternoon. He didn't want to appear pushy, but Sylvia had been on his mind ever since their first meeting. Seeing her wearing a dark green dress today let him know her year of mourning and black clothes had been set aside. However, it didn't mean she no longer mourned the death of her loved ones. That took time—possibly years. Dennis knew that firsthand. Even now, whenever he thought about his father's death, depression could set in. He was glad he'd let his guard down and shared the incident with Sylvia and her brother. Just talking about it had relieved some of his emotional pain.

"I would enjoy looking for birds with you." Sylvia's comment pulled Dennis's thoughts aside. "But would you mind very much if I went out to the greenhouse right now and talked to my mamm about it? I need to see if she's willing to—"

"I don't mind at all. In fact, I'd like to walk out there with you and meet her. It would also be nice to have a look around. I'd like to see what all you have available."

"Sure, that'd be fine." Sylvia led the way, and when they entered the building, she suggested that Dennis look around, while she spoke to her mother, who was currently with a customer.

"No problem." He smiled. "I would like to meet her before I leave, though."

"That's fine. I'm sure there will be time for it when she's between customers."

"Okay then, I'm off to wander around."

With raised brows, Ezekiel looked at Henry. "Is there something going on between Sylvia and that man?"

Henry squinted. "What do ya mean?"

"Is he lookin' to court her?"

Henry thumped Ezekiel's arm. " 'Course not. What a dumm question."

"It's not dumb at all. I have a hunch from the way that fellow eyeballed our sister that he has more than looking for birds on his mind."

Henry grunted. "Are you kidding me? He barely even knows our sister. Besides, Sylvia's not looking to be courted by anyone. She still loves Toby. I've heard her say so many times."

Ezekiel glanced toward the greenhouse. "That may be, but the bird-dog expression on his face made me think about the way I felt when I first met Michelle." He thumped Henry's back. "There's an interest, all right, but it may only be wishful thinking on his part, because you're right—Sylvia's love for Toby went deep."

"Well, if you feel that way, then why'd you say it was okay for us to go birding with him tomorrow afternoon?"

"Because, little brother, Sylvia has been too serious since Toby, Dad, and Abe were killed. She deserves to have some fun, and so do you."

Henry kicked at a clump of grass with the toe of his boot. "I have fun when I'm with my friend Seth."

"Jah, well from what I've heard, Seth is not a good influence on you."

Henry crossed his arms and gave a huff. "Is that so? Who told you that?"

"Never mind. The point is, you shouldn't hang around with a fellow who might try to steer you in the wrong direction."

"None of my friends have control over me. I'll have you know I can think for myself."

Ezekiel held up his hands. "Now don't go getting your feathers ruffled. I just felt the need to give you a word of caution. I know what it's like to be sixteen, and even when I got older, there was a time when I caused Mom and Dad all kinds of heartache."

"Ya mean when you bought a truck and thought you might not wanna join the church?"

Ezekiel nodded. "But God got a hold of my life and showed me otherwise, and I'm sure glad He did."

"What's God really done for you, Brother?" Henry's tone had an edge to it. "He let Dad, Abe, and Toby die, and He could have stopped the accident from happening."

Ezekiel put both hands on his brother's shoulders. "God gives everyone a free will, and if you'll remember, all three men wanted to get ice cream for Mom's birthday, even though she didn't want them to go."

Henry stared at the ground. "I remember."

"When they made that decision, they had no idea what their fate would be, but it was their choice, and perhaps even their time to leave this earth."

Henry slowly shook his head and walked off toward the greenhouse.

Ezekiel bowed his head. *Heavenly Father, please open my brother's eyes to the truth and help him come to terms with what happened. Blaming You for something that was an accident is not helping him recover from the anger he feels. Please help me to set a good example for him, and grant Henry peace of mind and the desire to serve You.*

Dennis stopped to look at primroses and a few other early spring flowers. Then he moved on to check out some of the outdoor items, such as birdbaths and solar lighting.

A birdbath might be a nice touch to my yard, he decided. Even though Sylvia's house didn't belong to Dennis, he still thought of it as home. Giving the birds that came into the yard a nice place to drink and bathe seemed like a good idea. He also planned to hang several bird feeders and houses. These would increase his chances of seeing a good variety of birds.

Dennis had made the complete tour of the greenhouse when Sylvia came up to him and said her mother was fine with her and Henry going with him Sunday afternoon. "She would like to meet you, though," Sylvia added. "And so would my sister, Amy."

"I'd enjoy meeting them too."

Dennis followed Sylvia to the front of the building, where a middle-age lady and a younger woman who looked close to Sylvia's age stood behind the checkout counter.

When Sylvia introduced Dennis to her mother and sister, he shook their hands. "This is a nice place you have here. There's a good variety of items for sale. And speaking of which. . . I want to buy one of your birdbaths today." He looked at Sylvia. "I'd like to put it in the front yard, near the big maple tree."

"That'd be nice." She smiled, although it seemed a bit forced.

"Are you sure you don't mind?"

She shook her head. "As long as you're living there, feel free to put whatever you like in the yard and also the house."

"Danki, I appreciate that." Dennis walked back to where the birdbaths were located and brought the one he liked up front to pay for it. He then visited with the three women until two more customers came in. "I'd better get going. It was nice to meet you, Belinda and Amy."

"We enjoyed meeting you as well," Amy said.

Belinda nodded and moved down the aisle behind the people who had come in.

When Dennis walked out with the birdbath, Sylvia accompanied him.

"Hey, what have ya got there?" Henry asked, stepping around the side of the building.

Dennis chuckled. "You mean you work here and have never seen a birdbath?"

Henry snickered. "'Course I've seen 'em. Just wasn't expecting to see you carrying one out of the greenhouse."

"I'm gonna put it in my front yard, and hopefully it'll lure in more birds." He started walking toward his horse and buggy and was pleased when Sylvia went with him.

Since the birdbath was in two pieces, he placed them both on the floor in the back of his buggy. "Is three o'clock a good time for me to pick you and Henry up tomorrow?" he asked.

"That should be fine."

"Okay, great. I'll see you then."

When Dennis pulled his rig out of the yard a few minutes later, he found himself whistling—not a tune to any song he knew—but the whistle of a young male mockingbird's song. He could hardly wait until tomorrow afternoon.

Chapter 19

"What are you looking at, Virginia? You're not spying on the neighbors, I hope."

She whirled around to face her husband, nearly dropping the binoculars she held. "For heaven's sake, Earl, don't sneak up on me like that. You nearly scared me to death."

He rolled his eyes and moved closer to where she stood at the living room window. "What were you looking at?"

"Just watching the King family and their guests. There's a group of them, and they climbed into two buggies and headed out down the road. I'm surprised you didn't hear the horses clomping their hooves on the pavement."

He shook his head. "I was in the bathroom, and the only thing I heard was the water running while I showered."

She glanced out the window again. "There's more horse and buggies coming down the road now, so tell me you can't hear those."

"Oh, I hear 'em all right." Earl peered out the window. "Looks like a whole procession."

"I wonder where they're all going."

"Probably church. From what I understand, the Amish worship in one another's homes every other Sunday."

Virginia lifted the binoculars for a better look. "Now that I think about it, there has been a string of Amish buggies going down the road on Sundays about this time of day, twice monthly." She lowered the binoculars and turned to look at Earl. "I wonder why they hold their worship service in people's homes instead of a church building. That seems strange, doesn't it?"

"It does to us, but I'm sure to them it's normal." Earl moved away from the window and motioned for her to do the same. "Come on, Virginia, that's enough spying for now."

She frowned. "What else do I have to do that's exciting?"

"Why don't you put on a sweater and we'll take a Sunday drive?"

"Where to?"

"I picked up a map the other day of covered bridges in the area. We could check those out."

"Okay, I'll get my sweater and meet you in the car." Virginia wasn't the least bit interested in looking at covered bridges, but it would be better than sitting home all day, listening to Earl snore up a storm when he fell asleep watching television.

🐦

Holding her children's hands, Sylvia entered the barn on Mary Ruth Lapp's property, where church was being held. She took a seat on a backless wooden bench, between Amy and their mother. They would both help keep the children quiet during the three-hour service.

Sylvia glanced at the men's side of the room, and noticed that Dennis wasn't there. Then she remembered that because he now occupied her old house, which was in another church district, today would be his off-Sunday. When Sylvia saw Dennis later today, if she didn't forget, she would mention that he'd be welcome to visit this church on his in-between Sundays.

She reached up and adjusted her head covering ties. *Listen to me—all worried about Dennis. I barely know him, so why should I be concerned about where he attends church?*

Sylvia thought about how she and Toby used to visit her parents' church whenever possible on their off-Sundays. Afterward they would go to Mom and Dad's house to visit and share a meal. Those were such happy times, although Sylvia had taken them for granted. She had believed that she and Toby would grow old together, raising their children, and someday becoming grandparents.

Thinking about all she'd lost caused Sylvia to choke up as she held

Rachel firmly on her lap. Tears pricked the backs of her eyes when she saw Allen holding his grandma's hand. How sad that her son was missing out on the joy of being with his Grandpa King and didn't see Grandpa and Grandma Beiler nearly enough due to them living in another part of the state.

At least my kinner have a grandma, an aunt, and one uncle who all live close by and will have a positive influence on them.

Sylvia glanced at Henry sitting beside his friend, Seth. *I hope my younger brother will put aside his curiosity with worldly things and set a good example for Allen and Rachel. I'd hate to think otherwise.*

Sylvia's thoughts were pulled aside when the first song from the Ausbund was announced. She swallowed past the thickening in her throat and forced herself to sing along.

Ezekiel rubbed a sweaty palm down his pant leg. As a guest minister, he'd been asked to deliver a sermon this morning, and he couldn't help feeling a bit nervous. *I hope what I plan to say will be beneficial to someone here today.*

Ezekiel had grown up in this church district and known many of the people for most of his life. It seemed strange to be put in a position where he'd be preaching to folks who'd known him during his running-around days. *I know people who go astray can return to the faith and be a good example to others.* Ezekiel hoped once again that he could prove this in the way he had cleaned up his own life and settled down.

He lifted his hand and rubbed the back of his neck, also wet with perspiration. *Can this congregation see me as a minister now, or to them will I always be the unsettled young man who'd once been dissatisfied with the Plain ways? Will they take me seriously and listen to what God has laid on my heart?*

Ezekiel would be preaching from the Book of Habakkuk on the topic of faith and trust in God during difficult times of unimaginable loss. The verses had helped him during unsettling times, and he hoped someone in the congregation would be helped by them today as well.

As he stood to deliver his sermon, Ezekiel gave a quick glance at the women's section. Michelle offered him a reassuring nod, as did his mother.

Lord, he prayed, *let the words that come from my mouth be Your words, not mine.*

As Ezekiel delivered his sermon, tears welled in Belinda's eyes. *If Vernon was here right now, he would be so pleased to hear his once-wayward son preaching God's Word.*

She glanced across the way to see if Henry's attention was where it should be. He sat with both elbows resting on his knees, and his chin cupped in the palms of his hands. Belinda couldn't tell what her teenage son was thinking, but she had a feeling he was bored and would probably tune Ezekiel's sermon out. Henry's thoughts might be on the time he and Sylvia would spend with Dennis Weaver this afternoon. He'd certainly mentioned it enough times since the plans had been made. Even Sylvia had brought up the topic this morning. Belinda felt a bit concerned by Sylvia and Henry's fascination with a near stranger.

Turning her attention back to Ezekiel, Belinda struggled to keep her tears at bay as he read several verses of scripture. One in particular, Habakkuk 3:18, spoke to her heart. "Yet I will rejoice in the Lord, I will joy in the God of my salvation."

"The prophet Habakkuk predicted that difficult times were on the way," Ezekiel declared. "Things sometimes get worse before they get better." He paused, as if to collect his thoughts. "How do we deal with unexpected financial problems, serious health issues, or the death of a loved one? Habakkuk stated that we need confident faith and trust in God, who is the source of our strength and salvation. In the end, we who trust Him will not be disappointed. When we go through difficult circumstances, God not only meets our needs, but He teaches us to encourage others when they are faced with a crisis."

When Ezekiel ended his sermon and returned to his seat, it was all Belinda could do to control her swirling emotions. Her husband, a son, and a son-in-law had been taken from them a year ago, and they had faced uncertain times concerning the greenhouse and whether their earnings would provide for them ever since. Vandalism and a threatening phone message had occurred, but nothing serious had happened, and no one had been hurt. Belinda had much to be thankful for, and like Habakkuk she could rejoice in the knowledge that during the past year, God had been with them and met all of their needs. Her only hope was that the rest of the family could see that and rejoice in the Lord too.

A sense of anticipation welled in Dennis's chest as his horse and buggy approached the Kings' place. Today had been his church district's off-Sunday, so he'd slept in this morning and spent the rest of the morning reading a recent issue of *Birds and Blooms* magazine. Tomorrow, Dennis would begin training a new horse his friend James had bought at an auction recently. Thanks to James's referrals, Dennis had two more people's horses he would begin working with soon. Dennis had already determined that he liked it here in Lancaster County, and unless something unforeseen came up, he planned to stay and make this area his permanent home. Whether he would continue renting from Sylvia or eventually buy her place remained to be seen.

Who knows, Dennis thought as he turned up the Kings' driveway. *If Sylvia doesn't want to sell her place, I might end up buying some other home with enough property for all my needs.*

When Dennis pulled his horse up to the hitching rail, he spotted two young children—a girl and a boy—on the front porch. They appeared to be fairly close in age. Dennis figured the children belonged to Sylvia's brother, Ezekiel, and his wife. He wondered if they had any other children besides these two.

Dennis had no more than gotten out of the buggy when Henry came running toward him. Sylvia followed, only at a slower pace. They both carried binoculars in their hands.

After greeting him, Henry got in the back of the buggy, and Sylvia rode up front. Then Dennis backed the horse away from the rail and headed off down the driveway.

Dennis gave Sylvia a sidelong glance and noticed that she sat stiffly in the passenger's seat, looking straight ahead. He cleared his throat. "I've been on the lookout for a hund, but so far I've come up empty-handed."

Sylvia remained quiet, but Henry spoke up. "You're tryin' to find a dog? Why not a puppy?"

Dennis jiggled the reins. "When I was a boy, I helped my daed raise some German shepherd pups, and it was a lot of work, which I don't have time for right now. If I could locate a fully grown German shepherd locally, that would be great."

"Maybe you oughta put an ad in *The Budget* or check at the animal shelter in Lancaster," Henry suggested.

"Jah, that might work."

Seconds ticked by before Dennis looked Sylvia's way again. *Why so quiet? She'd been talkative the last time I saw her. What could she be thinking about? I hope I didn't say anything to offend her.*

The silence between them felt awkward and seemed to be growing the farther they rode. *Why am I so tongue-tied right now? I deal with people all the time and always have something to say.*

Struggling to find a good topic, Dennis was about to ask Sylvia about one of the items he'd seen in her mother's greenhouse, when Henry tapped him on the shoulder and piped up with a question of his own.

"Have you seen any mockingbirds since you moved to Strasburg?"

"No, I can't say as I have. I am acquainted with the species though, because I saw some where I used to live in Dauphin County."

"Sylvia saw one the other day—or at least she thinks it was a mockingbird."

"Is that right?" Dennis glanced in her direction. "What'd it look like, Sylvia?"

She turned her head to look at him, then looked back at the road ahead when a car whizzed by. "The bird was in one of the trees in our yard, and I saw it while looking out a window in the house. It was hard to tell for sure, but it appeared to have a gray body and head."

Good. She's talking now. "Was the tail mostly black with white outer feathers?" he questioned.

"I think so, but I can't be sure."

"A male mockingbird has a silvery gray head and back, with light gray chest and belly. It also has white wing patches, and a mostly black tail with white outer tail feathers. Oh, and its bill is black," he added.

"You seem to know a lot about birds," Sylvia said.

"That's because I've been studying them for several years. Of course, that doesn't make me an expert by any means."

"Well, you know more than we do," Henry interjected. "I bet if we get together and go birding with you from time to time, we'll learn a lot more."

"You're right, Henry, but it'll be the birds that'll teach us, not me."

Sylvia couldn't remember the last time she'd enjoyed herself so much. Certainly not since Toby had died. Standing among trees and shrubs, listening to the call of various birds as she peered at them through the binoculars she'd brought along had transported Sylvia to a different world.

The rising whistle of *bob-white. . .bob-white*, caught her attention, and she pointed in the direction of the mostly brown stocky bird with a short gray tail. Upon closer examination through the field glasses, Sylvia realized the bobwhite had a prominent white eye stripe and white chin. She saw clearly that its sides and belly were reddish brown with black lines and dots.

She turned to look at Dennis and mouthed, "Isn't it beautiful?"

He grinned at her and gave a nod.

Henry was all-smiles as he watched the bird searching for insects on the ground.

"If I'd had any idea bird-watching would be so much fun, I would have taken up the hobby sooner," Sylvia whispered to Dennis.

"I agree with you. It's not only an educational hobby, but relaxing and entertaining too." Dennis moved closer to Sylvia. "Can we do this again next Sunday?"

"I'd like that. I'll need to check with my mamm first, but I'm pretty sure she'll be fine with Henry and me going birding with you again. By next Sunday, Ezekiel and his family will be gone, so maybe before or after we go bird-watching, you'd like to share a meal with us."

"That'd be great." There was no hesitation in Dennis's response.

Sylvia looked forward to next week and spending more time with this nice man who knew so much about birds. She hoped either Mom or Amy would be willing to watch Rachel and Allen so she wouldn't have to cancel her plans.

Chapter 20

A lump formed in Belinda's throat as she stood on the porch Monday morning, waving goodbye as Ezekiel and his family gathered their things to put into the driver's van. Even though she'd done this more than once, it never got easier. She craved to have the whole family together, and all this did was fuel the flames. Wonderful as it was to have them visit, it always took her a few days to readjust when they left. However, having her children and grandchildren together in one place made the sting of not having Vernon, Abe, and Toby with them seem a little less severe.

It's in my son's best interest to live where he does, Belinda reminded herself. Each time Ezekiel and his family returned to Clymer, the need to keep Sylvia and the children nearby held her more tightly in its grip. Belinda wasn't certain, but it might be because she felt insecure without a man in her life. She had grown used to Vernon being there by her side and making the heavy decisions around the house. It made things simpler to trust his judgment, sit back, and relax. There were times when they would disagree on some topics, but the waters usually calmed quickly.

Why can't things be easier for me now? I work hard and try to be considerate of others. Belinda rolled her shoulders a couple of times. *If only my husband could give me his sound opinion on things. He allowed more time in figuring out how to work through everyone's problems. I want answers now.* She leaned against the railing, her fingers drumming the wooden surface.

"Are you all right, Mom?" Amy slipped her arm around Belinda's waist. No doubt she sensed her mother's anxiety.

Belinda stopped tapping. "I'm fine, or at least I will be once we go to the greenhouse and get busy."

"Jah. The quicker we get to work, the sooner our minds will be on other things." Amy looked at Henry, along with Sylvia and the children, who had come out to tell Ezekiel and his family goodbye.

Soon they were waving to each other as the van started down the driveway. They all stood watching the vehicle head away from the house and onto the road.

"We'll miss them." Belinda's voice wavered.

Sylvia patted her arm. "Maybe someday we can all go to Clymer to visit them, Mom. Perhaps we could do it on a long weekend."

"I'd like that 'cause I've never been to the state of New York," Henry spoke up.

"That would be a fun trip," Amy agreed.

"I'd consider the plan, but it would have to be when the greenhouse is closed during the winter months. Of course, we'd need to ask someone to pick up our mail, take care of the animals, and check the house." Belinda looked at Amy. "We'll need to put the idea of the trip on hold until after your wedding, so if we go to Clymer, it'll have to be sometime after the first of the year."

Amy nodded. "I hope Jared and I will be able to join you."

Belinda patted her daughter's arm. "I hope so too."

They all remained on the porch for a while, looking out into the yard. The birds seemed to be enjoying the freshly filled containers Henry had taken care of earlier that morning.

Sylvia leaned against the railing by Amy and Belinda. Allen and Rachel came up to their mother, watching a barn cat give herself a bath near the porch. Things seemed somber for a time, as Belinda soaked up the quiet with her family. She looked toward the greenhouse before turning to face her children. "It's getting close to opening time, and even though our spirits are low, we need to get to work."

"You're right, Mom." Amy nudged Henry's arm. "Oh and you'd better get some honey. We're low on what we have available in the greenhouse to sell."

He sneered at her. "Don't be tellin' me what to do. You ain't my boss, you know."

Belinda stepped between them and spoke before Amy could respond to her brother. "Your sister is right—we do need more jars of honey. Would you please take care of that for me, Son?"

"Jah, okay." Henry stepped off the porch and headed for the outside entrance of their cellar, where they kept the raw honey from their bees in glass jars, along with other home-canned goods.

Belinda turned to Sylvia. "Amy and I will be heading to work now. We'll either take turns coming up to the house for lunch, or if we're too busy, one of us may run up and get sandwiches to take out to the greenhouse, which we'll eat whenever we can."

"Okay, Mom, but before you go, I need to ask you a question."

Belinda looked over at Amy. "Would you mind opening up this morning while I talk to Sylvia? I'll be there as soon as I can."

"Sure, Mom. No problem." Amy stepped down from the porch and hurried off in the direction of the greenhouse.

Belinda turned toward Sylvia again. "What did you want to say?"

"Umm. . .just a minute, please." Sylvia opened the door and ushered her children into the house. Belinda heard her instruct them to play quietly in the living room. Then she returned. "Could we take a seat while I talk to you about something?"

"Of course."

After they were seated, Belinda cleared her throat. "What's on your mind, Daughter?"

"Dennis asked Henry and me to go bird-watching with him again this Sunday, and I wondered if you'd be willing to watch the kinner while we're gone."

"Certainly. I always enjoy spending time with my grandchildren." Belinda wasn't thrilled about Sylvia spending time with this stranger they knew so little about, but she couldn't say no to her request. It was good to see that her eldest daughter had found something to get her out of the house. This new hobby was something she and Henry had in common. For the past year, Sylvia had rarely smiled or gotten excited about anything. A fascination with birds and a desire to learn more about them had given her something to look forward to.

"There's one more thing." Sylvia placed her hand on Belinda's arm. "Would it be okay if Dennis joined us for supper Sunday evening, after we get back from birding? I probably shouldn't have, without asking first, but I sort of invited him to join us for the meal."

Belinda's muscles tightened, and she had to consciously force them to relax. Had Sylvia become interested in Dennis Weaver, or he in her? If she saw him regularly, might they end up courting? Although a year had passed since Toby's death, Belinda couldn't accept the idea of her daughter being courted—especially by a near stranger. *I'd like to say what's on my mind right now, but I don't want to undo the progress she's starting to make.*

Belinda had to give Sylvia an answer, and she didn't want to create a problem, so she forced herself to smile and say, "Jah, that would be fine."

Sylvia smiled and gave her a hug. "Danki, Mom. I'll give Dennis a call on his cell phone and let him know about Sunday."

"Cell phone?" Belinda clutched her apron. "Why does he have one of those? There's still a phone shed on your property, right?"

"There is, but the phone's been disconnected since the kinner and I moved out."

"He could have it reconnected and get a new number."

Sylvia nodded. "And he probably will, but he needs the cell phone for business purposes."

"Puh!" Belinda flapped her hand. "We've run a business here for several years, and never needed a cell phone. As I recall, the church district you used to belong to didn't allow their members to own a cell phone."

"Maybe they've changed the rule."

"Or maybe the church leaders aren't aware that Dennis has one." *I'd hate to think so, but this young man we barely know could be a bad influence on my son and daughter.*

The sound and sight of a horse and buggy coming up the driveway put an end to their conversation. "I need to go." Belinda stood. "I'll see you at lunchtime."

🐦

Sylvia entered the house and was greeted with the shrill scream of her daughter. With her heart beating a staccato, she raced to the living room to see what had happened. Rachel sat in the middle of the room, tears coursing down her flushed cheeks, as her brother galloped a plastic horse in circles on the floor. Rachel's tiny baby doll had been draped over the horse's back. No wonder the poor thing was so upset.

Sylvia knelt on the floor, rescued the doll, and handed it to Rachel, who immediately stopped crying. Allen, however, pouted. "The horse has no rider," he said in Pennsylvania Dutch.

"He probably likes not having the dolly on his back." Sylvia reached for her son's hand. "Why don't you come with me to the kitchen? We'll bake some peanut butter *kichlin*."

Allen's eyes widened, and he didn't have to be asked twice. He took off on a full run, and Sylvia found him sitting at the kitchen table when she entered the room. Her son loved cookies and would often ask to taste some of the batter. Truth was, Sylvia liked to test the cookie dough too.

She got out all the ingredients and let Allen help stir the batter. Then she showed him how to drop spoons of dough onto the greased cookie sheet. While the tasty treats baked, Allen colored a picture Sylvia had drawn of a bird. It was supposed to look like the mockingbird she'd seen in the yard, but her son colored it brown instead of gray.

Sylvia smiled. *It doesn't matter what color Allen chose for the bird. At least it's keeping him occupied while his sister plays quietly with her doll by herself.*

Sylvia remembered how, when she was a child, she and her siblings had sometimes quarreled over certain toys. Their mother, in all her wisdom, always came to the rescue by giving each of the children something different to do. Sometimes it turned out to be an unpleasant chore, while other times Mom gave them something fun to do, like helping bake a cake, pie, or cookies.

Back then, Sylvia had no choice but to do whatever her mother said, and now she was a grown woman, with two children of her own to care for.

Sylvia sucked in her bottom lip. *I don't understand why Mom still thinks it's her job to tell me what to do.* She opened the oven door and removed a batch of cookies, placing them on the cooling rack. *Since Mom said it was okay, I need to let Dennis know that he'll be welcome to join us for Sunday supper.*

The first hour after opening the greenhouse they'd been busy, but now things had slacked off. Amy was about to go to the storage room to look for a few items they needed to replenish, when Mom called her up to the front counter.

"What is it, Mom? Did you need me to get something from the storage room?" Amy questioned.

Mom shook her head. "No, I wanted to tell you about the conversation I had with your sister before joining you here after the greenhouse opened."

"Is everything all right with Sylvia?"

"She's not sick or anything, but I am feeling a bit *bekimmere* about her."

"I don't understand. Sylvia seems to be doing a little better lately emotionally, so in what way are you concerned?"

"She and Henry have plans to go birding again this Sunday with that man, Dennis Weaver."

Amy smiled. "I'm not at all surprised. My brother and sister both seem to have found a hobby they really enjoy."

Mom put both hands against her hips. "It's not their new hobby I'm worried about. It's the man they're going bird-watching with. Why, did you know that Dennis owns a cell phone?"

"No, I did not, but I don't see why his having a cell phone would cause you to worry about Sylvia."

"I think he might be worldly and maybe even deceitful, since it's doubtful that he got permission from the leaders in his church district to have any kind of phone other than one that would be in a phone shed."

Amy was on the verge of telling her mother that whatever Dennis did had nothing to do with Sylvia, when Maude, the lady who lived in a nearby shack, came in.

Mom left her stool and went to speak with the unkempt woman. Before Maude left, she would probably be carrying a bag of groceries and whatever else Mom decided to share with her.

Amy pursed her lips. *Doesn't my mother even care that this elderly, eccentric lady has stolen from us?*

Since there was no one else in the building at the moment and Mom was busy talking to Maude, Amy hurried off to the storage room. When she stepped out several minutes later, she heard Maude criticizing the way Mom ran the greenhouse, saying that her prices were too high and the plants and flowers for sale needed to be rearranged.

Amy's finger curled into the palms of her hands. *Who does that woman think she is, talking to my mother that way?* Amy felt sorry for the elderly woman, but it was not good for business to have her here complaining about high prices and saying negative things about the greenhouse. If anyone else had come into the building while Amy was in the storage room, they might have heard Maude's grumblings and decided to take their business elsewhere.

Amy drew in a breath and blew it out with such force, the ties on her head covering swished across her face. *And that would certainly not be good. We need all the business we can get right now.*

Chapter 21

"Things are sure slow this afternoon," Amy commented as she and her mother sat behind the counter, eating ham-and-cheese sandwiches. "If we'd known things would taper off like this, we could have taken turns eating lunch in the house."

Mom took a drink from her bottle of water. "I don't understand it. Usually in the spring we're so busy we can barely keep up." Her neck bent forward as she released a heavy sigh. "Maybe the things Maude said to me earlier today are true. We might be losing customers to the other greenhouse."

"As many kind things as you've done for Maude, she had no right to upset you." Amy's elbows pressed against her sides. "We can't afford to lose any business, Mom. Maybe we need to advertise more."

"Running an ad in the newspaper means more money out of pocket," Mom replied. "Word of mouth has always been our best form of advertising, but if people aren't happy with our prices or the items we sell, they'll tell others not to shop here."

"Let's try not to worry about this." Amy tried to sound optimistic. "Today may just have been slow, and we can't put too much stock in what Maude has to say about things."

"I suppose you're right. Just the same, we do need to come up with some reasonable ways to bring in more business."

"I agree, and speaking of which. . .one of us needs to check with Sara's flower shop and see if there are some flowers her assistant might need. Since Sara's still at home with her new baby, Misty is most likely in charge of things in her absence."

"Why don't you go now, Amy? Since we're not busy and Henry's here to help, I'm certain the two of us can manage while you're gone."

"But Henry's not here, Mom. He went up to the house to eat lunch and hasn't come back yet."

"I'm sure he'll be here soon." Mom gave Amy's shoulder a tap. "Go ahead into town. A stop at the flower shop shouldn't take you long."

"Okay, I'll go get my horse and buggy ready." Amy stepped off the stool and went out the door.

On the way to the barn, she saw Henry coming out of the house with a pair of binoculars. "There's no time for bird-watching now, Henry. I'm going into town for a bit, and Mom will need your help in the greenhouse while I'm gone."

Henry kicked at a clump of tall grass, a reminder to Amy that it was in need of being mowed. "But we're not that busy today. Can't Mom get along without me for half an hour or so?"

"You'll have to take that up with her. Right now I need to get my horse so I can head for town."

Belinda had started a list of ways they might advertise reasonably, when Henry came in with a scowl on his face.

"How come Amy gets to go to town and I have to be in here when there ain't even any customers?" He leaned on the counter where Belinda sat.

She pointed a finger at him. "You know how I feel about that word *ain't*. I am sure you were never taught to say it in school."

"I ain't—I mean, I'm not in school anymore, Mom. Besides, all the fellows I hang around say *ain't*."

"What your friends say or do is none of my concern." She pointed at him again. "You, on the other hand, are still living at home and under my care, so you must do what I say as long as you're living here. Understood?"

Henry's features tightened as he gave a brief nod. "So since there are no customers right now, what do you need me to do?"

Belinda was about to respond when the front door of the greenhouse opened and Monroe stepped in. *Oh dear, I wonder what he wants. I hope he's not here to put pressure on me about seeing him socially. I thought we had that settled.*

"*Gut nammidaag*, Belinda." Monroe stepped up to the counter, almost bumping shoulders with Henry.

"Good afternoon," she responded. "Is there something I can help you with?"

"Not really. I came in to tell you that as I was going by your place, I noticed your sign by the front of the driveway is missing. Just wondered if you knew this and whether you may have taken the sign down for some reason."

Belinda's facial muscles slacked as her mouth dropped open. "The-the sign is gone?"

"That's what I said. I looked around in the tall grass but didn't see it anywhere."

"It was there last night when Seth dropped me off," Henry spoke up.

Belinda's face heated. "What were you doing with Seth? You said you were going out for a walk to look for unusual birds you could write about in your journal." She stared at Henry. "At no time did you mention that you'd be seeing Seth."

"I wasn't planning to see him, Mom. He just drove by as I was walking home and asked if he could give me a ride."

Belinda's mouth felt unexpectedly dry, so she took a sip from her water bottle. "Could Seth have taken the sign after he dropped you off?"

Henry shook his head. "Why would he do that?"

"He's still going through *rumschpringe*, right?" Monroe looked at Henry with wrinkled brows.

"Well, jah, but what's that got to do with anything?"

"Some young people going through their running-around time think it's funny when they pull a few pranks on someone—even a friend."

Henry sighed. "Think I'd better go have a talk with him."

Belinda held up her hand as she shook her head. "Not right now, Son. You have work to do here. Talking to Seth can wait."

"But what about the sign? If it's not hanging at the end of our driveway, how are folks gonna know we're here?"

Belinda massaged her forehead, hoping to stave off the headache she felt coming on. "I'll ask Sylvia to make up a cardboard sign that we can put out there temporarily until the old one is found."

"What if it's never found?" The question came from Monroe. "Maybe whoever has done some vandalism here in the past took the sign." His voice deepened as his brows drew together. "Someone wants to see your business fail, and I'm worried about you."

"There's no need for you to worry," Belinda assured him. "No harm has come to me or any of my family." She continued to rub her forehead. "It is obvious, however, that someone wants us to close the greenhouse permanently."

"I'm sorry this happened, Belinda. If you need anything let me know." Monroe reached across the counter and placed his hand on her shoulder, giving it several gentle taps. "I'll drop by again and check on you tomorrow."

Belinda was on the verge of telling Monroe that it wasn't necessary for him to come by, when one of their steady customers, Dianna Zook, entered the greenhouse.

"Did you know your sign is missing out front by the road?" Dianna questioned.

Belinda nodded, feeling her head throb with every movement. She wished she could go up to the house and take a long nap. Sometimes, sleeping was the only thing that would shake off a tension headache such as this. But with the possibility of more customers coming in, Belinda needed to stay here until Amy got home.

"Did you take the old sign down to repair it or something?" Dianna asked.

"No," Henry spoke up, "but we'll be putting up one in its place real soon."

Belinda managed a weak smile. "Jah, that's right." She slipped out from behind the counter and stood next to Dianna. "If you'll tell me what you came for, I'll be happy to show you where it can be found."

Before Dianna could respond, Belinda glanced over at Monroe and said, "Danki for stopping by, Monroe. I hope the rest of your day goes well." She hurried away with Dianna without waiting for the man's response.

When Amy pulled her horse and buggy up to the hitching rail, not far from the flower shop, she spotted the girl Abe used to date, Sue Ellen Wagler. She was walking down the street with a young Amish man Amy didn't recognize. No doubt he was from another church district. What caught Amy's attention the most, though, was that they were holding hands. Sue Ellen had no doubt found another boyfriend.

Amy felt a pang of regret. If Abe were still alive, he and Sue Ellen would be married by now. She couldn't really fault Sue Ellen for moving on with her life. Abe wasn't coming back, and she had every right to be courted by someone else.

I wonder if my sister will ever meet another man, fall in love, and get married. After all, Sylvia is still young, and her children need a father to help raise them.

Toby and Sylvia had been so happy together that it was hard to picture her with someone else.

Amy thought about her own wedding that would take place this fall. Sometimes she felt selfish for being so happy with Jared, especially when Sylvia had no one and still grieved her loss.

Amy loved Jared more than words could say, and she would be devastated if anything ever happened to him. He was all she'd ever wanted in a husband, and Amy felt grateful they'd been able to get their courtship back on track.

Her focus changed as the flower shop came into view. Two women came out of the building as Amy approached, and she stood off to one side, waiting for them to clear the door.

Once inside, she found Sara's helper Misty behind the front counter.

"Good afternoon," Amy said. "I came by to see if there are any flowers Sara wants you to order from our greenhouse this week."

Misty blinked rapidly and gave a sharp intake of breath. "Oh dear... hasn't Sara given you the news?"

Amy moved closer to the counter. "What news?"

"I'm in the process of buying her shop."

"We knew that might be a possibility, but I didn't realize it would be soon."

"So Sara hasn't said anything to you or your mother?"

Amy shook her head.

"I'm sure she hasn't kept the information from you intentionally." Misty tapped her pen against the invoice book lying on the counter. "With the adjustment of becoming a mother, Sara's probably been so busy she hasn't gotten around to contacting everyone yet."

"That's understandable." Amy smiled. "Congratulations on becoming the new owner of this business. We'll enjoy working with you the same as we did Sara."

Misty cleared her throat a couple of times as she pushed a wayward hair behind her left ear. "Umm. . .the thing is. . .I've already been approached by the other greenhouse in the area." She paused and swiped her tongue across her lower lip. "Since they are much closer to my shop here, and their prices are reasonable, I've agreed to purchase all my flowers from them."

Tilting her chin, Amy broke eye contact with Misty. "Oh, I see."

"I'm sorry, but I have to do what I think is best for my new business. I hope you understand."

No, I don't understand at all. Amy kept her thoughts to herself as she nodded. "Thank you for telling me. I'll pass the word along to my mother."

Amy's throat felt so swollen, she couldn't say another word. In order to keep her emotions under control, she turned and hurried out the door. *Oh boy. . .I dread telling Mom this bit of bad news. No sales to the flower shop will surely affect our finances.*

Amy wandered up the street a ways, feeling stunned. *Why do things have to change like this?* She was glad she'd had lunch before all this went down, because now her stomach was knotted up.

As she continued to absorb the news, she felt a light tap on the back of her shoulder. Amy turned.

Jared stood with his brows furrowed as he looked at her. "Is something wrong? You look umgerennt."

"I am upset," she admitted.

"Want to talk about it?"

"Jah." Amy explained about Sara selling the flower shop. "And I can't understand why she didn't let us know about it."

"But you knew it was a possibility, right?"

Amy nodded. "Never dreamed she'd go through with it and not tell us, though."

"I'm sorry, Amy." Jared stood close to her. "I wish there was something I could do for you. I'm sure your family appreciated having that account."

"Mom surely did. But there's not much we can do about it."

Jared's tone was gentle as he looked into her eyes with a tender expression. "Have you eaten yet?"

"Yes, and I don't think I could eat anything else." Amy placed both hands against her stomach. "I dread telling Mom this news."

"I was about to grab a bite to eat before heading back to work on the roof of a house nearby. Why don't you come along and keep me company?"

"Okay."

As they headed to the nearest restaurant, Amy released a lingering sigh. She wished she could stay here with Jared for the rest of the day, because she dreaded having to go home and share the bad news.

"Will this work as a temporary sign?" Sylvia asked Belinda the following morning. She lifted a wooden sign for the greenhouse that she'd painted the night before and placed it on the table.

Belinda smiled and gave an affirmative nod. "You did a good job, Daughter. In fact, since you painted the front and back of the sign with clear lacquer, it should be good enough to use as a permanent sign."

"You think so?"

"Definitely. I wouldn't have said so if it weren't true."

"But the letters I painted in green aren't nearly as nice as the original one we had professionally done."

"Doesn't matter. You made the letters clear and large enough to be seen from the road, so that's all I care about."

Belinda looked at Henry, who'd come into the kitchen, via the back door. "Your sister made a new sign for us. Would you please go out and hang it right now? I'll have breakfast on by the time you get back."

"There are a couple of spots that seem a bit tacky yet, so you'll need to be careful putting it up," Sylvia told him "As long as it has a chance to dry all the way, it should last us a long time."

Henry frowned. "I'll be careful, but can't it wait till after we eat? I'm real hungerich this morning."

Belinda handed him a sticky bun. "This should tide you over till you get back. By then, I'll be ready to serve breakfast."

"Okay, I'll take care of it now." Henry grabbed the sticky bun in one hand and the new sign in the other. When Belinda opened the door for him, he went out with a spring in his step.

She looked over at Sylvia and shook her head. "That brother of yours has more energy in his little finger than I do in my whole body. Think I must be getting old."

"You're not old, Mom." Sylvia gave her a hug.

"I feel like it sometimes."

"That's because you work so hard," Amy said when she joined them in the kitchen.

A flush of heat erupted on Belinda's cheeks. "You heard what I said?"

"Jah. And I'm right, Mom. You do work hard—in the greenhouse, in the garden, and here in our home."

"I do what needs to be done."

"But once in a while you ought to take a little break." Amy looked at Sylvia. "Don't you agree that our mamm should take it easy whenever she can?"

Sylvia replied with a quick nod.

"So fix yourself a cup of kaffi and take it to the table." Amy gestured to the chair their mother normally sat in. "Sylvia and I will fix breakfast this morning." She looked at Belinda with a smug expression. "We're perfectly capable, you know."

"I am well aware, but it's good for me to keep busy. Helps me not to focus on our current situation."

"You mean, Sara selling her shop and the new owner deciding not to order from us anymore?" Amy asked.

"Jah."

"And don't forget the greenhouse sign that someone took down yesterday," Sylvia interjected. "I hope they don't do the same to the one I made last night."

"Sure wish we knew who took the missing sign." Belinda drank some of her coffee.

"Too bad one of us isn't a detective. Then we might find out who is behind this mystery."

"We need to pray it won't happen again and that God will bring us all the business we need." Belinda clasped her hands together, placing them against her chest. She wouldn't say it to her daughters, but if things didn't get better, and fewer customers came in, by this time next year they could be out of business.

Dennis took a seat at the kitchen table and bowed his head for silent prayer. This was something he'd been taught to do at an early age, so it became a habit. The only problem was, he'd never been sure if his prayers made it to heaven. His mother and dad believed in the Bible, but for a long time after his dad passed away, the scriptures seemed like a fairy tale to Dennis—something someone had made up for the benefit of people who needed something to believe in that would give them a hope for the future.

Dennis had determined that his focus should be on hard work and a determination to make something of himself. He'd remained Amish because it was the only way he'd ever known, and he liked living plain. He went to church every other Sunday, but sometimes his mind was focused on other things.

Dennis wanted something better from life than merely working hard at a job he disliked. That's what his father had done, and it had taken him nowhere.

Who am I kidding? Dennis asked himself as he peeled a hard-boiled egg. *My daed was satisfied, even though farming might not have been his first choice.*

Dennis's stomach clenched as he relived the day his father had been killed. He still hadn't forgiven Uncle Ben for ending his dad's life and wasn't sure if he ever could.

Nausea replaced the pang of hunger he'd felt when he'd woken up this morning. He pushed his plate aside and stood. *If I take one bite of that egg, it may not stay down.*

After tossing the paper plate and its contents into the garbage can, Dennis grabbed his Thermos full of coffee and went out the back door. Looking around the yard, he thought once more about how nice it would be to have a dog.

Dennis had checked *The Budget* earlier, but there was nothing except some puppies being advertised. When he had some free time, he would make a trip to the local animal shelter and take a look at the potentials waiting for a good home. If he found nothing there, he'd check the newspaper again in a few weeks.

Walking across the yard, Dennis smelled the odor of coffee and looked down. *Oh great! The Thermos is leaking on my trousers. Guess I'd better fix the lid before more of it seeps out.*

As Dennis paused to tighten the lid, he heard the horses whinnying and nickering from the barn. There was always some excitement when he added a new horse to the group. His friend's new mare was in the barn, waiting for her first day of training. For the next few hours, Dennis would think of nothing else except teaching the horse how to pull a buggy by first getting her used to a jogging cart.

After Mom, Amy, and Henry went out to the greenhouse, Sylvia fed her children, did the dishes, and cleaned up the kitchen. She hoped to get some potholders made today that could be sold in the greenhouse. The material she planned to use had birds on it, which reminded Sylvia of the hobby Henry had introduced to her.

Sylvia looked forward to going birding with Dennis again this Sunday and sharing a meal with him and the family afterward. It would give them a chance to get better acquainted in a relaxed atmosphere. She hoped he would also share some stories about unusual birds he'd seen when living in Dauphin County.

Right now, though, she wanted to take a look at the sign she'd made and make sure it looked okay.

When Henry came in for a drink of water, Sylvia asked him to stay with the children while she went outside.

"Okay," he responded. "There ain't much happening in the greenhouse right now anyway, so I probably won't even be missed."

Sylvia resisted the urge to correct his English. She left the house and trotted down the driveway until she reached the sign.

It looks good, even if I do say so myself. She hoped this new sign, which she'd painted with a brighter color than the old one, would bring in some new customers.

Sylvia was about to leave, when she noticed Maude across the road, loitering near the neighbors' place. She wondered if the strange little woman would come by soon for more goodies from Mom, or if some other item might vanish from their property again.

Sylvia heard some birds overhead, squawking to each other. A few black crows, like the one Henry had taken an interest in last year, sounded off, which she found to be annoying. She started to turn back toward the house when Maude approached.

"I reckon you're open for business again?"

Sylvia's brows knit together. "Excuse me?"

"Your sign was gone yesterday, so I thought you may have closed down the greenhouse."

"No, we're still open, and we don't know what happened to the sign. But as you can see, a new one is up now."

The old woman snickered behind her weathered-looking hand. "I wonder how long till the new sign disappears."

Before Sylvia could comment, Maude hurried ahead to the greenhouse. She couldn't tell if the elderly woman was kidding or not, but Sylvia chose not to let it bother her long, because she spotted a pair of cardinals on one of their hanging feeders. They were gorgeous in their red attire, as one chirped a pleasant song.

Sylvia planted her feet and watched intently as the pair took turns eating from the feeder. *I wish Dennis could see this with me. What a pretty sight.*

She remained fixated on the cardinals for several more minutes, until the birds flew away. Sylvia couldn't help smiling. Watching the cardinals reminded her of the fun she'd had on Sunday with Dennis.

He appears to be such a kind man, and he's quite nice looking. It seems odd that Dennis isn't married, Sylvia mused as she returned to the house to relieve Henry of his duty. *Maybe Dennis hasn't found the right woman yet. Or, he could be so focused on trying to get his new business going that he has no time for love and romance.*

Sylvia paused on the porch and tapped her chin. *I don't know why I'm thinking about this. It's none of my business what Dennis does or why he's not married. My concentration needs to be on raising my children and trying to help Mom come up with new ways to keep people coming to the greenhouse and buying the items she has for sale. Hopefully the money I'm now earning because of renting out my home will help compensate for any loss of business.*

About an hour after Earl left for work, Virginia got dressed, climbed in her car, and went shopping. Her friend Stella had worn some nice outfits during her visit, and Virginia had been inspired to buy something. *I hope there's enough room on the credit card I'll be using today. Earl says we need to budget our finances, so I'll try not to get carried away.*

Virginia found a dress shop a few doors down from Miller's Smorgasbord and parked her car. It had been too long since she'd bought herself new clothes, and she was determined not to go home empty-handed. She'd finally cleaned out her closet of several outdated outfits and donated them to a thrift store.

Virginia spent the next hour trying on outfits and jewelry. So far everything either didn't fit, wasn't in a color she liked, or cost too much money. She scrutinized the sale rack and found a pair of black knit leggings, as well as a floral print tunic. Seeing that the size and price were right, she carried the clothes to the dressing room. After trying them on, and turning different ways in front of the fitting room mirror, Virginia convinced herself that the tunic and leggings were made for her. She put her old clothes on and took the new ones up to the register, where she discovered a velvet-beaded double strand necklace highlighted with crystals and gold links on display. It was the most unusual necklace she'd ever seen. The piece of jewelry cost almost as much as the tunic and legging, but Virginia knew she couldn't leave the store without it.

It's not like I'm spending a king's ransom in here. Virginia watched the sales gal finish with the lady ahead of her. *I bet when Earl sees me in this new outfit, he'll think I look so nice he will want to take me out for supper this evening. And if he asks which restaurant I would like to eat at, I'll say, "Miller's Smorgy."*

After a clerk came to wait on Virginia, she plunked down a credit card. "You sure have some nice stuff in here. The next time my husband gets paid, think I'll come back and look around."

The middle-age woman gave Virginia a wide smile. "You'd be welcomed."

When Virginia left the store, she chose to ignore the pain in her leg as she headed for her car. She clung tightly to the fancy gift bag the clerk had put her purchases in. *Wow, if I'd known I was gonna feel this good about myself, I'd have bought some new clothes a lot sooner. Too bad my one true friend isn't here to go shopping with me.*

Virginia got in her car and looked at herself in the rearview mirror. *If I had a friend here with me right now, I'd find some place to change into my new clothes and invite her to go out to lunch.*

Her shoulders slumped. *But I guess makin' a new friend is never gonna happen. Even if I did meet someone, who'd want to hang out with a woman who has a gimpy leg and doesn't have anything interesting to talk about?*

Chapter 23

"You look real nice this evening, hon." Earl grinned at Virginia when he stepped in the door. "Did you go shopping today?"

"I sure did, and I found these clothes on a sales rack." Making no mention of the necklace she'd bought at full price, Virginia turned all the way around so he could see the front and back of her new outfit.

"You did real well." Earl stepped forward and gave her a kiss. "I'm glad you tried them on for me, but you might want to change clothes before you start cooking supper."

Virginia put on her best smile. "I was hoping we could go out for supper tonight."

Earl tipped his head from side to side, as though weighing his choices. "Well now. . .let me think. . ."

She puckered her lips. "Come on, Earl, pretty please."

"Didn't you have something already planned for supper?"

She shook her head.

He jiggled his brows, then pulled Virginia into his arms for a hug. "Okay, sweetie, it's a date. Just give me a few minutes to clean up and change my clothes. Then we can go to the restaurant of my choice."

"Your choice, huh?" She poked his stomach.

"Well, sure. Since it was your idea to go out to eat, don't you think it's only fair that I should get to choose which restaurant we go to?"

"I suppose." Virginia smiled. *What a thoughtful husband I have. I can't believe I was lucky enough to find him. I still have to wonder what Earl ever saw in someone like me.*

"Where are you and Jared going for supper this evening?" Sylvia asked her sister.

Amy turned away from the living room window, where she'd been standing for the last five minutes. "I'm not sure yet. Maybe Diener's in Ronks, or we might eat someplace here in Strasburg. When Jared stopped by the greenhouse today and invited me to go with him this evening, I said he could choose the restaurant."

"That was gracious of you. I hope it's a place you like."

Amy smiled. "I'm sure it will be. There aren't many restaurants in our area that don't serve good food."

"You're right. Toby's and my favorite place to eat was the Bird-in-Hand Family Restaurant." A pang of regret shot through Sylvia as she thought of her dear husband, remembering more of the good times they'd spent together. She couldn't help feeling a bit envious of her sister. At the same time, Sylvia was happy for Amy. She deserved the chance to build a life with the man she loved. Someday Amy and Jared would have children and Mom would have more grandchildren to love and dote over.

Sylvia sighed inwardly. *Sure wish I could give Mom another grandchild or two, but I guess it's not meant to be. If Toby hadn't died, we'd surely have had more kinner.*

Ronks

"What made you choose this restaurant, Earl?" Virginia asked after they were seated at a table at Diener's Country Restaurant.

"I heard they have good food. In fact, I was told that it's a favorite of the Amish in the area."

"I can tell." She looked around the room where several Amish people sat at tables and rolled her eyes. "Don't we get enough Amish exposure at home? I mean, almost every time I look out the window, a horse and buggy is going by or turning up the Kings' driveway."

"We're living in Amish country, so we're bound to see Amish people." Earl leaned closer to Virginia. "And please keep your voice down. Someone might hear what you're saying and think you're prejudiced."

She shrugged her shoulders. "So what if I am?"

Earl had no chance to respond, because a middle-aged waitress came and asked what they would like to drink.

"I'll have a glass of water and a cup of coffee," Virginia replied.

"Make that two," Earl chimed in.

The waitress smiled. "Is this your first time visiting our restaurant?"

"Yes, it is. I heard about this place from my coworkers," Earl spoke up.

"That's good. I hope you both enjoy your meal."

He gave a nod. "I'm sure we will."

Virginia looked around and overheard a man at a nearby table say, "This restaurant is a bit of a landmark."

Virginia took in the minimal decor, as well as all the homey-looking wooden tables and chairs. The place grew busier, with more and more people being seated. The room soon became abuzz with constant conversations all happening at once.

Their friendly waitress went over the way things worked with where the different food counters were located as she held out menus. "Would you like to order off the menu or choose the items you want from the buffet?"

"I'll go with the buffet." Earl looked at Virginia. "How about you, dear?"

"Guess I will too."

"Feel free to help yourself whenever you're ready. I'll get your beverages and be back with them soon." The woman turned and walked away.

Earl pushed his chair aside and stood. "Okay, Virginia, let's go after some food."

As they joined a few others in line at the buffet bar, Virginia noticed an Amish couple at one of the tables across the room. *Oh great. It's Amy King and Jared, the roofer. I hope they don't see us.*

Once their plates were full, Virginia followed Earl back to their table.

"Say, isn't that the guy who did our garage roof?" Earl gestured in that direction. "And I think he's with one of the young Amish women who lives across the road from us."

"I believe you're right." Virginia picked up the chicken leg she'd placed on top of her buttered noodles, because her plate was so full.

"Oh, look, they must have seen us, 'cause they're coming this way."

Virginia put the chicken down and held her elbows tightly against her sides, wishing there was someplace she could hide. The last thing she needed was feeling forced to carry on a conversation with someone she didn't care about.

"It's nice to see you folks," Jared said as he and Amy stood beside Earl and Virginia's table. "Is this your first time eating here?"

"Yes, it is, and I've heard they have good food."

"We like it." Amy looked at Virginia and smiled. "I'm sure you will too."

"Maybe, if our food doesn't get cold before we have a chance to eat it," Virginia mumbled, barely glancing at Amy.

Amy nudged Jared's arm. "We need to get our dessert from the buffet and let my neighbors eat their meal in peace."

"You're right, Amy." Jared clasped Earl's shoulder. "Sorry for the intrusion."

"Not a problem." Earl reached out and shook Jared's hand. "Your stopping by has given me a chance to tell you once more what a good job you and your crew did when you replaced my garage roof. I've been telling some of the fellows I work with about you. So don't be surprised if you get a few phone calls from some of the people I told about you."

"Thanks, I appreciate that." Jared's cheeks turned a light shade of pink.

Amy gave Jared's shirtsleeve a little tug. "Let's get some dessert before it's all gone."

"Okay, okay." He looked at Amy and chuckled, then turned back to face Earl and Virginia. "I think my future wife is eager to satisfy her sweet tooth."

"Future wife?" Virginia repeated. "I didn't know you and Amy were engaged to be married. When's the big day?"

"The first Thursday of October." Jared spoke before Amy could form any words.

"Yes, and there's still much to be done before the wedding," she interjected.

"Thursday seems like an odd day to get married. Why not a Saturday?" Virginia asked.

"We Amish always choose a weekday for our weddings because the following day we need to clean up after the event," Jared explained. "A Saturday wedding would mean cleanup on Sunday, and since we don't work on Sundays. . ."

Virginia held up her hand. "Okay, I get it."

"Maybe you should save yourself the time and energy of all the fuss and preparations, and just elope." Earl snickered.

Jared shook his head. "Young couples who've joined the Amish church would never elope."

Amy nodded in agreement. "It's just not done."

"Perhaps you folks would like to come to the wedding service, or at least join us for one of the meals that will be served throughout the day."

"You serve more than one post-wedding meal?" Virginia thought this was a strange custom too.

"Yes," Jared replied. "We don't normally have enough room to accommodate everyone in the building where the wedding takes place, and having more than one meal afterward allows people who didn't come to the wedding to join the bride and groom, as well as their witnesses, in a meal. Of course," he added, "those who do attend the wedding are usually served directly after the service. Then later in the day, many people who did not attend the wedding come to the second meal."

Earl nodded, but Virginia merely looked down at her plate piled high with food. Amy figured her neighbor wasn't that interested in what had been said.

"So we'll make sure you receive an invitation in the mail—if not for the wedding itself, then for one of the meals." Jared looked at Earl, who bobbed his head once more.

Seeing her future husband's eager expression caused Amy to cringe internally. *What is he thinking? I'm not sure about Earl, but I seriously doubt that Virginia's interested in being a friendly neighbor, much less attending our wedding. I bet Jared was only being polite by bringing up the topic.*

"I hope you two will enjoy your meal." Amy inched her way farther from the table.

"Thanks, I'm sure we will." Earl picked up his knife and fork and cut into his piece of chicken breast.

Amy managed a smile before she and Jared walked away. "I don't think Virginia likes me," she whispered at the dessert bar as she took a piece of cherry pie with whipped cream on top.

"What makes you think that?"

"Really, Jared, couldn't you tell how disinterested she was when the topic of our wedding came up?"

He shook his head. "You might be a little overly sensitive when it comes to your English neighbor."

"I don't think so. Ever since our first meeting, Virginia has been standoffish."

"She might be one of those people who needs a little time to get acquainted with someone."

"Jah, especially someone like me and my family who live a completely different lifestyle than her."

"Just give her the chance to get to know you better." Jared put a large scoop of bread pudding on his plate and covered it with warm maple sauce. "Ready to go back to our table now?"

"Sure." Amy followed him across the room. She would need to check with her mother and see how many people they planned to invite to her wedding. Maybe the list would be too long and there wouldn't be enough room to include Virginia and her husband.

Virginia watched the young couple get some dessert and head back to their table. She looked at her plate and tried the noodles, followed by a bite of chicken. "Yum. . .this isn't bad at all. In fact the food here's pretty tasty."

Earl nodded as he shoveled in a mouthful of potatoes with gravy.

"You must like the food here too, 'cause you're taking big bites like there's no tomorrow." She snickered. "You'd better take it easy, Earl.

There's still plenty up there for you to have seconds."

He thumped his belly. "Yep, and I'm gonna take advantage of that very thing."

Virginia took a drink of water. "This place would have been fun to bring Stella during the time she was here. What a bummer she couldn't be with us right now. Sure wish there was a way to lure my friend back here for another visit."

"She did seem to be taken in by the Plain people in the area. And there's plenty of 'em here in this restaurant this evening." He picked up his roll and buttered it. "Stella asked me some questions about the Amish, but I don't know them that well, so I had no concrete answers for her."

"Same here. I don't know much except what I've seen of our Amish neighbors." Virginia picked up her fork again. "But I did see Stella purchase a book about the Amish from one of the shops we stopped at during the time she was here."

"Maybe being in Lancaster County whet your friend's appetite enough that she'll come back for another visit." Earl looked toward the buffet counter, where another long line of people had formed.

But who knows when that will happen? Stella may not be able to fit it into her schedule to come here anytime soon.

An idea popped into Virginia's head, and she gave Earl's arm a tap. "Hey!"

"Hey, what?"

She waited for him to face her. "If we should get an invitation to Jared and Amy's wedding, and I share the news with Stella, I'm sure she'd want to come along."

Her husband chuckled. "Woman, your mind is always at work, isn't it? But you're right, an invitation to an Amish wedding would probably prompt your best friend to come for another stay."

Virginia nodded. *Maybe I'll need to be a bit friendlier to our neighbors. Oh bother, this is sure not what I'd like to do, but I desperately want Stella to come here again.*

"I'm going back up for seconds." Earl pushed away from the table. "Would you care to join me?"

"Guess I could eat another piece of that chicken, and maybe some more noodles with gravy."

They left their used plates behind and headed for the counter for new dishes. Earl went ahead of her as he loaded up his plate again. The grin he wore reassured Virginia that they'd be back here another evening in the future.

She picked out some pickled beets to go along with the chicken and noodles. *I'm glad the pants I'm wearing are stretchy and my tunic will hide my expanding belly.*

Virginia peeked at Amy and Jared, before scooting over to join Earl in front of the desserts.

"If I've got any room after all this, I might get some of that chocolate cake with frosting." He pointed to it.

"Same here." Virginia followed Earl to their table.

A few minutes later, a large group of Amish came in and were seated at a long table near them. It looked like three generations of folks getting settled in their chairs. Earl chuckled and mentioned something about how big their bill would be.

Virginia tried to watch them without staring. *I wonder if I'll ever understand the Plain people. This wouldn't even be an issue if we were still living in Chicago.*

Chapter 24

Saturday morning when Amy went out to get the mail, she saw Virginia standing at her own mailbox.

"Good morning." Amy smiled.

"Morning." Virginia's response could barely be heard, and she avoided Amy's glance.

"Did you and your husband enjoy your meal at Diener's the other evening?"

"Yeah, it was good." Virginia grabbed her mail and was about to cross the road, but she stopped suddenly and turned to face Amy. "I noticed you have a new sign out front." She spoke louder and pointed in that direction. "What happened to your old one?"

"Apparently someone took it, so my sister made a new one."

"Bet I know who stole it." Virginia's lips pressed into a thin, flat line.

Amy moved closer. "Who do you believe it was?"

Virginia fiddled with one of her dangly earrings. "I think it was that scruffy-looking old woman who walks by here nearly every day." She looked directly at Amy. "I've seen her meandering up and down your driveway a few times too. She seems creepy to me, although I've never talked to her. Don't even know the woman's name or where she lives."

"You must be referring to Maude. She doesn't speak much, and we don't know a lot about her, other than that she lives most of the year in an old shack up the road."

"I see. Well, the other morning, around six o'clock, I saw her walking back and forth in front of your driveway. Her head was down, and she appeared to be looking for something. Then I noticed that it looked like she was holding an object behind her back."

"Could you tell what it was?"

"Nope, but I wouldn't be surprised if she's the guilty one who snatched your sign." Virginia shook her head slowly. "You need to keep an eye on that woman if she comes around again. A person like her can't be trusted. In fact, I'm gonna keep a watch out for her too. If she could lift your sign, then who knows what else might disappear from your place, or maybe ours next."

Amy thought about the things Maude had done previously, like taking some produce from their garden. Then there was the time she snatched some cookies they had setting out on the counter in the greenhouse. *Virginia might have a point. It's possible that Maude may have taken the sign out front and possibly the watering can that went missing last year.*

"Think I'd better get back to the house now and start a load of laundry." Virginia's comment broke into Amy's disconcerting thoughts.

"Okay, I need to take care of this mail." Amy tapped the envelopes against her other hand.

"See you around." Virginia smiled, looked both ways, and limped to the other side of the road.

Clasping the mail in her hands, Amy headed back up the driveway and turned toward the greenhouse. *If Maude did take our sign, what would she have wanted with it?*

Belinda had put the Open sign on the door and was about to check all the plants to see if any needed water, when Amy came in.

"I just talked with our neighbor across the road, and she thinks Maude may have taken our sign." Amy breathed heavily.

"The new one Sylvia made?"

"No. It was the old sign that went missing."

"What makes Virginia think it was Maude? Did she see her take the sign?"

Amy shook her head. "No, but she saw her walking back and forth in front of our driveway that morning, and then Maude bent down like she was searching for something. Oh, and Virginia said it looked like the elderly woman had something behind her back."

Belinda flapped her hand. "For goodness' sake, Amy, that's no proof that Maude took the sign. She could have dropped something that belonged to her."

"I suppose, but you know how strange Maude acts at times. And don't forget—we have caught her taking things before."

"We certainly can't accuse her unless we have some proof."

"True, but—"

"Is that the mail you have in your hands?" Belinda decided it was time for a topic change.

"Jah." Amy handed the letters to her.

"Danki. Now, would you mind checking the plants for water while I go through the mail?"

"I don't mind, but where's Henry? Shouldn't he be checking the plants?"

"I assume he's still in the barn, which is where he said he was going after we finished breakfast."

"Should I go get him?"

"It's not necessary. I'm sure he will come here when he's done. In the meantime. . ."

"No problem, Mom. I'll check on the plants." Amy turned and headed down the first row, while Belinda took a seat behind the counter.

I'm glad Amy had a pleasant time with Jared last night. He's a nice young man, and they get along so well—just like Vernon and I did.

Belinda sighed as she picked up a piece of mail. The first envelope she opened was a bill and there were two more after that. She clicked her tongue against the roof of her mouth. It seemed lately there were more bills than money coming in.

Belinda finished looking at the last piece of mail—an advertisement—when Monroe entered the greenhouse. *I wonder what he wants this time.*

"Morning, Belinda. I was on my way back from the doughnut shop and thought I'd drop some off for you." He set a sweet-smelling box on the counter and grinned at her. "I got busy at work and couldn't make it back here until today, but I wanted to come by and make sure no more vandalism has been done."

"Everything's fine. No more problems at all." Belinda lifted the lid and inhaled the delightful aroma of maple bars and chocolate-glazed doughnuts. "Danki, Monroe. It was thoughtful of you to think of us with these treats. I'll be sure to share the doughnuts with the rest of my family."

His smile widened. "I'll bring you more the next time I stop at the doughnut shop. Whenever I go there, I get the freshest baked pastries."

She held up both hands. "Oh, there's no need for that. If I ate treats like this too often, I'd surely get fat."

"No way!" He shook his head. "You still have the trim figure of an eighteen-year-old girl."

Belinda's face warmed. No man but Vernon had ever talked to her in such a personal way. It made her feel peculiar. If she wasn't careful, Monroe could end up worming his way in, making it harder to convince the determined man that she had no interest in a romantic relationship with him.

"Go on with you now." She waved her hand. "I look nothing like I did when I was a teenager."

"You look good to me."

Belinda's face grew hotter, and to her relief an English couple came in and asked if she would help them with something.

"Yes, I'll be right with you."

Before Belinda could step down from the stool, Monroe lowered his voice and said: "By the way. . . I went by that new greenhouse and checked it out the other day.

"You did?"

"Jah. It's big, and they carry a lot of different things, but not personal like your business. I was not impressed with it at all."

"Danki for sharing your thoughts. Now if you'll excuse me. . ."

"Oh, sure. Guess I'd best be going anyway." He leaned closer to Belinda. "Feel free to let me know if you have any more problems."

"I'm sure we'll be fine." She slipped out from behind the counter and gave the customers her full attention as Monroe went out the door.

Sylvia mouthed the words to one of her favorite hymns, then began to hum the tune. The house was full of sunshine, and the kitchen smelled of fresh-brewed coffee. She felt light-hearted and could almost sense God's presence. *Maybe it's because of the song that popped into my head,* she thought. *Or maybe I'm beginning to heal. Some of the scriptures Mom read during our family time of devotions have made sense to me, and my anger toward God and the man responsible for the accident that killed our loved ones seems to have dissipated some. Maybe in time I'll feel whole again spiritually.*

"Whatcha doin', Mama?" Allen asked when he darted into the kitchen where Sylvia stood, mixing the batter to make sugar cookies.

"I was humming while getting ready to bake some kichlin. Would you like to help?"

Allen bobbed his head.

Sylvia pulled a stool over to the counter and helped him climb up. Then she showed him how to dip the bottom of a cup in a bowl of sugar and flatten each blob of dough she'd placed on the cookie sheet. Sylvia did it a couple more times, and then guided Allen's hands through the process.

He caught on quickly, so Sylvia sat back and took a drink from her cup of coffee. The kitchen was so warm and cozy, as she relaxed, watching Allen at work.

Things went well at first, and her son seemed to be having a good time until his sister came into the room and started to fuss. Allen turned to look at her, and in so doing, his elbow hit the canister, sending it flying off the counter and landing on its side. Sugar went everywhere—including Rachel's hair. The sobbing child dashed out of the room, leaving a trail of sugar as she shook her head.

Allen remained on the stool with his mouth gaping open, and Sylvia didn't know whether to laugh or cry. She set the cookie sheet aside, helped Allen off the stool, and followed the trail of sugar in search of her daughter.

Sylvia found Rachel in the hallway, outside the bathroom door, no longer crying, as she sat with her legs crossed. Looking up at Sylvia, the child slid a finger across the top of her head and then stuck it in her mouth. "*Zucker.*"

"Yes, little one. You have sugar in your hair." Sylvia couldn't hold back the laughter bubbling in her throat. She had a mess to clean, but it could have been worse, and it felt so good to laugh about something. She needed to look at the humorous side of things more and not be so serious all the time.

Sylvia picked Rachel up and carried her to the back porch. The first chore was getting the sugar out of her daughter's hair, and then she would return to the kitchen to get the cookies baked. Hopefully they would turn out well and she could serve them when Dennis came over tomorrow to do more bird-watching and join them for supper.

When Dennis entered the house shortly after noon, he went to the bathroom and wet a washcloth. After wiping his sweaty forehead with it, and then scrubbing his hands with plenty of soap and water, he headed for the kitchen.

Once he'd fixed a peanut butter and jelly sandwich, Dennis poured himself a glass of milk and took a seat at the table. Since no one was here to see him, he didn't bother to offer a prayer, even though he did have much to be thankful for.

Dennis had spent the better part of the morning working with his friend's horse, and as soon as he finished eating lunch he had another person's gelding to work with. He'd hung several flyers around the area, advertising his business, and had run an ad in the local newspaper. Dennis hoped he'd soon have more business than he could handle.

He picked up one of his sandwich halves and took a bite. *Who knows, maybe I'll eventually be able to hire someone to help around the barn—cleaning the stalls, along with feeding and watering the horses. A helper could also brush down the horses after their training sessions.*

This morning, before Dennis had gone out to the barn, he'd called the bird-watcher's hotline and was pleased to hear a few people talk about some sightings in this area. One person from Gap had seen several turkey vultures, as well as a Cooper's hawk and a blue jay. Another person, from a different area, stated that they'd spotted a blue-winged teal and some black terns. Dennis planned to take Sylvia and her brother to that area tomorrow afternoon. With any luck, they would find some interesting birds too.

Dennis eyed his stack of reading material on the counter. *I should look up those birds in one of my books. That way, if we do catch sight of any of the species talked about on the hotline, I'll be more informed about what I'm hoping to see.*

He was eager to see Henry and Sylvia again. He'd enjoyed their last birding adventure and been pleased to see Sylvia smile and hear her laugh a few times. She'd seemed more relaxed than she had previously, and Dennis looked forward to joining her family for a meal when they got back from birding. It would be nice to get better acquainted with Sylvia's mother and sister. He was curious to see how well Sylvia got along with her family. The sit-down supper should help him see this.

Home-cooked meals weren't the norm for Dennis these days. It was a nice treat for him to be invited to eat with the King family. He was sure there would be some kind of a dessert to follow the meal—something else to anticipate.

Dennis bit into his sandwich and drank some milk. His world seemed to be filled with more happiness as he'd gotten better acquainted with Henry and especially Sylvia. He didn't understand why, but he was drawn to her—had been from the moment they'd met.

Maybe it's because I saw the hurt in her eyes and heard it in her tone of voice. Dennis knew all the signs of emotional pain, because he'd felt them too, ever since his father died. Truth was, he wasn't sure he would ever fully come to grips with Dad's death, but keeping busy seemed to help some. And of course, his hobby of bird-watching was a pleasant distraction, so maybe it would be for Sylvia too.

Chapter 25

Clymer

Michelle's heart swelled with joy as she sat in church, listening to her husband preach from Psalm 127:3–5. "Lo, children are an heritage of the Lord: and the fruit of the womb is his reward. As arrows are in the hand of a mighty man; so are children of the youth. Happy is the man that hath his quiver full of them. . . ."

Michelle looked at her daughter sitting beside her, so well-behaved, and then at the little boy in her lap. What a blessing and a privilege it was to be these children's mother.

Although far from perfect, Michelle did her best to be a good mother. She wanted her children to feel loved and safe—not hopeless and fearful, the way she'd felt as a child.

Michelle was thankful she'd married a good man who spent quality time with his children and gave them all the love and proper training they needed.

I wish my dad had been like Ezekiel. I'm sure I would have turned out differently if he'd been a loving Christian father. She reached into her tote and pulled out a couple of snack-sized bags for the children.

Michelle didn't think of her parents as often as she used to when she and her brothers were first put in foster care, but sometimes, like now, a vision of her mother and father came to mind. She wondered if they'd ever gotten help for their problems, or if they sometimes thought about her, Ernie, and Jack. Had her folks ever come to realize what bad parents they'd been? Were they sorry for the abuse their children had suffered?

Looking back on it now, Michelle was glad that she and her brothers had been taken from their parents. They were better off without them.

Her thoughts went to Ernie and Jack and what a nice visit they'd all had the last time they had gotten together. Michelle looked forward to the next opportunity for either of her brothers to come for a visit.

"Dennis should be here anytime. Would you two like to join us today for some bird-watching?" Sylvia looked at Amy and Jared, who sat on the porch swing. They'd all recently returned from visiting a neighboring church district.

"It's nice of you to ask," Amy replied, "but Jared and I have other plans. We've been invited to my friend Lydia's house to play some games and join a few other young people for a barbecue. We'll be leaving soon."

"So you won't be here for supper?"

"No," Jared spoke up. "Our get-together will probably last until late evening."

"Sounds about right. Guess I'd better let Mom know so she doesn't fix too much chicken."

"I already told her that Jared and I won't be here," Amy said.

"Oh, okay." *It's hard to believe that this fall we'll be adding another member to our family. Jared will be a nice addition.* Sylvia gazed out into the yard. *Although I'm feeling more alive these days, it would take a miracle for me to find the same kind of bond with another man that I had with Toby.*

"Dennis is here!" Wearing binoculars attached to a leather cord around his neck, Henry bounded off the porch and raced over to the hitching rail as Dennis's horse and buggy came up the driveway.

Sylvia opened the screen door and called: "Henry and I are leaving now!"

"Okay, I'll have supper waiting when you get back," Mom responded from the living room.

"I'll see you two later." Sylvia smiled at Amy and Jared, grabbed her binoculars and notebook from the wicker table, and hurried down the porch steps. It was hard to believe the thought of bird-watching could have her feeling so enthusiastic. *If I'm being honest, maybe there is more to it than just excitement over the birds we might see.*

"I can't believe we were fortunate enough to see a female northern harrier hawk today," Dennis said as they headed back to the Kings' place that evening.

"Think I've seen one before, but I thought it was an owl," Henry chimed in.

"Its face does have a distinctive owl-like look," Dennis admitted. "It's actually one of the easiest hawks to identify."

"Why is that?" Sylvia questioned.

"For one thing, harriers glide just above the ground while searching for food."

"What do they eat?" Henry asked.

"Snakes, insects, mice, and small birds. Another interesting fact about the harriers is that they used to be called marsh hawks because they hunted over marshy areas. The female harrier, like we saw today, has a dark brown back with a brown-streaked breast, large white patch on its backside, and narrow black bands across the tail. The tips of its wings are black, and it has yellow eyes."

Henry tapped Dennis on the shoulder, from where he sat in the back seat. "Do the males look like that too?"

"They have the same yellow eyes and black tips on their wings, but the male's body is silver gray and its belly is white."

"I can't get over how much you know about birds," Sylvia commented. "I bet you could write your own bird book."

Dennis laughed. "I've taken plenty of notes about the birds I've seen, but I don't have what it takes to put it all together in the form of a book." He snapped the reins to get his horse moving quicker. "And as much as I know about training a horse to pull a buggy, I wouldn't try to write a book about that either."

Sylvia smiled. "We all have different things we're good at, but it doesn't mean we could write a book about them."

"Very true." Dennis had to force himself to keep his focus on watching the road ahead and making sure his horse behaved. All he really wanted to do was look at Sylvia. She was a beautiful woman. What a shame she'd lost her husband at such a young age.

I wish there was something I could do to offer her comfort. Dennis also wished he had the nerve to ask Sylvia to go out for supper with him one night this week. If her brother wasn't sitting behind them, no doubt listening to every word being said, Dennis would ask her right now. Maybe he would have the opportunity sometime before the evening was out.

🐦

When they pulled up to the hitching rail at the King home, Henry hopped out and secured Dennis's horse.

"I hope you like cold, fried *hinkel,* because that's what my mamm said she'd be serving for our supper this evening," Sylvia said as Dennis walked between her and Henry.

He grinned. "Definitely. I mean, who doesn't like fried chicken, warm or cold?" All week Dennis had looked forward to having some home cooking. The bland sandwiches he'd been eating for lunch, or the so-so canned soups for supper paled in comparison to this.

"My brother Abe didn't care for hinkel," Henry said. "Fact is, he wasn't a chicken eater at all."

"Did he like eggs?" Dennis asked as they neared the porch.

"Yep. He liked 'em just fine." Henry's voice lowered. "I sure do miss my bruder."

"I'm sure you do." Dennis gave the boy's shoulder a squeeze. "It's never easy when you lose someone close to you." He glanced at Sylvia, wondering if she would say anything, but she was silent. No doubt she still missed her husband, brother, and father. A person never really got over a tragedy like that, although in time the pain became less raw and more bearable to deal with. Maybe a distraction from time to time could help them both to better cope with their losses.

Dennis looked up at the gutter on the front of the house and noticed the drain spout had come loose. He stepped under it and pointed. "Sometime tomorrow, with the aid of a *leeder,* I could put that back together."

"It's up there pretty high. Are you sure you want to do it?" Sylvia asked.

Before Dennis had time to answer, Henry jumped in. "I could help by holding the ladder for you, Dennis."

"That'd be great. I'd appreciate your help if you're available when I come over."

"I'll bring the matter up to Mom," Sylvia said.

"That's fine. It shouldn't take me long at all." Dennis moved toward the front door.

When they entered the house, Sylvia's mother came into the living room, and he shook her hand. "Danki for including me in your supper plans this evening."

"You're welcome." Belinda smiled, but it didn't quite reach her eyes. No doubt she still grieved for her deceased family members. Either that, or Dennis figured Sylvia's mother might not care much for him.

But how can that be? he wondered. *This is only the second time we've met.*

"If you'll excuse me, I need to get back to the kitchen and finish setting things out for our meal." Belinda hurried from the room.

Sylvia invited Dennis to take a seat on the couch, before excusing herself to help her mother. "We should have supper on the table soon, so just sit and relax with Henry. I'll call you both when the food's on the table."

"Okay, thanks." Dennis sat on the couch, and Henry seated himself in an overstuffed chair. *This is a nice house. It's bigger than the home I'm renting, but I don't need a place this big.*

"I sure had fun birding with you and Sylvia today." Henry looked over at Dennis and grinned.

"I enjoyed it too." *Henry's a good kid. I bet he could use a big brother in his life.*

"I'm always watchin' for different birds in our yard." Henry clasped his hands around one knee. "Birding's a lot more interesting than takin' care of *ieme.*"

"Are you a beekeeper?"

"Not by choice. It was my brother Ezekiel's job before he and his fraa moved to New York. After that, Abe took it over. When he died, I got stuck with the bees." The boy wrinkled his nose. "Can't tell ya how many times I've been stung."

"Don't you wear protective clothing?"

"Course I do, but sometimes those pesky insects find their way to my skin."

"It's a good thing you're not allergic to bees."

Henry bobbed his head. "That's for sure."

"Don't you also work in the greenhouse with your mother and sisters?" Dennis asked.

"Jah, only Sylvia doesn't work there 'cause she. . ."

Henry stopped talking when two young children darted into the room. The little girl hid behind the chair where Henry sat, but the young boy walked right up to Dennis and said in Pennsylvania Dutch: "Who are you?"

"My name is Dennis Weaver. *Was is dei naame?*"

The boy pointed to himself. "Allen." Then he pointed at the chair where the girl hid. "That's Rachel."

The child peeked out from behind the chair, her brown eyes growing large as she stared at Dennis. Then just as quickly, she ducked back again.

"Are these children your little brother and sister?" Dennis looked at Henry.

Henry shook his head. "No, they're. . ."

At that moment, Sylvia entered the room. When she approached the couch, the little girl came out from behind the chair and shouted, "Mammi!"

Dennis's jaw dropped. He had no idea the children were Sylvia's. She'd never mentioned anything about being a mother.

Sylvia bent down and picked Rachel up. Then she took hold of Allen's hand. "These are my kinner, Allen and Rachel."

"Your son greeted me already, but your little girl hid behind the chair until you came in."

"Rachel is shy around new people, so don't let it bother you." She kissed the girl's dimpled cheek.

Dennis reached around and rubbed the back of his neck. "I didn't realize you had children, but then since you were married, I guess it should be no surprise."

Sylvia smiled. "If you'll come with me to the dining room, supper is on the table."

Dennis stood, and both he and Henry followed Sylvia and her

children out of the room.

Moments before they bowed their heads for silent prayer, Sylvia noticed Dennis looking at her children. Allen sat on a booster seat at the table, and Rachel had been seated in the wooden high chair Sylvia's father had made. She'd spoken to her mother about the loose downspout near the front porch, and Mom said she was fine with Dennis fixing it for them at his convenience.

After the prayer and while Mom passed the platter of chicken around, Sylvia watched her brother's face light up when Dennis spoke to him. She thought about how well Henry and Abe had gotten along in the past. No doubt Henry still missed him and needed a big brother who lived close by. *No wonder he seems so drawn to Dennis, since they share the same hobby.*

If only Toby, Dad, and Abe could see how much the children have grown, Sylvia thought before closing her eyes. Although her prayer was a short one, she managed to ask God to keep her family safe, and to be with Dennis as he settled into the community.

When Sylvia opened her eyes, she was surprised to see Dennis looking once more at Allen and Rachel. She wondered if little ones made him nervous, or perhaps he wished he was married and had children of his own.

As they ate their meal, Dennis and Henry struck up a conversation centered around birds. Sylvia wasn't surprised, since Dennis knew a lot about birding, and Henry wanted to know more. As a matter of fact, so did she. Studying birds and writing down specific things about them was a nice break from household chores, cooking, and taking care of her children. Not that Sylvia minded those things. It was just nice to do something out of the ordinary that she found fascinating.

Although Sylvia would never admit it out loud, she enjoyed being with Dennis. It was too soon to say whether she could develop strong feelings for him or if he felt anything for her, but if Dennis should invite her to go bird-watching with him again, Sylvia would definitely say yes.

Chapter 26

Dennis paced, shuffling through the straw scattered across the floor in front of his horse's stall. It would be two weeks tomorrow since he'd had supper with Sylvia and her family. The food had tasted good, and he'd enjoyed spending time with Sylvia and her children, as well as Henry.

But her mother, who'd been less than friendly toward him, had excused herself and gone to her room soon after they'd finished eating, saying she'd developed a headache. He hoped she hadn't used it as an excuse.

A day later, Dennis and Henry fixed the downspout, and soon it was back together. The two of them talked more about birding. Henry was easy to talk to and full of curiosity.

Since that day, Dennis hadn't spoken with Sylvia or Henry. Between training three new horses and struggling with his fear of commitment, Dennis had decided it would be best for both him and Sylvia if he didn't see her socially anymore. That, of course, would mean no more outings to do bird-watching. With the decision made, it was probably for the best that he hadn't asked her to go out with him.

Or maybe, Dennis told himself as he made another pass by his horse's stall, *I should set my concerns aside, follow my heart instead of my head, and take a leap of faith.*

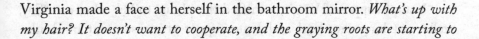

Virginia made a face at herself in the bathroom mirror. *What's up with my hair? It doesn't want to cooperate, and the graying roots are starting to*

show. I need to see a hairdresser, that's for sure.

Virginia turned off the bathroom light and headed for the kitchen. *I could sure use a cup of coffee right now.* She was glad to see that there was still enough in the pot Earl had started for himself before he left for work, and he'd left it on warm for her.

She grabbed a mug, and in the process of pouring coffee into it, some spilled onto the counter. Virginia pulled a paper towel off the cardboard roll and wiped it up. "No wonder I spilled it," she muttered. "The traffic on the road out front has increased again, and it's made me edgy. Wish we'd never moved here. Don't know what Earl was thinking, buying a place in the country."

Virginia's cell phone rang. She tossed the damp paper towel in the garbage and picked up her phone. When her friend Stella's number showed in the caller ID, Virginia wasted no time answering. "Hey, Stella, how are you doing?"

"I'm fine. How are you?"

"Except for being bored out of my mind, I'm okay."

"Have you made friends with anyone in the area yet?"

"Nope. Not yet." Virginia picked up her mug and drank the rest of her coffee.

"I'm sorry to hear that. I'd hoped you would have made a friend or two by now."

Virginia heaved a sigh. "Even if I had any friends in the area, I wouldn't like living here."

"I enjoyed my time there when I came to visit. It was fun going over to the greenhouse across the street too."

Virginia's gaze flicked upward. *Fun for you maybe, but not for me.*

"Are you going to plant a vegetable garden this year?"

"I don't think so. We can get all the produce we want at the local farmers' market." Virginia moved over to the kitchen window and looked out at the backyard. "Earl's working part of the day, so while he's gone I may go outside and do a little work in the flowerbeds."

"That should make the time go quickly," Stella said. "Fresh air and a little exercise are good for a person too."

"Yeah, I suppose." Virginia shifted the phone to her other ear. "Say, Stella, not long ago, Earl and I ate supper at a restaurant in Ronks.

While we were there we saw our neighbor, Amy King, and her fiancé, Jared. They spotted us and came over to our table. And you know what the best part was?"

"I haven't a clue."

"Jared invited us to their wedding, which will take place this fall."

"How nice. Are you planning to go?"

"Maybe so. Would you like to come along?"

"Are you kidding me?"

"Nope. I'm tellin' the truth." Virginia couldn't help but smile. This was one sure way to get Stella to come back for a visit.

"Wow! Once you know the exact date, let me know and I'll cancel anything I may have scheduled. I wouldn't miss going to an Amish wedding for anything. I'm so excited right now, you could knock me over with a feather."

"Glad to have made your day, my friend, and I already know the date. It's the first Thursday of October. I just need to wait for a formal invitation."

"That's great! Now what were we talking about earlier?"

"I seem to have forgotten, Stella."

"Oh. Now I remember. It was about you working in your flowerbeds. You should go over to the greenhouse and see what kind of plants they have. You might find something that would look nice in your yard."

Virginia's jaw clenched. Truth was, she'd prefer to do any shopping for plants at the new greenhouse across town. But she couldn't let on to Stella how she really felt, because if her friend knew the way she felt about the Amish family across the road, she'd probably say Virginia was prejudiced.

"Umm, Virginia, I'd better go. I have another call coming in."

"Oh, okay. I'll talk to you again soon, Stella. Bye for now."

When Virginia clicked off her phone, she went out to the utility porch and grabbed her gardening gloves, some hand-clippers, and a shovel. At least her friend would likely come to visit again in the fall, which made Virginia happy.

Now maybe a little time spent outdoors would help her work off some of her stress.

"Would you look at these beautiful daffodils in bloom? I think they're prettier than ever this spring." Sylvia's mother gestured to the flowers adorning the flowerbed near the front porch.

Sylvia, deep in thought, hung a pair of Allen's trousers on the line and gave a brief nod.

"You seem distracted this morning," Mom said. "You haven't spoken more than a few words since we came outside with the laundry basket."

"Sorry, Mom. I've just been thinking, is all."

"About what?"

"Nothing in particular. Just thoughts about life in general." No way would Sylvia admit that she'd been thinking about Dennis and wondering why she hadn't heard from him since he'd come over to fix the downspout. They'd had a pleasant time when they'd gone birding and he'd joined them for supper—at least Sylvia had, and Dennis had mentioned going bird-watching again. It seemed strange that he wouldn't have at least called or come by. Could training horses be keeping him that busy?

"Daughter, did you hear what I said?"

Sylvia turned abruptly when Mom bumped her arm. "Uh. . .no, sorry, I did not. What was it, Mom?"

"I wondered if you'd have time to make up some hanging baskets for us to sell in the greenhouse. You made some lovely ones last year, and they sold quite well."

"Of course, I'd be happy to make more. I enjoyed using my creativity, and I've been thinking about some new ways I could arrange some flowering plants this year." Sylvia picked up a towel from the laundry basket and gave it a snap before hanging it on the line. "I'll get started on them as soon as all the laundry is hung."

"Danki. I look forward to seeing what you come up with." Mom turned her head in the direction of a horse and buggy coming up the driveway. "Looks like Mrs. Yoder, our first customer of the day is here. I'm sorry to run off and leave you with the rest of the clothes to hang, but I really should go to the greenhouse and help Amy."

"No problem. You go right ahead." Sylvia hurried to finish hanging the laundry, and then she carted the empty wicker basket back to the house. Seeing that the children were playing happily in the living room, she went to the kitchen and sat at the table with a notebook and pen. Since Mom wanted her to make up some hanging baskets, Sylvia thought it would be a good idea to start by making a list of all the plants she might want to include. At least she had something to keep her busy and take her mind off Dennis.

Sylvia had only been working on the list a few minutes when she heard Rachel crying from the living room. She pushed her chair aside and hurried to the other room, where she found her tearful daughter pointing at the open door.

Sylvia looked out and saw Allen sprinting toward the greenhouse. She picked Rachel up and hurried out the door. *Sure hope I get to him before he enters the greenhouse.*

🐦

Preparing to wait on a customer who'd entered the building a few minutes ago, Belinda felt a tug on her apron. She looked down and was surprised to see Allen looking up at her with a rubber ball in his hands. *"Gleichscht du balle schpiele?"*

"Jah, Allen, I like to play ball, but Grandma is busy working right now." The boy's bottom lip protruded as he held the ball over his head.

Belinda glanced around hoping either Henry or Amy was nearby and could take Allen up to the house. Neither of them was in sight. She couldn't leave the greenhouse unattended, and hoped they were at least somewhere in the building.

Belinda bent down and scooped Allen into her arms, but it obviously was not what he wanted. Allen began to thrash around, and ended up knocking Belinda's reading glasses on the floor. The next thing she knew, the woman she'd been about to help stepped back and the glasses shattered.

Belinda gasped, and Allen started to howl. This was not a good way to begin the morning.

The woman apologized for ruining her glasses and offered to pay for new ones.

Belinda waved her hand. "They're an old pair, and I have another, so there's no need to worry about it."

The woman apologized again and headed down one of the aisles. By then, Allen had calmed down some. Belinda's only consolation was that she had another pair of reading glasses in the house. If she could only remember where she'd put them.

Sylvia entered the greenhouse in time to see Mom down on the floor, picking up the pieces of her broken glasses. Allen stood next to her, whimpering, which made Rachel's tears start up again.

"What happened here?" Sylvia questioned.

As Mom explained, Sylvia clasped her son's hand.

A few seconds later, Amy came around the corner. "Mom, what's going on?" She looked down at what was left of their mother's glasses.

While Sylvia tried to get her children calmed down, Mom repeated the story.

"Why don't you go up to the house and look for your other glasses?" Amy suggested. "Henry's in the storage room right now, but I'll get him. The two of us will wait on customers while you're gone, and make sure things go okay here."

"All right." Mom held onto the remnants of her glasses. "Oh, by the way. . .a lady came in a few minutes before Allen showed up, and I was going to see if she needed any help." She gestured to Aisle 2. "She went that way."

"No problem. I'll see if I can help her."

Mom disposed of the broken glasses, and then she left the greenhouse, along with Sylvia and the children.

They'd barely entered the house when Sylvia heard a horse and buggy come into the yard. She stepped out onto the porch to see if it was anyone they knew and felt pleasure, seeing that it was Dennis.

Sylvia remained on the porch until he secured his horse and joined her there.

"It's good to see you, Sylvia. How have you been?" he asked.

"Fairly well. How are things going for you?"

"Not bad at all. My business is picking up, so that's a good thing."

"I'm glad it's working out."

Dennis shuffled his feet and leaned against the porch railing.

Is it my imagination, or could Dennis be nervous about something?

He took a step toward her and cleared his throat. "This is kind of a last-minute invitation, but I wondered if you'd be free to go out for supper with me this evening."

Sylvia had mixed feelings about being alone with Dennis, but at the same time, the idea of having supper with him appealed.

"If you're not free this evening, then maybe some other time." Dennis shuffled his feet a few more times.

"It's not that," Sylvia was quick to say. "I'll just need to see if someone would be willing to watch Rachel and Allen for me."

"Wouldn't your mamm do that?"

"Probably." Sylvia smiled. "My kinner love spending time with her. Allen even snuck out to the greenhouse a while ago, just to be with his grossmammi."

Dennis chuckled. "I bet that little guy keeps you busy."

"He certainly does. Jah, both kinner keep me plenty busy."

"So how about it, Sylvia? Are you willing to go out for supper with me?"

She gave a quick nod. A few months ago she wouldn't have believed she'd be spending the evening alone with a man, much less one she found to be both interesting and attractive. Even though she felt a bit nervous about going out with Dennis, Sylvia looked forward to this evening.

"Okay, good. I'll come by around six to pick you up." Dennis took a few steps back, and then stopped. "Oh, by the way. . . I thought you might want to know that when I was coming up your driveway, I noticed that the greenhouse sign was no longer hanging—it was lying on the ground."

Sylvia was at a loss for words. *Oh, no. . . Not another act of vandalism!*

Chapter 27

After Dennis left, Sylvia went into the house, where she found her mother sitting on the sofa in the living room. Allen sat on one side of her, and Rachel was seated on Mom's lap.

"Did you find your glasses?" Sylvia asked.

Mom shook her head. "I haven't had a chance to look. Someone needed to watch the kinner while you were out there talking to that man."

"His name is Dennis, and I wasn't out there very long."

"What'd he want?" Mom set Rachel on the couch beside her brother and went over to the wicker basket by her rocking chair.

Sylvia felt the tension building in her mother's words. She'd been down this road once already, when Dennis came for supper and Mom acted so distant.

Rummaging through the basket, Mom spoke again. "Well, what did Dennis want?"

"One thing he mentioned was that he noticed our sign by the road was lying in the dirt when he came up the driveway."

Mom stood up straight, her eyebrows drawing together. "Was it intentionally cut down?"

Sylvia shrugged. "I don't know. Dennis just said it was down."

"I'll have Henry put it back in place. Maybe he didn't secure the sign you made tightly enough when he put it up."

Sylvia drew in her bottom lip. "I hope that's the case. It's upsetting to think that someone might be targeting the greenhouse by removing our sign."

"The worst part is, we don't know who or why." Mom sank into the rocking chair. "Nothing like this ever happened when your father was alive."

Sylvia nodded. "Everything was better for all of us before the accident."

"That's true, but God is still with us, and we must remember to depend on Him for all of our needs."

Sylvia gave no response. Even after a year of being a widow, her faith was still on shaky ground. There were still moments when she couldn't get past the anger she felt about Toby, Dad, and Abe having been taken away. She didn't see how any good could come from their absence. *I'd like to know the reason the Lord allowed their lives to be taken.* Sylvia pondered this a moment.

"I think I know where my other pair of glasses is." Mom stood up suddenly. "I believe I may have left them on the nightstand in my bedroom." She turned in the direction of the hallway.

"Umm. . .before you go, there's something I need to ask you."

Mom turned back to face Sylvia. "What is it?"

"Would you be willing to watch the kinner for me this evening?"

Mom blinked. "How come? Won't you be here to watch them?"

"Normally I would be, but Dennis asked me to go out for supper with him."

Mom's forehead wrinkled as she pinched the bridge of her nose. "Are you serious? You haven't known that man long enough to go anywhere alone with him."

"I may not have known Dennis long, but I think I'm a pretty good judge of character. And there's nothing to worry about, because Dennis and I are just friends. Besides, I thought you wanted me to get out more and do something fun."

"I do, but not with a man you barely know." Mom moved closer and placed her hand on Sylvia's arm. "There are other single men in our church district, you know. Please think about what I've said."

"I'm not interested in any of them, and none have shown interest in me." Sylvia shrugged her mother's hand away. "If you don't want to watch Rachel and Allen, that's fine. I'll see if Amy is free to do it."

"I did not say that. I'm always willing to spend time with my grandchildren, and if you are determined to go out with Dennis, then

I will watch the kinner."

"Danki. Now I'd better get back to my flowering plant list, and I'm sure you want to find your missing pair of glasses before heading back to the greenhouse." Sylvia gave her mother a hug. She hoped there were no hard feelings.

When Belinda returned to the greenhouse, she found Henry putting fresh jars of honey on the shelf. She stepped up beside him and placed her hand on his shoulder. "Those amber-filled containers sell well, that's for sure. So many of our customers like to buy raw, unfiltered, local honey."

"Beekeeping's a lot of work, and sometimes I get stung, but like Dennis said, at least I'm not allergic to bee venom."

Belinda nodded. "When you're done with that, would you please go out and rehang our sign by the road?"

His eyes widened. "The sign is down?"

"Jah. Dennis was here a while ago to see Sylvia, and he informed her that he'd seen the sign lying in the dirt. I'm sorry, Son, but you'll need to hang it back up again."

A flush of red erupted on Henry's cheeks. "I wonder how that happened. Sure hope it wasn't taken down on purpose."

"Maybe there's a simple explanation."

"Like what?"

"You might not have secured it tightly enough."

There was a visible tightness in Henry's jaw. "So now I'm to blame, huh?"

"I didn't say that. I just thought—"

"When I put the sign up I made sure it was secured."

Belinda held up one hand. "Okay, I believe you did your best. Now would you please go out and put the sign back in place? We can't afford to lose any customers for lack of a sign."

"Jah, okay. I'll go out to the tool shed and get what I need." Henry put the last two jars on the shelf and went out the back door.

Belinda heaved a sigh. *I didn't mean to imply that his work was inadequate, but I wanted to steer my son away from thinking it was vandalism.* Henry had been a little easier to deal with lately. She hoped he wasn't back to his old defensive ways.

Belinda straightened a few other items for sale and headed up front to the counter where Amy sat. Since there were no customers in the building at the moment, she said, "This day has not begun the way I'd hoped."

Amy tipped her head to one side. "What's wrong, Mom?"

"Well, for starters, our business sign out by the road is no longer hanging up. I just told Henry about it, and he's going to put it back in place."

"Do you think it was done intentionally? Could it have been the same person who took the other sign?" Amy leaned forward with both arms on the counter.

"I have no idea, but I hope not. With all the things that have been done over the past year, I'm a little skittish."

"Me too. If we knew who was responsible for the vandalism, maybe we could talk to them and find out what made them do those things."

Belinda readjusted her left apron strap. It was close to falling off her shoulder. "The sign being down isn't all that has me upset."

"What else is wrong?" Amy brushed some dirt off the counter. "What's going on?"

"Dennis asked your sister to go out to supper with him this evening, and she wants me to take care of Rachel and Allen while she's gone."

A wide smile spread across Amy's face. "I think that's great. Sylvia needs to get out once in a while without the kinner."

"I agree, but it's too soon for Sylvia to be seeing a man socially, especially one we know so little about."

"What did you tell her about watching the children?"

"I agreed to it, but I'm not happy about the situation. As I said, we know little or nothing about Mr. Weaver, and I still feel your sister was hasty in letting him rent her house." Belinda pinched the skin at her throat. "I can't put my finger on it, but there is something suspicious about that man. I hope he doesn't worm his way into Sylvia's life. She's been through enough emotional pain. It would be horrible if Dennis did anything to hurt her."

"What in the world are you doing, woman?"

Virginia jumped, nearly dropping the pair of binoculars she held in her hands. "For goodness' sakes, Earl, you shouldn't sneak up on me like that. I could have dropped these expensive things."

"Right, Virginia, and they're intended to be used for looking at wild-life, not spying on the neighbors. That is what you were doing, correct?"

"Maybe I was bird-watching. You know, birding is a hobby, and you need binoculars to do that." She held them back up to her eyes.

He patted her shoulder. "What kind of birds are you observing out the front window?"

"Umm. . . Well, okay, you caught me."

"I thought so. Who are you watching this time?"

"Henry King. He's out by the road hanging up their greenhouse sign."

"Good grief, you've become a red-haired spy. I can see what he's doing from right here standing next to you. Anyways, I thought they already had a sign."

"They did, but I guess somebody took it down. When he picked it up, it had been lying in the dirt." Virginia tapped her foot. "I can't blame whoever did it either. I'm sure no one who lives on this road appreciates all the heavy traffic or piles of smelly road apples."

He quirked an eyebrow. "You're sure about that?"

"Yep. Only a person who's hard of hearing could deal with the steady *clip-clop*, not to mention all the cars that go up the Kings' driveway." She clenched her fingers tightly around the binoculars. "I've said this before, and I'll say it again. I wish we'd never moved here, Earl."

He slipped his arm around her waist. "Oh, come on now. It's not so bad."

"That's easy enough for you to say. Those people aren't right, with their backward mode of transportation and the way they have to dress so plain. You're at work most of the time, and I'm left here all alone, putting up with that." Virginia pointed out the window. "It's not fair."

"If you'd get out more and try to make some friends, I'm sure you'd adjust and find some fun things to do."

She set the binoculars on an end table near the couch and folded her arms. "I'm never gonna be happy here, and I will probably never make any new friends."

"With that kind of negative attitude, you probably won't."

"I'm gonna try and be more accepting of the Kings. I want Stella to come visit again, and the only way I can keep my friend on board with the idea is to get that wedding invite from Amy and Jared."

"So you're going to try to win over the Amish neighbors?"

"Yep." *If I can find the determination and courage to do it.*

"What is your plan?"

"For starters, I need some plants for the yard. So I'm gonna make myself go across the street and pick some out." Virginia pointed to the greenhouse.

He let out a hearty chuckle. "I won't believe it till you're walking in that direction and returning with a flat of pretty petunias or some other flowers."

"Are you getting a big bang out of this, Earl?"

"No, not really."

"I'm flat out miserable, or can't you tell? I have to go to a place I don't wanna go, just to ensure that we'll get invited to that wedding."

"Why don't you simply try to be yourself and get along with the neighbors, like I'm sure you're capable of, instead of acting like you want to be their friend?"

She put one hand against her hip. "You plainly don't understand me. Guess I'm just a complicated person with strange needs and wants."

"I didn't say that. Just go ahead and do what you like, but they'll probably see through your deception." Earl turned and walked out of the room.

Virginia picked up the field glasses again and looked out the window. The greenhouse sign was back in place now, and Henry was out of sight. *I wish those people would move someplace else. At least that would be one problem resolved.*

Chapter 28

Sylvia felt a lightness in her chest as she waited on the porch for Dennis's arrival. She'd told Rachel and Allen goodbye before coming outside, as well as Mom and Amy.

Henry's friend Seth had come by in his car a short time ago to pick Henry up. They planned to go out for pizza. When Henry had told Seth about their greenhouse sign, Seth denied knowing anything about the one that went missing or the sign Sylvia had made that Dennis found on the ground.

Mom still wasn't happy about Henry's friendship with Seth, but Sylvia had heard her tell Amy that she didn't want to hold the reins too tightly on Henry, or he might rebel.

Sylvia figured Mom was probably right and had made the best decision letting Henry go with Seth. She hoped her brother would behave himself this evening.

Sylvia took a seat on the porch swing. Glancing into the yard, she heard a bird calling from the maple tree. Sylvia wondered if it was that mockingbird again. Since the sun had begun to set, she couldn't make out what the bird looked like.

She'd just gotten the swing moving when a horse and buggy entered the yard. Sylvia knew right away it was Dennis because she recognized his well-groomed horse. Before he had a chance to pull up to the hitching rail, she stepped off the porch and approached his buggy.

"*Guder owed.* I wasn't expecting you to be waiting for me outside," Dennis said when Sylvia took her seat on the right side of the buggy.

"Good evening." She turned to him and smiled. "Figured I'd save you the trip of coming up to the house to get me."

"I wouldn't have minded." Dennis guided his horse down the driveway and out onto the road.

Normally, when Sylvia rode in anyone's buggy, her nerves were on edge. She'd been like this ever since the accident that took her husband's life. But this evening, seeing how self-confident Dennis seemed to be, she allowed herself to relax while riding in a carriage for the first time in over a year. As long as Dennis's horse didn't act up or a vehicle came up behind them going too fast, she might stay in her relaxed state of mind all the way to the restaurant.

"Have you decided where we're going to eat?" she asked.

Dennis shook his head. "Thought I'd leave that up to you. What's your favorite restaurant?"

"There are many good ones in our county, but I'm kind of partial to the family restaurant in Bird-in-Hand. Have you been there since you moved here?"

He shook his head. "Not yet, but I've heard good things about the food. So that's the direction we'll head."

Sylvia clasped her fingers loosely in her lap as she drew in a deep, satisfied breath. It was difficult to explain, even to herself, but when she was with Dennis she felt like a different person. Although Sylvia hadn't forgotten that she was the mother of two small children, as the horse's hooves clopped along the pavement, she felt like a teenager again, going on her first date.

"Did you get the kinner settled in bed?" Amy asked when Belinda entered the living room and seated herself in the rocking chair.

"Jah and now I can relax. It took a little prompting to get Allen to fall asleep this evening. He said he wanted to see his mom, and I had to remind him that he'd see her tomorrow morning." Belinda reached into the basket near her feet to get the dishcloth she'd been working on in her free time.

Amy plumped up one of the throw pillows on the couch where she sat. "Sylvia's kinner are adorable, and I love them both, but they can be a handful sometimes."

Belinda nodded. "But I wouldn't trade any of my *kinskinner* for all the world."

"I hope when Jared and I have children that I'll be as good a mother as Sylvia. She's so patient with Rachel and Allen and always seems to know what to say and how to handle any situation that arises with them."

Belinda got the rocking chair moving as her knitting needles clicked together. "You're right, she is a good mudder. I just wish she would use common sense where Dennis is concerned."

Amy tipped her head. "In what way?"

"She barely knows the fellow, yet she agreed to go out to supper with him." Belinda stopped rocking and leaned slightly forward.

"Going out to supper is a good way for Sylvia to get to know him better, don't you think?"

Belinda shrugged. "Maybe so, but they could do that in mixed company, not alone. What if someone from our church district sees them together at the restaurant? Why, there could soon be a round of gossip and speculation about Toby's widow being involved with the *geheem fremmer* who came to our area."

Amy laughed. "Really Mom, Dennis is hardly a mysterious stranger. He seems like a nice man. Sylvia and Henry believe he is too. I've heard them both say so several times."

Belinda was going to say more, but a knock sounded on the front door.

"That must be Jared." Amy rose from the couch and went to let him in.

Belinda had forgotten Amy had mentioned earlier that her future husband would be coming by.

A few minutes later, Amy entered the room with Jared. Belinda couldn't help but notice the circle of red on both his and Amy's cheeks. She wondered if he and Amy had embraced and possibly kissed, when he'd entered the house, the way she and Vernon used to do when they were courting.

"Guder owen, Belinda." Jared came over to Belinda and extended his hand. "How did things go for you today?"

She shook his hand and smiled. "It went all right. At least there were no mishaps in the greenhouse, and we sold a fair amount of flowers."

"Good to hear." Jared took a seat on the couch beside Amy. They sat quietly looking at each other.

These two probably want to be alone to discuss their plans for the future. Belinda put her knitting aside and stood. "I'm kind of tired this evening. Think I'll head to my room and get ready for bed."

Amy didn't try to dissuade her. She merely smiled at Belinda and said, "*Gut nacht*, Mom."

"Good night, Daughter. Good night, Jared."

After Jared replied, Belinda left the room. *Oh, to be young and in love again,* she thought. *My dearest Vernon, I miss you ever so much, but I'll never forget the special bond of love we shared.*

"You were right about the food being good at the Bird-in-Hand Family Restaurant," Dennis said as they traveled back to the King home.

"I'm glad you enjoyed it."

Not as much as I enjoyed being with you. Dennis kept his thoughts to himself. It was too soon to tell Sylvia that he was beginning to have strong feelings for her. He'd never felt like this before, and no way did he want to scare her off.

Dennis couldn't believe he was setting his concerns aside about establishing a relationship with a woman that could possibly lead to a permanent relationship. Of course he was putting the buggy before the horse when it came to any future he might have with Sylvia. For all Dennis knew, she had no intention of falling in love or getting married again. The love she'd felt for her husband might be so deep that she could never love another man.

I need to quit thinking about this, Dennis chided himself. *I'll just take things slow and easy with Sylvia and see how it all goes.*

When Dennis pulled his horse and buggy onto the Kings' driveway, Sylvia surprised him by asking if he'd like to come in for coffee and dessert. "I made some whoopie pies earlier today," she added.

"That's tempting," he said, "but I'm too full from supper to eat anything else. Besides, it's getting late, and we both need to get up early for church tomorrow morning."

She turned in her seat to face him. "Didn't you say during our meal that tomorrow is your off-Sunday?"

"That's right, but I thought I'd visit your church district's service tomorrow. Would that be all right with you?"

"Of course. You are welcome any time." Sylvia gave Dennis the address of the place where church would be held in the morning.

Dennis cleared his throat. "There's something else I'd like to ask."

"Oh?"

"I was wondering if you would be free tomorrow after church to go birding with me again."

"That sounds wunderbaar, but I had planned to take my kinner on a picnic."

Dennis reached over and lightly touched her arm. "Would you mind if I tag along? Maybe we'll see some interesting birds while we're there."

"Of course, you're more than welcome to join us. If you'd like, you can come over here right after our church's noon meal."

"Think I'll go home and change clothes first. Then I'll be over to join you."

"Sounds good."

Dennis stepped down from the buggy, secured his horse, and came around to help Sylvia exit.

"I had a nice time this evening, Dennis. Danki for inviting me to join you for supper."

"You're welcome." He had to restrain himself to keep from leaning down and giving her a kiss on the cheek. *What am I thinking? That might scare her off.*

He said a pleasant, "Good night," and watched as Sylvia made her way to the house, using the flashlight she'd brought along to guide the way.

As Dennis directed his horse and buggy back down the driveway, he smiled. *Sylvia must like me a little bit, or she wouldn't have invited me to go on a picnic with her and the kids tomorrow.* He pressed his lips together. *Of course, I did actually invite myself. Even so, she was agreeable, so I'll take that as a positive sign.*

When Sylvia entered the house, the scent of freshly made buttered popcorn filled the air. This only added to her pleasant mood, and she couldn't wait to spend more time with Dennis. *I'm looking forward to going on a picnic and getting out with the children. They'll enjoy it, and creating fun memories is an added bonus.* She found Amy and Jared in the living room, working on a jigsaw puzzle. A bowl of popcorn sat between them.

Amy looked up and smiled. "Did you have a nice evening?"

"Jah. We ate at the family restaurant in Bird-in-Hand."

Jared looked at Sylvia and wiggled his brows. "Good choice. I enjoy their buffet."

"I ate a lot of my favorite foods there but got a little carried away, I'm afraid. Dennis must have liked it too, because when I invited him in for coffee and a whoopie pie, he declined, saying he was still full from supper."

Jared looked over at Amy and his chin dropped down slightly. "There are whoopie pies in the house and you never offered me any? Is that how you're gonna treat me once we're married?"

Amy giggled and tossed a piece of popcorn at him. "Sylvia made those whoopies to take on the picnic she and her kinner are going on tomorrow afternoon. If I'd offered you one, you'd probably have eaten so many there wouldn't be enough left."

"Not true." He shook his head. "If you'd have told me why Sylvia baked them, I'd have only taken one."

Sylvia got a kick out of watching her sister and Jared's playful banter. That was how it used to be with her and Toby. He often teased her, and she enjoyed it, because his teasing was always done in a fun, loving way. Dennis seemed more serious-minded than Toby, but Sylvia enjoyed being with him, nonetheless.

I can't believe I'm comparing my deceased husband to someone brand-new in my life. She scratched an itch near the side of her nose. *I never expected to have so much fun. Maybe a little too much. It doesn't make sense that I feel so comfortable with him. It seems like we've been friends for a good many years.*

"Mom put the kids to bed some time ago, and she went to her room soon after." Amy's comment broke into Sylvia's musings.

"Oh, good. Did they behave themselves for you and Mom this evening?"

Amy bobbed her head. "There were no problems, other than that Mom had to work with Allen to get him to go to bed. He wanted his mommy to say goodnight. Otherwise, thing went as usual around here."

"I'm glad." Sylvia leaned over the card table and put a piece of puzzle in place. "Say, I have an idea. Why don't you and Jared join us on the picnic tomorrow? I'm sure Dennis would enjoy some male company."

Amy's eyebrows squished together. "I thought it was just you and the kinner going on a picnic. When did Dennis come into the picture?"

"Tonight, when he brought me home, I mentioned the picnic, and he sort of invited himself to join us." Sylvia's cheeks warmed. "Of course, I could hardly say no."

Amy gave Sylvia a knowing look. "No, I'm sure."

"What do you mean?"

Amy waved her hand. "Oh, nothing."

"Well, would you two like to go with us or not? I'm sure it will be fun, and being outdoors someplace different would be a welcome change."

"I'm in," Jared spoke up. "I'd like to get to know this Dennis fellow."

"You'll like him. He's a very nice man."

Amy shot Sylvia another look, but she chose to ignore it. "When I see Mom and Henry in the morning, I'll invite them too. It should be a fun day for all of us."

"Speaking of Henry. . . You'll be happy to know that he came home from his evening with Seth about thirty minutes ago."

"I'm glad to hear it." Sylvia turned toward the door leading to the stairs. "It's getting late, so I'm turning in now. Good night, Amy. Good night, Jared."

"Gut nacht," they said in unison.

Sylvia smiled as she left the room. *I'm glad my sister is with the man she loves.*

Chapter 29

The sound of gunfire reverberated in Dennis's head, and he woke up with a start. Several seconds passed before he realized where he was. Thankfully, the gun going off had only been a dream—one he'd had too often.

Dennis tried to calm down. He had hoped these recurring episodes would fade away over time, but they had not. Some day he would like to look back and say he hadn't had that nightmare for a long, long time. *Just when I thought I was beginning to heal, my feelings of anger toward Uncle Ben have surfaced all over again.*

Dennis rolled out of bed and looked at the clock on his nightstand. It was nine o'clock. "Oh great, I've overslept." He thumped his head and groaned. "Must have forgot to set my alarm." Dennis picked up the clock and checked the back side. *I definitely did not set this alarm!* He set it back on his nightstand and squinted at the light breaching into the room through the partially open window shade.

He ambled over to the window and looked out. The sky looked blue, with only a few scattered puffy clouds. It should be a good day for a picnic. Unfortunately, Dennis would not have time to get dressed, eat breakfast, and make it on time to the home Sylvia told him would be hosting church in her district this morning. Since the service would have already started, he'd feel like a fool showing up so late. *I'll make it up to Sylvia and try to attend her church on my next off-Sunday.*

Dennis ambled over to the closet to pick out something to wear. He was low on clean clothes, and that meant doing laundry soon. Dennis didn't like washing clothes, but it had to be done. With the nicer weather, at least things would dry quickly. When he lived at home, Mom had taken care of his clothes, even mending tears or pressing wrinkles out of stubborn pieces.

I wonder how she's doing. It had been a while since Dennis had called home to check on things. He was surprised she hadn't called him. No doubt Mom and the rest of his family would be in church today. Dennis's family had been diligent about attending church services during his childhood.

Dennis found a shirt he liked and slipped it on. It would be better to forget about church and just show up at the Kings' place around two o'clock. He would have some explaining to do, but at least he'd get to spend the afternoon with Sylvia. At least, he hoped she'd still want to see him. She might be angry because he missed church.

Sylvia sat stoically on her bench, looking straight ahead. It was difficult to focus on the message being preached when all she could think about was why Dennis hadn't shown up for church. Had he gotten sick between last night and this morning? Or perhaps he couldn't find the place; although she thought she'd given good directions.

Sylvia shifted on the bench when Rachel began to squirm on her lap. Her mind went from one thing to the next, as she worried about why he hadn't come today. *Maybe Dennis changed his mind and decided not to come. If so, he probably won't show up for the picnic this afternoon either. That sure would be a disappointment. I've been thinking warmly about this since we made plans for the day.*

Sylvia's hands began to sweat as another thought popped into her mind. *What if Dennis was involved in an accident this morning?*

"I thought you said Dennis would be attending our church service this morning," Amy commented as she drove the horse and buggy on their way home that afternoon. Since the home their service had been in this morning was only a mile away, Henry had decided to walk. Otherwise, they would have taken two buggies, and either Mom or Henry would have been in the driver's seat.

"That was my understanding too, but I guess something must have happened to detain him." Sylvia's fingers tightened around her purse straps. "I hope nothing bad has happened."

Mom glanced over her shoulder, from her seat at the front of the buggy beside Amy. "Maybe he forgot or changed his mind about coming. Some folks can be unpredictable, you know."

Sylvia clamped her lips shut to keep from saying anything she might later regret. *Is Mom trying to put doubts in my mind about Dennis's dependability? If so, she needn't bother. I've been questioning it myself. I can't wait to find out the reason for him not coming to church. Hopefully, nothing serious occurred. I'd feel bad if something had.*

"Sylvia, did you hear what I said?"

"Yes, Mom, and when we get home I'll check the phone shed for messages. Maybe he left me one."

As they approached their driveway, Rachel began to fuss. No doubt it was time for a nap.

When they pulled up to the hitching rail, Henry came out of the house. He'd left soon after their noon meal following church, so it was understandable that he'd arrived home before them.

"I'll take care of the horse and put the buggy over by the barn for now. When Dennis gets here, and we're ready to go out for a picnic, I'll bring Dusty back and get him hitched to the buggy." Henry looked over at Amy. "Would you mind drivin' Mom's buggy so I can ride with Dennis?"

"It's fine if you want to ride in Dennis's rig," she responded, "but I'll be riding in Jared's buggy. "Did you forget that he was invited to our picnic?"

Before Henry could respond, Sylvia spoke up. "We're not even sure if Dennis is coming. He wasn't in church, even though he said he would be."

"No need to worry." Henry held up his hand. "Since I didn't see Dennis in church, I stopped at the phone shed on my way into the yard to see if he might have left us a message."

"And did he?" Mom asked.

"Jah. Said he forgot to set his alarm and woke up too late, but he'll be over in time for our picnic. Dennis also said he'd try to make it to our church service on his next off-Sunday."

Mom made a little grunting sound in her throat. "Waking up late on a Sunday morning doesn't sound like someone's who very dependable. I've always managed to get up in time to go to church."

Sylvia felt relieved, knowing Dennis was all right and still planned to join them, and by this time, she had the children out of the buggy. So rather than comment on her mother's judgmental statement, she headed straight for the house with her little ones. Rachel needed a diaper change, and both she and Allen were going down for a nap. Otherwise, they'd be cranky the rest of the day. Besides, Sylvia was eager to get inside before her mother said anything more about Dennis. Hopefully while they were on their picnic, Mom would get to know him better and realize what a nice man he was.

"Hmm. . . So far still no German shepherds being offered in *The Budget* or local newspaper." Dennis tapped his fingers against the table where he sat drinking a second cup of coffee. "I suppose I'll have to go to the animal shelter soon and have a looksee."

He glanced at the clock on the kitchen wall. It was about time to leave. Dennis pushed back his chair and went into the bathroom to see if his hair had been combed neatly enough.

I hope Sylvia forgives me for goofing up and sleeping in this morning.

Dennis moved away from the mirror and headed out the back door. When he entered the barn, he was greeted by friendly stomping and nickering of the geldings. Midnight looked in his direction, and the closer Dennis got to his stall, the more pawing his horse did.

"Okay, buddy, simmer down. You and I are going for a ride to the Kings' place." He led Midnight out of the paddock and got the animal geared up and hooked to the buggy.

"Sure hope Sylvia got my message." Dennis spoke out loud. Although his horse couldn't understand what he was talking about, the gelding's ears perked up.

Dennis chuckled. "You think I'm talking to you, don't you, boy?"

Midnight whinnied and flipped his tail.

"You're a schmaert one, huh?" Dennis climbed into the buggy, backed the horse up, and flicked the reins.

All the way to the Kings' house, his thoughts were on Sylvia. Would she be pleased to see him or upset because he hadn't shown up in church? He hoped it wouldn't be the latter. He couldn't help wanting to be with Sylvia. He'd gone out with other Amish women before, but no one had interested him until now. It frightened Dennis a bit, but not enough to stay away. His fear of commitment was beginning to wane.

As they traveled along, Dennis thought about his business and how he'd gained more clients. If he could keep things moving along at this rate, he should be able to support a wife and children.

Would I make a good father to Sylvia's kinner? He let go of the reins with one hand and pinched the bridge of his nose. *I shouldn't be thinking this way. We're still in the early phase of a relationship, and it's not in my nature to rush ahead.*

When Dennis started up the Kings' driveway, he spotted Henry in the yard, playing fetch with his dog. The boy threw the stick and raced over to Dennis's horse as soon as he pulled up to the hitching rail.

"I'll tie him up for you," Henry called.

Dennis nodded, and once Midnight was secure, he climbed down from the buggy.

"Glad you could make it." Henry spoke rapidly as he moved toward Dennis. "Sorry you didn't come to church, but we got your message."

"Good to hear." Dennis looked toward the house. "Is Sylvia inside?"

"Jah, and so are the others. I'll go let 'em know you're here. Then we can all head out for our picnic." Henry rushed inside.

Figuring it would be best not to barge into the house uninvited, Dennis took a seat on the porch swing.

Several minutes went by, and then Dennis caught sight of a male mockingbird sitting on top of a shrub in the yard. He recognized the bird's silvery gray head and back, with a light gray chest and belly. It didn't take long before it began to sing.

Caught up in the moment, Dennis's head jerked to one side when the screen door slammed. He turned and saw Sylvia standing in front of the door with a wicker basket in her hands. "I'm glad you could make it."

He gave a nod. "So am I. Sorry about missing church this morning. I'll have to try again in two weeks."

"That'd be nice."

He rose from the swing and approached her. "Want me to take that basket and put it in my buggy?"

"Yes, please." Sylvia handed it to him.

"So where's everyone else?"

"They're coming." She gave Dennis another heart-melting smile.

He drew in a quick breath. *Why am I so affected by this woman?* The fact that Sylvia had children didn't bother him in the least, which surprised him most of all.

🐦

As Sylvia sat on a blanket near the pond located a few miles from her mother's home, she breathed deeply of the wildflowers growing nearby. Lily pads floated on the surface of the water, and a pair of mallard ducks swam nearby. A bird flapped its wings overhead as it took flight, and Dennis leaned closer to Sylvia and pointed. "Did you see that Horned Lark?"

"I saw a tannish-brown bird but didn't know what it was called."

"Horned Larks are birds of open ground," Henry interjected. "They're common in rural areas like this and are usually seen in large flocks."

Dennis nodded. "I'm impressed with your knowledge, young man."

Henry grinned and grabbed another chocolate whoopie pie from the dessert basket. Although her brother had eaten more than his share of ham-and-cheese sandwiches, not to mention several peanut butter cookies, apparently he had room for more.

Sylvia glanced at her mother, sitting on a separate blanket with the children. They'd spread both blankets side-by-side, so they could all visit while enjoying the picnic lunch Sylvia, Amy, and Mom had prepared.

Sylvia couldn't help but notice how quiet Mom was today. When she did say something, it was directed to Amy and Jared, who sat close to her.

Sylvia felt a little guilty that her mother was stuck caring for Allen and Rachel, but she'd volunteered to oversee them while eating, so she must not mind.

Once everyone had finished eating, and the food had been put away, Dennis suggested that he and Sylvia take a walk.

"Just the two of us?"

"Jah. If no one else minds."

Sylvia looked in Amy and Jared's direction. Jared shrugged, and Amy smiled and said, "Go ahead. I'll stay here with Mom to keep an eye on the kinner."

Mom sat quietly, holding Rachel in her lap. Since she made no objection, Sylvia picked up her binoculars and stood. She looked over at Henry and noticed his wrinkled brows but didn't feel it was her place to invite him on the walk.

Dennis led the way down a path that followed the circumference of the pond. When her family was no longer visible, he stopped walking and placed his hand on her arm. "I. . .uh. . .don't quite know how to say this, Sylvia, but I really enjoy your company. Would it be okay if I stop by to visit you one evening this week?"

She moistened her lips with her tongue and swallowed hard. Was Dennis asking if he could court her? Did she want him to?

Chapter 30

Sylvia needed to answer Dennis's question, but she could barely find her voice as she stared at the ducks in the pond. *I'd like to see more of Dennis, and it's wonderful to know he enjoys my company.* The fact that Dennis wanted to see her again must mean he was interested in her. And if Sylvia were being completely honest with herself, she was interested in him too. She'd never imagined having feelings for anyone but Toby, but Sylvia felt drawn to Dennis.

She lifted her head and turned to face him. "I'd be pleased if you came over to see me. It would make me happy to spend more time with you."

A wide smile formed on his face. "What evening would work best for you?"

"How about Wednesday, and why don't you plan on joining us for supper?"

"That'd be great, if it won't be any trouble."

Sylvia shook her head. "Not a bit. Is there anything special you'd like me to cook?"

"Nope. Whatever you fix is fine. I'm not a picky eater."

"Neither am I, but my Allen sure is. I have to coax him to try new things."

Dennis chuckled and then pointed to another pair of ducks. "Look over there. In case you didn't know, those are called blue-wing teals."

"No, I didn't know. I've seen ducks like that before but never knew their name." Sylvia moved closer to the pond, watching as the male and female, both smaller than the mallards they'd seen previously, dipped their beaks in the water to catch a few bugs.

"The ducks' name comes from the fact that they have a blue wing patch, but it's usually only seen when they're in flight." Dennis squatted down in the grassy area. "These are some of the smallest ducks in North America. They are also one of the longest-distance migrating ducks."

"The female looks pretty plain," Sylvia commented. "The large, white crescent-shaped mark at the base of the mallard's bill certainly sets him apart."

Dennis nodded. "It does, as well as his black tail with a small white patch."

Sylvia knelt beside him. "I still can't get over how much you know about the birds in this state. You must retain everything you learn."

Dennis shrugged. "Maybe so, but I mostly remember things I care about." He looked at Sylvia intently.

Her heart beat a little faster than normal. She remembered how Toby used to look at her like that.

"Hey, you two—didn't you hear us calling?"

Sylvia looked over her shoulder and saw Jared heading their way.

Dennis took hold of Sylvia's hand and helped her stand. It was a good thing too, because her legs felt like they were made of rubber. She wasn't sure if she could take a step forward.

"What were you calling about?" Dennis asked.

"Sylvia's kinner are getting fussy, and it'll be getting dark soon. Your mamm thinks we should be heading for home."

Dennis looked up at the darkening sky. "She's right, and from the looks of things, we might be in for a storm. Sure don't want to be caught out here if it starts raining heavily."

"Me neither," Sylvia agreed as they turned and headed back to the place where they'd had their picnic meal.

Virginia washed the last of the lunch dishes by hand, since there weren't enough to fill the dishwasher. "I'll be glad to get this done so I can relax."

"I thought you were going over to the greenhouse to buy some plants or flowers today," Earl said when he came in from outside, wiping perspiration from his forehead.

"I was, and I'm still planning to go there, so don't worry." Virginia had hoped he wouldn't notice the empty flowerbed along the side of the house. "It's not like I can go there today, anyway," she added. "Since it's Sunday, their business is closed."

"Then lucky you, it seems." He chuckled.

She finished up her work at the sink and shut off the running water.

He took a glass from the cupboard and filled it with orange juice from the refrigerator. "After I drink this, I'm heading back outside to finish painting that trim I sanded yesterday."

"Okay." Virginia took a seat at the table. *I'm glad he quit bugging me about those flowers. But I still need to go over to the greenhouse and play nicey-nice, or we'll never get a wedding invitation.*

❧

Amy looked over at Jared and smiled. She felt fortunate to have him in her life, and it was hard to believe in just a few months she would become his bride. She couldn't imagine her life without him.

As the swaying of Jared's buggy threatened to lull her to sleep, Amy's thoughts turned to other things.

I wonder if Mom is right about Dennis. Could he be interested in Sylvia as more than a friend?

She looked toward a large home coming up on the right. *I'd like to have a place like that after Jared and I are married. But whatever size our home turns out to be, I plan on entertaining our family and friends.*

Switching gears, Amy recapped what her mother had said earlier. Soon after Dennis and Sylvia walked away together, Mom had begun talking about him and not in a good way. She'd mentioned one more time, with a look of disapproval, that she thought Dennis had set his cap for Sylvia. Amy saw nothing wrong with this, as long as he and Sylvia didn't rush into anything. They needed time to get to know each other well, and it would be good if Sylvia met Dennis's parents and siblings. Mom thought it was strange that he hadn't told Sylvia much about his family—only that they lived in Dauphin County.

To give Dennis the benefit of the doubt, Amy figured he probably wanted to get to know Sylvia's family first. *If he approves of us, then he'll surely want my sister to meet and get to know his parents too.*

Jared reached over and took Amy's hand. "You're awfully quiet. Are you feeling *mied* and anxious to get home?"

"I am a little tired," she admitted, "but I've mostly been thinking."

He stroked her hand with his thumb. "About us?"

"Jah, mostly." Amy thought it best not to mention her sister and Dennis—not with Mom in the back seat with the children. Although Rachel and Allen had fallen asleep, their grandmother was no doubt listening to Amy and Jared's conversation. If Amy brought up the topic of Dennis, Mom would want to add her two cents.

Amy leaned back against the seat and closed her eyes. She tried to visualize what it would be like on the day of her and Jared's wedding. All of their family and friends would be present. She hoped the fall weather would cooperate for their special day and everything would go as planned. *Oh, what a joyous occasion it will be.*

The entire way home, all Belinda could think about was how improper if had been for Dennis to ask Sylvia to go for a walk with him alone. *They should have had some supervision. When Vernon and I were courting, we followed the rules. We didn't step out of line and do things that might cause our parents to worry or fret over our actions.*

Her fingernails cut into her skin as she drew them tightly into her palms. *Why didn't Dennis ask my son to walk with them? He knows how much Henry enjoys bird-watching.* The longer Belinda reflected on the way things had gone, the more frustrated she became.

On top of my daughter agreeing to walk with Dennis alone, she hardly paid any attention to her children while we were eating lunch. The responsibility of looking after Rachel and Allen fell on me and Amy, and it wasn't fair. Belinda shifted on her unyielding seat as she sat between her precious grandchildren. *These two deserve their mother's full attention, and Sylvia should be riding back here with them, instead of in Dennis's buggy.*

Belinda craned her neck to look between Jared and Amy. She saw

Dennis's horse and buggy moving along at a pretty good clip ahead of them.

At least he invited Henry to ride in his rig. Belinda leaned her head against the seatback. *But then, what other choice did he have? There wasn't room in Jared's carriage for more people.*

Belinda hoped Dennis wouldn't come around too often. It wasn't good for Sylvia to be so distracted. She had two young children to raise, and that should come first.

Sylvia glanced over her shoulder, wondering why her brother was so quiet. He hadn't said a word since they'd begun their journey home. Henry sat slouched in the back seat with his arms folded and lips pressed together. Was he tired, or could he be upset about something?

Maybe he felt left out because Dennis and I took a walk by ourselves, Sylvia reasoned. *I probably should have invited him to go along.* Sylvia fiddled with the ties on her head covering. *But since it was Dennis's idea to go for the walk, and he only asked me, it wasn't my place to invite my brother. Besides, I enjoyed the time Dennis and I had alone. It gave us another chance to get to know each other better.*

Sylvia thought about how things could change in the years to come. Jared and Amy would be married this year. She and Dennis could even end up that way sometime in the future. Also, Mom might eventually find someone if she chose to. Of course, Henry would, in due time, find a special woman to court and sooner or later get married. Sylvia felt a little overwhelmed at the prospect of what could be, with the addition of new family members.

Marriage to Dennis was a silly notion, given the fact that they were so newly acquainted, but Sylvia found herself wondering if she might possibly have a future with him.

Would Toby approve if it did happen? she wondered. *And how would the rest of my family feel about it? Would Dennis be a good stepfather, and could my children accept him as such?*

It wasn't like her to think such thoughts about another man, much less the prospect of having a future with him. She felt relieved when

Dennis struck up a conversation about birds that included both her and Henry.

She glanced at Dennis, then looked quickly away. *I'm glad he can't get into my head and know my thoughts. That would be most embarrassing.*

As they drew closer to home, Sylvia caught sight of Maude ambling along the shoulder of the road. Keeping her head down, the elderly woman never even glanced their way. Surely she had to hear the horses plodding along.

I wish we knew more about that poor lady. Sylvia repressed a sigh. *Surely she must have some family somewhere.*

"Who is that woman?" Dennis asked. "Is she one of your neighbors?"

"Her name is Maude, and she lives down the road from us in a run-down shanty."

"That's sad." He slowed his horse before the turn. "Well, we're here. Glad we made it back before it got dark or decided to rain."

Dennis guided Midnight up the driveway. "What's that on the greenhouse?" He pointed. "It wasn't there when we left for the picnic."

As they approached the building, on the way up to the house, Sylvia's thoughts became fuzzy, and her ears began to ring. Every visible window on the side of the building had been splattered with black paint.

Oh my! Who could have done this, and why? Was it the same person who did all the other acts of vandalism?

Chapter 31

Sylvia stood with Dennis, Jared, and her family, staring at the black-painted windows. This was yet another unnecessary act for her and the rest of them to deal with. It seemed as though they were being targeted, and it was getting old. It bothered Sylvia that Mom had refused to notify the sheriff, but she understood why her mother didn't want Ezekiel to know.

This kind of thing gets me upset and makes it hard to trust the Lord, she thought. "Why did such a beautiful day have to be ruined like this?" Sylvia drew in a few raspy breaths as she looked at her mother.

Mom shook her head slowly. "This is our family's business—the way we make our living. I can't understand how or why anyone could be so mean."

"Unfortunately there are some not-so-nice people who like to do destructive things." Jared frowned. "I hope you're going to call the sheriff's office."

"No, we're not." Mom spoke in a low-pitched voice.

"Why not?" Dennis asked. "Don't you want the person who did this to be punished?"

"First of all, we don't know who did it." Mom looked at each of them with a serious expression. "We need to pray harder for God's protection and that the person who did this will fall under conviction."

"I bet it was Seth," Henry spoke up.

"Why would you think it was Seth?" Amy questioned. "He's supposed to be your friend. Right, Henry?"

"Jah, but Seth invited me to go someplace with him this afternoon, and I turned him down 'cause I was goin' on the picnic with all of you." Henry's eyes narrowed as he folded his arms across his chest. "And a lot of good that did me. Spent most of the day lookin' for birds by myself." He glanced briefly at Sylvia, then back at the painted windows.

Sylvia's chin dipped slightly. Although she had enjoyed her time alone with Dennis, it was rude of them not to include Henry—especially since he enjoyed birding so much. *I sure wasn't thinking, and my brother has good reason to be upset.*

Mom gestured to one of the windows. "I don't think Seth would do something like this just because you had other plans today."

"He might though." Henry frowned. "He was pretty miffed when I said I couldn't go with him."

"Where did he want you to go?" The question came from Jared.

Henry shrugged. "Don't know for sure. Just hang around with him and some of his friends, I guess."

"I'm afraid Seth's friends are not good company, Son." Mom put her hand on Henry's shoulder. "There's no telling where they would go or what they might do. You were better off with your family today."

"I suppose."

"If this is the sort of thing Seth and his friends deem as fun, then I'm relieved you were not hanging around them today." Mom's gaze remained fixed on Henry. "Have they done something like this before, or said anything to you about doing this sort of thing to anyone else?"

"No. I haven't heard anything." He shook his head forcefully. "I'm just suspecting them, is all, but I aim to ask Seth about it. If he and his friends had anything to do with painting the windows black, I'm gonna tell their parents." Henry's shoulders slumped. "Just makes me sick to think that my friend might have been involved in this."

Sylvia figured Henry felt betrayed by her for ignoring him at the pond, and also by his friend who was possibly responsible for blackening their windows. *My poor brother.*

When Sylvia heard Rachel fussing from the buggy, she realized the children were probably both awake. Since Jared's horse was secured well to the rail, Sylvia had thought it best to let them sleep while she and the others went to take a closer look at the greenhouse windows.

"Rachel's awake, and Allen probably is too." She looked at Dennis, who stood close to her side. "I'd better get those two out and take them up to the house." Sylvia glanced at the ugly windows again and frowned. *I hope what Mom is doing by not involving the sheriff isn't a mistake. I wonder how Dad would have handled this and all the other vandalism that's taken place.*

"I'll go with you," Dennis was quick to say. "I'll carry one of your kinner, and you can carry the other."

"Danki." Sylvia followed Dennis to the buggy. She appreciated his thoughtfulness so much. Once again, she couldn't help thinking about Toby and how Dennis reminded her of him in many ways.

"Let's take a walk around the rest of the greenhouse," Jared suggested, "Maybe not all the windows were painted."

"Good idea." Belinda led the way. To her relief, only the one side of the greenhouse windows had been painted black. All the others looked clear.

"Whew! That's a blessing." She reached out to Amy and clasped her arm. "This means we won't have quite so much work to do in the morning."

"You won't have to do it alone either," Jared said. "I'll be over bright and early to begin scraping."

"It's very much appreciated. Hopefully we can get the job done before any customers show up." Belinda's brows furrowed. "The last thing we need is for people to spread the word about the vandalism that's gone on here from time to time. If too many people know, Ezekiel's bound to find out. He still has some friends in this area, you know."

"Don't you think he has the right to know?" Henry grunted and folded his arms.

This was not the first time one of Belinda's children had asked this question.

She shook her head forcefully. "We've had this discussion before, Son, and my answer is always the same. If your brother knew what was happening here, he'd pack up and move back to Strasburg, no matter how much he'd be giving up by leaving his home there."

"I realize that, Mom."

Amy released a heavy sigh. "I can't believe anyone would do something like this in broad daylight."

"Maybe we should check with your closest neighbor and ask if they saw anything going on here while we were gone," Jared suggested. "Amy and I can go over there right now."

"That's a good idea," Henry said. "While you're doin' that, I'm gonna go check in the barn and the rest of our place to make sure nothing else is wrong."

I hope nothing else is amiss around here. We'll have our hands full enough trying to remove all that black paint. Belinda closed her eyes. *Please keep us from harm, Lord, and also, I pray that this would stop and the person responsible for the vandalism would fall under conviction.*

🐦

Amy remained close to Jared as they stood on her neighbor's front porch, waiting for someone to answer the door. She was glad he'd come with her, because something about Virginia made her feel uncomfortable. Although the woman had never said anything unkind to Amy, she always seemed a bit curt as if she couldn't wait to get away from her. Amy had a feeling the neighbor lady didn't much care for her and probably not the rest of the family either.

She held her breath a few seconds and released it slowly. *Maybe this is a mistake, coming over here. Virginia may not want to talk to us.*

After Jared's second knock, the front door opened, and Earl greeted them with a smile. "Well hello there, Jared. It's nice to see you." He glanced at Amy. "What brings you two by here this evening?"

Amy spoke first and quickly explained about the painted windows.

"We were wondering if you or your wife saw anybody hanging around the greenhouse this afternoon," Jared put in.

Earl shook his head. "I saw no one, although Virginia may have." He turned and called his wife's name.

A few seconds later, Virginia showed up. Her short red hair was in disarray—as though she'd just gotten out of bed. "What's up?"

"These people want to know if either of us saw anyone hanging around their greenhouse today."

Virginia pursed her lips. "From our house we can only see one side of the building."

"Did you see anyone in our yard at all?" Amy questioned.

"Nope. I've seen nothing out of the ordinary while we've been home. Course we weren't here all day. Earl and I went out for lunch this afternoon. When we got home, we took a nap—me in the bedroom and him in his easy chair while watching TV." Virginia picked at her thumbnail. "We were up late the night before, and so I ended up sleeping nearly two hours during my nap." She hesitated a moment. "I wouldn't be one bit surprised if that scruffy old woman—oh yeah, Maude—may have been hanging around your place. As I mentioned previously, I've seen her there before."

"Yes, I remember you saying that."

"Maude seems suspicious to me—the way she wanders up and down the road, like she's lookin' for something—or maybe ready to snatch something that doesn't belong to her." Virginia's bland expression changed to one of sympathy, and she spoke in a soothing tone. "Sure wish I could be of more help to you, and I hope you find out who's been messing around your place."

Amy gave a brief nod. "Thanks for your time." She and Jared said goodbye and stepped off the porch.

Amy walked along, holding tightly to Jared's hand. "Virginia seemed like a different person to me, especially toward the last of our conversation."

"What do you mean?" Jared asked.

"Like I mentioned before, she's usually not very talkative or friendly."

"People can change, right?"

"I hope so."

After they crossed the street, Jared stopped walking and looked directly at Amy. "Someone needs to convince your mamm to call the sheriff."

"That's a good thought, and I totally agree, but when my mother sets her mind on something, no one but my daed has ever been able to change it."

"Guess I'll have to start coming by here more often to check on things." Jared squeezed her fingers as they headed up the driveway. "It'll give me another good reason to see you."

Amy smiled. "How *glicklich* I am to have found a man like you."

"And I am lucky to have you, *mei lieb*."

A ripple of joy shot through Amy's soul whenever Jared referred to her as his love.

Virginia ambled into the living room and flopped onto the couch. "I'm having a tough time, Earl."

He looked at her with a curious expression. "What do you mean?"

"I need to speak kindly to those people, because if I'm nicer, they'll be more apt to invite us to their wedding. On the other hand, I wish they'd stop coming over here and bothering me. I mean, why would they think we knew anything about the vandalism?"

Earl looked at Virginia as if she'd lost her mind. "Because we live across the street."

A warm flush crept across Virginia's face. "Please don't look at me like that, Earl."

He took a seat in the recliner and picked up the remote. "Now can we stop talking? I'd like to watch one of my favorite TV shows."

"Sure, whatever!" Virginia got up and limped out of the room. She went out the back door and walked around the house, trying to imagine how it would look with more flowers. Even some hanging baskets on the porch would look nice.

She came toward the front of the house and shuffled across the driveway. Looking toward the greenhouse, she could see only one side of the building. So at least what she'd told Amy and Jared was the truth.

Virginia heard the blaring TV through the open living room window and cringed. "I'm sure Earl is napping in his recliner again, and he isn't even watching whatever program he has on."

As raindrops began to fall, she reached down and rubbed her leg, which hadn't hurt much earlier in the day. *I wish Stella was still here. At least then I'd have someone to talk to. Doesn't Earl even care how much I hate living here?*

Chapter 32

Early the following morning, before breakfast had even been started, a knock sounded on the back door. Sylvia hurried to see who it was. When she opened the door, she was surprised to see Dennis on the porch holding a scraper.

"I came to help scrape paint off the windows. Has anyone started on it yet?" he asked.

She shook her head. "We thought it would be best to eat breakfast first, which I'm about to start. Would you like to join us?"

"No, that's okay. I had a cup of coffee and a doughnut before I left the house, so I'll head on out to the greenhouse and get busy. Once all the windows are cleaned off, I'll need to get going. I got a call this morning from a man who needs his horse trained to pull a buggy, and he'll be bringing the horse later this morning." Dennis gave Sylvia a dimpled smile. "Am I still invited for supper on Wednesday?"

"Of course. Are you sure there isn't something special you'd like me to fix?"

He shook his head. "Whatever you decide to cook is fine, and I look forward to seeing you." Dennis tipped his straw hat and stepped off the porch. "See you soon, Sylvia."

She watched as he sprinted across the yard and disappeared around the corner of the house. *What a thoughtful man.*

When Sylvia returned to the kitchen, Mom, Amy, and Henry were there.

"Who was at the door?" Mom asked. "I heard someone knocking as I came down the hall."

"It was Dennis. He came to help scrape paint off the windows, and he's headed out to the greenhouse now."

"That's so kind of him." Amy looked at their mother. "Don't you think so?"

Mom moved her head slowly up and down and turned to look at Sylvia. "Did you tell him we'd planned to eat breakfast before starting on the windows?"

"I did, and I even invited him to join us, but he said he wanted to get started on them now. He has a horse to train today, so he'll have to leave here as soon as the windows are done," Sylvia replied.

"We could have gotten by without him." Mom grabbed a bowl of boiled eggs from the refrigerator and placed them on the table. "After all, Jared said he'd help with it, plus Amy, Henry, and I will be scraping. I'm sure we can manage to get the job done before any customers show up."

Sylvia said nothing as she set the table. Mom obviously didn't feel Dennis's help was needed, but it made no sense. The more hands working, the sooner they'd get the job done. Her fingers clenched around the glass she held in her hand. *Why is my mother being like this toward Dennis? He's trying to fit in and is acting out of kindness toward our family. What could be wrong with that?*

Sylvia wished she could help too, but the children would be getting up soon, and she'd have to fix their breakfast. Besides, she couldn't leave Allen and Rachel alone in the house or let them run around the yard while she was busy scraping windows.

Another knock sounded on the door, and this time, Amy went to answer it. She returned with Jared at her side.

"Guder mariye, Jared." Mom smiled when he entered the kitchen.

"Good morning, all."

If Mom can be so nice to Jared, why not be cordial to Dennis? Shouldn't they both be treated kindly and with respect? Sylvia greeted him, and Henry gave a nod in his direction.

"We're about to eat breakfast." Amy moved closer to Jared. "Would you like to join us?"

He shook his head. "I came here to work, not eat. Besides, I already had some breakfast."

"Dennis is here too," Sylvia spoke up. "He's out at the greenhouse, scraping windows."

"Is that so? Guess I'd better join him." Jared gave Amy a quick hug and headed out the door.

"How ya doin?" Dennis asked when Jared showed up.

"I'm fine. How about you?"

"Can't complain." Dennis gestured to the scraper Jared held. "Looks like you also came early to help clear off these windows."

"Jah. Amy and her family are getting ready to eat breakfast, but with the exception of Sylvia, they'll be out to help soon, I expect."

"No problem. We might have the project done by the time they show up."

They worked quietly for a while, and then Dennis pointed at the window he'd been working on and posed a question. "Has this kind of thing happened many times before?"

"More than it should have, unfortunately." Jared's forehead creased. "I think someone wants Belinda to shut down the greenhouse."

"How come?"

Jared shrugged. "Don't know. Maybe to be spiteful, or it could be someone who's just plain mean."

"Any ideas who may have done it?"

"Not really. But I have a hunch that it might be one of the owners of the new greenhouse on the other side of town."

Dennis stopped scraping and tipped his head. "You're kidding? Don't they believe in fair competition?"

"Maybe not. According to what Amy told me, the man who owns the other greenhouse came by here to check things out soon after his place opened for business." Jared pulled his scraper down the window in front of him. "The Kings' greenhouse has been around a good many years, and they have lots of steady customers. Also, with it being Amish-run, Amy has mentioned that the tourists seem to enjoy coming by and asking all sorts of curious questions."

Dennis pushed the brim of his hat upward. "May I ask what?"

"Oh things like, 'Why aren't you open on Sundays?' 'How come you use a horse and buggy instead of a car?' Sometimes they sneak pictures here." Jared's eyebrows rose.

Dennis shook his head "I know what that's like. I've had a few cameras pointed at me too."

"I wouldn't be surprised." As Jared scraped, the paint curled against his tool. "Anyways, the owners of the other greenhouse don't have that advantage. Even though their place is bigger and they sell a lot more things, they may not have gained a steady flow of customers yet."

"Hmm. . ." Dennis drew in a deep breath and released it slowly. "If it was the other greenhouse owner who did this, then he needs to be stopped. I think Belinda ought to notify the sheriff. Do you agree?"

"It doesn't matter what I think," Jared answered. "I'm not a member of this family yet."

"But you will be soon, right?"

"Jah, Amy and I will be getting married in early October." Jared glanced toward the house. "Here comes Belinda, Amy, and Henry, so we'd better drop this subject. Sure don't want to say anything that'll put me on the bad side of my future mother-in-law."

Belinda was surprised to see how much Jared and Dennis had already accomplished. Only a few windows were left to scrape.

"If you ladies have something else you need to do, Dennis and I can finish the rest of the windows," Jared said.

"Actually, I do have a couple of things I need to do in the greenhouse before opening it to the public this morning." Belinda smiled. "So danki, Jared."

"No problem at all." He grinned at Amy. "Do you want to stay and help, or do you also have something to do in the greenhouse?"

"Nothing that can't wait." She looked at Belinda. "Right, Mom?"

"Right. You can stay out here and enjoy yourself, Daughter. You too, Son," Belinda added, pointing at Henry.

He rolled his eyes. "Okay, Mom. There's nothin' I'd rather do than scrape off the black paint."

She gave him a gentle poke before heading to the front door of the building.

Once inside, Belinda set to work watering all the plants, while the noise of windows being scraped by metal tools sounded in the background. *I must say, more hands do make less work. At this rate, that job will be done in short order. My Vernon would be well pleased with the help we've received.*

By the time Belinda finished watering, Amy came inside. "The windows are all clean, and Jared and Dennis are getting ready to head out," she announced.

"What about Henry? What's he up to right now?"

"Said he had something to do in the barn."

Belinda's brows furrowed. "I thought he did all his chores before we had breakfast."

"Maybe he forgot something and decided to take care of it now."

"Or he could be in the yard looking at birds." Belinda shook her head. "I don't mind that he and Sylvia have a new hobby, but he sometimes gets so caught up in watching for birds that he forgets about the things I've asked him to do."

Amy laughed. "Mom, Henry did that even before he got into birding."

"True."

Belinda slipped behind the front counter just in time to greet their first customer of the day.

"Guder mariye, Belinda." Herschel Fisher reached across the counter and shook her hand.

Belinda smiled. "Good morning, Herschel. What can we do for you today?"

"I came to buy a nice plant for my mamm. She's been down with a bad cold for the last week, and I thought it might cheer her up."

"Sorry to hear she's not feeling well." Belinda made a sweeping gesture. "Why don't you have a look around? I'm sure you can find something to your liking down one of the aisles."

"Okay, I'll take a look, but first, I was wondering. . ."

Another customer came in, and it was Jared's mother, Ava. She smiled and came over to the counter. "I saw my son leaving here as I was coming in on my scooter. He told me last evening that he'd be at your place first thing in the morning."

"Jah, we appreciated Jared's help."

"Dennis was here helping too," Amy hollered.

Ava looked at Herschel and smiled, and then she patted Belinda's hand. "Just think, it won't be long until the wedding."

"I'm looking forward to it." Belinda pushed her reading glasses in place. "We still have lots of planning and work ahead of us though."

Ava nodded. "We'll help in any way we can."

Herschel leaned on the counter. "Before I go searching for a plant to give my mamm that will brighten her day..."

"Is she under the weather?" Ava questioned.

"Jah, but she's some better this morning." He looked back at Belinda. "I wondered if you know of anyone in the area who might want to rent my house."

"Are you leaving Gordonville?"

"Oh no. I have no plans of moving. I meant the little house I own here in Strasburg. It's the one Jesse Smucker used to rent from me before he married Lenore."

Amy left her job of sweeping the floor and stepped up to him. "Jared and I might be interested in renting the house. We'll be getting married in October, and we haven't found a place to live yet. We've been looking, but most of the homes come with a lot of property. With his roofing business, Jared doesn't have time to keep up a big place."

"Sounds like my rental might be just right for you then." There seemed to be a gleam in Herschel's eyes as he looked at Amy. "Can we set up a time for me to show it to you and your future husband?"

"That would be great. If you'll give me your phone number, I'll ask Jared to call and set up an appointment." Amy gave Herschel a wide grin. "I'm looking forward to seeing it. Can you tell me how much the rent will be?"

"We can wait and talk about that after you've toured the house. If you don't like it, that's okay too. But if it pleases you, then maybe Jared could move in right away. The previous renter moved out two weeks ago, and I'd prefer not to leave it vacant much longer." Herschel reached into his pocket and handed her a small card. "This has my bulk food store's number on it. It's probably the best number to reach me, because I check messages in the shed outside the store regularly."

Ava grinned. "Sounds like it might be something my son would be interested in."

"Danki, Herschel." Amy handed Belinda the card. "Would you put this on the shelf under the counter for me? I'll get it when I go up to the house at the end of the day."

Belinda took the card, and Amy went back to sweeping the floor. Ava went off to look at the selection of plants.

Not long after, Belinda noticed their neighbor Virginia come in.

"Well, I'd better get busy and choose a plant for my mamm," Herschel announced before hurrying down aisle 1.

Belinda stepped out from behind the counter and walked over to Virginia. "Hello. It's good to see you again. Is there something I can help you with today?"

Virginia nodded. "I popped in to see what kinds of flowers you have that I can plant along the side of my house."

"Most of the plants are in the first three aisles. Just take your time looking, and if you have any questions, I shouldn't be too hard to find. Amy is here too."

"All righty, then. Oh, by the way—did you find out who was on your property yesterday?"

Belinda shook her head.

"That's too bad. Well, hopefully you'll find out soon." Virginia lowered her voice. "I'm thinking that Maude lady might be responsible for what went on here."

"Oh?"

"Yeah, she seems suspicious enough to me. Maude wanders up and down the road quite often. In fact, I've been keeping an eye on her." Virginia caught her breath. "I bet she's the one who took your original sign that went missing."

Feeling the need for a change of subject, Belinda rested one hand on her hip and said, "One of these days, when things slow down a bit here, we'll have you and your husband over for a meal."

"That'd be real nice, Mrs. King." Virginia turned and headed toward the first row of flowering plants.

Belinda's thoughts turned to the offer Herschel had made to Amy, and her heart clenched. Although she was happy her daughter had found a wonderful man to marry, the thought of Amy moving out of the home she'd grown up in was difficult to accept. Ezekiel had already left the nest, and soon Amy would be gone too. *At least she won't be living in another state.* Belinda consoled herself with that thought. *But what will happen when she and Jared have a family of their own? She won't be able to help in the greenhouse anymore. And what about Sylvia? What if she ends up marrying Dennis, or some other Amish man?* Belinda's eyes teared up. *Someday Henry will be grown and ready to start a new life too. What then? Will I have to give up the greenhouse and live on this property all by myself?*

Chapter 33

Dennis had spent the better part of the morning working with an unco-operative horse, and he was exhausted. He'd brushed the animal down in its stall and then gotten things ready for the next client's horse.

Tired and frustrated, Dennis came into the house to take a lunch break before going back out to continue with his schedule. He wouldn't let his fatigue, however, interfere with his plans to have supper at the Kings' house this evening. Dennis found himself thinking about Sylvia more and more, and he looked forward to spending time with her this evening. Hopefully he'd have an opportunity to be alone with her, even if only for a short time.

Dennis took his boots off by the back door and headed for the kitchen. He was in need of something cold to drink to help his parched throat. After filling a glass with water from the sink, he opened the refrigerator, took out two hard-boiled eggs and a slice of ham, then sat down at the table. Dennis required the extra protein to ramp up his energy. He would work until four, and then clean up and get ready to head to the Kings' place by five. Dennis had already laid out his clean clothes to wear after he showered and shaved at the end of his workday. He'd gone shopping the other day and purchased a cou-ple of new shirts, including two white ones he would wear for church services.

While Dennis ate with one hand, he reached for his cell phone with the other. *Think I'll check the birding hotline. Maybe there'll be some interest-ing bird sighting I can tell Sylvia and Henry about this evening.*

Ever since she'd finished breakfast, Sylvia had been scurrying around the house, making sure everything was clean and orderly for Dennis's visit this evening. The kids' toys were still out in the living room, but she could wait to pick those up until closer to Dennis's arrival. Sylvia had made a new dress, which she would wear this evening. The color was a dark purple—one of her favorite shades.

"Is lunch ready?" Henry asked, bursting into the kitchen where Sylvia stood at the counter slicing a loaf of bread.

"It will be soon, but if you can't wait, grab a knife and make your own sandwich."

"No, I can wait. We're not that busy in the greenhouse right now, so I'm in no hurry to get back." Henry flopped into a chair at the table. "I'd rather be in the barn, looking out the hayloft window and watching for birds."

"You'll have time for that later, Henry." Sylvia frowned. "Don't you think you ought to wash your *hend* while you're waiting?"

He held up his hands. "Already done. I washed 'em at the sink in the greenhouse."

"Okay." Sylvia went to the refrigerator and took out the chicken-salad spread she'd mixed up earlier.

She thought of Dennis, and wondered what he was having for lunch. Being a bachelor, there was no telling what he'd make—probably something quick and easy to fix.

Sylvia blinked. *Why am I always thinking of him? Dennis is on my mind so much of the time.*

"Will Mom and Amy be coming up to the house to eat, or do they want you to take their lunch out to them?" she asked, needing to focus on something else.

"I'll take Mom's lunch out to her after I eat, but Amy won't be here for the noon meal."

Sylvia turned to face him. "How come?"

"Jared came by a while ago to pick her up. They're meeting Herschel Fisher at the house he owns not far from here."

"Oh, that's right. I forgot about that. I didn't see his buggy pull in, but I've been busy with the kinner and getting some chores done." Sylvia pulled the cutting board with the sliced bread closer and put the sandwiches together. "I hope they like the place and it works out for them to rent it."

"Me too. If Amy lives close after they're married, she'll be able to keep workin' at the greenhouse and not so much will fall on me." Henry scrunched his face. "But I don't know what'll happen once Amy and Jared start havin' *bopplin*. If you would help out things might go better."

Her spine stiffened. "You know I'm needed here to take care of my kinner as well as cook, clean, and keep up with the laundry."

"You could hire someone to watch Rachel and Allen. I think you just don't wanna work in the greenhouse."

"That's right, I don't, but it's none of your concern." Sylvia hurried to finish Henry's sandwich and handed it to him. "You can eat it in here if you want, but let's not talk about me working in the greenhouse anymore."

Henry wrapped his sandwich in a napkin, stood up, and tromped across the room toward the back door. "I'll tell Mom she can come eat her lunch now."

"I thought you were going to take it out to her." She handed him a lunch basket with food for Mom.

Henry's face flushed. "Oh, yeah, that's right. See you later."

When her brother left, Sylvia blew out an exasperated breath. She felt guilty enough for not helping in the greenhouse without having a reminder from her brother of the fact. *I wish Mom could afford to hire another pair of hands to work in there. Especially with my sister soon to be married and eventually having children of her own. The pressure of me being next in line to work in the greenhouse is stifling.* Sylvia tapped her foot. *And then there would be the expense of getting someone to watch Rachel and Allen. If that should be expected of me, then why not Amy? When the time comes, she could get a sitter for her kinner too.*

"My children come first," she mumbled. "They're better off having me take care of them than they would be with a sitter."

Another thought popped in Sylvia's head. *If it doesn't work out for me or Amy to work in the greenhouse after she's married, then what will Mom do?*

Amy's skin prickled with excitement as Jared pulled his horse and buggy onto the driveway at the address Herschel had given them. From the outside, the small white house looked cozy and inviting. She could hardly wait to see the inside. This just made it more real to her. Here they were, about to look at a place in hopes of setting up their new lives together as the future Mr. and Mrs. Jared Riehl.

Herschel's horse had been secured at the hitching rail, and Jared pulled his horse alongside it and got out, while Amy held onto the reins. Once his horse was secured, she climbed down from the buggy, and the two of them headed for the house.

They'd no more than stepped onto the porch when Herschel came out the front door and greeted them. "Did ya have any trouble finding the place?"

Jared shook his head. "Not a bit. I've been by this house many times. Just never been invited to see the inside till now." He glanced at Amy and smiled. "We're excited to see it."

Herschel opened the door wide. "Come on in. As you can see, the front door leads right into the living room."

When they stepped inside, Amy tried to take it all in at once. A comfy-looking recliner sat near an upholstered sofa. Both appeared to be in fairly good condition. Built-in bookshelves graced either side of the fireplace, and two end tables were positioned on both sides of the couch, as well as another one alongside the recliner. A battery-operated lamp sat on each of them.

"Nothing fancy, but it should serve your needs," Herschel said. "Of course, you'd be free to buy furniture of your own if you don't care for what's here."

"It's adequate for me." Amy looked at Jared and was pleased when he nodded.

"Should we move on to the bedrooms and bathroom?" Herschel asked.

Amy and Jared both nodded and followed Herschel through a narrow hallway, where the two bedrooms and bathroom were located.

Each of the rooms was furnished with a wooden-framed bed, dresser to match, and a closet with a door. In one of the rooms there was also a small desk. No doubt that would be the room Amy and Jared would claim for themselves.

The bathroom had a tub-shower combination, as well as a toilet and sink, with a mirror above the vanity.

"Are you ready to see the kitchen?" Herschel asked.

"Jah." Amy was the first to respond, and Jared nodded.

Back down the hall they went, and they soon entered a spacious kitchen. It was nearly the size of the two bedrooms put together. The layout reminded Amy of Sylvia's kitchen. The cupboards were different and the color was lighter than her sister's place, but it gave off a comfortable feeling that she liked.

Amy smiled. She enjoyed cooking, and this kitchen with a propane-operated stove and refrigerator would be perfect for fixing meals. The table was quite large, so even though the house had no dining room, they could easily eat in the kitchen and serve several guests at one time.

Amy leaned close to Jared and whispered, "I like the house. Do you?"

He nodded. "We'd be pleased to rent this from you, Herschel, and I'd like to move in as soon as possible."

"Don't you want to know the price I'm asking for the rent?"

"You told me when we talked on the phone to set up this meeting."

Herschel's cheeks flushed pink above his beard. "So I did." He moved toward the back door. "Maybe you should take a look at the yard and also the washhouse for doing laundry. There's an older model ringer-washer in there, but it could be replaced with a newer one if you choose."

"We'll take a look, but I don't think we're going to change our mind about renting the place." Jared grinned at Amy. "Right?"

She bobbed her head.

As they stepped into the backyard, Amy spotted a wooden table with benches on either side, situated near a fire-pit. "Oh, this would be perfect to use year-round. What a nice place for entertaining our friends and family."

"I agree." Jared clasped her hand and gave her fingers a tender squeeze.

Amy's words felt rushed as she told Herschel how much she appreciated the chance to rent this cozy home. "We'll have you over for supper one night after Jared gets settled in."

He smiled but kept his gaze toward the ground. "That'd be real nice."

Amy wandered across the yard to a small garden patch. *Maybe I'll invite Mom to join us when we plan an evening to have Herschel for supper. He may be a little shy, but he's such a nice man. I believe they might enjoy each other's company. Of course, I won't say anything to Mom about it right now. It could even turn out to be a surprise.*

After returning from a relaxing evening at the Kings' house, Dennis was ready to call it a night. The meal had been good and he'd been able to spend a few minutes alone with Sylvia, so the evening couldn't have gone much better. He'd even enjoyed sitting on the floor, playing with Allen and Rachel for a while before the meal. Except for Belinda's cool tone whenever she spoke to him, Dennis had almost felt like part of the family.

I don't think she cares much for me, he thought as sat on a chair in the kitchen and removed his black dress shoes. *What I can't figure out is why. Could she be worried that I might ask for her daughter's hand in marriage some day?* He rubbed his chin. *Is that a possibility?*

Dennis continued to contemplate things until his cell phone rang. He recognized the number and figured he may as well answer it or she'd keep calling until he finally responded.

Dennis swiped his thumb across his phone. "Hi Mom, how are you?"

"More to the point, how are you and why haven't you answered any of my calls lately? Neither I nor any of your siblings have heard from you for several weeks." Her shrill voice made Dennis's pulse quicken. Mom hadn't been like this before Dad died. At least not with Dennis. Maybe the fact that he was the youngest of five children made her more possessive of him.

"Sorry for not responding to your messages," he said, struggling to keep his voice calm. "I've been super busy with my new business and some other things."

"To busy to call your mamm?"

"I said I was sorry." His excuse for not returning her calls was weak, but listening to her carry on about him moving away from her and the rest of the family was hard to take. Especially when she had no understanding of his reasons for leaving Dauphin County.

Dennis shifted on his chair. *Don't I have the right to make a new start?*

"You broke Sarah Ann's heart when you moved, you know. She'll probably never recover from the hurt."

Mom's ridiculous statement caused the muscles in Dennis's face to tighten. "There is no reason Sarah Ann's heart would be broken. She and I weren't even courting."

"But you were friends since childhood, and I'm sure she assumed—"

"Mom, is that why you called—to talk about a relationship that never developed into anything romantic?"

"Well, uh. . .no. . ." There was a pause. "Your brother has some business in Lancaster next week, and I'm planning to come with him. Does the house you're renting have room for the two of us to stay with you a few nights?"

I know where this is leading, and boy, it doesn't leave me with a lot of time to get things ready for company. He bit down on his bottom lip. *I'll need to get the beds ready and stock the cupboards and refrigerator with enough food.*

Dennis's face warmed, and he fanned himself with the back of his free hand. "Umm. . .yes, there are enough bedrooms, but—"

"Good. Gerald and I will see you next Monday, sometime before noon."

"Mom, I don't think—"

She said goodbye and hung up before Dennis could finish his sentence.

Dennis felt like his chest had caved in. The last thing he needed was company to interrupt his work schedule—not to mention all the unwanted advice he'd no doubt get from his mother.

But I'll get through it, he told himself. *After all, it'll only be for a few days.*

Chapter 34

On Monday, when Dennis headed for the house to wash up and fix lunch, a black van pulled into the yard. It caught him off guard at first. Then he realized the vehicle belonged to his brother. Gerald had never joined their Amish church and attended a Mennonite church, so he'd owned a vehicle since he'd turned eighteen. Both of their parents had made an issue of it, but their eldest son had a mind of his own.

Just like me, Dennis thought as he moved toward the vehicle. *Only I chose to remain Amish and join the church.*

A few seconds later, Dennis's mother and his tall, gangly brother got out.

"It's so good to see you," Mom shouted as she hurried toward Dennis. The short, slender woman could certainly move fast for a woman in her early sixties.

Dennis met his mother halfway and gave her a hug. "It's good to see you too, Mom."

Tears welled in her blue eyes and she sniffed. "It's been far too long."

Dennis didn't bother to remind her that he hadn't been in Strasburg all that long. "Why don't you go on up to the porch and wait for me while I help Gerald with the luggage?"

"Okay." She reached in her handbag and pulled out a tissue, dabbing at her eyes, before heading toward the house.

Dennis greeted his brother with a hearty handshake. "It's good to see you."

Gerald grinned and gave his neatly trimmed beard a tug. "Same here."

"So what kind of business do you have here in Strasburg?" Dennis asked.

"It's not in Strasburg. It's in Lancaster, but I figured if I was gonna come this close to you I oughta bring Mom along." Gerald placed his hand on Dennis's shoulder. "She really misses you, and so do the rest of us, for that matter."

"I miss my family too, but I needed to start over—someplace where there was a lot of horses and people who needed them to be trained." *And where there weren't so many reminders of Dad.*

"I understand, but Mom thinks you left because of Dad's untimely death. She believes you might blame yourself, somehow."

Dennis's spine stiffened. "Why would I be to blame for him getting shot? That was Uncle Ben's fault, not mine."

"But you were out hunting with him that day. Have you ever wondered if you'd been paying close attention to what was happening, things might have gone differently?"

"You're right, I was there, and of course, I've wondered how I might have made things turn out different somehow. But I had no idea when Dad invited me to go hunting with him and Uncle Ben that an accident would occur. If I'd known, I would have tried to prevent it from happening somehow, or at least talked Dad out of going into the woods that day."

Gerald shook his head. "No one could stop our daed from doing anything he set his mind to. Dad liked to hunt, and he'd go out as often as he could to find his next trophy. Some folks in our community said he was the most adventuresome person they knew."

Dennis kicked at the gravel beneath his boots. "You're right about that. Dad loved to get out into nature, even when he wasn't hunting for deer. He enjoyed showing people his collection of antlers too. I used to like listening to his stories when I was a boy."

"Same here."

Dennis reached into the van and grabbed a small suitcase, along with a tote bag, which he recognized as his mother's. Glancing back at his brother, he asked, "So what kind of business dealings will you be having in Lancaster?"

Gerald took out his suitcase and they began walking toward the house, where their mother still waited on the porch. "I'll be talking with a Realtor about the possibility of buying a couple of vacation homes that have come on the market near Bird-in-Hand."

Dennis stopped walking and turned to face his brother. "Why would you want to buy vacation homes? If you, or any of the family, wants to vacation in Lancaster County, you'd be welcome to stay here."

"No, the homes aren't for us. It would be an investment, and I would give part of the proceeds to Mom, so she never has a need."

"What needs would she have that aren't already being met?" Dennis asked. "She's still living with Dorcas and her family, right?"

Gerald bobbed his head. "But it would be nice for our mother to have some money of her own and not have to rely on others when she wants to buy something. Don't you agree?"

"Jah, I suppose." Dennis wasn't sure their mother would accept such a gift from Gerald, but what his brother chose to do was none of his business.

Clymer

"I talked to my sister today," Ezekiel said as he took a seat at the kitchen table to eat the lunch Michelle had prepared.

"Which one? You have two sisters you know." Michelle chuckled and poked Ezekiel's arm.

The children followed suit with giggles of their own. Angela Mary may have understood what was so funny, but surely not little Vernon.

Ezekiel tweaked the end of his daughter's nose. "The sister I spoke to was your aunt Amy."

"What did she have to say?" Michelle questioned.

"I'll tell you as soon as we've finished praying." Ezekiel bowed his head. *Dear Lord*, he prayed silently, *Please bless my family back home, as well as our family here. Help us to be receptive to Your will at all times. Thank You for this food, as well as the hands that lovingly prepared it.*

Ezekiel opened his eyes and cleared his throat, at which point, Michelle also opened her eyes. The children's eyes were already open, and he wasn't sure if they'd ever closed them. He supposed it didn't matter that much, as long as they learned the importance of prayer and thanking God for His many blessings. As Angela Mary and Vernon grew older, they would understand more about traditions.

"So what did Amy have to say?" Michelle prompted as she handed Ezekiel a plate of cold chicken left over from last night's supper.

"She said that she and Jared met with Herschel Fisher last week and toured the home he has for rent."

"Oh, that's right. You did mention when you talked to your mother last week that she'd told you Herschel offered them the opportunity to rent the house he owns in Strasburg. It's the same one Jesse used to rent from him, right?"

Ezekiel nodded and put some macaroni salad on his plate.

"Did they like the house?"

"Jah, and Jared's already moved in."

"That's good news. I bet Amy's excited." Michelle forked some of the chilled salad into her mouth.

He nodded. "That's an understatement. When I listened to the message Amy left, her voice was at least an octave higher than normal. My poor ear is still vibrating from the experience. Oh, and wanna know what else she told me?"

"Sure."

"She's going over to Jared's this evening to cook supper, and they've invited two guests who don't know the other one is coming. I think my sister is up to something."

Michelle tipped her head, looking at Ezekiel through half-closed eyelids. "Who are the guests?"

"My mamm and Herschel." He took a bite of chicken.

Michelle's eyes widened. "Why would they invite them both without telling the other?"

Ezekiel shrugged. "Can't say for sure, but Amy did say the meal is to thank Herschel for letting them rent the house for a reasonable price."

"And the reason for your mamm's invitation?"

Ezekiel leaned closer to his wife and whispered, "I believe my sister may have matchmaking on her mind."

"Between Herschel and your mother?"

"Jah. He's a kind person. You never know—Herschel Fisher might be just what my mamm needs."

Michelle put her hand up to her mouth. "Oh my."

Strasburg

"I still don't understand why you felt the need to invite me to supper this evening. Honestly, I'm going to feel like an extra wheel on the buggy being with you two," Mom said as she and Amy headed with Mom's horse and buggy toward the rental where Jared was staying.

"Please don't feel that way, Mom. We like having you around. Besides, I wanted you to see the homey place and maybe give some ideas on how we might make it even cozier."

"I'm sure you and Jared can figure that out on your own without my opinion."

"Bouncing ideas off you could help with some decisions I'm not sure about. Also, I thought you deserved a night off from helping cook supper and doing dishes." From the driver's seat, Amy glanced at her mother. She noticed a smile form on Mom's lips.

"That's nice of you, but don't expect me to sit idly and watch you cook the meal this evening and not offer to help."

"You can offer, but Jared and I will be doing the cooking."

Mom's eyebrows lifted slightly. "You are blessed if your future husband likes to cook. I could never get your daed to do any kind of cooking except when it came to using his outdoor grill."

"I do remember, but Dad had many other good qualities."

"How well I know." Mom released a lingering sigh. "I still miss him so much, Amy. Life has been different without your daed around. But with the Lord's strength and the help of my loving family, I've been able to keep going."

Amy held the reins with one hand and reached over to clasp her mother's hand. "Of course you do. The love you and Dad had was strong and true. A part of him will always be with you and with us too."

"Jah, that is for certain."

They rode quietly for a while, and then Amy asked a question. "Do you think if the right man came along that you would ever remarry?"

Mom didn't respond for several seconds, and then she said in a near whisper: "Perhaps, but it's doubtful. He'd have to love me deeply, and I, him."

"Do you think Monroe might be in love with you?"

"I believe so—or at least he thinks he is."

"How do you feel about him?"

She wrinkled her nose. "He's just a friend from the past. I have no strong feelings for him, but I suppose that could change down the road."

"I see." Amy decided it was best to move on to another topic. "It was good to see that business in the greenhouse picked up a bit today."

"Jah, and it helps to make the time at work move along faster when we keep busy. I am hoping as the summer progresses we'll see even more customers."

Amy relaxed her shoulders. "In spite of the new greenhouse moving into the area, it hasn't really hurt our business that much, thanks to the tourist trade."

"True. Even so, we need to come up with more things people would be interested in purchasing. Maybe we should run an ad in the local paper when we have our next sale. Since we can't count on business from the flower shop Sara used to own, we need to think of other ways to increase our business."

"And even though ads cost money, they usually pay for themselves in sales," Amy said.

"Agreed."

Amy loosened her grip on the reins a bit. "Mom, there's something else I've been meaning to talk to you about."

"Oh, what's that?"

"Jared and I have been talking about whether I should work or not after we're married."

Mom sat very still, looking straight ahead. "What have you decided?"

"We agreed that I should continue working at the greenhouse until we're expecting our first child. After the boppli is born, my responsibility will be to take care of my family, and I can't do that and work in the greenhouse too."

"I understand, and when the time comes, we'll just have to make do." Mom's voice trembled a bit.

Amy couldn't help feeling guilty, but at the same time, her responsibility would soon be to Jared and any children they had. She was about to mention that perhaps her mother could hire someone outside the family to work in the greenhouse, but the rental house came into view.

As Amy turned the horse and buggy up the driveway, she spotted Herschel standing in the front yard, talking to Jared.

"I see Herschel is here," Mom commented. "Did you know he was coming?"

Amy nodded. "Jared invited him for supper to say thank you for allowing us to rent this place for a reasonable fee."

Mom's cheeks colored a bright pink. "I hope Herschel doesn't mind me being here. He's quite shy around women, you know."

Amy reached across the seat and patted her mother's hand. "I'm sure it'll be fine. Let me get the horse secured, and then we can go inside and I'll show you around."

Chapter 35

Seeing Herschel's surprised expression when he looked her way, Belinda could only assume that he had no idea she'd been included in their supper plans. She noticed the dressy, aqua shirt he wore. It made his silver-gray hair and beard stand out more than usual. Belinda didn't mean to gawk, but this was the first time she'd realized what a handsome man he was.

Hoping he hadn't seen her staring, she looked in the direction of the house her daughter and future son-in-law would occupy once they were married. Feeling a bit unsure of herself, Belinda stepped up to Herschel. "Good evening. I hope you don't mind that I'm joining the three of you for supper. Amy extended the invitation, and I presume you didn't know."

"No, I did not, but it's nice that you're here." He offered her a timid smile as well as a warm handshake.

Belinda thought it was kind of cute how a grown man could have such a shy streak.

"Why don't the three of you go inside while I put your gaul away?" Jared gestured to Belinda's horse. "You're going to be here a while, and he'd become too restless if he remained at the hitching rail."

"I'll help you," Herschel was quick to say.

"Danki, I appreciate that."

When the men headed for Belinda's horse, she followed Amy into the house. She stopped in the living room and peeked out the front-room window, watching as Herschel and Jared began leading the horse to the barn.

"So here's the living room." Amy made a sweeping gesture with her hand. "It's nowhere near as big as our living room at home, but it should be adequate for Jared and me, don't you think?"

"Jah, I would say so." Belinda moved over to stand beside the fireplace. "You'll enjoy this during the winter months, I imagine."

Amy bobbed her head. "Oh, yes. I can picture a nice fire burning, and its heat warming up this area. Now let's go down the hall, and I'll show you the bedrooms. These rooms aren't large, but they'll certainly serve our needs."

"Sounds good." Belinda followed her daughter out of the room.

By the time Amy showed her mother the rest of the house, Jared and Herschel had come inside. She found them sitting in the living room. Herschel kept his gaze toward the floor, and Jared looked at Amy with a wrinkled forehead as he bounced one leg over the other.

"Jared and I are going into the kitchen now to prepare supper." Amy looked at Mom. "You and Herschel can make yourselves comfortable and visit while we get the meal prepared."

Herschel nodded, but he didn't look up or even glance at Mom. Amy's mother, however, folded her arms and shook her head. "Jared, why don't you sit here and relax? I can help Amy with the meal."

"No way." Jared stood with his feet firmly planted. "Amy and I invited you and Herschel for supper, and we're going to do the cooking." As though the matter was settled, he marched out of the room. Amy hurried behind him.

It was quiet in the living room, with neither Herschel nor Mom saying anything. Amy listened from the kitchen, near the doorway, and it wasn't long before she heard her mother try to get the ball rolling.

"I've been by this place many times, Herschel, and never imagined that one day my youngest daughter might be living here. The house seems to be in good shape, and the layout is nice."

"Jah."

"I like the built-in shelves on either side of the fireplace. That's an extra feature you don't see in many newer homes."

"Uh-huh."

Amy grimaced and moved away from the door. "I hope we didn't make a mistake by leaving those two alone," she whispered to Jared. "So far, things don't seem to be going so well. Mom is doing most of the talking and Herschel's only said a few words."

Jared kissed Amy's cheek. "Just give it some time. I'm sure Herschel will open up and say more. He's kind of shy, you know."

Amy was hopeful as she moved over to the refrigerator to take out the chicken, while Jared heated the frying pan on the stove. Maybe once everyone began eating the meal, they would all relax and have a good time.

"This is a good meal." Dennis cut into another piece of succulent roast beef. "Danki for taking the time to fix it, Mom."

She looked across the table at him. "And why wouldn't I want to feed my sons a nice meal?"

"You're my guests," Dennis replied. "I should be the one serving you."

Gerald rolled his eyes. "Since when did you learn how to cook?"

"I admit, I don't know my way around the kitchen very well, but we could have gone out to eat supper. There are some pretty good restaurants here in Lancaster County."

"I'm sure there are, but I enjoy cooking, so there's no reason for us to go out. Besides, you don't often get many leftovers when you eat at a restaurant." His mother sprinkled some pepper on her food. "How about the nice meatloaf sandwiches with the toasted rolls you like? I could make those for supper tomorrow."

Gerald nodded with a mouthful of potatoes Mom had mixed with sour cream.

"I'd like that." Dennis forked the piece of meatloaf into his mouth, and as he chewed, he mulled over the idea of whether he should say anything about Sylvia or not. He wanted to tell his mother about the feelings he'd begun to develop for Sylvia but wasn't sure of her reaction.

"So what have you been up to other than horse training since you moved to Strasburg?" Gerald asked.

Dennis placed his fork on the plate and wiped his lips with his napkin. "I'm still doing some birding when I have the time."

"Good to hear." Mom smiled. "Everyone needs an outlet that doesn't involve work."

Dennis fiddled with his knife handle a few seconds and took a drink of water. "The young widow who rented me this home is also a bird-watcher and so is her youngest brother."

"That's nice." Mom dished some scalloped potatoes onto her plate and took a bite.

"We've gone birding together and shared some meals at her mamm's place."

"Sounds like they're a hospitable family," Gerald commented.

"They are, and Sylvia has the cutest kinner. Rachel's kind of shy, but I think Allen's taken a liking to me." Dennis paused for a breath. "Oh, and I recently asked Sylvia if I could court her."

Mom's brows shot up. "You're courting a widowed woman with children?"

"Correct."

"Congratulations for taking such a big step!" Gerald reached over and gave Dennis's shoulder a squeeze. "By this time next year you could be a married man. That'd be great news."

Dennis shrugged. "You never know, but I don't plan to rush it. Sylvia's been through a lot, losing her husband, father, and oldest brother all in one accident."

"Wow! Just goes to show we're not the only family dealing with a loss." Gerald's face sobered.

Mom looked around the cozy kitchen, where Sylvia's touches could be seen. "So this is the place she and her husband lived before his death?"

"Jah, but she and the kinner have been living with her mamm."

"I'm surprised she didn't sell it."

"I believe the thought occurred to her, Mom, but she decided to rent the place out instead."

"Is there any chance that we could meet her before we head back home before the end of the week?" Mom asked.

"Umm. . .I don't know. . .maybe. I'm not sure what her schedule is like."

Dennis wasn't sure that his mother meeting Sylvia was such a good idea, but when Mom pressured him on it, he agreed to see if Sylvia would be free tomorrow evening. "I'll make the call when we're done with supper."

Well, at least my family is interested in meeting the woman I'm courting. That's a step in the right direction and a positive sign.

"I hope she's free," Gerald interjected, "because I'd like to meet the young lady who could end up being my sister-in-law."

Dennis lifted his gaze to the ceiling. "Let's not get ahead of ourselves. There's been no talk of marriage yet." He reached up and rubbed the back of his much-too-warm neck. *I hope if Mom and Gerald do get to meet Sylvia that neither of them says anything to embarrass me. They can both be pretty blunt at times.*

⟨⟨⟨ ❦ ⟩⟩⟩

"Has anyone checked for phone messages today?" Sylvia asked as she sat in the living room with her mother and sister after they returned from having supper at Herschel's rental. The children were in bed, and so was Henry.

"I went to the phone shack this morning before the greenhouse opened," Amy said. "There was a message from Toby's folks, checking to see how things are going, and there was also one from Sara. She apologized for not telling us that she'd sold her business. Sara said her only excuse was how busy she's been taking care of the baby and trying to keep up with church-related functions. She also thought Misty would notify all of her customers."

Mom frowned. "I can understand her busyness, but I wish we hadn't heard the news second-hand. It would have nice if she'd been the one to tell us."

"Were there any other messages besides the one from Sara?" Sylvia asked, quickly changing the subject. She'd been hoping she might hear something from Dennis today. The last time she'd seen him, he'd said something about wanting to get together with her this week.

Amy nodded. "They were all related to greenhouse business."

"Oh, I see." Sylvia couldn't hide her disappointment.

Sylvia saw a gleam in her sister's eyes as she turned in her chair to look at her. "Why don't you go out right now and see if there are any new messages? He may have called since I checked earlier today."

"He?" Mom tipped her head. "Are you referring to Dennis?"

"Jah. That is who you were hoping to hear from. Right, Sister?" Amy gave Sylvia's arm a gentle poke.

Sylvia's face heated. "Jah. Think I'll go check for messages."

Amy smiled, but Mom pressed her lips tightly together as she pushed her feet against the floor to get the rocking chair moving.

Sylvia stood. "I'm going to grab a flashlight and head out to the shed now." She ambled out of the room. *Mom still seems to have concerns about me and Dennis as a couple.*

Belinda fanned her face with her hand. "Does it feel hotter than normal in here to you?" She looked over at Amy, who appeared to be quite comfortable on the couch.

"Maybe a little. Should I open another window? If a breeze has come up, it would surely help cool this room."

"Jah, that might help." Belinda took the corner of her apron and blotted the perspiration from her forehead. *I wish my daughter hadn't agreed to let Dennis court her so soon. For all we know he could have a girl-friend up in Dauphin County.*

Amy got up and went to open the second window.

"If you ask me, your sister is too eager to see Dennis. She needs to keep her focus on the children. Don't you agree?"

"She's not neglecting them, Mom, if that's what you mean." Amy returned to her seat. "Sylvia's a good mother, but she deserves to have some happiness that doesn't involve the kinner."

"I thought she enjoyed her new hobby of bird-watching."

"She does, but she likes—maybe even loves—Dennis, and Sylvia has the right to develop a relationship with him."

Belinda's hands went limp in her lap. "If she knew him better, I might agree, but things are happening too fast for me."

"Dennis knows what Sylvia has been through, so I'm sure he will take it slow."

Or maybe he'll lose interest in her and move on to someone else.

Rather than dwell on this topic, Belinda let her mind focus on the nice evening she'd had with Amy, Jared, and Herschel. Things had been a bit awkward between her and Herschel at first, but Belinda had managed to think of several things to talk about, and he'd seemed to relax some too. After supper, Jared had gotten out a game of Rook and they played that while eating chocolate cake for dessert. Belinda hadn't admitted it to herself until now, but she had not enjoyed herself so much in a long while.

Perhaps I need to get out and socialize more, she told herself. *Maybe in the next week or two, I'll get together with one of my friends.*

Dennis was relieved when his phone rang and he recognized the Kings' phone number on his screen. "Hello."

"Hi, Dennis, it's Sylvia."

"It's good to hear from you."

"Same here."

"I assume you got my message." Dennis moved over to his bedroom window to breathe the fresh air blowing in.

"Yes, I did, and I would be pleased to meet your mother and brother."

"Would it be okay if we came by tomorrow evening after supper?"

"That will be fine." Sylvia was tempted to invite them to join her family for a meal, but figured that might not go over too well with Mom. It stressed her out when they had last-minute guests, the way it had when Monroe used to come by close to suppertime.

"Would seven-thirty work for you?"

"That should be fine. I'll fix something special to serve for dessert."

"Don't go to any trouble on our account."

"It won't be any trouble," she said.

"Okay then. We'll see you tomorrow evening. Bye, Sylvia."

"Goodbye, Dennis."

Dennis couldn't help but smile. *She wants to see me tomorrow and meet some of my family. I see that as a good sign. Sure hope Mom and*

Gerald like Sylvia and her family. For that matter, I hope Sylvia likes my family too.

He set his device on the counter and frowned. *I'm a bit worried though. Can't help but wonder how Mrs. King will respond to Mom and Gerald, since she tends to be so cold toward me.*

Chapter 36

Last night, Virginia had bumped her previously injured knee on the coffee table, and this morning, her leg hurt so bad that she needed to use her cane. She'd pulled a bag of frozen peas from the freezer and iced her knee while lying on the sofa. Virginia had whined to Earl about how much it hurt, but the cold soon made the soreness diminish. As long as the bag cooled her knee, Virginia felt pretty good. After a while, though, the pain returned. But she wouldn't let it keep her from making another trip to the greenhouse today to put on a friendly front.

Think I'll get some jars of honey this time, Virginia told herself as she cautiously crossed the road. One never knew when a horse and buggy or some motorized vehicle might approach.

On the other side, she made her way slowly and painfully up the driveway. Of course she had to dodge some horse droppings. *Why can't someone take a shovel and clean up these gross landmines? I feel like I'm wasting time here, limping around all these useless piles of yucky debris.*

It was a relief when she finally made it to the front door of the greenhouse. Stepping inside, she spotted Belinda seated behind the front counter, thumbing through some paperwork.

"Good morning, Mrs. King." Virginia spoke in what she hoped was a cheerful tone.

Belinda looked up and smiled. "It's nice to see you, Virginia. And please call me, Belinda."

"Okay, sure." Virginia leaned against the counter. "How are things going with your business?"

"Fairly well, all things considered. We manage to keep busy."

"I bet."

"Did you make a trip over here for something specific?" Belinda asked.

Virginia bobbed her head. "Came to get some more of that tasty honey—if you have any, that is."

"Yes, we have a few jars left. They're right over there." Belinda pointed to the shelves across the room. "Would you like me to get you a jar?"

"Actually, I'd hoped for two. My husband and I both enjoyed the honey you gave us previously, and it went real quick."

"I'm glad you liked it, and we can certainly spare two jars for you."

"Do you have a sturdy bag for me to carry them in? I am using a cane today and can only carry with one hand."

Belinda's brows furrowed. "Oh, I'm so sorry. Did you suffer an injury recently?"

"Well, sort of. I bumped my knee on our coffee table, and it aggravated an old wound I had from long ago."

"I can see if my son Henry is free to carry your purchase over to your home for you."

Virginia flapped her hand. "Naw, that's okay. I can manage." She turned and made her way over to the shelf where the jars of honey stood. Once she'd chosen two glass containers, she realized she couldn't carry them both in one hand and manage her cane in the other.

Belinda must have realized her predicament, because she stepped out from behind the counter and came right over. "Here, let me carry them for you."

Back at the counter, where Belinda had set the jars, Virginia pulled a twenty dollar bill from her jeans pocket. "I believe the sign above the bigger jars of honey stated that they are ten dollars per jar."

"That's correct." Belinda took the money and put it inside the cash register drawer.

While she wrapped the jars with bubble wrap and placed them in a brown paper sack with handles, Virginia contemplated what her next move should be.

She cleared her throat and plunged ahead. "Say, I heard that Amy and Jared will be getting married this fall."

Belinda gave a nod. "Yes, that is correct. The wedding will take place the first Thursday of October."

"How nice." Virginia managed a fake smile. "I've never been to an Amish wedding. I imagine they are quite different from an English one."

"Yes, our weddings are similar to one of our regular church services, with the addition of sermons being preached specifically for the benefit of the bride and groom. And of course, there's a time for the wedding couple to say their vows as they answer certain questions presented to them by the bishop."

"Sounds interesting." Virginia was on the verge of telling Belinda that Jared had mentioned they might get an invitation, when a tour bus pulled into the parking lot, and several enthusiastic-looking people rushed into the building.

"Things are going to get kind of hectic right now," Belinda said, "but we'll talk some other time."

"Umm. . .yeah, okay." Virginia picked up the sack and headed out the door. *I'll come back some other time,* she told herself. *Maybe I'll ask when the wedding invitations will be sent out. At least then I would have some idea when to watch for ours to come.*

Sylvia stood with one arm holding the other at the elbow as she looked at the clock. She and the family had eaten supper, and the dishes were done. Now all she had to do was wait for Dennis and his family to arrive. It was hard not to be nervous. Sylvia had never been comfortable around strangers—even more so since Toby died. But oddly enough, she hadn't been nervous around Dennis, not even the day they'd first met.

I hope his mother and brother approve of me. Continuing to stare at the clock, she tapped her foot. *And I hope I like them. If they're anything like Dennis, then things should be fine. We'll sit around and get to know each other while we eat the dessert I prepared for this evening.*

"Sister, are you fretting?" Amy bumped Sylvia's arm, causing her to jump. "Oh, sorry if I frightened you. Thought you knew I was still here in the kitchen."

Sylvia turned to face Amy. "A part of me is eager to meet some of Dennis's family, but another part is a nervous wreck. If they don't like me, Dennis might decide to pull away."

Amy slipped an arm around Sylvia's waist. "I'm sure they'll like you, and even if for some reason they don't, Dennis will not pull away."

"How can you be so sure?"

"I've seen the way he looks at you. That man is smitten."

"How does he look at me?"

"With shining eyes and a silly grin that hardly leaves his face. I realize you two haven't known each other very long, but I recognize two people in love when I see them looking at each other with rapt attention." Amy moved her hand from Sylvia's waist to the small of her back and gave it a few pats. "Jared sees it too. In fact, he told me the other day that he believes Dennis is head over heels in love with you."

Sylvia's face heated. "I don't know about that, but I do think he cares for me. And the truth is, I have strong feelings for him too."

"Then stop thinking negative thoughts, try to relax, and enjoy being with him this evening. Keep your focus on Dennis and quit worrying about what his family may or may not think of you."

Sylvia gave her a sister a hug. "Danki, Amy. You're always full of good advice."

I must have lost my mind to agree to this, Dennis thought as he headed for the Kings' with his mother and brother. Gerald sat up front with Dennis, and Mom was seated in the back of the buggy. Midnight seemed well-behaved as he trotted along at an easy pace. Gerald had said he would drive them there in his van, but Mom insisted they go by horse and buggy.

The rest of the day had gone well. Dennis's brother had come out to watch him train a horse for a while, and then Dennis talked Gerald into driving him to the animal shelter in search of a German shepherd. While there, Gerald had pointed out a few different breeds, but Dennis kept looking until he found the right dog.

After the arrangements were made, and the black and tan shepherd had been loaded into the van, they went to buy dog food and some other needed supplies. Dennis was glad he'd finally found the right dog and felt it had been worth the wait.

Dennis's thoughts brought him back to the present, and the closer they got to the Kings' place, the more nervous he became. To get his mind off that, he brought up the topic of his new dog.

"I'm gonna need some help putting a pen together for my hund." He glanced at his brother. "I don't want him getting out and possibly being hit by a car when I'm not with him."

Gerald groaned. "I know where this going. I'll help you while I'm here, so don't worry."

"That would be much appreciated."

"Does the mutt have a name?" Mom tapped Dennis on the shoulder. "Or will you have to come up with one?"

"No, I'll need to name the dog."

"How 'bout Goliath? He's certainly big enough to be considered a giant." Gerald chuckled.

Dennis shook his head at his brother's suggestion. "I'll figure it out soon. Maybe after we get back from the Kings', and I let the hund out of the barn."

The closer they got to Sylvia and her family, the more stress Dennis felt. *What if Mom says something to Sylvia that embarrasses me? I don't understand why she was so desperate to meet the young woman. It's not like we're planning to get married or anything.*

A trickle of sweat rolled down his forehead as the Kings' place came into view. All Dennis could do was hope and pray that things went well here this evening, because there was no turning back now.

🐦

After the introductions had been made, Sylvia invited everyone except the children, who were already in bed, to take seats around the dining room table. Once they were all seated, she excused herself to get the dessert.

Dennis was quickly on his feet. "I'll go with you. I'm sure you'll need help bringing everything in."

Sylvia smiled. "Danki."

When they entered the kitchen, she got out her Cherry Melt-Away bars as well as a plate with two kinds of cookies on it.

"Looks like you've been busy today." Dennis stepped up to her. "I hope you didn't go to all this trouble on account of me bringing my mamm and bruder over to meet you and your family."

A pink flush crept across her cheeks. "Well I'll admit I did hope the desserts would help, in case they didn't care for me as a person."

"Are you kidding?" It was all he could do to keep from taking her into his arms. "You're the kindest, sweetest woman I've ever met, and I'm sure it's obvious to others too."

Sylvia lowered her gaze. "I'm not always kind or sweet. For the first several months after Toby, my daed, and my bruder died, I was quite difficult to live with."

"It's understandable. After my dad was accidentally shot, I felt full of rage. Some of my family avoided me because they never knew when I would say something unkind." He placed his hand on her arm. "We've all been through difficult times, and when someone we love dies, there are several stages of grief we must go through."

"I know." Her chin trembled, followed by tears in her eyes, and it was almost his undoing.

Unable to control his own swirling emotions, Dennis put his arms around Sylvia's waist and pulled her into an embrace. It seemed right for him to hold Sylvia like this. At this moment, Dennis felt that God had brought her into his life for a reason, and they were meant to be together. He was on the verge of kissing away her tears, when someone entered the room. Dennis let go of Sylvia and turned around.

"What's goin' on in here? Mom sent me to see if—" Henry stopped talking and stared at Sylvia. "Have you been cryin' Sister?"

She nodded.

Henry pointed at Dennis. "Did you say something to make her cry?"

"I suppose I did," Dennis replied. "But it wasn't intentional. We were talking about grief, and how hard it is to deal with the loss of a loved one."

Henry pressed a fist against his chest. "Ya don't have to tell me about it."

Dennis rested his hand on the boy's shoulder. "You still miss your daed and bruder, don't you?"

"Jah."

"It's okay to grieve for them, Henry, but your dad and brother would want you to move on with your life." Dennis's skin tingled. This was the first time he'd realized that he was actually beginning to move on with his life. *Guess I really have forgiven my uncle and accepted the fact that the accident wasn't his fault. Now maybe I can somehow help Henry to work through his pain.*

Henry looked up at Dennis. "I'm glad God brought you into our lives 'cause I really like you."

Dennis gave Henry's shoulder a squeeze. "I like you too."

Sylvia sniffed and reached for a tissue to blow her nose. "Guess we'd best get the desserts taken out before someone else comes looking for us."

🐦

"My son tells me you're also a bird-watcher." Dennis's mother, Amanda, looked across the table at Sylvia.

"Yes, that's right. It's a fairly new hobby for me. My brother Henry is also into birding. In fact he got into it before I did."

"That's right," Henry interjected. "Sylvia and I were out looking at birds the day we met Dennis."

"It's nice you three have that in common. Don't you think so, Belinda?" Amanda turned to look at Sylvia's mother.

Sylvia held her breath, waiting to hear Mom's response.

Mom nodded slowly. "Yes, I am happy that my son and daughter found a hobby they can both enjoy."

Since there was no mention of Amanda's son, Sylvia felt the need to say something on his behalf. "Dennis has taught Henry and me a lot about the various species of birds in our area. I think we have learned more from him than from the bird book Henry has."

Amanda smiled as she looked at Dennis with a gleam in her eyes. "My son's interest in birds began when he was a young boy, and he's learned a lot over the years."

"My mamm's right," Gerald spoke up. "Whenever my bruder went missing, we always knew he was off looking at birds somewhere on the farm."

Dennis held up his hand. "Okay, that's enough talk about me. Let's move on to some other topic, shall we?"

"We could talk about the wonderful way you have with horses," his mother said. She looked at Sylvia's mom. "He's had that ability since he was a boy as well."

"Yes, Sylvia's told me that Dennis trains horses." Mom's smile didn't quite reach her eyes. Sylvia figured she was only being polite.

Abruptly, Mom changed the subject. "My daughter Amy is planning to be married this fall. It's too bad her fiancé couldn't be with us tonight."

"Jared's a roofer, and he had an out-of-town job so he wouldn't have gotten back in time to be here," Amy explained. "Perhaps some other time when you come to visit Dennis, you can meet Jared."

Amanda smiled. "I'll look forward to that."

As the conversation around the table changed to talk about the weather, Sylvia's thoughts turned inward. *What do Dennis's mother and brother think of me and my family? Are they okay with their son courting me?*

She glanced at her mother, sitting straight in her chair. *Will Mom ever accept the idea of me seeing Dennis and making him a part of my life? Sometimes I wish I'd never moved back into her house and had toughed it on my own after Toby died. Then she wouldn't know so much of my personal business and might be more accepting of my new friend.*

Today, Dennis had brought out his new dog from the pen he and Gerald had put together. The shepherd seemed timid around the horses, but Dennis kept him nearby while working. He hoped in due time the dog he'd named Brutus would be fine around Midnight and any other horse.

It had been a week since Dennis's mother and brother left, and she'd called him nearly every day since. Gerald had called once, just to tell Dennis that the deal had fallen through on the vacation home he'd wanted to buy. He'd also mentioned that their mother had seemed kind of out-of-sorts since they came home and kept asking him what he'd thought of Sylvia.

Dennis's mother could get curious at times about certain topics. And when it came to her boys getting involved with a potential mate, her antenna went up in a hurry. He couldn't believe how interested she was, so sometimes he'd go off the topic and talk about his dog, or some of the things going on with his work.

Mom said she had more questions about Sylvia and his intentions toward her. Dennis didn't say much, other than that he was taking it one day at a time and would let her know if anything serious developed.

Dennis grunted as he combed Midnight's mane. "How am I supposed to respond to my mamm's questions about my relationship with Sylvia when I don't have any answers myself?"

The horse's ears perked up, and he let out a noisy nicker.

"Yeah, I know, boy. You don't have any answers for me either." Dennis patted Midnight's flanks and looked over at the dog. "What do you think, Brutus?"

The dog tilted his head and watched.

"I feel like I've got a little family of my own right here." Dennis paused to clean out the comb he'd used on the horse.

"I can't even consider marriage until my business is making enough money to support a real family." Dennis continued his one-way conversation with both the horse and his black and tan dog. "After all, it wouldn't just be me and Sylvia to worry about—she has two children."

Midnight stomped his hooves impatiently when Dennis kept combing the same section of his mane. Dennis couldn't help it—Sylvia, Allen, and Rachel were forefront on his mind. He wanted to be a good provider for them. His biggest concern was how long it would take before that chapter in his life began.

"Well boy, I can't stay here all day—I've got work to do." Dennis put the curry comb away. "And tonight I'm taking my best girl and her kinner on a picnic supper at the park." He reached down and patted Brutus's head. "Maybe I'll take you along. The kids might enjoy being introduced to you."

After a busy day in the greenhouse, Amy had decided a warm shower would be a perfect way to wind down. Now as she sat at the kitchen table, working on her guest list for the wedding, her long, damp hair hung down her back. "Who, besides family, do you think we should invite to the wedding?" she asked her mother.

Mom looked up from the two-page letter she'd been writing. "Well, our close friends, of course, like Mary Ruth, as well as Lenore, Jesse, and their little family. We'll also include the families in our church district. I think you'll have a good amount of members present for your service and also for the afternoon and evening meals."

Amy picked up a tube of lotion she'd placed on the table and squirted some into her hand as she thought about their neighbors across the street. While she wasn't particularly fond of Virginia, Jared had extended them a verbal invitation, so they should probably be included. After rubbing the lotion in well, she wrote Virginia and Earl's names on the evening meal list.

"What about Herschel?" Amy asked.

"He's not in our district."

"I realize that, but he's a friend, and if it weren't for him, Jared and I wouldn't have a place to live after we're married."

"I'm sure you would have found something else." Mom tapped her pen against the writing tablet. "I hope I haven't left anything out."

Amy inhaled the lavender-mint scent of her lotion, lingering on her skin. "That's a good-sized letter you're working on. Who are you writing to?"

"Ezekiel and Michelle. I'm filling them in on our local news, here and in our community." Mom set her pen aside. "I wouldn't mind using some of that lotion too. It sure smells nice."

"Help yourself." Amy passed it to her. "So how come you don't just call them and leave a message?"

"It's easier to write it all down." Mom placed a dollop of the moisturizer on her hands and rubbed it in. "Besides, we don't do enough letter writing these days."

"True." Amy glanced at her list. "So what do you think—is it okay if I invite Herschel?"

Mom shrugged her shoulders and grabbed her pen. "It's your wedding, so it's up to you. It would be a nice gesture, I suppose."

"Okay, I'm going to add him to the list." When Amy finished writing Herschel's name, she looked back at her mother. "Can I ask you something else?"

"Of course."

"Did you enjoy the time we spent with Dennis and his family last week?"

Mom put her pen down and looked directly at Amy. "They seem nice enough, and I don't think Dennis is a bad person, but I believe he's pushed your sister into a relationship too soon."

"It's not too soon for Sylvia to be in a relationship, Mom. She's been widowed over a year, and I don't think she would have agreed to let Dennis court her if she didn't feel ready to begin again."

"I've been without my mate the same time as her, and I'm not ready to be courted by anyone." Mom shifted on her chair. "Monroe would like me to be, but I'm not in love with him."

Amy bobbed her head. "I agree. No one should begin a serious relationship with someone unless there is love—or at least the beginning of those feelings."

"You're right, and I have a feeling Sylvia still loves Toby. She may only be looking for a father for her kinner, which is ridiculous since Dennis has never had any children."

"He does well when he's around Rachel and Allen, and I believe they—especially Allen—are drawn to him," Amy argued.

"That doesn't mean—"

Mom stopped talking when Henry entered the room. "Seth just pulled up in his car, and I wanna go talk to him. I've been trying to connect ever since the greenhouse windows were painted black, and he hasn't answered any of my messages."

"You can go out and talk to him," Mom replied, "but please do not get into his *fuhrwaerick*."

Henry shook his head. "Don't worry—I'm not gonna get in Seth's vehicle. I just want to ask if he's the one who did that to our windows."

"Okay, go ahead, but don't stay too long. We'll be starting supper soon."

Henry glanced around. "Where's Sylvia? Figured she'd have supper started by now."

"She and the kinner went out with Dennis this evening, remember? And we met his new dog, Brutus, right before they left. Where's your head, Son? Are you sure it's on straight today?"

"Of course it is. My mind's just preoccupied with getting some answers out of Seth." Henry turned and raced out the back door.

Amy scrunched her face. "Poor guy. He's definitely upset over this."

"Do you think one of us should go with him?" Mom asked. "Maybe he'll need some help convincing Seth to tell the truth."

Amy shook her head. "Seth is a closed-mouth kid. He's not likely to admit anything to either of us."

"Guess you're right." Mom heaved a sigh. "Let's just hope if Seth is the one responsible for the vandalism that he owns up to it and promises not to do anything like that again."

Sylvia was glad Dennis had decided that they should go on a picnic, rather than eating in a restaurant. Rachel got fussy if she was made to sit very long, and here at the park, both children could run and play after they ate. Of course, they would still need some supervision.

Allen and Rachel seemed to take a liking to Brutus right away. He was a big hit and kept the children well entertained. Sylvia watched Allen running around with the dog, while Rachel stood on the sidelines clapping her hands.

"Brutus is a friendly, nice-looking hund." She looked over at Dennis.

"I agree. He's a beautiful dog and a keeper. His personality around the horses is still somewhat timid, but I think he will eventually toughen up," he responded.

"At least he isn't the other way—aggressive around anyone or anything."

Dennis shook his head. "I couldn't afford to have a dog that would be unsafe—especially when I'm running a business with people coming and going."

Sylvia felt contented as she soaked up the nice view here at the park. The children laughed at Brutus chewing on a stick he'd found. It was a warm evening, and the birds seemed to be everywhere.

Dennis pointed to a couple of doves. "It's interesting that they're related to pigeons."

"I never thought about that, but they do look similar."

"I hope it was okay to come here and have a picnic."

Sylvia nodded, and then looked over at the children again. Between all the activity her son and daughter experienced here this evening, as well as the hearty picnic fare they would eat soon, she felt sure they'd both sleep well tonight. Dennis had furnished the picnic food from a local deli and included peanut butter and jelly sandwiches that the children would enjoy.

If only my mother could understand my needs and how Dennis makes me feel. Sylvia let her thoughts wander as she sat back until she could rest comfortably against the bench where she and Dennis sat. *She thinks my only priority should be raising my kinner, and I'm doing that. Doesn't Mom see that being with Dennis brings me joy? I don't see anything wrong with it. Maybe I'll be like my sister in the near future, planning for a wedding. I wonder what my mamm would say about that.*

"I enjoyed meeting your mother and brother last week," Sylvia said as they watched the children run around. Brutus ran with them, playfully barking and wagging his tail.

Dennis looked over at Sylvia and smiled. "Mom and Gerald were pleased to have met you and your family. Every time my mamm's called me this past week, she's asked about you."

"That's nice to know." Sylvia sat quietly for a few minutes and gathered up her courage to say something that had been on her mind since she and Dennis had begun courting. "I want to apologize for my mother's curtness toward you."

Dennis shifted on the bench so they were directly facing each other. "I had noticed it, and I think I know why."

"Oh?"

"Your mamm probably thinks our relationship is moving too fast."

"That is part of the reason," Sylvia admitted. "But I believe there's more to it."

"Such as?"

"Mom's afraid I might end up getting married someday, and then it would be just her and Henry to run the greenhouse."

"Married to me?"

Sylvia's cheeks warmed. "Well, she might think that, I suppose."

Dennis reached for her hand. "And she might be right. I've thought about it a lot, in fact."

"You. . .you have?" Sylvia's skin tingled beneath his gentle touch.

"Jah." Dennis stroked the top of her hand with this thumb. "Even though our relationship is still fairly new, I feel like I've known you all of my life."

"I feel the same way about you."

"The thing is, I can't really think about marriage until I'm making more money. I need to build up my business, so it's successful. But in the meantime, I'd like to continue our relationship, making it stronger."

Sylvia licked her lips, feeling cautious hope. "I'd like that."

Belinda had finished mixing the ingredients for the macaroni and cheese she'd planned for supper, when Henry burst into the room. "I talked to Seth, and now our *freindschaft* is over. *Sis nau futsch.*"

She turned to face him. "In what way is your friendship ruined now?"

"Seth said he's not the guilty one, and he's mad at me for thinkin' he would do something like paint the greenhouse windows black." Henry sank into a chair at the table and groaned. "I apologized to him for making the accusation, yet he refused to forgive me. There's no doubt about it—I've lost my good friend." He held his fist against his chest. "Something right here told me he wasn't the one who did it, but I had to ask, just the same."

"Don't be so dramatic," Amy said from across the room, where she stood making a tossed green salad. "If Seth was ever a friend, he won't hold it against you because you asked if he had anything to do with the vandalism."

"Your sister is right." Belinda put the casserole dish into the oven. "And if he does break your friendship off, then maybe it's because he was in fact guilty and refused to admit it. Some people are like that, you know. When they're caught doing something they shouldn't have, they try to lie their way out of it and can even go so far as to put the blame on someone else."

Henry shook head. "Seth didn't blame anyone else, Mom. He just said he didn't do it. Now I don't have my friend to hang around with anymore." His shoulders slumped.

"You really weren't spending much time with Seth anyway, Son," Mom said.

"That's 'cause I'm workin' so much around here and in the greenhouse."

"Well, the fact that he got angry with you tells me there's something amiss. Maybe I should speak to Seth's mother about this matter."

Henry rubbed his sweaty forehead. "Please don't do that, Mom. It would make Seth even more umgerennt with me."

"If he's innocent, then he has no reason to be upset." Amy put the finished salad in the refrigerator then she came over to the table and put her hand on Henry's shoulder. "If Seth's not guilty of anything, then give him a little space. I bet by this time next week, he'll come around and resume his friendship with you."

Henry shrugged his shoulders. "We'll see, but I'm not holding my breath. Seth was pretty upset, and he basically told me to leave him alone."

Belinda's heart went out to her son. She watched him as he shuffled up the stairs. *I have a feeling Henry will go up to his room and mope around over this now.* He did what he thought was right by talking to Seth about the blackened windows, and now he has to worry about losing his friend.

Belinda sighed. *I hope for Henry's sake that he is right and his friend is innocent, because it's not easy to watch my boy suffer. But if Seth was responsible for the damage, then my son is better off without him.*

Chapter 38

Sylvia went blissfully through the summer months as she and Dennis saw each other more frequently. They went to church together, spent time with the children, and continued birding—most times together and sometimes by themselves or with Henry. These adventures brought them even closer, as they compared notes, sightings, and messages they'd heard on the bird-watcher's hotline—like the buff-breasted sandpiper someone had seen near the end of August.

Sylvia felt certain that Dennis was the right man for her, and she thought if Toby could look down from heaven, he would approve of the special relationship she'd found herself in. Sylvia looked forward to the day Dennis would feel ready to propose marriage and knew her answer would be yes.

Her mother still hadn't fully accepted Dennis, but Sylvia continued to hope that would change once Mom realized what a good husband and father he'd make.

Today was the first Monday in September, and Amy's wedding was only a month away. Sylvia looked forward to the occasion and especially to being one of her sister's witnesses, along with Amy's friend Lydia. She felt honored to have been asked.

Jared's best friend was Gabe Fisher, whom he'd known since he was a boy, so he had asked him to be one of his witnesses, as well as Jared's younger brother Daniel.

This morning, Sylvia had gotten up early to do some baking while the kitchen was cooler than it would be later in the day, and with the children still in bed, there would be no interruptions.

Sylvia heard a bird creating a racket outside the window. She opened it wide and peered out. There sat that silly old mockingbird chirping out a song.

"Hush now. It's too early to be making a nuisance of yourself."

Chirp. . .chirp. . .chirp. . .

Sylvia put a hand on her hip. "Are you mocking me?"

The bird flitted to another tree and continued to warble.

Sylvia couldn't be sure what a mockingbird really sounded like, because according to what she'd read in Henry's bird book, these birds often took on the tone of other birds in the yard. *I sure enjoy being able to identify the species around our yard. I couldn't do such a thing a few months ago. Thank you, Henry and Dennis, for your encouragement.*

"What are you doing?"

Sylvia jerked at the sound of her brother's voice. "*Ach*, you scared me, Henry. I didn't think anybody else was up."

"Just me, as far as I can tell. I thought I was the only person up till I came in here and found you." Henry went to the cupboard and took out a glass. "How come you got out of bed so early?"

"I wanted to get some baking done before the kitchen gets too hot and everyone is up and about."

He sniffed and looked around. "Don't see or smell anything yummy."

She poked his arm playfully. "That's because I haven't started anything yet, silly."

"Well hurry up. I'm hungerich." Henry opened the refrigerator and took out a jug of apple cider Jesse Smucker had given them recently. It had been frozen when he'd brought it over, and he'd said it was the last of the previous fall's squeezing that he'd put in the deep freezer he rented. With autumn around the corner, it wouldn't be long before Jesse would get out the cider press, and there'd be plenty of apple cider to share with others.

"What's your reason for being up so early?" Sylvia asked as her brother poured cider into his glass.

"Wanted to check all the feeders. They're probably getting low. I need to keep our feathered friends happy and coming back to visit." He grinned. "I'll probably spend some time just lookin' at birds after I'm done with the chore."

"Here in the yard, I hope. Mom wouldn't like it if she found out you went somewhere without asking."

He crossed his arms and frowned. "I don't think our mamm trusts me. Truth be told, she probably still thinks I'm the one responsible for all the vandalism that's been done here since Dad, Abe, and Toby died."

"Don't be silly Henry. It's been a long time since Mom's suspected you, and since you weren't at home when some of the things were done, she has no reason to believe it was you."

He pulled out a chair and sat down. "Guess you're right. As soon as I drink my cider, I'm going out in the yard to look for birds—or maybe I'll climb up into the loft like I've done before. I prefer goin' up there, 'cause it's got a nice soft place with loose hay to sit and lean into." Henry gulped some cider and licked his lips clean. "The vantage point is nice because I can see into the big tree in our yard. There can be a lot of bird action goin' on in that old maple."

"That explains why you like to go up there more than not." Sylvia opened the pantry door and took out the ingredients needed to make cornmeal muffins. *If we could get to the bottom of who's responsible for the vandalism, no one would be a suspect anymore.*

Virginia pulled open the door to her mailbox. After retrieving the mail, she stood thumbing through each piece. She couldn't help glancing up her neighbors' driveway to take a look around. Her thought was to catch someone outside to chat with about the upcoming wedding. Hopefully it might lead to a verbal invitation.

Virginia saw no one in sight. The place appeared quiet and still. *Think I've done a decent job of playing nice to these Amish neighbors, and I really want Stella to come for another visit.*

Her forehead wrinkled. Still no invitation in the mail from the Kings, and that wedding was just a month away. Virginia had gone over to the greenhouse a few weeks ago, and dropped a couple more hints about the wedding, asking when they'd be mailing out invitations. Belinda had been really busy that day and hurriedly said, "About a month before the wedding."

Virginia slammed the flap shut, and after looking both ways, she limped back across the street. *I wonder if they forgot about us. This really stresses me out.*

Virginia drew in a couple of deep breaths and tried to calm herself. *Of course, maybe one of them might come over and deliver the invitation in person.* "At least I can console myself with that," she mumbled as she made her way up to the house.

A robin flew past and landed on the garage roof. Virginia watched it preen itself for a minute. She thought the Kings' yard and the feeders they had hanging brought a lot of bird activity.

I should buy myself a few of those bird hoppers to draw more birds into our yard, but Earl might think it's silly and too expensive.

Once inside, she tossed the mail on the coffee table. She'd hoped she might catch one of the King family members outside, but that hadn't panned out.

Virginia's fingers trembled as she pulled them through the ends of her hair. *I've got to calm my nerves. Maybe some coffee would help, but I know something else that would take the edge off.*

Virginia went to the hall closet and took out a metal box where she'd hid a carton of cigarettes. If Earl knew she had started smoking again, he'd have a conniption.

She took one cigarette out and put the rest back, then walked out to the kitchen and looked at the clock. "I've got plenty of time to ease my stress before starting supper." She stepped over to her mug, filled it with creamer from the refrigerator, and then topped it off with coffee.

After grabbing a book of matches, Virginia went out the back door and took a seat at the picnic table. Once her cigarette had been lit, she took a puff and inhaled deeply before blowing out the smoke. "Ah, that's better. Now I feel more relaxed."

Virginia propped her bum leg on a nearby chair. As the sunshine warmed her up, she admired the pretty flowerbed that held an abundant array of flowers. The hanging baskets she'd put up also added a splash of color up under the eaves of the house. She'd bought all the plants from the greenhouse across the street. So far they looked happy, slowly putting on more buds. "At least these plants should do well, since I didn't add any of that dumb horse manure to the soil. My poor tomato plants—now that was sure a waste last year." Virginia took another puff from her cigarette.

Virginia had quit smoking nearly a year ago, but since moving to a place she didn't like, she'd started up again whenever she felt testy. Virginia kept the evidence well-hidden and always smoked outside and made sure her clothes were aired out or washed before Earl came home from work. She used mouthwash and toothpaste to freshen her breath and either washed her hair or applied a lot of hairspray and perfume to mask the smoky odor. So far Earl hadn't caught on, and she aimed to keep it that way.

After I finish my cigarette, think I'll get out the binoculars and watch whatever birds come into the yard. If that gets boring, I may sit on the front porch and spy on the neighbors.

Clymer

"Look what came in the mail today," Ezekiel said when he entered the kitchen, where Michelle had breakfast waiting for him. He held an envelope out to her and grinned.

She looked at the return address. "It's from Amy, right?"

He nodded. "Go ahead and open it."

She opened the flap carefully and removed a card. "It's our invitation to her and Jared's wedding." Michelle put her arms around Ezekiel and gave him a hug. "I can hardly wait to witness their marriage and see all the rest of our family and friends in Strasburg."

"Same here. It's been five months since we last saw them, and by the time we arrive for the wedding, it'll be six."

"Will we get to go a few days early so we can help out? As you well know, there's a lot to be done those last few days before the big event."

"You're right, and we will definitely want to be there for that."

Excitement bubbled in Michelle's soul. *How wonderful it will be to see not only Ezekiel's family but Mary Ruth, Lenore, and maybe even Sara as well.* Until then, Michelle would count off each one of the days. The first Thursday of October couldn't come soon enough.

Strasburg

Virginia remained at the picnic table, drinking more coffee, while working on a crossword puzzle. This one was harder than most in the book she'd purchased last week, but she was determined to finish the puzzle, even if she had to get out the dictionary for help.

As she sat trying to decide what a word meant for "someone who complains a lot," something rubbed against her leg.

Virginia looked down, and her eyes widened when she saw a gray-and-white cat with its furry tail flipping back and forth across her leg.

"Now where'd you come from?" She leaned over and pet the critter's soft head. Virginia had never seen the cat before and wondered if it was a stray.

"You lookin' for food?" She continued to stroke the cat. "I'm sorry, but I have nothing for you except maybe a bowl of milk or a can of tuna."

She pulled her hand back and thumped the side of her head. "What am I thinking? If I feed the stray, he's bound to keep coming around. Nope, not a good idea. I need to use some common sense."

"Common sense about what?"

Virginia whirled around. "Earl, what are you doing home so early?" She glanced at her cell phone. "It's only two o'clock."

"I've been fighting a headache all day, so the boss said I could go home." He gestured to the metal-framed hammock he'd bought earlier this summer and set up on the patio. "I thought maybe a cold beer and a nap in that might help."

"It's too hot to sleep out here. Why don't you go inside and lie on the bed?"

"Because I want to take my nap outside."

Meow!

Earl looked toward Virginia's feet, and his brows shot up. "Where'd that mangy cat come from?"

"It's not mangy, and it just showed up here a few minutes ago. I have no idea where it came from."

"Well it's not staying." Earl clapped his hands as he took a few steps toward Virginia.

The poor cat took off like it had been shot out of a cannon.

Virginia scowled at him. "Now look what you've done. I bet that poor animal will never come back."

"Exactly." Earl put his nose in the air and sniffed. "What's that putrid odor?"

She shrugged. "I don't smell anything."

"Smells like cigarette smoke." He sniffed again. "Virginia, have you started smoking again?"

"No, Earl."

He leaned close to her head and took in some air. "Phew! Your hair reeks of cigarette smoke. I'd recognize that aroma anywhere."

With rushed speech, Virginia made up a story about having gone shopping this morning. "And when I came out of the store, there was this guy smoking like a diesel. That man blew smoke curls everywhere. Guess the odor must have stayed with me."

Earl rolled his neck from side-to-side then massaged his forehead. "You'd better be telling the truth. Need I remind you that when you quit smoking, you said it was for good?"

"I don't need any reminders." Virginia gathered up her empty mug and puzzle book. "I'm going to the house to get more coffee. Want me to get you some?"

"No thanks. I'm just gonna lie in the hammock. If I'm not up by suppertime, give me a holler." His forehead wrinkled. "On second thought, don't holler. Better give me a gentle shake instead."

"Okay, Earl. Have a good nap."

Virginia went inside and closed the back door. *Whew, that was a close one. I wasn't expecting Earl to come home early or I'd have taken my shower sooner. I'll need to be more careful next time I decide to have a cigarette.*

Chapter 39

"Well, if that doesn't beat all." Virginia stood in front of the living room window, shaking her head. She turned to face her husband.

"What's wrong?" Earl asked from where he sat putting on his work shoes.

"You should see all the horses and buggies, as well as some cars, pulling into the Kings' driveway."

"More greenhouse traffic, huh?"

She shook her head. "Today is Jared and Amy's wedding, don't ya know? And of course, we didn't get an invite to it, which is why Stella didn't come."

"It's not the end of the world, Virginia. We barely know those people, and we're not Amish, so they might not want outsiders at the occasion."

"I realize that, but if you'll recall, Jared said we would be invited." She tapped her foot, as anger flooded her soul. "I have half a notion to go on over there and crash that wedding. I wonder how that would go over."

"Not very well, I imagine. So just get the idea right out of your head." Earl stood. "And for crying out loud, get away from the window. It's doing you no good to spy on those folks."

"If we can't go, then I may as well see what I can from here." Virginia moved over to the coffee table and picked up the binoculars. *I wonder if there's a way to get a better look over there. If I could find a spot to see into their property well, maybe then I'd be satisfied.*

Earl moved toward her. "Listen, I don't think. . ."

She waved him away. "You'd better get going, or you're gonna be late for work."

"Yeah, okay. But promise me you'll be good today and find something constructive to do."

She gave him a salute. "Will do."

Virginia waited until she heard Earl's vehicle pull out before she went back to watching the goings-on across the road.

Amy paced the living room floor, every once in a while stopping to draw a quick breath. This was the most exciting, but nerve-racking day of her life. It felt like she'd been waiting for this special event to take place forever—certainly since she'd fallen in love with Jared.

I wonder if he's feeling as nervous as I am right now. Oh, I hope the love of my life has no regrets.

"You need to stop pacing, or you'll wear a hole in the floor."

Amy stopped walking and turned to face her oldest brother. "I can't help it, Ezekiel. I'm a nervous wreck."

"Of course you are. All brides and grooms are *naerfich* on their wedding day. I sure was, and if you ask Michelle, she'll admit to having been nervous too."

"How did you get through it without falling apart?"

"I prayed for peaceful thoughts and did a lot of deep breathing."

Amy gave him a hug. "Danki, big brother. I'll try to do both throughout the wedding service." She turned toward the hallway as the rest of their family entered the living room.

"You look pretty." Michelle came over and gave Amy a hug. "I'm so glad we could be here to help celebrate your marriage."

Amy smiled. "It wouldn't be the same without all of my family." Her smile faded and tears welled in her eyes. "Oh how I wish Dad, Abe, and Toby could be here. I never expected to be getting married without their presence."

Mom got teary-eyed and so did Sylvia. The three of them gathered in a group hug.

"We need to get control of our emotions," Mom said. "There are a lot of people waiting outside the barn, and they'll soon be seated. Are you ready to head out now, Daughter?"

"Jah." Amy gave a nod.

Mom took Allen and Rachel's hands and led them out the door. They would sit with her during the service. Ezekiel, Michelle, and their two children went next, followed by Henry.

Sylvia came alongside Amy and clasped her hand. "I am honored to be a part of your special day."

"And I'm happy you are one of my witnesses." Amy paused and said a quick, silent prayer. It was hard to believe, but in the next few hours she would become Mrs. Jared Riehl.

Sylvia sat up straight in her chair as she listened to the message being preached on the topic of husbands and wives. She remembered her own wedding with Toby and how excited yet nervous she felt sitting across from her groom as they waited to say their vows. She also recalled how all of her family and friends had been there to offer their blessings and approval. The thought that she might lose her husband in a few years was the furthest thing from Sylvia's mind. As a young bride, she'd been full of hope for the future and felt certain that she and Toby would be together for a long time.

A lump formed in Sylvia's throat. She would never forget what she and Toby had together, but she couldn't bring him back, and she had no regrets about her decision to move on with her life. *Toby would not have wanted me to mourn for him indefinitely. He'd want me and the children to be happy and cared for.*

Sylvia glanced at Dennis sitting in the men's section of the barn. She felt more convinced than ever that he was the right man for her.

As Jared and Amy stood before the bishop to say their vows, Dennis watched Sylvia. He wouldn't say anything today, of course, but he wondered if it was too soon to ask her to marry him. His business had grown throughout the summer months, and he had some money saved up. He would wait until he had the approval of Sylvia's mother, however, before asking Sylvia to become his wife.

My mamm would be excited if Sylvia and I got married, although probably disappointed because we'll stay here in Strasburg. No doubt she would like me to move back to Dauphin County, but she'll have to accept the fact that I've established a new home here.

Dennis snapped back to attention when the bride and groom returned to their seats. He'd missed hearing the rest of their verbal commitment to each other. He glanced at Sylvia again, and saw her wiping tears on her cheeks. *Are they tears of joy for her sister, or could Sylvia be thinking about her deceased husband and the years they spent together? Is she ready to commit to me, or am I fooling myself to believe she's truly in love with me?*

His fingers curled into his palms. *I have to know, and it needs to be soon.*

Belinda could hardly control her emotions as Amy and Jared said their vows. She was happy her daughter had found happiness with the man she loved, but she would miss Amy so much when she moved into Herschel's rental with Jared.

I'm glad Jared doesn't have a problem with Amy working at the greenhouse until she becomes pregnant with their first child. Belinda patted Rachel's back as the little girl leaned against her chest and slept. *I am concerned, little one, as to what will transpire if your mammi should marry Dennis. Will she move you and your brother back to her old place, or could Dennis decide to pack up and move back to Dauphin County where his family lives? It's hard enough having Ezekiel living in New York. It would really be difficult if Sylvia and the children moved away too.*

Try not to think about it, she told herself. *No one but God knows what the future holds.*

Sitting beside her groom at the *Eck*, or the corner table, Amy felt like pinching herself. It was hard to believe she had finally become Jared's wife. What a joyous occasion. Everything had gone just as planned. Now as she and Jared ate a delicious wedding meal with their guests,

Amy tried to absorb it all. Since there would be no pictures taken, Amy wanted to instill everything about this wonderful day into her memory so she would never forget it.

"Are you enjoying the meal?" Jared leaned close to Amy, brushing his lips against her ear.

"Oh jah, very much."

"Me too." He looked out at all the people sitting at the long tables beneath the tent. "Too bad your neighbors couldn't have made it today."

"Which neighbors?"

"Earl and Virginia. Remember the night we met them at Diener's, and I said they would probably get an invitation to the wedding or at least one of the meals afterward? Did you include them?"

Amy blinked. "I'm sure I put them on the invitation list for the second meal. Maybe they were unable to come." *Or maybe, they weren't interested in attending the event.*

🐦

Virginia walked out to get her mail, limping all the way. She'd brought the binoculars, but in her hurry, she had forgotten to bring her cane along and now regretted it. As she approached the box, she heard the sounds of laughter and people talking from the Kings' yard. Before getting the mail, Virginia decided to walk up the driveway a bit, curious to see what was going on. Earlier, she'd heard singing and figured it must be part of the wedding service. Now with the laughter and chattering, she felt sure the wedding must be over.

Virginia moved slowly toward the event and pulled the binoculars up to her eyes. She still didn't have a good spot to do any viewing. *I'll walk closer until I can see something. It's unfair that I'm reduced to this, slinking about to get a glance at what I should have been able to attend. At the very least, I'd like to have something to tell Stella about.*

Halfway up the driveway she spotted a couple of large white tents set up near the barn. This was an area of their yard she couldn't see from her house. Open flaps on the canvas gave her a clear view of some of the guests, but she couldn't see any sign of the bride and groom. Behind Virginia, she heard someone humming and the sound grew closer. Her first instinct was to hide, so she ducked behind some shrubs and peeked out. Not long after, she saw that odd, gray-haired woman wearing shabby clothes and ambling up the driveway. Virginia watched Maude walk toward the greenhouse. *I wonder what she's up to. Hmm. . . she definitely isn't going to the wedding looking like that.*

In a crouched position, Virginia continued to watch Maude. A few minutes went by, and she saw Mrs. King come out of the tent and hand the old woman a plate full of food. Virginia couldn't believe her eyes as Maude took a seat on a wooden bench and gobbled up the fare.

"Now that certainly takes the cake. They're eating a meal, and now Maude's getting in on it too." Virginia spoke quietly through clenched teeth. *A meal that I should be sitting down eating right now—along with Stella and Earl.*

Virginia smelled the food from where she hid, but her knees were beginning to go numb and might buckle if she didn't stand up soon. *I need to get out of here before someone sees me.*

As Virginia tried to stand, she lost her balance and fell backward into some kind of bush with vines, and her arm got tangled up in it. *Oh great. Now what should I do?*

After a few failed attempts at trying to get up, she was finally on her feet. However, as her left foot came down, it landed in something strange. *Oh boy. What did I just step in?* Virginia looked down at her sandal, enveloped in a pile of fresh dung. *Oh sugar. . .this can't be happening to me. I shouldn't have even bothered coming over here.*

Virginia shook her foot, trying get rid of the stuff, and even tried wiping it in the grass. Worried that someone would see her, she limped toward home. *I've got to either clean this well or throw the sandals away. I can't let Earl know I've been out spying on the neighbors and on their property, no less.*

She looked over her shoulder. No one seemed to have taken notice of her. She made her way to the mailbox and grabbed the contents. Now her hip hurt as well as her bum leg.

Once she was in her own backyard, Virginia placed the mail on the picnic table and grabbed the hose to wash off the mess on her sandal. Most of it came off, but now it looked stained. *I'm gonna have to throw them both out. This really bums me out. Those shoes are my favorite because they're so comfy.* With a groan, Virginia walked over to the garbage can and tossed them in.

Once inside the house, she put the mail on the counter and suddenly realized the binoculars hadn't made it back home with her. She figured she must have dropped them in the weeds when she fell. *When can I go back over there and get them?*

She stepped up to the front window and saw Maude moseying down the driveway like she didn't have a care in the world. No doubt she was quite satisfied after that meal she'd eaten.

Guess I could try to go back over there and fetch them now, but I'd be taking a chance of that wedding gathering being over soon, and then people getting into their rigs would surely see me.

Virginia thought about Stella again. She still felt bad having to tell her best friend that they hadn't received an invitation to Amy and Jared's wedding, but she had asked Stella to come visit anyway. "We can sit on the front porch and listen to the festivities," she'd told her friend. But Stella had declined, saying she'd made other plans for this week.

"Other plans my foot," Virginia muttered. "I bet the only reason she backed out of coming is because we wouldn't be going to an Amish wedding."

She kicked at a stone beneath her feet and groaned as a searing pain shot up her leg. "A lot of good it did me to try and be friendly with those Plain people. Think I'm gonna have a cigarette to help me calm down."

Chapter 40

"I wish we didn't have to go back home so soon," Michelle complained to Ezekiel as they put the children to bed that evening. "The wedding was wonderful, and we got to visit with several people, but I didn't get to spend enough time talking to Mary Ruth or Lenore, and I was sort of hoping we could stop by to see Sara, Brad, and the baby since they couldn't make it to the wedding."

"We can stay through tomorrow, but we'll need to head back to Clymer Thursday morning as planned. If there's time tomorrow evening, maybe we can see if our driver would be free to take us over to see the Fullers." Ezekiel patted their son's back before putting him in the portable crib they'd brought on this trip.

Michelle tucked Angela Mary in and bent to kiss the little girl's forehead, and then she and Ezekiel tiptoed out of the room.

Standing in the hall outside the guest room, her voice lowered to a whisper. "Isn't it hard for you to come here for special occasions and then have to leave, knowing it might be several months before we see any of your family again?"

"Jah, but I'm happy living in Clymer." Ezekiel looked at her pointedly. "I thought you were too."

"I am for the most part, but it's always hard to say goodbye to our loved ones here."

"Just think about how the pioneers must have felt when they left their families and homes to travel to lands unknown in the West. Some of them never saw any of their relatives back home again. At least we only live one state away and get to see our family several times a year."

"You've made a good point, and I'll try not to get so emotional when we say goodbye this time." After their last visit, Michelle had shed tears most of the way home.

"Let's go back to the living room and visit with the others for a while before it's time for bed," Ezekiel suggested.

"Okay." Michelle breathed a heavy sigh and started down the hall toward the living room, where the rest of the family had gathered. Amy and Jared had left to spend their first night as a married couple in their rental. They would be back in the morning to help with the clean-up and putting things away that had been set up for the wedding. In a few weeks or so, they planned to take a trip out West by train. Michelle had never been to the West Coast, but hoped someday after Angela Mary and Vernon were older she and Ezekiel could make such a trip. If it was off-season for the greenhouse, perhaps Ezekiel's mother would be willing to watch the children.

"Virginia, what is this?" Earl marched into the living room, where she sat on the couch reading a magazine about birds in the state of Pennsylvania.

She put the magazine down, and when she looked up at him, her eyes widened. "Where'd you get that?"

"Found it in the hall closet, inside a box." He held up a carton of cigarettes. "So you haven't started smoking again, huh?"

"Well, umm. . ." Virginia squirmed on the couch.

"How long has this been going on, and how come you lied about it?" Earl's stern tone caused Virginia to cringe. She feared he might become violent and hit her. Although he'd never done anything like that in the past, this was something Virginia feared could happen if Earl became angry enough.

"I started smoking again because I'm a nervous wreck, and I didn't admit it to you, because I knew you'd be disappointed in me." Virginia's lips quivered and tears sprang to her eyes as she lowered her head. "Guess I'm nothing but a big failure, and you probably regret having married me."

"Not true, Virginia." Earl came over and sat down beside her. "I am disappointed that you're smoking again, but I don't regret marrying you."

Virginia sniffed and leaned her head on Earl's shoulder. "I don't know what I did to deserve a wonderful man like you." She gestured to the carton of cigarettes. "I'll try really hard to quit smoking, but I can't promise. As long as we're living among the Amish here in Strasburg, my nerves will be on edge." She nodded her head toward the living room window. "Those people over there can't be trusted."

"Are you still fretting about not getting an invite to that wedding?"

"Uh-huh. I can't help it, Earl. It was my ace in the hole to get Stella back here for a visit." Virginia wiped her tears away. "Now I'm stuck here with no friends at all."

He put his arm around her. "Not true, Wife. I'm here with you, and I thought we were friends."

"We are, Earl, but I need someone I can hang out with when you're not at home." She sniffed. "Even a dog or a cat would be nice."

"Well, if it means that much to you, then we can go looking for a dog at the animal shelter on Saturday."

"How about a cat? That gray-and-white one that rubbed my leg would make a nice pet if it shows up here again."

"I'm sure that cat belongs to someone. What you need is a pet that doesn't already have a home."

"Yeah, maybe." Virginia was pleased that Earl cared enough to get her a pet—especially when he wasn't that fond of cats or dogs. Still a critter couldn't take the place of a human friend—at least not for her.

What continued to weigh heavily on Virginia's mind, though, were the binoculars she'd dropped in the weeds across the street. She needed to fetch them before Earl realized they were missing, so she wouldn't have to explain the whole stupid story of her spying on the Kings. Earl would be ready for his after-supper nap pretty quick. He already had his favorite TV show on, and it wouldn't be long till he was out like a light.

Virginia limped to the kitchen and poured herself some coffee. She had previously cleaned up everything from their meal. Despite the gnawing pain in her leg, she felt determined to sneak back over to the neighbors as soon as possible.

Virginia returned to the living room with the coffee in hand and took a seat again on the couch. Sure enough, like clockwork Earl reclined in his chair, engrossed in his show. *Wild horses couldn't rouse him out of that chair right now.* She covered her mouth to keep from snickering.

Earl glanced in her direction briefly but didn't say anything. He turned his head back to his favorite program, while Virginia waited for his nap to start.

As she looked through her magazine, her mind got to thinking that it was getting later and darker outside. She'd probably need a flashlight in order to see. Virginia hoped no one would catch her shining the beam of light around their driveway. *I just need to be careful, is all, and make sure I'm not seen.*

It didn't seem that long before Earl was slouched in his chair and snoring. He had mentioned during supper that he'd been busier than normal at work today and felt more tired than usual.

Now was Virginia's chance to take care of the task. She grabbed a flashlight, put on an old pair of shoes, and crept out the back door. It was dark, and she needed both hands to carry things, so again, she left her cane behind. *I'll get those binoculars quickly and will be back in no time.*

Virginia paused to wait for a passing car, then headed across the road. She shined a beam of light in front of her, and halfway up the Kings' driveway, she headed for the side she'd last had the field glasses.

"Okay, it was about here that I was crouched," Virginia whispered as she kept the light pointed directly at the ground. "Ah, that must be it." She caught sight of something shiny on the ground, but it turned out to be an aluminum can, so she gave it a kick. *Ouch! That was dumb.*

As Virginia kept searching, her leg started hurting again. *Come on—where are those binoculars? I'm pretty sure this is where I was before.* She continued to search, but was interrupted when a couple of horse and buggies pulled in. Virginia ducked behind a tree and waited until they passed.

What's the deal? Are they having more people coming to this event? Oh, yeah, I bet it's the second meal Jared and Amy had told us about.

Others followed in both cars and Amish rigs. Her nerves were about shot from hiding and waiting for the guests to quit flowing in. *Why did I decide to do this? If Earl wakes up and I'm not there, he'll come looking for me.*

When the coast was clear, Virginia did more hunting. After a few minutes, she bumped something hard with the toe of her shoe. At last she'd found the binoculars, so she leaned down and grabbed them up. Now the goal was to head back home quickly, but her leg throbbed even worse, making walking more difficult.

Virginia was almost to the mouth of the driveway, when another buggy came down the road. She moved into the shadows, out of sight, but managed to slip and fall. Her knee took the brunt of it, and when the rig went past, she clambered to her feet and, despite the pain, made a beeline straight for her house and in through the back door.

Breathing a sigh of relief, she put away the flashlight and carried the binoculars into the living room.

Earl sat up in his chair and looked at her. "What are you up to, woman?"

"What do you mean?" Virginia's heart pounded so hard she worried Earl might hear it from across the room.

"You're holding those field glasses. Are you spying on someone again?"

"I could be." She sat down on the couch.

He pointed at her knee. "What's that on your pant leg? It looks like dirt and grass stains."

"Um, well. . .maybe." She tried to brush it away.

"You red-headed spy. Were you outside in the dark, trying to see what our neighbors are doing?" He shook his head. "Woman, we need to find you a better hobby."

"I was bored, Earl, that's all."

"That is an understatement." He sat back and grabbed the TV remote.

Virginia was glad her husband didn't know any of the details about what had really happened. She still couldn't help feeling cheated by those Amish people. How could they have forgotten to send her an invite?

She crossed her arms and frowned. *I can't help being mad over the whole thing. I wish we lived somewhere else right now.*

Sylvia tried to relax and enjoy the evening, but she was tired from the long day and felt a headache coming on. She'd put Allen and Rachel to bed half an hour ago and wished she could join them, but didn't want to be impolite. After all, it wasn't every day they got to visit with Ezekiel and Michelle. Since they would be returning home the day after tomorrow, she wanted to spend as much time with them as possible.

"Would anyone like more cake or coffee?" she asked.

Mom yawned as she shook her head. "I'm too full and tired to eat anything more. How about the rest of you?"

"No thank you. I'm full too," Michelle said.

"Same here." Ezekiel looked at Henry. "I bet you've got room for some more cake. Am I right, *bissel* bruder?"

Henry blew out his breath in a noisy huff. "I ain't your little brother. I'm almost a man, and I work full time in the greenhouse and other places around here, so in my book, that makes me a man."

Mom lifted her hand toward Henry from across the room, where she sat in her rocker. "You're right, Son. You do the work of a man, and it's much appreciated."

Henry shrugged in response, then got up out of his chair. "Think I'll go up to my room." He hurried off before anyone could say goodnight.

Sylvia felt sorry for her brother. He had a lot on his young shoulders and had been cheated out of being able to fully enjoy his teenage years. She was thankful Dennis had come into their lives, because he'd filled a void in both her and Henry's lives.

She leaned back in her chair and closed her eyes, remembering how handsome Dennis had looked today. She'd invited him to stay awhile after everyone else went home, but he said he'd better go and tend to his dog and the horses. Dennis did promise to return in the morning to help clean up and put everything back together.

Her lips formed a smile. *What a kind and thoughtful person he is.*

"What are you grinning about, Sylvia?"

Her eyes snapped open at the sound of Ezekiel's question. "Oh, nothing much—just reflecting on what a nice day we all had." She wasn't about to admit that her focus had mostly been on Dennis. Quite likely her brother would start in with some teasing, which Sylvia didn't feel like dealing with right now.

"It was a good day, wasn't it?" Mom spoke up.

Michelle bobbed her head. "Yes, it was great. Amy and Jared make such a nice couple. Their faces glowed with the happiness they shared on their wedding day." She looked over at Ezekiel and smiled. "And I know exactly how it feels."

He grinned back at her. "Same here, Fraa. Being married to you has made me so happy."

"Michelle, you have been a welcome addition to our family," Mom said. "We all love and appreciate you."

Patches of pink erupted on Michelle's pretty face. "Danki, Belinda. I love and appreciate all of you too."

Sylvia's thoughts turned to Dennis. *Why can't Mom be as accepting toward him as she is with Michelle? Of course,* Sylvia reasoned, *it wasn't always that way. In the beginning of Ezekiel and Michelle's relationship, Mom made no bones about how absolutely she opposed their courtship. My sister-in-law had to prove herself before Mom would let her in. Hopefully Dennis will eventually do or say something that will cause my mamm to see him in a positive light.*

Around midnight, after Belinda and the others finally retired for the night, she lay in bed, unable to sleep. Too much excitement from the day might be part of the reason, but mostly Belinda couldn't turn off the thoughts swirling through her head concerning her family and the situations each of them was in. Her oldest son seemed content living in Clymer, New York, while she sensed his wife would rather they still lived in Strasburg. But Michelle had agreed to be content living away from the friends she'd made here and seemed supportive of her husband and his business aspirations.

Amy was now a married woman and would settle into a routine as Jared's wife. No doubt children would come in the next few years.

Henry still struggled with the turmoil of losing his father and brother. Even when he smiled and things seemed to be going along okay, Belinda sensed a battle raging inside her son.

Then there was Sylvia, who had made progress in accepting her husband's death, and now appeared to be looking to the future with another man.

Belinda reached back and clutched the edges of her pillow. *I just wish things weren't moving so fast between Sylvia and Dennis. I still don't think she knows enough about him to make a permanent commitment, and I hope Dennis doesn't push her into a marriage she's not ready for.*

A fiery orange shone through Belinda's bedroom window, putting an end to her musings. *Could the sun be coming up already? Could I have fallen asleep and not realized it?*

She pushed her covers aside and crawled out of bed, then padded over to the window and lifted the shade. She froze, rooted to the spot, before she let out an ear-piecing scream and ran from the room. "Fire! Our barn is ablaze!"

Chapter 41

Belinda stood with tears rolling down her cheeks, staring at what was left of their barn. She still couldn't believe it was gone. *Oh Vernon, you sure liked that old building, and so did I.*

She plucked a tissue from her sweater sleeve. In the light of day it looked worse than it had in the blackness of night.

After she'd seen the fire and called out to her family, they'd all rushed outside, and Henry dashed to the phone shed to call for help. In the meantime, Belinda, along with Ezekiel, Michelle, and Sylvia made every effort to put out the fire with the hose and buckets of water. By the time the fire trucks arrived, nearly half the barn was gone. Ezekiel and Henry had managed to get the horses out in time, and Henry's dog, as well as the barn cats had all escaped danger.

Belinda had left a message on Amy and Jared's voice mail, but she couldn't be sure when they might check it and learn the sad news. *Maybe they won't know until they get here.* Belinda gripped her face on both sides. *Oh my. . .what a shock it will be.*

Sylvia stepped up to Belinda and reached for her hand. "How could this have happened, Mom? Was the fire set on purpose, or could a gas lamp have gotten knocked over?"

Belinda shook her head. "The only evidence the firemen found was an empty pack of cigarettes outside the barn."

"Who do you know that smokes and might have been in our barn? Could it have been someone who attended the wedding yesterday?" Michelle asked. She'd been in and out of the house several times, checking on the baby, who lay sleeping in the living room in his playpen. The other children played outside by the house, where it was safe, while the adults stood around the site of the damage.

"I know of nobody specifically," Belinda responded, "but I suppose the empty package could have been from one of our guests." She crossed her arms as she looked at her youngest son, who appeared to be fidgeting. *What's going on with my boy?* Henry wasn't looking at her much, which seemed odd to her.

"Seth smokes," Henry finally spoke up.

"What was that, Son?" Belinda blinked.

"I said, 'Seth smokes.' Of course he wasn't at the wedding." His brows furrowed. "Seth has been in the barn before, and maybe he came here late last night after everyone else had gone home."

"Why would he show up that late and drop a pack of cigarettes outside the barn?" Ezekiel looked at Henry.

"He's mad at me right now."

"Oh? How come?" Ezekiel tilted his head.

Henry explained Seth's reasons, and Belinda quickly spoke up. "I don't believe Henry's friend would deliberately set our barn on fire. It was probably some kind of an accident that started the blaze." Belinda turned her head as Jared's horse and buggy entered the yard. He brought it to a halt at the hitching rail, then both he and Amy jumped out of the carriage.

"What in the world?" Amy's ashen face reflected her shock. "Did this fire happen during the night?" She pointed to what was left of the barn.

Belinda nodded. "We discovered it shortly after midnight."

"I wish you had notified us," Jared interjected. "We would have come over right away."

"I left a message on your voice mail but not until the fire had been put out," Belinda explained.

Jared pulled his fingers through the back of his hair. "Amy and I slept longer than we expected, and I forgot to check for messages before coming here."

Amy's cheeks colored a bit as she nodded. "Yesterday was a long, busy day, and we were pretty tired."

"And it turned out to be a long night." Ezekiel gazed down with his hands clasped behind his back.

"I hope this was not another act of—"

Belinda looked at Amy and put a finger to her lips. No way did she want Ezekiel or Michelle to know about any of the damage that had been done on the property.

"We'll need to have a work party to clean this mess up." Jared gestured to the debris. "And also build a new barn."

"We'll stay long enough to help clean things up and also come back to help with the reconstruction."

"There's no need for that," Belinda was quick to say. "I'm sure we'll have more than enough help when it's time to have a barn raising."

"Maybe so, but I wouldn't feel right about not being here for that, so I'll try to make sure it will happen." Ezekiel gave Belinda a hug. "You know, Mom, I'm still willing to move back here if you want me to."

She shook her head determinedly. "Not a chance! I won't ask you give up the life you have created for your family there in New York. Is that understood?"

He bobbed his head.

Belinda drew in a sharp breath. She hoped no one else would bring up any of the things that had previously been done to their property.

When Dennis showed up a short time later, Sylvia felt like running to him and throwing herself into his arms to release her pent-up emotions. But she held herself in check when he joined them in front of the devastation and stared with incredulity.

Sylvia noticed her mother's quick look of disapproval toward Dennis. Did she think he shouldn't have come to help out?

"What happened here?" He looked at Sylvia and placed his hand on her arm. "I came this morning to help clean up after the wedding but never expected to see something like this."

Sylvia didn't trust her voice to respond to his question, but she was saved from having to answer when Mom spoke up. "During the night, someone or something started the fire in the barn."

"Oh my!" His mouth opened slightly.

"We did our best to put the fire out," Ezekiel interjected, "but on our own we couldn't do much until the fire trucks arrived. Even then, they couldn't save much of the barn."

"I'm so sorry." Dennis's words were spoken in a kind, soothing tone.

Sylvia felt better with him being there, and it gave her heart pleasure, despite the charred remains that lay in front of them.

"We'll be having a clean-up frolic and later a new barn will be raised," Jared said. "I'll get the fellows who work for me to help put on the new roof when the structure's ready."

"I will help in any way I can." Dennis slipped his arm around Sylvia's waist. "Are you okay? Was anyone hurt?"

"I'm fine, and so is everyone else. Thank the Lord for that."

"Yes, indeed."

Sylvia felt comforted by Dennis's presence, and his arm around her waist made her feel protected and loved. *I'm certain that he loves me,* she thought. *I love him too. I hope as Mom sees how much Dennis cares about all of us that she'll change her mind about him.*

Sylvia looked up when that crazy mockingbird began to carry on. "Go away, you silly bird." Once again, she thought it seemed as if the feathered fowl had been mocking them.

Virginia stood at the living room window with her binoculars. She tried to see, but it was hard with the amount of trees and bushes covering part of their neighbors' property. She looked up their driveway intently. *Sure wish I could see into their yard better. I know where there's a good place to see things, but I'd have to go back to the spot where I was yesterday.*

"Are ya lookin' at the devastation caused from the fire across the road?"

She whirled around. "Earl Martin, do not sneak up on me like that."

"I wasn't sneaking. Just wandered into the room to get my empty mug from last night. And big surprise, I found you here snooping again."

"I wasn't snooping. Just wanted to get a better look at what we couldn't see last night when those blaring sirens woke us out of a sound sleep."

"I'm not sure how sound it was. You were rolling around in that bed like a mouse was crawling up your leg." Earl took the binoculars from her and set them on the end table by the couch. "If you can tear yourself away from the window long enough, I'd appreciate some breakfast before I leave for work."

Virginia's toes curled inside her slippers. "No problem, Earl. I'll get your breakfast going right now."

Once in the kitchen, she heated up the skillet. "Are you fine with some hash browns and eggs?" she called.

"Yeah, that sounds good. Do we have any ketchup for the potatoes?"

Virginia opened the refrigerator and grabbed the bottle, along with a carton of eggs. "Yep, there's plenty of ketchup," she hollered back.

"Good deal!"

While Earl showered and got dressed for work, Virginia made their breakfast and had it warming in the oven. She then returned to the living room with a hot cup of coffee, to which she'd added her fancy creamer.

As she waited for her husband to come down the hall, her thoughts took her down a negative path. *If we'd only gotten an invite to that wedding, Stella would be here with me. She and I would be doing something fun today, like going out to lunch and shopping for clothes.*

When Virginia heard Earl coming, she headed back to the kitchen and pulled the food from the oven.

"Breakfast smells good, and I can't wait to eat." Earl poured some coffee and took a seat at the table.

She set the skillet and the small casserole dish on potholders. "We'd better get started while the food is hot."

"I'm ready to eat. I'll go ahead and dish up."

Virginia waited for him before helping herself. "Guess I'll do some bird-watching today."

Earl chuckled. "I'm sure you will, except I should remind you that birds don't wear bonnets or straw hats. If you really want to know what happened, go on over there and ask. I'd go myself if I didn't have to head for work in a few minutes."

"Very funny. You don't have to believe me, but I'm gonna look for birds today." Virginia spooned some eggs and hash browns on her plate.

As Earl ate his food, Virginia nibbled on the hash browns and stared out the window. After her husband left, she'd be bored and lonely. It was too bad they had a fire last night, but she couldn't help feeling jilted by those Amish folks.

Maybe they think they're better than me. She grimaced. *I can't believe I fell for Jared's promise of an invite to their wedding when we met at Diener's.*

"What's got your smile turned upside-down? You're not still upset about not going to that wedding, are you?"

"Of course I am. Everything would've been perfect if we'd received an invitation and gone across the street for Jared and Amy's big day. Stella would have loved it. That much I know." Virginia took a drink of coffee.

"They have a teenage boy over there, you know. I'm sure there'll be a wedding for him sometime in the future. Maybe we'll get invited to that." Earl stood and carried his dishes to the sink.

Virginia wasn't impressed with that bit of news. Mrs. King's son might wait years to get hitched, and there was no guarantee that they'd get an invitation to his wedding either.

I should feel bad about those people's barn burning, but they don't care a hoot about me, so why should I care about them?

Amy and Jared walked together around the rubble. Her heart sank while looking at the remains of the old barn that once stood large and tall on her parents' property. Some recognizable things lay among the black-ened remains, but none of it looked usable. Amy felt the burden of it all. If she'd been here at the house last night, she could have helped out.

"I'm sorry about what happened to your family's barn," Jared said.

"So am I, but I can't help feeling bad that I wasn't here instead of—"

"Instead of where? Being with me at our new place?" Jared's tone had an edge to it.

"Oh, come on now, Jared. That's not what I meant."

"It sounded like it to me." He took off his hat and fanned his face with the brim. "Do you really think you could've done something to prevent this from happening or made it better somehow?"

"I could have tried to do something." Amy's hand went to her hip.

He frowned. "It still would have turned out like this."

They stood silently for a few moments. The sunshine felt nice as it shone down upon them. Amy's family had headed off in the direction of the large tents that needed to be dismantled and ready to be returned to the place where they'd rented them.

Amy's arm fell to her side as she turned to face Jared. "I just feel bad for not being here to help out is all—not because I was with you." She looked up at him. "I love you, Jared."

"I love you too." He grinned and let out a chuckle.

"What's so funny?"

"I do believe we've just had our first tiff."

Amy smiled and laughed too. "Jah, I guess we did."

"We'd better go help the others now, don't you agree?"

"Most certainly." Amy walked alongside Jared. *I'm sure there will be more misunderstandings in our marriage, but we'll talk them through, just like we did now. How thankful I am for such a loving husband. I surely hope my sister finds that kind of happiness with the man she loves.*

Chapter 42

Holding her binoculars in front of her face, Virginia stood poised at the living room window. She shook her head in disgust as the steady *clippity-clop, clippity-clop* pounded the pavement in front of her house. Every single one of those horses and buggies turned up the Kings' driveway. Earl had said he'd talked to Belinda's teenage son yesterday and learned they'd be having a new barn built today. He'd also stated that many from their community would be at the event, so the constant flow of buggy traffic was no surprise. That didn't make it any easier to deal with.

Virginia's nerves were on edge, and she couldn't wait for Earl to leave for work so she could light up a cigarette. Although she'd promised to give up smoking, Virginia couldn't seem to help herself. Her habit was a strong crutch, and she wasn't sure she could quit. Her life now was easy compared to how it used to be during her first marriage, but since coming to Amish country, she'd been uptight most of the time. Earl had told her once that her aversion to living here made no sense, yet his statement had done nothing to change the way Virginia felt. If she'd known what it would be like before moving here, she never would have agreed to leave Chicago. At least there, she had Stella to talk to. Now all she had was Goldie, the fluffy orange cat she'd brought home from the animal shelter a week ago.

Virginia continued to watch the activity across the road. *I would love to see what's happening even better over there. It's too bad the fire didn't burn some of those trees down, so I could see into their whole yard.*

"Ah-hem." Earl cleared his throat. "Since I don't detect any pleasant aromas coming from the kitchen, I can only assume that breakfast has not been started."

She lowered the binoculars and turned to face him. "It's still early. Figured I had plenty of time to start breakfast."

"Well, you don't. I told you last night that the boss called a special meeting at work this morning, and I need to go soon."

"Sorry. I must've forgot. I'll get something going now. Maybe I've got enough pancake mix to make some flapjacks."

He shook his head. "Don't bother. I'll pick up a doughnut and coffee on the way to Lancaster." Earl gestured toward the window. "I hope you can find something meaningful to do with your time and don't spend the whole day staring out the front window. Gazing through those field glasses is not going to change the fact that our neighbors are Amish and they still live across the road."

She scrunched up her face. "That's not funny, Earl."

"It may not be funny, but it's a fact." He stepped up to Virginia and kissed her cheek. "Have a nice day, dear, and don't forget to feed the cat."

"Yeah, you have a good day too." She reached down and petted Goldie's head. *Well, at least I'm not alone anymore.*

As soon as Virginia heard the back door open and shut, she picked up the binoculars and resumed her snooping. *If I keep watching long enough, I might see something that will pique my interest.*

Belinda stood on the front porch of her home, watching and listening to the work going on in the yard. The soon-to-be structure was currently just a concrete-block foundation, but it wouldn't be long before a new barn stood tall. Men had gathered into small groups, and after a few minutes, those who'd come to work broke up and everybody found a job to do. Soon, the air was filled with the pounding of hammers, along with the hum of saws cutting wood.

Belinda was awed by the large number of people from their community who had come to help out. Monroe Esh was among them. Herschel Fisher came even though he was from outside their church district. Jared arrived with his crew of roofers. Dennis was also among the men who were already working up a sweat. Belinda noticed that he would glance back at the house from time to time—no doubt hoping to catch a glimpse of Sylvia. Both of Belinda's daughters would be inside most of the day, getting a noon meal ready for the workers. Other women from their community had also come here today to help cook and serve the men.

Belinda looked toward the road and heaved a sigh. Too bad Ezekiel couldn't be here. Michelle had come down with a nasty flu bug, and even though one of his wife's friends had offered to help out, he didn't want to leave her when she wasn't feeling well. Belinda had assured her son that they would have plenty of help today and reminded him that his place was with his family. He'd sounded relieved when she'd assured him that she'd let him know how things went once the new barn was done.

"Sure is a good turnout today, jah?" Jared grinned at Dennis as they worked alongside each other.

Dennis nodded. *Sylvia's mamm is still giving me the cold shoulder, though. I said, "Hello, Mrs. King" to her this morning, and she barely responded to my greeting.* He let out a huff. *Sure wish I knew how to break the ice with her so we could become friends. Even with Sylvia's reassurances that eventually her mother will come to like me, I have my doubts.*

"You've been awfully quiet this morning. Is everything okay?"

"Let's just say they're not the way I'd like them to be." Dennis's breaths came faster as he continued to hammer.

"Hey, slow down. There's no need to rush." Jared put his hand on Dennis's shoulder. "If there's something bothering you, it might help if you get it off your chest."

Dennis glanced at the men working nearby. "I'd rather not talk about it right now."

"Then let's take a break. We've been working hard, and sitting for a few minutes with some cold water to drink will help." Jared pointed to the table that had been set up in the yard with cups and glasses for water and coffee.

"Okay, sure." Dennis set his tools aside and joined Jared at the table. After they'd poured water into their paper cups, they walked around to the side of the house and took a seat on a wooden bench.

"So what's on your mind?" Jared asked.

Dennis swiped a hand across his sweaty forehead. "I think it would be better if I wasn't courting Sylvia anymore."

Jared's eyes widened. "How come?"

"Her mudder doesn't like me, and I don't want to come between Belinda and Sylvia." Dennis paused and took a drink. "And then there's my mamm. She keeps saying that she wants me to get married, but I need to make sure Sylvia's the right woman and that I shouldn't rush into things."

"What are you going to do?"

Dennis shrugged. "I don't know. My head tells me the right thing to do is break things off with Sylvia, and. . ." His voice trailed off. There was no point in talking about this, because he couldn't make Belinda like him, no matter how hard he tried. He gulped down the last of his water and stood. "Guess we need to get back to work."

Jared nodded. "If you need to talk about this again, I'll listen and offer my advice if needed. I'll also be praying for your situation. I'm sure this can't be easy, but take heart—the Lord can work out problems, no matter how big they seem."

"Danki." Dennis tossed his paper cup in the trash and hurried back to the construction site. Putting his tool pouch back on, he looked around at the other busy men. *I shouldn't have opened my big mouth and spilled some of my personal business to Jared. And then he goes and brings up the Lord. I've felt sometimes like the heavenly Father has forgotten about me since I've refused to forgive my uncle for accidently shooting my daed. Thought all I needed was a happy life with the woman I love. I'm beginning to realize I can never find true happiness until I've learned to forgive.* He closed his eyes briefly. *Lord, please help me to do that and give me a sense of peace. I'm sorry for holding a grudge against Uncle Ben. Please forgive me for that. I'll give my uncle a call as soon as I can and make things right with him.*

Sylvia's hand felt tired from cutting so many sliced cucumbers, carrots, and celery sticks to go with the ranch dip one of the ladies had brought this morning. Hearing voices outside the house, she dried her hands and stepped up near the open doorway, where she caught sight of Jared and Dennis engaged in conversation.

Her ears perked up when she heard her name mentioned and listened to what else was said. Sylvia stood frozen, with her hands clenched at her sides. She had lost interest in going outside to see if more water and coffee was needed. Dennis was going to break up with her, and there was nothing she could do about it.

It's Mom's fault, she fumed inwardly. *If she'd only accept the fact that I'm in love with Dennis and welcomed him as she did Jared, he would not be having second thoughts about us.*

The more Sylvia thought about it, the more frustrated she became. *I need to talk to Mom about this when there's no one else around and make her see how miserable I'd be if Dennis broke things off with me. She wouldn't have liked it if her mother had tried to come between her and Dad when they were courting. Surely she must remember what it was like to fall in love and look forward to a promise of marriage. As much as she loved Dad, she couldn't have forgotten it by now.*

Fighting tears that threatened to spill over, Sylvia turned and went to the living room to check on Allen and Rachel. She found Allen playing with some toys by himself.

"Where's your sister?" Sylvia asked in Pennsylvania Dutch.

Allen shook his head. "Don't know."

Thinking her daughter may have gone to her room, Sylvia headed up the stairs. The door to Rachel's bedroom was open, and when Sylvia walked in, she found the room empty. *That's strange. I wonder where the little rascal could be.*

Sylvia went quickly to each room on the upper level and checked all of them thoroughly, calling her daughter's name. At the end of her search on the second floor, it was apparent that her daughter wasn't there.

She went back downstairs and searched every room in the house, calling Rachel's name. When she entered the kitchen and asked her mother if she'd seen Rachel, Mom shook her head. "I thought she was playing with Allen in the other room."

"No, she's not, and I can't find her anywhere in the house."

"We'd better check outside." Mom dried her hands on a towel, told the other women she'd be back soon, and followed Sylvia out the back door.

They both ran around the yard calling Rachel's name. It was hard to hear if she'd answered them or not, because of the amount of noise coming from the workers. They also checked the greenhouse to see if she might have found an open door and gone inside. But there was no sign of the little girl there either.

"I'm really worried." Sylvia clutched the hem of her apron. "What if we can't find her? What if she left the yard and is walking down the road somewhere all alone?"

Mom caught hold of Sylvia's hand. "Let's go up to the worksite and see if any of the men have seen Rachel."

"Jah. That's what we should do all right."

When they approached the new barn that was taking shape, Sylvia asked every person she met if they'd seen her daughter.

One of the English men, whom Sylvia didn't recognize, said he'd seen a young girl who fit Rachel's description talking with a ragged-looking English woman.

"Where are they now?" Sylvia questioned.

The man shrugged, then pointed toward the driveway entrance. "They walked out of the yard about an hour ago. The woman she was with had gray hair, walked stooped over, and wore tattered-looking, baggy clothes."

"Why, that sounds like Maude." Mom's brows drew together. "Oh my! Do you think she kidnapped Rachel?"

Sylvia covered her mouth, trying to gain control of her swirling emotions. *No, no, no. . .this can't be happening! That woman has taken other things from our yard. Could she possibly have stolen my precious little girl?*

Chapter 43

"What's going on?" Amy asked, rushing up to Sylvia and their mother. "I heard you calling for Rachel."

Sylvia's voice cracked. "She's missing, and a man over there said he saw her heading out of the yard with Maude." She shivered. "At least we think it was her. I'm so afraid for my daughter. I just want her back in my arms."

Sylvia's mother stepped right over and put an arm around her. "It'll be okay. We'll get her back. You'll see."

Amy's mouth opened wide. "Oh dear. Do you think Maude may have taken Rachel to that old shack she lives in?"

"I don't know, but I aim to find out. I'm going there right now."

"Someone should go with you," Mom put in.

"I'll go."

Sylvia turned and saw Dennis and Jared walking toward them at a fast pace.

"Amy and I can go one way down the road, while you and Dennis go the other way."

"Maybe we should call the sheriff." Mom's chin quivered as she released her embrace of Sylvia.

Sylvia shook her head firmly. "Not until we see if we can find her first."

"Sylvia's right." Dennis looked at Mom and spoke softly. "Give us an hour, and if we aren't back with Rachel by then, I'll call the sheriff myself." He reached into his pocket and pulled out his cell phone.

Mom nodded. "I'll be praying."

"Same here." Sylvia prayed silently, *Lord, please let my little girl be safe. Allow us to bring Rachel safely home, and forgive me for the lack of faith I've had in You. I trust You, Lord, and I believe You will take care of my daughter.*

Dennis and Sylvia hurried out of the yard and turned right at the end of the driveway, while Jared and Amy went left. About halfway to Maude's place, Sylvia paused to catch her breath.

"I don't know what I'd do if something happened to my precious little girl. Rachel and Allen mean the world to me, and I can't imagine my life without either of them."

"We'll find her." Dennis's tone was reassuring. "I promise, we won't return without Rachel."

Sylvia didn't see how he could be so sure, but she'd prayed for her daughter's safety and needed to trust God to answer that prayer.

They started walking fast again, and a short time later, Sylvia spotted a rundown shack, not much bigger than some people's chicken coops. "There it is." She pointed with an unsteady hand at the dilapidated shanty. "That's where Maude lives."

Dennis's forehead wrinkled as he squinted at the wooden hovel. "Seriously?"

She nodded as her pace kept up with his until they reached the border of Maude's overgrown yard. Dennis led the way on a worn path. Sylvia didn't like the eerie feeling this place gave her. It was so neglected, and it didn't seem possible that anyone could actually live here.

"How does she survive the winters in there?"

"I believe Maude goes someplace else during the colder months. We've never seen her during the wintertime."

They approached the small building cautiously, and Sylvia reached out with a trembling hand to knock on the door. When no one answered, Dennis pushed the squeaky door open. There sat Maude and Rachel at a small table with wobbly legs, eating cookies.

In addition to the table and two folding chairs, the sparsely-furnished cabin had only an old cot with a faded, torn quilt; an antiquated woodstove; a dry-sink; and two unpainted boards used for shelving. A beat-up looking suitcase sat at the foot of the cot. Sylvia also noticed a pile of things on the floor that Maude had no doubt stolen from people in their neighborhood, including a watering can like the one that went missing last year outside the greenhouse.

Before Sylvia had a chance to say anything, Dennis bent down and lifted Rachel from the chair. She looked up at him with wide eyes, called him, "*Daadi*," and then turned her head in Sylvia's direction. "*Kichlin* is gut."

"Jah, I'm sure the cookies are good, but it's time for us to go home." Sylvia glanced in Maude's direction. "It's wrong to take things or people that don't belong to you, Maude. We were worried about my little girl." Sylvia spoke quietly, in a gentle tone. She wasn't sure what Maude might be capable of doing and didn't want to rile the woman.

Maude mumbled something Sylvia didn't understand, and then the old woman spoke again, more clearly. "Rachel's a pretty girl. We were havin' a tea party but without the tea."

Sylvia tried to hold it together as she talked more with Maude, and a feeling of compassion filled her soul. "From now on if you want to spend time with Rachel, you will need to ask me first. Maybe sometime we can all have a tea party with cookies at the picnic table in my mother's yard. Would you like that, Maude?"

The elderly woman nodded her head and bid them goodbye.

As Sylvia and Dennis walked back to the house, with Rachel clinging to Dennis's neck, Sylvia blurted out a question that was heavy on her mind. "I heard you talking earlier with Jared. Are you planning to break things off with me?"

He stopped walking and turned to face her. "I have been thinking about it because your mamm doesn't approve of me. But I don't think we should talk about this right now, do you?" He reached up and touched Rachel's arm, still held firmly around his neck.

"You're right. I don't know what I was thinking. I need to take my daughter home and get her cleaned up. Her face and hands are smeared with chocolate from the iced cookies she and Maude were eating." Sylvia wondered if the cookies had been stolen from someone's home or perhaps a store in Strasburg. She kept that thought to herself, however. Sylvia had already said too much in front of her young daughter. Even though Rachel was still quite young, there was no telling how much she understood—especially when they spoke in Pennsylvania Dutch, as they had since leaving Maude's shack.

When they arrived home, Sylvia's mother ran out to greet them. "Ach, I'm so relieved that you found her. Where was our precious Rachel?"

"She was with Maude in her little shack, but I'll explain later. I don't think Rachel was frightened by her, but she clung tightly to Dennis the whole way home. Even called him Daadi when we found her."

Mom reached out and stroked Rachel's back. "I'm so glad to see that she's okay." She looked at Dennis with a sincere expression. "Danki for helping Sylvia find her daughter."

"You're welcome. When I heard that she was missing, all I could think about was getting her back. Rachel is a special child, and I love her and Allen as if they were my own."

Amy came out of the house and clapped her hands when she saw Rachel. "I'm so glad you found her. Jared and I looked and called, and when we saw no sign of her, we came back here to wait for you, hoping you'd had success." She hugged Sylvia. "Where did you find her?"

"In Maude's shanty."

Amy blinked rapidly. "What was she doing there?"

Sylvia explained the details, including what she'd said to Maude before they came home.

"We're going to have to watch that woman more closely," Mom said. "Stealing cookies and produce from our garden is one thing, but taking a child is another matter—one that could have involved the sheriff."

"We could still call him," Amy asserted. "It's possible that Maude's the one responsible for the vandalism here and maybe even the fire. I personally think she should be investigated."

"No way! We are not going to involve the sheriff in that matter." Mom shook her head vigorously.

Sylvia put her finger to her lips. "Can we talk about this later? Rachel needs to get cleaned up and fed a nourishing lunch." She looked at Dennis. "Maybe when I come back out, we can finish our talk."

"I can take her inside and see to her needs," Amy offered.

"Okay, thank you."

When Amy reached for Rachel, the child went willingly into her arms. Sylvia watched with gratitude as her sister carried Rachel into the house. She closed her eyes briefly. *Thank You, Lord, for helping me and Dennis find my daughter, and Thank You for my kind, loving family.*

"It won't be long before we'll need to feed our helpers who are working so hard on the new barn. I should get back to my kitchen duties and helping the other women soon," Mom said. "But before I go, there's something I'd like to say to Dennis." She looked directly at him. "I am sorry for being so cold to you all these months. I. . .I didn't think you were the right man for Sylvia, but I can see now that I was wrong." She paused and swiped at the tears trickling down her flushed cheeks. "My daughter loves you, and I can see that her daughter does too. I give you my full blessing to court Sylvia, and if the two of you decide someday to get married, you'll have my blessing for that too."

Dennis's face broke into a wide smile. "Thank you, Belinda. What you have said means a lot to me." He looked at Sylvia's shining eyes, then back at her mother. "I love your daughter very much, and if she'll have me, after an appropriate time and once I'm sure I can support her and the children, I will make a formal proposal of marriage."

"And my answer will be yes." Sylvia smiled as she reached for Dennis's hand, not caring in the least who might be witnessing her act of love.

A bird twittered from a nearby tree branch, and Sylvia looked up and smiled. *Go ahead, little mockingbird, sing your song.* She no longer felt as if the bird mocked her. Instead, Sylvia simply enjoyed the bird's melodic song as she and Dennis held hands. She didn't know what might lie ahead, but if they held tight to their faith and trusted in God, she felt confident that He would see them through anything they had to face in the days ahead.

Sylvia thought of Psalm 30:5, the Bible verse she'd read last night: "Weeping may endure for a night, but joy cometh in the morning." *Thank You, Lord, for restoring my faith and filling my heart with joy again.*

Recipe for Sylvia's Cherry Melt-Away Bars

2 cups flour

2 eggs, separated

1½ cups sugar, divided

1 cup margarine or butter

2 (21 ounce) cans or
  1 quart cherry pie filling

Dash of cream of tartar

1 teaspoon vanilla

½ cup chopped walnuts

Preheat oven to 350 degrees. Cream together flour, egg yolks, 1 cup sugar, and margarine. Press into 9x13-inch pan. Spread pie filling on crust. Beat egg whites with cream of tartar until very stiff. Gradually beat in ½ cup sugar and vanilla. Spread over pie filling. Sprinkle with nuts. Bake for 30 to 35 minutes. Cut into bars once sufficiently cooled.

Discussion Questions

1. Sylvia became afraid to drive a horse and buggy after the accident that killed her husband, father, and brother. She also didn't go out or socialize much during the first year after their deaths. Do you think that was a normal reaction? Would you react in a similar way and not drive again because of an accident that happened to a family member or close friend?

2. Sylvia and her younger brother, Henry, were angry at God for the accident, and even after a year, it had affected their faith. Why were their reactions so different from their mother's and other siblings? Some went to God for comfort, while others turned their backs on Him. Which would you do?

3. Sylvia rented her house to Dennis Weaver, a man she didn't know and who gave her no references. Do you think that was wise? Would you rent your home to a total stranger?

4. Belinda started trying to control her children's lives—especially Sylvia's. Why do you think she did this?

5. The Kings' neighbor, Virginia, didn't want to connect with the Amish family. She thought they were strange and that she had nothing in common with them. Have you ever felt reluctant to reach out to someone who is different from you? What were your reasons?

6. Belinda couldn't seem to say anything nice about Dennis. Why do you think she was negative toward him? Could she have been jealous of Sylvia or simply overly protective? Should she have been happy that her daughter found a new friend and was getting out of the house more?

7. Dennis struggled with commitment and with forgiveness toward the person responsible for his father's death. What do you think caused his lack of commitment and his inability to forgive?

8. Virginia was stressed over not getting an invitation to Amy and Jared's wedding, so much that she started smoking again. Why was going to the wedding so important to her?

9. Sylvia and Dennis's relationship grew quickly. Do you think she should have waited longer to get involved with a man who could possibly become her husband?

10. With all the trouble at the greenhouse and then the barn fire, do you think Belinda should have called the sheriff? Why do you think she didn't?

11. Was it right for Belinda to hide their problems from her oldest son, Ezekiel? Was her reason for doing it justified?

12. Amish weddings are not the same as English weddings. Based on what you read in this story, how are they different? Have you ever attended an Amish wedding? If so, what were your thoughts?

13. When Sylvia's youngest daughter disappeared, do you think the elderly woman, Maude, thought she was doing something wrong? Did you agree with the way Sylvia handled it? Do you know someone like Maude? How would you reach out to her?

14. Were there any scriptures or spiritual insights in this book that spoke to your heart or helped you in some way?

15. Like Sylvia and her family, every person is faced at one time or another with difficult situations. What are some things we can do to strengthen our faith when it becomes weak due to a hardship or loss we have faced? How can we help someone who has suffered a loss and seems to have lost their faith?

Amish Greenhouse Mystery
Book 3

The
ROBIN'S
GREETING

Chapter 1

Strasburg, Pennsylvania

Belinda. . .Belinda. . .Belinda. . .

She opened her eyes, still heavy with sleep, sure that the voice she'd heard was her beloved husband, Vernon, calling out to her. But that couldn't be. He'd been gone nearly two years—killed in a tragic accident that had also taken the lives of her son Abe and son-in-law, Toby. The voice Belinda heard must have been a dream, or just the howling November wind outside her bedroom window.

Belinda lay there, with the quilt on her bed pulled up to her chin. The lovely covering with the Wedding Ring pattern had been made by her mother and given to Belinda and Vernon the day they'd gotten married. To her, it was a priceless treasure.

Belinda remained still as she reminisced about days gone by. While there'd been some tough times over the years, nothing she had faced compared to the agony of losing three family members in the same day. Her struggles had increased with the responsibility of running the greenhouse without Vernon's help. Belinda didn't know what she would have done without the help of her daughters and teenage son. They'd needed the greenhouse for financial support, and even more they'd needed each other for emotional support.

Now that Amy was married to Jared, and Sylvia was in a relationship with Dennis, things had changed once again. Belinda was okay with all of that. What she wasn't okay with was the senseless vandalism on her property, most recently the barn. Seeing the building her husband built go up in flames had pierced her heart like a dagger. No one knew how the fire had started. It may have been arson, but if someone had been smoking in or near the barn, the fire could have been an accident.

Unable to resume her sleep, Belinda fluffed her pillows and sat up in bed. How grateful she was for all the help they'd received a few weeks ago when they built a replacement barn. English and Amish friends, neighbors, and family members came together and gave of their time. Now Belinda and her family were ready to begin again, with the hope and prayer that things would settle down and there'd be no more vandalism or tragedy. Given all the needless attacks they'd experienced, Belinda felt certain someone wanted to put them out of business, and perhaps do enough harmful things so Belinda would become discouraged and move somewhere else.

She swiped her tongue across her parched lips and swallowed. At one time, Belinda had believed that her youngest son might have been responsible for the vandalism that had occurred in and around the greenhouse. After his father and brother died, Henry had let it be known that he did not want to take over the beekeeping job Abe used to do. Nor did Henry wish to help in the greenhouse. But he'd assured Belinda that he was not responsible for any of the destruction to their property. She had no reason to doubt him. Henry had proved himself many times with all the help he'd done around here. If the greenhouse folded, Henry would have as much to lose as Belinda and her daughters, since it was the sole means of their livelihood.

Belinda's eldest son, Ezekiel, a minister who lived in Clymer, New York, had offered to give up his bee-raising supply business and move back to Strasburg to help in the greenhouse. But Belinda insisted that he and his family stay put in the community that had become their home.

Bringing her thoughts to a halt, she turned on the battery-operated light resting on the nightstand beside her bed and looked at the alarm clock. It was almost 5:00 a.m. She turned off the alarm, pulled the covers back, and climbed out of bed. It was time to begin another day.

When Belinda entered the kitchen, she found her eldest daughter in front of the stove. The light from the gas lamp hanging on a ceiling hook illuminated the room, and except for the whistle of the wind outside, all was quiet.

"*Guder mariye*, Sylvia." Belinda placed a hand on her daughter's shoulder. "You're up early this morning."

"Good morning, Mom." Sylvia turned the propane gas burner on under the tea kettle. "The howling wind woke me, and I couldn't get back to sleep."

Belinda nodded. "Same here." She moved across the room and lifted the dark green shade that covered the kitchen window. It would be another hour or so before the light of day replaced the darkness in their yard.

Once the water heated, Sylvia made a small pot of tea. "Why don't we get out our favorite teacups and sit until it's time to fix breakfast?" she suggested.

"Good idea. A cup of warm tea is what I need right now." Belinda got out the cups and joined Sylvia at the table. A few minutes later, she poured tea for both of them. It was nice to have some uninterrupted time with her daughter. With Belinda running the greenhouse, and Sylvia taking care of her two children, they didn't get many moments alone.

"It's hard to believe November is here already," Sylvia commented. "Seems like just yesterday when Amy and Jared got married."

Belinda smiled. "Thanksgiving will be here in a few weeks, and next thing we know, it'll be Christmas."

"*Jah.* Too bad Ezekiel and his family won't be coming down for Christmas like they did last year."

"But we're all planning to go to their place to celebrate the holiday this year, and that will be nice."

Sylvia picked up her spoon and swirled the amber liquid in her cup. "I had hoped they would come here instead."

"How come? I figured you and the *kinner* would enjoy getting out of Strasburg for a few days and seeing where your brother lives."

Sylvia drank some tea and blotted her lips with a napkin. "At first I wanted to go, but now that I'm seeing Dennis regularly, I'll feel bad about leaving him to celebrate the holiday alone."

"I would think he'd want to spend Christmas with his mother and siblings."

"I'm sure he would enjoy that, but if Dennis leaves the area for the holiday, he will have to get someone to watch his dog, not to mention the horses he's recently bought for breeding purposes."

Belinda tipped her head. "So what are you saying, Daughter—that you would like to stay here so you can spend the holiday with Dennis and cook him Christmas dinner?"

Sylvia smiled wistfully. "If the children and I went to New York with you, I wouldn't enjoy myself knowing Dennis was all by himself."

Belinda stared into her cup of tea, evaluating her daughter's last statement. She couldn't blame Sylvia for wanting to be with Dennis, especially since they were courting. She had a hunch that it wouldn't be long before Dennis asked Sylvia to marry him. Things would surely be different around here, if and when that event occurred. Sylvia, along with her daughter, Rachel, and son, Allen, had been living with Belinda since the tragic accident that took her husband's life. It was hard to think of how things would be if they moved out of the house to begin a new life with Dennis Weaver.

"Would you mind if the children and I don't go with you to Ezekiel's for Christmas?"

Sylvia's question pushed Belinda's thoughts aside. "If you feel you should stay here to spend Christmas with Dennis, it's fine with me. I'm sure Ezekiel and Michelle will be disappointed, but they'll also understand." The words didn't come easy for Belinda, but it was the correct thing to say. She had no right to interfere in Sylvia and Dennis's relationship. If Belinda were in her daughter's place, she'd no doubt make the same choice.

"*Danki*, Mom, for understanding." Sylvia took another sip of tea.

The two women spent the next hour talking about other things. When a ray of sun shone through the kitchen window, Belinda got up. "Guess we ought to get busy and fix breakfast before the kinner wake up." She glanced toward the hallway door. "I'm surprised Henry isn't up already and outside doing his morning chores."

"He came in pretty late last night, after spending time with some of his friends. Maybe he forgot to set the alarm and overslept."

"That could be." Belinda glanced at the clock on the far wall. "I would call up the stairs to see if he's up, but I don't want to wake your children."

"If you like, I'll go upstairs and knock on his door. It's about time to get Rachel and Allen up anyway."

"That might be a good idea," Belinda said. "He needs to get the chores done so we can eat breakfast and get the greenhouse open on time."

After Sylvia left the room, Belinda cleared the table and put their cups in the sink. As she glanced out the window, she was taken by surprise when a male robin flew out of a tree in the yard and bumped the kitchen window. Believing it was just a fluke, and that the bird would return to the tree, Belinda merely shrugged and turned on the water. She'd no more than filled each cup when the robin was back again. This time he bumped the window a little harder.

Belinda shook her head. "What in the world?" She assumed with cooler weather setting in, most of the robins in their yard would have moved on to warmer territory by now.

As Belinda stood watching, the robin kept hitting the window, then returning to the tree.

She shook her head. "What a silly *voggel*."

"What bird are you talking about?" Henry asked when he sauntered into the room.

"That one." Belinda pointed to the robin as it made another pass at the window. "The crazy thing acts like it wants to get into our house."

"He probably sees his reflection in the window and thinks it's another bird." Henry moved closer to the window and looked out.

"Well, I can think of a better way to be greeted this morning than watching that poor bird beat himself up." Belinda rolled her eyes. "Wouldn't you think with the colder weather we've been having that Mr. Robin would have moved on to a warmer climate by now?"

Henry shook his head. "Not necessarily, Mom. Robins can withstand very cold temperatures. It's not that unusual to see some of 'em in the wintertime, although they survive off a different kind of food than the worms and seeds they eat during the warmer months," he added.

Belinda stared at Henry with her mouth slightly open. "I had no idea you knew that much about robins. How'd you gain such wisdom?"

With a single raised eyebrow, he cocked his head. "Do I have to remind you that I've been bird-watching for some time, not to mention reading up in that bird book of mine. I can tell you a lot more about robins if you're interested."

"Maybe another time." Belinda pointed to Henry's hat and jacket, hanging on a wall peg near the back door. "Right now you need to get out to the barn to do your chores, and I need to get breakfast ready so we can eat when you come back in."

"Jah. I'll go right now." Henry slipped into his jacket and slapped the straw hat on his head. Once the weather got colder, he'd no doubt wear his knitted stocking cap instead.

Henry had no more than gone out the door when the robin smacked against the window again.

Belinda reached up and pulled the shade down. If the crazy bird was determined to keep that up, at least she didn't have to watch it.

🐦

After Sylvia got Rachel in her high chair and Allen on a booster seat, she joined Belinda and Henry at the kitchen table. Belinda took hold of her grandson's hand as they all bowed their heads for silent prayer.

Heavenly Father, she prayed, *please guide and direct our lives today. We ask that You would provide for our needs and help us to set a good example for others. Bless this food and bless all who are seated at my table. In Jesus' name I ask it. Amen.*

Once Sylvia and Henry raised their heads and opened their eyes, Belinda forked a pancake from the platter in front of her and put it on Allen's plate. After passing the platter on to Henry, she poured a small amount of maple syrup over Allen's pancake.

The young boy looked over at her and grinned. *"Gut pannekuche."*

"Jah," she replied, "The pancakes are good."

"Think I'll have some *hunnich* on mine instead of *sirrop.*" Henry passed the bottle of syrup to Sylvia and reached for the jar of honey. "Since I work so hard at beekeeping, I deserve the fruits of my labor."

Belinda couldn't argue with that. In spite of the fact that beekeeping was not her son's favorite thing to do, he'd been expected to take over the job after his older brother was killed. He still complained about it at times, but not as much as he had at first.

As they ate their meal, the conversation centered mostly around the sale they would be having at the greenhouse next week. In addition to fall plants and flowers, many other things they sold in the greenhouse, like honey, jam, solar lights, and several outdoor decorative items, would be on sale. Belinda hoped they would do well and make enough to put some money away for the winter months when the greenhouse would be closed.

They were getting close to finishing their meal when a knock sounded on the back door. Belinda went to answer it. Monroe Esh stood on the porch, holding a bakery box.

"I brought you some glazed *faasnachtkuche*." He grinned and held the box out to her. "Figured you might like them for breakfast."

"It was kind of you to think of us, but we're already in the middle of eating." Belinda paused, unable to maintain eye contact with this attractive fifty-two-year-old Amish man. When they had been teenagers, Monroe had been interested in Belinda. She'd been flattered by his attention but chose Vernon instead. Monroe had moved away from Strasburg and returned to the area several months ago. He had been coming around ever since, offering to help out if needed. He clearly wanted to renew a relationship with Belinda, but she was unsure of her feelings for him and not nearly ready to make any kind of commitment.

Belinda took the offered doughnuts. "Danki. If you haven't eaten this morning, why don't you come in and have some pancakes with us? Or you could eat one of your doughnuts."

Monroe offered her a wide smile. "Don't mind if I do."

Belinda led the way to the kitchen, and Monroe kept in step with her. When they entered the room, he walked up to the table and greeted Sylvia and Henry.

Sylvia said hello, but Henry just sat with his arms folded. This was not the first time Belinda's son had given Monroe the cold shoulder. He clearly did not care for the man.

"Please, take a seat, and I'll get you a plate." Belinda set the box of doughnuts on the table, and then gestured to an empty chair.

"Sure thing." He hung up his jacket and hat on the wall peg next to Henry's.

Monroe bowed his head for a few seconds, then opened his eyes and forked three pancakes onto his plate and covered them with plenty of syrup. After his first bite, he grinned at Belinda. "These are sure tasty. You're a good cook, Belinda."

"I can't take all the credit," she responded. "Sylvia mixed the batter. I'm only responsible for making sure the pancakes cooked all the way through and didn't get too brown."

"Well, all that being said, they're delicious." He smacked his lips.

When Belinda glanced at Henry, she couldn't miss his look of disapproval. *What was I supposed to do?* she asked herself. *I couldn't take the box of doughnuts from Monroe and shut the door in his face. I'm not trying to encourage this man, but I won't be unkind to him either. Henry needs to get over his irritation whenever Monroe comes around. I may have to remind him that the man was very helpful during our barn raising. That ought to count for something.*

Chapter 2

The greenhouse had only been open a few minutes when their first customer showed up. Belinda smiled as Herschel Fisher came in and stepped up to the counter. "Good morning, Herschel. Is there something I can help you with today?" she asked.

"Not particularly." He shifted his weight from one leg to the other. "I was in the area and thought I'd stop by to see how you're doing. There's been no more problems around here I hope."

Belinda shook her head. "Not since the barn burned, but then we don't know if that was a deliberate attack or an accident caused by someone's carelessness. We appreciated your help the day of the barn raising." She fidgeted with the pen beside her notepad on the counter, wondering why she felt so nervous in this man's presence. It made no sense, really, since Herschel had never done or said anything to cause Belinda to be tense or apprehensive. He was one of the kindest men she knew—not to mention good looking for a man approaching his sixties. Herschel's silver hair and striking blue eyes made him quite attractive, in fact.

Clasping the brim of his straw hat, Herschel tipped his head slightly. "I was glad to do it. If there's anything else you need to have done around here, don't hesitate to let me know."

"Danki, I will." Herschel's offer of help was the second one Belinda had received today. Before Monroe left, after consuming half a dozen pancakes, he'd mentioned once again that if Belinda needed anything she should give him a call. While Belinda appreciated both men's offers, she would only call upon them as a last resort. Henry was able to do many things around the place, and both Dennis and Jared came by to help out as often as they could. Of course, Dennis kept busy most days with horse training, and Jared had his roofing business, which took up a good many of their weekly hours.

Herschel stood near the counter a few more seconds, with his head tipped down. There was no doubt about it—this mild-mannered man was most definitely shy. At least he seemed to be whenever he spoke to Belinda. She'd observed him talking to other people before, like Jared or Amy, and he'd never appeared to be timid. It seemed a bit odd that he would be shy around her, but Belinda shrugged it off. She had too much to do today without trying to analyze Herschel's response to her.

Belinda felt relieved when he moved away from the counter and mumbled a quick, "Have a good day."

"Goodbye, Herschel. It was nice of you to stop in."

Shuffling his feet and with head down, Herschel went out the door.

A few minutes later, Amy showed up. "I saw Herschel Fisher get into his buggy, but he had nothing in his hands. Are we out of whatever he came here to buy?" she asked, joining Belinda behind the counter.

Belinda shook her head. "Herschel said he didn't need anything, just came by to see how we're doing and offer his help if we needed anything done."

"Ah-ha! I see how it is." Amy's eyes widened.

"You see how what is?"

"My *mamm* has two suitors."

Belinda lifted her gaze toward the ceiling and gave a little huff. "Don't be silly, Daughter. I have no suitors."

"I believe you're wrong about that. We've all known for some time that Monroe's set his cap for you. And now Herschel has shown interest too."

Belinda waved the thought aside. "That's not true. Where did you get such an idea anyway?"

"I've seen the way Herschel looks at you—kind of shy-like and with a crimson blush on his face. Also he seems to have trouble finding the right words whenever he's talking with you." Amy offered Belinda a dimpled grin. "I recognize all the signs, because that's how Jared acted when he was getting up the nerve to ask if I would let him court me."

Belinda clicked her tongue against the roof of her mouth. "That's *lecherich.* Herschel has no interest in me beyond a casual friendship, and I'm sure he has no intention of asking if he can court me."

"I don't think it's ridiculous at all." Amy shook her head. "And I'm gonna say, 'I told you so,' when he finally gets the courage to ask if he can begin seeing you on a regular basis."

"We're done with this nonsensical conversation, so let's get to work." Belinda pointed to the hose across the room. "Would you please water all the plants while I set out some fresh jars of honey?"

"No problem, Mom." Amy stepped out from behind the counter and paused. "Oh, I almost forgot. When I rode in on my scooter a short time ago, Henry was heading into the phone shed—no doubt to check messages. He hollered at me and asked if I would tell you that he'll be here in the greenhouse soon."

"Danki for relaying that message."

"You're welcome. There's something else I was going to mention."

"What's that?"

"Before coming here, I stopped at the house to drop off some banana bread I made last night. While I was in the kitchen, I noticed that the shade on the window was pulled down. When I opened it up, you'll never guess what happened."

"A robin flew out of the tree and smacked the window?"

Amy's eyes opened wide. "Well, jah. How did you know?"

"Because the silly voggel was doing that while I was in front of the sink. He kept at it so hard that I finally closed the window shade, thinking it might dissuade him."

Amy shook her head. "Well, for goodness' sake. I wonder what flying into the kitchen window is all about."

Belinda repeated Henry's explanation of the strange occurrence. "I was impressed with how much your *bruder* knows about robins."

"Well we've both noticed his fascination with birds ever since that pesky crow showed up in our yard back when..." Amy's voice trailed off. "Sorry, Mom. I didn't mean to open up old wounds by mentioning what occurred after the death of our loved ones."

"Don't worry about it. The accident happened, and we can't change the past, so there's no point in trying to avoid mentioning it."

Amy nodded. "That's true, but I always feel bad for bringing up a topic that still hurts whenever we talk about it."

Belinda had to admit that it was painful to talk, or even think about, but not nearly as much as it had been when the accident first happened—and on her birthday, no less. What had started out to be a happy celebration with their whole family had turned out to be one of the saddest days of Belinda's life. Since that dreadful evening, she'd done her best to maintain a positive attitude, put her trust in the Lord, and make the best of every situation. No one's life was free of trials, but it was important not to give in to self-pity or succumb to depression, the way Sylvia had done until she met Dennis. Both of Belinda's daughters had found love since the tragic day that changed their lives so dramatically. But Belinda remained certain that love and romance were not in her future, for no one could ever replace dear Vernon.

Sylvia sat at the kitchen table, adding to the grocery list her mother had started last evening. This was a good time to do it, as the house was basically quiet, since Rachel was taking her nap and Allen played happily by himself in the living room across the hall.

"Let's see now. . ." Sylvia tapped her pen against the table as she studied the list. Toothpaste, mouthwash, deodorant, facial tissues. . . Those were all necessities, but it would be nice to buy something that was not particularly needed. She tapped the pen again. "Think I'll add some ice cream to the list. We haven't had any frozen dessert in quite some time."

Thoughts of ice cream drew Sylvia's thoughts back to the day they'd been celebrating her mother's birthday. Everything had been going along fine until the topic was brought up that they had no ice cream to go with Mom's cake. Mom had insisted that she didn't need ice cream, but Dad had been equally determined to go to the store and get some. When he asked who would like to go with him, Sylvia's brother Abe and her husband, Toby, had agreed to accompany him, never guessing that they would only make it a few feet past the driveway.

Tears welled in Sylvia's eyes as she remembered with clarity how the accident had occurred. A vehicle coming down the road rammed into the back of her father's buggy so hard that the impact killed all three passengers, as well as Dad's horse. What a shock it had been for the whole family to lose their dear loved ones in such an unexpected, tragic way.

As more tears came, Sylvia's vision blurred so that she could no longer read the grocery list. Just when she'd thought she had put it all behind her, a little thing like adding ice cream to the list had brought back the pain of that day.

Sylvia got up from the table and went across the room to get a tissue from the box sitting on the desk. "I need to get a hold of myself," she murmured. "I can't change the past or bring back my loved ones with a simple wish—as much as I would like it to be so. I need to keep my focus on the here and now and be thankful for the wonderful man God has brought into my life." Although there would always be a place in Sylvia's heart for the memories she held of Toby, there'd be lots of new memories to make with Dennis.

Sylvia dried her eyes and blew her nose before going back to the shopping list. No one knew what the future held, but they should live every day as if it were their last. This is what Sylvia had decided to do. She appreciated each member of her family and felt a sense of peace and joy when she spent time with Dennis. How grateful Sylvia was that she and Henry had met Dennis when they'd been out bird-watching one day. They'd made an instant connection, and each opportunity Sylvia had to spend time with Dennis caused her fondness for him to grow. It was probably too soon for him to propose marriage, but she knew that if and when he did, her answer would be yes.

A thump against the window halted Sylvia's contemplations. She turned and was surprised to see the robin Mom had mentioned earlier, smacking its little body against the glass.

Although she knew a little about robins from what she'd read in the bird book Henry owned, Sylvia had never seen one do this kind of thing before. Could the bird be trying to get in the house, or was it simply trying to say hello?

Unsure of what else to do, Sylvia reached up and closed the shade. *That ought to take care of the bird. At least for now.*

Chapter 3

Amy turned the gas burner down on the stove and went outside to call Jared for supper. Seeing that he was chopping wood across the yard, she cupped her hands around her mouth and shouted, "Supper's ready, Jared!"

Apparently he hadn't heard, for he made no response.

Amy stepped off the porch and made her way across the yard. A chilly wind had come up, causing her to shiver. *If I'd known I was going to have to walk all the way out to the woodpile, I would have put on a sweater.*

She paused by the woodshed and waited for him to finish with the piece of wood he'd placed on the chopping block. "Supper's ready, Jared."

He grinned. "That's good, 'cause I've worked up quite an appetite out here with all this." Jared gestured to the pile of wood he'd already cut.

Amy smiled. "We'll certainly stay warm during the coming months. It'll be nice to have a cozy fire in the fireplace during the cold winter evenings."

Jared put the axe away and swiped his hand across his sweaty forehead. "Just think, Amy, Thanksgiving and Christmas will be here soon, and we'll get to spend them together as husband and wife." He slipped his arm around her waist and pulled her close to his side.

"Are you wishing we could spend the holidays alone, without either of our families?"

Jared shook his head. "Although in some ways, it would be nice to have a quiet Thanksgiving and Christmas with just the two of us, it'll be nice to share a meal with your mother and siblings on Thanksgiving."

"Are you still willing to spend Christmas at Ezekiel's place in New

York?" Amy asked as they made their way to the house.

"Sure. It'll be nice to see where they live, and the change of scenery will probably do us all some good."

"I hope your parents won't mind."

"I'm sure they'll miss us, but we can celebrate with them when we come back to Strasburg."

Amy thought this was a good idea. She would never want to leave her husband's family out.

As they entered the house, Amy's sense of smell was filled with the delicious aroma coming from the kettle of chicken and dumplings simmering on the stove. How thankful she felt to be married to a wonderful man like Jared. She looked forward to spending the rest of her life with him and growing old together. Amy also felt thankful for the opportunity they'd been given to rent this cozy home from Herschel Fisher. While it might not be big enough to raise a large family, it was a place to call home for the immediate future. When they'd saved up enough money, they would either buy or build their own home.

A third thing Amy felt thankful for was Jared's willingness to allow her to work every other day at the greenhouse. In addition to the extra money it gave them, Mom needed the help. On Amy's off day, she watched her sister's children so that Sylvia could assist their mother and Henry in the greenhouse. Until Amy and Jared became parents, this arrangement should work well. After that, Sylvia might have to consider hiring someone else to watch the children while she helped Mom in the business.

Jared tapped Amy's shoulder. "Is there any reason we're standing in the middle of the kitchen when there's good-smelling food on the stove waiting to be dished up?"

Amy jerked her head. "Sorry. I was just thinking."

He tipped his head in her direction. "Mind if I ask what you were thinking?"

"For one thing, I was thinking about how lucky I am to have married you."

"I'm the lucky one." Jared pulled Amy into his arms and gave her a kiss. *Ich liebt du unauserschprechlich.*"

"I love you beyond measure too."

Virginia Martin curled up on the couch with a glass of apple cider and her cat, Goldie. All day long she had listened to cars going by and horse and buggies making ruts in the road, while stinking up the crispy fall air with their manure droppings. Living across the street from an Amish family was bad enough, but the excess traffic due to their greenhouse customers made it seem even worse. Virginia hated living here in Amish country, a feeling she'd had ever since she and her husband, Earl, had moved here. She wished he'd never gotten the bright idea to apply for a job as a sales representative at one of the large car dealerships in Lancaster.

Virginia had been perfectly happy living in Chicago near her friend Stella. She hadn't made any new friends here and had very little to do other than clean house and putter around in the yard. She had taken up bird-watching, plus neighbor-watching, using Earl's binoculars, but that didn't compare to sitting down with a cup of coffee and enjoying a long chat with a close friend. Neither she nor Earl had any family living in the area, so it was just the two of them for holidays, and they never went to any social gatherings like they'd done in Chicago.

Goldie purred and nuzzled Virginia's hand, pulling her thoughts aside. She set the glass of cider down and gave the cat's head a few gentle strokes. "Are you feelin' lazy today, girl? Are ya content to just lie here with me?"

The cat's purr increased in volume.

"Okay, I get it. You want me to keep petting you, right?"

Goldie licked Virginia's finger with her sandpapery tongue.

Virginia had chosen the female feline from the local animal shelter a few months ago. It wasn't like having Stella to talk to, but at times Virginia carried on a conversation with Goldie. It was better than talking to herself and foolishly answering in response.

She relaxed and thought about how she'd gone through her closet yesterday, pulling out the summer things and replacing them with all fall/winter items. It wasn't too hard for Virginia to make the transition since she'd stored them in a tote in the guest-room closet.

Today she'd chosen to wear a peach blouse with a rust-colored cardigan. Virginia liked it because she'd gotten some compliments in the past while living in Chicago, so she hoped Earl would like it this evening.

As she looked down at her shirt, the cat moved away for a moment. Virginia noticed a lot of loose fur clinging up and down the front of her sweater. *Oh Goldie, look what you're doing to my nice clothes.* Virginia tried to brush off the hairs while the cat nuzzled into her. "Look you." She picked Goldie up and placed the feline at the end of the couch. But the animal was insistent and headed right back to her.

"Come on, kitty." Virginia placed the cat back in the same spot. This wasn't working, for the animal seemed determined to seek attention. Virginia chuckled in defeat and let Goldie have her way.

"Guess I'll have to resort to using the lint roller that's in the kitchen drawer." Virginia patted the cat's head as it laid down in a contented manner.

She picked up the magazine lying nearby and thumbed through the pages until she spotted a young model with bold red hair. "Well that's a fancy color that pretty woman's wearing. I'd sure like to give that shade of red a try. Since I've got nothing better to do tomorrow, maybe I'll go shopping and see if I can find the right color to try on myself."

A few minutes later, she went to the kitchen to check on the chicken baking in the oven. Earl would be home soon, and he'd no doubt be hungry.

Virginia glanced toward the kitchen door to see if Goldie had followed her in, like she often did, but apparently the lazy cat had chosen to remain on the couch. That was fine with Virginia. At least she could fix the rest of the meal in peace, without Goldie begging for food or rubbing against Virginia's leg.

Seeing that the chicken was done, Virginia turned the oven to low. Instead of mashed or baked potatoes, she'd made a cold potato salad earlier today and put it in the refrigerator to serve with the meal. She had also baked an apple pie for dessert, which she would serve with vanilla ice cream. She hoped by fixing Earl's favorite pie, he'd be willing to listen to her request about spending Thanksgiving in Chicago. She hadn't mentioned it to Stella yet, but Virginia felt sure her good friend would be open to the idea and welcome her and Earl to join her family for the holiday meal.

After she set the table, she headed back to the living room. Since

Goldie was still sleeping soundly, she picked up Earl's binoculars and went to the front window to look out. Traffic had slowed on the road—probably because the greenhouse was closed for the day. Virginia caught sight of Henry King out in the yard. He appeared to be searching for something.

"Probably looking for his dog," she muttered. "I hope the mutt doesn't come over here and start trampling my bushes."

"Who's looking for his dog?"

At the sound of Earl's voice, Virginia whirled around. "For heaven's sake, Earl, you shouldn't sneak up on me like that. I didn't know you were home."

"If you'd quit spying on the neighbors you might have more awareness of what's going on around you." He stepped up beside her. "Is supper ready? I didn't take time to eat lunch today, so I'm starving."

"Yes, everything's ready. I just need to set it on the table."

He gave her a peck on the cheek. "Okay, then I'll go wash up and meet you at the table."

"Sounds good." Virginia put the binoculars away and returned to the kitchen.

A short time later, she and Earl were enjoying their meal. "I made your favorite apple pie for dessert." She smiled at him from across the table.

He nodded. "That's good, but I may want to wait awhile to eat it, 'cause I'm gonna be plenty full from this meal."

"Is the chicken done to your liking?"

"Yep, sure is. The potato salad's good too."

Virginia wiped her mouth with the napkin and decided not to wait till they'd had dessert to ask her question.

"Say Earl, I've been thinking how nice it would be if we had Thanksgiving at Stella and Joe's place this year."

His brows rose. "You mean drive all the way to Illinois just to eat dinner?"

"Actually, I thought we could go a few days early, or until the day after Thanksgiving. I haven't seen Stella since she came here to visit all those months ago, so. . ."

Earl held up his hand. "Not gonna happen, Virginia."

"How come?" Her spine stiffened.

"Because I have to work."

"On Thanksgiving?"

"No, the day after. You should know by now that the day after Thanksgiving is one of the biggest shopping days of the year. If it goes anything like it did last year, there'll be lots of people coming in to the dealership to buy a new car at our sales prices." He glanced at her, then back at his food. "So going anywhere for Thanksgiving is out."

Virginia swallowed around the constriction that had formed in her throat. She'd lost her appetite for the food on her plate and didn't think she could eat another bite.

My life stinks—it's boring and it's not fair that I can't spend time with my best friend anymore. I feel like getting on a bus and going to Chicago for Thanksgiving without Earl. I wonder how he'd like that.

She released a sigh. *Guess I won't do it, but I will go into town tomorrow to find a brighter red hair color. Maybe that will make me feel a little better about myself.*

Belinda stepped out the back door and rang the dinner bell to let Henry know that supper was ready. He'd been in the barn for some time, and she figured he must be done with his chores by now.

I'll give him a few more minutes and then ring the bell again. Belinda stepped back inside and went to the stove to stir the pot of stew that was plenty done and just keeping warm.

"Where's Henry?" Sylvia asked when she entered the kitchen a few minutes later. "With his voracious appetite, I figured he'd be in here by now asking if supper was ready."

"I rang the dinner bell, so hopefully he will be in shortly." Belinda pointed to the kitchen table. "You may as well bring the kinner in and get them seated. Then we can eat as soon as Henry comes in and washes his hands."

"Okay." Sylvia went out of the room and returned a few minutes later with Allen and Rachel. After getting them situated—Rachel in her high chair and Allen on his booster seat, she filled a pitcher with water and placed it on the table.

Belinda glanced up at the clock. "Still no sign of Henry, so I guess I'd better ring that old bell again." She moved toward the door, but as she was about to reach for the nob, the door opened and Henry rushed in. A sheen of sweat covered his forehead, and his cheeks were bright red. Belinda had a hunch it was not from the cold.

"What's wrong, Son? You look *umgerrent*."

"I'm very upset." He swiped a hand across his forehead. "Two of our best laying hens are gone. I can't find them anywhere, Mom. They just vanished from the coop." He scrunched up his face. "I bet the vandalism's started up again."

"Now calm down, Henry. The chickens may have found a way out of the pen. Did you check to see if there were any holes or tears in the chicken wire?" Belinda spoke quietly, so as not to rile him more. The last thing she wanted was for her son to start shouting and upset the children who'd been waiting patiently at the table for their supper.

"Of course I checked, and everything was fine. Someone let themselves into the pen and took those hens." Henry pulled his fingers through his sandy brown hair repeatedly. "We need those chickens for the eggs they produce, and I aim to find out who took them. The bad stuff that's been going on around here ever since Dad, Abe, and Toby died has gone on long enough. And by the way. . .I ain't hungry!" He whirled around and stomped down the hall.

Belinda turned to look at Sylvia to gauge her reaction, but her daughter merely shrugged and said, "Should we start eating supper without him?"

"I suppose so." Belinda drew a quick breath and blew it out. There had to be some explanation for the missing hens. But if someone had come into the yard today and taken the chickens, they may never learn who that person was. She hoped Henry wouldn't go around the neighborhood and start accusing people. *My boy's making a big deal out of nothing. I'm sure there's a perfectly reasonable explanation for the missing chickens.*

Chapter 4

With his binoculars in position, Henry sat cross-legged inside the large open window near the top of the barn. He'd done this every morning and evening since two of their hens had vanished. So far he'd seen nothing suspicious, nor had any more chickens disappeared. Even so, Henry felt sure the hens had been stolen, because if they'd been eaten by some critter, he should have seen some feathers left as evidence.

Today was Thanksgiving, and except for Ezekiel and his family, all the Kings would be together. Mom had also invited Jared's parents to join them, but Ava and Emanuel had made plans to visit one of their daughters.

Thankfully, Monroe had not been included in their Thanksgiving plans. Henry had no tolerance for the irritating man. He hoped Monroe would never succeed at worming his way into Mom's heart, because Henry couldn't imagine her being married to anyone but Dad. Just the thought of Monroe becoming his stepfather left a bitter taste in Henry's mouth. If that ever happened he didn't know what he would do. He sure couldn't live in the same house with Monroe.

Maybe Jared and Amy would take me in. Henry lowered the binoculars into his lap.

"What are ya doin' up there with those field glasses—looking for birds?"

Henry looked down and spotted Dennis on the ground below, pointing up at him. "Not the kind of birds I normally watch," he called in return. "I'm watchin' my chickens."

"Can't you do that from down here?"

"I'll be right there." Henry moved away from the window and climbed down the ladder. Before he could make it to the barn door, Dennis stepped in.

"So what's this about you watching chickens?" he asked with a grin.

Henry explained about the missing hens and said that in addition to making sure no others disappeared, he was on the lookout for the thief who stole the chickens.

Dennis pulled a stubble of hay from one of the bales close by. "Are you certain they were stolen?"

"Jah. I looked the chicken wire over really good, and there was no way those hens could've gotten out by themselves." Henry frowned. "I think whoever set our barn on fire and did all those other acts of vandalism to our property ripped off our *hinkel*, and they might try to take more of them again."

Dennis placed his hand on Henry's shoulder. "You can't sit up in the hayloft like a security guard twenty-four hours a day, so why don't you come out in the yard with me, and we'll do a little bird-watching until dinner is ready."

Henry hesitated but finally nodded. He wasn't sure if Dennis agreed with his theory or not, but since Blackie was roaming freely in the yard today, he figured the dog would bark out a warning if anyone who shouldn't be there came onto their property.

Clymer, New York

Ezekiel left the phone shed where he'd called his family in Strasburg. Even though it didn't happen very often, he'd hoped someone might be nearby to speak with directly, but all he got was the message machine, so he'd recorded his Thanksgiving greetings.

Ezekiel wished he and Michelle could have taken their son and daughter to Strasburg for the holiday, but it was nice that Michelle's brothers could be here. Because she and her siblings had been taken from their parents and put in foster care when they were children, Michelle, Jack, and Ernie had missed out on so much. Being reunited a few years ago had seemed a miracle, and Ezekiel was pleased whenever Michelle and her brothers could get together. Besides, his side of the family would be here for Christmas, and he looked forward to that.

I wonder how my little brother is doing these days, Ezekiel thought as he made his way back toward the house. *Sure hope he's not giving our mamm any trouble like he did for so many months after Dad, Abe, and Toby were killed.*

Ezekiel stopped walking long enough to throw a stick for Michelle's dog, Val, and watched as the mutt chased after it, barking all the way. He still remembered the joy he had seen on Michelle's face when he'd presented the dog to her on Valentine's Day, back when they were courting. Ezekiel enjoyed every opportunity to bring a smile to his wife's pretty face.

After tossing the stick to Val a second time, Ezekiel reflected a bit more. Michelle had grown up in an English environment, and he still marveled at how well she had adapted to the Amish way of life. In fact, she seemed to flourish—as if she'd been destined to live as one of the Plain people.

He reached under his hat and scratched his head. *It's hard for me to believe sometimes that I once had it in my head to go English so I could drive a motorized vehicle and own modern things. Michelle was a good influence on me in that regard. She helped me realize that material things are not important. It's the relationship I have with God and my family—those are the things that count the most for me now.*

Ezekiel still couldn't believe he'd been chosen by lots to be one of the ministers in their church district. He felt humbled and unworthy but also blessed to be able to minister to others through the preaching of God's Word. Sometimes, like last week, Ezekiel was called upon to counsel a couple who were struggling in their faith. In his younger days, he would never have imagined being put in a position where he'd have to preach, teach, and counsel. But with total commitment and reliance on God, Ezekiel's calling had become a blessing to him as well as to others.

"Ernie and Jack have arrived with their wives," Michelle called from the back porch. "Are you coming inside to greet them?"

"I'll be right there." Ezekiel tossed the stick to Val one last time and hurried up the steps to the back porch. A day of good food and fellowship was about to begin, and he looked forward to every moment.

Strasburg

Virginia stood in front of the hallway mirror, staring at her reflection. She had colored her hair days ago, and the red was far more vibrant than ever before.

Earl had noticed her hair as soon as he'd come through the door and hadn't seemed to mind it. In fact he gave Virginia a compliment about the newer, brighter shade. Virginia felt good and was delighted that she had gone to the trouble to do it. Her crooked bangs, which she'd cut herself some time ago, had grown out, but it was time for another haircut. This time, though, she wouldn't tackle it herself. She'd tried making an appointment at the styling salon in town, but couldn't get in until Tuesday of next week. Virginia could have tried some of the other salons outside of her area, but didn't want to start over with a new stylist. Since she and Earl were going to a nice restaurant in Lancaster for Thanksgiving dinner, Virginia wanted to look her best.

"You look great, honey, so stop fretting and get away from that mirror." Earl stepped up behind Virginia and put his hands on her shoulders. "You've got the prettiest red hair in all of Lancaster County."

She rolled her eyes. "Yeah, right."

"It's true. Your carrot top is one of the reasons I married you, didn't ya know?"

He nuzzled the back of Virginia's neck. "The perfume you're wearing is real nice too. You smell like a rosebush in full bloom."

"Thanks, Earl. Now we'd better get going before we miss our reservation."

"Yep. I'll get our coats right now."

Virginia felt relieved that Earl hadn't asked if she'd quit smoking, like she had promised. The truth was, she hadn't quit and had used the perfume to cover up any telltale odor from the cigarette she'd snuck this morning. She'd also brushed her teeth twice and swished plenty of mouthwash around in her mouth before getting dressed. Virginia wanted to quit smoking because it wasn't good for her health, but her nerves were frazzled, and having a cigarette was one of the few things that helped. Hopefully she could keep Earl from finding out that she'd started up again, because Virginia couldn't tolerate it when he began nagging.

"That was sure a good dinner, Belinda. Danki for all your hard work." Jared patted his stomach. "I ate so much I don't think I'll have to eat again for at least a week."

Amy poked her husband's arm. "I've heard you say that before. Why, I bet by tomorrow you'll be saying, What's for *friehschtick, fraa*?"

He chuckled. "You're probably right. I can't see going through tomorrow without my supper."

"I'm glad you enjoyed the meal," Belinda said, "but I can't take all the credit. Sylvia helped with most of the cooking, and as you know, your wife brought two pumpkin pies."

"I stand—or should I say, sit—corrected." Jared's gaze traveled from Amy to Sylvia and then back to Belinda. "I appreciate each one of your efforts."

"Same here," Dennis spoke up. "We men would have gone without food if it weren't for you kind ladies today."

Smiling, Sylvia gave him a sidelong glance. "I'm sure you would have managed to fix yourself something to eat."

"True, but it wouldn't have been near as tasty as this Thanksgiving treat."

Belinda glanced at Henry to see if he would comment, but he sat fiddling with the knife beside his empty plate. Except for a bit of conversation with Dennis, when he told him about the robin that had kept hitting their kitchen window for several days in a row, her son hadn't joined in much of the conversation going on around the table. She hoped he wasn't still sulking about the missing chickens. None of the other hens had turned up missing, so he ought to just leave it alone. She wouldn't force Henry to be more verbal today. Sometimes he simply needed time to think about and deal with things in his own way. She couldn't deny that the hens weren't important to the family, since they provided eggs, but two missing chickens did not signal the end of the world.

Perhaps, she thought, *Maude, the homeless woman, took the hens so she would have something to eat for her Thanksgiving meal and beyond. We have plenty of hens out in the coop laying eggs, and with the cost of their feed bill each month, it wouldn't hurt to have a few less chickens to feed.*

Belinda sipped the rest of her water. *If the poor woman felt the need to snitch cookies that had been set out in the greenhouse, and take produce from our garden last summer, then she could very well be the reason the chickens went missing.* Of course, Belinda was not about to offer this suggestion to her son. He would no doubt get right on his scooter and head over to the shanty where Maude stayed most of the year and confront her with his suspicions.

Amy stood and began clearing the table. "Should we bring out the pies for dessert or wait till we've done the dishes?"

"I'm too full to eat anything more right now," Jared said. "But I'll watch the rest of you eat dessert now if that's what you want to do."

Dennis shook his head. "I'd rather wait too."

Belinda looked at Henry. "What do you think, Son?"

He shrugged and mumbled, "It ain't up to me."

Rather than correcting his English, Belinda looked at Sylvia and then Amy. "Are you two in agreement with waiting awhile to bring out the pies?"

They both said yes.

"All right then, let's get the table cleared and the dishes done. Then we can all relax in the living room with the warmth of the fireplace while we watch Rachel and Allen play." Belinda rose from her seat, and was about to pick up the first plate when a knock sounded on the front door. "Now I wonder who that could be. We weren't expecting more company today." She glanced over at Henry, slouched in his chair. "Would you please answer the door?"

"Okay." Henry pushed back his chair and shuffled out of the room.

Belinda stacked several plates but decided not to take them out to the kitchen until she found out who was at the door. A few seconds later, Henry came back with Monroe at his side.

Her son's narrowed eyes and tightly pressed lips said it all. He was not happy to see Monroe.

"Sorry for the intrusion." Monroe looked at Belinda and smiled. "I bought a mincemeat pie at the bakery yesterday, and since it's one of your favorites, I wanted you to have it." He handed the dessert to Belinda.

"Oh, well...um...danki, Monroe. It was nice of you to think of me." She placed the pie in the center of the table. "We just finished our dinner and won't be eating dessert until the dishes are done, but you're welcome to join us if you like."

A wide grin spread across Monroe's clean-shaven face. "I'd be pleased to join you. That'd be real nice."

Belinda glanced at Henry and wasn't surprised to see the whitening of his knuckles as he clasped his hands tightly at his sides. Her son had never made it a secret how he felt about Monroe. But that didn't excuse his rude behavior whenever the man came around.

Belinda gestured to the adjoining living room. "Monroe, why don't you make yourself comfortable with the other men while we women do the dishes? Afterward, we'll bring out the rest of the pies."

Monroe didn't have to be asked twice. Following another big smile in Belinda's direction, he headed to the living room with Jared, Dennis, and the children.

Belinda picked up the stack of plates but paused to see what Henry would do. True to form, wearing a frown, he left the dining room and clomped up the stairs. She figured they wouldn't see him again until Monroe went home. It was too bad Henry couldn't be a little more cordial to the man. If he gave Monroe half a chance, he might discover that he wasn't so bad—a little pushy, perhaps, but with some good qualities too.

Chapter 5

Virginia limped out to the kitchen to pour herself a cup of coffee. She'd slept later than usual this morning and barely remembered Earl telling her goodbye when he left for work. With colder weather setting in, her bum leg hurt more than usual. She was fairly sure that arthritis had set into her old leg injury where several bones had been broken. Other parts of Virginia's body felt stiff too, but none as bad as the pain she felt nearly every day in her leg.

After filling her coffee cup, she opened a can of cat food and called for Goldie.

"Here, kitty, kitty. . . Come get your breakfast."

When there was no immediate response, Virginia went to the living room to see if the cat might be sleeping on the couch. But there was no sign of Goldie.

"Goldie. . .where are you, kitty?" Virginia stood still and listened. Normally when she called for Goldie, the feline would come running, no doubt believing she was going to be fed or cuddled.

"That's sure strange." Virginia limped her way through the house, calling the cat's name, but Goldie could not be found.

Puzzled and more than a bit frustrated, Virginia returned to the other side of the house. The only place she hadn't checked was the utility room. When she stepped in there it felt chillier than usual.

"Oh no." Seeing the back door was open a crack, Virginia groaned. *Earl must not have closed it tightly when he left for work this morning.* Her muscles tightened. *If Goldie got outside and ran off, Earl will never hear the last of it!*

With no thought of fixing herself something to eat, Virginia went to her room to get dressed. She would start by going across the street in search of her cat. Since the King family had cats, Goldie may have gone there to bond with them.

A short time later, Virginia found herself limping up the Kings' driveway with her cane as she scanned their property in search of Goldie. She hobbled along with a watchful eye, not wanting to step in a fresh pile of horse droppings.

Virginia thought back to that fall evening when she'd lost her binoculars in the grass, trying to spy on the wedding she hadn't been invited to at the Kings' place. "I think I should've gotten an invite to Jared and Amy's ceremony—or at least the meal following the nuptials," Virginia mumbled as she looked ahead.

Two horse and buggies, along with one car, were parked near the greenhouse, but there was no sign of Virginia's cat.

She kept going until she entered the Kings' yard, where many plain clothes, towels, and sheets flapped in the chilly breeze on the clothesline. Virginia shook her head. *I could never hang my laundry outside in cold weather like this. How thankful I am for an electric washer and dryer. Sure wouldn't want to hang my clean clothes outdoors all the time.*

As Virginia approached the barn, she saw two black-and-white cats run from the building. *Hmm. . . .I wonder if Goldie went in there.*

She paused and looked up at the new structure. It sure didn't take those Amish folks long to build a new barn after the old one burned down. From what Virginia had seen through Earl's binoculars on the day of the barn raising, it looked like every Amish person living in Strasburg had come to help construct the new building. *Must be nice to have so many people who care about you. Wish I could say the same.*

Redirecting her thoughts, Virginia stepped inside and called the cat's name. No response from Goldie, but a few seconds later, a voice called down from the hayloft: "Who's there?"

"It's Virginia, your neighbor from across the street. My cat's missing, and I came over to see if she wandered in here."

"I don't think so, but I'll come down and take a look."

Virginia watched as young Henry descended the ladder from above. When he stepped off the last rung, he turned and brushed some straw off his trousers.

"What's your cat look like?" Henry questioned.

"She's kind of orangeish-yellowish. Her name is Goldie. She's an inside cat, but my husband left the back door partway open when he left for work this morning, so I'm sure she got out."

"I haven't seen any cats that color around here, but I'll have a look-see." Henry began moving about the barn, looking behind boxes and calling for the feline.

Virginia followed, but there was no sign of Goldie.

Henry tipped his hat off his forehead. "Guess your cat didn't come in here, 'cause there's sure no sign of her."

Virginia sighed. "Okay, I'll head back home for now, and then go out looking for her again after I've rested awhile."

"I'll let you know if I see a cat that looks like the one you described," Henry said.

"Thanks." Virginia shuffled out the door and made her way slowly down the driveway toward home. She hated the thought of never seeing Goldie again, but if she didn't find the cat soon, it might end up that way.

"My only friend, and now she's gone," Virginia lamented as she entered her house.

She sat at the kitchen table several minutes, drinking a second cup of coffee and eating a glazed doughnut Earl had brought home from the bakery yesterday. Although the coffee warmed her insides, and the doughnut tasted good, neither did anything to lift Virginia's spirits. *Think I'll go get my cigarette stash.*

Virginia left the kitchen and headed down the hall to the linen closet. She'd found a new hiding place for her cigarettes—under a small box inside the closet.

Virginia was almost to the closet when she heard a slight *meow*. She tipped her head and listened. The sound seemed to be coming from the closet where they kept their coats. The desire to find Goldie took precedence over smoking, so Virginia turned back and opened the door of the hall closet. There sat Goldie inside a box filled with gloves and scarves for wearing in cold weather. The poor feline looked up at Virginia and gave a pathetic *meow*.

"Oh Goldie, I'm so glad I found you." Virginia leaned down and scooped the cat into her arms. "Why didn't you meow when I called for you earlier? If you had, it would have saved me the trouble of going over to that smelly farm across the road."

Goldie's only response was another *meow*, followed by plenty of purring.

At noon, Belinda left the greenhouse and headed down the driveway to get the mail and check for any phone messages that may have come in. As she approached the mailbox, she spotted her neighbor across the road, standing in front of her living-room window. It looked like Virginia held a pair of binoculars up to her face.

I wonder what she is looking at. Could Virginia be watching me? Belinda smiled and lifted her hand in a wave. The red-haired woman lowered the binoculars and moved away from the window.

Belinda opened her mailbox and sighed. She'd tried on several occasions to strike up a conversation with her neighbor, but Virginia had never been very receptive. Belinda could only assume the woman either didn't like her or wasn't the friendly type. Either way, Belinda would pray for Virginia and keep trying to be a good neighbor.

After retrieving the mail, Belinda walked halfway up the driveway and entered the phone shack. She found two messages from customers asking if they had any poinsettias left in the greenhouse, and another message from Ezekiel, wondering if Belinda knew what time she and the family might arrive the day before Christmas.

Belinda responded to all three messages, and was about to leave the shed when the telephone rang. Pleased that she was here and the caller would not have to leave a message, Belinda picked up the receiver. "Hello."

A cold chill swept over her as a muffled voice said: "I've warned you before—you need to close up the greenhouse and move. If you don't heed my advice, you'll be sorry."

Belinda sat in stunned silence. This was the second time an unidentified person had called and demanded that she close the greenhouse and move.

"Who is this?" Her voice quavered.

Click! Whoever the caller was, they'd hung up.

Belinda's grip tightened on the phone. *Who would make such a threat as this, and why? Could the muffled-voice caller be the one responsible for starting the fire in our barn? Did they think that would be enough to get us to move?*

Belinda closed her eyes and lowered her head. *Heavenly Father, please protect my family, as well as every bit of the property our home and greenhouse sit upon. Convict the person responsible for all the vandalism and threats that have been done so they will see the error of their ways and stop doing it. In Jesus' name I ask this, amen.*

As Belinda remained in the phone shed, trying to compose herself, she made a decision. She didn't want to frighten her family, so in addition to not telling Ezekiel, she wouldn't mention the muffled phone call to any of them at this point. She would, however, continue to pray about this matter and also ask her good friend Mary Ruth Lapp to join her in prayer.

"In fact," she murmured, "I'm going to call and leave a message for her right now."

"Hey, Mom, since there are no customers in the greenhouse right now, is it okay if I quit for the day?" Henry asked, stepping up to the counter where Belinda stood.

She shook her head. "We still have another hour before closing, so there could be more people coming in, looking for things on their Christmas list." She gestured toward the shelves where they sold honey, jams, and some other gift items. "Would you please set a few more things out? The next week will no doubt be busy, since we'll be closing soon for Christmas and the remainder of the year."

"Jah, okay. I'll go to the storage room and get out some more jars." Henry glanced around. "Where's Amy? I haven't seen her for a while."

"She's not done with her Christmas shopping yet, so since we've been slow this afternoon, I said she could leave a little early today."

He frowned. "If she got to leave early, then why can't I?"

"Because someone needs to be here with me, in case we do get busy."

Henry mumbled something Belinda didn't understand, before he headed to the storage room.

Belinda took a seat behind the counter and rubbed her forehead. Ever since the phone call that had upset her this morning, she'd been struggling with a headache. It was ever so difficult to hold this inside and not tell someone.

She glanced up at the clock. It would be closing time soon, and then she could go up to the house and lie down for a while before it was time to start supper. Maybe while she rested, Sylvia might cook the meal, which she often did on the days when she didn't work in the greenhouse.

A short time later, with only a few minutes left before it was time to put the CLOSED sign on the front door, Belinda told Henry he could do his chores in the barn and that she would lock up the building.

"Okay, Mom. I got everything put on the shelves, like you asked me to do," Henry said before he went out the door.

Belinda remained in the greenhouse and spent the next half hour straightening a few items and going over some paperwork. She was about to leave the building when a horse and buggy pulled in. Opening the door, she saw Mary Ruth and her granddaughter, Lenore, get down from their buggy.

"I got your phone message saying you wanted to talk to me." Mary Ruth stepped up to Belinda. "Lenore volunteered to come along with me, while Jesse watches their kinner."

Belinda wasn't sure what to say. As much as she wanted to talk with her friend, she didn't want Lenore to hear it, because she might repeat it to Sylvia. The young women had been friends since they were children, and Lenore might feel that Sylvia had the right to know.

Belinda felt relief when Lenore said she would go up to the house and visit with Sylvia while her grandmother and Belinda talked.

"Danki, dear one." Mary Ruth gave Lenore's shoulder a pat. "I hope you two will have a nice visit."

As Lenore headed for the house, Mary Ruth entered the greenhouse with Belinda. Once inside, she turned to Belinda and said, "I could tell by the tone of your voice that something was troubling you. The fact that you asked me to pray but didn't say why, made me wonder if something might be seriously wrong."

Belinda drew a quick breath and released it slowly. "I don't know if it's serious or not, but something is definitely wrong. If you'd like to take a seat on the stool behind the counter, I'll tell you about it."

Mary Ruth did as she suggested and sat quietly waiting.

Belinda rubbed her forehead as she leaned against the front of the counter. "I received a disturbing phone call this morning while I was in the shed."

"Oh?"

"The voice was muffled, so I have no idea who the caller was, but they said. . ." Belinda paused and swallowed hard. "The person said we should close up the greenhouse and move, and if we don't, we'll be sorry."

Mary Ruth's fingers touched her parted lips. "Oh my. Did you call the sheriff?"

"No, I did not, and I haven't told any of my family about it." Belinda shifted her weight. "This is the second time I've received such a message, and I have to wonder if the person who called isn't the one who's done all the vandalism to our property."

"This is very disconcerting, Belinda. I really think you should call the sheriff."

She shook her head. "I don't want the law involved. For that matter, if word gets out and too many people know what's been happening around here, they might say something to Ezekiel. I'm sure he still keeps contact with some of his friends from our area."

"Are you still worried that if he were to find out, he'd move back to Strasburg in order to help out in the greenhouse and make sure that you and the rest of the family are okay?"

"Jah, and I don't want him to make that kind of sacrifice for us. My son has established a good life there in New York, and I won't take that away from him."

"It's your decision, but if it were me, I'd want my son to know what's been going on."

Belinda shook her head vigorously. "Promise you won't tell anyone what I've shared with you today? I just need your prayers, that's all."

Mary Ruth got off the stool and came around to give Belinda a hug. "I will definitely be praying for all of you, as well as the person behind the senseless, destructive acts. In fact if it's all right, I'd like to pray with you now since we're alone in the shop."

Belinda murmured her agreement.

Although most Amish didn't pray out loud, Mary Ruth took hold of Belinda's hands and prayed out loud with an understanding that touched Belinda's heart. She felt comforted by what was said as her dear friend asked the Lord to give Belinda and her family strength and protection. When she finished, Mary Ruth expressed her willingness to help out in any way she could.

A few tears escaped from under Belinda's lashes and she reached up to wipe them away. "Danki, Mary Ruth. You're such a good friend."

Chapter 6

The next day after enjoying a visit with Sylvia's children and Amy during lunch, Belinda returned to the greenhouse with a plate of Amy's cookies.

"Are those peanut butter *kichlin*?" Henry asked after she placed the plate on the counter.

"Yes, you're welcome to have a couple, but don't eat too many. Amy and I sampled a couple right after lunch. She did a good job, because they're sure tasty. I brought them out to share with our customers."

Henry's brows lifted as he looked around. "What customers, Mom? There's only been a handful of people come into the greenhouse this morning, and I doubt we'll see many more this afternoon either."

"You never know." Belinda stepped around behind the counter where Sylvia sat. "You're free to go up to the house and eat lunch now. And no doubt you'll want to check on the kinner."

Sylvia smiled. "I'm sure Amy has everything under control, but I am getting hungry, so I'd better go fix something to eat."

Belinda smiled. "Your sister has things all ready to go. You just need to show up with an appetite."

"That sounds good to me." Sylvia stood up and walked toward the exit.

After she left the building, Henry grabbed a cookie and took a bite. "Yum! This is sure tasty. You and my sisters make the best cookies, Mom."

"I'm glad you like it." Belinda pointed to a row of Christmas cactus and poinsettias. "Could you please make sure those got watered this morning?"

"I think they did, but I'll check just in case." He took another cookie and shuffled down the row.

Belinda shook her head. *That boy! Seems like he's always hungry.*

A short while later, Maude entered the greenhouse, wearing a heavy black coat with a hood. It looked almost new, and Belinda wondered where the woman had gotten it, since she'd never seen her wear it before.

Pushing the hood off her head, Maude stepped up to the counter and snatched a cookie from the plate without asking.

"Would you like me to put the rest of the cookies in a plastic sack so you can take them with you?" Belinda asked.

Maude bobbed her head with an eager expression.

Belinda reached under the counter, took out a plastic sack, and put the cookies inside. "Your coat looks nice and warm. Is it new?"

"It's new to me. Got it at the thrift store in town." Maude wiped her mouth on her coat sleeve. "I wear it in my cabin when I have no wood for heat."

"Do you have any wood now?"

"Nope, sure don't. Haven't got enough money to buy any either—not till the dinky pension I get comes, but the next won't be for several weeks."

"Do you have any family living in the area? Perhaps they could help with your needs."

Maude shook her head. "Nope. I'll manage on my own—least till winter."

Belinda's heart went out to the poor woman. They needed to do something to help her—especially now, with colder weather setting in. *I should have asked Maude more questions sooner. I really know so little about her.*

"I'll ask my son to bring you some wood as soon as the greenhouse closes today."

Keeping her gaze toward the floor, Maude said, "Okay."

Although the older woman had not offered any words of thanks, Belinda was certain that Maude appreciated the gesture. Considering she had so little and lived in a shanty, surely she would see any offer of help as kindness.

"Think I'll take a look around before I head back to my hovel," Maude mumbled. Still holding the bag of cookies, she turned and shuffled down the aisle where Belinda had sent Henry to check on the plants.

Several minutes elapsed before the woman returned to the counter.

"Does your boy know where I live?"

"Yes, I'm certain he does. You can expect to see him there in a few hours."

Maude put her hood back on and shuffled out the door.

"Think I know who stole our chickens, Mom." With narrowed eyes, Henry stepped up to Belinda.

"Oh?"

"It was Maude."

"How do you know? Did she admit that she took the hens?"

He shook his head. "Nope, but I saw the evidence."

"Really? And what evidence would that be?"

"There was chicken manure on her shoes."

"Maybe she stepped in some as she walked up our driveway."

Henry slapped both hands against his hips. "My hinkel do not roam around our yard, Mom. You know I always keep them in their pen."

"Good point, but I suppose she could have picked up the manure from someone else's yard, or even along the side of the road, where she's often seen walking."

"I haven't seen anyone else with chickens in our area, and we are the only ones that are close enough to Maude."

Belinda tilted her head. "That's true, Son. You've made a good point."

Henry moved his hands from his hips to his pockets. "As soon as we close the greenhouse today, I'm gonna head over to her place and see if she has my chickens. Okay?"

"As a matter of fact, I planned to ask you to go over there anyway."

"How come?"

"Maude has no firewood, and I'd like you to fill up our wheelbarrow and take her some."

Henry's brows lowered. "If that woman has our hinkel, she doesn't deserve any firewood."

"This is not about deserving, Son." Belinda shook her head. "It's about being kind and helping out a neighbor in need."

Henry pulled his hands out of his pockets and turned them palm-side up. "Okay, I'll do whatever you say."

"And Son, please don't accuse poor Maude of stealing our chickens."

He shrugged, before heading toward the back of the greenhouse.

Half an hour after Maude left, Monroe entered the greenhouse. He sauntered toward Belinda, steeped in heavy cologne and wearing a big smile. "How are things going? Have you been busy today?" He stepped up to the counter where she sat.

Why does Monroe think he needs to splash on so much of that overpowering fragrance? He wears enough for himself and at least one other man. "A little slower than I expected," she replied, looking at Monroe. "With Christmas only a few weeks away, we normally have more customers coming in to buy gift items and indoor plants."

"Maybe people are shopping at the new greenhouse across town." He gave his left earlobe a tug. "They do have a lot more available there."

Belinda cringed inwardly. She didn't need the reminder of their competition. Before the new greenhouse opened, their family business was the only one in the area that sold plants and flowers, and they'd been doing so well. They were still managing, despite all the vandalism that had taken place, but things could be a lot better.

"What are your plans for Christmas?" Monroe asked, detouring Belinda's thoughts.

I wonder if he wants to spend the holiday with us. Surely Monroe would enjoy spending Christmas with his parents and siblings. "We're all going to New York to see Ezekiel and his family," she replied.

His brows furrowed. "For how long?"

"Three or four days. We'll leave here on Christmas Eve day."

"Who's gonna feed the livestock and watch the place while you're gone?"

"We'll probably ask our neighbors to the right of us, or maybe see if our friend Jesse Smucker would come by."

Monroe shook his head. "There's no need for that. I'd be more than happy to come by every day and do whatever you need to have done."

Belinda shifted on her stool. "Oh, I couldn't ask you to do that."

"You're not asking. I'm volunteering." He leaned a bit closer. "I'd like to do this for you, Belinda, so please don't say no."

She tried not to choke on the strong musky odor as it wafted her way. "Well, since you put it that way. . .I don't have much choice but to accept your kind offer."

Monroe's clean-shaven chin jutted out a bit as he gave her a wide smile. "I'll come by the day before you leave to get a *schlissel*."

Belinda tipped her head. "For what, Monroe? Why would you need a key?"

"So I can put your mail in the house."

"Our mailbox is the locking kind, so any mail we get should be fine in there until we get home." *I really wouldn't feel comfortable with him looking through our letters, but I'm sure Monroe only means well and is just trying to be helpful.*

"Oh, I see." He folded his arms. "What about any plants you might have in the greenhouse or inside your home? Those might need to be watered, don't you think?"

Belinda tapped her knuckles gently on the counter as she thought through Monroe's request. "If we have any plants that don't sell before Christmas, those will need to be watered, so we'll put our houseplants in the greenhouse, and you can check on those too."

"I'll need a schlissel for the greenhouse then."

"Jah, and when you come by for the key, I'll have Henry show you what needs to be done with his *hund*, and also the *katze* and *gaul* in the barn."

"Don't you worry about anything, Belinda." Monroe looked directly into her eyes. "I'll make sure the dog, cats, and horses are well taken care of while you're away."

Belinda hoped allowing Monroe to check on things while they were gone was the right decision, and that the rest of her family would be okay with it.

Pushing a wheelbarrow full of split wood, Henry headed in the direction of Maude's run-down cabin. When he arrived, he looked on all sides of the small building, but there was no sign of any chickens on the overgrown property. *Could I have been mistaken?*

Henry stacked the wood on the dilapidated, uneven porch and then knocked on the door. When Maude didn't answer, he knocked again.

After a few more tries, with no response, Henry was about to give up until he heard a familiar, *Bawk! Bawk! Bawk!*

Scooting over to the only window in the front of the cabin, he peered through the dirty-looking glass. Henry couldn't see anything until a chicken startled him by jumping up on what looked like a wooden box and began pecking at the window. He felt sure it was one of his hens, but couldn't figure out what it would be doing inside Maude's old cabin. Was it possible that Maude let them run all over the place, and that's why she had chicken manure on her shoes?

Henry knocked one more time then tried the knob, but the door appeared to be locked. Could the eccentric old woman be inside, choosing to ignore him?

He tried two more times but finally gave up. If Maude was at home, she obviously wasn't going to let him in.

Henry's facial muscles tightened. *I need to get home and tell Mom about this.*

Belinda stood at the stove, stirring a pot of chicken noodle soup, while Sylvia made a tossed salad. Dennis would be coming over soon to join them for supper, which Belinda felt sure was the reason for the radiant smile on her daughter's face.

Although she hadn't approved of Sylvia and Dennis's relationship in the beginning, Belinda had come to realize that Dennis was exactly the man her daughter needed. He was kind, polite, a hard worker, attentive, and good with Sylvia's children, who both seemed to like him. Belinda hoped in time Dennis would feel ready to marry Sylvia and become part of their family.

"Are you looking forward to spending Christmas with Ezekiel and his family?" Sylvia asked.

Belinda turned toward her daughter and smiled. "Jah. I can hardly wait to see them all again, and hold those cute little grandchildren in my arms."

"It was nice of Ezekiel to leave a message the other day, inviting Dennis to join us. It'll give him a chance to get to know Dennis better.

I'm sure my boyfriend would like to become better acquainted with my brother and his family, so it was good he asked a neighbor to feed his dog and horses, in addition to keeping an eye on the place while he's gone."

Belinda was about to respond when Henry stepped into the kitchen. His nostrils flared as he breathed noisily through his nose and mouth, as though he'd been running.

"Did you get the wood delivered to Maude?" Belinda questioned.

"Sure did, and you'll never guess what I discovered."

Belinda tipped her head in question.

"Our missing hinkel. They're in that old shack where she's been livin'. I heard 'em cackling, and then when I looked in the window, I saw one of the hens." His lips pressed into a white slash. "I knocked on the door, but Maude either wasn't at home or she was hidin' in there—probably afraid I'd take those chickens away from her."

"Oh dear." Belinda's fingers touched her parted lips.

Henry tromped across the room and stopped in front of her. "I was right all along about the manure on her shoes. Figured for sure that she had our chickens."

"When did you see manure on Maude's shoes?" Sylvia asked.

"Today, when she was in the greenhouse. I told Mom that I thought Maude was the one who took our hens." Henry shook his head. "That *verrickt* old woman's not to be trusted, and I think we should notify the *schrief*."

Belinda shook her head. "No, Son. We will not report this to the sheriff, and I don't think Maude is crazy. That was not a nice thing to say."

"Okay, but let's go get the chickens. It wasn't right for Maude to take them. She's a thief."

"Henry has a point, Mom," Sylvia interjected. "This is not the first time that woman has taken things from us without asking."

"Maybe if we'd been more giving and helpful to her, she would not have been desperate enough to steal."

"Taking things that ain't yours is wrong, plain and simple," Henry said.

"That is true, and I will have a talk with Maude."

"When?"

"Tomorrow morning, when I take her a sack of groceries," Belinda replied.

Henry's brows shot up. "You would give her groceries after she's stolen from us?"

"Yes, because it's the charitable thing to do."

Pink spots erupted on Henry's cheeks before he whirled around and headed for the back door.

"Where are you going?" Belinda called.

"Out to feed my hund." He swung the door open, and it clicked shut behind him before she could say anything more.

Belinda looked at Sylvia and released a sigh. "That bruder of yours has a lot to learn about forgiveness and being a good neighbor."

Chapter 7

New York State Line

"I still don't see why you asked Monroe to take care of things while we're gone," Henry mumbled as their driver's van left Pennsylvania and entered New York.

"I did not ask him," Belinda replied. "He volunteered."

Henry grunted. "I don't trust that fellow. I bet the only reason he offered was so he could snoop around."

Belinda turned her head to look at him in the seat behind her and frowned. "We've been over this before, Son, and I don't want to discuss it now."

"Jah, well, I think you're too nice sometimes, Mom." Henry shook his head. "I still can't believe after Maude stole our chickens that you went over there and gave her a sack of groceries."

"Our mamm did what she felt was right," Sylvia interjected.

"Maybe so, but I bet that old woman didn't even say thank you."

"That's not true," Belinda said. "When I handed Maude the paper sack, she said thank you."

"She shoulda said more than that." Henry's gaze flicked upward. "Maude should have apologized for stealing those hens and been willing to give them back. But no—you let her keep 'em."

"This discussion is over." Belinda turned back around and stared out the front window of their driver's van. She hoped her son's disposition would improve once they got to Ezekiel's. Otherwise it could ruin everyone's Christmas.

Clymer

As their driver pulled into Ezekiel's yard and parked his van, the doors opened. Everyone piled out, and they were almost immediately joined by Ezekiel and Michelle, who rushed out the front door to greet them.

Belinda's heart swelled with joy. It was so good to see this part of her family again.

After everyone had received a welcome hug or handshake and their luggage had been taken from the van, they all headed for the house. Belinda went straight for her grandchildren. Vernon stood in his playpen, and Angela Mary sat on a blanket nearby. Bending down and swooping the little girl into her arms, she gave her granddaughter a kiss. Angela Mary giggled as she wrapped her arms around Belinda's neck.

"I've missed you, little one," Belinda said in Pennsylvania Dutch.

"Can I hold my niece now?" Amy stepped forward and held out her arms.

"Of course." Belinda handed the child to Amy and lifted Vernon out of the playpen. "Oh, my sweet grandson, I can't believe how much you've grown." She lowered herself into the rocking chair and held the little guy in her lap. His smile reminded her of Ezekiel when he was a young boy. She felt warm inside as memories stirred from within to a time when she and Vernon had held their own children when they were about the age of her sweet grandchildren. *I'm so glad to have those images saved from a long while ago to reflect on. I am even more grateful for new opportunities with my loved ones here and now.*

Everyone else took a seat, and as they visited with each other, contentment filled Belinda's soul. How wonderful it was to have family together to celebrate this special holiday remembrance of Jesus' birth.

"Can I talk with you in private?" Henry whispered to Ezekiel, who sat beside him on the living-room sofa.

Ezekiel glanced around the room, where the rest of the family and

Dennis sat visiting. "Can it wait awhile?" he quietly asked. "You've only been here a short time, and I don't want to be rude by leaving the room."

Henry leaned closer to his brother. "I need to talk with you now. Can't we go outside or someplace else? Everyone's talking a mile a minute, so I bet we won't even be missed."

"Okay, if you insist." Ezekiel gave another quick glance around the room, and then he stood. Michelle looked at him and smiled before she continued to share with his mother about what baby Vernon had done the other day.

Henry was immediately on his feet and followed his brother to the utility room, where everyone's outer garments had been hung. After putting on their jackets they stepped out the back door.

"It's too cold out here to stand around and talk. Let's go out to my shop," Ezekiel suggested. "You might enjoy seeing all the *iem* supplies that I sell."

Henry wasn't the least bit interested in looking at bee supplies, but he gave an agreeable nod. At least they'd be out of the cold and away from listening ears.

When they entered the building a short time later, Ezekiel lit one of the gas lamps and motioned toward his supplies. "I'm sure happy with the amount of interest the bee stuff generates. I've added more hives outside and have been able to keep up with the amount of honey needed to sell to the tourists as well as the locals. Even Michelle likes to help out when she can, and she often shares the feedback she gets from our customers."

"That's nice." Henry's impartial tone fell from his lips as he waited.

Ezekiel told Henry to take a wooden stool near his desk. "I sense you want to get something off your chest. So what's on your mind?" He seated himself behind the desk.

Henry took a deep breath and released it slowly. *I'm hoping since Ezekiel is a minister it won't influence his thoughts about this situation. I want my brother to agree with me and nip in the bud any chance of Monroe winning our mother over.*

Henry folded his arms and looked directly at Ezekiel. "You're not gonna believe this, but Mom gave Monroe permission to feed our animals, water the plants, and keep an eye on our house while we're here."

He uncrossed his arms and gave his jacket collar a tug. "He even had the nerve to ask her for a key to the house so he could bring the mail inside and check on things."

Ezekiel leaned forward, with his arms resting on the desk. "How did Mom respond to that?"

"She said since the mailbox locks, whatever mail we may get while we're gone should be fine in there till we return." Henry paused and swiped his hand across his forehead. "And she said there wasn't anything in the house that needed to be checked, so all he has to do is take care of the animals, water everything in the greenhouse, and make sure everything on the property looks okay."

Ezekiel tapped his fingers against the surface of his desk. "I don't understand how this took place. It was my understanding that Monroe had quit coming around, so why would our mamm ask him to do anything while you're gone?"

Henry felt a sense of tightness in his jaw and facial muscles. "She didn't ask him. He suggested it. And even though Mom did not encourage him, he's started coming around again, asking how we're all doing and if there's anything he can do to help out."

"I see."

Henry frowned. "Is that all you have to say about this, Brother? Can't you see what that irritating man is up to?"

"I suspect he's still trying to win Mom's *hend*."

"Jah, well, if I have anything to say about it, Monroe's not gonna win Mom's hand." Henry got up from the stool and stood in front of Ezekiel's desk. "I don't trust that man; *Er is en missdrauischer mensch.*"

"How do you see him as a suspicious person?"

"I can't put my finger on it, but Monroe's not to be trusted. In fact, he's on my list of suspects."

Ezekiel's brows lifted. "Suspects for what?"

With eyes closed, Henry pinched the bridge of his nose. *What am I thinking? I almost blurted out the fact that we've had some vandalism at our place since Dad, Abe, and Toby were killed. If I let it slip to my brother, he'll ask Mom about it, and then I'll be in trouble with her for blabbing what she doesn't want him to know.*

"What is your list of suspects for?" Ezekiel asked again.

Henry opened his eyes and pulled his fingers through the back of his hair. He had to think quick and come up with some kind of believable explanation. "Umm. . .I guess suspects isn't really the word I shoulda used. What I meant was the list of men I believe might be interested in our mamm."

Ezekiel's eyes widened. "There are others, besides Monroe?"

Henry nodded.

"Have some other men been hanging around, asking Mom if they can court her?"

"Well, not exactly."

"What then?"

Henry shuffled his feet on the concrete floor. "I've seen a couple of widowed men in our church district eye-balling Mom lately. And then there's Herschel Fisher, who drops by sometimes too. He was there to help raise the new barn, and. . ."

Ezekiel held up his hand. "Even if there are some men who are interested in Mom, it's none of your *gscheft*."

"Why isn't it my business?"

"Because it's up to our mother to decide if she's interested in a relationship with another man."

"You've sure changed your tune. I thought you didn't care much for Monroe."

"He did come across as a bit irritating, but if Mom should decide to let Monroe, Herschel, or any other man court her, then we need to accept it and do nothing to stand in the way of her happiness."

Henry's face warmed. "I cannot stand by and do nothing if Mom chooses Monroe, or even Herschel. She still loves Dad and no one can ever replace him, plain and simple!"

He turned and stomped out the door.

I shoulda never brought this up to Ezekiel. He didn't care for Monroe when he met him before, but apparently he's changed his mind. Henry moved briskly through the path leading back to the house. *Sure am glad I didn't say what was really on my mind concerning Monroe. He's definitely high on my list of suspects and could only be showing interest in Mom to get his hands on our greenhouse.*

Strasburg

Virginia stood in front of her living-room window looking through Earl's binoculars again. Sometimes it was to get a closer look at the birds in their yard, but most often she used the field glasses to spy on the neighbors across the road. *I wonder what those Amish folks are up to today. They're always busy, and I'm sure I'll see something going on over at the Kings' place.*

The first thing she'd noticed early this morning was when an oversized passenger van drove into the yard. She had watched with interest as the King family came out of the house with suitcases and piled into the van. She had no idea where they were all going but figured it was probably somewhere to spend the Christmas holiday. Why else would they have loaded suitcases into the back of the vehicle?

As Virginia continued to stand there, her bum leg began to throb—a sure sign that she'd been on it too long. She took a seat in the recliner and tried to rub the pain out, but it did little to help the discomfort.

Goldie leaped onto of the arm of Virginia's chair. "You silly cat—come here." She scratched behind the animal's ear while a chorus of purring began. Virginia tried to relax in the recliner with Goldie, but her leg continued to ache. "I'm sorry to disturb you, sweet kitty, but your mommy needs to take care of something." Virginia moved the cat to the carpeted floor.

Rising from the chair, she limped into the kitchen. After pouring herself a cup of coffee, Virginia took an ice pack from the freezer compartment of the refrigerator, then back to the living room she went.

She was about to take a seat when her ears perked up at the sound of a horse and buggy coming down the road. *Well, at least it's not heading to the greenhouse, because thankfully, it's closed for the winter season.*

As the sound grew closer, Virginia glanced out the window and caught sight of the horse and buggy turning up the Kings' driveway. *Hmm. . .that's strange. The sign out by the road says the greenhouse is closed for the winter, so who would be going there today?*

Virginia sat her coffee mug on the end table, along with the ice pack, and then she picked up the binoculars and stood in front of the window, ignoring the pain in her leg.

Her interest piqued when she watched an Amish man with no beard get out of the buggy and tie his horse to the hitching rail near the house. Virginia had seen this same man come to the greenhouse on several occasions, but she didn't know his name, or if he had any kind of relationship to the King family. Since the man was here now, she figured he either hadn't seen the sign or, if he knew the Kings personally, didn't know they were leaving.

Virginia continued to observe until the Amish man disappeared around the side of the house where the new barn had been built to replace the old one. *He's not heading to the greenhouse, or the Kings' home, so I wonder what he's up to.*

She was tempted to put on her warm jacket and go over there to see what the man was up to, but in addition to the colder weather that had set in, her leg hurt too bad to walk that far. She returned to her recliner and put the ice pack against her leg again. She wished Earl could have stayed home from work today. It wasn't fair that he had to show up at the car dealership this morning. After all, who would be looking at new vehicles on Christmas Eve day?

Maybe some rich guy wanting to buy a new car for his wife or spoiled teenager, she thought. *But then why would anyone wait till the last minute to get a big Christmas gift like that? And who has that kind of money anyway?*

She reached for her cup of coffee and took a drink. While she and Earl were getting by financially, they were far from rich and never would be. It was hard not to be envious of people who could afford the finer things in life.

Virginia glanced at the small Christmas tree on the other side of the room. *Big deal! What's a holiday without a family to spend it with? As usual, Christmas Day will be just me and Earl, watching TV and eating a meal by ourselves. Oh, how I wish we were back in Chicago and could get together with Stella and her husband for at least a part of the holiday. We could visit, eat snacks, and play one of our favorite card games, like we did in the past.*

The longer Virginia stewed about this, the worse she felt. And the worse she felt, the more tempted she was to light up a cigarette.

Virginia's thoughts were pulled aside when she heard a horse whinny. She got up and made her way over to the window again, in time to see the Amish man undo his horse and climb into the buggy. Whatever he'd come over to the Kings' place for, he'd obviously figured out that they weren't home.

"Good riddance," she mumbled. "I hope I don't see or hear anymore Amish buggies on our road the rest of the day." Of course, Virginia knew that was not likely to be the case. Like every other day since she and Earl had moved to this area, she was sure to see horses and buggies. The only good thing was that now, with the greenhouse closed until spring, there would be a lot less traffic on this road. At least she had something to be thankful for on this boring Christmas Eve.

Chapter 8

Clymer

Christmas morning, after breakfast and a time of devotions, the women did the dishes while the men went outside to look at Ezekiel's shop and tour the property.

Jared took a sip from his cup of coffee and then looked over at his brother-in-law. "Thank you for leading us in the devotion after the meal earlier."

"Jah," Dennis agreed. "It was a timely reminder of how God sent His Son to earth as a baby, in order to later die and rise again so that those who believe on His name will be saved from their sins."

"I remember when my *daed* was the one leading our morning devotionals in the past," Ezekiel said. "Then after his death, Mom took over for him to keep the family who lived in her home moving on the right path."

Jared's gaze drifted toward the floor of the shop. "It's important to spend time in God's Word, and I'm thankful that He helps us through the good and bad times."

The men agreed, and Ezekiel continued showing them around the shop.

"This is quite an operation you've got going here," Dennis commented after Ezekiel described some of the supplies he either made in the shop or sold from where he purchased them at wholesale prices. "Do you also raise bees and sell honey?"

"While beekeeping is not my primary business, we do make some extra money by selling jars of honey to several local stores." Ezekiel smiled. "Growing up in Strasburg, I became interested in raising bees for honey when I was a teenager. Although I helped in my parents' greenhouse, it was never my favorite occupation. I preferred selling the honey my bees made, and jumped at the chance to move here when I learned of this business that was for sale. Let's go outside now so I can give you a tour around the property."

With eager expressions, the men headed out the door.

"I've always thought it was important to work at a job I enjoyed," Jared interjected. "When my uncle Maylon taught me the roofing business, I knew I'd found my niche."

"I feel the same way about training horses," Dennis put in. "Even when I was a young boy, I was interested in them. When I got my own horse after turning sixteen, I could get him to do most anything." He chuckled. "My older brother always teased me and said the only reason my gaul did what I wanted was because he knew there'd be a lump of sugar as a reward."

"Makes sense to me." Ezekiel smiled. "Everyone—even a horse—needs a little incentive to get certain things done."

"True." Dennis glanced from where he stood facing the backside of the house. "Guess I'd better go find Henry. He's supposed to be in the front yard waiting for me. There's a little project the two of us need to work on." Dennis looked at Ezekiel, and then Jared. "I'll see you two back at the house."

After Dennis left the shop, Ezekiel looked over at Jared. "I can't figure out what kind of project those two would need to do in my yard."

Jared lifted his broad shoulders in a shrug. "I have no idea, but one thing I can tell you is that your young brother has sure taken a shine to Dennis."

"Since I can't be there for Henry, I'm glad he's found a friend in Sylvia's new boyfriend. From what I can tell, Dennis has been good for my sister as well as my brother." There was a part of Ezekiel that wished he could be the person to help his brother. But the Lord had provided Dennis, and Ezekiel would trust him to take good care of Henry.

Soon after the men came inside, the family gathered in the living room to open gifts. The room seemed to be filled with excitement and anticipation. The pretty red-and-green wrapping on some of the gifts added to the expectancy.

Sylvia smiled, seeing the look of joy on Henry's face when Dennis presented him with a gift subscription to a well-known birding magazine.

"Danki, Dennis." Henry grinned as he thumbed through the first issue, which accompanied the subscription notice. "Bet I'll learn a lot while looking at this magazine when a new issue arrives in our mailbox every month."

"You're welcome, Henry." Dennis turned to Sylvia and handed her a package. "I hope you like what I got for you."

The present had been wrapped nicely, and Sylvia wondered if Dennis had done the work or asked someone else to wrap it for him. The package felt a little weighty. She couldn't begin to guess what was inside. Curious to see what it was, she hurriedly opened the gift and discovered a pair of binoculars.

She looked at Dennis and smiled. "Danki. It's nice to finally have a pair I can call my own." Sylvia inspected the field glasses and placed the leather strap over her head to try them out.

"They have a stronger power than many of the binoculars I looked at," Dennis explained. "Looking through these, you should be able to see most birds easily, even from quite a distance."

Sylvia held them close to her chest. "I can hardly wait to go birding again so I can put these to good use."

"Why wait till then? Let's go over to the front window and you can try them out now." He winked at her. "You never know. . .there might be something in the front yard worth looking at."

Sylvia wasn't sure there would be any birds in Ezekiel's yard to look at, but she didn't want to disappoint Dennis, so she left her seat and followed him to the window. When she held the field glasses up to her face, Dennis said, "Scan the whole front yard now, and look for anything interesting that might catch your eye."

Sylvia did as he asked, and nearly dropped the binoculars when a large heart-shaped sign came into view. Painted in bright red letters was a surprising message: "Will You Marry Me?"

Sylvia had never seen nor heard of such an unusual marriage proposal, but then she'd never met a man quite like Dennis before. Happy tears pricked the back of her eyes, as she turned to him and said: "Jah, Dennis, I will marry you."

Sylvia had no sooner said the words, when her whole family clapped and gathered around them, offering hearty congratulations.

Sylvia felt a sense of weightlessness as she shed more tears of joy. It had been a long time since she'd felt so happy. Oh, how she looked forward to becoming Dennis's wife, but first they'd need to set a wedding date and do a lot of planning in the days ahead.

After everyone gathered around the tables Ezekiel had set up in the dining room, all heads bowed for silent prayer. Although Belinda missed her husband, son, and son-in-law's presence at this meal, she felt a sense of calm being here with the rest of her family. As the platters and bowls of food were passed around, she studied each person's face, committing their happy expressions to memory. Even Henry, who looked like he'd been forced to eat a bowl of sour grapes on the trip to Clymer, wore a pleasant expression on his face. No doubt the happiness he felt was because of his friendship with Dennis. Belinda felt pleased that Sylvia's future husband had taken her son under his wing. Since Ezekiel lived too far away to spend much time with Henry, it was good that he had a special bond with Dennis.

Belinda's attention turned to Sylvia. The transformation in her eldest daughter since Dennis had come into her life was wonderful to witness. Sylvia seemed more sure of herself these days, and Belinda noticed a spring in her step and a brightness in her eyes that hadn't been there since Toby died.

She looked across the table, where Amy and Jared sat. Both wore happy smiles as they dished up their food and made conversation with Michelle and Ezekiel.

My eldest son and youngest daughter are both happily married, and soon my eldest daughter will be too, Belinda mused. *I'm happy for them, but I can't help thinking that it'll only be me and Henry running the greenhouse by ourselves once Sylvia and Dennis are married. After Amy has a baby and perhaps Sylvia has more children, neither will want to work away from their homes.* Belinda helped herself to some gravy, which she ladled over the mashed potatoes on her plate. *I've reflected on all of this too many times, and I need to focus on the treasured moments I'm making with my family today. My thoughts should be on the present, not the future, which is out of my hands, for only God knows what lies ahead for each of us.*

Strasburg

Virginia frowned as she watched her husband sleeping in his recliner a few feet from where she sat on the couch. "Merry Christmas," she mumbled. "What a quiet, boring day."

Earl didn't open his eyes or move a muscle, but his snoring increased. He'd fallen asleep soon after they'd finished eating the ham and baked potatoes Virginia had fixed for their holiday meal. She'd even gone to the trouble of making a green bean casserole and sweet potatoes with melted marshmallows on top. Earl had eaten more than his share, which had no doubt contributed to his sleepy state.

The television blared with some action movie playing in the background. This sort of thing happened more often than not in the evenings after dinner. *How in the world can that man of mine sleep through all the noise?*

Virginia went over quick enough to turn down the volume on the set and return to her seat without disturbing Earl. *That's better, even though I'd rather be watching something else that has to do with Christmas today.*

She looked around the room for the cat, but Goldie wasn't in sight. *I'm sure she's asleep on our bed. It's one of her favorite spots, especially on top of my pillow.*

Hearing a horse and buggy coming down the road, Virginia rose from her seat and went over to the front window to look out. The buggy looked the same as most of those she'd previously seen, but she recognized the horse as it turned up the Kings' driveway.

Virginia picked up Earl's binoculars for a better look and watched as the same Amish man she'd seen before got out of his rig and secured the horse. *I wonder what he's doing back here again.*

She couldn't help watching as the man walked in the direction of the barn and disappeared from her sight. *Drats! Sure wish I could see what he's up to. If some of those trees weren't blocking my view, I'd have a front row seat into their yard.*

"Hey, why'd ya turn the volume down?" Earl sputtered. "And what are ya doin' with those binoculars, Virginia?"

She whirled around. "Earl, you about scared me to death. I thought you were sleeping."

"Nope. I was listening to the TV while resting my eyes."

"Puh!" She flapped her hand in his direction. "People don't snore unless they're sound asleep. I don't see how anyone can rest their eyes the way you do with the volume up so loud."

"It doesn't bother me." Earl let out a yawn and pointed at the binoculars Virginia still held in her hands. "Who are you spyin' on this time?"

"If you're really interested, there's an Amish man who's been over at the Kings' place since they left to go somewhere yesterday morning."

"Maybe he doesn't know they're not home." Earl got up and moved over to the window. "Or maybe he's checking on the place while they're gone. They do have some critters that would need to be fed and watered, you know." He took the binoculars from her and motioned to the couch. "Why don't you sit down and relax, before your leg starts to hurt from standing so long?"

Virginia gave a huff. "I am tired of sitting, and on top of that, I'm bored. Except for our scrawny little tree, and the few lights you put up outside, it doesn't even feel like Christmas to me."

"Didn't you make a chocolate mint cake for our dessert?"

She put a hand on her hip. "Is that a hint that you have room for more after eating our big meal?"

"I could handle a piece of your delicious cake. Also a cup of hot coffee would go real good with it too."

"Okay, whatever you want." Virginia headed for the kitchen.

Once there, she got out some holiday plates and a couple of matching mugs. At least the dessert would add a little cheer to the hum-drum day. *I wouldn't mind having a few grandchildren to spoil today, or at least some family around to make the season brighter.*

Virginia grabbed a tray to set the plated desserts and coffee mugs on. She returned to the living room and served Earl his dessert. With an eager expression, he gobbled it down, while Virgina ate hers slowly.

"Let's watch one of those sappy Christmas movies." Earl remained in the recliner as he picked up the remote. "That oughta be enough to put you in the holiday spirit."

Virginia took a sip of her coffee and wrinkled her nose. "Yeah, right."

After she returned to the couch, another thought popped into her mind. *If the Kings are away on a trip, I wonder why they didn't ask me and Earl to keep an eye on the place instead of some fellow who lives so far that he has to travel over there by horse and buggy. I bet they don't think we're trustworthy enough to take care of their place while they are gone. Amy, and probably Mrs. King too, must not care much for us, or we'd have gotten an invitation to Amy and Jared's wedding.*

Dwelling on this topic for too long caused Virginia's stomach to knot up. She still held a grudge and didn't think she could get past the feeling of rejection she'd felt.

"How 'bout some more cake and coffee?"

Earl's question halted Virginia's negative thoughts. "Sure, why not? Your wish is my command, Earl." She pulled herself up from the couch and limped out to the kitchen. Maybe another piece of cake would make her feel better too. At least for a little while it might squelch her self-pity.

Chapter 9

Virginia watched out the living-room window as a van pulled onto the Kings' driveway. As near as she could tell, it was the same one that had left the place with the King family the day before Christmas. Now, here they were, two days after the holiday, returning home.

Earlier this morning, shortly after Earl left for work, Virginia had seen the old woman, Maude, standing near the mailboxes across the road. She'd been about to open the front door and holler out, asking Maude to move along, when the scraggly-looking woman finally ambled on down the road. With the way her mouth moved as she shook her head, Virginia figured Maude must have been talking to herself.

She's probably senile, or maybe has some kind of mental problem, Virginia told herself. *A person like her can't be trusted. I wonder if she went onto the Kings' property while they were gone. I wouldn't be surprised if she took something.*

Purring like a motor boat, Goldie rubbed against Virginia's leg, swishing her fluffy tail.

"Okay, okay, you determined cat. Let's go out to the kitchen, and I'll get you some food." As Virginia made her way to the kitchen, Goldie pranced beside her. While the cat couldn't converse with Virginia, at least she was good company.

She grabbed a can of food from one of the lower drawers and opened it. The aroma of fish and chicken permeated the room. "This stuff doesn't smell too bad." Virginia lowered her glance at Goldie as she plopped the food into the cat's dish. "Here you go. Enjoy your breakfast."

Virginia noticed a bit of the food had remained in the can. *I wonder what this stuff tastes like. What would it hurt to sample a bit?* She took her finger and ran it around the inside of the can. But before she could retrieve it some blood began dripping from her finger.

"Oh no! That wasn't a good idea." Virginia went to the sink, rinsed off her hand, and took a closer look at the wound. It was still bleeding, but at least it wasn't a deep cut that might require stitches.

She went to pull off a paper towel, but the way she'd yanked it, with only one hand, sent the roll from the counter onto the floor. Goldie jumped when the towels landed near her, and Virginia moaned. "This is turning out to be a bad morning." She left the mess where it lay and grabbed a damp dish rag from the sink to wrap her finger in. Then Virginia limped off to the bathroom to find the right bandage to tape the cut closed.

She fumbled about, working to get her finger taped up, and when she finished she brought back the stained rag to the kitchen. Goldie had eaten all of her food and now lay on the throw rug, bathing herself. "At least you are satisfied and happy."

Virginia picked up the unwound roll of paper towels and tore off the long tail from it. She hung up what was left and threw away the rest in the garbage. Her finger hurt and some blood seeped through the bandage. The can of cat food remained on the counter, along with traces of blood. Virginia, still curious after everything that occurred, picked a spoon from the utensil drawer and gave the cat food a taste. It didn't linger long in her mouth before she rushed to the sink and spit it out. "This stuff tastes nasty! How can it smell one way and taste so bad? Well, at least no one but me will know I gave Goldie's food a try."

Virginia picked up the can and tossed it in the garbage on top of the wad of paper towels. Then she retrieved the used blood-stained rag and tried to rinse it out. It wouldn't come clean, so she used it to wipe away the rest of the blood droplets and threw it away too. *At least Earl won't find out what happened, since I did a good job of taking care of things.*

After Henry helped bring everyone's luggage inside, he said goodbye to Dennis, Jared, and Amy before they climbed back into the van to be driven to their homes.

"Want me to check for phone messages?" he asked his mother.

"That would be helpful. And please get the mail too." She handed him the key.

"Sure, I'll do that first, and then after I leave the phone shed I'm gonna let my hund out of his dog run for a bit while I make sure the horses and chickens are okay."

"I'm confident that they're all fine. Monroe knew we'd be home today, so he probably came over early this morning to take care of things."

Henry resisted the urge to say something negative about Mom's would-be suitor. She didn't like it when he bad-mouthed someone— even Monroe, who no one in the family particularly cared for, except maybe Mom. Henry couldn't be sure how she really felt about her old boyfriend, since she treated him kindly whenever he came around. But she had stated on more than one occasion that she had no romantic interest in Monroe Esh. While that might be true, Henry was concerned that the persistent man might keep trying to charm his mother until she finally gave in and allowed him to court her. That, of course, could lead to a possible marriage proposal, which Henry could not stand for.

He gripped the mailbox key in his hand so hard it dug into his palm. *Don't know what I'd do if Mom ended up marrying that irritating fellow. I couldn't live in the same house with him, that's for sure.*

Forcing his thoughts aside, while shivering against the harsh wind that had begun to blow tree branches about, Henry hurried through some scattered leaves the heavy breeze had pushed down along the driveway. When he came to their mailbox and opened it, Henry discovered only a few advertising pamphlets inside, along with a couple of bills.

Holding tight to the mail in one hand, he made his way back up the driveway to the phone shed. Upon entering the small building, Henry shut the door, took a seat, and clicked on the answering machine. It was good to get out of the wind even if it had to be in the tiny, cold cubical. The first message was from Herschel Fisher's daughter, Sara, saying she wanted to wish the King family a Merry Christmas because she didn't have time to send out cards this year. The next message was from Mary Ruth Lapp, inviting Mom to join her and some other ladies in their church district to a quilting party that would take place next week in Mary Ruth's home.

Henry paused the answering machine and wrote both messages on the tablet beside the phone. When he finished, he clicked the button again to see if anyone else had called.

The third and final message caused Henry to freeze in place. He was so stunned in fact that he had to replay it again, to be sure of what he'd heard.

The voice sounded muffled, but the message was clear: "You've been warned before, but chose to ignore. You need to sell your place and move before it's too late."

Henry's ears rang as a knot formed in his stomach. Warned before? Had there been a similar message he didn't know about? If so, who'd listened to the muffled voice, and why hadn't they said anything? Whenever the earlier threatening message had come in, it had obviously been deleted because there were no other muffled voices left on the answering machine.

Why didn't anyone tell me about this? I'm not a child. I can't help but feel hurt by being left out of what is going on around here. Henry needed to let go of the disappointment and focus on the matter of his family being threatened. He listened to the message one more time, trying to decipher who the person was, but to no avail. The man or woman who'd made the call had done a good job masking their voice.

He remained in the phone shack a few more minutes, mulling things over. The frightening message made him even more determined to find out who was responsible for the damage that had been done to their property. He felt sure that whoever had made the call was the person who'd done it, and might even be responsible for their barn burning down.

Henry saved the message so his mother could listen to it, and then he left the phone shed. He would go inside and talk to her once he'd let Blackie out for a run and gone out to the barn to check on the horses. Henry needed the extra time to think things through before talking to Mom.

After letting Blackie out of his pen, Henry started for the barn. The dog, however, had other ideas. Barking and nipping at Henry's heels, Blackie continued to carry on until Henry stopped walking. "Knock it off you crazy hund. I know ya missed me, but I don't have time for this right now."

When the dog continued to bark, Henry picked up a stick and gave it a toss. Blackie gave another excited *woof*, and took off after the stick. Henry took advantage of this brief reprieve and made a dash for the barn.

He'd barely entered the building when he spotted a note tacked up on the wall near the double doors. It said: *"Sell Out or Face the Consequences!"*

Henry's heart pounded as he grabbed a bright-beamed flashlight to check every area of the barn. He hoped he would find some sort of evidence as to who had hung that sign. Someone who wanted them gone had not only left the muffled message, but they'd been in the barn.

Henry couldn't shake the uneasy feeling. He wanted to catch this person so his family could have peace again. After his father, brother, and brother-in-law passed away, he and the rest of the family had enough to deal with. They certainly did not need this type of problem on top of everything else.

After looking in the horses' stalls and all the other areas in the lower half of the barn, Henry felt defeated because he'd found no clues. *I'd like to see this person be held accountable for his or her actions.*

With jaw clenched, he climbed up the ladder to the loft. There had to be a clue somewhere that would let him know who had come to the barn and hung that sign. The only person Henry knew for sure had been in the barn while they were gone was Monroe, since he was supposed to feed and water the animals.

Henry snapped his fingers. *That's it! Why am I looking for clues when the answer's so clear? That aggravating man has been up to no good ever since he came back to Strasburg and started hangin' around Mom. Monroe needs to be confronted, and I aim to do it as soon as possible.*

<hr />

With her suitcase lying on the bed, Belinda was busy unpacking when Henry stepped into the room. "Was there any mail or phone messages waiting?" she asked, barely glancing his way.

"Jah, there was some mail, and. . ."

"Where'd you put it?"

"Umm. . .I must have left it in the phone shed."

"Could you go back and get it, please?"

Henry's gaze darted around the room as he blew out a series of short breaths.

"What's wrong, Son? Is something bothering you?"

"Jah, and I am very *verlegge*."

"What is it? What has you so troubled?"

"There was a muffled message on our answering machine and a threatening note tacked to the barn wall near the double doors."

A rush of adrenaline passed through Belinda's body as she listened to Henry explain what both messages said.

Henry moved closer to the bed. "This has happened before, hasn't it, Mom?"

She nodded. "Not the note on the barn, but the muffled voice on the phone."

"Why didn't you say something about it?"

"I didn't want to upset you."

"Well, it's too late for that. I'm umgerennt now, and I woulda liked to have known about this sooner."

"How would that have done any good, Son? We don't have a clue who's behind all of this, and the truth is, we may never know."

Henry planted his feet in a wide stance and stared at her. "There's only one person who could've done it, Mom."

"Oh? And who would that be?"

"Monroe. He went in the barn to feed the horses and cats while we were gone."

"I realize that, Henry, but it doesn't mean Monroe is responsible for the note you discovered." Belinda put both hands on her hips. "Monroe's never given me any reason to believe that he would want us to sell and move out. In fact, he's been kind enough to drop by regularly to see how we're doing and ask if there's anything he can do to help out."

Henry's eyes narrowed as he reached up to rub the back of his neck. "He's pretending to care about us, Mom. Can't you see that? For some reason that man has been trying to frighten us so we'll move out."

"What reason would he have for doing that?"

"Maybe he wants the greenhouse for himself, and since he hasn't been able to win you over, he's changed tactics and decided to use threating messages to get what he wants. He could also be the one responsible for all the vandalism that's been done around here."

Belinda held up her hand as she lowered herself to the bed. "That's enough, Henry. I don't want to hear any more of your *narrisch* theories."

"It's not foolish." Henry shook his head vigorously. "That man is not to be trusted, and I aim to prove it. Right now, though, I'm goin' back out to the phone shed to get the mail."

Henry turned and tromped out of the room before Belinda could form a response. Monroe might be a lot of things, but she couldn't believe he would stoop so low as to frighten them so he could get his hands on the greenhouse. After all, what did he need it for? He had his own furniture business to run. *It sounds like my son wants to find out who's behind this and so do I. I'm sure Monroe isn't the person but that still leaves my family in a precarious situation.*

Belinda picked up the dresses from the suitcase and hung them in her closet. She did not want to move from her home. *Dear Lord, please help me to have the faith that You will take care of all this.*

"You look *umgerrent*, Mom. Is something wrong?" Sylvia asked when she entered the kitchen where Belinda paced the floor.

She stopped pacing and turned to face her daughter. "As a matter of fact, I'm very upset." Belinda relayed everything Henry had told her before he'd rushed back outside in a huff. She also told Sylvia about the muffled phone call she'd received previously and apologized for keeping quiet about it.

Sylvia's brows drew together as she lowered herself into a chair. "Oh dear. That's so frightening. Do you think Henry could be right about Monroe? Is it possible that he's the one responsible for the muffled phone calls and all the other negative things that have happened around here?"

Belinda took a chair across from her daughter. "I can't imagine why he would do such a thing. Monroe claims to care for me, so I wouldn't think. . ." Her voice trailed off as she placed her fingers across her forehead and massaged the pulsating parts.

"Are you going to talk to Monroe about this?"

"I. . .I don't know what I would say, other than to come right out and ask if he's responsible for any of what's been done."

"If he is, he'd probably deny it."

"Maybe it would be better if I tell Monroe about the phone message and note tacked to the barn wall. Then I'll wait and see how he reacts."

Sylvia bobbed her head. "That might be the best approach."

At the sound of a horse and buggy coming up the driveway, Belinda got up from her chair and stepped into the hallway to look out the small window on the front door. *I guess there's no time like the present, because Monroe just pulled in. I need to speak with him right away, before Henry sees him and makes an accusation that is most likely false and could make things worse.*

Chapter 10

Belinda waited until Monroe stepped onto the porch before she opened the door. "I saw you coming, so—"

"It's good to see you. When did you get home?" he interrupted.

She glanced in the entry where Henry's suitcase sat. Belinda slid it against the wall to be out of the way. Her face warmed, feeling a little embarrassed. "A few hours ago. I was going to call and leave a message for you, but now I won't have to." Belinda opened the door wider. "Would you like to come in and join me for a cup of *kaffi* and some kichlin?"

A wide smile stretched across his face. "Coffee and cookies sounds good to me." He stepped inside and joined her in the hallway. Monroe seemed to be in good spirits, and his gaze never left Belinda as he slipped off his shoes by the door.

"Sylvia's in the living room with her kinner, so let's go in the kitchen where we talk in private." Belinda gestured in that direction.

"Okay, that's fine with me." Monroe followed Belinda to the kitchen and took a seat at the table. "Everything went fine here while you were gone." He grinned at her. "I had no problems with any of the animals, and I remembered to water all the plants." He reached into his pants pocket and handed Belinda the key to the greenhouse.

"Danki." Belinda poured them both a cup of coffee, set a plate of ginger cookies on the table, and took a seat across from him. "There's something I'd like to talk to you about, Monroe."

"Sure, no problem. I always enjoy talking to you." He reached for a cookie and gobbled it down, then followed it with a drink from his cup. A look of contentment showed on Monroe's face as he stared at her. As usual, his appearance was neat as a pin, and his hair had been combed back from his face. The aftershave or men's cologne he wore had a light musky odor. She caught his boyish grin before he took another sip of coffee. "Belinda, your place is kept up nice, but I don't know how you manage to run your business and keep up with this big house."

"I have a lot of help. My children pitch in; especially when things get hectic around here." She dropped her gaze. *I've known this man for a good many years and he's never shown any signs of contempt. In fact, since Vernon's death Monroe has been nothing but supportive.*

She added some cream to the hot liquid and gave it a stir. *But my children haven't warmed up to him and have expressed their lack of fondness toward Monroe many times. Are the negative things they've complained about enough reason to think he would be capable of vandalizing, leaving threatening notes, or making muffled phone calls?*

Belinda sat a little straighter in her chair. She cleared her throat, and was about to ask if he knew anything about the note tacked up in the barn, when Henry came into the kitchen with a stack of mail in his hand. A sheen of sweat formed on Henry's face as he glared at Monroe. "You're just the person I wanna see."

"Oh?" Monroe tipped his head. "I'm glad to see you too."

Henry dropped the mail on the counter and pulled a folded piece of paper out from the stack of envelopes. Then he marched across the room, unfolded the paper, and placed it on the table in front of Monroe. "What do ya know about this?"

Belinda held her breath as she waited to hear Monroe's response. While this wasn't the way she would have brought up the topic, at least now they would know whether her ex-boyfriend had written the note, and if so, what made him do it.

Monroe stared at the piece of paper several seconds before he spoke. "Where did you get this?" He looked right at Henry.

"In the barn. It was tacked up on the wall near the double doors."

A muscle on the side of Monroe's neck twitched. "That's sure strange." He tapped the piece of paper with his index finger. "I never saw this while I was in the barn feeding the horses and cats."

"So you didn't put it there?" Henry's eyes narrowed as he continued to stare at the man.

"Of course not! Are you suggesting that I wrote the note?" Monroe's mouth slackened.

"That's how it seems to me," Henry stated.

Monroe looked over at Belinda. "Surely you don't believe I would do something like this. I mean, why would I, for goodness' sake?"

Belinda opened her mouth to respond, but Henry cut her off. "Did you leave a muffled message on our answering machine?"

"What? No!" Monroe's cheeks colored. "I have no idea what you're talking about."

"Someone left a threatening message while we were gone, and we couldn't tell who it was because their voice sounded strange—barely audible," Belinda explained.

"And you think I did that?"

Belinda blinked rapidly. "Well, I—"

"I can't believe you would even suggest that I'd be capable of doing such a thing. I care about you, Belinda, and would not do anything to hurt or upset you. I've never been anything but helpful and kind where you and your family are concerned." Monroe's jaw clenched, causing his lips to form into a white slash. He stared at Belinda and then pushed his chair away from the table. "Think I'd better go."

As he walked briskly toward the door, Belinda called out to him. "I'm sorry, Monroe. We didn't mean to offend you. It's just that. . ."

"Enough said. I guess our friendship is purely one-sided." He rushed out the door before Belinda could try to stop him.

She turned to Henry and said, "I wish you hadn't accused him, Son. I was only going to ask if he had seen the note or might know if anyone besides him had been on our property while we were gone." She heaved a sigh. "Now he's offended and will probably never come around here again."

"That's good." Henry gave a shrug. "Maybe now that I've confronted him with what I've suspected, he'll finally leave us alone."

Monroe snapped the reins and got his horse moving at a good pace down the road. "I can't believe the way Belinda talked to me. And that son of hers—well, he should be seen and not heard. If he were my boy, he'd get a good tongue-lashing and plenty of extra chores to do for being so disrespectful to me."

Every muscle in Monroe's body tensed. "At this rate I'll never convince Belinda to marry me." He pressed one fist against his mouth and puffed out his cheeks. "And just when I thought I was gaining ground with her. Now I'm not sure what to do. Should I wait a few days and then go back over there—try to make her listen to reason and convince her that I'm not the enemy? Or would it be better to stay away longer and hope that she'll make contact with me? I lost Belinda once to Vernon. I won't lose her again."

As he headed down the road, Monroe got to thinking about what Henry had said. *I can't allow them to believe I had anything to do with the things that have happened to them.*

Sylvia got up off the living-room floor where she'd been rebraiding Rachel's hair and went to the kitchen. She found her mother sitting at the table with her head bowed and hands folded, as though praying. She waited quietly until Mom lifted her head.

"Is everything okay?" Sylvia asked. "I heard you talking to someone awhile ago, and it sounded like Monroe."

Mom moved her head slowly up and down. "He was here all right, and he may never be back."

"How come?"

Sylvia took a chair and listened as her mother repeated everything that had been said between her and Monroe, as well as what Henry had accused the man of.

"Monroe denied knowing anything about the note or threatening phone calls." Mom's chin quivered. "He seemed sincere, not to mention deeply hurt by the accusations. Monroe's final words were that he thought our friendship has been one-sided."

"That's good in a way, Mom. He obviously realizes now that you don't care for him."

Mom shook her head. "I never said that, Daughter. While I don't think of Monroe in a romantic sort of way, he has been a good friend, who I felt sure cared for me."

Sylvia sat quietly for a few moments, carefully forming her next words. "I'll admit that I don't care much for Monroe, but he doesn't seem the type who would do anything malicious to you or anyone in our family."

"I agree. But I doubt we could convince Henry of that. He's sure Monroe is the one responsible for the phone message and note left in the barn, and for that matter, all the rest of the things that have happened to us since your daed, Abe, and Toby were killed."

"And you think it's not *meechlich*?"

"Anything's possible, but I've known Monroe since we were youngsters, and if he cares for me the way he's often stated, then I am quite certain he would not do anything to knowingly hurt or upset me."

"So now what?" Sylvia asked.

"The first thing I'm going to do is have a talk with Henry." Mom rapped her knuckles on the table. "Then I am going to call Monroe and say that I'm sorry for anything we said that may have hurt his feelings." She looked at Sylvia and smiled. "And you, my dear daughter, don't need to worry about this. After that very original marriage proposal you received from Dennis on Christmas Day, all you should be thinking about is planning for and looking forward to your wedding."

"Oh, I am looking forward to the day I become Dennis's fraa, but we haven't set a date yet, so I can't do much planning." Sylvia spoke in a subdued tone.

"I understand. It would have been difficult for you to do much planning with all the commotion we had during the few short days spent at Ezekiel and Michelle's place."

"We had a nice time though, and I was pleased that my bruder and his fraa welcomed Dennis into their home and everyone got along so well. I was a little worried about Henry at first because he seemed kind of sullen when we arrived." Sylvia took a cookie from the plate in the center of the table. "After he opened his Christmas gift from Dennis, Henry's attitude improved."

"Jah. Henry looks up to Dennis, there's no doubt about it. His coming into your life has been good for both you and your young brother."

Sylvia couldn't deny it. The part of her soul that she never thought would heal had been brought to life again. She looked forward to seeing what God had in store for her, Dennis, and the children in the days ahead. She'd continue to pray for the protection of her family. And if, for some unimaginable reason, Monroe was to blame, her prayer would be that God would convict him of his wrongdoings and the attacks and threats would end.

"I enjoyed our trip to your brother's place in New York, but it's good to be home," Jared commented as Amy got out some bread to make them both a sandwich.

She nodded. "I was glad for the opportunity to finally see where he and Michelle live, and having our whole family together for Christmas made it even more special."

"True." Jared joined her at the counter. "Is there anything I can do to help?"

"You can get out the lunch meat and cheese while I slice the bread and spread some butter."

"Not a problem." Jared opened the refrigerator and took out what Amy had asked for. "Would you want some *sellaat*, a *tomaets*, or the jar of *bickels*?"

"Lettuce and tomato might be nice, but I don't care for a pickle on mine. Feel free to get them out if you want one though," Amy responded.

"Naw, I don't need a bickle either."

After the sandwiches were made, and they took seats at the table, Amy and Jared bowed their heads for silent prayer.

Heavenly Father, Amy prayed, *thank You for keeping us safe on our trip home from Clymer, and for giving us such a wonderful Christmas with our family. Bless this food we are about to eat, and please bless and protect each member of our family in the days ahead so we may better serve You. Amen.*

Amy kept her eyes closed and head bowed until she heard the rustle of Jared's napkin. When she opened her eyes and looked at him from across the table, she smiled. "After all the commotion that went on at Ezekiel's place the last few days, it seems kind of quiet in here with just the two of us."

Jared bobbed his head before taking a bite of sandwich. "Someday, when the Lord blesses us with kinner, it won't be so quiet in this home."

Amy placed one hand against her stomach. She hoped it wouldn't be long before they were expecting their first child. While it was nice to spend time with her nieces and nephews, it wasn't the same as having children of their own.

"Getting back to our conversation about the time we spent with your brother and his family"—Jared paused for a drink of milk—"I enjoyed seeing Ezekiel's shop and listening to him talk about all the bee supplies. From some of the things Ezekiel said, I'd guess he's quite *zufridde* living in Clymer."

"You're right, but my brother wouldn't be so contented if he knew about all the vandalism that's been done at Mom's place." Amy blotted her mouth with a napkin. "I still think he has the right to know, and it's getting harder to keep it a secret. I'm surprised Henry hasn't blurted it out already."

"Nothing's happened recently though, right?" Jared asked.

Amy shook her head. "Not that I'm aware of. I'm sure Mom would have said something to us if anything new had occurred, if for no other reason than to ask for our prayers."

Chapter 11

"Is that another *amschel* I see in the yard?" Belinda turned to face Henry, who'd come into the kitchen after doing his outside chores.

He stepped up to the window next to her and peered out. "Yep. That's a robin, all right."

"But it's cold outside and heavy frost is on the ground. I wouldn't expect to see any robins in the middle of February. They usually don't greet us until the beginning of spring," Belinda commented.

"That's true, Mom, but as I've mentioned before, not all robins are the same."

She pointed into the yard. "At least this one isn't banging against our window, like that poor one did a few months ago. I found that to be quite stressful."

"Guess the amschel got tired of abusing himself. Either that or he finally realized no matter how many times he hit the window, he wasn't gonna get in." Henry continued to watch out the window. "Even though robins are considered migratory, some of them stick around and move about in northern locations."

"But what do they eat? I doubt they'd be able to find many worms or insects this time of the year."

"You're right, but they can survive off fruit and berries that are still on trees and bushes."

"Another interesting fact."

"That's not all. Robins can handle very cold temperatures. To keep warm, they fluff up their feathers, which makes 'em look really big. I read about this in the latest birding magazine." Henry sounded enthusiastic.

Belinda was glad to see this side of her son. She smiled and gave his shoulder a tap. "You certainly know a lot about birds."

"Wouldn't know near so much if it weren't for the birding magazine I'm getting thanks to Dennis. I've gotten two issues already."

"It was a thoughtful gift. Your sister's future husband is a good man."

"Jah, not like Monroe." Henry's mouth turned down at the corners. "Sure am glad he quit coming around. Even though he said he wasn't the one responsible for the note on the barn wall or the muffled phone message, I don't believe him."

"Do you really think he would lie about it?" she asked.

Henry shrugged. "If he is the guilty one, I doubt that he'd admit it."

"Maybe not, but he said he didn't do it, so we need to give him the benefit of the doubt."

"You can if you want to, Mom, but I'm gonna keep an eye on things. If Monroe Esh shows up here again I'll watch him like a hawk."

Belinda rolled her eyes. *Does my boy think he's a detective now?* "I don't believe you have to worry about Monroe coming around again," she said. "When he stormed out of here after hearing your accusations, I called and left him a message, apologizing for both of our comments. I also said I appreciated him looking after things while we were gone." Belinda released a heavy sigh. "That was a month and a half ago, and Monroe hasn't come around since. He didn't even call me back to say he accepted my apology."

Henry sagged against the counter. "It's just as well. Even if Monroe isn't responsible for any of the bad things that have been done around here, he's had his eye on you, and I don't like it one bit. If Dad was still here, he wouldn't like it either."

Belinda pressed a hand against her chest. "If your daed was alive, this wouldn't be an issue. We'd still be happily married and Monroe wouldn't even be in the picture."

Henry lowered his gaze. "I wish that was the case. I'd give anything to have Dad, Abe, and Toby back in our lives."

Belinda slipped her arms around Henry and gave him a hug. "I would too, Son, but since that's not possible, we need to move on with our lives and look to the future. We can't change the past."

"It figures you'd say somethin' like that." Henry turned toward the door. "Want me to go out and check for the mail? Nobody got it yesterday, so there's bound to be some."

"That would be most appreciated."

"I'll be back soon."

When Henry went out the door, Belinda's thoughts returned to Monroe. It bothered her that he hadn't returned her call, and she couldn't help wondering if Monroe would ever talk to her again.

Belinda's thoughts switched to Herschel. At least he was an easygoing person, although a little shy. And from what she had witnessed whenever he'd come into the greenhouse with his mother, Herschel appeared to be an attentive son.

Belinda opened the pantry door and took out a box of oatmeal. On a chilly morning such as this, a hot breakfast would be most welcome.

"That Monroe fellow really gets under my skin," Henry fumed as he tromped down the driveway to get their mail. "I can't believe Mom apologized to him for asking questions that needed truthful answers."

Regardless of Monroe's denials, Henry felt sure the man was up to no good. He hoped for everyone's sake that Mr. Esh would never come around their place again. Since they hadn't seen or heard from him since they'd gotten home from Ezekiel's, Henry took it as a good sign that he'd finally gotten the message and wouldn't bother them again. There had been no more muffled phone messages or threatening notes since then either, so maybe things would be normal again.

As normal as they can be, Henry thought.

When Henry stepped up to the mailbox, he nearly collided with the redheaded neighbor lady from across the street. Apparently Virginia had been unaware of his presence and stepped in front of his family's mailbox at the same moment he did.

"Excuse me." Virginia's cheeks reddened and she took a step back. "I should've been watching where I was going instead of looking at my mail." Virginia held up a stack of envelopes. "Turns out they're mostly advertisements."

"It's okay. No harm done." Henry unlocked their mailbox and pulled the flap down. There were only a few pieces of mail, which he didn't bother to identify. After taking the envelopes out, Henry closed the box and turned to face her again. "Say, do you mind if I ask you a question?"

"I guess not." Virginia shifted her weight from one foot to the other. "What is it you want to know?"

"I was wondering if you or your husband noticed anyone hanging around our place while we were gone over the Christmas holiday."

Her forehead wrinkled. "You're asking me about something that happened almost two months ago?"

"Yes, well. . ." Henry gave his earlobe a tug. "I hadn't thought to ask you before." *Duh, stupid me. Why didn't I think to ask any of our neighbors that question?*

"I doubt that Earl saw anything out of the ordinary, since he works most days and spends his evenings in front of the TV. But now that I think about it, I did see someone at your place while you were gone."

Henry blinked. "Did you recognize the person? What'd they look like?"

Virginia shook her head. "It was an Amish man, but I didn't recognize him. He came over by horse and buggy a couple of times while you were gone. I figured he was either being snoopy or had been asked to check on your place."

"His name is Monroe, and my mom asked him to feed our animals and water plants while we were visiting my brother and his family in New York. Well, actually," Henry corrected, "she didn't ask—he volunteered and she agreed."

"I see."

"Was Monroe the only person you saw on our property while we were away from home?"

"Yeah, except for that old woman, Maude. I didn't see her in your yard, but she walked by a couple of times and even stopped once at the entrance of your driveway." Virginia frowned. "That unkempt woman is strange."

Henry thought so too, but he chose not to respond. "Well, I'd best get back to the house with the mail."

"Sure, okay."

When Henry said goodbye, the red-haired neighbor mumbled something he couldn't understand and limped her way across the road.

More than once Henry had been on the verge of asking about the leg she favored, but he figured it was none of his business and she might take offense. If he and the rest of the family knew her better, it might be okay to ask, but Virginia and her husband pretty much kept to themselves. Since they weren't Amish, they probably wouldn't have much in common to talk about anyway, so the least said the better.

Henry started back up the driveway, pausing briefly to admire a ruffed grouse. The brown, chicken-like bird with a long, squared tail had a tuft of feathers on its head that stood up like a crown. The black ruffs on the bird's neck were what it had been named for. Since the grouse was nonmigratory, it wasn't uncommon to see one or more of them during the winter months.

Once the bird skittered into the bushes along the left side of the driveway, Henry moved on. When he entered the house a short time later, he went to the kitchen and handed his mother the mail.

"You can put it over there." She gestured to the desk on the other side of the room. "I'll look at it while we're eating breakfast."

"Okay." Henry did as she asked, then he went down the hall to wash his hands in the bathroom. When he returned, Sylvia, along with his niece and nephew, were in the kitchen. Rachel had been put in her high chair, and Allen was seated on his booster seat up at the table.

"The oatmeal is ready, and we can eat now." Mom pointed to the chair where Dad used to be seated. "Henry, why don't you sit there this morning?"

He swallowed hard as he did what she suggested. Sitting in Dad's chair was an honor for Henry, but at the same time he felt humbled. Even though Henry was almost a man, he could never measure up to his father.

Once Mom and Sylvia were seated, it was time for silent prayers to be said. Henry bowed his head and closed his eyes, but the words he wanted to say to God wouldn't come. He sat quietly until his mother cleared her throat, indicating that she'd finished her prayer.

Using a large metal spoon, Mom put oatmeal in everyone's bowls, while Sylvia gave her son and daughter each a piece of toast with some of Mom's special strawberry-rhubarb jam.

Henry took a piece of toast and put plenty of honey on it. The tasty but gooey amber treat was the best part of raising bees. In fact, it was the only thing Henry liked about it.

As they ate, the little ones chattered and made a mess with their food, and his mother and sister talked about Sylvia's engagement to Dennis.

Henry really liked his sister's fiancé. He had no problem with Sylvia marrying Dennis. He thought it would be great to have a brother-in-law who shared his interest in birds. Henry still missed his father and Abe being around to talk to and learn things from. But as of late, spending time with Sylvia's boyfriend had filled in some of those empty places in his life, and Henry felt like he and Dennis had become good friends.

Henry swallowed the spoonful of oatmeal he'd put in his mouth. *I wonder where Sylvia and Dennis will live after they're married. Would she be comfortable moving back into the house she used to share with Toby, or will they buy a new place somewhere in the area and start over? Guess it wouldn't be right to bring up the topic. It's something Sylvia and Dennis must decide upon themselves.*

"Want me to bring the mail over to you?" Henry asked, pushing his contemplations to the back of his mind. "When I brought it in, you said you'd look at it while you ate breakfast, and you're about done now, so. . ."

"You're right, Son. I almost forgot about the mail." She looked over at him and winked. "Who knows? There could be a big check in one of those envelopes."

Sylvia laughed. "Now wouldn't that be a nice surprise?"

Henry got up and went over to the desk. When he returned, he placed the letters next to his mother's bowl. "Here you go."

Mom picked up the first envelope and opened it. "Just another advertisement." She set it aside. The second piece of mail was a larger envelope—the kind a person would use if they were sending someone a card.

Henry watched as Mom opened it.

"Well, for goodness' sake. This is sure unexpected. I'd forgotten that today is Valentine's Day, and I certainly never expected this."

"What is it, Mom?" Sylvia leaned to the right as she moved her chair a bit closer.

"It's a Valentine card from Herschel Fisher."

"This certainly is a surprise," Sylvia commented. "I wonder why he sent you a card."

"I wonder that too," Henry interjected.

Their mother blinked tears from her eyes, while staring at the card. "I don't know, but it was a thoughtful gesture."

Henry couldn't help noticing the blotches of red that had erupted on his mother's cheeks. This had clearly come as a surprise to her, and no doubt she felt embarrassed.

The more Henry thought about it, the more confused he became. *Herschel doesn't know Mom very well. So what reason would he have for sending her a Valentine card?* Henry squinted as he rubbed his forehead. *At least it wasn't from Monroe. If it had been, I hope Mom would've thrown it out. Think I'd better keep a closer watch on the mail from now on.*

Chapter 12

After the breakfast dishes had been washed, dried, and put away, Belinda picked up the Valentine she'd received from Herschel and read it again. In addition to a picture of a pretty red rose and red heart on the outside of the card, inside, after a Valentine's greeting, was a hand-written note. Belinda read it silently for the third time.

> *Dear Belinda:*
> *I hope you and your family are doing well. I'd meant to stop by the*
> *greenhouse before you closed for the winter, but things got really busy*
> *for me at the bulk-food store before Christmas, and I couldn't seem*
> *to get away. In addition to seeing how you are doing, I'd wanted to*
> *buy a nice indoor plant for my mamm's Christmas gift. I ended up*
> *giving her a set of towels for the bathroom instead, which I found at*
> *the variety store not far from where I live.*
> *Things have slowed up at my store now, so if there's anything I*
> *can do to help you, please let me know.*
>
> *Most sincerely,*
> *Herschel Fisher*

Belinda put the card aside. It seemed a bit odd that Herschel would send her a Valentine card. Even his note was a surprise, because whenever she'd seen him in person, he'd been a man of few words. She remembered the meal she and Herschel had shared when Amy and Jared were courting and they'd moved into the small home Herschel owned and offered to rent to him and Amy. Herschel had been friendly but kind of quiet the first part of the evening. He'd become a bit more vocal during the meal while talking with Jared, although some of his conversation had been directed at her. Once Herschel seemed to relax, Belinda had too, and she'd enjoyed the rest of the evening.

Belinda glanced at the battery-operated clock on the kitchen wall and mumbled, "I'd better get started on mopping this floor. It could sure use a good cleaning."

A knock sounded on the front door, and Belinda went to answer it since Henry had gone bird-watching and Sylvia was upstairs with the children.

Monroe stood on the porch holding a box of chocolates in one hand and a big red balloon in the other. "Happy Valentine's Day, Belinda." His smile stretched wide. "I hope you don't mind me dropping by without calling first, but I wanted it to be a surprise." He held the balloon and chocolates out to her.

Belinda was almost too dumbfounded to think of what to say. After all these weeks of hearing nothing from him, now he was here with Valentine's Day gifts? She wondered what was behind his sudden appearance.

"You. . .umm. . .caught me by surprise," she murmured. "I wasn't expecting you to come by today—much less with gifts."

He continued to look at her, still smiling. "I couldn't let Valentine's Day go by without letting you know how much I care. Also I wanted to clear the air with you regarding the insinuations that I might be responsible for the threatening phone message and note on the barn wall."

"Didn't you get my message, apologizing for the things that were said?"

"Jah, but I thought it best to let some time pass before I came over here again." He took a step toward her. "I really hope you don't believe I had anything to do with what happened. I'd never intentionally hurt you or any of your family, Belinda. I've always had your best interest at heart."

Seeing his sincere expression caused Belinda to weaken a bit. "Why don't you come in out of the cold and have a cup of coffee or tea with me?" She was glad to be able to clear the air in person. Despite Henry's disapproval of Monroe, Belinda remembered back to the days when she was young and had been fond of him.

"That'd be real nice," Monroe said. "I'd appreciate a warm cup of kaffi."

When they entered the kitchen, Belinda placed the candy on the counter and attached the string on the balloon to the back of a chair. Since it had been filled with helium, it floated up, nearly touching the ceiling. It reminded Belinda of her childhood days, when her parents took her and her siblings to various activities in the area where balloons and souvenirs had been sold. At one event a man dressed in a clown costume made animal figures by twisting long, skinny balloons. Those were carefree days when she had so little to worry about. If only her life could be simpler now.

Monroe pulled off his hat and coat and hung them up. Then he took a seat at the table while Belinda poured coffee for both of them. He looked well-groomed, as usual, and smelled of that same musky-scented cologne he'd worn when he'd been to her place on other occasions. "It's a little chilly out there, but it feels nice and comfortable here in your kitchen," he commented.

Belinda stepped over to the cupboard and retrieved a mug. "It will be nice when spring arrives and we can enjoy the warmer weather. Here you go." She placed Monroe's cup in front of him and set a plate of peanut butter cookies within his reach. He wasted no time in helping himself to two of the biggest ones.

"You're sure a good cook," Monroe said after he'd eaten the first cookie. "It's no wonder Vernon wanted to marry you."

A warm flush spread across Belinda's cheeks. "Vernon often said he appreciated my cooking, but his desire to marry me came from the close friendship we developed during our days of courting. Not only that, but Vernon and I both loved flowers, and that gave us a common bond that eventually prompted the opening of our greenhouse."

"Yes, yes, I understand. I just meant..." Monroe sputtered, as though trying to find the right words. Instead of finishing his sentence, however, he reached for his cup and drank some coffee.

Barely hearing Monroe speak again, Belinda glanced at the clock, wondering how long he planned to remain at her table and hoping Sylvia wouldn't come into the kitchen. It would be even worse if Henry got home and saw her visiting with Monroe.

Monroe cleared his throat. "Belinda, did ya hear what I said?"

"Uh. . .no, sorry. . .my mind had wandered a bit. What did you say?"

"I asked when you would be opening the greenhouse."

"Not until the middle of March," she replied.

"Just another month then, huh?"

"Jah, but I have a lot of planning to do in order to get the business ready to open, and time can get away from me in a hurry." She rose from her chair. "I don't mean to be unhospitable, Monroe, but I have some things I need to get done yet today. So if you'll excuse me. . ."

Monroe snatched two more cookies and pushed back his chair. "No problem. I should be on my way anyhow. I have some errands to do before going back to the house. Just wanted to drop by to wish you a Happy Valentine's Day and make sure there are no hard feelings between us."

"None on my part." Belinda offered him what she hoped was a reassuring smile. *I'm glad we are back on good terms again. I would've disliked it if I'd spoiled a friendship because of an assumption.*

Monroe hesitated a moment, then moved toward the back door. He put on his coat and grabbed the straw hat from the wall peg. "I'll stop by again once the greenhouse opens and check things out. You might have something for sale that would look good in my yard."

"Do you mean your parents' yard, or are you expecting to get a place of your own now that you've settled back here in Strasburg again?"

"Actually, since my plans are to remain in the area, I've been thinking about either buying a house or getting some land and having my own place built." Monroe wiggled his brows. "I'm not a kid anymore, so I can't remain at my mamm and daed's home indefinitely. One way or the other, I plan to make Strasburg my home, and if things go well, I'd like to own another business or two."

"Are you wanting to open a second furniture store?" Belinda questioned.

He shrugged. "Maybe, if it was located someplace other than this town. It would be rather foolish of me to compete with myself." He plopped his hat back on his head. "Have a good rest of your day, Belinda, and I hope you'll enjoy the *schochlaad* candy I brought."

She gave a heartfelt smile. "Danki, I'm sure I will. However, since everyone in my family likes chocolate candy as much as I do, I'll willingly share some with them."

"Tell 'em I said hello." He lifted his hand in a wave before going out the back door.

She waved back, and then watched out the window as Monroe headed to his buggy. In a small way he reminded her of Vernon, but she wasn't sure how. Even though some time had passed since Belinda lost her husband, something stirred within her as she remembered how she and Vernon had spent some of their Valentine's Days together. *You and I made sure to make the time for romance, didn't we? Even though I remember the ups and downs in our marriage, I wouldn't trade one moment of them for anything.* She brushed a tear from her cheek, and it landed on her dress sleeve.

Belinda looked toward the entrance of the kitchen, hoping she had this private moment alone. She collected herself quickly, not wanting to trouble her daughter or son by acting sappy.

Her gaze went to the box of candy and then the red balloon. When Sylvia and Henry saw the gifts, they were bound to ask questions. *Would it be wrong to say nothing and just take them to my room?* Belinda pursed her lips. *Guess I'll have to tell them, because I certainly don't want to eat all that candy by myself.*

Henry had been out bird-watching for over an hour when he spotted his friend Seth's car through his binoculars. With this close-up view he was able to see a couple other fellows in the vehicle too.

Henry waved, but apparently no one saw him, for the car sped on down the road.

I wonder what they're up to today. Henry lowered his binoculars and frowned. *Wouldn't be surprised if Seth and the other fellows are stinkin' up his car with cigarette smoke. Sure am glad I never got hooked on any kind of tobacco.*

Henry thought about the package of cigarettes that had been found outside the barn after it burned. He hoped Seth wasn't the one responsible for the fire or any of the vandalism that had been done at their place. Henry's friend would remain on his list of suspects until the mystery had been solved and the person responsible was punished.

"Monroe, Seth, Maude, Virginia, or the owner of the new greenhouse across town." Henry counted with his fingers. "I'm sure it's gotta be one of those people—unless I've missed someone. I really oughta start lookin' for more clues."

When Henry returned home a short time later, he entered the kitchen to get a glass of water. Despite the cold weather, he'd worked up a sweat walking to and from the meadow where he'd gone to search for birds.

None of his family was in the room, but he noticed a box of candy sitting on the counter, plus a red balloon tied to the back of a chair and floating toward the ceiling. Henry assumed Dennis must have come by while he was gone and given the gifts to Sylvia for Valentine's Day.

Henry was on the verge of opening the heart-shaped box when Sylvia entered the room.

"Oh, you're back." She smiled at him. "How'd the bird-watching go?"

"It went okay, but I didn't see anything special today. Just a couple of bobwhites, and one hawk. Nothing I haven't seen before." Henry gestured to the box of candy. "Looks like Dennis must have been by with a gift for you, huh?"

Sylvia shook her head. "I won't be seeing Dennis until this evening. He's taking me out for supper."

Henry's brows squished together. "That's nice, but then where did these come from?" He pointed to the candy and then the balloon.

"Mr. Esh."

Henry's head jerked back. "Monroe was here?"

"Jah. He came by awhile ago, when I was upstairs with the kinner," Sylvia replied. "Mom told me about it when I came down and found her in here with the gifts."

"Oh, great! I thought we'd seen the last of him." Henry smacked the side of his head. "So now the determined fellow comes back with gifts, hopin' to win Mom over with his fake smile, heavy cologne, and sickening comments." He shook his head. "Wish I'd been here when he showed up. I would have told him that Mom's not interested in any of his gifts."

Sylvia placed her hand on Henry's shoulder. "You need to calm down. I don't care for Monroe any more than you do, but it's Mom's place to decide if she wants to accept a gift from him. My advice is to keep quiet and let our mamm handle things with Monroe however she thinks is best."

"I'm having a hard time doing that, Sylvia." Henry folded his arms and gave a huff. "If Mom was handling things right, Monroe wouldn't still be comin' around."

Henry's mother came into the kitchen. "Oh good, Son, I'm glad you're home. I was hoping you might hitch my horse to the buggy and go to town to get a few things I need at the store."

"Okay, yeah, I can do that. Is your list ready?" he asked.

"Not quite, but I'll finish it while you get the buggy out of the shed and prepare the horse for travel." She moved over to the counter and opened the heart-shaped box, revealing a layer of chocolates. "Would you like one before you go?"

Henry shook his head. "I heard they're from Monroe."

"That's right. He came by to clear the air with me and—"

"So does that mean he'll be comin' around all the time, like he used to?" Henry's face tightened.

She shook her head. "It just means there are no hard feelings between us."

Henry felt some relief. He glanced at Sylvia as she pressed a hand against her chest. No doubt she felt a sense of relief too. Maybe their mom hadn't been taken in by Monroe's sappy gifts after all.

Chapter 13

"I see you've started *nachtesse* already," Jared commented when he arrived home from work that evening and joined Amy in the kitchen.

"Jah, there's a ham and two nice-sized potatoes baking in the oven for our supper." She lifted her face toward him and waited for the expected kiss.

Jared lifted Amy's chin and caressed her lips with his own. "If I'd known you were going to cook this evening, I would have told you before I left for work this morning that I was planning to take you out for supper." He kissed her again. "I'd hoped it would be a nice Valentine's Day surprise."

Amy put her arms around Jared's waist and gave him a hug. "I have an even bigger surprise for you, and I don't want to share it in a public place."

Jared tipped his head to one side. "Oh? And what surprise do you have for me, Fraa?" Amy placed both hands against her stomach and smiled up at him. "I'm expecting a *boppli*. The doctor confirmed it today when I went in for an appointment."

Jared's mouth opened slightly. "Oh Amy, that's *wunderbaar!*" He put his hands on her shoulders. "I didn't know you had a doctor's appointment. Why didn't you say something?"

"Because if what I'd suspected wasn't true, I didn't want to disappoint you. And if it was true, then I wanted it to be a surprise."

He pulled Amy even closer and gently rubbed her back. "So when will we become *elder*?"

"According to the doctor's calculations, and mine, we should take on the role of parents the first or second week of September."

"This is such good news. I can hardly wait to tell both of our families."

"I'm sure they'll be happy for us," Amy said, "but can we wait until later in the week? I'd like us to savor this information awhile—at least for tonight."

"I have no problem with that. Maybe tomorrow evening, if the weather holds, we can visit our parents' homes and share the good news."

Tears sprang to Amy's eyes and she blinked to keep them from escaping onto her cheeks. "If only my daed and brother were still alive. I know they would be happy to hear our good news. For that matter, Toby would have been pleased too, since he would have been the boppli's uncle.

"I can't pretend to know what goes on in heaven, but maybe our loved ones who have passed and entered the pearly gates are allowed to see or even hear about some of the good things that happen on earth."

Amy took comfort in her husband's words. *Whether my father, brother, and brother-in-law are aware of anything that's happened down here, the one thing I feel confident in is that they were true believers and had accepted Christ as their Savior, which means they had the promise of heaven.*

Virginia sat on the living-room couch with her arms folded across her chest. If it weren't for the nice card and note she'd received in the mail earlier today from her friend, Stella, it would hardly seem like Valentine's Day. Earl hadn't sent her flowers, like he had in years past, nor had he made any mention of what day it was before he left for work this morning.

He must have forgotten. Virginia shifted her position on the couch. *Either that or he's too cheap to buy me anything this year. Maybe he's still irritated because I bought a new outfit for Christmas, which he said was pretty, but not something I needed.*

Virginia thought about the horse and buggy she'd seen drive onto the Kings' property earlier today. She'd noticed a big red balloon poking out of the back of the rig, where the flap had been open. It appeared as if someone might be getting a gift for Valentine's Day.

Virginia speculated on who the lucky recipient had been. She couldn't help feeling envious.

Goldie purred like a motorboat as she came up and nuzzled Virginia's chin.

"I'm upset right now, so this isn't a good time for you to try and butter me up." Virginia remained rigid, but her cat seemed determined to melt away any resistance. Each time Goldie cuddled she released a soft *meow*, and Virginia couldn't help smiling.

"Okay, you win. I can't stay mad anyways with you being so sweet to me."

Virginia uncrossed her arms to pet Goldie after the feline curled up in her lap. "At least you still love me, don't ya, pretty girl?"

The cat's response was another *meow*, followed by rhythmic purring. The pleasing sound calmed Virginia's nerves for a bit, until she observed an advertisement on TV where a handsome man presented a lovely young woman a heart-shaped box of chocolates. Another ad followed, showing an older woman receiving a beautiful necklace with matching earrings from a gentleman with silver hair.

"Must be nice to know that someone besides your cat cares about you." Virginia glanced at the card lying on the coffee table from her Chicago friend. "I guess Stella cares about me too, or she wouldn't have sent the note. Of course," Virginia reasoned, "I sent her a card with a letter, so maybe she was only reciprocating."

Virginia grinned despite her melancholy mood. Reciprocating was not the kind of word she would normally use, but because of the crossword puzzles she often did, she'd discovered the word in the thesaurus while trying to find an answer to the question: *"To do for someone after they've done something for you."*

Virginia stopped petting Goldie and lifted both hands over her head as she yawned. It would be time to start supper soon, but she had no desire to cook even a simple meal this evening. After all, why should she fix a nice supper for Earl when he couldn't even remember to get her something for Valentine's Day?

She suppressed another yawn then she put Goldie on the floor and reclined on the couch. It wasn't long before the cat jumped back up and curled into a ball on Virginia's chest. The vibration of the cat's purring put Virginia into a drowsy state. She soon closed her eyes and gave in to slumber.

"Hey, wake up, sleepyhead."

Virginia's eyes snapped open and she sat up so quickly Goldie jumped down. "Wh–what are you doing here, Earl?"

He lifted his gaze toward the ceiling. "I live here—remember?"

"Don't be funny." She flapped her hand. "I mean, what are you doing here when you should be at work?"

"It's five thirty, and I'm done for the day." Earl leaned over and placed his hand on her shoulder, giving it a little shake. "I figured you'd be all dressed up and ready to go by now, but since you're not, it'll give me enough time to shower and change my clothes into something more presentable."

"Presentable for what?"

"For supper."

"Since when do you worry about looking presentable for any of our meals?"

"I do when we're going out to eat."

She gave a bark of laughter. "We're going out to a restaurant?"

"Yep. Thought I told ya that this morning when I kissed you good-bye. Said a meal out would be your Valentine's gift from me this year."

Virginia shook her head. "If you said it, I must have been asleep because I have no memory of it at all." She pulled herself up off the couch. "While you're taking your shower I'll look through my closet for something nice to wear."

"Sounds good. I'll meet you back here in half an hour." Earl kissed Virginia's cheek and sauntered out of the room.

Virginia couldn't take the smile from her face. It was nice to know Earl hadn't forgotten about Valentine's Day after all, and wanted to surprise her, no less.

Bird-in-Hand, Pennsylvania

"I still can't believe you agreed to marry me." Dennis reached over and took Sylvia's hand, as they sat beside each other in a booth at the

Bird-in-Hand Family Restaurant. "Every day since you accepted my proposal I've had to pinch myself to make sure I'm not dreaming."

Sylvia smiled. "I feel the same way, and I'm truly looking forward to becoming your wife."

He grinned back at her. "We still haven't set a date, and we need to do that soon."

"Agreed."

"I don't see any reason to wait till fall, when many other Amish couples will be getting married."

Sylvia nodded. "Since this is a second marriage for me, there's no reason to wait that long." She paused for a drink of water. "We do have some planning to do that will involve the wedding, though, and it will take some time. Would the first Thursday in August work for you?"

"I'd like it to be sooner, but the time between now and then will probably go fast." Dennis added a spoonful of sugar to his coffee and stirred it around. "Speaking of planning. . . We haven't discussed where we're going to live after we're married. Even though it's become like home to me, I would understand if you didn't want to live in the house you once shared with your first husband."

Sylvia's throat constricted. "Can I pray about it for a few days before I decide?"

"Of course. In the meantime, though, can we tell our families that we've set a date for the wedding?"

"That's fine. Why don't you come over to my mamm's place tomorrow evening? We'll tell her and Henry, and then I will call Amy the following day to let her and Jared know about our plans."

"Sounds good. I'll call my mamm tomorrow too. She can relay the information to the rest of my family there in Dauphin County. I'm sure everyone will be happy for us." Dennis took hold of Sylvia's hand again and gave her fingers a gentle squeeze.

Sylvia looked down at her unfinished plate of food. It would be difficult to share a home with Dennis that had once been meant for her and Toby. However, the land and even the outbuildings were perfect for Dennis's horse training business as well as for raising horses, which he'd already begun to do. It might be difficult and time consuming to find another place for them to live—not to mention expensive. Then there would be the chore of selling Sylvia's home, and it could take time to find the right buyer. If she and Dennis were going to be married by August, it might be best for her and the children to move into her old home with him after the wedding. Maybe it wouldn't be as hard as she imagined. And if it was too difficult an adjustment, they could look for another home with plenty of acreage that would work well for Dennis's business.

Sylvia would pray about it, of course, and do whatever God laid on her heart. One thing she had learned over the last several months was that everything went better when decisions were made following prayer.

"We're eating here? I thought we'd be going to Miller's Smorgy." Virginia couldn't hide her disappointment when Earl pulled into the parking lot at the Bird-in-Hand Family Restaurant.

"What's wrong with this place?" Earl turned off the engine. "They serve good food."

Virginia wrinkled her nose as an Amish couple walked past and entered the restaurant. "Those Plain folks like to eat here. Don't think I've ever seen any Amish or Mennonite people eating at Miller's."

"I'm sure some of them do." Earl reached across the seat and gave Virginia's arm a poke. "Are you ever going to get over your prejudice against people who don't look, dress, or think the way you do?"

Virginia gave the collar of her heavy jacket a tug. "I'm not prejudiced. I am just not comfortable around people who—"

"Are different than you? Is that what you were going to say?"

She sighed. "Those old-fashioned people are so different than you and me. The way they live is strange, and to me it makes no sense."

"Maybe not, but it's the way they choose to live, and as far as I know, we're still living in a free country." He tapped the steering wheel. "Now are we going inside, or would you rather go home and throw something in the microwave for supper?"

Virginia's shoulders slumped as she gave a dejected sigh. "Okay, have it your way." She opened the car door and stepped out. *Happy Valentine's Day, Earl.*

When they entered the restaurant and had been seated at a table, a young waitress came and handed them a menu. Then she asked each of them what they'd like to drink with their meals and wrote it down on her tablet. "The buffet is also available, if you'd rather choose from that. There are many items to choose from there," she stated.

"I'll have the buffet." Earl handed the menu back to the waitress then he looked at Virginia. "How 'bout you?"

She perused the menu briefly before handing it to the young woman. "Guess I'll go with the buffet as well."

The waitress smiled. "Feel free to go up whenever you're ready. I'll bring your beverages to the table while you're getting your food."

Earl looked over at Virginia. "Are you ready?"

"I guess so, but I wish we would've been seated in a booth instead of a table."

"What's wrong with this spot? It isn't so bad." He grinned. "We're close to the buffet, so it won't be too far of a walk for you."

"Okay, let's get in line for the food." Virginia waited until Earl got up from his chair, and when she did the same, she bumped her bad knee into the table leg. "Ouch."

"Are you okay?"

She remained beside the table, massaging the sore spot and hoping to relieve the pain. "I'll be all right. Let's go on up so we can eat."

This is not the way I'd hoped to spend the evening. Virginia pursed her lips as she followed Earl over to the buffet. On the way there, they passed an Amish couple sitting in a booth. When Virginia realized it was her neighbor Sylvia sitting with an Amish man she'd seen at the Kings' several times, she hastened to look away. No way did she want to engage them in conversation. They had nothing in common, and as far as Virginia was concerned, her Amish neighbors were rude. She still hadn't forgiven them for not inviting her and Earl to Amy and Jared's wedding last fall. At this point, Virginia didn't care about going across the street for anything except to get her mail.

Chapter 14

Strasburg

Fully intending to leave a message, Dennis punched in his mother's number. He waited as the phone rang several times, meanwhile, picking at a sliver embedded in his thumb. Dennis was surprised when Mom answered the phone. She was obviously in the phone shed either making calls or checking for messages.

"Hi, Mom. It's Dennis."

"Well hello, Son. How are you doing?" Her tone sounded upbeat.

"I'm doing okay. How about you and the rest of the family?"

"Everyone's fine here, although the weather's cold, so we're all eager for spring to arrive."

"Same here." Dennis reached for his cup of coffee and took a drink. "The reason I'm calling is to let you know that Sylvia and I have set a date for our wedding. It's going to be the first Thursday of August. I wanted to give you advance notice so you could make plans to come down here for our big day."

"We wouldn't miss it for the world, and I'm happy you've found someone you care about, Son. My only concern is the responsibility you'll be taking on by marrying a widow with two *kinner*."

Dennis blew out a noisy breath. "Not this again, Mom. You've brought this topic up to me a few times already, and my answer is still the same. I love Sylvia and her children, and I'm not concerned about becoming their stepfather. In fact, I'm looking forward to my new role."

"But can you financially afford to provide for a readymade family?"

Dennis reached up with his free hand and rubbed the back of his tight neck muscles. "Can't you just be *hallich* that I've found the woman of my dreams and I'm eager to make her my fraa?"

"Of course I'm happy. I'm just afraid you might be taking on more than you can handle."

Dennis clenched his teeth. If he didn't hang up now, he might say something he'd later regret. "It'll be fine, Mom. You'll see. Listen, I'm sorry for cutting this short, but I need to go. In addition to grooming the horses in my barn, I have several errands to run yet today. I'll talk to you again soon, though, okay?"

"Jah, sure. Tell your intended I said hello."

"I'll do that when I see her this evening. Bye, Mom."

When Dennis hung up, he closed his eyes and said a quick prayer. *Lord, please give my mother a sense of peace about me marrying Sylvia. Also guide and direct me and Sylvia in the days ahead as we make decisions about our future together.*

Amy's pulse quickened as Jared's horse and buggy approached her mother's house. They'd just come from telling his parents their good news. Jared's mother and father, Ava and Emanuel, had expressed their happiness at becoming grandparents and said they'd be praying for an easy, healthy pregnancy for Amy. She felt thankful to have loving, caring in-laws. Some people, like a young woman she knew in their church district, weren't so fortunate. Kara's mother-in-law had never approved of her, and sometimes said hurtful things to her. Amy wondered if Kara's husband, Ronald, had ever spoken up and put his mother in her place.

She glanced over at Jared as he gripped the horse's reins securely in his hands. *I'm sure my man would stand up for me if his mother ever said hurtful things. I bet Jared would even put my own mom in her place if she spoke out of turn and caused me grief.*

When he guided the horse up her mother's driveway, Jared looked over at Amy and smiled. "Are you ready to relay our good news a second time?"

She reached across the seat and squeezed his arm. "Definitely."

When a knock sounded on the front door, Sylvia got up from her seat on the couch in such a hurry that Belinda had to laugh. No doubt it was Dennis on the porch, since Sylvia had mentioned during supper that he'd be dropping by this evening. It was a joy to see her daughter so enthused about her future husband coming for a visit.

Belinda remembered how eager she'd always been when she and Vernon were courting and he'd come to her parents' house to see her.

Those were such happy days, she mused while patting Rachel's back as she attempted to rock the fussy girl to sleep. Allen sat on the couch, next to where his mother had been, engrossed in a picture book.

Sylvia returned to the living room, but not with Dennis. Belinda smiled as Jared and Amy came fully into the room. "Well, this is a nice surprise. We didn't know you two would be dropping by this evening."

Amy chuckled. "That's what Sylvia said when she answered the door. Apparently she'd been expecting Dennis." She looked over at Jared. "Should we wait till he gets here to tell them why we came by?"

"That's a good idea."

Sylvia took their outer garments and said she'd hang them on the coatrack in the hall. "Would anyone like a cup of hot chocolate or some warm apple cider," she called from the hallway.

"Hot chocolate sounds good to me, if it's not too much trouble." Jared looked at Amy. "Does that appeal to you?"

"I think I'd rather have the cider," she replied. "I'll go out to the kitchen and help Sylvia with that. But first, what would you like, Mom?"

"Cider for me." Belinda looked at Henry, who had just entered the room. "How about you, Son? Would you like to join us for hot chocolate or apple cider?"

"Sure." Henry meandered over to the couch and sat down beside Allen.

"Sure what?" Amy asked. "Do you want cider or hot chocolate?"

"I like them both, but if I'm given a choice, guess I'll take a cup of hot chocolate." Henry patted Allen's knee. "I bet he'd like some too."

"Okay, I'll go put in our orders, and then Sylvia and I will bring the beverages out to you soon."

Belinda stroked Rachel's soft cheek. Her precious granddaughter had finally settled down and fallen asleep. "Think I'd better put this little one to bed," she whispered.

"Would you like me to do it?" Jared offered.

She hesitated but then nodded. Amy and Jared would no doubt have children of their own someday, so this would be good practice for him.

After Jared took the child in his arms, Belinda got up from her chair. "I'm going out to the kitchen to help Amy and Sylvia," she told Henry, who'd picked up one of his birding magazines. "Would you please keep an eye on Allen? I don't want him going upstairs and waking his sister."

"Sure, Mom. I'll make certain he stays put while you're gone."

"It might be good for you to remain on the couch beside him." Belinda had spoken all this in English so Allen wouldn't understand. She didn't want the little fellow to know they were talking about him or what was being said.

Henry's eyebrows lowered and pinched together. "Don't see why I have to stay next to him if I decide to sit someplace else." He gestured to one of the recliners. "I can see him just fine from over there."

"Not with your nose in that magazine. If you're sitting right beside Allen you'll be more aware if he decides to get up."

"Okay, whatever." Henry reached over and tousled Allen's thick crop of hair.

The young boy looked at him and grinned. Then he pointed to the page he had opened in his children's book. *"Bussli."*

"Jah, that's a kitten," Henry responded in Pennsylvania Dutch.

Belinda figured Allen would keep Henry busy for a while, showing him pictures and pointing to each one, so she hurried out of the room. Belinda was almost to the kitchen when another knock sounded on the door. She went to answer it and found Dennis on the porch.

"Good evening." Stepping into the hallway, he smiled. "Looks like I'm not the only visitor you have here this evening." He turned and pointed at the other horse and buggy parked next to his horse and carriage at the rail.

"Amy and Jared stopped by." Belinda took his hat and jacket. "My daughters are in the kitchen getting ready to serve warm apple cider and hot chocolate. "If you'll tell me which one you'd like, I'll let the girls know."

"Cider sounds delicious."

"Okay. Henry's in the living room with Allen, and Jared's putting Rachel to bed. I'm sure he will join them soon, so why don't you go in and make yourself comfortable?"

"I will, danki."

As Dennis headed for the living room, Belinda entered the kitchen. "Dennis is here," she announced, stepping up to the counter where Sylvia stood, cutting slices of banana bread.

"Oh, good. Did you ask if he'd like something hot to drink?"

"Jah. He'd like warm cider. Why don't you take the bread to the dining-room table and ask the men to join us there?" Belinda suggested. "I'll help Amy bring in the beverages."

Sylvia smiled. "Okay, Mom." She picked up the plate of bread and hurried from the room.

Amy looked at Belinda and chuckled. "I do believe my sister is eager to see her future husband."

Belinda gave a deep, gratified sigh. "Jah, and I'm ever so happy for her." She felt joy in seeing one daughter married, and the eldest with a suitor who was a good man. Her loved ones were all healthy and doing well in their lives, so there was much to be thankful for.

I wonder what the future holds for me. I have suitors of my own, or so my daughters believe, even though I don't have any notion at this point of letting things get serious with either man. Belinda slid the tray closer to the stove and began loading it with the hot beverages. *I could use some help with Henry though. I can't help feeling concern because my son doesn't have a true, constant male figure in his life. Over the next few years, while he's still living at home under my care and guidance, I need to do what is right by him.*

🐦

When Belinda followed Amy into the dining room, both carrying trays with everyone's beverages, she noticed Dennis and Sylvia standing close together in one corner of the room. He appeared to be whispering something in her ear. They made such a nice couple, and Belinda felt good about their relationship.

Now I'm curious. What could Dennis have to say to my daughter that he doesn't want us to hear? Belinda pondered this question for a few seconds. *Is he telling Sylvia how much he loves her?*

She remembered how things had been between her and Vernon during their courting days. Belinda couldn't imagine anyone as handsome or grounded in his faith as her special man had been. She reflected on the way Vernon used to plan their dates to go places, and how special he had treated her. He would often whisper tender words of love, sometimes even when they weren't alone. She'd thought his sweet actions were endearing. Once again, Belinda felt a pang of regret at losing her dear husband.

Refocusing, she invited everyone to take a seat at the table. Once they were all seated, the hot beverages were handed out and Sylvia passed the nice-sized plate of freshly made banana bread around.

They chatted for a bit about the weather, with Dennis bringing up how strange it was that they'd only had a few light dustings of snow so far this winter.

"You're right," Belinda agreed. "Usually by the middle of February we've had a foot or two—sometimes more—of snow on the ground."

Everyone but Allen agreed. He was busy poking at the marshmallow in his cup of hot chocolate.

Dennis looked at Sylvia, and when she smiled at him, he cleared his throat real loud. "Sylvia and I have an announcement to make."

All heads turned in their direction.

"We've decided to get married on the first Thursday of August."

Everyone clapped—even Allen with his sticky fingers.

"Can you get all your plans made and everything put together by then?" Belinda asked. She'd really thought after Dennis proposed to Sylvia on Christmas that they would have set their wedding date right away so it would give them plenty of time to plan everything out.

"I'm sure it can be done," Sylvia replied. "It won't need to be a big occasion, since it's a second marriage for me."

She heard in her daughter's voice the determination driving their decision. "But it's Dennis's first marriage." Belinda looked over at him. "Are you okay with keeping things small?"

"All I care about is marrying your daughter," he said. "Nothing else matters to me."

Belinda saw sincerity in the young man's expression and heard it in the tone of his voice. She took another sip of her beverage. *At this point I can tell their minds are made up, so I'll let that subject rest.*

"We'll all help out as needed," Amy said.

All heads bobbed in agreement.

"Now it's our turn to share some news." Amy looked at Jared. "Would you like to tell them, or shall I?"

His smile was directed at her. "Why don't you go ahead?"

Amy's cheeks colored as she placed one hand against her belly. "Jared and I are expecting our first child. He or she is due to make an appearance in early September."

More hand clapping ensued and everyone, including Henry, extended hearty congratulations.

Belinda closed her eyes briefly and lifted a heartfelt prayer. *Things are swinging to the positive side for our family, Lord. Amy and Jared are expecting their first child, and I'm ever so happy for them. Sylvia and Dennis have set their wedding date, and I look forward to having him as my son-in-law. Also there's been no more vandalism, threatening notes, or muffled voice messages aimed at us this winter, and I thank You for that as well. Please continue to be with us in the days ahead. Amen.*

Belinda opened her eyes, looking fondly at each of her family members. She hoped all of their lives had turned the corner toward a happier life.

Her gaze landed on Henry. *Now if my youngest boy would just let go of his negative attitude, and turn his worries over to God, the future will look even brighter.*

Chapter 15

Today was the first day of spring, and the greenhouse had been open for a week. The weather was chilly, and the sky seemed full of gray clouds. Belinda wondered how this umbrella-type day would impact the number of customers they'd see. Although mid- to late-March was never as busy as April through November, they'd had some customers last week, so she felt sure things would pick up. They needed money coming in to pay bills, not to mention the expense of her oldest daughter's upcoming wedding.

Belinda carried a small lunch with her, just half a sandwich and an orange. The baked oatmeal she'd eaten for breakfast had filled her up good. Besides, she needed to reorganize some of the seed packets on the rack, since they'd gotten in some new ones. Belinda figured she'd stay put and eat her lunch in the greenhouse today.

As she entered the building and put the OPEN sign in the window, an image of Sylvia's smiling face at breakfast came to mind. It did Belinda's heart good to see the change that had come over Sylvia since she'd met Dennis. She was more positive and less fearful. Last week she and Dennis had taken her horse and buggy out, and for the first time since Toby's death, Sylvia had been in the driver's seat, taking control of her mare. She'd admitted to being nervous, but with Dennis by her side, patiently coaxing and guiding along the way, the experience went surprisingly well. They drove several miles down the road to a fabric store, where Sylvia had purchased thread and material for her wedding dress. She'd also purchased some scraps of colorful fabric to make potholders to sell in the gift side of the greenhouse.

Henry had painted and decorated some horseshoes to put in there too, and on the shelves sat jars of amber honey, along with apple butter Belinda and Sylvia had put up last fall.

I wish there was enough money in my bank account so we could add on to the greenhouse, Belinda thought as she put her insulated lunch bag behind the counter. She looked over at the seed rack. *I need to take care of those, but first I should check on the plants to make sure they're well-watered.* Belinda turned on the hose and uncoiled it as she went down the first aisle to water all the plants and shrubs. *Even a separate building where we could sell only gift items would be nice.*

While home-canned jams, jugs of cider, and honey were not traditionally sold in most greenhouses, they made a nice addition to offer their customers—especially the tourists who often came in by the busloads. Those people were usually interested in potholders, solar lights, and other small items her family had come up with to sell. Every sale, big or small, helped. She'd even gotten some cute birdhouses in a couple of sizes and styles to sell that she'd ordered last month.

"A delivery truck came up to the house with a big box filled with bags of potting soil," Henry said when he entered the greenhouse.

Belinda saw by her son's squinted eyes and the slight tilt of his head, that he was unhappy about this. And rightly so. The man who delivered their planting supplies always brought the boxes and packages to the greenhouse and dropped them off. "Was someone new driving the truck?" she questioned.

Henry shrugged. "Beats me. I was in the barn when the vehicle pulled in and didn't see the driver."

Belinda gave a weary sigh. This was only the second time it had happened. Apparently it had been a new driver today, and he didn't know to bring the packages out to the greenhouse.

"You'll need to open the boxes and then haul all the bags of potting soil down here in the wheelbarrow."

Henry groaned. "Aw, Mom, that's gonna take me several trips, and who's gonna be here to help you while I'm doin' that?"

"I'll be fine when Sylvia gets here. She needs to wait until Amy comes to watch the kinner."

"I wonder how long she'll be able to keep doin' that. With her bein' in a family way, I'd think she would need to stay home and rest."

Belinda gave his shoulder a few pats. "It's nice of you to be concerned about your sister, but Amy's feeling fine, and she's agreed to watch Allen and Rachel as long as she's doing well."

"But not after she has the boppli, right?"

"Correct. And by then Sylvia and Dennis will be married, so neither one of your sisters will be working here in the greenhouse."

Henry's pinched expression made it appear as if he'd eaten something distasteful. No doubt he felt some bitterness about being stuck helping here and doing the kind of work he'd often said was not what he wanted to be doing for the rest of his life.

Ezekiel felt that way once too, Belinda reminded herself. *That's why I'll never say anything that would encourage him to move back.*

"Look, Son. . ." Belinda spoke quietly, in a reassuring tone, "When you are old enough to move out on your own and you wish to find some other means of employment, then I'll either learn to manage by myself or hire someone else. But for now, and until you're at least eighteen years of age, you are my responsibility, and you'll be expected to do as I say. Is that understood?"

Henry's posture slumped as he lowered his head. "Jah, Mom, I get it." He turned and shuffled out the door.

Belinda walked with slow, heavy steps up the next aisle. This work day had not begun well.

She'd finished watering all the plants and headed for the front counter when a middle-aged English man entered the building. "May I help you?" she asked as he approached.

"Are you the owner of this establishment?"

"Yes, I am." Belinda smiled. "Are you looking for anything particular today?"

"Actually, I need a lot of things." The man opened his jacket and pulled out a card from an inside pocket, which he handed to her. "My name is Brian Rawlings, and I own Rawlings' Landscaping Service. We're located about halfway between here and Lancaster, and our business has been growing by leaps and bounds."

Belinda moved to the front counter, where she studied his card. While she'd had no contact with his business previously, a few customers had mentioned having some work on their property done by Mr. Rawlings's company.

"The thing is," Brian continued, "I've been looking for a local supplier, and someone suggested you. If you have the time right now, could we talk about what you have available here, and then discuss the cost?"

Belinda felt a sense of excitement over the prospect of being able to sell more plants, shrubs, and trees. If things worked out, this would make up for them having lost the contract with the flower shop in town after Sara Fuller sold it. She was about to respond to Mr. Rawlings when Henry came in with one of their shopping wagons piled high with bags of potting soil. He looked her way, pulled the wagon off to one side, and joined her behind the counter.

"Everything okay?" Henry leaned close to Belinda's ear.

"It's fine." She introduced the man to Henry and explained why he was there.

Henry asked Brian several questions.

A pleasant warmth spread through Belinda's chest. It pleased her to see Henry taking the initiative to ask pertinent questions, but she hoped the man would not be put off by them. He didn't appear to be, as the three of them discussed a suitable arrangement for providing the landscaping service with many items they would need. Before the man left, she gave him her business card.

"Thanks, I'll give you a call when I'm ready to place my first order." He gave them a wide smile before heading out the door.

"Danki for your input." Belinda placed her hand on Henry's shoulder. "For a young man who doesn't want to take part in this business, you sure know what you're talking about. Also the questions you asked were things I may not have thought to ask."

"Sure you would, Mom. You and Dad began running this greenhouse a long time before I became involved."

"That's true, but you've caught on fast in regard to the business end of things, not to mention your knowledge of the plants, flowers, shrubs, and trees we have available here. I'm proud of you, Son."

A crimson flush spread across Henry's cheeks. "Aw, Mom, it ain't nothin'."

Belinda was tempted to correct his English, but instead, she put her arm around him and gave him a hug.

Henry didn't pull away until a customer came in. Then he stepped out from behind the counter, grabbed the handle of the shopping wagon, and pulled it toward the area where potting soil and fertilizer were sold.

"Before you head out to bid on some roofing jobs today, could I ask you a question?" Amy asked Jared when he came into the kitchen to get his lunch pail.

"Sure, ask away."

"I was wondering what you would think about us having a bonfire supper here this Friday evening, with hot dogs and marshmallows."

He tipped his head. "Just the two of us?"

"Actually, I would like to invite my family, as well as Herschel Fisher, to join us."

"It's a nice idea, Amy, but I'm worried about you doing too much. You're already watching Sylvia's kinner so she can help your mamm in the greenhouse, and that can be quite tiring for you."

Amy shook her head. "It's not really. I rest when they're napping, and I'm doing fine physically. And remember, we had your folks over for a meal last week, and I didn't overdo." She moved over to where he stood leaning against the counter and placed her hand on Jared's arm. "I promise to keep things simple for the bonfire meal. It would be so nice to sit outside under the moon and stars while we enjoy a time of eating and fellowshipping with my family."

Jared quirked an eyebrow. "But Herschel isn't part of your family."

Amy bit on her lower lip, then released it and smiled. "No, but he might make a nice addition."

Jared's eyes widened. "Are you hoping your mamm and Herschel will get married someday?"

"Mom needs a man in her life. After Sylvia and the kinner move out, it'll just be her and my bruder living in that big house and trying to run the greenhouse by themselves."

"I think you're forgetting something, Amy." Jared held up one finger. "First and foremost, your mother may have no desire to get married again." He lifted a second finger. "And even if she were thinking about remarrying someday, she might have no interest in Herschel."

"Are you finished, or do you have another point to mention before I make a comment?"

"Just one more." A third finger came up. "If your mamm, with Henry's help, is not able to manage the greenhouse, she can always hire someone to work full-time or even part-time."

"That might be okay for a while, but eventually, Henry will reach the age where he'll be looking to find a wife and get married. Then my dear mother will be completely on her own."

Jared leaned away from the counter and crossed his arms. "She may decide to sell the greenhouse and move in with us or Sylvia and her family. I'm sure we'll have a bigger house by then, and hopefully, the home Sylvia and Dennis choose to live in will have plenty of bedrooms. Another option would be for a *daadihaus* to be added on to one of our places."

"While those ideas are all possible—that is, if Mom wanted them—I truly believe she would be happier if she got married again." For emphasis, Amy tapped the edge of the counter where she'd been making Jared's sandwich. "I think Herschel is the right man for her."

"There's a fourth thing to consider," Jared was quick to say. "Herschel may have no romantic interest in your mom, or even want to get married again. As you know, he's been a widower for a good many years, and if he wanted to get remarried, he'd have most likely done so by now."

"Maybe he was waiting for the right woman to come along."

Jared snickered and tweaked the end of Amy's nose. "Such a little matchmaker I married."

She swatted at his hand playfully. "Neither Herschel nor Mom will know if they're meant for each other if we don't get them together more often." She wiggled her brows. "Besides, I think he is interested in her. He sent her a Valentine's Day card, remember?"

Jared's shoulders rose as he lifted both hands in obvious defeat. "Okay, okay, feel free to invite Herschel to join us for the bonfire meal. If he doesn't want to come, he can always say no."

"Do we need to tell him that my mamm is going to be here?"

"I think that would only be fair, don't you? The last time you invited your mother and Herschel to join us for supper, without either knowing the other would be here, it seemed a bit awkward for both of them."

"Only for a short time though," Amy argued. "As the evening progressed they seemed to relax, and I'm sure they enjoyed themselves."

Jared bent to kiss Amy's forehead, then her cheeks, and finally his lips touched hers. "You have my blessing to do whatever you like, but please let both parties know that the other person has been invited."

Amy grinned up at him. "Danki, Jared. I have a good feeling about this."

He kissed her again, and then placed his hand against her stomach. "And I have a good feeling about you and our boppli. I can't wait to take part in raising this child."

She finished putting his sandwich together, placed it inside the lunch pail next to the apple she'd put there earlier, and handed it to him. "I feel real good about it too."

Chapter 16

Gordonville, Pennsylvania

Herschel stood in front of the bathroom mirror inspecting his face. He'd finished shaving above his upper lip, which Amish men always kept free of hair. Now it was time to do something with those unruly hairs sticking out at odd angles from his beard.

Picking up the comb, Herschel ran it down the length of his nearly gray beard a couple of times. He paused. "Hmm. . . I have to say my hair could use a good trimming too. I might as well speak to Mom about givin' me a quick haircut. She and Dad have been after me to get it taken care of anyways."

Until recently, he hadn't thought too much about his appearance, since he wasn't married and no longer had a wife to come home to each evening. When Mattie was alive, Herschel had always made sure he smelled nice and looked well-groomed. Before leaving his bulk-food store, he would wash up good and put on fresh deodorant so that when he came into his house and greeted his dear wife, she would find him appealing. But until recently, he'd let himself go, mostly worrying about his appearance on church Sundays, and if he attended a wedding, funeral, or some other special event.

Things were different now. While Herschel had not admitted it to anyone, he'd become interested in Belinda King. The first time he'd seen her in a different light was last year, when Jared and Amy invited them both for a meal. He'd been surprised when, soon after he arrived, Belinda showed up. However, what had surprised Herschel even more was how much he'd enjoyed her company, despite feeling a bit shy in her presence.

Is she interested in me at all? Herschel asked himself. Although Belinda had always been friendly to Herschel, she'd never given him any indication that she might see him as anything other than a casual friend.

Word had it on the Amish grapevine that Monroe Esh had set his cap for Belinda King. Herschel's mother had mentioned recently that while attending a Mud Sale, she'd overhead two women talking, and Monroe's name was brought up. One of the women said he'd been actively seeking to court the Amish woman who owned the greenhouse in Strasburg. Since the only greenhouse in Strasburg run by an Amish woman belonged to Belinda, Herschel knew exactly who that woman had been talking about.

He snipped off some of the stray hairs on his beard, then stopped and mused. *It has been awhile since my wife passed away, and I had a hard time letting her go. But the change that's been coming over me is like an awakening of sorts. It might be time to start over with someone I can share my life with.*

Herschel gave his facial hair some combing. *I'm only a couple of years older than Belinda, and truth be told, most people guess me to be younger than I look. But that's not a bad thing. I kinda like it.*

He grinned at his reflection in the mirror, but his smile faded as the reality of competing against another man for Belinda sank in. Herschel wondered how crafty Monroe would be if he made it known that his hat was set on Belinda too. The awful doubt that crept in seemed to yank at Herschel's confidence.

"What chance do I have against him?" Herschel spoke out loud. "Monroe's younger than me, and his furniture store is always busy, so he's probably doing well financially. Not only that, but he's quite a talker. I bet it wouldn't take much for him to win Belinda over."

Herschel reached around and scratched the back of his head. "Maybe she would think I'm too old for her anyway."

He picked up the scissors and made a few snips. *I need to quit worrying about all this and just relax and enjoy my time at Jared and Amy's this evening. If it's meant for me and Belinda to have a connection, then it will happen in God's time, not mine.*

Strasburg

When Herschel guided his horse and buggy up the driveway leading to the home he'd rented to Jared and Amy, he saw two other carriages parked there.

Everyone must be here already. I hope I'm not late. Herschel stepped down from the buggy and hurried to get his horse secured to the hitching rail. Once that chore was done, he reached inside the carriage and pulled out a paper bag. Even though Jared had said Herschel didn't need to bring anything, he wanted to do his part, so he'd purchased a bag of chips to contribute to the meal.

Herschel was glad his mother had taken the time to cut his hair. It really needed it, and Dad had even gotten Mom to trim a little on his hair too. Herschel hoped he would make a nice impression on Belinda and her family by having taken more interest in his appearance.

He looked down, making certain that his attire was in order and his dark trousers were free of any dust or smudges from the buggy. *If I'm going to the trouble of making sure my hair and beard look good, then everything else should too.*

Hearing voices coming from the backyard, Herschel headed in that direction. Upon rounding the corner of the house, he spotted a glowing bonfire in the pit he'd made a year after he'd bought the house as a rental. Jared, Amy, Belinda, and Sylvia, holding Rachel on her lap, sat on folding chairs. On the other side of the yard Dennis and Henry played catch with Allen, using a large rubber ball. Everyone appeared to be content, and he almost hated to interrupt. A pang of envy shot through him. How nice it would be to have a large family. For Herschel, it was just him and his parents living in the same area. When they got together, things were pretty quiet.

Jared must have seen Herschel coming, for he looked his way and motioned him over.

"*Guder owed,*" Herschel said when he joined the group.

"Good evening," came their responses.

"I brought some chips." Herschel placed the paper sack on the picnic table.

"Danki, that was nice of you." Amy smiled. "In addition to the hot dogs we'll soon be roasting, we have a tray of cut-up veggies. Oh, and there's also a big pot of savory baked beans. I'm sure you'll enjoy those as much as we all do."

Herschel's chin dipped slightly as he glanced in Belinda's direction. Her cheeks looked a little pink, but then that could have just been from the glow of the fire. "It's a recipe my *mudder* used to make."

Herschel's mouth felt awfully dry all of a sudden. He didn't understand why he felt so nervous or at a loss of words in Belinda's presence.

"Why don't you take a seat over there?" Amy pointed to the empty chair beside Belinda.

Herschel waited to see if Belinda would object, and when she gave a little nod, he quickly sat down. "Nice evening, jah?"

She turned to him and smiled. "It certainly is. And I'm glad you could join us."

"I appreciate the invite." Herschel undid the top button of his shirt. It felt like it was choking him.

"How's your mother getting along these days? I haven't seen her in some time."

"She's getting by okay. Same with my daed." Herschel held his hands out toward the warmth of the fire. *Sure wish I could think of something interesting to talk about—a topic that might be of interest to Belinda.* He cleared his throat a couple of times. "How are things going at the greenhouse?"

"It's been kind of slow since we reopened, but as the weather improves, people normally start thinking about gardening and spending more time in their yards." Belinda glanced at her granddaughter, still sitting contently on Sylvia's lap, and then she turned her attention to Herschel again. "A man who owns a local landscaping business came to the greenhouse earlier this week. He talked with me about supplying some of the plants, trees, and flowers he would like to offer his customers."

Herschel scratched an itch behind his left ear. "Sounds like it could be a good thing for both of you then."

"Jah. I hope it works out."

"Okay, everyone, the fire's died down enough so we can roast our hot dogs," Jared announced. "Let's gather around to offer thanks, and then I'll pass out the roasting sticks."

Dennis, Henry, and Allen stopped playing ball and ran over to join the group. Dennis shook Herschel's hand. "It's nice you could join us."

"Danki. I'm glad I was invited."

At Jared's lead, all heads bowed for silent prayer. In addition to thanking God for the food they'd be eating soon, Herschel said a prayer on Belinda's behalf. *Lord, please bless Belinda and her family. Provide for them through the money the greenhouse brings in. And if it's meant for me to develop a deeper friendship with Belinda, then please give me some sign that she's interested so I won't barge ahead and make a fool of myself.*

🐦

Henry held his stick with a hot dog on it close to the embers and listened to the conversation between his mother and Herschel. They'd been sitting by each other since Herschel arrived, and now the man was roasting a hot dog for Mom. *She knows how to roast her own wiener, for goodness' sake. She's had plenty of practice over the years and doesn't need anyone's help.*

Henry angled his stick in a different direction so the hot dog wouldn't burn on one side. *I wonder why Mom didn't tell Herschel that she could manage on her own. He glanced at Amy and noticed a big smile on her face. What in the world is my sister so happy about? Is it because she's expecting a boppli? Maybe she just enjoys having our family together.*

Henry rotated his stick again. The hot dog had begun to brown quite nicely. *Or maybe Amy's glad to have Herschel visiting. He was nice enough to rent them this house at a reasonable price. Amy might feel beholden to him.*

Then another thought crossed Henry's mind. He'd heard his sister tell Mom on more than one occasion what a nice man Herschel was and that she was surprised he'd never remarried. *Is it possible that Amy invited Herschel here tonight so he and Mom could get better acquainted?* He looked in Mom's direction. She too wore a smile as she leaned closer to Herschel, while pointing at the two wieners on the stick he held close to the glowing embers. *Could my sister be plotting to get Mom and Herschel together? If so, is she succeeding?*

"Look out, Brother! One side of your hot dog is turning black." Sylvia pointed.

"You may have been holding it in one position too long," Dennis interjected.

Henry flipped the stick over and grimaced. Sure enough, part of the meat looked like charcoal. "It's okay," he mumbled. "I like it well done." He grabbed a bun from the table, put the hot dog inside, and then squeezed on plenty of ketchup and mustard. *There, that should make it taste better.*

"Who made the *gebackne buhne*?" Herschel asked after he'd finished roasting his and Mom's wieners.

Before Mom could respond, Amy and Sylvia both pointed to her. "You should try some," Amy said. "Our mamm makes the best baked beans of any I've ever tasted."

"That's right," Sylvia agreed. "I always have more than one helping."

No wonder she mentioned they were a recipe of her mamm's. "I'll be eager to try them." Herschel got their hot dogs ready, and then he spooned some baked beans onto his plate.

Meanwhile, Henry watched, while he chomped on a handful of chips.

Herschel ate the beans in short order, then helped himself to more. "I have to say, your daughters are right, Belinda. Your gebackne buhne are *appeditlich*. If there's enough to go around, I may have to eat three helpings."

Mom tilted her head to one side. "Why thank you, Herschel. I'm glad you think the baked beans are delicious."

Henry glanced at Dennis. Allen sat beside him, chattering away like a magpie. Every once in a while, Rachel, while sitting on her mother's lap, reached over, giggled, and touched Dennis with her grubby little ketchup-stained hand. Those two kids had really taken a shine to Dennis, but as far as Henry was concerned, they monopolized too much of his time. He had wanted to talk to Dennis about some unusual birds he'd seen the other day, but it didn't look like he'd get the chance.

At the sound of Mom's laughter, Henry looked her way again. Apparently Herschel had said something she thought was funny, because she'd just thanked him for sharing such a humorous story.

What story? Henry's hand tightened around his bun so hard that part of it crumbled and fell apart. He picked up the hot dog with his bare fingers and gobbled the rest of it down.

Henry remembered the Valentine card Herschel had sent to his mother last month and wondered once again if he had a personal interest in Mom. *Even though Herschel isn't nearly as irritating as Monroe, he should not be makin' a play for my mamm. He's been a widower for a good many years, and apparently remained content, so why the sudden interest in Mom?*

Henry spooned some baked beans onto his plate. *I'd better get 'em while the gettin' is good.* He ate the beans quickly, barely able to enjoy the savory flavor, while his thoughts remained on Herschel. *Hopefully Mom will say something to let the man know that she's not interested in a relationship with him. If she doesn't, then at some point, I may need to let him know that fact myself. I'll just tell Herschel that my mamm's still in love with my daed and has no plans of ever remarrying.*

Henry nearly choked on the forkful of beans he'd put into his mouth. *At least I don't think she does. Maybe Mom is looking to get married again and hasn't said anything to me.* The thought of it put a sick feeling in the pit of Henry's stomach, diminishing his appetite. Unless he got it back at some point this evening, he probably wouldn't bother roasting any marshmallows. What would be the point? If his mother and Herschel kept talking and laughing with each other, anything Henry ate from here on wouldn't have much of an exciting taste. Not even the chocolate brownies Sylvia had made for dessert.

Chapter 17

Monroe sat at his mother's kitchen table, eating a late supper after his folks had gone to bed. He'd worked later than usual on some paperwork at his furniture store and then gone over to the Kings' place to see Belinda. He had anticipated visiting for a while with the special woman he admired, but that didn't work out the way he'd planned.

Monroe wouldn't have minded being in Belinda's presence this evening and possibly getting to eat some of her delicious and hearty cooking. To his disappointment, she wasn't at home, and apparently neither was anyone else in her family, because nobody had answered the door. He'd been tempted to stop at Belinda's neighbors across the street and ask if they knew where she was, but decided against it. Belinda probably didn't keep her English neighbors informed of her whereabouts, and he couldn't fault her for that. On more than one occasion when Monroe had dropped by the greenhouse or up to Belinda's house, he'd caught sight of the red-haired English woman on her front porch, looking across the street with a pair of binoculars.

That woman is a snoop, he told himself. *She's probably a big gossip too.* Monroe had met plenty of people like her—busybodies who liked to stick their noses in someone else's business.

"Whatever goes on at Belinda's place should be my business," Monroe muttered, reaching for his glass of milk to wash down the sandwich he'd eaten a few minutes ago. He felt reassured that there wasn't anyone else to compete with to win Belinda's heart—at least not so far. He hadn't seen or heard about any of the other single men his age from their Amish community going over to her place or asking her out.

As his body relaxed, he muttered some more. "I'm the fella for Belinda, and in time I'll win her and we'll be setting the date for our big day." If there was one thing Monroe wanted more than anything, it was to become Belinda's husband. He'd wanted it when they were young people, and his desire to have her as his wife had never died, not even after she'd married Vernon. Dejected and hurt by her betrayal, Monroe had left the area. He'd hoped to start a new life and put the pain of losing her aside. But when he heard from his mother that Vernon had been killed, Monroe couldn't wait to move back to Strasburg. Fortunately he'd had enough money saved up to start his new business, which had turned out to be a good investment. Many people living in the area and even from other places wanted expertly crafted furniture built by the Amish. So Monroe made sure everything his employees turned out was top-notch. Through some good advertising strategies and word of mouth, it hadn't taken long for Monroe's business to become successful.

Monroe felt a tingling sensation on his arms and the nape of his neck. *Now if I can just get Belinda to see that we're meant to be together, everything will be as it should, and my life will finally be complete.*

"What's for dessert?" Earl asked from his easy chair across the room. He'd come home from his job at the dealership sounding a little defeated. But before he'd changed from his nicer clothes into the comfy attire he had on, he'd shared the details of what had happened. Earl and another salesman had been trying to sell the same vehicle to make a potential sale. He admitted that they were both after their commissions. Unfortunately, the customer Earl dealt with didn't have enough money up front to purchase the car, like the other patron did. Rebounding from his wound, Earl seemed to be craving extra attention, and what helped him through it was being waited on. However, Virginia wasn't sure if her patience at this point could accommodate his mood.

Virginia groaned. She and Goldie had just gotten comfortable on the couch, and the thought of getting up so soon to get dessert held no appeal. *I know he's the breadwinner, but I've been busy today with ongoing chores here at the house. And things haven't been perfect around here either—especially when Goldie threw up on my pillow after I got up this morning.* Virginia petted the cat. *It's not your fault I gave you a new brand of cat food that was cheaper than the normal stuff.*

Virginia felt annoyed, and her limbs were growing rigid as she looked over at her husband. "Why didn't ya say something before I sat down, Earl?"

"Didn't think about it till now."

"Can't you go out to the kitchen and get something yourself?"

He shook his head and pouted. "Besides having a lousy day, I'm in the middle of my favorite show right now, and I don't want to miss the ending. Come on, honey. . .pretty please."

Wow! He is sure being a big baby. I suppose he'll keep it up if I remain here on the couch with Goldie.

Virginia set the cat aside and rose from the couch. "All right, Your Majesty, your wish is my command," she mumbled on the way to the kitchen.

Virginia pulled out the cookie jar and set several on a plate. *It's a good thing I made the time to bake these earlier today.* She replaced the lid and slid the jar back to its spot. *That ought to last Earl awhile, at least till the end of his show.*

She took the plate out to the living room and set it on the TV tray beside his chair. "Here you go—chocolate-chip—your favorite kind."

"Thanks, hon. Do we have any coffee in the pot?" He gave her a sheepish grin. "That would go real good with these yummy cookies."

Virginia stepped back. "Yes there's plenty in the carafe. I'll get you a cup." Before she had moved a step from his recliner he spoke again. "How about a bowl of ice cream to go with the cookies?"

Virginia poked her tongue into the side of her cheek and inhaled a long breath. "Won't the cookies and the hot cup of coffee be enough? You don't wanna get fat, ya know."

He swatted the air with his hand. "I am not overweight, Virginia, and a little ice cream won't tip the scales." Earl glanced up at her, and then looked quickly back at the TV. "You ought to have some too. Maybe a bowl of ice cream will cool you down."

"I am not hot. If anything, this room is a bit chilly."

"I didn't mean physically warm. I was talking about your disposition.

You've been hot under the collar ever since I came home from work today." Earl raised his eyebrows. "And if anyone should be hot, it's me, because I'm the one who had a rough day."

She clenched her teeth.

"Could you please get me some ice cream? It'll help me feel better, my pretty red-headed doll."

Ignoring his compliment, Virginia couldn't deny her crankiness. She'd spent a good portion of her day cleaning and baking, as well as listening to and watching the traffic out front. And most of it was because of that stupid greenhouse across the road. But of course, Earl probably wouldn't care about any of that.

"You know what, Earl? I have good reason to be irritated this evening. You should know by now that all those horses and buggies on our road really get on my nerves. Not to mention all the messes those smelly horses create and leave behind." Virginia looked toward the front window. "It'll be another year just like the last one we had. You'll have to hang those sticky fly catchers outside near the exterior doors. And I have to say that we never had flies in the big city of Chicago like we have out here in this rural country." She turned to see if her husband was involved in the conversation.

Earl made no comment as he leaned forward with his elbows on his knees, looking intently at the TV.

Shaking her head and muttering to herself, Virginia returned to the kitchen for Earl's coffee and a bowl of ice cream. *That man doesn't give a hoot about my feelings. He has no problem with our neighbors and all the noise and icky smelling road apples on the road, because he's not here all day.*

Virginia felt a sense of tightness in her chest. *I wish there was something I could do to put a stop to it once and for all!*

🐦

From the passenger seat of her buggy, with her horse being driven by Henry, Belinda reflected on the wonderful evening they'd had at Jared and Amy's. She couldn't get over how enjoyable it had been—especially spending time with Herschel and getting to know him better. Although at first he'd seemed slow in taking part in a conversation, once he had opened up and become more talkative, Herschel had proved to be quite an interesting man. He'd told Belinda, as well as those who sat nearby, some humorous stories about when he was a boy. One in particular caused Belinda to laugh out loud. According to the story, when Herschel was about six years old, he'd begged his mother to let him eat some of her baking chocolate. She had told him that it was quite bitter, not sweet like the chocolate bars sold in a candy shop. After Herschel's insistence and lots more begging, she finally gave in and cut off a chunk for him. One bite and Herschel raced for the garbage can to spit out the bitter-tasting chocolate. He told Belinda that it had taken him a long time until he could eat anything made with chocolate.

"What are you thinking about, Mom?"

Henry's question pushed Belinda's thoughts aside.

"Just reflecting on what a nice time we had this evening sitting around the bonfire. I'm glad Amy and Jared planned the event and invited Herschel too."

Henry didn't comment as they headed down the road toward home, with Dennis's horse and buggy following not too far behind. Sylvia and the children had ridden with him, and since it would have been a bit crowded with four adults and two children in one buggy, Belinda opted to take her own horse and carriage, allowing Henry to take charge as the official chauffeur. Her son was a careful driver and had good night vision, so she felt comfortable letting him take control of her horse.

"Did you have fun tonight?" Belinda asked, looking over at Henry.

"It was okay, I guess. Didn't get to talk to Dennis much though."

"He was kept pretty busy with your niece and nephew. He'll make a good father for Sylvia's children. I've even heard Allen call him 'Papa' a few times."

"But he's not their daed, and if you got married again, your new husband would not be my daed either."

Belinda couldn't mistake the angry tone in her son's voice. "Now what brought on that statement, Son?"

"Just saying, is all."

"If you're worried about Monroe—"

"Seems to me you might have two suitors vying for your hand in marriage."

"What suitors?"

"I saw how cozy Herschel was with you tonight, Mom. He monopolized all your time, making it hard for you to talk to anyone else. He even roasted a hot dog for you."

"For goodness' sake, Henry, Herschel was just being friendly and polite. I enjoyed his company, yes, but I am not thinking our friendship could end in marriage."

"You might not think so, but I bet he does. And it don't take no genius to figure out what Monroe has on his mind."

Belinda reached across the seat and placed her hand on Henry's knee. "You may be right about Monroe, but I seriously doubt that Herschel has anything more than a casual friendship with me on his mind. And you needn't worry about me getting married again, because I have no desire for that at this time."

"Well that's good."

Belinda sighed as she crossed her arms over her chest. *I don't think my girls would have a problem if I should ever decide to remarry. Why does Henry have to be so opposed to the idea? Doesn't he realize that someday he'll get married and leave home? Would he not care that I'd be in my big old house all alone and would most likely try to keep the greenhouse running by myself?*

Maybe by then, she consoled herself, *he will have changed his mind about me getting married again. And perhaps by that time I'll be ready to consider it as well.*

A short time later, Henry turned the horse and buggy up their driveway. The moon was out fully tonight, and Belinda thought she saw something dangling from one of the trees in their front yard. She didn't think too much about it until they were out of the buggy and Henry made a comment just moments after she'd heard the hoot of an owl.

"Look, Mom, there's something up in that tree." Henry reached into the buggy and grabbed his flashlight. When he shined the light on the spot, where the *hoo-hoo* had come from, Belinda gasped.

"Oh no. . . Someone draped toilet paper from the branches, and maybe other trees in our yard as well."

Henry shined the light around. Sure enough, the rest of the trees had also been done.

About that time, Dennis's horse and carriage pulled in. Belinda waited until Sylvia and Dennis got out with the children, and then she pointed to the white streamers, clearly seen under the beam of light from Henry's powerful flashlight. "Someone came onto our property and did this while we were gone," she exclaimed. "Just when we thought the acts of vandalism were behind us, now we're faced with this."

"It's so frustrating." Sylvia's voice quivered a bit. "Why would someone want to do such a thing?"

"It gets worse. Look there." Henry moved closer to the house, shining the light back and forth across the front living-room windows.

Belinda cringed when she saw that raw eggs had been thrown at the glass, creating a real mess on both windows.

Dennis stepped forward, holding Rachel in his arms. "This kind of thing needs to be stopped. Belinda, you really need to call the sheriff."

"What good would that do?" she asked. "Unless someone saw the person who did this, we have no witnesses, and how likely is that? It was probably just some rowdy kids going through their *rumschpringe*. I'm sure they meant no harm, and most likely our home wasn't the only one they targeted." She looked at Henry. "We'll clean up this mess in the morning when we have better light. Right now, we need to get the kinner inside and ready for bed."

As they approached the front door, Belinda's heart pounded. A note had been taped on the door. It read: *"When are you going to give up and move?"*

Chapter 18

What kind of clues should I be looking for? Henry asked himself while he cleaned off the windows early the following morning. *Almost every time we've had an incident at our place, we were away for a while. That would mean someone is casing the property and knows when we're not here.*

Henry sprayed more cleaner on the window and rubbed at the dried egg yolk stuck to the glass. *I shoulda cleaned this mess off last night.* He'd already taken down all the toilet paper. "What a waste," he'd said when he threw it away.

He scowled at the eggshells beneath his feet. *This could have been done by anyone who decided to come in here last night.*

Henry gritted his teeth and squatted down to pick up the cracked shells. *I'm sure gettin' sick and tired of all this. It's gone on too long, and if Mom won't call the sheriff or even tell Ezekiel about it, then I have no choice but to find out who is responsible.*

Henry continued to fume and analyze things as he finished cleaning up the windows. So far he'd seen no evidence near the house that would give him any clues, but after breakfast, before it was time to help out in the greenhouse, he would do a more thorough search around the property. Surely there had to be a clue somewhere.

🐦

Belinda had a difficult time keeping her mind on the business of running the greenhouse. *I should be fertilizing some of the plants. I'll have to go back and grab the watering can and the mix.* She looked out toward the parking lot. *I'll take care of it after Sylvia returns, because Henry is already busy in the back. Besides, someone should be up front. I don't want the customers coming in and it appearing as if we're not here.*

They'd been open about an hour, and a few customers had come in, but it had been a challenge for Belinda to converse with any of them. Sylvia came to work with her today, and she seemed quieter than usual as well. If only their lives could be peaceful again, without having to worry about if or when another act of vandalism may occur.

Henry had been out looking for clues earlier but found nothing out of the ordinary. Since part of last night's mess involved eggs, he'd mentioned the prospect of Maude being the culprit. "After all," Henry had told Belinda shortly before she'd opened the greenhouse, "the old woman probably has eggs now, since she stole two of our hens. Maude is one strange lady, and I wouldn't put anything past her."

Belinda looked toward the storage room, where Henry had gone to get a broom to sweep up some dirt that had been spilled in aisle 1. *My son is really concerned about this, and I am too, but I don't know how to put an end to it.*

Belinda fingered the tablet lying on the counter where she sat. *Would it help if I wrote a note and tacked it up someplace where the person doing the vandalism might see it if they came back again? I could ask what they have against us and suggest that we meet in person to discuss the situation.*

She tapped her pen against the tablet. *I suppose that wouldn't work if the person feels vindictive toward us for some reason. They obviously don't want us to know or they would have come to me and spoken their feelings face-to-face.*

Belinda closed her eyes and said a prayer for the man or woman who had made it clear that they wanted her to close the greenhouse and leave the area.

Her eyes snapped open when she heard footsteps approach. Thinking it was Sylvia, returning to the greenhouse after going to the house to check on Amy and the children, Belinda was surprised to see Herschel standing on the other side of the counter. She'd been so engrossed in her prayer that she hadn't even heard the bell above the door jingle, indicating that someone had entered the building.

"Guder mariye, Herschel." She offered him what she hoped was a welcoming smile.

"Good morning, Belinda." Grinning back at her, he removed his straw hat and held it by the brim. Herschel appeared to be less shy than usual. "I sure enjoyed myself last night at Jared and Amy's."

"I did too." *At least until we got home and found a mess, along with a note, waiting for us.* She wanted to tell him about the vandalism but decided it was best not to mention it. Herschel might say something to his parents or someone else, and then the news could travel quickly around their community.

Herschel shifted his weight and leaned against his side of the counter. "I came by to ask you a question."

"Oh?" She tipped her head slightly.

He glanced toward the front door, then back at her. "I. . .umm. . .was wondering if you might be free to go out to supper with me one evening next week. It would give us a chance to get better acquainted."

She touched her cheeks, which felt quite warm. "Well, yes, that would be nice. What night did you have in mind?"

"Would Friday work for you?"

"I think it would. In fact, I'm sure nothing else is going on that evening, so jah, I'd enjoy going out to supper with you, Herschel."

"Okay, good. Should I come by to get you around five thirty, or would that be too early?"

"The greenhouse closes at five, so could we make it six? The extra half hour would give me a little more time to get ready."

"Six it is. I'll see you then. Have a nice rest of your day, Belinda." Herschel put his hat back on his head and went out the door.

The corners of Belinda's lips twitched. *Did I just agree to go out on a date with Herschel? I'm surprised he came right out and asked me to go out with him. Herschel wasn't being shy at all and I'm glad.* She touched her ever-warming cheeks again. *Oh my. . .I wonder what my children will say when I tell them—especially Henry. This might not set well with him. It's a good thing my son wasn't here when Herschel extended the invitation. He may have spoken on my behalf and said no to Herschel, and that would have been most embarrassing.*

Monroe pulled his horse and buggy into the greenhouse parking lot in time to see Herschel Fisher come out of the building and approach his own rig. The man wore the biggest grin. Monroe had never seen the fellow look so happy.

"How are things with you these days?" Monroe asked, stepping down from his buggy.

Herschel gave his mostly gray beard a tug. "Fine and dandy. How about you?"

"Can't complain." *Things would be better if Belinda would let me court her though.* Monroe kept his thoughts to himself. Whatever happened or didn't happen between him and Belinda was none of Herschel's business.

Monroe scrutinized Herschel, noticing that he was empty handed. "You came from the greenhouse, but it doesn't look like you bought anything," he commented in a nonchalant tone.

Herschel shook his head. "Didn't come to buy anything. Came to talk to Belinda."

"Mind if I ask about what?"

"Oh, just wanted to see how she's doing this morning and ask if she'd like to go out to supper with me next week."

Monroe blinked rapidly, and his mouth nearly fell open. Until this moment, he'd had no idea Herschel was interested in Belinda. "Uh, what'd she say?"

"She agreed to go." Herschel pulled his shoulders back a bit and gave a crisp nod. "I'll be taking her out Friday evening."

A burning sensation traveled across Monroe's chest and all the way up to his neck. *Belinda's agreed to go out with Herschel but not me? What's going on here anyway? I'd bet Herschel's at least eight or ten years older than her. What in the world would she see in him?*

Struggling to keep his composure, Monroe forced himself to offer what he hoped was a pleasant smile. "Well, I need to head into the greenhouse and state my business, and then I'll be on my way."

"Have a good rest of your day." Herschel released his horse from the hitching rail, climbed into his carriage, and backed away.

As Herschel's horse and carriage started down the driveway, Monroe made a beeline for the greenhouse, ready to give Belinda a piece of his mind.

He stopped short, just outside the front door and sucked in several breaths of air. It wouldn't do to go charging in there like a jealous fool. He needed to use some common sense and try to stay on her good side. The last thing Monroe wanted to do was rile her up. Then she'd never agree to let him court her.

So while he collected himself, Monroe assessed the situation. *It's obvious I'm not the only eligible man interested in Belinda. I'd thought this would be easy and that I had her all to myself. That's all right though. I'll just have to use my wit and come up with a way to win my gal. To start with, I'm younger and more financially sound than Herschel, so that could be to my advantage.*

Belinda was about to leave her place behind the counter and see what was taking Henry so long, when he showed up.

"Things were gettin' disarranged in there," he told Belinda. "So I took some time to straighten all the items on the shelves and make sure all the boxes were set so we can easily see the labels on what's inside each one."

"That's good. I appreciate it, Son." Belinda gave his shoulder a squeeze. This was the first time he'd seemed worried about disorganization. Maybe it was a sign that he had gained some maturity.

"I swept up the dirt you asked me to, so now what do ya want done?"

She was about to respond to Henry's question when Monroe entered the shop and stepped between them. "Can I talk to you for a few minutes, Belinda?"

"Well yes, I suppose, but. . . ."

"Before you do, I'd like to ask a question." Henry looked right at Monroe, narrowing his eyes.

"About what?" Monroe asked.

"I was wondering what you were doing last night."

"I did several things. For one, I dropped by here to see your mamm, but no one was home." Monroe looked right back at Henry. "Do you have a problem with that, young man?"

"It all depends."

"On what?" A muscle on the side of Monroe's cleanly shaven face twitched.

"On how you answer my next question."

"And that would be?"

"What'd you do when you found out we weren't home?"

"Henry, please. . ." Belinda's elbow connected with his arm. Her son's behavior was embarrassing. She couldn't imagine what Monroe must be thinking. It seemed as though Henry thought Monroe might be guilty of something. Did he believe this man was responsible for hanging toilet paper from the trees in their yard, egging the front windows, and leaving the note on the door? If so, Belinda felt certain her son was wrong. Besides, it wasn't right to make accusations with no evidence whatsoever. She hoped Henry would not say anything more, because things were already uncomfortable.

"It's okay. I don't mind answering," Monroe said. "I went home. Why do you ask, son?"

Henry folded his arms and grunted. "I ain't your son."

"It was only a figure of speech." Monroe took a step closer to Henry. "Why did you ask?" he repeated.

"Did ya see anything out of place in our yard or anyone hangin' around the house while you were here?"

Monroe gave a hearty shake of his head. "The only person I saw at all is your red-headed neighbor lady across the road."

"Virginia came over here?" Belinda questioned.

"No, I saw her standing on her front porch. It looked like she had a pair of binoculars in her hands."

"That's no big deal." Henry shook his head. "Sylvia and I are bird-watchers, and we use our binoculars a lot."

Monroe shrugged. "Well, you asked if I'd seen anyone, and that woman is the only person I saw."

"Okay, whatever." Henry moved toward the front door. "I'm goin' out to check on the beehives, Mom. Give a holler if you need me." Henry was out the door before Belinda could respond.

"Well, good. I'm glad we have a few minutes to talk while there's no one else in the building."

"What did you wish to speak with me about, Monroe?" Belinda moved back toward the counter and stood behind it. She needed to be ready in case another customer came in.

Monroe followed. "I would like to take you out for supper one night next week. Are you free on Friday?"

Belinda's face warmed and she swallowed hard. "Um. . .well. . .I've already made plans."

"What kind of plans?"

Trapped. Now what should I say? Belinda glanced at the door, hoping Sylvia or a customer would come in. *What is taking my daughter so long in the house? She must know her help could be needed out here.*

"Belinda, are you going to answer my question?" Monroe looked at her pointedly.

She moistened her lips, feeling ever so anxious. "If you must know, I agreed to have supper with Herschel Fisher that evening."

His facial features tightened. "Oh, so that's how it is. You'll go out with that man, who has so little to offer, but not with me." Monroe tapped his foot and glared at her. "You know how much I care for you, Belinda, and yet you're choosing an older man who hasn't much of a personality, over me." He pressed one fist against his chest. "Do you have any idea how badly my feelings have been hurt?"

Belinda dropped her gaze to the floor. She hadn't meant to upset him. She felt pain in the back of her throat as she tried to come up with the right thing to say to Monroe. Somehow Belinda had to make it better.

"How about Saturday night? Would that be okay?"

He placed both hands on the counter and leaned in closer to her. "Are you saying that you'd be willing to go out for supper with me on Saturday?"

"Jah."

With a wide smile, Monroe clapped his hands. "All right then, it's a date. What time would you like me to pick you up?"

"Would six o'clock work for you?"

His head bobbed quickly up and down. "I'll see you then, Belinda, and be prepared to have a wunderbaar evening."

When Monroe went out the door, with a spring in his step, Belinda sank to the wooden stool behind the counter. *Oh my! What have I gotten myself into? Two meals out with two very different men, and all in the same week? What in the world was I thinking?*

Chapter 19

"Do I have any stray hairs sticking out of my bun or the sides of my head covering?" Belinda asked Sylvia when she entered the living room Friday evening to wait for Herschel.

Sylvia left the chair where she'd been sitting with a notepad and pen. She stepped behind Belinda and walked around to check both sides and the front. "Everything looks fine. You did a good job with your hair, but then you usually do. And you'll have a nice time, so please relax, Mom, because you seem a little nervous for your date."

"Jah, guess I am. It's because I'm a little rusty since my courting days, so I'm not sure how to act."

Sylvia took hold of Belinda's hand. "I have the best mamm a daughter could want, and I'm sure you'll get along fine with Herschel this evening."

Belinda's face warmed. "In some ways it feels like I'm a young woman again, until I look in the mirror." She laughed. "It's funny how, after all this time, those feelings can be stirred up again."

"Here, let me fix your apron tie. It's a little crooked." Sylvia leaned in and took care of the problem. "There you go—now you're ready."

"Danki." Belinda motioned to the writing tablet Sylvia still held. "Have you been working on your wedding plans?"

"Yes, and just when I'm sure all the details are covered, I think of something else to add."

Belinda chuckled. "It'll all come together. It has to, since you only have four-and-a-half months till the big day."

"True." The gleam in Sylvia's eyes couldn't be missed. No doubt, she'd been counting the days until she would become Mrs. Dennis Weaver.

Belinda glanced at Henry, slouched on the couch with one of his bird magazines. He hadn't said more than a few words to her all day. Her son had said plenty earlier in the week, however, when she'd let him and her daughters know about her two supper dates. Amy seemed pleased about Belinda going out with Herschel, but said nothing concerning Monroe. Sylvia's only comments were she hoped Belinda would enjoy herself and that she deserved an evening out now and then, giving her a break from having to help cook a meal. Belinda, however, couldn't miss her son's look of displeasure when he had said, "I can't believe you'd agree to go for supper with either of them, Mom."

Belinda had defended her right to spend time with anyone she chose and told Henry it was not his concern. All he needed to worry about was staying out of trouble and setting a good example for his impressionable niece and nephew.

She smiled when Rachel climbed up on the couch with a picture book and sat close to Henry, leaning her head against his side. Not to be outdone, Allen pranced across the room and took a seat on the other side of Henry.

Someday my youngest son will get married and have children of his own, Belinda thought. *So it's nice to see how well he gets along with Sylvia's kinner, and Ezekiel's too on the occasions we get to see my eldest son and his family. I could be happy and feel blessed if our entire family lived close by so I could see them more often.*

Belinda moved to the front windows and looked out. *No sign of Herschel's rig yet. Maybe he left his bulk-food store later than he'd planned.*

Herschel gripped the reins a little tighter as he urged his horse to move faster. He'd left the store later than he wanted and then taken a few extra minutes at home cleaning up and making sure he looked respectable. He had not taken a woman out to supper since Mattie died and rarely went out to eat alone. He had, on a few occasions, eaten at a restaurant with his mom and dad, but most of the time his meals were eaten at home or his folk's house.

What if I can't think of anything sensible to talk about? He lamented.

Maybe if I keep my mouth full of food, I won't have to say much of anything while we're at the restaurant.

Herschel's lips pressed together in a slight grimace. *But I won't be eating any food on the ride to and from Dienner's Country Restaurant. I sure can't travel all the way to Ronks and back without talking to Belinda. She'd probably wonder why I even bothered to ask her out.*

Herschel let go of the reins with one hand and thumped the side of his head just below his straw hat. *Why am I thinking like this, anyhow? Last week at Jared and Amy's I conversed with Belinda without too much problem. And even when I went into the greenhouse the following day, things were okay. I just need to relax and enjoy my time spent this evening in the company of a very pleasant woman. I'm sure if I stop fretting about it, the words will come.*

"Supper's ready, Henry!" Sylvia called from the kitchen. "Would you make sure the kinners' hands have been washed before you bring them in to eat?"

"Already done. We've just come from the bathroom." Henry led the children down the hall and into the kitchen. He lifted Rachel into her high chair and made sure Allen sat securely on his stool, before taking his own seat.

Sylvia seated herself in her normal chair, and when she instructed the children, they all bowed for silent prayer.

Henry often wondered why he bothered to say any prayers. It seemed that God hadn't answered many of them, which was discouraging. He'd heard their bishop and the ministers from their church district say that God hears everyone's prayers and answers according to His will.

Henry curled his fingers into the palms of his hands. *Am I supposed to believe it was God's will for Dad, Abe, and Toby to be killed? Is God okay with someone vandalizing our place and makin' us worry?* Henry struggled to understand why God would allow any of those things. It didn't seem fair.

Henry figured Sylvia should be done praying by now so he opened his eyes. He found her staring at him with a strange expression.

"What's the matter?" he asked.

"Nothing. I've just never seen you pray at the supper table so long before."

Henry shrugged. No way would he admit to his sister that he hadn't been praying—just trying to figure out why God didn't always answer like he wanted Him to. For that matter, Henry wondered why the Lord allowed so much suffering to go on in the world.

Sylvia spooned some macaroni and cheese onto her children's plates, while Henry helped himself to one of the plump Polish sausage links she'd baked in the oven. There was also a fruit salad to accompany the meal.

Henry looked over at the chair where Mom normally sat and grimaced. It didn't seem right for her place to be empty, much less that she would be out on a supper date.

"What's wrong, Brother?" Sylvia questioned. "Isn't the sausage cooked to your liking?"

"It ain't that." Henry shook his head. "I was just thinkin' that our mamm oughta be here."

"She's entitled to an evening out, don't you think?"

"I suppose, but not with Herschel."

"Why would you say that? Herschel is a nice man, and I'm sure he's quite lonely."

"I don't see why he should be. His folks don't live too far from him, and his English daughter, along with her husband and baby, are in Lancaster, so could visit any of them whenever he wanted." Henry's neck and shoulders tensed up. "I don't understand why he'd need to spend time with our mudder. He's quite a bit older than her, you know. They don't have much in common either, and there's probably very little for them to talk about."

Sylvia's voice lowered as she spoke. "Did you ever stop to think that Mom might be happier if she got married again? It's not fair to expect her to live alone for the rest of her life."

With forced restraint, Henry spoke through his teeth. "You know what? I didn't expect you to understand. All you ever think about is your upcoming wedding and how happy you're gonna be being married to Dennis."

Sylvia glanced at the children, then back at Henry, and put her finger against her lips. "Let's not talk about this anymore."

"Okay, sure. . .whatever you say." Henry looked down at his plate. He had enough on his mind trying to figure out who'd been threatening them without having to worry about their mother falling for one of the men in their community and getting married.

Amy and Jared stood at the kitchen sink doing their supper dishes. Jared had volunteered to wash, stating that Amy could dry and put them away, since she knew exactly where she wanted everything to go.

"I'm pleased that my mamm agreed to go out to supper with Herschel this evening." Amy looked over at Jared and smiled. "It must mean there's an attraction on both of their parts. Otherwise Herschel wouldn't have asked Mom out." She paused for a quick breath. "And if my mamm hadn't wanted to go, she would have politely said no."

"I'm sure you're right, but please don't meddle. You've already plotted to get them together on two occasions, so it's time now to sit back and see what happens. If it's meant for your mother and Herschel to be together, it will happen, all in good time."

"You're right," Amy agreed. "All in God's good time." *But that doesn't mean I can't be on the sidelines to encourage things along. With Herschel being kind of shy, and Mom not sure she wants to get married again, one or both of them might need a little nudge now and then to keep things moving in the right direction.*

Amy finished drying another dish and placed it in the cupboard. *One thing's for sure—Herschel would make a better husband than Monroe ever would. I doubt there's a woman in our community who'd want to be married to a man like him.*

Ronks

Belinda sat across from Herschel at a table inside Dienner's, enjoying every bite of food on her plate. She tried not to stare at how nice his periwinkle-blue shirt brought out the color in his eyes.

"The buffet here certainly has plenty to offer, doesn't it?" Herschel asked.

"I was just going to say the same thing."

He offered her a cute, almost boyish smile. As attractive as he was at the age of fifty-eight, she could only imagine what a handsome fellow he must have been in his twenties.

Belinda hadn't known Herschel back then. Besides their age difference, they'd both attended different schools as well as different church districts. Although she'd learned a few years ago that Herschel had fathered a child out of wedlock, Belinda had never cast judgment on him. From what her friend, Mary Ruth Lapp had told her, Herschel and Mary Ruth's daughter, Rhoda, used to go with each other when they were teenagers. Rhoda had run away from home when she realized she was pregnant, and didn't tell Herschel about the baby because she believed he was going to break up with her because he had another girlfriend. So the Lapps' daughter had taken off one day, leaving a brief note for her parents stating that she was leaving, but without a truthful explanation. From that day on, Mary Ruth and her husband, Willis, never heard from their wayward daughter again. It wasn't until Rhoda passed away that her daughter, Sara, read a note in her mother's Bible, telling of her grandparents from Strasburg and providing their address. Sara had been stunned when she arrived at her grandparents' home and found out that Michelle had impersonated her and wormed her way into the Lapps' lives. What a transformation in Michelle's life since then. It was hard to believe she'd once been a deceitful English girl, who later committed her life to the Lord, joined the Amish church, and married Belinda's son Ezekiel. It just went to show that no matter what sins had occurred in people's pasts, if they accepted Jesus as their Savior and turned from their sinful ways, they could become a new person in Christ.

Belinda watched Herschel eat the drumstick on his plate and thought about how he'd discovered that Sara was his daughter because of a note in an old jar found hidden at Mary Ruth's. It was a surprise to everyone to learn of this—Herschel most of all.

Our Lord works in mysterious ways, she thought. *And now, here I sit, having supper and enjoying myself with Sara's biological father.*

Belinda's musings were halted when Herschel pointed to her plate.

"I'm guessing by what I see still there that you must be full and won't have room for dessert."

Belinda snapped to attention and picked up her fork. "I am getting full, but not so much that I can't finish the food I took from the buffet." No way would she ever admit that she'd stopped eating because her mind had wandered toward the past, and that most of her thinking had involved information about him and the child he'd fathered. If Herschel ever decided to talk about that time in his life, it would be his decision, not come about because she'd brought it up or asked for explanations. The truth was, Belinda had done a few things during her running-around years as a young woman that she wasn't proud of. But she'd sought forgiveness, and God had set her feet on a solid path in the direction of wanting to say and do things that pleased Him.

"If you're willing, I'd like to do this again sometime," Herschel stated. "And next time we can go to the restaurant of your choice."

"That sounds nice, but I was thinking maybe you'd like to come to my house for a home-cooked meal. There won't be nearly as much food as we've had here this evening, but if you'll tell me what you'd like, I'd be happy to fix it for you." Belinda could hardly believe her boldness in inviting him to supper.

Herschel rested both elbows on the table and leaned forward. "That suits me just fine, Belinda. Just name the day and time, and I'll be there." He paused and gave his beard a tug. "As far as what to fix, it doesn't really matter, because when it comes to food I'm pretty easy to please."

Belinda smiled. "How about a week from tonight? I'll invite Amy and Jared to join us too. Would that be all right with you?"

"Of course. It'll give me the opportunity of getting to know your whole family better."

"All but Ezekiel, his wife, and their two kinner," Belinda interjected. "It's not likely that they could come down from New York on such short notice. Maybe some other time it'll work out for them to join us."

"I'll look forward to that." Herschel pushed back his chair. "Now, if you don't mind, I'm goin' up to the dessert buffet and choose something sweet. Want me to get you a piece of cake or some pie?"

Belinda looked down at her plate. "Think I'd better finish what I have here and skip dessert this evening. You go ahead though. I'll enjoy watching you eat whatever you choose."

"Okay then, I'll be back soon."

As Belinda watched him walk away, her thoughts went to Monroe. *I seriously doubt that I'll have as good a time with Monroe tomorrow night as I'm having with Herschel this evening. But I said I would go out to supper with him, and I won't go back on my word.*

Chapter 20

"I went out to the phone shed and checked for phone messages," Henry said when he entered the kitchen Saturday morning.

Belinda turned from the stove. "Danki for doing that, Son. Were there any?"

"Only one. It was from that man who owns the landscaping business. He said he'd be by sometime today to see what we have in stock and to place an order."

She smiled. "That's good news. I'd hoped we would hear something from him soon."

"How long till breakfast?" Henry asked. "Just wondered if I have time to feed the chickens."

Belinda's brows lowered. "You haven't done that yet?"

"Huh-uh. Wanted to check for phone messages first."

"I see. Well, I've just started the bacon and still have eggs to fry, so if you hurry, I should have breakfast on the table by the time you get done tending the chickens."

"Okay, I'll snap to it." Henry hurried out the back door.

Belinda had a hunch that Henry went to the phone shed first in case there had been another muffled threatening message. She was well aware that he hoped to discover who was behind all the vandalism but doubted he'd have much success. Up to this point the person responsible had been clever enough not to leave any clues. Of course, there was the cigarette pack they'd found outside the barn after it caught fire, but that could have been accidentally dropped there by someone who'd attended Amy and Jared's wedding.

"Both of my kinner are up and dressed now, so can I help with breakfast?" Sylvia asked when she entered the kitchen.

"Let me see now. . . Would you mind setting the table?"

"Of course not." Sylvia moved closer to the stove and pointed to the bacon Belinda had been cooking. "That looks about done. Would you like me to take over at the stove and fry the eggs after I've set the table? You seem a little preoccupied this morning."

"I am a little," Belinda admitted. "Guess I have too much on my mind."

"Are you reflecting on your date with Herschel last night, or thinking about going out with Monroe this evening?"

Belinda's face filled with warmth. "I was actually thinking about your bruder when you came in."

"Which brother—Henry or Ezekiel?"

"Henry, but I won't go into that right now." Belinda removed the bacon strips from the frying pan and placed them on paper towels to absorb some of the grease. "If you don't mind frying the *oier*, I'll set the table."

"Okay. I'll scramble the children's eggs though. They like them best that way."

While Sylvia took over at the stove, Belinda got out the dishes and silverware.

"Did you enjoy yourself with Herschel last night?" Sylvia asked, glancing over her shoulder.

"Jah, we had a pleasant evening."

"I'm glad. You deserved some time away from your responsibilities here."

"I've never minded cooking. In fact, I invited Herschel to join us for supper next Friday evening, and he said yes."

"Oh did he now?" Sylvia looked at Belinda again, only this time with a smirk.

"Please don't read anything into it. Herschel and I are just friends."

"How about Monroe? Do you consider him a friend too?"

"Well yes, I do—although not in the way Monroe would like me to."

Sylvia cracked three eggs into a bowl and stirred them with a fork. "Do you suppose that Herschel would like you to be more than a friend?"

Belinda blinked. "I doubt it very much. I'm sure he's just lonely and in need of companionship."

Sylvia kept stirring the eggs.

Belinda finished setting the table and was about to take some apple juice from the refrigerator when Henry came in with a basket of eggs.

"If you need any oier for our breakfast, here's some fresh." He set the basket on the counter.

"We already have eggs out for this morning, so the ones you got can be washed and put in the refrigerator." Belinda placed the pitcher of juice on the table. "Sylvia will have the eggs fried soon, so why don't you go wash up and bring Rachel and Allen in from the living room?"

"Will do."

When Henry left the kitchen, Belinda heard his boots clomping down the hall. "Well, wouldn't you know? He forgot to remove his *schtiffel* and should have left them in the utility room. Guess he's got other things on his mind this morning."

Sylvia laughed. "What else is new?"

That evening, when Belinda heard a *clippity-clop* sound, followed by a horse's whinny, she went to the front window and peered out. As expected, her escort to supper had arrived with his well-groomed prancing horse and an equally nice buggy.

Belinda couldn't help smiling. Even back when they were young people, Monroe had taken pride in his horse and carriage. When he had brought her home from some of their youth singings, the inside of his rig had always been spotless.

"Guess some things never change," she murmured.

"What was that, Mom?" Sylvia asked from her chair across the room where she sat with Rachel in her lap. Sylvia and the children, along with Henry, had eaten an early supper this evening. This gave Sylvia an opportunity to enjoy doing something with Allen and Rachel before it was time to put them to bed.

"I was just thinking out loud," Belinda responded to her daughter's question. "But now I need to quit musing, because Monroe is outside."

"I figured as much, with the horse noises going on out there." Sylvia pointed to the clock on the mantel. "And he's right on time."

"Jah, Monroe's always been the punctual type. There's no need for him to come up to the house, so I'll just grab my shawl and outer bonnet, then head outside." Belinda came over and kissed Rachel's soft cheek. "Be good for your mamma now." She looked at Allen, sitting on the floor with his wooden horse and a small cardboard box he'd been using as a barn for the horse. "You be good too, little man."

Belinda had spoken in Pennsylvania Dutch so the children would understand what she said. They both grinned and bobbed their heads.

"Have a pleasant evening, Sylvia."

"I will, Mom. I hope you have a nice one too."

Belinda put on her outer wrappings and was almost to the door when she paused and turned back around. "Henry went out to the barn after you four finished eating supper. When he comes back in, would you tell him I said goodbye?"

"Jah, Mom, I'll do that." Sylvia pointed at the door. "Now don't keep your date waiting."

Belinda rolled her eyes. "Monroe's not really my date. We're just two old friends going out for supper."

"Okay, Mom. Whatever you say."

Belinda stepped outside and hurried out to Monroe's buggy.

He'd just gotten out and said he wanted to assist her, but Belinda insisted that she could get in by herself. "After all, I've been doing it for a good many years." She gave a small laugh.

"I suppose you have." Monroe climbed in and backed his horse up. Soon they were heading down the driveway. Before turning onto the main road, he looked over at her and smiled. "You look very nice this evening, Belinda. Seeing you sitting here in my buggy makes me think back to when you were a young woman and we were heading out on our first date."

Belinda's face burned with the heat of embarrassment. *He would have to bring up the past.*

Henry sat cross-legged in front of the open double doors of the hayloft overlooking their front yard. He'd seen Monroe pull up with his well-maintained rig and needed something to take his mind off the dislike he felt for this man.

Henry looked away and pondered where someone or, more to the point, the vandal could watch his family from. Henry's desire to figure out who the culprit was grew more intense each day, even though he didn't always talk about it with anyone. There seemed to be many spots where a person could observe his mother's home as well as the greenhouse.

Tapping his chin with his finger, he thought about a few of his suspects. *If it were say Seth or one of his buddies, it wouldn't be hard for one of 'em to hide behind a tree on our property. If it's old Maude, she's always walking by out front of our place, but of course she's too old to be climbing any of our big trees.*

Henry snickered a little over the idea, and then tensed up as he looked back at Monroe. *I'm leaning toward him, 'cause I believe he's hiding something. Just wish I could prove my theory. It don't help that Mom's in his corner. Apparently she thinks highly of him, because now she's lettin' Monroe into our lives again.*

He watched in disgust as his mother got into Monroe's buggy and struggled with the urge to shout down at her, "Please stay home!"

But what good would that do? he asked himself. *Mom promised she would go out to supper with Monroe, and she's always tried to keep her promises.*

It was wrong of Henry to think this way, but he couldn't help it. *Maybe Mom will have a bad experience with him while they're out to supper, and then she won't go on any more outings with Monroe. I wonder how he'd react to that. Would the persistent fellow finally give up, or would he keep comin' around, trying to worm his way into Mom's life?*

Henry's heart felt heavy as he watched Monroe's buggy lurch out onto the pavement with Mom in the seat beside him. *It's hard to see her being courted by anyone—especially Mr. Esh.*

Henry stood up and closed the doors. It would be dark soon, so there was no point in staying up here any longer. The problem was, he didn't feel like going back in the house.

"I sure miss Abe," Henry muttered as he made his way down the ladder. "If my brother was still alive, I bet he'd help me figure out who's behind the vandalism, threatening phone messages, and notes." Abe had been smart, and Henry had looked up to him ever since he was a boy. Henry had no doubt about his older brother's ability to search for important clues.

Once again, Henry ran over the list of suspects he'd come up with. *The red-haired woman across the road; Maude the chicken stealer; my friend Seth or one of his friends; the owner of the other greenhouse; and last, but certainly not least, Monroe Esh.* For the time being, at least, Mom's old boyfriend was at the top of Henry's list. The irritating man might pretend to be nice, but Henry felt sure that Monroe was only after the greenhouse.

Before leaving the barn, Henry stopped to pet Mom's horse. "I believe the fellow my mamm's out with tonight wants one of two things. Monroe would be happy if Mom agreed to marry him. That would make it easy for him to take over her business." He scratched the mare behind her ears and gave her neck a few pats. "And in case being nice to Mom doesn't work out the way he planned, then he will rely on the pranks he's been doing, hoping we'll all get so scared that we'll pack up and move." He shook his head. "Well, that's never gonna happen."

Bird-in-Hand

"How'd your day go, Belinda?" Monroe asked after they were seated in a booth at the Bird-in-Hand Family Restaurant.

"It went quite well," she responded, fidgeting with her silverware.

Monroe wished he could reach over and take her hand, but that would be too bold—especially here in a public place. "Lots of customers then?"

"Yes, we did have a fairly good turnout, but the best part of the day was when one of the local landscapers came in and placed a large order of bedding plants for several of his customers. He also bought a selection of our smaller fruit trees." A pleasant smile spread across Belinda's face. It was good to see her relax in his presence. On the trip here, she'd seemed preoccupied and hadn't contributed much to his conversation.

There has to be something I can say or do to win her over. Monroe pretended to study his menu, which was a waste of time, since he planned to choose his food items from the buffet. *If we were married, there isn't anything I wouldn't do for Belinda. I'd take her anywhere she wanted to go and buy her whatever she asked for.*

"How was your day?" Belinda asked, pushing Monroe's thoughts aside.

He looked away from the menu and put his focus on her. "It went well in the store during the morning hours when I was there. I didn't go in this afternoon, though, because I had some important things to do in town."

Their waitress came to take their orders, and Monroe told her he'd be going to the buffet. "How about you, Belinda?"

"I'll do the same."

After the waitress took their beverage orders, Monroe looked at Belinda and posed another question. "How'd your Friday evening plans go?"

Belinda tipped her head as she gave several rapid blinks. "My plans?"

"Jah. When I asked you to go out to supper with me, I mentioned doing it on Friday, remember?"

She nodded.

"Then when you said you had plans to have supper with Herschel that night, I suggested Saturday."

A rosy blush erupted on Belinda's cheeks. "Oh, umm. . .yes. . .my plans went okay."

Monroe balled his fingers into the palms of his hands beneath the table. *She's not going to tell me how her date went yesterday with Herschel. I'm thinking maybe it didn't go so well and she'll have a better time with me.*

"Shall we pray before we go to the buffet or would you prefer we wait until we come back to the table?" Belinda's question halted Monroe's contemplations.

"We can do it when we return to the table."

Belinda slid over and got up from the bench, and Monroe did the same. He decided not to say anything more about Friday night, because he didn't want her to know how jealous he felt.

Monroe smoothed the front of his black vest. *I will, however, whenever the opportunity affords itself, let it be known to my competitor that I'm the better man for Belinda. Herschel just needs to step aside.*

Chapter 21

Strasburg

The following Friday, Belinda woke up to the sound of a rooster crowing as daylight approached. Tonight Herschel would be coming over for supper, and she hoped things would go well. Jared and Amy planned to come over as well. Of course, since Amy would be watching Allen and Rachel while Sylvia helped in the greenhouse today, she'd already be at the house, so Jared would join her once he finished working for the day.

Belinda looked forward to having most of her family for a meal. Her only concern was whether she'd done the right thing by being so bold and inviting Herschel. He might take it wrong and think she was interested in him, which was ridiculous. Or was it? She had enjoyed his company last week—more so than she was willing to admit.

Belinda climbed out of bed and ambled over to the window to lift the shade. The sun peeked through the clouds, signaling a new day was about to begin.

Belinda remained at the window for a few minutes, reflecting on her supper date with Monroe. The evening had gone better than expected, and she had no complaints. The only thing that concerned her about seeing Monroe socially was the fact that he'd made it clear he had a personal interest in her. By agreeing to go out with him, he may have seen it as an encouragement on her part.

She touched her warm cheeks. *Oh dear, what have I done? There's no way I can go back and undo it, so I may as well put the matter aside and go forward from here.* The only problem was that part of going forward involved cooking and sharing another meal with Herschel. *After tonight, though, I won't take things any further by going anywhere socially with either of the men.* She bobbed her head. *That definitely seems like the smartest thing to do.*

Around noon, before Belinda went up to the house to get lunch, she made a trek down the driveway to the mailbox. She'd no more than retrieved a pile of envelopes from the box when she saw her neighbor preparing to cross the street.

Belinda waved, before thumbing through her mail, and was reminded that she still hadn't invited Virginia and Earl to their home for a meal. It wasn't like Belinda to make a promise and not follow through, and she felt guilty about it.

I need to extend an invitation to them now. Belinda waited for Virginia to cross the road, and then she approached her. "Good morning, Virginia. How are you and your husband doing?"

"We're gettin' along okay." Her dangling butterfly earrings twinkled in the sunlight while she pulled each envelope from her mailbox.

"Are you enjoying the beautiful spring weather we've been blessed with this week?"

"It's all right. Better than harsh winds, rain, or cold snow of winter. Makes me shiver just to think about it."

"I agree. I've always preferred warmer weather." Belinda took a few steps closer. "I was wondering if you and your husband might be free to come to our house for supper one evening next week."

Virginia looked at her with an incredulous stare. "Seriously?"

"Yes. I've wanted us to get together ever since you moved here, but our life gets so busy, and I've kept putting it off. Is there an evening that might work for you?"

Virginia dropped her gaze to the mail in her hands. "I. . .uh. . . would need to talk to my husband about it, so I can't give you an answer right now."

"That's perfectly understandable. Once you've had a chance to discuss it with him, would you please let me know?"

"Yeah, sure, I'll be in touch." Virginia looked both ways and made her way back across the street.

Belinda shut and locked her mailbox door and headed up the driveway. Now that she'd finally extended an invitation to supper, she hoped her neighbors would be able to come.

"Well, if that don't beat all," Virginia muttered. "Sure never expected to get an invite to the Kings' for a meal. I wonder what brought that on anyway. If they didn't care enough about me and Earl to invite us to their daughter's wedding last fall, why would Belinda want us to eat a meal with them now?"

Virginia looked down at Goldie, curled up on the throw rug in front of the sink. The cat had followed Virginia to the kitchen after she'd come back with the mail.

Virginia put the stack of envelopes and advertising flyers on the counter and took a seat at the table to drink a cup of coffee.

Maybe I should give Earl a call and see what he thinks about the supper invitation. He will probably think it's pretty strange to be getting an invite now, after living across the street from that Amish family all these months. She blew on her coffee and took a cautious drink. *I bet Belinda only asked out of obligation, or maybe it was a spur of the moment decision.*

Virginia picked up her cell phone and punched in Earl's number. It rang several times before he answered.

"Hey, Earl, it's me. Guess what happened when I went out to get the mail a short time ago?"

"I have no idea, but unless it's something critical, I don't have time to talk. A customer walked in a few minutes ago and I need to speak to him before I lose a potential sale."

Virginia took another drink from her cup; this time without blowing and she burned her tongue. "Ouch!"

"What's wrong, Virginia?"

She grimaced. "Burned my tongue on some hot coffee."

"You shoulda blown on it first."

"I did when I took my first sip, but then I—"

"Gotta go, Virginia. We can talk later, when I get home from work." Earl hung up without saying goodbye.

Virginia pressed her lips together and frowned. "I don't want to wait till you get home, Earl. I wanted to talk now!"

"Now that you're here, and there's food on the table, can I tell you what I called about earlier?" Virginia tapped her husband's shoulder.

"Go right ahead." Earl reached for the bowl of spaghetti and plopped a good-sized mound on his plate. Following that, he sprinkled a hefty amount of Parmesan cheese over the top.

"I saw Belinda King this afternoon, when we were getting our mail."

His eyebrows squished together. "Was that worth bothering me when I was at work?"

"You don't understand. There's more."

Earl grabbed two slices of sourdough bread and slathered them with butter. "Go ahead."

Virginia told him about the supper invitation for one night next week. "Now isn't that something, Earl? I mean, we've been living here all this time, and never once have they invited us for a meal. They didn't even have the decency to include us in one of the suppers following Amy and Jared's wedding."

"Not that again. You shouldn't hold it against them, because you may have misunderstood when Jared said we'd get an invitation."

"I did not!" Virginia's posture stiffened as she scrunched her napkin into a tight ball. "But all that aside, I just don't get why Belinda would want us to come for supper now. Does she really believe we would be willing to go over there and be all neighborly with them?"

"I think it's a great idea. I hope you told her we'd come." Earl dipped a piece of bread in the spaghetti sauce and took a bite.

"You can't be serious." She frowned at him. "After the way those people have treated us, and you think we should go over there and play nicey-nice?"

"Yep."

"What for? You know I'm not comfortable around those Plain folks—we have nothing in common at all." Her lower lip protruded. "I wish Stella could come visit me again."

"Now, where did that comment come from?"

"Don't you remember, Earl, how interested she was in those Amish people? Stella was excited about the prospect of going with us to the wedding across the street. I bet she'd be just as thrilled to come with us on an invite into their home for dinner."

"I don't see how that's gonna happen. Stella can't come racing out here on a moment's notice."

"You never know. Maybe she could. I'll call and let her know of our plans. I will just say to Stella, 'It's too bad you can't be here when we hang out with the Amish and enjoy their home-cooked dinner.'"

"You should drop the silly notion of including your friend, because she was not invited." Earl spun a good-sized amount of spaghetti onto his fork and shoved it into his mouth.

"Like I said before, I have nothing in common with them. Besides, they make me feel uncomfortable."

"It would be rude not to accept their invitation," Earl mumbled around his mouthful of spaghetti.

She shook her finger in his direction. "Didn't your mother teach you that it's not polite to talk with your mouth full?"

"She tried, but I'm not a kid anymore, so I'll do as I please." Earl swiped his napkin across his lips, then picked up his glass of water and took a drink. "So what'd you tell the neighbor lady?"

"I said I'd need to speak with you."

"And now that you have, you can graciously let her know that we'd like to come, and find out what day and time." He bit off a piece of his bread. "Also, you might ask if there's anything we can bring."

Virginia's shoulders curled forward. Her chest felt like it was ready to cave in. The last thing she wanted to do was share a meal in that Amish home. Virginia wished her friend could be there, but Earl had poured cold water all over the topic, so she'd let the matter go. There was no telling what kind of weird thing they might be expected to eat at the Kings' house though. *And, oh my. . . What in the world will there be to talk about?*

With her appetite all but gone, Virginia rubbed her forehead and thought once more, *I wish we had never moved here.*

Monroe had left his store early, planning to stop by Belinda's place to ask her a question. If he could catch her before she started supper, she might agree to go out for another meal with him. He felt that the more time he spent with Belinda, the better his chance would be of winning her over.

I deserve a second chance with her, he told himself as he guided his horse and buggy up the Kings' driveway. *I'll buy her gifts, butter up to her family, and do whatever it takes till she finally agrees to become my fraa.*

When Monroe stepped onto the porch, a delicious aroma wafted out the partially open kitchen window. He couldn't be certain, but it smelled like baked cabbage rolls, one of his favorite meals. Belinda or her daughter must have started fixing supper.

His lips pressed tightly into a grimace. *I should have gotten here sooner.* Then another thought popped into Monroe's head. *If I knock on the door, and Belinda invites me in, I'll mention how good the food she has cooking smells.* Monroe smiled. *Then maybe Belinda will be kind enough to invite me to join her family for the meal.*

With that decided, Monroe rapped on the door. When no one answered, he knocked again, a little louder this time.

Soon the door swung open and Sylvia greeted him. "Hello, Monroe. What can I do for you this evening?"

"Uh nothing, I came to say hello to your mamm."

"She's in the kitchen."

"Okay, guess I can talk to her there."

Sylvia led the way, and after Monroe entered the kitchen, he spotted Belinda in front of the sink, peeling potatoes.

"You have a visitor, Mom," Sylvia announced.

Belinda turned, and when she looked at him, her head jerked back slightly. "Oh, it's you, Monroe. I thought. . ." Her voice trailed off.

He took a few steps toward her and gave a wide smile. "I came by to see if you'd be free to go out for supper with me." Monroe gestured to the potatoes. "But I can see that you've already started fixing your meal. Truth is I could smell the delicious aroma from outside."

Her slightly pink cheeks turned a deep red. "We have company coming for supper soon, so Sylvia and I have been busy trying to get everything ready before their arrival."

He dipped his head slightly. "Oh, I see." Since it sounded like more than one person would be coming, they probably wouldn't want to include one more, so Monroe decided not to try and wangle an invitation to join them. It would seem too pushy and might not set well with Belinda. He needed to stay on her good side, no matter what.

"I'd best be on my way now, but would there be an evening next week when we could go out to a restaurant again?" he asked.

Belinda glanced at her daughter, and then looked back at Monroe. "Next week is pretty full for me. I'm sorry, Monroe."

"Oh, I see." His gaze flicked upward as he tried to hide the disappointment he felt. Was she looking for an excuse not to go out with him? He turned toward the door. "I'll check back with you in a few weeks. Have a nice evening, ladies."

Monroe barely heard their response as he rushed out the door with his ears ringing. "One step forward and two back," he mumbled. "Something needs to change, because this isn't working out the way I want."

When Monroe headed down the driveway in his rig, another horse and buggy pulled in. He was stunned to see that the driver was none other than Herschel Fisher.

Monroe clenched his teeth. *So Herschel gets an invitation to supper, but I'm left out? What's up with that anyway?*

He snapped the reins and got his horse moving at a good clip. *For ten cents, I'd turn right around and have a talk with that man.*

Chapter 22

As Herschel began his approach to Belinda's house, he felt less nervous than when he'd taken her out to eat. It was either because he'd become more comfortable in her presence or the fact that this evening they wouldn't be in a public place where someone they knew might see them and start a round of gossip. As it was, when Herschel told his folks of his plans, he'd asked them not to mention it to anyone. News traveled fast in Lancaster County, and Herschel didn't want to put Belinda or himself in a position to answer a bunch of curious questions. If and when a stronger relationship developed, he wouldn't care if word got out that an old widower, pretty much set in his ways, and a lovely middle-aged widow lady had begun courting.

Herschel snorted. Since Mattie died, in his wildest dreams, he'd never considered the idea of courting anyone else. But after getting to know Belinda better, a spark had ignited, and the thought of seeing her more often was quite appealing. He hoped she felt the same way about being with him.

After setting the brake, Herschel stepped down from his buggy and tied the horse to the hitching rail. *I wonder what topics of conversation will be discussed this evening or what Belinda has fixed for supper.* He hoped the evening would turn out well and that he wouldn't mess up and say something wrong.

He patted his horse and looked up toward the house with its pretty baskets of hanging flowers. *Come on, Herschel, don't overthink things. All you need to concern yourself about is trying to relax and having a nice time.*

As Herschel moved swiftly across the lawn, Henry rounded the corner with his dog at his side. One look at Herschel and the animal rushed toward him, barking and wagging his tail.

Henry clapped his hands and hollered, "Blackie, you come back here, right now!"

Herschel chuckled when the dog stopped in front of him and pawed at his pant leg. No sign of viciousness here. Blackie clearly demanded some attention.

Herschel bent down and patted the dog's head. "Hey, Blackie. Nice to meet you." He looked up at Henry and smiled, despite the young man's scowl. "Your hund's a nice-looking Lab. Have you taught him to do any tricks?"

"A few." Henry barely made eye contact with Herschel.

"Wanna show me?"

Henry shrugged. "Don't know if he would be willing. Looks like he'd rather be petted right now, but I guess I could try."

Herschel straightened to his full height.

"Okay, Blackie, now do what I say." Henry called the dog and told him to sit. Blackie hesitated at first, but then did as the boy had asked.

"Du bescht en schmaerder buh." Herschel pointed at the dog.

"He's only a smart fellow when he feels like it, or if he thinks I have a treat waiting for him."

Blackie nuzzled Henry's hand. "See what I mean?"

Herschel nodded. "Yep. He's one *schmaert* hund."

"Yeah, but my mutt took off yesterday morning, and I ended up chasing him clear up to old Maude's shanty." Henry frowned. "Had to practically drag him home."

"Who's old Maude?" Herschel asked.

"She's a weird lady who lives in a shack up the road most of the year. Maude vacates the place during the cold winter months, but we don't know where she goes." Henry reached under the brim of his hat and rubbed his forehead. "She's taken some things from our yard and even the greenhouse before. I don't trust her at all."

"Has your mamm called the authorities?"

Henry shook his head. "Naw, she thinks Maude is harmless and has even given her food, not to mention two hinkel."

"Were the pieces of chicken fried or baked?"

"Neither. They were alive when Maude snatched them out of our coop. When we discovered that the old woman had the laying hens, Mom said she could keep them." Henry shrugged. "Maude probably thinks the chickens will lay enough eggs to provide for her breakfasts, but I'm sure she'll be back here again sometime, looking for something else to steal."

Herschel wasn't sure how to respond. If Belinda had no problem with the old woman taking without asking, there wasn't much he could say about it. She might not appreciate him butting in.

"Something smells mighty good coming from the house." Herschel pointed to the partially open kitchen window from where the aroma wafted toward them.

"Yeah. Mom made cabbage rolls for supper, and I guess we'd better get inside, 'cause I think it must be about ready. First though, I need to put Blackie in his pen. Otherwise, he's likely to wander off again." Henry called his dog and the animal went obediently with him.

Herschel watched as they approached the dog's pen. *Should I go knock on the door or wait for Henry?* He decided on the latter and took a seat in one of the wicker chairs on the front porch.

The cloudless spring evening gave way to the dimming blue sky. It seemed so serene and quiet outside. Herschel looked toward the tilled garden with its deep brown soil and rows of rich green plants. He then surveyed the layout of the property. Everything seemed well thought out.

Herschel pulled a mint candy from his pocket and pulled off the wrapper. *It can't be easy for Belinda and her family to stay up with all this work, plus keep the greenhouse running.*

When Henry returned a few minutes later, he paused by the chair and looked down at Herschel with a quizzical expression. "How come you're sittin' out here? Figured you would have gone inside."

"I could have, but I thought it was best to wait for you. Plus I was admiring how nice your family keeps this place up."

"Oh, I see." Henry grabbed hold of the doorknob. "Let's go in then. I'm *hungerich.*"

As he followed the boy, Herschel heard one of the children asking in Pennsylvania Dutch if they could have milk with their supper. *That does sound good. When I was a boy, I used to drink milk with my suppers.*

Herschel had to admit, with that great smell coming from the kitchen, he too was hungry. And he was glad Belinda's son had warmed up to him just a bit.

Belinda greeted Herschel when he and Henry entered the house and suggested they both take a seat in the living room. "Just make yourself comfortable, Herschel," she said. "We'll eat as soon as Dennis and Jared arrive."

"Sure."

Belinda waited until Henry and Herschel headed for the living room before she returned to the kitchen to help her daughters with the final supper preparations.

She pulled the large baking pan from the hot oven. *This is the first time I'm having Herschel over to my house. I hope he's comfortable and will enjoy the meal we've prepared.* Belinda opened the lid to check the contents which looked nicely done, and then she placed the container on top on the stove.

It wasn't long before Jared showed up, and a few minutes later Dennis arrived. While Sylvia rounded up her children, Amy went out to the living room to let the men know they could wash up and join them in the dining room.

Everyone had barely taken their seats around the table and were about to bow their heads for prayer when a knock sounded on the front door.

"Would you like me to see who it is?" Jared directed his question to Belinda.

"Yes, please. We'll wait to pray until you come back."

"Okay."

When Jared reappeared a few minutes later with Monroe at his side, Belinda's eyes widened. Since he'd been here a short time ago, she couldn't figure out why he'd come back.

"Sorry to interrupt your meal, folks, but after I left here earlier, I got to thinking that I must have dropped my *backebuch* in your yard somewhere because it was no longer in my pocket." He shifted his weight from one foot to the other. "So I came on back to look for it, and lo and behold, I discovered the billfold not far from the hitching rail."

Belinda's mind felt a bit fuzzy. *If Monroe came back to look for his wallet and he found it, why'd he feel it was necessary to come up to the house and tell us about it?*

As though he could read her thoughts, Monroe looked right at Belinda and said: "I figured I should come on up to the house to let you know in case someone saw me outside and wondered what I was up to."

"Although it wasn't necessary, danki for letting me know." Belinda tapped her foot under the table. The food was getting cold, and they still hadn't prayed, but she couldn't come right out and ask him to leave.

Monroe sniffed deeply and made a sweeping gesture of the table. "Looks like you're all in for a real treat 'cause those cabbage rolls, and everything else, sure look and smell good."

Belinda's tapping foot went suddenly still. With Monroe standing there with a hungry expression, she could hardly do anything but invite him to join them.

"Umm. . .would you like to join us?" The words almost stuck in her throat.

"Jah, that would be nice, but I don't want to intrude."

"It's fine, really." Without bothering to suggest that he might want to wash up first, Belinda pointed to an empty chair. She just wanted to get on with their meal. "Please, take a seat, Monroe."

A big grin spread across his face as he lowered himself into the chair. Then all heads bowed for silent prayer.

Bless this food and all who sit around my table, Belinda prayed. *And, Lord, please help this evening to go well and pass quickly. Amen.*

🐦

After everyone's prayer had been said, the meal began with the passing of bowls and dishes. Monroe took over the conversation almost immediately. Herschel, feeling quite anxious since Monroe had showed up, quickly realized that he'd lost his appetite. He could see by the sappy look Monroe gave Belinda that the overly talkative man most definitely had a keen interest in her.

So now that I'm aware of my competition, I need to figure out what to do about it. Herschel picked up his fork, stabbed one of the cabbage rolls, and put it on his plate. *Would it be best to back off, or should I keep pursuing Belinda and hope that I'm the one she chooses? Of course,* he reasoned, *she may not be interested in either me or Monroe. The invitation I received to join Belinda and her family at this table may only have been made because she's such a nice woman or felt like she owed me the favor because I treated her to supper at a restaurant.*

As the meal came to a close and dessert was served, Monroe became even more obnoxious. Herschel couldn't believe what a braggart the man was, especially when it came to his furniture business.

"Of course," Monroe said with a smug expression, "I've always had a good business head. Fact of the matter—my goal is to own several businesses, which will secure a strong financial future for me and the woman I will marry someday." He looked at Belinda and gave her another sappy grin.

Herschel nearly choked on his piece of shoofly pie. There was no doubt in his mind. Monroe had his sights set on marrying Belinda.

His jaw clenched. *And I guess there isn't much I can do about it. The question is: Does she feel the same way about him?*

As the evening progressed, Belinda's anxiety had advanced to the state of near exhaustion. She couldn't help wondering how the evening would have gone if it had only been Herschel and her family there. *I wish it would've been just him. I'm the one who initiated the invite for Herschel to come over this evening—unlike Monroe, who hadn't been invited at all.*

Belinda went into her room and closed the door. *I felt like Monroe made it impossible for me to say no. I should've gotten up from my seat first thing, led him out to the front door, and sent him on his way.* She felt sure that if Monroe had not been there things would have gone better. Not only had he monopolized all of her time, but poor Herschel had barely gotten a few words in to express his appreciation for the meal. He'd been the first one to leave, and Monroe was the last person out the door. Before he left, he'd mentioned taking Belinda out for supper again. She'd politely said she wouldn't be free anytime soon and told him goodnight.

Now, as Belinda sat on the edge of her bed, she reflected on other things that had gone on this evening. The situation reminded Belinda of her younger days when she was being courted by Monroe and Vernon had come into the picture. She hadn't wanted to hurt Monroe, but her heart lay with Vernon. Fortunately that wasn't the case this time, as she felt no romantic love for Herschel or Monroe. It would take time to get better acquainted with each of them, and Belinda wasn't in any rush to remarry, which meant that she was in control. It didn't make it any easier, though, since both men were obviously interested in her. On top of that, Henry had been even more sullen than usual this evening. No doubt he didn't approve of either man.

Oh my. . . Belinda lay back on the bed. *What am I supposed to do? I don't want to hurt Monroe or Herschel, but I can't allow either of them to think they have a chance at a relationship with me,* she reminded herself. *I can't accept any more supper invitations from either of them, nor will I extend an invitation for them to join us for a meal here. I have to nip this in the bud now, before it gets out of hand.*

Chapter 23

When Belinda stepped into the greenhouse the following morning, she was greeted with a pretty sight. A whole row of impatiens bloomed brightly. It was a cheery display, in spite of the uncertainty hovering over her.

Since only she and her eldest daughter were in the building at the moment, Belinda motioned for Sylvia to step behind the counter with her. While Henry was tending the beehives, she would take this opportunity to talk to Sylvia without anyone listening.

"What is it, Mom?" Sylvia questioned. "Is there something specific you need me to do here today?"

"No, I wanted to talk to you about last night but didn't want to say anything at breakfast, especially since Henry was there and would no doubt want to put in his two cents' worth."

Sylvia placed a hand on Belinda's arm. "What's wrong? You look so serious right now. Has more vandalism been done?"

Belinda shook her head as she took a seat on the wooden stool. "It's about Monroe and Herschel and their behavior last night. I wish I hadn't invited either of them to join us for supper." She released a heavy sigh. "It was a big mistake."

Sylvia's dark brows lifted. "Both men are obviously smitten with you, although they each show it in different ways." She emitted a giggle behind her hand.

"It's not funny." Belinda groaned. "I couldn't believe their expressions every time I spoke to one of them. You'd think I was some prize to be won."

Sylvia laughed a little louder this time. "You'll have to admit, it is a little funny. I mean, when was the last time you had two men vying for your attention?"

"When I was a young woman being courted by Monroe, and then your daed came along and swept me right off my feet." Belinda gave a quick shake of her head as her face heated. "I was flattered back then and felt quite special, but now at my age, it's embarrassing." She glanced at the door to be sure no one had come in and then looked back at Sylvia. "I need to put a stop to this nonsense before it gets any worse."

"Why would you need to stop it, Mom?" Sylvia questioned. "Why not just enjoy the attention you're getting from Herschel and Monroe. If you spend more time with both of the men, you may come to realize that you care deeply for one of them." She wrinkled her nose. "Although, I can't imagine you falling in love with Monroe. He's too full of *hochmut*, always bragging about himself and his accomplishments."

Belinda's head moved up and down. "He's always been that way, even when we were teenagers. But Monroe does have a certain charm. He's adventurous and says nice things to me." She paused and touched her hot cheeks. "I can't believe I'm admitting this, but I feel youthful when Monroe's around."

"And Herschel? How do you feel when you're with him?"

"Herschel is the quiet type, but he's kind and gentle. I feel relaxed when I'm with him."

"Would you like my advice?"

"Certainly."

"If I were you, with one man making me feel relaxed and the other giving me the feeling of being young again, I'd make an effort to spend time with them both—at different times, of course. That's the only way you'll ever reach a decision about which man is right for you."

"There's one problem with that, Daughter. I don't want a serious relationship with Herschel, Monroe, or any other man. I'm content being a mudder and a *grossmammi*. I don't need a romantic relationship."

"Are you sure about that?"

Belinda gave a decisive nod. "I think it's best if I don't see Monroe or Herschel socially any longer."

Sylvia opened her mouth, as if to say something more, but when the bell tinkled above the greenhouse door, she pointed and mouthed the word, "Monroe."

Belinda turned in that direction. *Oh dear. This is not what I need this morning.*

When Monroe walked toward the counter, Sylvia moved away. "I'm going to put out some of the new potholders I made on display, but I'll be available to assist any customers who may come in needing assistance."

"Sounds good. Danki, Sylvia." Belinda turned her attention to Monroe. "Good morning. May I help you with something?"

"I don't need anything from the greenhouse," he replied. "I came by to say how much I enjoyed being with you and your family last night, and I'd like to return the favor."

Belinda gave a brief shake of her head. "As I told you last night, there's no need for that. Besides, I'm going to be quite busy for the next several weeks." She released a frustrated breath. *This man is so persistent. I don't want to be rude to him, but I'll need to figure out a way to deal with his exuberance.*

"Then tell me what you'd like from one of the restaurants that does take-out orders, and I'll bring a meal to you one evening."

"There's no need for that, Monroe. Sylvia and I don't mind cooking."

"But I must insist. It's the least I can do to repay your kindness."

Belinda's resolve weakened. "All right, Monroe, I accept your offer."

He gave her a wide grin. "How about if I bring a couple of pizzas over to your house tonight? Would six o'clock be a good time?"

"That'll be fine. I will see you then." Belinda gestured to the English couple who'd come into the greenhouse. "If you'll excuse me, I need to see what my customers want."

"Sure, no problem. See you this evening, Belinda." With a spring in his step, Monroe left the building.

I hope I haven't made a mistake. Belinda bit the inside of her cheek. *But as Sylvia mentioned, I really haven't given Monroe or Herschel a fair chance. I suppose it's possible that after some time, I might develop feelings for one of them.*

Shaking her troubling thoughts aside, Belinda stepped out from behind the counter and went up to her customers. "Are you looking for anything in particular?"

"We saw your sign along the road and thought we'd pop in for a look around."

"That's good. If you have any questions, don't hesitate to let me know."

The woman appeared to be a tourist, carrying a camera in one hand, while the man munched on a soft pretzel. Belinda saw the wedding bands on their fingers and guessed they were married. It wasn't uncommon for the curious English to visit her greenhouse, and they were usually full of questions. She and Vernon had plenty of years dealing with English folks who came in to look around or snap photos without asking.

Belinda returned to her place behind the counter and watched the couple chatting away as they looked at the plants. She wondered what they might be talking about as she got out a rag and cleaned off some soil from the counter. The two of them made their way over to the gifts, looking at Sylvia's homemade pot holders and some other things. Soon they brought up a few items, setting them near the register.

"I have a question," the woman said.

Belinda could only guess what that might be as she rang up each item. "What is it you'd like to know?"

"Are there other Amish businesses in this area?" She reached into her purse and took out a wallet. "My husband thought I should ask you since we are from out of town."

Belinda pointed north. "There's a shoe shop down this road about a mile. Beyond that is an Amish-owned furniture store, but they do sell other things there as well."

"Good to know. My husband and I will have to go by there and check them out." She handed Belinda the money to pay for her purchases.

"My wife will no doubt want to return to this area sometime in the future. She's fascinated by the Amish culture and has a good many questions," the man interjected.

His wife blushed as Belinda bagged up the items she'd purchased. "I can't help it. Your Plain ways are intriguing to me. I'm especially fascinated with your mode of transportation and how you get around with a horse and buggy."

"It's part of our heritage," Belinda responded.

"It is certainly an interesting way of life."

The couple stepped away from the counter, but the wife turned back around. "Thank you for telling me about other Amish businesses that are nearby. And by the way, you have a nice greenhouse here." She looked at her husband. "If I didn't have to put my things into a suitcase for our flight home, I'd be tempted to pick out some plants here today."

Belinda watched as the man and his wife left the building. *Sylvia will be happy when she finds out that some of her pot holders sold. No doubt, she'll get busy making more.*

Virginia put on a heavy sweater, picked up her cane, and went out the front door. She dreaded going across the road to speak with Belinda King, and even more so this morning, since her bum leg was acting up.

"I don't see why Earl insisted that we accept Belinda's supper invitation," Virginia muttered as she stood on her side of the street, waiting for a horse and buggy to pass. The thought of spending an evening with the King clan caused a tingling sensation in her chest. It would be a miracle if she made it through the ordeal.

Virginia looked both ways before crossing the road. As she made her way slowly up the driveway, a car passed her, coming down from the direction of the greenhouse.

She clenched her teeth. *I hope there aren't a bunch of customers milling around the building right now. I just want to say a few words to Belinda and get out of there as quickly as possible.*

When Virginia entered the building a few minutes later, she spotted Belinda's oldest daughter sitting behind the front counter but saw no sign of Belinda.

"Is your mother here?" Virginia asked.

The dark-haired woman, whose name Virginia did not recall, shook her head. "Not at the moment. She went up to our house to get something. Is there anything I can help you with, Virginia?"

"Umm. . . I came over to speak with your mother."

"You can either wait here for her or go on up to the house."

"Think I'll wait outside on the bench I saw in the area where you sell birdbaths and other yard decorations." Virginia shuffled out the door and made her way over to the bench. She'd only been sitting a few minutes when the old woman, Maude, came along and stopped in front of the bench Virginia sat upon. "Whatcha doin'?" She pointed a bony finger at Virginia.

"I'm waiting to speak to Mrs. King." *Not that it's any of your business.*

"She's probably in there." Maude gestured to the greenhouse.

"Not at the moment, but she should be back soon."

Maude folded her arms and took a seat next to Virginia. "Guess I'll wait here too."

How nice. The last thing I need is some nosey old lady sitting beside me. Virginia shifted to the far side of the bench. *If Belinda doesn't show up soon I'll go back inside the greenhouse and wait for her there. I'd go up to the house like her daughter suggested, but the unkempt woman next to me would probably follow.*

"Where ya from?" Maude asked.

"My husband and I live across the street."

"No, I meant where'd ya live before you moved here?"

"Chicago." Virginia's lips pressed together. *I wish she'd stop asking me questions.*

Maude reached into her coat pocket and pulled out a partial roll of toilet paper. She then proceeded to pull off a few pieces and blew her nose.

After watching the old woman toss the pieces on the ground, Virginia grimaced. *Surely there has to be a trash can around. If not, then Maude should have put the pieces she used to blow her nose in another pocket to dispose of when she got home. If that old shack she lives in could even be called a home.*

"You come here often?" The old woman's question pulled Virginia out of her musings.

"Sometimes."

"I come here a lot. I like to get things from the woman who runs this place." Maude looked at Virginia with furrowed brows. "I think she feels sorry for me, but I don't need no one's pity. I've been on my own ever since. . ." Maude stopped talking when Belinda approached.

"Good morning, ladies." Belinda gave them a pleasant smile. "I'm surprised to see you sitting outside on this chilly spring day."

"I've been waiting to talk to you." Virginia stood up.

"Certainly. Should we go inside, or would you rather have our conversation out here?"

"I'd prefer to speak to you in private." Virginia was not about to talk to Belinda in front of Maude. The old woman didn't need to hear anything they said.

"Okay, I can take a hint. You can have my seat here." Maude got up and ambled into the greenhouse.

Once Belinda was seated on the bench, Virginia got right to the point. She had no plans of sticking around here any longer than necessary.

"I came to tell you that my husband said we will be able to come for supper whatever evening is convenient for you."

"Would Friday at six o'clock be okay?"

"Yes, and is there anything I can bring?"

Belinda shook her head. "Just a good appetite. There will be plenty of food."

"Okay, we'll see you at six then." Virginia stood, and as she headed out of the parking lot, a busload of tourists pulled in. *I sure don't understand what the big attraction is for these English people. I wonder what any of them would say if they knew Earl and I will be eating supper this Friday with the Amish family who run the greenhouse.* Her chin jutted out. *Makes no sense to me, but I bet they'd be jealous.*

"Each to his own, I guess," Virginia mumbled as she made her way across the street. *All those crazy tourists may be fascinated with the Amish people, but not me. I just want to live a peaceful life without all the bad odors their horses put out, not to mention the disturbing noise.*

Chapter 24

Gordonville

Herschel sat in his office at the bulk-food store, eating a sandwich and thinking about how Monroe had showed up at Belinda's last evening, right when they were getting ready to eat.

That man is so full of hochmut, Herschel fumed. *I hope Belinda isn't taken in by him. Even if she isn't interested in me, she deserves better than a braggart like Monroe.*

He shifted his arm to the right and knocked a stack of papers off the desk. "If this is how my afternoon is starting, then I'm in for a tough time." Herschel groaned as he bent over to pick up the mess he'd made. *Monroe may have more money than me, but that doesn't mean he's a happier man. Some Bible verses talk about a person's riches and pride getting the best of them.*

Herschel's half-eaten roast beef sandwich beckoned him to eat. As he began to chew, his mind conjured up questions. *Do I have any chance to win Belinda from Monroe? Can I let myself envision us together as Mr. and Mrs. Herschel Fisher?*

It would be a challenge to go up against Monroe. Not quite like David and Goliath, because from what Herschel had learned, this fellow had been turned down by Belinda before, and she'd married the other guy. But now that Monroe had money and made it apparent to anyone who would listen, maybe Belinda would consider him the right man to make her happy.

Herschel couldn't forget how thick Monroe poured it on while discussing his accomplishments during supper. All the guy did was dominate each topic, and it seemed like he wanted to be the first to respond to every comment.

Herschel nearly choked on his last bite of food, thinking about the pride Monroe emitted. *How does Belinda put up with him? I can't imagine her liking that guy's personality. But if she does, I'm in trouble.*

Herschel felt like giving up, but as he mulled things over, he reached a decision. He would wait a few weeks and then invite Belinda out for supper again. If she turned him down without a valid excuse, Herschel would take it as a sign that she wasn't interested in him and bow out graciously. But if Belinda said yes and they had another pleasant evening together, Herschel would continue to pursue a relationship with her.

Strasburg

When Sylvia came into the house to take her turn at fixing something to eat for her lunch, she found Amy washing dishes.

"Have you and the kinner eaten already?" Sylvia asked.

"Jah, and they're both playing quietly in the living room right now." Amy gestured to the refrigerator. "Would you like me to fix you a ham and cheese sandwich?"

"No, that's okay. I can fend for myself. Besides, you probably need to take a break about now."

"I'm fine, really."

Sylvia opened the refrigerator and took out what she needed. "When I was pregnant with my little ones, I tired easily—more so with Rachel, since Allen was a toddler and always into things. Ever since my son learned to walk, he's kept me busy."

Amy chuckled. "He's a livewire, all right. Always full of energy and eager to investigate things."

"Jah, but he's never gone out of the yard with a stranger, the way Rachel did last year." Sylvia set her sandwich makings on the table. "She sure gave us a scare, and it was even more frightening when Dennis and I found her inside Maude's rundown shack."

"That woman had some nerve taking your daughter out of the yard. If it had been my daughter, I would have reported the incident to the sheriff." Amy tapped the side of her head. "I believe that old woman might be a bit touched."

"She is a strange one all right."

"Our mamm's always been good to Maude though."

Sylvia nodded. "Speaking of Mom, she and I talked privately this morning, before any customers showed up at the greenhouse."

"About the business?"

"No, it concerned Herschel and Monroe."

Amy dried her hands and took a seat at the table. "Sounds interesting. Would you mind filling me in on what was said?"

"Not at all." Sylvia sat in the chair opposite her sister, and as she prepared her sandwich, she told Amy everything their mother had said.

Amy's brows went up. "And so it begins."

"What begins?"

"The race between the two men who are smitten with our mamm, to see who will win the prize." Amy snickered. "Never thought I'd see the day."

"Me neither."

"Who do you think will win Mom's hand?"

"Maybe neither. Mom says she's not interested in getting remarried, but she also said she would be open to seeing both men, so maybe she'll change her mind."

"Hmm. . ." Amy tapped her fingers on the table's surface.

Sylvia leaned forward. "I know it's wrong of me to dislike someone, but I'm hoping Mom doesn't choose Monroe. In any event, it's our mother's decision." She glanced at Amy, who seemed to be in deep thought. "What are you thinking?"

"Oh nothing, just wondering how we might be able to give Herschel a little edge."

Sylvia took a small intake of breath. "I think it would be best if you didn't meddle. Our mamm's old enough to make her own decisions."

"True, but there's a fifty-fifty chance she might choose Monroe, and those odds could turn in the man's favor because of his strong will to win our Mom. In my opinion, that would be a big mistake."

"Maybe so, but it's still Mom's choice." Sylvia covered two slices of bread with mayonnaise and added a piece of ham. "Speaking of Monroe, he's bringing pizza over here tonight and joining us for supper again."

"Another meal with Monroe carrying on about himself? Can you imagine if he were to become our stepfather?"

"No, I can't." Amy's brows furrowed. "How did this invitation come about?"

"He came by the greenhouse this morning and made the offer. Mom told me about it before I came up to the house." Sylvia added some cheese, lettuce, and a pickle slice to finish off the sandwich. "Why don't you and Jared join us?"

"As much as we enjoy eating pizza, we can't come because we've already accepted a supper invitation for this evening from Jared's parents." Amy gave an unladylike snicker. "Guess you'll get to enjoy Monroe's company without us."

"I'll admit he's not my favorite person, and we both know he's not Henry's either. I really hope if Mom chooses one of the men, that it ends up to be Herschel."

"He has my vote too," Amy agreed. "I'm seeing already that his and Mom's personalities blend better."

Henry sat at the dining-room table, staring at the piece of pepperoni pizza on his plate. Normally he would have gobbled it down, but this evening his stomach churned so badly he didn't think he could take one bite. Henry wished he could excuse himself and head to his room or go out to the loft. Instead, he was stuck here, like Sylvia and the kids, being forced to sit through the meal. Henry still hadn't come up with anything that would pin the vandalism on Monroe, even though he was convinced this man had to be the one behind the damage.

Henry filled his glass with root beer and took a long drink. Setting the glass aside, he glanced out the window facing the front yard. *Maybe someday he'll be told by someone that he needs to stop being so into himself. Why did Mom let Monroe bring pizza over here for supper?* He continued to fume. *Doesn't she care how much I don't like him? Truth be told, unless Sylvia has changed her mind, she doesn't care for Monroe either. I can't figure out why Mom is so kind to him. She's gotta see that he's not as nice as he pretends to be.*

"Business was booming at my furniture store today. The customers commented on what finely crafted furniture I carry."

Monroe's loud voice drew Henry's thoughts aside. He picked up his glass of root beer and took a drink. *At least it was Mom who furnished the cold drink, as well as a tossed green salad, so guess I can eat that.* Henry sat stiffly in his chair. *I won't give that man the satisfaction of knowing pepperoni pizza is my favorite. I sure hope he doesn't stay long tonight.*

When the meal was over, Monroe jumped up and began clearing the table. "I'll put the paper plates and cups in the garbage." He smiled at Belinda. "Since you won't have any dishes to wash, maybe we can go outside and sit awhile. It's the perfect night for stargazing."

"I suppose we could." Belinda looked at Sylvia. "Would you and the kinner like to join us?"

"I need to give them both a bath, and then it'll be time for bed, so why don't you go outside without us?" Sylvia responded.

Belinda had a feeling her son would decline the invite, but she decided to ask him anyway. "How about you, Son? You could bring your binoculars out and—"

"Yeah, that's a good idea. I might see an owl or even a *schpeckmaus*."

Belinda was surprised at her son's positive response, but at the same time she shuddered. "I hope we don't see any bats. I remember once when I was a girl, a bat got in our house and my daed had a terrible time trying to catch it. The whole house was awakened by the time he finally shooed the critter out the door."

Monroe snickered. "The only encounter I've had with a schpeckmaus was during a young people's singing when I visited my cousin Timothy's family up in Perry County one summer." His gaze went to Belinda. "Don't think I ever told you about it, but stop me if you've heard this story."

Belinda listened with interest as Monroe gave a vivid account of a bat swooping into the barn where the singing had been held. She couldn't help but laugh when he ducked his head way down and squealed as he emphasized how some of the young women had reacted to the bat. Sylvia laughed too, which caused Allen and Rachel to laugh. But Henry just sat with a stony expression.

"Did the bat fly out of the barn of its own accord?" Sylvia asked.

He shook his head. "My cousin and a couple other real tall fellows chased after the critter, swatting at it with their straw hats. Then one of 'em knocked the bat to the floor."

"Was it dead?" Belinda questioned.

"Nope, just stunned. After that, using two hats, Timothy scooped up the bat and took him outside."

"What were you doing all that time?" Henry spoke up.

"I was sitting there holding my sides from laughing so hard."

"Figures."

Henry's words were spoken softly, but it didn't keep Belinda from hearing what he said. No doubt Monroe did too. Her son's rude behavior whenever Monroe came around did not set well with her. She would need to speak with Henry about it later.

Monroe turned toward the kitchen. "Guess I'd better get the paper dishes put in the trash so we can head outdoors."

Belinda picked up the silverware and followed.

"Mom's not happy with you. Couldn't you tell by her expression?" Sylvia whispered to Henry.

He folded his arms and frowned. "I'm not happy with her either. She shouldn't have let Monroe bring pizza tonight. He's only after one thing, and I—"

Sylvia put a finger against her lips. "Let's take the kinner into the living room. You can read to Allen while I give Rachel her bath."

"Okay, sure. I have nothin' else to do, and it'll be better than sitting outside looking at the stars and listening to Monroe acting all nicey-nice with Mom." Henry pushed his chair away from the table and trudged into the adjoining room.

"Are you sure?" Sylvia asked. "I thought you were going to take your binoculars out like Mom suggested at supper."

"I changed my mind. Decided to stay in the house to help you, and I'm fine with that."

Once his niece and nephew had been bathed and put to bed, Henry planned to spend the rest of the evening alone in his room.

❧

Monroe sat next to Belinda on the porch swing, tempted to reach for her hand. He remembered their courting days, and how the two of them had sat on her parents' porch with no interruptions. His heart felt full this evening, but he wished he felt free to talk about planning a future with her. The only thing that stood in his way was Herschel. *I'm not going to let him steal my girl the way Vernon did. I'll do whatever it takes to make her mine.*

They visited quietly as the swing moved gently back and forth. Monroe was tempted to lean over and give her a kiss. Instead, he kept his composure and folded his hands in front of him.

A cool breeze came up and Belinda shivered. "Are you cold?" Monroe asked. "We can go back inside if you want."

"I am a bit chilly, but I'm in no hurry to quit looking at the twinkling stars and bright moon." Belinda rose from the swing. "Think I'll go in the house and fetch a jacket to wear over my sweater. Can I get you something to drape over your shoulders?"

"No thanks. I'm fine."

Monroe watched as Belinda went back into the house. She was still a fine looking woman. He pulled his shoulders straight back and looked up at the sky. *I will not give up until she agrees to marry me.*

Chapter 25

Belinda glanced at the clock. In thirty minutes, the greenhouse would close for the day and she could go up to the house. Sylvia had already gone up to help Amy start supper. Virginia and Earl would be joining them for the meal and would be there at six o'clock. Since Belinda had invited Amy and Jared as well as Dennis to join them, there would be eight adults and Sylvia's two children. It would give them all a chance to get to know their neighbors better.

Belinda still felt bad that she'd procrastinated in extending an invitation to the Martins, but it was better to do it now than not at all. She wasn't looking for the neighbors to reciprocate—she simply wanted to do the right thing.

Belinda gazed at the row of indoor plants she had for sale. African violets seemed to be everyone's favorite, but other flowers such as orchids and shamrock plants sold well too.

The local landscaper had come by earlier today and placed another order. At the rate things were going, Belinda might be able to hire someone to either add on to the greenhouse soon or perhaps put up another building. The only problem was more room for items to sell meant more work to be done. Once Sylvia and Dennis got married in early August, Belinda and Henry would be on their own. When Amy's baby was born, she'd be a stay-at-home mother. Unless Sylvia found a sitter for the children or brought them to the greenhouse with her, she wouldn't be helping anymore either.

If anything, I should be downsizing, not thinking of adding on. Belinda sighed deeply. *Maybe I should sell out and move to Clymer to live with*

Ezekiel and Michelle. Another option would be to ask Ezekiel to move back here to help me run the greenhouse.

The idea of asking Ezekiel to move from a place where he'd established a new business and seemed content held no appeal for Belinda. Just thinking about it made her stomach clench. *No, I will not ask my son to make that sacrifice. If Henry and I can't handle it on our own, I'll see about hiring someone outside the family to help.*

Belinda heard a horse and buggy pull into the parking area and looked toward the door. *Just what I don't need—a last-minute customer.*

She waited behind the counter, and was surprised when Herschel entered the store.

"Hello, Belinda. How are you doing?" That expected little shy smile formed on his lips as he approached her.

"I'm doing fine. How are you?"

"Doin' all right. I came by, hoping you were still open. I want to get a nice plant or something else for my folk's yard, because today is their sixtieth wedding anniversary."

"That's wonderful. Please relate to them my hearty congratulations."

"I certainly will. I'm taking them out to supper at Shady Maple this evening to celebrate the occasion."

Belinda smiled, remembering back to last April, when her children had surprised her with a birthday supper at Shady Maple in East Earl. She'd been even more surprised when Ezekiel and his family showed up unexpectedly.

"Do you have an idea what you would like to get your parents, or should I offer some suggestions?"

"I don't have a clue what they might like," Herschel admitted, "so I'm open to any ideas."

"Is there a particular flower they favor?"

He shrugged his shoulders.

"Do they like solar lights for the yard?"

Herschel bobbed his head. "As a matter of fact, they do."

"Then how about a pretty metal flower that lights up for your mamm? I also have some metal chickens and ducks your daed may like."

"Those are both good options. Jah, I'd like to take a look at them."

Belinda went out the door with Herschel and walked over to where all the solar lights were displayed. "What do you think of those?" She pointed at the flower and then to one of the chickens.

Herschel bent down to check the prices and announced that he'd take a purple flower for his mother and a large rooster for his father.

Belinda led the way back inside the greenhouse. After Herschel paid for the items, she wrapped each one carefully in bubble wrap and placed them in a cardboard box. Belinda didn't voice her thoughts, but she wished she could be there to see Herschel's parents' reaction to the gifts he'd gotten for them. She'd met his mother, Vera, a few times when she'd come into the greenhouse but had not made his father's acquaintance.

Herschel picked up the box and opened his mouth, like he was about to say something more to Belinda, when Monroe stepped into the greenhouse. It took Belinda by surprise because she hadn't heard his horse and buggy come in. Perhaps he'd pulled his rig in while she and Herschel were outside on the other side of the building, looking at solar lights.

Herschel glanced at Monroe, nodded, and then mumbled to Belinda: "I'd better go." Before she could form a response, he was out the door.

Belinda felt a keen sense of disappointment. She'd hoped to talk with Herschel awhile longer.

Turning her attention to Monroe, Belinda wondered what he was doing here at this late hour. Surely he had to know she would be closing the greenhouse momentarily.

"I'm about to close the greenhouse for the day, but if there is something you need, I can wait a few minutes." Belinda smiled, despite her irritation. *It was nice seeing Herschel and it's too bad our chat got interrupted. Monroe always seems to know when Herschel is here. How can I get better acquainted with Herschel if Monroe keeps dropping in whenever Herschel's here?*

"I realize it's a last-minute invitation again, but I stopped by to see if you might be free to go out for supper with me tonight." He put both hands on his side of the counter and leaned a little closer to her. "Or I could head over to the pizza place and bring supper to you. No doubt after working all day, you're not feeling up to cooking."

"Actually, we have company coming this evening, so I won't be able to see you tonight, Monroe. And as I've stated previously, I would appreciate some advance notice if you want to include me in your plans."

"Sorry. It was a spur-of-the-moment decision." Monroe turned toward the windows facing the parking lot. "It's that Herschel fellow, isn't it? He's the one you invited for supper." A visible flush erupted on Monroe's cheeks. "Isn't that why he's still out there talking to your son?"

Belinda glanced in the direction Monroe pointed. Sure enough, Henry stood with Herschel, next to his horse and buggy. She wondered what they might be talking about.

I guess it would be good of me to clear things up, so he'll settle down. "Herschel is not coming to our home for supper. If you must know, we invited our neighbors across the street to join us for a meal."

"Oh, I see." Monroe's eyes brightened a bit. "It's good to be neighborly once in a while, jah?"

Belinda bobbed her head.

"Umm. . . Is it the neighbor with the bright red hair?"

"Yes it is. Why do you ask?"

"When I came by to check on your place when you all were gone to New York, I caught that gal outside on her porch with a pair of binoculars. I couldn't help feeling that I was being watched."

Belinda flapped her hand. "Oh yes, I believe she must have been bird-watching. It seems harmless to me."

"Well, anyway, it's nice of you to be a good neighbor." He straightened his hat.

"Did you come by for anything else?" she asked. "Because if not, I need to close things up and head to the house. I want to get cleaned up and help my daughters start supper."

"Sure. I'll let you get to it then. Maybe in another week or so, you and I can get together. I'd like to take you somewhere special."

"I'll have to wait and see how it goes."

"Okay."

Belinda felt relieved when Monroe said goodbye and went out the door. She wanted to give him a chance, but she'd feel much better about seeing him if he wasn't so overbearing.

"What's taking you so long, Virginia? It's almost six o'clock." Earl stepped into the bedroom and narrowed his eyes as he pointed at her. "Are you stalling?"

She shook her head, although to tell the truth, Virginia was in no hurry to walk across the street and share a meal in an Amish home.

She stared at her reflection in the full-length mirror attached to the front of their closet door. "I want to make sure I look presentable." Virginia reached down and rolled the lint brush she held across the front of her dark green slacks. "Can you check the back, to make sure none of Goldie's hairs are sticking to me?" She handed Earl the brush.

He stepped behind Virginia, made a few swipes, and gave it back to her. "Okay, let's go."

"Just a minute; I need to put my earrings in."

Earl groaned. "Are you kidding me? We're not goin' out to eat at a fancy restaurant. Those people across the road are Plain folks. In case you haven't noticed, they all dress in simple clothes, and none of the women I've seen wear jewelry."

"I don't care. I am not Amish, and I don't feel fully dressed unless my earrings are in." Virginia walked over to her dresser, opened the jewelry box, and took out a pair of white earrings with blue polka-dots. Once they were in place, she slipped on a sweater and picked up her cane. "All right, Earl, I'm ready to go."

"Someone just knocked on the front door, Mom. Would you like me to answer it?" Amy asked.

"Yes, please. I'm sure it must be our neighbors, since Dennis and Jared are already here." Belinda set the bowl of shredded lettuce on the kitchen table between a bowl of cut-up tomatoes and some chopped onions. "You can escort Mr. and Mrs. Martin to the living room and let them know that I'll be out there soon."

"Okay." Amy hurried from the room.

Belinda looked at Sylvia, who'd been busy chopping olives. "I'll go out and greet our guests and explain that we'll be eating in the dining room but serving from the kitchen."

"No problem, Mom. I should have the rest of the things set out in the next few minutes." Sylvia touched Belinda's shoulder. "You look kind of stressed. Take a few deep breaths and try to relax."

"You're right. I do need to calm myself a bit before greeting our guests."

"Are you nervous about having Virginia and Earl here for supper?"

"A little. It's the first time they've been in our home, and they may feel uncomfortable with our simple surroundings compared to their modern furnishings."

"It'll be fine, Mom. You'll see." Sylvia's confident tone did little to relieve Belinda's nervousness. The few encounters she'd had with Virginia had caused Belinda to believe her English neighbor didn't care much for her. Hopefully the evening would go better than she expected.

Virginia sat stiffly on the couch beside Earl, wondering if she'd lost her mind agreeing to come here and eat supper with these Plain people with whom she had nothing in common. Belinda had entered the room a few minutes ago and introduced Virginia and Earl to each of her family members. "It's too bad our son Ezekiel and his wife and two small children couldn't be here as well," she said.

"I didn't realize you had other family living in the area," Virginia commented.

"Ezekiel moved to Clymer, New York, a few years ago, not long after he and his wife got married."

"My brother's wife used to be English," Henry spoke up. "But she decided to give up her worldly ways and join the Amish church."

Virginia rubbed the bridge of her nose. *Who in their right mind would want to leave all their modern conveniences and stylish clothes in order to live the Plain life?* She glanced around, gazing at each of the Amish people gathered in this simply decorated room, devoid of a television or electric lights. *No way could I ever live like this, especially in the summertime with no air-conditioning.*

"It must have been a difficult transition for your son's wife to become Amish," Earl said.

"It was," Belinda responded, "but my daughter-in-law seems to have adjusted quite well."

What's this conversation have to do with anything? Virginia reached up and fingered the necklace matching the earrings she wore. *We came here to eat supper, not discuss Belinda's family members, who I care nothing about. I'd just like to get this evening over with so we can go home and maybe watch an hour or so of TV before it's time for bed.*

"New York, huh?" The question came from Earl. "That must mean you don't see your son too often."

"Not as much as we'd like, but we try to get together as often as we can." Belinda gestured to the adjoining dining room. "We'll be eating in there, because our table is quite large, but we will put the food on our plates from the items set out on the kitchen table. So Virginia and Earl, if you'll come with me, you can dish up first and the rest of my family will follow. Then once we are all seated around the table, we can pray."

Pray? Virginia glanced at Earl and struggled to keep from rolling her eyes. She hadn't uttered a prayer since her mother made her attend Bible school one summer when she was a girl. Virginia and Earl had never really talked about it, but she felt fairly sure he'd never been a praying man either. If he had, he'd chosen to kept it private.

I hope they don't call on me or Earl to recite a prayer, because I have no idea what either of us would say.

When they entered the kitchen, Virginia was surprised to see a stove and refrigerator, not that much different than hers. Other than the absence of a dishwasher or microwave, Belinda's kitchen didn't look too terribly plain. A calendar with a colorful sunset picture hung on one wall, and a pretty vase with pink flowers in it sat on the roll-top desk across the room.

When Belinda directed their attention to the items on the table, Virginia's brows squished together.

"Are you folks familiar with haystack?" Belinda questioned.

Virginia looked at Earl, and when he shrugged his shoulders, she shook her head. "Never heard of it before."

Belinda explained that they should choose from whichever food items they wanted and layer them on until their plate was full, making it resemble a haystack.

"I'm guessing it must be similar to a taco salad." Virginia looked at Belinda. "Is that right?"

"Yes, only some of the ingredients we're offering tonight are not included in any taco salad I've ever eaten."

"Well, it sounds good to me." Earl rubbed his hands together with an eager expression. "Should we start filling our plates?"

"Please do. Once you have everything you want, go ahead to the dining room and take a seat. The rest of us will join you shortly."

Virginia went first, starting with some crushed corn chips, forming the bottom layer of her haystack. Following that, she added lettuce, tomato, a few onions, several sliced black olives, and some of the ground beef mixture. On top of that she poured some melted cheese, added a dollop of sour cream, and topped it off with a spoonful of picante sauce. Carrying her plate, she hobbled into the dining room without the aid of her cane, which she'd left propped inside the entryway near the front door.

She took a seat on one side of the table and picked up the glass of water sitting there to take a drink. *I'll be glad when this evening is over and Earl and I can go back to the comfort of our home.*

Chapter 26

The next few weeks went by in a blur, with many more customers coming to the greenhouse in preparation of planting their gardens. Despite the fact that the big garden center in town absorbed a good many customers, it hadn't seemed to have hurt Belinda's family business. Now that it was April and more tourists were arriving, her greenhouse attracted people from far and wide. She'd had a customer the other day visiting from Canada. The gentleman stated how intrigued he was with the Amish and said he'd been to a couple of communities close to where he lived.

An older couple had come in yesterday from Texas. They'd driven up for a book signing to meet their favorite author who wrote about the Amish and also to see the Plain people. The man seemed as interested in what was being said as the woman. They'd asked Belinda about the Pennsylvania Dutch language, and she'd answered their questions. But as the greenhouse continued to fill with more customers, she'd had to excuse herself and tend to others who needed assistance.

So far today they'd been exceptionally busy, but Belinda had no problem with that. It kept her mind off the fact that today was her birthday, and how two years ago, her husband, son, and son-in-law had been killed. It was hard to think of celebrating anything when painful memories surfaced. She'd hoped her birthday might go unnoticed, but it was not to be. Sylvia had fixed Belinda a special ham-and-egg omelet this morning. Then when Amy arrived to watch the children, she'd informed Belinda that she and the rest of the family would be going to her house for supper that evening.

A lump formed in the back of Belinda's throat. While she looked forward to spending time with her loved ones, she wasn't in the mood to celebrate. The card she'd received in the mail this morning from Ezekiel and Michelle wished her a happy birthday and said they hoped she would have a good day. Belinda missed them so much, and the distance between them didn't help.

It would be better if they could be with us this evening, she thought. *But for my family's sake, I must put a smile on my face and try to have a pleasant time.*

Belinda glanced at the clock and heaved a sigh. Several people wandered up and down the aisles, and it would be another two hours before quitting time. She wished she could go up to the house, stretch out on her bed, and take a nap. But she had to keep pushing until the last customer left the greenhouse.

An English lady came up to the cash register with an outdoor plant and several pot holders that Sylvia had made. After the woman paid for her purchases and left, Belinda got up from the stool where she'd been sitting behind the counter. She'd noticed the give-away containers for the customers to use for their plants were running short.

Belinda headed to the area where the surplus was stored, but on the way back, something caught her eye. Henry was watering some plants while visiting with an Amish girl about his age. Belinda had seen the young lady and her family last week at church. She'd met the girl's mother and found out they were visiting from outside the area.

Belinda stepped up next to Henry and smiled at the girl. "I didn't see you come in, but it's nice to see you have found our place."

"Jah, I took a walk after breakfast and spotted this place. The hanging baskets on display out front look beautiful."

"Thank you." Belinda looked at her son. "I should get back up to the counter and take the supplies I came here for. When you're done watering, I'd like you to bring in more bags of potting soil."

He nodded. "I'll take care of it, Mom, as soon as I'm done talkin' to Anna."

It did Belinda's heart good to see Henry socializing with someone his age. He spent long hours working in the greenhouse and doing chores around the place.

She returned to the counter and added the containers to what was left. An English woman stood near the register, ready to pay for her things. "I'm glad I came here today. You've got some cute birdhouses. I'm getting one for my sister's birthday next week. The second one I will keep for myself."

The word *birthday* was another reminder to Belinda that she would be getting together with her family this evening. She rang up the items, and when the lady left the greenhouse, Belinda walked down the aisle where she'd last seen her son. He seemed to be taking his time getting done with the plants, and there was only one bag of potting soil left. *I wonder if he's still talking to that girl.*

She walked over to the area where Sylvia stood putting more pot holders on the gift items shelf. "Your homemade things have been selling well."

"Henry's sold a few of his painted horseshoes too," Sylvia reported.

"Business has been booming all right. I'm sure it'll be even busier throughout the summer months."

"Yes, and I've been thinking about that. In fact, Dennis and I have decided to change our wedding date from August to October, when things have slowed down here a bit." Sylvia put a few more pot holders in place. "There won't be as many customers in the fall, so you and Henry won't be quite as busy and can hopefully handle things okay without me by then."

Belinda swallowed hard. The thickening in her throat had returned. As much as she dreaded the day Sylvia would no longer be working here, she did not wish to stand in the way of her daughter's happiness by making her wait two extra months to get married.

"I do not want you and Dennis to change your wedding date because of me."

"It'll only be a few months later than planned, Mom. And it'll give Dennis more time to make some changes to my house before the kinner and I move in with him after the wedding."

Belinda's eyes widened as she touched the base of her throat. "You're going to move back to your old house?"

"Jah."

"But I thought you weren't comfortable with living there since it had once been yours and Toby's home and it holds so many memories."

"That's true, but with all the changes Dennis and I have in mind, it'll be like a new house. Plus, there will be more bedrooms for guests and children, should the Lord bless us with babies."

Belinda gave a closed-lip smile. Her daughter's announcement came as a surprise, and she hardly knew what to say. For many months after Toby's death, Sylvia could not even go to her house without falling apart. When she forced herself to go there, someone in the family always went along to offer their help and emotional support.

"So you're okay with us waiting till the first Thursday in October?"

Belinda slipped her arm around Sylvia's waist and gave her a hug. "Whatever decisions you make, regarding your wedding date or where you'll live after you and Dennis are married, are between you and him."

Sylvia smiled. "Danki, Mom. I was certain you'd understand and accept our reasons for waiting."

"A final note: if you need help painting any rooms or cleaning down the walls, please let me know."

"I will."

When Belinda heard someone come into the greenhouse, she made her way back to the counter. She was surprised to see Monroe walking toward her with a huge green gift bag and a bouquet of roses. "*Hallich gebottsdaag*, Belinda."

Her cheeks warmed as he handed her the flowers and placed the gift on the counter. "Danki, Monroe, but you didn't have to do that. I wasn't expecting anything from you."

He shook his head. "There was no way I could let your birthday go by and not give you a gift."

Belinda sniffed the roses. "They smell delightful."

He gestured to the other bag. "Go ahead and look in there."

Belinda placed the roses on the counter, reached inside the pretty bag, and withdrew two large battery-operated candles—the kind that looked like the flames were real. She'd seen them for sale in some of the stores in town and knew they were more expensive than the average candle with batteries.

"They're very nice, Monroe. Danki for thinking of me with these lovely gifts."

With his chin held high, and both thumbs positioned under the front of his suspenders, he gave her a wide smile. "You are most welcome. And now I have a question to ask."

"Oh?"

"May I help you celebrate by taking you out for supper?"

Belinda blinked. *Why does he keep asking me out for supper at the last minute? I thought I'd made it clear that I would prefer some advance notice.*

She looked at him and said: "It's kind of you to offer, but my family and I have already made plans for this evening."

His shoulders sagged. "Guess I messed up again by not asking sooner. Sorry about that."

"Maybe we can do it one night next week. How about Friday? Would that work for you?"

He reached out and touched her arm. "Jah, that'd be great. I can finally take you someplace special where they serve really good food."

Belinda couldn't imagine where it might be. Most of the restaurants in their area served simple fare—nothing fancy. Well, she'd only have to wait a week to find out where the location of the special place was.

When Belinda and her family arrived at Amy and Jared's that evening, she noticed two carriages parked in the yard. She was quite sure one belonged to Dennis, which was no surprise, since she'd assumed he would be included in their plans for tonight. The other buggy, she wasn't sure about. Had Amy invited someone else to this gathering?

Belinda stepped down from the carriage, and while Henry took care of putting the horse in the barn, Sylvia handed Rachel to her.

Belinda began walking toward the house with her granddaughter, until Sylvia called out: "Would you mind waiting for me and Allen? That way we can all go in together."

"Okay." Belinda thought her daughter's request was a little odd, but she came back to the buggy and waited for Sylvia to help Allen down. It was also a bit strange that Sylvia hadn't brought anything to contribute to their supper. It wasn't like her to allow Amy to provide everything for a meal—even one that took place in Amy and Jared's home.

"Let's take a walk out to the barn before we go up to the house,"

Sylvia suggested. "Amy mentioned that one of their barn cats had a batch of kittens last week. It'll be fun for the kinner to see them."

"Maybe we should wait and do that later," Belinda suggested. "Amy may have supper ready, and I'm sure she would appreciate it if we ate the food while it's warm."

"I believe she's making *hoischtock*, so there's really nothing involved that needs to be kept warm."

The mention of haystack caused Belinda to think of the evening they'd had their neighbors over for supper. Earl had eaten the meal heartily, and even complimented Belinda and Sylvia. Virginia hadn't said whether she enjoyed it or not. In fact, she hadn't contributed much to the conversation that evening and kept checking her watch. Belinda figured Virginia may have felt uncomfortable in a home lacking modern conveniences. Although she hadn't admitted it to anyone, Belinda had felt relieved when the Martins returned to their own home. It wasn't that she was prejudiced against English folks. She just didn't feel comfortable around Virginia, because she had very little in common with her neighbor. *Even so*, Belinda told herself, *I will try to be a good neighbor to Virginia and her husband.*

"Allen, wouldn't you like to see the new kittens in the barn?" Sylvia's question had been spoken in Pennsylvania Dutch, and it halted Belinda's musings.

The boy bobbed his head and took off running in that direction.

Sylvia looked at Belinda. "Looks like we have no choice but to go after him."

When Sylvia began walking quickly toward the barn, Belinda felt obliged to follow—especially since Rachel had begun shouting that she wanted her mamm.

Sylvia had a head start, and by the time Belinda got there with Rachel, both Sylvia and Allen had entered the barn and shut the door. It made sense that they would close it to keep so many flies from getting inside, because even in April the pesky insects could be a problem for the horses.

When Belinda entered the building, with the exception of horse whinnies, everything was quiet. Belinda glanced around the dimly lit barn but saw no sign of Sylvia, Allen, or Henry.

Holding tightly to Rachel's hand, she made her way toward the sound of the horses, where she assumed her daughter, son, and grandson had gone.

As Belinda approached the first stall, a chorus of voices shouted, "Surprise! Happy Birthday!"

Astonished, Belinda teared up when Ezekiel stepped out of the shadows and gave her a big hug. She looked around and saw Michelle smiling while she held on to little Vernon. Their daughter, Angela Mary, wearing a big grin, stood beside her mother. The rest of Belinda's family stood there too, along with Herschel.

"Did we surprise you?" Ezekiel asked. "Did we get ya good?"

"Oh jah, you fooled me again, just like last year when you showed up at Shady Maple." Happy tears welled in Belinda's eyes. She looked at both of her daughters. "Did you two plan this?"

Sylvia and Amy nodded. "It wasn't easy to keep you from finding out, but things fell together quite well, and we're glad you were surprised." Amy slipped an arm around Belinda's waist, and Sylvia did the same.

"Danki for making me feel so special." It was difficult for Belinda to convey her emotions without breaking down. The only thing that would have made this gathering more special would be if their departed loved ones could be there too.

"I hope you don't mind my being here, since I'm not part of your family," Herschel spoke up. "Amy and Jared invited me, and I sure didn't want to say no."

"It's perfectly fine, Herschel. I'm glad you're here." Belinda went around to each family member and gave them a hug. She could hardly believe they were all here. This was the first time she had seen Ezekiel, Michelle, and the children since she and the rest of their family had gone to Clymer for Christmas. This birthday had turned out to be joyful after all.

Chapter 27

"Should we take a look at the *busslin* before we go in the house?" Jared asked Belinda.

"Of course. That is the reason I was told we were coming out to the barn." She gave a small laugh.

"Okay everyone, follow me." Jared led the way to a wooden box near the back of the barn. Within the crate, a silver-gray mama cat lay next to her kittens. The children squealed with obvious delight, while the adults looked on.

It pleased Belinda to see her family so happy. Even Herschel wore a grin when each child was given the chance to pet one of the six kittens. Mama cat didn't seem to mind, as she lay in the box with her eyes closed. No doubt she was in need of a nap.

As she watched her young grandchildren interact with the squirming, meowing kittens, Belinda recognized again how much joy they brought to her heart.

She closed her eyes and lifted a silent prayer: *Heavenly Father, thank You for the privilege of being a part of my grandchildren's lives. Please bless and protect each member of our family and keep us from wandering off the narrow path. Help me, as well as the other adults in our family, to be a Christian example to the younger ones in all we say and do. Bless and protect Herschel too. He's such a kind man, with a servant's heart. Please be with us all in the coming days as You guide and direct each of our lives. Amen.*

When everyone headed into the house a short time later, Herschel held back and brought up the rear. The look of joy he had seen on Belinda's face when she'd entered the barn and discovered the surprise her children had planned for her caused Herschel to be filled with happiness too. Oh, what he wouldn't give to be part of a family like this.

If I were married to Belinda. . . But it's too soon in our relationship to be speaking of that to her. I wouldn't want to say anything that might scare her off. Besides, I have no idea how she feels about me. He pulled his fingers through the back of his hair. *Sure wish I could ask, but it would be too bold, and Belinda might think I was trying to push her into a relationship she isn't ready for or may not even want.*

In addition to his desire to respect Belinda's feelings, Herschel was concerned about his rival. A man like Monroe, with good looks, charm, and plenty of money, might succeed in winning Belinda's heart.

As Herschel drew closer to the house, he paused and looked around the yard. Despite Amy dealing with pregnancy and babysitting Sylvia's children sometimes six days a week, the young woman managed to find the time to keep her lovely flowerbeds from being overrun by weeds. *She must get up early in the mornings to do it, or maybe Jared helps out. I was smart to rent this house to them,* Herschel thought as he stepped onto the porch. *It's clear that they've been maintaining it well.*

When Herschel entered the house, he hung his straw hat on the coat rack in the entryway. Jared, Henry, and Ezekiel's hats were there too.

Amy asked everyone to wash up and meet in the dining room, where she'd placed the ingredients for haystack on an extended side table positioned on one side of the room.

A short time later, everyone gathered around, with the adults at the longer dining-room table and the children at a smaller folding table. Belinda's two youngest grandchildren were seated in high chairs.

When Jared announced it was time for prayer, Herschel bowed his head, along with the others. *Dear Lord,* he prayed, *please bless this food and the hands that prepared it. Bless those who are gathered in this room. And most of all, give Belinda a special blessing, for she is certainly a woman who follows after You.*

The evening went by too quickly, and Belinda enjoyed every moment of her birthday celebration. Today had turned out better than she could have imagined. Still full from supper, she could barely eat the piece of birthday cake Sylvia had cut and put on her plate.

Belinda mentioned the work Amy had done to make the evening happen, but her daughter brushed the compliment aside. "I can't take all the credit. Sylvia came over yesterday evening when you thought she went to visit Lenore Smucker. She helped me clean the house, baked your birthday cake, and prepped most of the ingredients for our haystack meal. She's also the one who got in touch with Ezekiel about hiring a driver to bring them here so they could be part of the celebration."

Belinda gave Amy a hug. "I appreciate everything you both did to make tonight possible."

"Are ya ready to open your birthday presents, Grandma?" Angela Mary tugged on the sleeve of Belinda's dress.

Belinda tweaked the young girl's nose. "I most certainly am."

"Why don't you open ours first?" Ezekiel handed Belinda a box wrapped in pink paper. "Sure hope you'll like what we got for you."

Belinda pulled the paper off and opened the lid. A pretty teapot with red roses on it was cushioned in tissue paper. Also in the box was a tin filled with mint-flavored teabags—Belinda's favorite kind. She smiled. "Danki, Ezekiel, Michelle, and grandchildren."

"We chose that teapot because we know how much you like roses," Michelle responded.

"Yes, I certainly do."

Next came a gift from Amy and Jared. Belinda was pleased to discover a plastic tote filled with material in various colors. "Danki. These pieces of cloth will come in handy the next time I need to make a new dress or apron."

"Here's a gift from me, Dennis, and Henry." Sylvia handed Belinda a box covered with bird-designed wrapping paper. "There's a picture inside too that Rachel colored with the help of her big brother." Sylvia placed her hand on top of Allen's head.

When Belinda opened the box, the children's drawing was on top, so she pulled it out first. "Well, isn't this nice? It's a picture of a robin, right?" She reached out and touched Rachel's arm, and then Allen's.

"Amschel!" Rachel declared.

Allen bobbed his head and spoke in Pennsylvania Dutch. "It's a robin all right."

Everyone laughed.

"Did you see what else is in the box?" Dennis questioned.

Belinda reached inside and withdrew a pair of binoculars. With a slight tilt of her head, she looked at her eldest daughter.

"You enjoy feeding the birds that come into your yard, so we thought you might like to take up bird-watching," Sylvia explained.

"That's right, Mom," Henry interjected. "Just think how much fun it'll be when we go on picnics this spring and throughout the summer. "You, Dennis, Sylvia, and I all have field glasses to look through now, so you can officially become a bird-watcher."

Belinda had never considered taking up bird-watching, but thought it might be kind of fun, and she didn't want to disappoint the three people who had chipped in on this gift. "Danki," she said with enthusiasm as she held the binoculars up for everyone to see. "I'll be eager to try them out."

"Here's my present." Herschel handed Belinda a small gift bag. "It's not much compared to the rest of your gifts, but I hope you'll like it."

Belinda reached inside and withdrew an alarm clock.

"It plays a hymn, instead of waking you with an irritating beep, beep." Herschel gave her one of his shy grins. "I have one, and waking up to Christian music helps to put me in a good mood before I get out of bed."

"Thank you, Herschel." Belinda smiled at him. "What a thoughtful gift. I'm sure I'll enjoy waking up to the inspirational music too."

"Hey, Mom, sorry for the change of subject," Ezekiel interjected, "but is it okay if we go home with you tonight and then spend a couple of days?"

"Of course." Belinda's cheeks grew warm with pleasure. "You're welcome to stay as long as you like."

Angela Mary hopped up and down. "We're goin' to Grandma's house to spend the night!"

Belinda scooped the little girl onto her lap. "And tomorrow you can visit me in the greenhouse."

"It's not just our daughter you'll be visiting, Mom," Ezekiel said. "I'm planning to help Sylvia and Henry so you can take the day off to enjoy all four of your *kinskinner.*"

Belinda released a gratifying sigh. "That would be wunderbaar, Son."

"How are things going for you these days?" Ezekiel asked as he and Henry fed the livestock in the barn the following morning.

"Not that great."

"How come?"

Henry kicked a clump of straw beneath his feet and closed the bag of oats they'd just given the horses. He wished he could share his frustrations over the vandalism that had gone on since their loved ones died, but Mom would be upset if he said anything. He'd also like to mention his decision to try and figure out who was behind the terrible things that had been done, but that was also out of the question.

"What's bugging you, Henry?" Ezekiel put both hands on his hips. "Come on. . .out with it now."

"Umm. . . Well, one of the things bothering me right now is that our mamm has two suitors."

"I assume you're referring to Herschel and Monroe?"

"Jah." Henry removed his hat and swatted at an irritating fly that began buzzing around his head. "If something isn't done soon, one of those men is likely to talk her into marrying him."

"Would that be such a bad thing, Henry?"

"Jah."

"How come?"

"Because Mom's still in love with Dad, and she don't need another husband."

"Maybe she wants one. Did you ever think of that?"

Henry shook his head vigorously. "I don't see why."

Ezekiel put his hand on Henry's shoulder. "Our mother might want the companionship that goes with marriage. She may also develop strong feelings for one of the men. If she does choose to remarry, we should be happy for her."

Henry's shoulders slumped as he dropped his gaze to the floor.

"Don't think I can. The thought of her gettin' married again makes me feel *grank*."

"That's *lecherich*. You should not feel sick if our mamm falls in love and chooses to get married again."

Henry looked up at his brother and frowned. "It's not ridiculous. I have a right to feel this way, and nothin' you say is gonna change my mind. Anyway, there's been enough changes around here for me to last a lifetime."

Henry left the horse's stall, poured some food into the cats' dish, and stormed out of the barn. *Sure hope Ezekiel doesn't say anything more about this while we're working in the greenhouse today. I can't believe he thinks it's okay for Mom to be courted by another man—let alone two! Doesn't he care how this affects me?*

Belinda smiled as she stood behind Angela Mary and Allen, watching as they drew pictures and colored them in. Michelle was in the living room with Rachel and Vernon, keeping them occupied with some age-appropriate toys. Amy had stayed home today, since Michelle had mentioned at the party last night that she'd be happy to keep an eye on Sylvia's children. Belinda could have watched them, but with Michelle here, it gave her the opportunity to bake some cookies for everyone to enjoy. She also relished this chance to be with all of her grandchildren.

"Your pictures look nice." Belinda put one hand on each of the children's shoulders.

"Danki," Allen and Angela Mary said in unison.

"How would both of you like to walk down the driveway with me so I can get the mail?" Belinda asked.

"Okay." Again, the children spoke at the same time.

Belinda bit back a chuckle. She didn't want Angela Mary or Allen to think she was laughing at them. "When we come back to the house, who wants to help me bake some oatmeal cookies with raisins?"

"I do! I do!" The children clapped their hands.

"All right then, let's head out the front door."

Virginia looked both ways before heading across the road to get her mail. She'd no more than stepped up to her mailbox when Belinda showed up with two young children—a girl and a boy. The boy she recognized, because she'd seen him playing outside several times and had met him personally the evening she and Earl had eaten supper at Belinda's. She didn't think she'd seen the girl before, but she was a cute little thing with rosy cheeks and braided reddish-brown hair.

"Hello, Virginia." Belinda smiled. "How are you this fine spring morning?"

"Doin' okay. How about you?"

"Very well. I'm privileged to have my son Ezekiel and his family visiting with us for a few days. Today my eldest son is taking my place in the greenhouse so I can spend more time with my grandchildren."

"How nice." Virginia reached down and rubbed her throbbing leg. She'd left her cane in the house and wished she had it right now. Not that it took away the pain she often felt in her bum leg, but it did offer some support when she walked.

"You've met Sylvia's son, Allen, already, and this is Ezekiel's daughter." Belinda gestured to the girl. "Her name is Angela Mary."

"Pretty name." Virginia opened her mailbox and took out the contents. *She's a cute girl. It's a shame these kids will have to grow up in such a sheltered environment. I wonder when they get older if they might decide not to join the Amish church, like some of those Amish young people I saw on that reality TV show some time ago.*

"When we get back to the house, we're going to bake cookies. You're welcome to come over in a few hours and have some," Belinda said. "Or I could bring them over to your house."

"Thanks anyway, but I'm trying to watch my weight these days." Virginia gave her stomach a few pats.

"Okay, but if you change your mind, let me know. Perhaps your husband would like some cookies."

"Earl's on a diet too." *Or at least he should be.* "Well, have a nice day." Virginia turned and limped to the other side of the road.

When she entered her house and took a seat on the couch to go through the mail, Virginia thought about her own childhood and what a rebellious teenager she had been. She'd grown up as an only child in a dysfunctional home and gotten married to the first man who asked, so she could get away from her parents. But getting married hadn't changed much of anything in Virginia's life. Her first husband had been physically and mentally abusive, and she'd been relieved when he died. Until Virginia met Earl, she'd never felt truly loved. Even with her husband's quirks and sometimes stubborn ways, she felt certain that he loved her.

"Although my marriage to Earl is better than the first one," Virginia mumbled, "I'd give almost anything to have even one grandchild right now. At least then I'd have someone besides Goldie to dote over."

Tears escaped Virginia's eyes, splattering onto the envelope she held in her hand. *Guess I need to quit feeling sorry for myself and find something sensible to do. Maybe I'll give my friend Stella a call and see how things are going in Chicago. That would be better than sitting around here giving in to unwanted tears that won't change a thing.*

Chapter 28

Belinda stood on the back porch, looking at the birds in their yard through her new binoculars. She spotted a baby robin and watched it for a while. The homely little bird couldn't fly well yet, but it wouldn't be long before it would be soaring from tree to tree in her yard.

Belinda reflected on the wonderful birthday she'd had with her whole family there to celebrate. She looked forward to Ezekiel, Michelle, and the children coming back for Sylvia and Dennis's wedding in October.

Before going home, Ezekiel had mentioned that if they could get away, he and his family might come sooner—maybe when Amy and Jared's baby was born. Otherwise, they would come a few days before the wedding so they could help with the preparations.

Shifting gears again, Belinda focused the lenses of her field glasses on something else in the yard, and her mouth opened slightly. So many goldfinches flew toward the new feeders Henry had put up recently, it looked like a bunch of leaves falling from the trees. She watched in awe for several seconds before going back into the house to help with breakfast. Today was likely to be busy in the greenhouse again, and this evening was her promised date with Monroe. She was eager to see where the special place was that he said he'd be taking her for supper.

Belinda was almost to the door when a vehicle pulled in. She turned and watched as Amy got out of her driver's car and began walking toward the house.

"I hope I'm not late," Amy said after she joined Belinda on the porch. "I got up a little later than planned and it set me back a bit."

"Not a problem." Belinda gave her daughter a hug. "We haven't had breakfast yet."

"Oh good. Guess I wasn't as late as I thought."

"You're welcome to join us at the table. Sylvia's fixing pannekuche at Allen's request."

"That little man does enjoy pancakes." Amy grinned. "Jared and I only had toast and tea this morning. His driver picked him up early to bid on a job in Lancaster, so there wasn't time to fix a big breakfast."

"Then you definitely need some pancakes." Belinda opened the door for Amy, allowing her to go in first, and then she stepped in behind her. Oh, how she would miss seeing her daughter every day once the baby came, but she understood the importance of Amy staying home to be a full-time mother.

When Henry entered the phone shack and shut the door, he drew in a couple of deep breaths to steady his nerves. Mom had asked him to go out and check for messages, but he'd gotten waylaid until now. On the walk down the driveway earlier, he'd discovered a whole bunch of nails had been scattered about. Henry felt certain they had not been there the evening before when he and Blackie played fetch. Someone had obviously come onto their property during the night and dumped out the nails.

Since the greenhouse would be open for business in less than an hour, Henry had gone to their storage shed for a cardboard box to put the nails in. It had taken him awhile to gather all the nails. He probably should have gone up to the house and asked Mom or Sylvia to come out and help, but he'd done it himself. This gave Henry an opportunity to check for clues. But the only thing he'd found were some shoe prints, which could have been anyone's, since some local people came to the greenhouse on foot.

Wish I knew who threw all these nails out. Henry rubbed his damp forehead and set the cardboard box on the counter inside the phone shed. *No doubt it was the same person who did all the other destructive things.*

Henry eyed the blinking light on the answering machine, indicating that some messages had come in.

His finger came down on the button and he listened to the first message. It was from Ezekiel, calling to see how they were all doing.

Henry paused the answering machine. *I wonder what my bruder would have to say if I told him our mamm's going out to some fancy place with Monroe this evening. Maybe Ezekiel wouldn't care. He might think it's fine and dandy that Mom's acting like a teenage girl with two fellows hanging around all the time, trying to impress her.*

Henry stared at the box of nails. *Bet he'd really be upset if I told him about these. Sure don't like keeping secrets from my brother.*

Henry wrote Ezekiel's message on the tablet but froze when he heard the next one: "When are you going to listen? I told you to get out. You have until the end of the year, and there will not be too many more warnings."

The voice sounded muffled, but Henry understood every word. He listened again and wrote the message down exactly as he'd heard it. Without waiting to hear any other messages, he grabbed the tablet and the box of nails and flung the shed door open. He needed to share this with Mom right away. Maybe now she'd wake up and call the sheriff.

Belinda had entered the greenhouse and was about to put the OPEN sign in place when Henry rushed in. One look at his sweaty, flushed skin and wide eyes and she knew something was wrong.

"What is it, Son? You look like you've encountered a *schpuck*."

"Not a ghost, Mom, but more *druwwel*."

Belinda's throat constricted. "What kind of trouble?"

Henry showed her the box. "I found all these *neggel* in the driveway and had to take the time to pick them all up. Sure wouldn't want some car to drive over the nails and end up with a flat tire."

She blinked several times. "I wonder how they got there."

"I'm pretty sure the person who left this message on our answering machine threw the nails all over our driveway sometime during the night." Henry handed the notepad to Belinda.

She barely took notice of the message from Ezekiel. It was the second message that caught her attention. "Was the voice muffled, or could you hear the person who spoke clearly?"

"It was muffled, but I understood every word they said." With the back of his hand, Henry wiped the sweat off his forehead. "Whoever's been doing all these things wants us gone. They expect us to get out by the end of the year."

The back of Belinda's neck prickled. "I can read, Son. You don't have to repeat what's written on the tablet."

"Sorry, I was just trying to make sure you got the point." Henry pointed to the nails. "Are you ready to call the sheriff now?"

She shook her head as determination welled in her chest. "We will not be run off our property because someone, for some reason, dislikes us. Involving the sheriff would make all of this public knowledge, because I'm sure the word would get out." She made little circles on her forehead, hoping to ward off a headache. "The thing we have to do is hold steady and not give in to this person's demands. We must be steadfast in our prayers and trust God to protect us and our property." She stepped closer to Henry and put one hand on his shoulder. "Let's keep this latest event to ourselves, okay? I don't want to upset your sisters."

Henry sighed. "I won't say anything to Amy or Sylvia, but I will keep a closer watch on things, even if it means sleeping outside at night until the weather turns cold."

Belinda shook her head. "There's no need for that, but we could let Blackie sleep in your room, since it faces the front of the house. If anyone enters our yard, the dog's bound to alert us with his super-loud barks."

"Okay, if that's what you wanna do, but I'm still gonna keep my eyes and ears open anytime I'm awake."

"Good idea, and I shall do the same."

Belinda turned the OPEN sign over and took a seat behind the counter after she instructed Henry to take the box of nails outside to the shed. She sat looking at the tablet he had brought in from the phone shed until Sylvia came in. Belinda quickly tore off the page with the messages, folded it, and put it under the front band of her apron.

"Looks like there are no customers yet," Sylvia commented.

"Right, but I'm sure we'll have people here soon."

Sylvia stepped up to the counter. "Did Henry come back from the phone shed? Dennis was supposed to call with a message about what time he'd be by to pick me and the kinner up so he can show us the colt that was born two days ago."

"Henry did come back," Belinda responded. "But he made no mention of a message from Dennis."

"Maybe I'll go see. He may have called and left a message after Henry came out of the phone shed."

"If you'll take my place behind the counter, I'll go check for you. I need to make a few phone calls anyway." The last thing Belinda wanted was for her daughter to hear the threatening message.

"Sure, no problem." Sylvia came around and seated herself on the stool as soon as Belinda stood up. "Where's Henry?" she asked. "I figured he'd be in here by now."

"He was, but he went out to the storage shed to put something away for me. He should be back soon I expect."

"Okay." Sylvia picked up the tablet Belinda had left on the counter. "Isn't this the one we keep in the phone shed to write messages on?"

"You're right, it is. Henry brought it in when he told me that Ezekiel had called to see how we're all doing. I'll call him back while I'm in the phone shed." Belinda took the notepad and started for the door, glad she'd torn off the page with the messages on it. She'd barely opened the door when Maude stepped in.

"Ya got anything set out in here to eat?" The old woman pressed a gnarly hand against her stomach. "There ain't much at my place for breakfast 'cause those fat hens you gave me haven't laid any eggs for a couple of days."

Belinda felt compassion for Maude. She couldn't imagine what it must be like for her to live all alone and in such poor conditions. It was a wonder she could even survive.

"I don't have anything here at the moment, but if you'll wait in the greenhouse a few minutes, I'll bring you something from the house."

"I can stay here." Maude lifted both hands and let them fall to her sides. "There ain't no other place I need to go anyways, so I'll just wander around here till you come back with some food."

Belinda glanced at Sylvia. She had a pretty good guess of what her daughter was thinking by the way her gaze flicked upward.

When Maude wandered down one of the aisles, Belinda returned to the counter and whispered to Sylvia, "I'll be back soon with something for Maude, and then I'll check the answering machine in the phone shed."

After Belinda gave Maude a box filled with a dozen cookies, several apples, a loaf of bread, a package of cheese, and a jar of honey, she hurried down the driveway to the phone shed. She would listen to all the messages, including the threatening one Henry had told her about, and then she'd make a few calls. One would be to Ezekiel, letting him know they were all fine, and the other would be to Monroe. After beginning her day with such stress, there was no way she could go out to supper with him this evening. Undoubtedly she would be thinking about the threat off and on all day, and by this evening she would not only feel tired but also wouldn't be good company. The best thing to do was cancel right away and make plans to see Monroe some other time.

Belinda clicked the button to retrieve messages. The first one was from Ezekiel, just as Henry had said. Next, came the muffled threatening call, which sent a chill up Belinda's spine. She deleted that message before moving on. A potential customer called, asking if they had any birdbaths for sale. The last message was from Dennis, telling Sylvia that he would be there around five thirty that evening. He said he'd take Sylvia and the children out for supper first and then head over to his place to see the colt.

Belinda wrote Dennis's message on the tablet for Sylvia and called Ezekiel. She left a message saying everyone was fine and she hoped that he and his family were doing well too. After that, she called the lady who'd asked about buying a birdbath, and finally she punched in Monroe's number. She hoped he wouldn't answer and that she could simply leave a message, but as luck would have it, Monroe picked up and said, "Hello."

"Good morning, Monroe. It's Belinda."

"It's good to hear your voice. What a nice way to begin my day." He spoke in a bubbly tone.

Belinda fanned her face with the tablet. *When he hears what I have to say, his mood will probably change.*

"I called to let you know that I'm not feeling up to going anywhere tonight, so we'll have to postpone having supper out." She sat quietly, waiting for his response.

"Are you grank?"

"No, I'm not sick. Things have been quite hectic around here this morning and I've developed a *koppweh*." It wasn't a lie. She truly did have a headache.

"Sorry to hear that, but it might be better by this evening. Maybe relaxing and enjoying a tasty meal at a nice restaurant is what you need."

Belinda clenched and unclenched her fingers. This was not going well. It would have been easier if she could have left Monroe a message. "When I get a bad headache, it rarely gets better until I've gone to bed."

"Why don't you go up to the house right now and take a nap? Then by the time I get there with my driver to pick you up. . ."

"Sorry, Monroe, but I need to cancel."

Several seconds went by before he spoke again. "Is something wrong? Have I done anything to upset you? Is that why you don't want to go out with me?"

Belinda pressed her lips together in a grimace. *Why does he have to be so persistent? And now he's caused me to feel guilty. Would it be better if I forced myself to go out for supper with him, or should I stick with what I first said?*

"Have I done something to upset you?" Monroe asked again.

"I am not upset. I'm just not feeling my best, and I would not be good company tonight."

"I understand if you're not feeling up to it. I only hope that when we make plans again you won't need to cancel."

"I hope not too, Monroe, and I appreciate your understanding." Belinda closed her eyes briefly.

"Goodbye for now. I'll talk to you soon."

When Belinda hung up, she sagged against the chair. Perhaps the next time Monroe contacted her, she'd feel better about things.

Chapter 29

Throughout the rest of April and the first half of May, Blackie slept upstairs in Henry's room. Not once had he awakened Henry with barking, nor had any more vandalism been done. Mom saw it as a good sign, but Henry figured it was just a calm before the storm. If his mother didn't put her place up for sale and move somewhere else, there was no telling what might happen.

"I've gotta figure out who's responsible for the vandalism, threatening phone calls, and notes," Henry muttered as he put on his protective gear in preparation of checking on the bees and the prospect of gathering more honey. He'd talked to his mother about all this two days ago, and she'd said that if she knew for certain who'd done all the mean things to them, she would either notify the sheriff or try to convince the guilty party not to do any more harm to her property.

Yeah, right. Henry kicked a small stone and sent it flying into the field that bordered their yard. *I don't think anything Mom could say would put a stop to the attacks. Whoever this person is, they need to be fined and put in jail.*

When Belinda left the register and started down aisle 1, she tripped on the end of the hose, nearly losing her balance. "Whew, that was close! I need to do a better job of putting that away so that no one gets hurt." She yawned and recoiled the green tubing out of the walkway.

Belinda figured the reason for her fatigue was because she had lain awake last night thinking about this evening's supper date with Monroe.

She wondered how it would go, trying to keep things on a strictly friendship basis.

Before she'd turned in last night, Belinda had set the musical alarm clock she'd received from Herschel. She thought of him often and his sweet personality. *I had a nice time when we were together for my surprise party. Herschel is so easy to get along with. Even though he's older than Monroe, he keeps himself in good shape, and I've noticed he likes to eat healthy too.*

Belinda smiled while cleaning the dirt left from putting the hose away as she thought once more about the clock Herschel had given her. *I think his gift is perfect, and it's nice to be woken up in the morning by its cheerful songs.*

Since there were no customers at the moment, Belinda walked to the back of the greenhouse where Sylvia had been putting some new plants in place.

"How are things going?" Belinda asked.

"Good. I'm just about done. How are things up front?"

"There are no customers right now, but I'm sure there will be more before the day is out."

"Are you looking forward to your supper date with Monroe this evening?" Sylvia asked.

"It will be nice to eat out, and I really couldn't put off Monroe any longer. He's waited several weeks to take me out, but we've had to put our plans on hold because things have been so hectic around here." Belinda made a sweeping gesture with her hand.

"It's true, Mom, and we're just as busy as we were three weeks ago."

"I know." Belinda yawned. "And I'm as tired as ever. But with Monroe's continued insistence, I felt I had no choice but to go out with him tonight."

"Can I give you some advice?" Sylvia looked directly at Belinda.

"Jah, of course."

"I sense that you're not in love with Monroe."

"That's true."

"So why go out with him at all?"

Belinda dropped her gaze. "I do consider him to be a friend, and friendship should always come first, but falling in love takes time."

"Good point. With me and Toby it wasn't love at first sight. But the more time we spent together, the more we both realized how much we cared for each other. It was the same way for Dennis and me," Sylvia added.

Belinda's shoulders loosened slightly as her tension ebbed. "Guess I need to stop worrying about this and just wait and see how things go." She reached over to pluck a dead bloom off one of the African violets. "What's the latest with the remodeling project on your old house? Has Dennis hired a contractor to do the work, or is he trying to do most of it himself?"

"He's doing the things he feels capable of, but he's had several horses to train of late and doesn't have time for much else."

"Has he considered having a work frolic to help with the remodel?"

"I'm not sure. He hasn't said."

"Probably many people from our community would be willing to help out."

"When Dennis comes over to join me, Henry, and the kinner for supper tonight, I'll mention the idea of a work frolic." Sylvia pointed to the row of plants ahead of them that still needed pruning. "Right now though, I'd better get back to work."

"Same here," Belinda agreed. "I hear a vehicle pulling in, which means another customer to wait on."

"So you and your woman-friend will be going to a fancy restaurant in Lancaster, huh?" Monroe's driver, Bill, glanced over at him and grinned. "Must be a pretty special woman, huh?"

Monroe bobbed his head. "I've been in love with Belinda since I was a teenager."

"But she married someone else, right?"

"Yeah, Vernon King." Monroe's fingers clenched around the brim of his hat, which he'd taken off when he got in Bill's car and placed on his lap. "Belinda's a widow now, and I've been courting her for a while."

"I'm guessing your plan is to marry the woman?"

"Yes."

"Gonna ask her tonight?"

"Nope. It's too soon for that. I'm just layin' the groundwork is all."

Bill chuckled. "I heard someone say once that they didn't think Amish men were romantic, but you're proving them wrong."

"I hope so." Monroe puffed his chest out as he mentally encouraged himself to succeed. He was aware that there were other romantic Amish men, but he didn't believe Herschel Fisher was one of them. During the times Monroe had spent in Herschel's presence, he'd perceived that the quiet man was rather boring. Monroe felt pretty smug about that. He'd convinced himself that after tonight, he would have a definite edge over Belinda's other suitor.

Monroe stared out the window at the passing scenery and smiled. *When Belinda sees how romantic I can be, she is bound to realize that the two of us are meant to be together.*

"I wonder where our mamm and Monroe ended up going for supper this evening." Sylvia passed the steaming bowl of spaghetti over to Henry.

His features tightened as he forked some noodles onto his plate. "I'm not in the mood to talk about Monroe, and I have no idea where they went. Mom's never made any mention of where he planned to take her."

"I don't think she knew. According to her, Monroe was planning to keep it a secret until they arrived at their destination." Sylvia sprinkled some Parmesan cheese over her spaghetti and then wiped a glob of red sauce off Rachel's face. "The only thing I know for sure is that Monroe said it was someplace special."

Henry looked over at Dennis and rolled his eyes. "That Monroe fellow is not the man for our mudder."

Sylvia slid the bowl of spaghetti sauce between them and ladled some onto hers and Rachel's pasta. "I know you aren't a fan of his, and I'm not sure about him either."

Henry remained quiet as he went next and spooned a fair amount onto his plate, and then passed it on to Sylvia's boyfriend.

Dennis glanced at Sylvia then back at Henry. "Not to change the subject or anything, but there's something I wanted to share with both of you."

"What's that?" Henry's tone sounded less than enthusiastic.

"I called the birding hotline this morning and listened to several reports on some local sightings of the ruby-crowned kinglet."

"I'm not familiar with the name. What kind of bird is it?" Sylvia questioned.

"It's a small, teardrop, greenish-gray bird with two white wing bars and a hidden ruby crown."

"Think I read about that species in one of the birding magazines." Henry's eyes brightened as he sat a little straighter. "Isn't it the second smallest bird in the state of Pennsylvania?"

"That's right." Dennis winked at Sylvia. He'd definitely succeeded in catching Henry's attention and altering his mood.

"The ruby-crowned kinglet is usually seen during migration in the spring and fall. You should look for it flitting around thick shrubs that are low to the ground."

"Where does the name *kinglet* come from?" Sylvia asked after she'd given Allen another piece of sourdough bread.

"It's from the Anglo-Saxon word *cyning* or 'king,' which refers to the male's ruby red crown," Dennis explained. "And the *let* part of the word means 'small.'"

"That's quite interesting."

They discussed some other birds Dennis said he had heard about while listening to the birding hotline, and then the topic changed to the prospect of a work frolic to help with the additions being made on Sylvia's old house.

"Things always get done quickly whenever there's a work frolic." Sylvia smiled at Dennis. "You sure can't be expected to remodel our house alone."

He grinned back at her. "I will if I have to, but I think a frolic might be a good way to go."

"I'm sure Jared, as well as Lenore's husband, will be there to help, and I wouldn't be surprised if Herschel and Monroe show up too." She laughed. "If for no other reason than to make an impression on Mom."

"Do you think there's a possibility your mamm could end up marrying one of those fellows?" Dennis helped himself to some bread.

"I don't know. . .anything's feasible. I'm pretty sure both men are hoping Mom will choose soon."

"I'm done eating, and I've heard enough of this conversation." Henry picked up his empty plate and stomped off to the kitchen.

Dennis looked over at Sylvia with raised brows. "I wonder what's wrong with your bruder. Normally he likes to sit and talk whenever I'm here."

"He's upset because Mom has two suitors. The idea that she might end up marrying anyone doesn't set well with Henry."

"No one can ever take his daed's place," Dennis said. "I understand that quite well. Thankfully, my mamm has never shown any interest in a prospective husband since my dad died. But if she had, I'd probably have a hard time with it too."

Sylvia heaved a big sigh. "I'm not thrilled with the idea of my mother getting remarried either, but if I had to choose which man she would marry, it would not be Monroe."

Lancaster, Pennsylvania

The minute Belinda entered the Greenfield Restaurant with Monroe she knew why he'd referred to it as special. The main dining room, which she assumed was where they'd be seated, offered a cozy fireplace, and that suited Belinda just fine, since it had become a bit chilly this evening. However, as their hostess walked with Belinda and Monroe, she did not escort them to a table in the dining room. Instead, she led them downstairs to a table near the wine cellar. "I'll give you two a chance to look over the menu and then your waitress will be here shortly to take your orders."

"Thank you." Monroe pulled out a chair for Belinda and waited until she was seated before seating himself across from her.

Such a gentleman, Belinda thought. *He does know how to court a woman.*

"This is the perfect spot for a special occasion." Monroe smiled at Belinda in such a tender fashion that she felt like a young woman on her first date. "That's why I requested it when I made the dinner reservations," he added.

She tipped her head slightly. "What are we celebrating, Monroe? I didn't realize this was a special occasion."

"Anytime is special when we're together. You make my heart sing, Belinda. When I'm with you, I feel like I did when I was a young man and first fell in love with you." He leaned closer. "Don't you feel it too?"

A warm flush spread across Belinda's cheeks, and her fingers trembled as she fumbled with her menu. *How do I respond to that? I can't tell Monroe what he wants to hear. Why has he put me in this awkward position and with no place to hide or escape?*

For a diversion and change of topic, she glanced at her menu. "Some of the entrées are a bit expensive."

"Not a problem. Money is no object, so go ahead and choose whatever you want. And if you'd like an appetizer before the main meal, that's fine and dandy too."

"Maybe I'll just have a *zelaat.*" She pointed to the menu. "The Farmer's Market Salad sounds pretty good."

Monroe shook his head. "No way! You can have a salad anytime. Why don't you order a steak, the grilled pork chop, or one of the seafood items?" He pointed to himself. "Think I might try the South African rock lobster tail."

Belinda scrutinized the listed items some more, until a waitress came to take their order. At that point, Belinda figured she'd better choose something, so she pointed to the grilled petite filet mignon and said, "I'll try this."

The young woman nodded. "How would you like it cooked?"

"Medium-well, please."

"It comes with a fresh tossed salad. Would you like to add some steamed broccoli or fingerling potatoes?"

Belinda shook her head. "No, thank you. Steak and salad will be plenty for me."

The waitress turned to Monroe. "What would you like to order, sir?"

"I'm in the mood for lobster tail."

"That's a good choice. Would you like one or two?"

Monroe chuckled. "If one's good, then two's bound to be better."

Belinda looked at the menu again and noticed that the price for two lobster tails was sixty-eight dollars. In all the times she'd gone out to eat,

Belinda had never spent that much on a single meal. Apparently money was no object for Monroe. Either that or he was simply trying to make an impression on her. And for the moment at least, he truly had.

Just relax and enjoy the evening, Belinda told herself. *It's not every day you get to eat at such a fancy place.* Belinda had to admit, she did feel kind of special this evening.

Chapter 30

Strasburg

By the middle of July, life was busier than ever for Belinda—working in the greenhouse, tending the garden, doing household chores, and socializing. She'd continued to see Herschel and Monroe as regularly as possible during what little free time she had. Her friendship with the men had deepened, but so far, Belinda's feelings had not turned to love.

And maybe they never will, Belinda thought as she guided her horse and buggy in the direction of her dear friend Mary Ruth Lapp's home. The older woman had come home from the hospital a few days before, after a right knee replacement. It was definitely time to drop by and see how Mary Ruth was doing.

Belinda glanced over at Sylvia, sitting on the front seat beside her with Rachel in her lap. Allen sat in the seat behind them, remaining quiet, which was unusual for a boy who often talked nonstop. It was a good thing his sister wasn't sitting next to him, because he'd probably be teasing her all the way to Mary Ruth's house.

"The wind's picked up, and the clouds have darkened," Sylvia spoke up. "I wonder if a summer storm might be coming."

"Could be. It's been dry here of late, so the crops and gardens could use a good dousing of *rege*."

"True. I only hope if it does bring rain that it won't go on for too many days. There's laundry to be done, and I'd prefer to hang things outdoors instead of in the basement."

"Same here, but unfortunately, we don't always get what we want."

Sylvia reached over and placed her hand on Belinda's arm. "I know, Mom. I know."

They rode in silence until the driveway leading to Mary Ruth's home came into view. "Come on, girl," Belinda coaxed, "This is where we make our turn." With the skill from many years of managing a horse and buggy, she guided her mare up the driveway to the hitching rail.

Sylvia placed Rachel on the seat beside Belinda, stepped down, and secured the horse to the rail.

A short time later, they walked with the children up to the house. "I hope you got my message about us coming by this evening," Belinda said when Mary Ruth's granddaughter Lenore greeted them at the door.

"I did, and my grandma has been looking forward to seeing you ever since I told her you'd be coming." Lenore let them in, and after Belinda handed her a container of brownies, she led the way to the living room, where Mary Ruth reclined on the couch with her leg propped on a pillow.

A wide smile graced the older woman's face as she beckoned them to come closer. "It's ever so nice to see you both. Danki for coming over."

Belinda reached down and took her friend's hand. "How are you feeling? Is there much *schmatze*?" She gestured to Mary Ruth's leg.

"To be honest, recovery from the surgery is not without pain, but thanks to the medicine I was given, I'm managing okay." Mary Ruth motioned to the two closest chairs. "Please take a seat so we can visit awhile."

"While you're doing that, I'll go to the kitchen and fix us all a cup of tea." Lenore smiled. "We can enjoy some of the brownies Belinda and Sylvia brought." She looked down at Allen and Rachel, hiding shyly behind their mother. "My kinner are at the kitchen table, coloring pictures. Why don't you two come along and join them?" As usual, Pennsylvania Dutch was spoken to the children.

Allen followed Lenore right away, but Rachel hung back.

"Guess I'd better walk out there with her," Sylvia said. "I'll come back with Lenore when the refreshments are ready. By then, my daughter will be happily coloring with the other children, and probably enjoying a brownie too."

After Sylvia left the room, Belinda pulled a straight-back chair close to the couch. "How long will you be convalescing, Mary Ruth?"

"I'm able to get up and move around with that." Mary Ruth pointed to the walker parked within her reach. "I'll start physical therapy soon, but it'll be several weeks before I'm pronounced to be good as new." The wrinkles in her forehead deepened. "If my dear husband was still alive, he'd probably keep me under his watchful eye, afraid I'd try to do too much too soon."

"I bet he would."

"So tell me, what's new with you?" Mary Ruth placed her hand on Belinda's knee.

"I've been working in the greenhouse, helping with household chores, and trying to keep up with the weeds in our vegetable garden. Sylvia's a big help, but since she began working in the greenhouse, she's just as busy as I am."

"Sounds like you have your hands full." Mary Ruth's voice lowered. "I hear tell you have two eager suitors hanging out at your house a lot these days. Has one of them stolen your heart or are you still trying to decide?"

It's funny how much she knows when we haven't spoken to each other for a spell. I'd say the grapevine in this community is healthy and strong. Belinda moistened her lips with the tip of her tongue and swallowed a couple of times. She'd rather not talk about this, but knowing Mary Ruth, she wouldn't stop questioning until she had some answers. "They're both quite different, but each has some good qualities that I admire."

"Enough to marry one of them if they should ask?" Mary Ruth tipped her head.

I think my friend here would make Monroe a good companion. They both seem to possess the strong desire to make me feel pressured. Belinda shuffled her feet against the hardwood floor while rubbing the back of her warm neck. It was embarrassing to be put on the spot, but it was just like Mary Ruth to ask lots of questions and say whatever was on her mind.

"If you'd rather not talk about it, I understand." Mary Ruth reached up and plumped the pillow behind her head. "It's really none of my business."

Belinda leaned closer and whispered, "When I'm with Monroe I feel like a young woman enjoying her boyfriend's attention."

"And Herschel? How do you feel when you're with him?"

Belinda lowered her hand and gave her dress sleeve a little tug. "He makes me feel calm and relaxed."

Mary Ruth's brows moved up and down as a playful smile spread across her face. "Well, there you have it—all you need to do is decide whether you want to spend the rest of your life enjoying your husband's attention or feeling calm and relaxed."

Belinda lowered her hand. *If it were only that simple. And who said anything about a husband?*

Henry wandered around the yard with Blackie at his side. It was kind of nice having Mom, Sylvia, and the kinner gone for a few hours. It gave him time for some things he wanted to do without having to worry about someone asking him to do something he'd rather not do. That seemed to have become his way of life since his dad and brother died.

"Work. . .work. . .work. . ." Henry muttered as he picked up a stick and tossed it for Blackie.

The dog took off on a run and came back soon with the piece of wood in his mouth. He promptly dropped it on the ground and, with tail wagging, looked up at Henry as if to say, "Throw it again."

"Enough already! We've done it too many times. Go lie down now, so I can sit and think awhile." Ignoring the stick, Henry pointed to the porch and headed that way himself. His faithful dog followed.

Blackie flopped onto the porch with a grunt, and Henry went inside to get them both some water. When he returned, he placed a plastic bowl, brimming full of water, beside the dog and took a seat on the porch swing with the glass he'd filled with ice and cold water.

Henry took a drink and grinned when Blackie began lapping thirstily from the bowl. It had been a hot, humid day, and now the wind had begun to blow, while the sky darkened with ominous-looking clouds. Off in the distance Henry heard the rumble of thunder. He watched the sky in anticipation of a bright flash appearing. Not long after, it happened.

"Oh, wow. . .that was a good one!" Henry heard Blackie's whimper. Soon a loud boom echoed across the landscape. The wind picked up, and the trees swayed even more. Henry felt the temperature drop and smelled the essence of rain in the air. He watched another flash, and not long after, the crack of thunder boomed.

Blackie got up and came over to Henry. "Aw, it's okay, boy. I'll take care of you." He combed his hand down the dog's back a few times and patted him.

Henry took another drink and set his glass on the small table next to the swing. *Oh boy, I bet we're in for a summer storm, and from the looks of that sky, it could be a bad one. Sure hope it doesn't hit hard—at least not till Mom, Sylvia, and the kinner get home.*

Belinda clung tightly to her horse's reins as a torrential rain poured from the sky, making it difficult to see out the buggy's front window, even with Sylvia working the hand-operated window wipers.

The poor horse looked soaked to the bone as it pulled them home. Belinda felt bad for the animal. It seemed as though they were right in the middle of this terrible storm.

A gust of harsh wind rocked the buggy as a clap of thunder boomed. Rachel and Allen both screamed.

"Maybe we should pull over and wait the storm out." Sylvia's voiced trembled. "The children are frightened, and the rain's coming down harder. The wind's grown stronger too. If we keep going, your buggy might topple over."

Speaking in short, strong sentences, Belinda said, "We're not far from home. We need to press on. If the weather gets worse, we'll be safer there."

Sylvia turned in her seat and spoke in a reassuring tone. "It's okay, little ones. Soon we'll be back at Grandma's."

As they continued on, although the sky had darkened, Belinda saw some trees on her side of the road that had been uprooted. If they didn't get home soon, there was a good chance her carriage could be upended.

Dear Lord, she prayed, *Please help both me and my horse to stay calm, and protect us from harm. Also please be with others who are out on the road this night too.*

As Belinda's prayer ended, a sheet of lightning lit up the sky, enabling her to see several feet ahead. To Belinda's surprise, she saw someone bent over and appearing to be struggling against the wind. Upon closer look, it became clear that the person was Maude.

Belinda leaned closer to Sylvia. "We need to stop and give her a ride. On foot, it'll be a miracle if she makes it back to her shanty in one piece."

"It's certainly the right thing to do," Sylvia responded, "but listen to my kinner and their terrified whimpers. They might be as afraid of Maude as they are the storm."

"Rachel wasn't scared when Maude took her to the shanty last year. I'm sure they'll be fine." With no further discussion, Belinda guided the horse and buggy to the side of the road. Although opening the door of the driver's side meant she'd be drenched within seconds, Belinda did it anyway. "Maude, it's Belinda King!" she shouted against the howling wind. "We've stopped to give you a ride to your home."

Maude didn't have to be asked a second time. Sylvia got out of the carriage and climbed in back with the children. Then Belinda instructed Maude to take the seat up front beside her.

"What are you doing out on a night like this?" Belinda asked once she got the horse moving again.

Maude looked over at her. "I could ask you the same thing."

She smiled. "Good point, but why don't you explain first?"

Maude shifted on the seat. "I went for a walk. Didn't realize bad weather was comin'."

When Maude spoke, Belinda had to hold her breath, for the pungent odor of garlic permeated the buggy. It was so bad Belinda figured the obnoxious smell was not only coming from Maude's breath but also leaching out of her body. No doubt this near-homeless woman had eaten a lot of garlic, either for the sake of her health or to ward off insects.

I wonder if Maude's been taking garlic from my garden. Belinda had noticed that it seemed to be disappearing rather quickly, but she figured Sylvia might have picked more than normal to use in upcoming suppers.

"So how 'bout you folks? What are you doin' out on a night like this?" Maude bumped Belinda's arm with her elbow.

"We were visiting some friends, but the weather didn't turn bad until we began our journey home."

The elderly woman made a clicking noise with her tongue. "I see."

Rain continued to pelt Belinda's buggy as stronger winds made it more difficult to stay on the road. When Belinda's mailbox, near the beginning of her driveway, came into view she directed her horse to go right.

"You turned too soon." Maude leaned closer to Belinda. "My little cabin is farther up the road."

"I'm aware of that, Maude, but the weather has turned so frightful, I don't think we should chance going any farther."

"Okay, well then, I'll get out and walk the rest of the way." Maude coughed a couple of times, making the odor of garlic permeate the carriage even more.

Belinda reached over to touch the woman's arm. "If the storm gets worse, you may not make it to your place. I would like you to come to my house and sleep in the guest room tonight."

Even with the wind howling, Belinda heard Sylvia's intake of breath from the back of the buggy. However, Belinda held firm in her decision. *Surely my daughter must realize the importance of helping out a neighbor, or anyone else, during a time such as this.*

Chapter 31

Henry had settled into a chair in the living room with the latest birding magazine, when Sylvia and her children entered the room with wide eyes and flushed faces.

Sylvia stopped in front of his chair. "How can you sit here so calmly when there's such a wicked storm outside? Haven't you seen the damage it's doing?"

"Where's Mom?" Henry asked without answering his sister's questions.

"She's outside trying to get the horse unhitched and put in the barn. Maude's with her."

His brows shot up. "Maude? What's she doin' here?"

"She was walking and got caught in the storm, so we picked her up and Mom decided to bring her here to spend the night."

Henry's mouth dropped open. "Why would she do something like that?"

"She feels sorry for Maude and wants to do right by the poor woman," Sylvia whispered. "Now would you please go out there and help her so they can get inside where it's warm and dry? While you're doing that, I need to get my little ones put to bed."

"Okay." Henry set down his magazine and stood. He didn't mind helping to put the horse away, but the thought of Maude spending the night in their home didn't sit well with him. His finger's clenched. *Just a few hours in this house and that old woman might steal anything she can get her hands on.*

Henry wished he could stay up all night to keep an eye on things, but his mother would never go for that. *Think I may sneak downstairs with Blackie and sleep on the couch after Mom, Sylvia, and Maude go to bed. That way, if the old woman comes out of the guest room and tries anything funny, the dog will let me know, and I can hopefully catch her in the act.*

The following morning, when Belinda woke up, the first thing she did was go to her bedroom window and look out. The sky was overcast, but at least it wasn't raining. The harsh winds had subsided too. However, the sight that greeted Belinda was disturbing. Two of the smaller trees in their yard had been uprooted. It made her feel sad, because those were the ones Vernon had planted the same year he'd died.

As she continued to scan the property it became apparent that broken branches lay scattered across the yard and one section of their fence had been knocked down. It would take some doing to get it all cleaned up, and it certainly wouldn't happen today.

Belinda stepped away from the window. *I can only imagine the state of other properties around our area. I pray no one was injured due to the storm that went through here last night.*

She hurried to get dressed so she could check and see if any damage had been done to the house.

When Belinda passed through the living room, she was surprised to see Henry sleeping on the couch, with Blackie lying on the floor nearby.

"Wake up, Henry." She shook his arm.

Henry rolled over and opened his eyes. "Morning, Mom."

Her brows furrowed. "Why are you and your hund sleeping down here?"

Henry sat up and yawned as he averted his gaze. "I. . .um. . .thought it would be good if I slept on the couch."

"How come?"

He pointed in the direction of the guest room down the hall.

She glanced that way then looked back at him. "What are you talking about?"

"I wanted to make sure our overnight guest didn't help herself to anything during the night." Henry spoke in a near whisper. "Don't think she came out of her room while I was sleeping though, 'cause I'm sure I woulda heard her."

Belinda's jaw tightened as she folded her arms. "Why must you be so suspicious?"

"Because Maude's given us plenty of reasons not to trust her."

"We'll talk more about this later. Right now, while I start breakfast, I'd like you to get dressed and go outside. Last night's storm left our yard in a terrible mess, and a good deal of the debris is blocking the parking lot of the greenhouse." Belinda bit down on her bottom lip. "If the building is still standing, that is."

Henry got up, grabbed his binoculars, and hurried over to the living-room window. "Wow, Mom, you're right, the yard is a mess, but from here, I can't tell much about the greenhouse except that it's still there."

She sighed softly. "That's a relief. Even so, I'd like you to walk down there and check on things. For today, at least, we'll need to keep the Closed sign on the greenhouse door. There is too much work to be done in the yard today, and I don't want anyone to get hurt with all the mess scattered around. Also, please take a look at all sides of our house," Belinda added.

"Okay, I will let Blackie out right now, and then I'll get dressed."

"At least the damage from the bad weather we had last night isn't due to another senseless attack," Belinda stated. "There have been no more incidents for quite a while, so I think maybe whoever did those things may have given up or realized what they were doing was wrong."

Henry shook his head. "I'm not sure about that. I think the person behind the attacks is waiting to see if we'll take his or her threats seriously and put our place up for sale."

Belinda's thoughts raced as she remembered the last threatening message they'd received. She hoped and prayed the person behind the message had changed his or her mind, because she had no plans to sell her home or the greenhouse she and Vernon had worked so hard to establish.

Henry tapped Belinda's shoulder. "Mom, did you hear what I said?"

"Jah, I did, but I don't want to talk about this right now." She glanced toward the guestroom door, noticing that it was partially open. "While you're outside, I'll get breakfast started and check on Maude. She'll no doubt be hungry and ready to eat."

Henry opened his mouth as if he wanted to say something more, but instead he called his dog and let him outside.

Belinda shook her head. *That boy of mine; I can't believe he slept down here to keep an eye on Maude.*

She moved across the hall to the guestroom and rapped on the door. When there was no response, Belinda pushed the door open a little farther and peaked in. The bed had been made, and the nightgown Belinda had given the old woman to wear last night lay at the foot of the bed, but there was no sign of Maude.

"Well, for goodness' sake." Belinda hurried down the hall to the bathroom to see if Maude may have gone there, but that door was open and no one was inside.

Belinda checked the kitchen next, but Maude wasn't there either. When she spotted a note on the table, she slipped on her reading glasses and read it aloud: "Thanks for the soft bed to sleep in. I helped myself to four cookies and an apple before I left. —Maude."

Belinda felt a tight sensation in her throat. *I wish there was something more I could do to help that poor woman. I can't imagine what it must be like to live in that old shack with barely any furnishings and no family around. There must be something our Amish community can do to help her out.*

Belinda tapped her chin. *The next time I see Maude, I'll ask her some questions. Surely she must have some family somewhere who would be willing to take her in. If not, then I'll speak to some of our church members and see who might be willing to do something to help out.*

🐦

"Would you look at that mess!" Virginia pointed out the kitchen window at their backyard. "That horrible storm we had last night left our yard in shambles."

Earl set his coffee cup down and joined her at the window. "We did lose a lot of tree branches, but at least my garage roof is still intact." He turned to face Virginia. "I'll pick up the larger branches when I get home from work this evening. In the meantime, maybe you can gather the smaller ones."

Virginia's fists tightened and her fingers curled into the palms of her hands. "I'd planned to do some shopping today, and there's also a batch of laundry that needs to be done. I'm tellin' you, Earl, if we still lived in Chicago, my life would be much easier and I wouldn't be expected to pick up tree branches today. It's like I'm a pioneer woman having to gather wood up to start a fire."

He rolled his eyes at her. "For heaven's sakes, woman, we had storms in Chicago."

"Yeah, but we didn't have a yard full of trees. Besides, I see myself as more of a city gal who's used to not doing unnecessary work."

Earl picked up his cup, took a drink, and then placed it in the sink. "I'm glad you've figured out that you're a city girl, Red, and that's all right by me. But it would still be helpful if you moved your caboose and got busy with those branches. I've gotta head out now. I'll see you when I get home." He grabbed his cooler and went out the back door.

Virginia flopped into a chair at the table, looked down at her cat who curled up near her feet, and groaned. "I think Earl's irritated, Goldie. I didn't even get a goodbye kiss. I long for the good ole days when picking up wood meant I'd be going to the store to buy a few Pres-to-Logs for the fireplace." She reached down and stroked the cat's fur. "But on a positive side, my bum leg has eased up some in the last day or two. Of course that'll probably change after I'm done working in the yard."

Virginia remained at the table until she'd finished her coffee, then ambled into the living room and picked up her binoculars. *I may as well look out front and see how things held up in the neighbors' yard across the road.*

Holding the field glasses up to her face, she was stunned to see that two trees in the Kings' yard had been uprooted. There were also plenty of limbs lying around.

Guess we were the lucky ones with only tree branches down. It's strange how a storm that hits the same area can do different kinds of damage from one individual's property to another's.

Continuing to observe through the binoculars, Virginia was even more surprised when she spotted a woman on the lower roof of the house that extended out under part of the second floor. She couldn't be sure if it was Belinda or her daughter, Sylvia, but whoever it was, they were sweeping off debris, no doubt left from the storm.

"What a foolish thing to do," she mumbled. "You couldn't pay me enough to go up there. It's bad enough Earl expects me to clean up some of the fallen debris in the yard." Virginia's brows knitted together. "Sure hope I don't have to witness that woman taking a tumble. Even if she survived the fall, she'd no doubt be seriously injured."

Herschel's eyes widened when he guided his horse and buggy into Belinda's yard and saw so many downed tree limbs, branches, and even a couple of uprooted trees. Apparently this part of Lancaster County had been hit pretty hard by last night's storm.

Herschel brought the horse up to the hitching rail, got out and secured the animal. When he turned toward the house, he pressed a fist to his mouth. *Oh my. . .what on earth is Belinda doing on that flat roof? Just one slip and she could be on the ground.*

Herschel saw Henry in the yard, picking up branches and loading them into a wheelbarrow. He hurried over to him and pointed to the roof where Belinda stood. "What's your mamm doing up there?"

Henry glanced in that direction and shrugged. "She's sweepin' the roof to get rid of everything the wind blew on it."

"Well, she needs to come down. It's not a safe place for her to be." The concern Herschel felt for Belinda was almost overwhelming. He hadn't experienced this feeling of protectiveness since Mattie died. "Is it okay if I go up?"

"On the roof?"

"Jah."

The teenage boy shrugged his shoulders. "Suit yourself, but I don't know what you're so worried about. My mamm's been on that flat roof before and she's never had a problem."

"What room is she near, and how do I get there?" Herschel didn't care what Henry said. With every second that passed, his concern for Belinda grew. His heart beat twice as fast as normal, while looking up at her and thinking about what might happen.

"Once you enter the house, go partway down the hall and then up the stairs to the second level. The room Mom is working from will be the first door to your left." Henry went back to picking up branches.

Herschel hurried up the front porch steps and knocked on the door. A few seconds later, Sylvia answered. "Hello, Herschel. How are you this morning?"

"I'm fine, but I saw your mudder up on the flat roof, and I'm worried about her. Henry said I could go on up."

"Of course, but—"

Herschel didn't wait for Sylvia to finish her sentence. He hurried down the hall and raced up the stairs. When he reached the second floor and found the door Henry had mentioned, he jerked it open, nearly colliding with Belinda.

"Oh my! You scared me, Herschel. I didn't know you were here, much less in this room."

"I saw you on the roof and was worried you might fall."

Belinda gestured to the partially open window. "I went out there to sweep off the debris from last night's storm."

"So you crawled out through a *fenschder*?"

She bobbed her head. "It's not the first time I've crawled out that window, so there's no need to look so serious."

"I—I can't help it. I'd feel terrible if you fell and got hurt or. . ." Herschel's voice trailed off and he blinked several times, hoping to control his swirling emotions. He'd never admitted it to himself until now, but he had fallen in love with this sweet woman and was on the verge of telling her so. The question was, how would she respond?

Chapter 32

Plink! Plink! Something wet landed on Herschel's arm. "What in the world?" He looked up just as another drop of water came—this one targeting his nose.

Herschel stepped aside and Belinda did the same. "Oh dear, it looks like there may be a leak in my roof. I bet it's from all the rain we had last night."

"Yes, and we had a lot of wind too. Maybe your shingles took a beating from it, like some of the other houses I spotted on the way over here this morning." Herschel went to the window and looked out. "Jah, and it's raining lightly right now." So much for declaring his love for Belinda. The matter of her roof in need of repair took precedence over anything else at the moment.

"If you have an extension ladder I can go up there and take a look," he offered.

Belinda shook her head. "My son-in-law's a roofer by trade, so I'll ask him to come over and look at it as soon as he's able."

"Are you sure? I don't mind going up there to check things out. I could patch any holes temporarily."

Before Belinda could respond to Herschel's question, her daughter hollered up the stairs: "Amy left a message on our voice mail, Mom! There's a fallen tree blocking the road between their place and here, so unless it gets cleared soon, she won't be able to make it over today to watch the kinner."

Belinda cupped her hands around her mouth. "I'll be right down!" She turned to face Herschel again. "I'd better go downstairs and talk to my daughter."

"Of course." Herschel followed Belinda down the stairs. When they reached the bottom step, he placed his hand on her arm. "It may be awhile before the road gets cleared, which means Jared might not be able to take a look at your roof today, or even tomorrow. So if you don't mind, I'd really like to go up there and see what I can do to stop the water from coming in."

"Very well, but only if you allow Henry to hold the ladder for you."

Herschel smiled. "I have no problem with that."

After Herschel went outside, Belinda sought Sylvia out. She found her at the kitchen sink, washing a batch of canning jars.

"Did you respond to Amy's message about not being able to come over?" Belinda asked.

"Jah. I said it was fine because we're not opening the greenhouse today."

"That's good, but I'm going out to the phone shed again to leave an important message for Jared."

"Oh?" Sylvia turned to face Belinda. "Is something wrong?"

"Apparently there's a leak in our roof. When I was talking to Herschel upstairs, we discovered water dripping through the ceiling."

"Do you think it will require putting on a whole new roof?"

Belinda shrugged. "I don't know. Herschel went out to ask Henry to get the tall ladder, and then he plans to go up on the roof to check things out."

Sylvia's brows lowered. "Henry?"

"No, Herschel. Your bruder will hold the ladder."

"That's fine, but it might be better if we waited until Jared can come over. Herschel's not a young man anymore. He might lose his footing and fall off the roof."

Belinda pinched the skin near the base of her throat. "I hope not. I would feel terrible if something bad happened to him."

"That's interesting, because Herschel was concerned about you being on the lower flat roof. He couldn't wait to get upstairs and see if you were okay." Belinda detected a gleam in her daughter's eyes as she leaned closer to her. "I think that nice man is in love with you, and I have a hunch the feeling is mutual."

"Now, don't be silly." Belinda's chin dipped down as she tucked her arms against her sides, unable to look her daughter in the eye. She couldn't deny that strong feelings for Herschel had begun to surface, but she wasn't willing to admit it to Sylvia or anyone yet. Truth was, Belinda could barely admit it to herself.

Her thoughts went to Monroe and how she felt whenever he was around. At times she enjoyed herself, but her feelings for him had not developed into anything close to love at this point. *I doubt they ever will,* she told herself. *In all fairness, I should let Monroe know that there's no hope of us having a future together, before he becomes too serious and proposes marriage. I'm not quite sure how to bring up the subject or form the right words.*

Belinda removed a wicker basket from the storage room and placed it on the kitchen counter.

"What are you going to do with that, Mom?" Sylvia questioned. "It's still drizzling outside, so this isn't picnic weather."

"Since Maude left before any of us got up this morning and didn't have breakfast with us, I want to take her something to eat."

"I'm sure she must have some food in her shanty."

"That could be, but it's probably not enough." Belinda placed a loaf of bread in the basket, along with a jar of honey, and some home-canned fruits and jellies.

"Do you think that poor woman has some sort of mental problems?" Sylvia asked.

"Perhaps, which is all the more reason she needs some help."

"Henry thinks she could be the person who has done the vandalism around your property."

"I know." Belinda rubbed at an itch on her arm. "Do you realize your bruder has made a list of suspects, but without any proof?"

"I'm well aware." Sylvia gave a small laugh. "But at least Henry playing detective keeps him occupied and out of trouble. And maybe he will discover who's been responsible for all the upsetting things that have happened."

"That would be nice, but right now we have other things to worry about." Belinda moved toward the back door. "The rain seems to have let up, so I'm going outside to leave a message for Jared, and then I'll see how Herschel and Henry are doing. Afterward, I may pick up a few of those branches that are scattered all over our yard before I head to Maude's."

"I know it's a mess out there because the children walked with me earlier to the phone shed. We had to make our own pathway to it, and the little ones were sure intrigued with the branches and the fallen trees." She continued to fill the basin with warm water. "I'd like to help you but I can't leave Allen and Rachel alone in the house." Sylvia grimaced. "No telling what kind of mischief they'd get into while I was outdoors. And I certainly can't allow them in the yard by themselves until everything's been cleaned up." Sylvia set the last jar in the sink and added more soap and water. "I also need to get started preparing the tomatoes we want to can."

Belinda flapped her hand. "Not a problem. If you decide you want to come outside later on, we can switch places."

"True, but you probably won't want to come inside until Herschel is gone." Sylvia gave Belinda a little smirk, and then plunged her hands into the water to begin her task.

Belinda ignored her daughter's last comment and went out the back door. She had no more than stepped onto the porch when she spotted Monroe's horse and buggy coming up the driveway. *Oh boy. . .both men are here at the same time. I wonder how this will play out.*

As Monroe pulled his rig into Belinda's yard, he noticed another horse and buggy at the hitching rail. He wondered if it belonged to a family member or if Belinda had company. Her yard was sure a mess. Last night's storm had done a number on the trees in Belinda's yard. No doubt she would need help cleaning it up, and he planned to volunteer his services.

Once Monroe stepped down from the buggy and secured his horse, he looked toward the house and noticed Belinda on her front porch. She wasn't the only person he saw, however. Her son, Henry, held a ladder against one end of the house.

Monroe's gaze traveled up to the roof. There stood Herschel, looking as though he was about to descend the ladder.

Monroe's lips pressed together. *Oh great. What's he doing here? Probably came over to see if Belinda needed anything. If I had gotten here sooner, I'd be the one fixing her roof instead of Herschel. I wonder if he's capable and can do a good job.*

Monroe approached the house and stepped onto the porch. "Morning, Belinda. I came by to see how you are doing after last night's unexpected storm." He turned slightly and gestured to the yard. "It looks like your place got hit pretty hard."

"It did, and now we have quite the mess to clean up. I'll need to find a good place to pile all this debris until we can dispose of it."

"That shouldn't be too hard since you've got plenty of property to keep it out of the way until then." He smiled. "I'm available for part of the day, so just tell me what you'd like done first and I'll get started."

"Well, umm..." A pink flush appeared on Belinda's face and neck as she looked over at Herschel, who'd just stepped off the ladder.

Before either of them could say anything more, Herschel walked past Monroe and stood in front of Belinda. "I found the problem. Several shingles were blown off, so that's why water's been getting in."

"I figured as much. I'll head out to the phone shed and leave a message for Jared."

"Would you like me to see what's in your toolshed and take care of patching it for now?" Herschel asked.

"I suppose it would be good to get something in place, because Jared might not be able to come over anytime today."

"No problem." Herschel looked over at Henry who had joined them on the porch. "Would you mind coming with me to the shed to get the supplies we need?"

Henry glanced briefly at Monroe, then back at Herschel. "Sure, I can do that, and I'll go up on the roof to help you too." The boy pointed to the barn on the other side of the yard. "I sit up in the hayloft sometimes and look out the front opening to watch for birds and other things, so I ain't scared, 'cause I'm used to being up high."

"All right, if your mamm has no objections, neither do I." Herschel gave Henry's shoulder a few taps.

Oh brother, this fella is too much. Monroe almost gagged. It seemed obvious that Herschel was trying to win over Belinda's son. He probably thought if he succeeded with that, he'd win Belinda's hand in marriage. *Well, I've got news for him. I'm the better man for Belinda. Besides, we have a history, and the fact is, she would've picked me to be her husband if Vernon hadn't come along and snatched her away.*

Monroe's fingers twitched as he held them behind his back. *Well, Herschel can try all he wants, but he will never succeed. I'm not about to let him steal my girl.*

Herschel looked down from the roof and frowned. Monroe pushed a wheelbarrow full of branches he'd picked up in the yard, and Belinda appeared to be helping him. "I'm glad I came by to check on you, and see how things are here," Herschel heard the man say. Monroe stopped briefly to pick up more branches. "You definitely need some help, and I'm the right man."

"That man," Herschel mumbled behind clenched teeth. Using the back of his hand, Herschel wiped sweat from his forehead.

"You talkin' about Monroe, by any chance?"

Herschel looked at Henry and nodded. "He seems to know everything and is always bragging. When we came out of the toolshed I heard him telling your mamm that even at the age of fifty-three, he could work twice as hard as any man half his age."

Henry's nose wrinkled. "Monroe says all that stuff, hopin' Mom will be impressed. He thinks that because he used to court her before she married my daed, it gives him an edge with her now." Henry handed Herschel another roofing nail. "Don't know what I'm gonna do if he talks her into marrying him. The last thing I want is a stepfather—especially a man like Monroe."

What about me? Herschel was tempted to ask. *Would you be okay if your mother and I got married?* Herschel's good sense kept him from asking that question. He wasn't about to let on to Belinda's son that he would like to marry his mother—especially since he hadn't asked Belinda yet.

As Herschel began patching the roof, he heard Monroe down below, bragging about his new open buggy. *Here we go again.*

When he looked down another time, and saw Monroe move closer to Belinda, Herschel's stomach tightened. *If I don't get my courage up soon and declare my feelings for Belinda, she'll be married to Monroe before I ever have a chance to ask for her hand in marriage.* He set a nail in place and lifted the hammer. *I need to act fast.*

Chapter 33

Monroe tossed a few more branches into the wheelbarrow, then reached into his trousers pocket and pulled out his timepiece. "Sorry, Belinda, but I need to go. I have a meeting soon with a Realtor about a home I may be interested in purchasing."

"No problem. I appreciate the help you've done here this morning. Before you go, though, let me run into the house and get a container of applesauce-raisin cookies for you."

A pleasing smile crossed his face. "Danki, Belinda. That's kind of you." He glanced across the yard, where Herschel was busy cutting limbs off one of the uprooted trees. "I figured Herschel would be gone by now. Doesn't he have a store to run in Gordonville?"

Belinda blinked. "Well, jah, but he also has employees who can run the store while he's away. Isn't that how it is with you?"

With a tight expression, Monroe gave a brief nod. "I'll wait over by my horse and buggy for you to bring me the cookies," he added, then left before Belinda could comment. The reality hit her that Monroe was jealous of Herschel. She felt sure it had nothing to do with his business dealings either.

Belinda went into the house and filled a disposable plastic container with cookies, then hurried outside and handed it to Monroe. "Thanks again for coming over to help out."

"It was my pleasure." His lips formed into another wide smile. "I would do most anything for you."

She swallowed hard. *I hope he doesn't say anything more. I'm not ready to tell him how I feel today.*

Belinda felt relief when Monroe said goodbye, untied his horse, and got into his carriage. She waved and watched until he was out of sight, then walked over to the section of yard where Herschel and Henry worked. "I have an errand I need to run," she said, looking at Herschel. "When I get back, I'll help Sylvia start lunch preparations, and I'd be pleased if you would join us for the meal."

Herschel brushed the cuff of his shirtsleeve across his damp forehead. "Between what I did on the roof, and now down here, I've worked up quite an appetite, so I won't turn away your invitation for lunch. Danki, Belinda."

"It's me who should be thanking you." She gestured to the tree he'd been cutting. "There's no way Henry and I could have accomplished this much by ourselves today, and we truly appreciate all your help." She looked at Henry. "Right, Son?"

Henry gave a weak smile as he bobbed his head. "Uh-huh, right."

"I'll let you two get back to work now. I shouldn't be gone long—just walking over to Maude's place."

Henry's forehead wrinkled. "What are you going there for?"

"I have a food basket for her."

Henry's mouth slackened before his gaze turned skyward. "You must be kidding, Mom."

The heat and humidity of the day accentuated the warmth she felt on her cheeks. "I most certainly am not."

"As many times as that woman has stolen from us, and you wanna give her some food? I still don't understand why you let her sleep here last night."

"The Bible says in Mark 12:31, that we should love our neighbors as ourselves." Belinda paused before continuing. "And in Luke 6:35 we are reminded to love even our enemies, and lend, hoping for nothing."

"But Maude ain't borrowin', Mom. She's taking and you're giving to her. That strange old woman's done nothing but cause us trouble."

"I don't believe you quite understand the concept of the scriptures your mamm speaks of," Herschel interjected. "God wants us to love others and do good to people, whether they have done good to us or not."

Henry's facial features tightened. Mumbling under his breath, he moved away and began picking up more limbs that had been scattered on the other side of the yard.

"I don't think your son appreciated my words on the matter," Herschel said to Belinda, "Guess maybe I spoke when I should have kept silent."

She shook her head. "What you said was the truth, based on God's Holy Word, and Henry needs to take those words to heart."

"Hopefully, someday he will." Herschel placed his hand on her shoulder. "In the meantime, Belinda, I'll be praying for your son and you as well—that God will give you words of wisdom and guidance as you continue to set a good example to each of your family members."

"Danki." Belinda's body felt weighed down. Being a single parent was a huge responsibility. There were many days when she didn't feel up to the task. If only she had a husband to share in the responsibilities and offer wise counsel the way Herschel just did. He truly was a good friend. She looked into the depths of his blue eyes and saw sincerity. Was it any wonder she'd fallen in love with him? If only she knew how he felt about her.

Belinda was halfway to Maude's when she saw a horse and buggy going down the road in the opposite direction. She blinked several times, barely able to believe her eyes. A full grown sheep sat in the front seat next to the Amish man who drove the rig. What a humorous sight to behold. Belinda remembered hearing that one of her English neighbors had planned to buy a new ewe. She figured this sheep might be on the way to its new owners, but having it ride in the front of the Amish man's buggy was a strange way to make a delivery.

"Each to his own, I guess." She chuckled. It was good to witness something humorous once in a while. Life often became too serious, and sometimes it was difficult to find anything to laugh or even smile about.

Belinda felt grateful for the two grandchildren who had lived with her since their daddy was killed. Rachel and Allen did cute or funny things almost every day. Other things in life brought joy to her too, such as the martins who had taken up residence in the martin boxes her husband had built before his untimely death.

Another thing that always brought a smile to Belinda's lips was watching the hummingbirds busy at the feeders she'd hung on shepherd's hooks near the front porch. Sometimes as many as five or six hummers tried to feed at the same time, which often meant some of the little birds tried to fight each other off. Belinda would miss their frenzied activity when it came time for the hummingbirds to leave, just like she would miss Sylvia and her children when they moved in with Dennis after the wedding in October.

But life moves on and we always have changes to deal with, Belinda told herself. *I'll need to keep my focus on keeping the greenhouse running, even if it means hiring someone outside the family to help out.* She stopped walking as another thought popped into her head. *What if I got married again? Would it mean giving up the greenhouse?*

As Belinda approached Maude's rundown shack, she wondered once more where the elderly woman went during the harsher winter months. She'd checked the cabin a few times last winter and found it empty, so Maude must have gone someplace until she returned in the early spring. The chickens were gone too. She'd either cooked and eaten them, or taken the hens with her—which seemed unlikely. *Maybe I'll ask her about that when I drop off the basket of food.*

A short time later, the shanty came into view and Belinda saw Maude sitting outside on a rickety-looking wooden chair. In her lap lay a beautiful cat with golden-colored hair.

"Hello, Maude. I brought you a few items of food you might enjoy." Belinda held out the basket. "I would have given them to you after breakfast this morning, but you left my house before I got up."

"I woke up early and didn't want to disturb ya." Maude put the feline on the ground and stood. "I'll take the food inside and put it away. Then you can have your basket back." She motioned to the cat. "Would you mind watching her for me so she don't run off?"

"I didn't realize you had a cat." Belinda bent down, and when she picked the animal up, it let out a loud, *Meow!*

"Didn't have it till this morning. The critter was here when I came back from your place. I think it must be a stray."

"That's possible." Belinda knelt down and stroked the cat's silky head. She wasn't much of a cat person, but this one seemed quite tame and lovable.

"Have a seat." Maude motioned to the chair she'd been sitting in. "I'll be back soon." She quickly disappeared into her sad-looking dwelling.

When Belinda sat down, the cat began to purr. All the cats she had were either outside or in the barn. Although it might be nice to have a cat inside for companionship, it would also mean having to stay on top of all the cat hair that would most likely get on the furniture.

Belinda stopped petting the cat when Maude came back out and set the basket on the ground by her feet.

She got up and offered Maude the chair and then handed her the cat. "I need to get home, but before I go, there's something I've been meaning to ask you."

The older woman sat down and placed the feline over her shoulder, like a baby. "What do ya wanna know?"

"I've noticed that you're not here during most of the winter and wondered where you spend the colder months."

"I stay with my late sister's daughter, Bonita. She lives in South Carolina." Maude stroked the length of the cat's body, which brought about more purring.

"I'm glad to hear you have someplace warmer to go. Our winters here can get pretty cold."

"Yep." Maude placed the cat back in her lap, and it began licking its paws.

The beautiful katz *might be just what this poor woman needs,* Belinda mused. *Of course, what will she do with it during the winter months when she's gone? Will Maude take the cat with her? Surely she wouldn't leave it here to fend for itself. Speaking of which. . .I still haven't asked about those* hinkel.

"I have another question." Belinda looked directly at Maude. "What happened to the hens you had in your possession?"

Maude blinked several times. "Well, I put 'em back in your coop, and got 'em out again when I returned from South Carolina."

Belinda's mouth nearly fell open. "Oh, I–I see." *How odd that Henry never said anything about the return of those chickens, or the fact that they were missing from the coop again. He must be too focused on playing detective these days.*

Belinda bent down to pick up the basket. "I'm glad there wasn't much damage done to your yard from last night's storm. It sure caused a mess in our yard."

"Yeah, I saw that this morning." Maude motioned to her shanty. "Figured when I arrived here I'd discover that not much of my place was left. But for some odd reason, the only damage I saw was a few places on the roof that were leaking."

"We had a leak in our roof too." Belinda put two fingers under her nose, to hold back a sneeze. When the feeling passed, she asked another question. "Would you be okay if some men from my Amish community came over and put a new roof on your cabin?"

Maude shook her head. "I don't have enough money to pay 'em."

"No, no. Their work would be free." Belinda clamped her mouth shut. *I shouldn't have said anything until I talked with Jared. He might be too busy to replace or even repair Maude's roof and may not appreciate me volunteering him to do it without pay. I should have thought things through before I spoke.*

Maude looked up at Belinda with her chin dipping slightly. "I'd be much obliged."

"All right, I will talk to my son-in-law who's a roofer, and either he or I will get back to you about it."

"Thanks." Maude picked up the cat and nuzzled it with her nose. "It's nice to know that some folks care about someone besides themselves."

Belinda reflected on the scripture verses she had shared with Henry awhile ago. This was an opportunity for some members in her church to do something good for someone in need.

🐦

With a sense of urgency, Virginia called Goldie's name over and over as she went from room to room. Shortly after Earl left for work this morning, she'd discovered the cat was missing. Goldie had disappeared one other time, and Virginia had been relieved to find her still in the house. This time, however, she'd looked high and low but had seen no sign of Goldie.

Virginia always kept the cat indoors, so if Goldie had gotten out, she probably ran off and wouldn't know how to find her way home. The idea of her furry companion being out on her own caused Virginia's chin to tremble. "Oh Goldie, what will I do if I can't find you?"

She stepped outside, checking both the back and front yards, while calling numerous times for the cat.

Virginia was about to look in the front yard again, when she spotted Belinda walking up the road. "Have you seen a gold-colored cat anywhere?" she hollered.

"As a matter of fact, I have." Belinda crossed the street and stepped into Virginia's yard. "I stopped by to see Maude, who lives in that old shack down the road, and she was holding a cat with gold-colored hair when I got there. She said it showed up at her place this morning."

"Oh, what a relief. It must be my Goldie. I'll get in my car and head over there right now." Virginia hurried to the garage without saying goodbye to Belinda.

A short time later, she pulled up to Maude's rundown shack. There was no sign of the old woman, or Goldie, so Virginia got out of the car, walked across the brown patches of grass, and knocked on the rickety front door. She'd only seen the cabin from the road before, and seeing it up close, she was appalled at the condition it was in. She could only imagine what the inside must look like.

I bet the old woman who lives here is a squatter, using the shanty without permission of the owner. Virginia pursed her lips as she waited outside the door. *How could anyone live in this place? I bet there's no indoor plumbing or electricity.*

Virginia's thoughts were stalled when the squeaky door swung open. There stood Maude with Goldie in her arms.

"Who are you, and what do ya want? If you're selling something, I ain't interested." Maude's gruff-sounding question caught Virginia off guard.

"I came here looking for my cat." Virginia pointed at Goldie. "That's her. She escaped from my house sometime this morning—probably when my husband left for work."

"Can ya prove she's yours?" Maude stroked the top of Goldie's head.

Virginia's muscles tightened. She was tempted to snatch her cat right out of the old woman's hands. "Can you prove she's yours?"

Maude looked down at Goldie, then back at Virginia. "Well, she's been with me since early this morning, so that oughta prove something."

Virginia poked her tongue against the side of her cheek as she released a long breath. Things were not going as well as she'd hoped. "I don't know why Goldie ended up on your doorstep, but I assure you, she is my cat. I've had her for several months, and if you'll put her on the ground right now, I'll prove that she belongs to me."

Maude hesitated a few seconds but finally did as Virginia asked.

Virginia took a few steps back, held out her arms, and called, "Come here, Goldie. Come to me, sweet kitty."

The cat let out two loud meows and pranced over to Virginia.

Without another word, Virginia scooped Goldie up, limped over to her car, and climbed in, placing the cat on the seat beside her.

Maude began walking toward the vehicle, but Virginia put her key in the ignition and backed out of the dirt driveway before the old woman could make it halfway across the unkempt yard.

"Don't you ever run off like that again." Virginia reached down and stroked Goldie's head. The contented cat curled up in Virginia's lap, and she felt the vibration of the feline's purring. She was ever so happy to have her furry friend back.

Chapter 34

As Amy made her way to the phone shed, she paused in the front yard to take in the damage left from last night's storm. No trees had been uprooted, but many branches lay scattered across the lawn. Jared had already cleared out the ones in their driveway and was out back, picking up more debris.

Amy had wanted to help her husband clean the yard, but he'd insisted that he could do it himself and said he didn't want her doing any strenuous work. Although Amy had assured him she wouldn't pick up anything too heavy or overdo it, Jared remained insistent.

Even though some people might believe Jared was too protective, Amy respected his decision, knowing he had her best interest at heart as well as that of their unborn child.

Amy entered the phone shed with a small pillow, and placed it on the chair before taking a seat. At Sylvia's suggestion, Amy had decided to sit on a soft pillow so she'd be more comfortable on the hard stool.

After Amy sat down, she placed both hands on her belly and gave it a massage, while thinking about the baby she carried and how exciting motherhood would be. Although her nieces and nephews were special, Amy looked forward to having her own precious child to love and care for.

She glanced out the open door and watched a robin outside of the shed as it hunted for a worm. The red-breasted bird hopped along until it grabbed hold of a worm and flew off. Amy continued to watch other robins in the grass and finally clicked on the answering machine. *I hope Mom and everyone in my family are doing well after the storm we had last night.*

Hearing her mother's voice, Amy leaned closer to make sure she would hear everything correctly. She felt relieved when she heard that the rest of the family was okay. It was too bad about the uprooted trees and leaky roof though. As soon as she listened to the rest of the messages, Amy would tell Jared that Mom had asked if he would come over at his convenience to check on the roof. Mom had also mentioned that Herschel had patched one section where water had gotten in due to last night's heavy rains.

The fact that Herschel had gone over to help was a confirmation to Amy that he cared about Mom's welfare as well as the rest of the family's.

Amy tapped her chin with the end of the pen she'd used to write down her mother's message. *I wouldn't be surprised if not too far in the distant future Herschel declares his love for my mamm.*

🐦

"How'd things go when you went over to Maude's?" Sylvia asked as she and her mother prepared sandwiches for lunch.

"Fine. She took the food inside, and when she came back out we talked for a bit." Mom opened four cans of tuna fish and emptied them into a bowl. "I learned that Maude spends her winters in South Carolina with a relative, but I didn't think to ask a few other questions I've been wondering about."

"Like what?" Sylvia took a jar of sweet pickles from the refrigerator and cut several into small pieces, which she would add to the tuna Mom had begun mixing with mayonnaise.

"I wanted to ask if she's ever been married, and more importantly, how she came to acquire the rundown shack she's been living in, but it slipped my mind. Guess with everything that's gone on here today, I'm feeling kind of befuddled."

"Those questions would be worth knowing. I'm surprised none of us have thought to ask her about it before."

"I get busy in the greenhouse, but the next time she drops by, I'll try to remember to question her more." Sylvia's mother added some diced onion to the tuna mixture. "That old shack needs some repairs, so I'm going to talk to Jared and some of the other men in our district about fixing the place up to make it more livable."

"What if you find out she doesn't own the rundown cabin?"

"Then we'll ask who the owners are and find out if it would be all right if our men make some repairs on the building." Mom sighed. "I should have tried to get the poor woman some help long ago, but I suppose it's better late than never."

Sylvia added the pickles she'd cut up to the bowl of tuna fish. "You're always doing kind things for others. Inviting Herschel to join us for lunch today is just one example."

"It was the least I could do to thank him for coming all the way over here to check on us and help out this morning." Mom kept her gaze on the tuna salad, while speaking in a quieter tone than normal.

"Did Herschel say how things were at his parents'?" Sylvia asked.

"No, and I didn't think to ask." Mom thumped her head. "I don't know what's wrong with my memory today. I hope it's not a sign of old age creeping in."

"You're just a bit rattled because of all the cleanup due to the storm on top of everything else that's been happening around here."

"Jah, I suppose."

Sylvia felt certain that her mother's problem today was feeling giddy with Herschel around. She was sure showing gratitude wasn't the only reason Mom had invited him for lunch. Mom's relaxed posture and smiling face whenever Herschel came around was enough for Sylvia to believe something special had developed between the two of them. Truth was, Sylvia figured Mom might have fallen in love with the nice man, and she was almost certain the feeling was shared.

At least it wasn't Monroe who won my mamm's heart. Sylvia's lips twitched. *I've never seen Mom respond to him the way she does to Herschel. I'm sorry, Mr. Esh, but I think you've lost out on your quest to gain my mother's favor.*

🐦

Belinda heard a familiar *clip-clop. . .clip-clop* and looked out the kitchen window. She was pleased to see Jared's horse and buggy come into the yard, and glad that Herschel and Henry had gotten the driveway cleared.

Belinda watched as Jared brought the horse up to the hitching rail and was happy to see Amy step down from his buggy as well.

She turned to face Sylvia. "Jared and Amy are here. I'm going out to greet them and see if they'd like to join us for lunch."

Sylvia smiled. "That'd be nice. I'll set out some other sandwich fixings, in case anyone prefers something other than tuna."

"Okay, we'll be in soon." Belinda wiped her hands, and hurried out the door, where she met Jared and Amy on the lawn.

"We got your message," Jared said. "The road between our place and yours has been cleared, so I'm here to do a check on your roof." He grinned at his wife. "As you might expect, Amy wanted to come along."

"Danki, I'm glad you're both here." Belinda gave them each a hug. "We're getting ready to serve lunch, and if you haven't eaten already, we'd like you to join us for the meal."

"Sounds good to me." Amy looked at Jared. "Is that okay with you?"

"Of course. After we eat, I'll climb up on the roof and take a look."

"I'll let Herschel and Henry know that it's time to wash up, and then we can all gather around the dining-room table."

"I can tell them," Jared offered. "It'll give me a few minutes to talk to Herschel about the condition of the roof and what all he found." He gave Amy's arm a squeeze and started across the yard.

Belinda turned to her daughter. "Did the storm do much damage to your yard?"

Amy shook her head. "A few tree branches came down, but nothing major. I'm sure Jared will be getting lots of calls from people in the area who had roof damage though."

Belinda looped her hand through the crook of Amy's arm. "Speaking of damage, I went to see Maude earlier today, and that old cabin she lives in could sure use some repairs. Some of it probably came because of the heavy winds and rain we had, but the building has been neglected for a long time and needs sprucing up. I'd like to ask Jared and some other men in our church district to have a work frolic over at her place sometime in the near future."

Amy bobbed her head. "Good idea, Mom. We need to help others in our area, and not just our Amish community."

While Herschel ate his tuna sandwich, all he could think about was the joy he felt sitting here at Belinda's table. With the exception of Henry, Herschel felt fully welcomed by her family members. Since he and his late wife had never had children, Herschel hadn't experienced the joy of raising a family. And since he hadn't known about his daughter, Sara, until she was an adult, he hadn't fully understood what fatherhood was about. Sara had a baby now, which made Herschel a grandfather, but he didn't get to Lancaster to see Sara, Brad, and the baby very often. They came by to see him whenever they could, but Brad's job as a minister kept him pretty busy.

Herschel looked across the table at Belinda and smiled. *If I married her, I'd have a ready-made family as well as a loving wife. If only I could work up the nerve to express the way I feel about Belinda.*

Herschel's biggest concern was not in finding the words to convey his love, but how he would deal with it if she didn't return his feelings. His chest tightened as he shuffled his feet underneath the table. The thought of her rejection lay heavy on his mind. After Mattie died, Herschel had been sure he could never fall in love again, and now that he had, he felt fearful and more than a bit overwhelmed. He'd spoken to his mother about it the other day, and she'd encouraged him to tell Belinda how he felt about her. He just needed to find the courage.

"Danki for the meal, ladies, but now it's time for me to go up on the roof to check things out."

Jared's statement brought Herschel out of his musings. "Would you like me to tag along? I can show you the spot that I patched."

"That would be helpful."

Herschel slid back his chair. "The sandwiches hit the spot." He looked right at Belinda, forcing himself not to lose eye contact with her. Sometimes in her presence, Herschel felt like a shy, tongue-tied schoolboy with a crush on a pretty girl.

"When I come off the roof, would you mind if I take a closer look at your garden?" Herschel shifted from one foot to the other as he continued to look at Belinda. "I glanced at it earlier, when I picked up some debris nearby, and was surprised at how well everything looked in spite of last night's storm."

"I don't mind at all." Belinda smiled. "Let me know when you're ready, and I'll join you in the garden."

"Will do." Herschel hesitated a moment, wondering if he should say something more, but decided he'd said enough and followed Jared out the door.

While Sylvia took her children down the hall to wash up after the meal, Belinda and Amy cleared the table.

When they entered the kitchen, Amy placed her stack of dishes in the sink and turned to face Belinda. "Is there something happening between you and Herschel? I'd sure like to know."

Belinda placed both hands against her warm cheeks. "What made you ask such a question?"

Amy held up one finger. "Let's see now. Herschel gets a bird dog expression whenever he looks in your direction." A second finger came up. "And you, Mom, blush, like you're doing now, when you're talking to, or even looking, in his direction."

"It could just be the heat. It's quite warm in the house today, you know."

Amy shook her head. "Today was not the first time I've seen blotches of pink on your cheeks when Herschel's been present."

Belinda dropped her gaze for a few seconds before looking up. "If you must know, I have come to care for Herschel."

"I am glad to hear it." Amy moved closer to Belinda. "Have you told him how you feel?"

"Of course not. That would be too bold. Besides, if I were to admit it, and he doesn't feel the same way about me, it would be quite embarrassing for me as well as Herschel. It might even be the end of our friendship."

"Are you willing to take the risk?"

"No, I'm not. If Herschel and I are meant to have a serious relationship, then he has to make the first move."

"I guess that would be more proper." Amy grinned. "Maybe I'll ask

Jared to speak to Herschel. He might need a little nudge."

Belinda held up her hand. "Please don't involve Jared. This is between me and Herschel, and I'm sure he wouldn't appreciate your husband or anyone else trying to get us together."

"Okay, Mom. I just want you to be happy, and I'm sure you wouldn't be with a man like Monroe."

"I have come to the same conclusion. I've tried to give Monroe a chance by spending time with him and even accepting his gifts, but I know in my heart that I will never feel anything more for him than a casual friendship."

Amy wrinkled her nose. "Sometimes Mr. Esh can be so irritating. I doubt that any *weibsmensch* could fall in love with him."

"You never know. . . He does have some good qualities, and the right woman might see things about him that would appeal to her." Belinda filled the sink with warm water and added liquid detergent. "And if things don't work out between me and Herschel, I shall keep my focus on running the greenhouse and being a loving, helpful mother and grandmother until God chooses to take me home."

Amy gave Belinda a hug. "I hope you'll be around for a good long time."

"Me too, my precious daughter." The back of Belinda's throat thickened. *Me too.*

Chapter 35

Virginia sat on the front porch with a cup of coffee. She'd raked up the last of the fallen leaves and picked up a bunch of smaller branches, all the while grumbling about it. Earl would take care of the large limbs that had come down during last night's storm when he got home.

"My life stinks," Virginia muttered. "Nothing's been right since Earl and I moved to Lancaster County. Why couldn't he have been happy to remain in Chicago?"

She looked across the street and saw two men on the roof of Belinda's house. *I bet they had some damage. I wonder if our roof is okay. Maybe Earl oughta climb up there and check.*

She set the cup down on the small table beside her chair and folded her arms. *We'll probably have to call that Amish roofer, Jared, and end up using the money we've been saving for a vacation to fix the stupid roof.*

Virginia glanced at the sign near the front of the Kings' driveway. A large piece of tape with black lettering had been placed over the greenhouse sign, letting people know that the business was closed for the day. No doubt it was due to the storm and the mess it had created in most people's yards.

When she saw Maude walking up the road, her jaw clenched. *I still can't believe that silly old woman treated my Goldie like she belonged to her. I think she would have kept my cat for herself if I hadn't shown up.*

Virginia limped inside to the kitchen, where she poured herself another cup of coffee, adding extra vanilla creamer to it, and placed it on the table. She smiled when Goldie rubbed against her leg. "Hi, pretty kitty." Virginia reached down and scooped up the cat. "Are you hungry?

Well don't worry, because I'll put some food in your bowl in a little bit." Goldie rubbed against Virginia's chin and purred like a motor boat. "You're one of the few good things that has happened to me since Earl and I moved here."

Virginia thought about how the Kings had all that help over at their place. *You'd think they would have asked us if we could use some help. Maybe they figure Earl is a capable man who can get things done around here.*

She drank her coffee and went outside again to take another look at the house. Tipping her head back, Virginia noticed some branches hanging from the roof. *I think it's possible for me to get a few of them down. I just need something long enough so I can reach them.*

Virginia went into the garage to see what was there that she might be able to use. She dug through the section where Earl kept all the lawn tools and frowned. *My husband sure isn't organized. How does he manage to find anything in this mess?*

Virginia located a metal rake. The handle looked long enough, so she went back to the yard and tried to reach one of the dangling branches. With a little determination, Virginia managed to hook it and pulled the branch down. "Now how 'bout that?" She looked up and saw another one hanging farther down from her. "I'll get that one too." As she stepped forward, Goldie zipped in front of her and ran across the yard.

Virginia looked toward the door that hung open. "Oh boy, look what I've done. I can't believe I forgot to shut the door."

She laid the rake on the ground and headed for her cat. "Here kitty, kitty. Come on, Goldie. It's time to go back inside." Virginia felt relieved when the cat stopped running and came over to her. She went to grab Goldie and noticed that her slacks had gotten grease on them from something in the garage she must have rubbed against. *Guess this is what I get for trying to be helpful. Sure hope these pants aren't ruined.*

"Jared and Herschel are off the roof now." Amy pointed out the kitchen window. "Should we go see what they found out?"

"Jah, let's do." Since the dishes had been done, Belinda drained the sink and dried her hands. She stepped into the living room to let Sylvia know that she and Amy were going outside, and then the two of them went out the back door.

"Herschel did a good job patching your roof, and I didn't see any other serious issues." Jared looked at Belinda. "I don't think we'll have to do any more work on it right now."

Belinda smiled. "That's a relief, but I do have something else for you to consider."

"What's that?"

She explained about the condition of Maude's shanty. "When you have time, could you take a look at it and let me know if you, and maybe some of your crew, would be willing to make the place more livable?"

"I can do that, and I'm sure others in our community will make themselves available when we let it be known that there's going to be a need for workers."

"I'd be happy to assist with the project," Herschel put in. "I've given my store manager more responsibility at the bulk-food store lately, so I have some free time to do other things."

"We'll take all the help we can get." Jared turned to face Amy. "I need to stop at a few other places before going home. Do you want to ride along, or would you rather wait here and have me pick you up in a few hours?"

Amy yawned. "I'm feeling kind of tired, so maybe I'll stay here and rest."

"Good idea." He gave Amy's shoulder a few pats and headed toward his horse and buggy. "Danki for lunch, Belinda," Jared called over his shoulder.

"You're welcome." Belinda looked at Herschel. "Do you still want to take a look at my garden?"

He bobbed his head. "You bet."

Before heading into the house, Amy looked at Belinda with a smirk, and Belinda could guess what her daughter was thinking. *She's probably hoping I'll tell Herschel how much I've come to care for him. I can't believe she would even suggest such a thing. It wouldn't be right.*

The day had turned hot and humid, and Herschel undid the top button of his shirt as he walked beside Belinda along the outer edge of her garden. "All of your vegetable plants look healthy," he commented. "You must be quite the gardener, because you sure have a knack for it."

"I don't know about that, but my interest in growing vegetables and flowers began when I was a girl, helping my grandma plant things in her yard."

"I've always wanted a big garden with lots of fresh veggies." Herschel's shoulders lifted then lowered. "But then, who would I be growing it for, when it's just me and my hund livin' in my house?"

"I'd be happy to share some of our produce," Belinda offered. "In fact, we can pick some now for you to take home."

"That'd be nice, but can we talk awhile first?"

"Certainly. Let's have a seat over there." Belinda motioned to the picnic table.

Herschel ambled over and took a seat on the closest bench. His nervousness increased when Belinda seated herself next to him. Did he have the courage to say what was on his mind?

"Was there something specific you wanted to talk to me about?" Belinda asked. She sat so close that Herschel felt her soft breath on his face, making it all the harder to think of the exact words he wanted to say. "Jah, I. . .umm. . ."

"Is something wrong?" Belinda's brows drew together. "You seem a bit *naerfich* right now."

Herschel's knuckles whitened as he pulled all eight fingers into his palms. *Of course I'm nervous. Who wouldn't be when they're about to blurt something out that could ruin a perfectly good relationship?*

Belinda sat quietly, and then unexpectedly she laid a hand on his arm. "What was it you wanted to tell me?"

Herschel's muscles twitched at her gentle touch. "I hope you won't think I'm being too forward or hold it against me if you don't like what I say."

She touched the base of her throat and gave a slight shake of her head. "I can't imagine what you could say to me that I might not approve of." Belinda looked at him with sincerity and spoke in a kind, gentle tone, which helped relieve some of his anxiety.

"The thing is. . ." Herschel paused and swallowed a couple of times. "I enjoy your company very much."

"I like being with you too."

Enough to marry me? Herschel almost bonked himself on the head. *Don't be stupid. I can't blurt that out—at least not till I find out how Belinda feels about me.*

Herschel pulled in a quick breath and started again. "The truth is, I've fallen in love with you." There, it was out. Now all he had to do was wait for her response.

Belinda stared at him with her mouth partially open.

I wish she would say something, even if it's not what I want to hear. Anything would be better than her silence.

A few seconds passed, which seemed like hours, and then Belinda finally spoke. "I'm pleased to hear you say that, Herschel, because I love you too."

A sense of relief flooded his soul as he clasped her hand. "I'm so relieved. I didn't think I stood a chance against Monroe. He has a lot more to offer you than I do."

Belinda shook her head. "Monroe's a friend, nothing more."

"I bet he doesn't see it that way. It's obvious to me that Monroe is determined to have you as his own, and I doubt he'll be willing to give up on his quest."

"I chose Vernon over Monroe when we were courting many years ago, and now I choose you."

A new sense of joy and hope sprang into Herschel's chest, such as he'd not felt in a long time. "After a proper time of courting for us, would you consider becoming my fraa?"

"I would be honored."

Herschel wanted so much to take Belinda into his arms and give her a kiss, but someone might be watching from the house. Instead, he gave her fingers a gentle squeeze and said, "You've made me the happiest man in Lancaster County."

A short time later, after Belinda told Herschel goodbye and sent him on his way with a sack full of freshly picked produce, she headed into the house, feeling as though she was floating on a cloud. It didn't seem possible that Herschel had declared his love for her or that he'd proposed marriage. Even more surreal was the fact that she'd admitted her love for him and said yes to his proposal. In her wildest dreams Belinda had never imagined she could love any man but Vernon or that it would happen so quickly.

It's been over two years since I became a widow, she reminded herself. *So that part didn't occur quickly. The fact that I've fallen in love with Herschel in such a short time is what amazes me.*

While it was true that Belinda had been acquainted with Herschel Fisher a good many years, she hadn't really gotten to know him until the last year or so. It amazed her that in the few short months Herschel had been coming around more often, she'd allowed herself to be drawn to him, like a moth attracted to light. Herschel was a good man—patient, helpful, and easy to be with. He'd never pressured her or tried to make an impression, the way Monroe always did. Herschel had won Belinda's heart just by being himself.

It wouldn't be easy, but she would have to let Monroe know that she and Herschel were planning to get married. He'd likely do everything he could to try and change her mind, just as he had when she'd picked Vernon over him. But Belinda would hold fast to her decision, because deep down in her heart, she knew Herschel was the man God had chosen for her.

She opened the front door. *And now I must tell my family.*

When Belinda entered the living room, she found Amy sprawled out on the couch, but she wasn't asleep. Sylvia sat in the rocker, with a stack of pot holders in her lap, while Allen and Rachel played on the floor nearby.

"Where's Henry?" Belinda asked. "I have something to tell all of you, and then I'll be going to the phone shed to call Ezekiel."

"What's wrong, Mom? Has something bad happened?" Amy sat up, and with wide eyes, she turned to face Belinda.

"I think Henry's in the barn," Sylvia said. "Should I go get him?"

"Please do."

Sylvia set the pot holders aside and went out. She returned several minutes later with Henry.

"What's up, Mom? Sylvia said you wanted to talk to us."

"Yes, I do." Belinda sat down and pointed to an empty chair. "Please take a seat."

Henry flopped onto the couch instead. "What's this about?"

There was no easy way to say this, so she just blurted it out. "Herschel has asked me to marry him, and I said yes." Belinda folded her arms and waited for their response.

It didn't take long, and Amy was the first to say something. "That's wonderful news. Congratulations, Mom!"

"Danki." Belinda looked at Sylvia.

"I think you chose well, and I'm happy for you." Sylvia smiled. "When's the big day? Will it take place before my wedding to Dennis or a few months later?"

"We haven't had a chance to talk about that yet." Belinda turned to face Henry. "What about you, Son? How do you feel about Herschel and me getting married?"

He pressed his knees together and shook his head. "I ain't one bit happy, and I hope you change your mind 'cause I'll never accept Herschel or any other man as my stepfather."

Before Belinda could respond to her son's outburst, he jumped up and raced from the room. She cringed upon hearing heavy footsteps clomp up the stairs and pressed a fist to her lips when his bedroom door slammed.

"Don't let Henry's attitude get to you," Amy said. "He'll come around when he realizes what a wonderful man Herschel is and how much you love each other." The joy on her face was evident when she got off the couch and came over to give Belinda a hug. Sylvia quickly followed suit.

Tears welled in Belinda's eyes. While it did her heart good to witness her daughters' acceptance of Herschel, she couldn't help but be concerned about her son's reaction. She hoped Henry would change his mind but wasn't sure what to do if he didn't.

I'll need to pray about it, Belinda reminded herself. *Pray and ask God to soften my son's heart so he will see for himself what a kind, loving man Herschel truly is.*

Chapter 36

With summer came lightning bugs and sweet corn, and by August, Lancaster County had plenty of both. Belinda enjoyed eating fresh corn on the cob with plenty of melted butter, salt, and pepper. She also liked spending her evenings sitting outside with her grandchildren watching the fireflies rise up from the grass.

Except for Henry's sour-grapes attitude toward her engagement to Herschel, things were going along well in Belinda's life. It bothered her that Henry wouldn't let Herschel into his life, but she continued to hold out hope that after more time her son's attitude would change.

Surely Henry can see Herschel's attributes, Belinda thought as she went down one of the aisles in the greenhouse, giving each of the potted plants some liquid food to help them grow and remain healthy.

Her thoughts went to Monroe. He'd been out of town on business for the past week, so she hadn't had a chance to tell him about her engagement to Herschel. Belinda dreaded the encounter when it came but knew she couldn't avoid it. She hoped she could say it in a way that wouldn't hurt Monroe's feelings. He had, after all, been kind to her in many ways, but he also had qualities and mannerisms that got on her nerves. Belinda couldn't pretend to be in love with Monroe or keep seeing him socially now that she'd given her heart and a promise of marriage to Herschel.

Pushing her concerns to the back of her mind, Belinda finished her plant-feeding project and went up front to take Sylvia's place at the counter so she could go to the house and eat lunch with her children.

"All done with your chore?" Sylvia asked as she picked up her drink container.

"Jah, and I'm here now to take over for you."

"Okay, but before I go up to the house, can I talk to you about something?"

"Of course."

"While you were checking phone messages this morning, after Amy came to watch the kinner, she mentioned that Jared's concerned about working on the shanty Maude lives in."

Belinda's brows lowered. "Really? He hasn't said anything about it to me, other than that he would put the word out and get things lined up for the repairs. Do you know what he's worried about?"

"Jah. He can't proceed with any repairs to the building without the owner's permission." Sylvia shrugged. "As far as I know, Maude has never mentioned to any of us about who owns the cabin. I've just always thought the place had been abandoned and she decided to take refuge there during the warmer months."

"You're right. We don't know who owns it. I'd planned to ask, but things have been so busy here in the greenhouse lately, it's been hard to focus on too many things at once. Also with Herschel coming by every evening since he asked me to marry him, talking to Maude slipped my mind yet again."

"Dennis and I could go over and talk to her," Sylvia offered. "She responded fairly well to him the last time we were there when we found out she had Rachel with her."

"If Dennis is willing, I'd be most grateful." Belinda smiled. "I can't believe how many exciting things will be happening for us in the next few months. The birth of Amy and Jared's baby is only a month away, and then yours and Dennis's wedding will take place in October."

"Two months after that, you and Herschel will get married." Sylvia clasped Belinda's hand. "I'm so pleased for you, Mom. Having both lost your mates, you and Herschel deserve to find happiness in love and marriage again. And I believe you are well suited."

"I'm happy to hear that, but do you think I'm rushing into things, getting married so soon?"

Sylvia shook her head. "Herschel's declared his love for you, and you have admitted that you love him, so what's the point in waiting to begin your new life together as husband and wife?"

"But you postponed your original wedding plans in order to help me here during the busiest season." Belinda paused to moisten her parched lips. "Maybe I'm being *eegesinnisch*, and perhaps a bit narrisch, trying to plan a wedding by December."

"You're not selfish or foolish, Mom. You deserve to be happy with the man you love. If Dad could look down from heaven, I am sure he'd approve of your choice for a second husband."

"You really think so?"

"Jah, I do. And don't forget—Ezekiel and Michelle are happy for you too. They made that clear when you called to give them your news."

Belinda's voice cracked as tears dribbled down her cheeks. "Danki, Daughter, for your words of affirmation and encouragement."

"You're welcome." Sylvia rose from the wooden stool behind the counter. "I'll head up to the house now, but before I go, I'll give Dennis a call and find out when he might be free to go with me to see Maude." Sylvia started for the door, but stopped walking when a horse and buggy came into the parking lot. "It's Monroe, Mom. Would you like me to stay here while you talk to him? I'm sure it won't be easy to tell him your news."

"No, that's okay. Telling him that I've accepted Herschel's marriage proposal is something I need to do alone. And as long as no customers come in who might overhear us, it's time for me to face Monroe and tell him the truth."

Monroe walked with a spring to his step as he made his way to Belinda's greenhouse. He could hardly wait to share his good news and hoped she'd be as excited about it as he was.

Upon entering the building, he was pleased to see her sitting behind the front counter. Since there were no cars or other horse and buggies parked in the lot, he assumed she didn't have any customers at the moment, which was good. *I'll have my bride-to-be all to myself,* he thought with confidence. *And none of her children appear to be around, especially that unfriendly son of hers. If I become Henry's stepfather I'll have my hands full. But I'm not worried. I'm sure things will work out in time.*

Unable to keep from smiling, he stepped right up to the counter and said hello. Then with feet pointed forward and shoulders straight back, Monroe announced: "I have some good news that could affect both of us."

Belinda squinted as she pushed her reading glasses up to the bridge of her nose. "Really? What kind of good news?"

"While I was gone this past week, I made a lucrative business transaction in the outskirts of an Amish community near Harrisburg."

"I see."

"Aren't you interested in what it was?" Monroe shuffled his feet. *Something seems off, but maybe it's my imagination playing tricks on me.*

"Certainly, if you wish to tell me."

Monroe leaned slightly forward, resting his hands on the counter. "I bought another furniture store, and the business is thriving, so I'll soon be making even more money than I am now." He grinned at her. "I'm becoming a real entrepreneur." *Herschel doesn't have a chance. Belinda must see that I'm the perfect man and only true love for her.*

"Well, I guess you are."

Belinda's placid expression had Monroe worried. Wasn't she excited for him? "Would you like to hear more?" he asked.

She nodded slowly. At least she hadn't said no.

"I've been looking for houses in the Strasburg area, and I think I've found the perfect one for us."

Belinda's eyes widened. "Us?"

He pointed to her and then himself. "You and me, for after we're married."

"Oh. . .uh, Monroe. . .where did you get the idea that you and I were going to get married?"

"I just assumed, since we've been courting for a while. . ."

She held up her hand. "We've gone to supper a few times, and you've come here fairly often, but we haven't been officially courting."

"Really, well, I thought we were." Monroe turned his palms upward. "But okay, whatever. The point is, I've spent a good many months trying to prove my love for you, and I figure it's about time for us to get married."

Belinda glanced around, as though looking for someone, and then her facial muscles went slack.

What's going on here? His gaze rested on Belinda. *I've done everything right. Has something changed between us while I've been away?* "Say something, please."

The silence deafened Monroe's senses as he waited for her response. This was supposed to be a most happy moment, but things weren't going the way he'd hoped. He looked around, making sure they were still alone and hoping they could continue their private conversation.

"I am sorry, Monroe, but I cannot marry you."

Monroe stood frozen, unable to digest this information. *Belinda's rejection brings me right back to the day she turned me down for Vernon. It hurt then, and it is just as painful now.*

"How come? Haven't I proven my devotion to you? Don't you realize that I can provide well for you?" He made an arc with his arms, as he turned in several directions, and then back to face her. "You'll be faced with running this place with only the help of your teenage son after Sylvia is married. Think about it, Belinda. If you marry me, you won't have to do that anymore. We'll be co-owners of this business and we can hire someone else to run it." Monroe leaned in closer. "I love you, Belinda. I always have, and if you'll think it through, you'll realize that we were meant to be together."

Belinda covered her mouth with her hand as she slowly shook her head.

He reached over and pulled her hand away. "Please don't say no. It's okay if you don't love me as much as I love you. In time, after we've been married awhile, you could develop stronger feelings for me. I'm sure if you think about it, you'll come to realize that I'm the best man for you."

Belinda pulled her hand back. "I can't marry you, Monroe, because I'm in love with Herschel, and I've promised to marry him in December."

"What?" Monroe felt like his eyes were about to bulge right out of their sockets. "You can't be serious, Belinda. This must be a joke!"

"I am telling you the truth. Herschel proposed to me a week ago, and I said yes."

"A week ago?"

"Yes, it was the same day he came here to help clear away the debris left from the storm."

"Is that so? Guess it must have taken place after I left then, huh?"

"Yes, Monroe. Herschel and I were sitting in my yard after lunch, and—"

His face heated, and he slapped his hand on the surface of the counter. "That's lecherich! He is not the man for you."

"It's not ridiculous. I love Herschel very much, and he loves me."

Monroe shook his head determinedly. "Not as much as I do. Besides, what does that boring old man even have to offer you?

"Herschel is not boring or old. He's a fine person, with kind, gentle ways."

"Are you implying that I'm not a good person?"

"You have many fine attributes." Belinda's voice softened as she lowered her gaze. "I don't want to hurt your feelings, Monroe." She paused a few seconds before continuing. "I'm not in love with you, and I am sorry if I've said or done anything to make you believe we could be anything other than friends."

Monroe's muscles quivered and his heart pounded in his chest. "You'll be sorry you chose him over me, Belinda. Jah, you can count on my words." Monroe whirled around and stomped out the door. All this time he'd worked so hard to win Belinda's heart and hand, and now she'd chosen an older man with a graying beard?

He gritted his teeth. *That woman must be touched in the head.*

Henry stood inside the back door of the greenhouse, wondering if he should have made himself known and said something to Monroe the minute he started pressuring Mom about marrying him.

Henry's toes curled inside his boots. *The nerve of that man expecting my mamm to accept his proposal—such as it was. Monroe's pushy and arrogant, and he's still on my list of suspects.* He wiped the sweat from his brow. *With Monroe's tone when he basically told Mom she'd have regrets if she married Herschel, I have to say that her ex-boyfriend has some serious issues. Since he's so upset, I bet we'll have more problems, because I still think he is the one behind all our troubles.*

Although no vandalism had been done to their place recently, Henry remembered the last threatening phone message they'd received, saying they had until December to put the place up for sale and move. Mom hadn't done it, of course, and Henry couldn't blame her. She and Dad had started the greenhouse together, and there was no way she'd let it go and move off this land.

Henry had given up playing detective for the time being, since there'd been no more attacks, but if anything else should happen again, he'd be more determined than ever to find out who was behind their problem.

Henry's thoughts returned to Monroe. He was glad Mom had stood up to the man, letting him know she didn't love him and couldn't accept his proposal.

Henry bit the inside of his cheek. *I wish Mom would do the same with Herschel. She needs to break things off with him, and I have to think of some way to make it happen, because I can't stand the thought of Herschel moving into our house and trying to replace my dad.*

Henry's face heated as another thought popped into his head. *What if Herschel expects Mom to sell this place and move to Gordonville to live with him? Just where would that leave* me?

More sweat formed on Henry's forehead and dribbled onto his face. *There's no way I'm moving into that man's house. If necessary, I'll leave Strasburg for good. I wonder if Ezekiel and Michelle would take me in. If not, then I'll get a job and strike out on my own, 'cause I won't be any man's stepson.*

Chapter 37

Clymer

"I still can't believe your mamm and Herschel are engaged," Michelle said to Ezekiel as they sat at the supper table with their children.

"I know. I was surprised myself when I listened to Mom's voice-mail message, telling us about it."

"Surprised in a good way though, right?"

"Jah. I think Mom made the right choice when she picked Herschel over Monroe. He's a nice fellow, and his personality is better suited to hers."

Michelle smiled. "We will go down for their wedding in December, I hope."

"Definitely. Wouldn't miss it for the world." Ezekiel reached for a piece of bread and spread creamy butter over it. "We'll go to Strasburg in September after Amy's baby is born, and make another trip for Dennis and Sylvia's wedding in October."

Michelle's face broke into a wide smile. "Oh good. That certainly gives us a lot to look forward to."

"It sure does. I'll see about hiring a driver for the first trip as soon as we get word that my sister's had her baby."

Michelle reached over and wiped little Vernon's messy face. "I wonder if she and Jared are hoping for a boy or a girl."

"I'm sure they'll be happy with either one, but Jared might like a son who he can eventually train to join him in the roofing trade."

"And Amy may want a daughter she can teach to cook, sew, tend her garden, and do many other things." She placed her hand on Angela

Mary's shoulder and gave it a squeeze. "We are fortunate, Ezekiel, because God gave us one of each."

Strasburg

"It's too hot out here, and the flies are bad," Virginia complained as she and her husband sat at the picnic table in their yard, eating the evening meal. "I'd rather be in the house where it's air-conditioned."

"Aw, don't be such a sissy. It ain't summer unless a person enjoys a meal outside now and then." Earl grabbed another hot dog and slapped it in a bun. "You oughta be happy sitting out here where you can listen to the birds carrying on." He gestured to an area across the yard. "And just feast your eyes on all those pretty white posies over there."

Virginia turned her head to look in the direction he pointed. "Those aren't posies, they're daisies, and boy, do they stink!"

His brows furrowed. "Really? I thought most flowers smelled sweet, like perfume."

"Not those. Their odor is worse than the horse droppings on the road out front." Virginia plugged her nose. "Phew!"

"If they're so bad, why don't you remove 'em from the flowerbed?"

"I pulled them out last year after they'd finished blooming, but some must have reseeded."

"Well the next time you yank out the smelly daisies, let me know and I'll spray some weed killer all over the spot where they'd been growing."

"That might work, but then nothing else will grow there either."

"Guess you'll have to decide what's more important to you—an empty flowerbed or flowers that look pretty but stink." Earl snatched up his hot dog and held it close to his mouth. "Now can we quit talkin' long enough for me to eat this?"

"Sure, Earl, enjoy yourself while I try to eat the potato salad I worked so hard to make today. Just be careful you don't end up eating one of those pesky flies that's been buzzin' our heads ever since we sat down."

He snorted and shrugged his shoulders. "If I do, it'll be a little more protein added to my meal."

Virginia rolled her eyes at him. Earl might think what he'd said was funny, but she thought it was gross—enough to ruin her appetite.

"I'm glad that bad storm we had didn't damage our roof," Earl commented after he finished eating his hot dog. He eyeballed the pan of hot dogs and forked another. "Sure do like this brand of dogs you bought us, but now back to the topic of the roof. I'm relieved that it all stayed intact and we're not stuck with more expenses."

Virginia took a sip of her iced coffee. "Me too. I felt relieved when Jared looked at it and said the roof was fine. That means we won't have to use any of the vacation money we've been saving up."

Earl grabbed a handful of potato chips and dropped them onto his plate. "About that, Virginia—"

"Are you planning a surprise trip for me?"

He shook his head. "How would you feel about foregoing our vacation plans and buying a big-screen TV instead?"

Her jaw clenched. "Oh, so you can waste more time sitting in front of the TV with the volume blaring until it gives me a headache? I don't think so, Earl. I want us to take a trip so we can get out of this boring place for a while."

Earl patted her hand after taking a swig from his sweaty glass of cola, apparently unshaken by her outburst. "We both have our favorite shows on TV, and just think how much more enjoyable it would be to watch them on a bigger screen."

She grimaced and wiped her hand with a napkin. "Can't we go on vacation and get a new TV too? I don't think they're that expensive."

"The really good ones are over a thousand dollars."

He'll never budge from that television set if we get the big expensive one. "That's ridiculous, Earl. We don't need anything that fancy."

"We do if we wanna keep up with the latest technology. You have a smartphone, right?"

"Yeah, but what's that got to do with—"

"The television I have my eye on is a smart TV. We'd be able to go on the internet with it and access YouTube and many other places where you can watch all kinds of movies."

Virginia groaned. "Let's forget the TV and go on a nice vacation to the shore this fall like we've talked about. We can rent a little cottage and stay for a week."

"We can discuss this later. Right now, I'd like to eat the rest of my meal in peace." Earl's shoulders pushed back, and Virginia saw the determined set of his jaw. No doubt he would win out and buy a new television, but if she had anything to say about it, they'd be going to the beach too.

"I'm a little nervous about talking to Maude and wondering how we should bring up the topic of who owns the old cabin," Sylvia said to Dennis as they walked along the shoulder of the road in the direction of Maude's rundown shack. She wondered if the older woman might not be straightforward with them.

Sylvia looked over at him. "Mom has been the one person that Maude seems to like. I sure hope we don't offend her with our questions."

"Would you like me to bring up the topic?"

Her tone perked up. "If you don't mind. I'd probably end up saying the wrong thing, and then she might clam up and refuse to tell us anything."

He agreed. "That might be especially true if she is living there without the permission from the person who owns the place. Maude may not even know who the owner is."

"I hope that's not the case. I don't think we can do any renovations without the proper person's approval."

"We're almost there, so we should know something soon." Dennis pointed up ahead when the shanty came into view. "This place could use more than just some work on the roof. It looks like it's been neglected for a long time and in need of much care."

As they drew closer, Sylvia spotted Maude sitting outside on a tattered-looking wicker chair that looked like it should have been thrown out with the trash. It had definitely seen better days.

"Hello, Maude," Sylvia said as she and Dennis approached the woman.

"Howdy. What are you two doin' over here?"

"We came by to talk about the cabin you live in," Dennis responded.

"Yeah, well, it ain't much, but a least it's a place for me to sleep, eat, and get outa the weather when it rains." Maude gestured to a wooden bench that didn't look much better than the chair she sat upon. "Take a seat."

Sylvia looked at Dennis, wondering if it was strong enough for them both to sit on, but when he sat down, she did the same. The bench didn't give way, so she figured they might be okay.

Dennis cleared his throat. "As Sylvia's mother mentioned to you previously, we would like to spruce the cabin up so it's more livable, but we need to know who the owner is so we can ask their permission."

Maude carved her fingers through the ends of her shoulder-length hair, pulled it away from her face, held it back, and then released it. "The place is mine, fair and square."

"Oh, so you bought it from someone?" The question came from Dennis.

"Nope. It belonged to my grandparents, on my daddy's side." Maude paused and flapped her hand in front of her face. "Whew, it sure is hot this evening. Thought it woulda cooled down some by now."

Sylvia gave Dennis a gentle nudge, hoping he would turn the conversation back to the cabin. He must have gotten her message, for he looked at Maude and said, "Did they leave it to you legally?"

"Yeah, it was in their will. Grandpa died first, and then a year later, Grandma followed, but I didn't come here to stay in this place till a few years ago. I'd been living with a friend at that time and didn't have any need to hurry here and settle down. I suppose I should admit that in my younger days my life took off in a bad direction." Maude paused once more—this time to blow her nose on a hanky she'd pulled from the pocket of her faded trousers. "I ain't got much money, except for the small monthly pension I've received since my husband, Fred, died five years ago." She sniffed and blew her nose again. "I manage to get by, though sometimes it's slim pickings for me."

Sylvia's heart went out to Maude. She couldn't imagine what it must be like to live all alone with so little money in this small, dilapidated shanty. She figured it must be hard for the poor woman to talk about it to people she hardly knew.

"Did your grandparents live in this cabin at one time or were there other buildings on the property?" Dennis asked.

Maude pointed to the shack. "This is where they lived, but I'm sure it looked better at that time than it does now. From what I've been told, they planned to build a bigger home, but that never happened because they ended up movin' to Minnesota when my great-grandpappy died."

"Thank you for sharing the information." Dennis spoke in a kindly tone. "We'll be on our way now, but someone will be over to see you soon about when we can begin fixing some things in and around your cabin."

Maude gave the hint of a smile. "Sounds good."

Sylvia rose from the bench. "If you need anything between now and then, please let us know."

"Okay."

"We'll see you later, Maude. I hope you have a pleasant rest of your evening." Sylvia gave a wave and followed Dennis across the overgrown yard.

"It sure is nice to have some time alone with you and chat," Belinda said as she and Herschel sat together on her front porch swing. He had stopped by shortly after Sylvia and Dennis left to talk to Maude, and they'd been visiting for the last forty-five minutes or so, while Allen and Rachel chased after the fireflies rising up from the grass.

"Monroe dropped by the greenhouse today." Belinda looked over at Herschel to see how he would react.

"I'm guessing he didn't come to buy anything?"

"No, he wanted to talk to me." Belinda fingered the front of her apron. *Should I tell him everything Monroe said or just the basics?* She opted for the latter.

"He asked—no pretty much stated—that he and I should get married and was quite upset when I told him that I'd accepted your marriage proposal."

"I'm not surprised." Herschel reached over and clasped Belinda's hand, giving her fingers a gentle squeeze. "I still can hardly believe you chose me over him."

"It was an easy choice, because you're the man I love." Belinda smiled. "I could never be as happy with Monroe as I am with you."

The blue in Herschel's eyes deepened as his gaze remained fixed on her. He pulled Belinda into his arms and gave her a kiss on the mouth that felt as soft as butterfly wings.

Belinda's pulse raced as she melted into his embrace. Although her love for Herschel was different than what she'd felt for Vernon, it was equally strong. She knew without a shadow of a doubt that he was the man for her.

Their lingering kiss was interrupted when Belinda heard Sylvia call out to her children: "How many *feierveggel* have you caught?" Belinda quickly pulled away from Herschel.

Oh, I hope she and Dennis didn't see us kissing. Belinda felt heat on her cheeks as she rose from the swing and was glad when Herschel followed her into the yard.

"How'd it go at Maude's place? Did you have a chance to talk to her?" Belinda asked.

"Yes we did," Sylvia responded.

"Why don't we all take a seat on the porch and then we can talk about it," Dennis suggested.

As they stepped onto the porch, Sylvia came alongside Belinda and whispered in her ear: "Was that the first time Herschel's kissed you?"

Belinda's face grew hotter as she nodded.

"I'm glad you've found such a nice man. You deserve to be happy, Mom." Sylvia gave Belinda's arm a tender squeeze. "And don't let anything Henry says discourage you."

"I'll try not to," Belinda responded. *But my son's making it quite difficult for me,* she admitted to herself. *I hope he changes his attitude toward Herschel.*

Chapter 38

Things moved along quickly during the remainder of August. Maude's cabin got a makeover, and the remodels to Sylvia's house were almost finished.

On the first day of September, before she opened the greenhouse, Belinda went to the phone shed to check for messages. To her delight there was one from Jared, letting them know that Amy had delivered a baby boy at two o'clock that morning. The home birth with the aid of a midwife went well. Both mother and son were doing fine, and they would welcome company later today when Amy felt more rested. The name they'd chosen for their baby boy was Dewayne Aaron, named after Jared's and Amy's paternal grandfathers.

Tears welled in Belinda's eyes, almost blurring her vision. *Thank You, Lord, for my new grandson's safe delivery.*

She lifted the cover on the notepad, to write down the baby's weight, length, and his name. Seeing that something had already been written on the new page, she wiped the tears from her eyes and slipped on her reading glasses.

"Oh my!" Belinda's body broke out in a cold sweat as she stared at the words: *"Are You Ready to Sell? Your time's running out."*

There had been no vandalism for some time, nor more threatening notes or voice-mail messages. Belinda shivered. *Someone must have come into the phone shed during the night or earlier this morning and written this note. But why? What were they trying to prove?*

Wondering if the person responsible may have also left a message on her answering machine, Belinda clicked the button and listened. The only message besides Jared's was from the man who owned the land-scaping business, wanting to place another order.

Belinda sat in the chair, rocking back and forth, as she tried to figure out what to do. *Should I tell anyone in my family about this note or keep quiet?*

Thinking how someone had entered her phone shed and written the threatening message caused another chill to course through Belinda's body. *Guess I ought to at least let Henry and Sylvia know about this so they can help me figure out what, if anything, we should do. Telling Ezekiel is out of the question, because if he knew what has been going on the past two-plus years, he'd not only be upset with me for keeping him in the dark, but would insist on selling his place and moving back here.*

She shifted on the chair. *I don't want to feel this way, but I am wondering if Monroe has something to do with this because I chose Herschel over him.*

Belinda sat quietly for a while, thinking things through and praying for God's guidance. Finally, she picked up the notepad, stepped out of the shed, and headed for the house. Her excitement and joy after hearing Jared's message had been dampened, but at the same time, it was something positive to focus on.

"What took you so long?" Henry asked when his mother returned to the house. "I thought you wanted to go over a few things with me and Sylvia before we head out to the greenhouse this morning." He noticed the notepad in his mother's hand. *Why does Mom have the tablet from the phone shed? Usually we write down the information from the answering machine on it and tear off the page to bring into the house, not the whole pad.*

"Sylvia won't be working with us today after all," Mom answered. "Jared left a message saying Amy had her boppli earlier this morning, so she obviously will not be coming to watch Allen and Rachel today."

"How exciting!" Sylvia gave Mom a wide grin.

"What'd she have?" Henry asked.

"Is the baby healthy? Is Amy doing okay?" More questions from Sylvia.

Mom held up her hand. "Please slow down, you two. I can only answer one question at a time."

"Sorry." Sylvia took a seat at the kitchen table, and Henry did the same. After their mother joined them, she replied to each of their questions.

When finished, she looked over at Henry and said, "We'll close the greenhouse at four o'clock this afternoon so we can have an early supper, and then we'll all go over to Amy and Jared's to see the new boppli."

"That sounds good," Sylvia said, "but if I don't work in the greenhouse, you'll be shorthanded."

"Henry and I can manage by ourselves today," Mom replied. "But before Monday, we will need to find someone else to either watch the kinner or help in the greenhouse."

"It would take time to train someone to work in the greenhouse, unless they'd had experience working in that capacity," Sylvia responded. "I'll call Lenore and see if she'd be willing to watch Rachel and Allen so I can keep working in the greenhouse. Maybe I can take them over to her place, which would make it easier for Lenore, since she needs to stick close to home to help with chores Mary Ruth is not able to do."

Mom smiled, but Henry noticed that her eyes held no sparkle. He figured she'd be so excited about Amy and Jared's new baby that she wouldn't be able to stop smiling.

Mom put the notebook on the table. "The thrill of hearing the news that I have a new grandson was dampened when I read this note someone had written on the tablet we use in the phone shed for messages."

"Someone?" Henry tipped his head. "You mean one of us?"

"No, this was written by somebody who must have gone into our phone shed during the night or very early this morning." Mom pushed the notepad over to Henry. "Open it to the first newly written page."

Henry did as she asked, and his eyes widened as he stared at the printed message.

"What does it say?" Sylvia asked. "Your *gsicht* is bright red."

"Your face will be red too after you read this." He pushed the tablet over to her.

When Sylvia spoke again, her voice trembled. "Who keeps doing this to us? Just when we think there will be no more vandalism or threats, another one comes." She heaved a sigh. "This is so discouraging."

Henry looked at his mother. "Know what I think we oughta do?"

"What's that? And please don't say I should call the sheriff."

"Instead of letting Blackie sleep inside the house, wouldn't it be better if he stayed outside at night? That way, if an intruder comes onto our property while we're sleeping, my hund's bound to see them and bark out a warning."

"That might be advisable, but I'm beginning to think it may be best if I sell the greenhouse as well as our home."

"You're kidding, right?" Henry couldn't believe his mother would say such a thing. The business had been part of her life for a good many years, and she'd said many times that she would not let it go or be run out of here by somebody who obviously didn't like them.

"Since your daed died, I've held on to the business for sentimental reasons and to provide for my family," Mom said. "But the fact is, once Herschel and I are married, my needs will be provided for, and yours too, Henry. I'm sure my husband will want us to sell this place and move to his home in Gordonville."

"That's too much change for me. My life is here, where I was born." Henry slapped the palm of his hand against the surface of the table. "I don't wanna move to Gordonville, and I don't need Herschel to provide anything for me."

"Calm down, Henry, and please lower your voice." Sylvia pointed to the door leading to the living room across the hall. "It upsets my kinner when people shout, so please try to control your emotions."

His tone lowered. "I'm weary of this family going through the trial we seem to be facing. I just want it to end and things to go back to normal." Henry's mouth clamped shut, and he tapped his fingers along the tabletop. *I wonder who wants us to sell out and move away. I still think it must be Monroe.*

He sat up tall in his chair as once more, his thoughts took him down the list of suspects he'd created. Whether it was Monroe or not, Henry was more desperate than ever to find out who was behind all of this.

Although Virginia had seen the mailman's vehicle go by a few hours ago, she'd waited until after lunch to cross the street and get it. Now, back in her yard, she took a seat on the front porch and shuffled through the letters. One in particular caught her eye because it had the Kings' address in one corner.

Now why would they send anything to me and Earl? Maybe they're planning some sort of get-together and have invited us to attend.

Virginia tore the letter open and nearly dropped the card when she realized it was an invitation to Sylvia and Dennis's wedding, which would take place the first Thursday of October. "Now this is a surprise."

Continuing to stare at the invitation, Virginia wondered if she ought to call her friend Stella and tell her the news. She held the card against her chest and pondered the situation. *When Earl gets home, I'll talk to him about this. If he says we can go to the shindig, I'll let Stella know. She was fascinated with the Amish way of life when she was here visiting the last time. I'm sure she would jump at the chance to attend an Amish wedding.*

She placed the invitation in her lap and focused on the house across the road. *For that matter, it might be kinda interesting for me and Earl to see up close what the Plain people's wedding is like.*

Belinda's throat clogged as she gazed at her newest grandson, resting peacefully in his mother's arms.

"He's a beautiful boppli," she whispered. "Welcome to the world, Dewayne Aaron Riehl."

"Such a big name for a little guy. I assume everyone will just call him Dewayne?" Sylvia looked at Jared.

"I guess so, unless Amy prefers to call him Aaron. We haven't really talked about it."

Although Amy looked tired, her smile was radiant as she stroked the top of her son's downy dark head. "Either one is fine with me, but I kind of favor the name Dewayne."

"Have Jared's parents been by to see the boppli yet?" Belinda asked. "I'm sure they're as thrilled as I am about having a new grandson."

"I spoke with my mamm earlier," Jared responded. "Dad developed a pretty bad headache today, so she said they'd come by sometime tomorrow. Oh! I called Ezekiel too, but young Vernon has a cold, so they won't be coming to see the baby right away."

"I can't believe your little guy came almost a week earlier than your due date." Sylvia touched the baby's wee hand. "Both of mine came nearly a week late."

Amy shrugged. "Maybe we miscalculated."

"Well it doesn't matter. He's here and is healthy, which is all that counts." Sylvia turned to face Henry. "You're awfully quiet. What do you have to say about your new nephew?"

"He's sure *bissel*."

"You were that small once too," Belinda said.

"That's right. All *bopplin* are little when they're first born." Jared chuckled and bumped Henry's arm. "You need to know things like this, because someday you'll get married and have some babies."

"Yeah, right," Henry muttered. "I ain't never gettin' married."

"Bet you'll change your mind once the right girl comes along." Amy looked at her brother and grinned. "First comes love and then marriage."

"Yeah, I know. . .and sometime after that I'm stuck pushing a baby carriage."

Everyone laughed, including Rachel and Allen, although Belinda felt sure they didn't know what was so funny.

They visited awhile, and all the adults except Henry took turns holding little Dewayne.

Belinda couldn't help but notice her son's placid expression as he sat cross-legged on the floor by the children. She figured he might be thinking about the note she'd found in the phone shed earlier today. It had been on her mind too, but Belinda refused to let it ruin her day or suck the joy out of being here right now as they welcomed a new member of their family.

She closed her eyes briefly and prayed. *Heavenly Father, please bless Jared, Amy, and their precious little boy. May he grow up with the wisdom and knowledge that the only way to heaven is through Jesus Christ, Your Son.*

Chapter 39

September went by quickly, and Belinda divided her time between the greenhouse, working in her garden, spending time with the family, and helping Sylvia with all the final wedding preparations. Belinda also saw Herschel several times a week, and with each visit, she fell more deeply in love with him.

When Belinda shared with Herschel about the vandalism that had been done in various places on her property, he suggested putting some bright motion-activated solar lights around the yard. Belinda didn't know why she hadn't thought of the idea herself, since she sold several kinds of solar lights in one section of the greenhouse.

I could see the look of concern on his face, and when he spoke to me, his tone was calming to my ears. I'm blessed to have a man I love and who cares for me and my family. And Herschel is determined to get to the bottom of the vandalism, Belinda thought as she made her bed.

She hoped the reason there hadn't been any problems on the property lately was because Blackie had been sleeping outside in his pen and would surely have warned them if anyone came into the yard.

Something else that hadn't been resolved was whether Belinda should hire someone to help in the greenhouse or try to manage things on her own with only Henry's help. She thought it might be doable, since she'd be closing the business for the winter by the end of November and possibly indefinitely. It would depend on where Herschel wanted them to live after they got married. This was a subject they had not yet talked about, but would need to do so soon.

Lenore had agreed to watch Sylvia's children, but in just a few weeks that would no longer be necessary. Once Sylvia and Dennis were married, she would stay at home with the children instead of helping in the greenhouse. Many changes were happening within the family, giving her so much to think about.

Monroe hadn't come around since the day Belinda told him that she and Herschel planned to be married. Belinda had been concerned that he might try to persuade her into choosing him over Herschel. But the more days and weeks that passed, the better Belinda felt. She hoped he had accepted her decision and would move on with his life. Belinda wished she had never agreed to see Monroe socially because it had caused him to believe he had a chance at winning her hand in marriage.

After Belinda got dressed for the day, she opened up the window shades in her room before leaving. *I pray that a good woman will come into Monroe's life. He is deserving of someone, and only You, Lord, can provide a suitable mate for him.*

As Belinda entered the kitchen to prepare breakfast, she glanced out the window by the sink and gasped. A good portion of their vegetable garden had been trampled, leaving only one section untouched. *So much for solar lights and a dog that didn't bark. Of course,* Belinda reasoned, *it may not have been a person who destroyed part of the garden. It could have been some animal tromping on the vegetable patch.*

That idea had no more than flitted through her head when she heard a familiar *m-a-a. . .m-a-a. . .m-a-a. . .*

What is going on outside? Belinda wondered. A few seconds later, three frisky goats pranced across the lawn, heading toward the garden. *Oh no, you don't. You've done enough to our nice garden that we've worked hard to grow.*

Belinda grabbed a broom from the utility porch and raced out the back door. Shouting and shaking the end of the broom at the ill-mannered animals, she hoped they would have enough sense to go back to the yard from which they had apparently escaped.

"What is all the ruckus about?" Sylvia asked, leaving the house and joining Belinda in the yard.

Before Belinda had a chance to response, Henry came around the corner of the house and turned the hose on. He directed the stream of water at the goats but ended up spraying Sylvia instead.

"Yikes, that's cold!" Sylvia raced up the back steps and took shelter on the porch.

"Oops, sorry about that." Henry aimed the hose at the goats once more, and this time Belinda ended up getting wet.

"For goodness' sake, Henry, please watch what you're doing!" Belinda was tempted to grab the hose from his hand and give him a good dousing. If she hadn't been so angry at the goats for ruining one section of the garden, Belinda might have thought the whole thing had been funny.

When the feisty animals kept kicking up their heels and frolicking about, she grabbed the hose from Henry and shouted, "Let Blackie out of his pen. I'm almost certain he will chase those crazy critters out of the yard."

Henry handed the hose to Belinda and hurried across the lawn. Soon the dog was out of his pen, leading the goats on a merry chase. A few trips around the yard with Blackie barking and nipping at their heels, and every one of the goats made a hasty exit from Belinda's property.

Still holding the hose, and with the water turned on, she shot a little spray in Henry's direction.

"Hey! What'd ya do that for, Mom?"

"Thought you might need to cool off." She chuckled. "This day is starting off to be rather warm."

"It ain't funny." He leaped onto the porch and stepped behind Sylvia.

Belinda let loose with another laugh, only this one more boisterous. "At least that cold water got our blood pumping this morning, jah?"

"What about the poor garden?" Sylvia pointed to the trampled plants. "What those *gees* did to it pretty much puts the kibosh to us canning the last of the tomatoes."

Belinda turned off the water and joined Henry and Sylvia on the porch. "It's okay. With your wedding coming up in two weeks, we really don't have time to do much more canning."

Sylvia sighed. "Even so, it would have been nice to have the tomatoes and other produce to eat. Our neighbors down the road who own those goats should make an effort to keep them penned up."

"Some gees can be pretty crafty," Henry interjected. "They're good at figuring their way out, even when they're fenced in."

Belinda nodded. "Which is why we don't own any goats. They'd just be one more thing to worry about."

Sylvia opened the front door. "Guess we'd better go inside and get breakfast started. Allen and Rachel will be up soon, and before you know it, Henry will need to take them over to Lenore's so we can open the greenhouse."

A short while after Belinda entered the greenhouse, she spotted a beautiful Monarch butterfly hovering over one of the flowering bushes. She stood watching for several minutes, almost mesmerized by the flying insect's gorgeous colors and delicate, fluttering wings.

Belinda moved on down the row, pausing to pluck some dead leaves off a rust-colored dahlia plant. *People plant flowers for different reasons,* she thought. *Some enjoy the beauty of the blossoms, while others like the sweet fragrance that many flowering plants give off. Then there are people who plant flowers for the fun of simply watching them grow.*

She placed one hand on her chest. *And I plant* blumme *for all of those reasons.*

Belinda couldn't imagine not owning this greenhouse, with so much floral beauty around her each day. After she and Herschel were married, she would miss the joy of working with her hands and watching things grow before putting them on the shelves to offer her customers. If only there was some way she could continue to run the greenhouse after they became husband and wife. But that would be a challenge, since Herschel's home was in Gordonville, which would mean a commute every day. Besides, if she moved to her new husband's place, she'd have to sell her own home, and whoever bought the house might also want the greenhouse. This was an issue she should have talked with Herschel about before agreeing to marry him or at the very least soon after they became engaged.

Belinda turned and reached the front counter as the front door opened. She was surprised when Herschel entered the building. Normally, he came by later in the day and then stayed for supper.

"Guder mariye," she said with a smile. "I wasn't expecting to see you here at this time of day."

"Good morning to you too." He moved over to stand beside her. "I hope you're not disappointed."

"Of course not." Her face warmed. "I'm always pleased to see you." It was silly and made Belinda feel like a schoolgirl, but sometimes merely looking at her intended caused her to blush.

"I came to talk to you about something, and I thought if I got here early enough, you might not have any customers yet."

"You're right. Henry and Sylvia aren't even here yet, although I do expect they'll be along soon."

"Well good, then no one will be embarrassed when I do this." Herschel embraced Belinda and kissed her gently on the lips. Now she felt like a giddy teenager.

When they pulled apart, he smiled and said. "There's something we haven't talked about that needs to be discussed."

"Oh, what's that?"

"Our living arrangements once we are married."

"It's funny you should bring that topic up because I was thinking about that very thing before you arrived."

Herschel cleared his throat. "I was wondering what you would think of the idea of me selling my business in Gordonville and helping you run the greenhouse after we're married. Would it bother you to live in the same home with me that you once shared with Vernon?"

Belinda felt an unexpected release of all tension as she slowly shook her head. "I wouldn't have a problem with that at all."

Herschel grinned and gave her a second kiss. "That's what I was hoping to hear."

Belinda felt such a sense of exhilaration it was hard to keep from bouncing on her toes. She'd never expected Herschel would want to be part of the greenhouse or that he'd be willing to sell the bulk-food store and move here to Strasburg. Her only concern was how Henry would react to the arrangement. He still hadn't accepted the idea of Belinda marrying Herschel, and what if he never did?

Virginia picked up the cell phone and dialed her friend's number. Stella answered on the second ring. "Hi, Stella. How's it going?"

"Good. How are things with you?"

"Pretty much the same—except for one thing."

"What's that?"

"We got an invitation to the wedding of Belinda's oldest daughter, and I figured you might want to come here for a visit and go to the event with us."

"Sounds like fun. When will it take place?"

"Two weeks from today, at nine o'clock in the morning."

There was a brief pause before Stella responded. "Sorry, Virginia, but I won't be able to make it."

"How come?" Virginia couldn't hide her disappointment.

"Joe and I already have plans on that day as well as the weekend that follows."

"Can't you change them? It's a pretty big deal to be invited to an Amish wedding, and it sure would be nice if you could be there with me."

"I'd like to attend, but our trip to the shore was planned some time ago, and we'd lose money if we cancelled the reservations we made to rent a house that is practically on the sandy beach."

"Yeah, okay, I understand." Virginia gave a frustrated shake of her head. *So my friend gets to spend time at the beach, and Earl and I probably won't make it there this year—especially since he spent a good chunk of the money we were saving on a big-screen TV.*

"I'd like to talk more, Virginia, but I have a dental appointment in an hour and I can't be late. We'll catch up again after my mini-vacation, and you can tell me all about the Amish wedding."

"Okay, sure. Bye, Stella." Virginia clicked off the phone and lowered her head. She wasn't that enthused about attending Sylvia's wedding, but if she and Earl went, at least she'd have something interesting to share with Stella. Maybe it would even entice her friend to come back to Strasburg for another visit.

Virginia sagged against her chair. *At least I can hope for that.*

She felt Goldie's soft fur against her leg and reached down to pet her. Virginia was rewarded with a soft *meow* and some gentle purring. How thankful she was for the cat, because there were times like now when Virginia felt like she didn't have a friend in the world. Tears sprang to her eyes. *I have no family except Earl and no friends who live close by. Maybe I deserve the situation I find myself in, because I've made so many bad choices in my life.*

Chapter 40

"I can't believe we are about to attend an Amish wedding," Virginia commented to Earl as they were ushered into Belinda King's barn through tall double doors.

He nudged her arm. "Please keep your voice down. I feel conspicuous, and some people are already looking at us."

"Stop it, Earl," Virginia whispered. "They're looking because we're not one of them."

"Yeah, okay, whatever you say."

Virginia felt relieved when they were invited to take seats on folding chairs in an area where three other non-Amish couples sat. *At least Earl and I aren't the only ones not wearing Plain clothes.*

Virginia looked down at her own attire. With Earl's help she had chosen a pair of bright blue slacks that blended well with a coral-and-blue-patterned blouse. Her gold-and-blue jewelry was bold and bright, to accentuate the outfit. Virginia had also recolored her hair a few days ago, and the red was most vibrant.

As other people arrived and took their seats, Virginia studied the large building. The wooden walls were rustic and rough-looking. Behind her, she noticed a ladder leading up to a loft. How odd it seemed to have a big wedding inside of a barn.

Virginia sniffed. Despite all the cleaning and clearing away of the animals this barn would normally house, she detected the faint aroma of horseflesh and manure. It seemed that no amount of scrubbing could completely dispel such putrid odors.

Virginia fiddled with her wedding ring, wondering when things would get started. She hoped the service wouldn't take long, because the metal chairs that she and Earl sat upon were hard and unyielding. She couldn't imagine how the Amish people sitting on backless wooden benches might feel by the end of a wedding, funeral, or church service. Virginia's back, and even her bum leg, would probably be stiff and sore from sitting more than thirty minutes on one of those benches.

"Look, Earl, here comes the bride and groom." Virginia bumped Earl's arm with her elbow as Sylvia and Dennis entered the barn and took seats in chairs facing each other near the center of the room. Two other couples had walked in behind them. The women sat on either side of the bride and the two young men did the same with the groom. Sylvia's sister, Amy, was one of the women, but Virginia didn't recognize the other young woman. Virginia presumed she might be a friend of Sylvia's, or maybe a cousin. She knew Sylvia's teenage brother, who had accompanied Dennis, but Virginia couldn't remember having met the young man sitting on the other side of Dennis. Maybe he too was a relative or friend.

Virginia noticed Belinda sitting behind Sylvia and her attendants. She held a baby in her arms. After talking to Belinda at the mailbox a few weeks ago, Virginia had learned that Amy had given birth to a baby boy. No doubt the infant Belinda held belonged to Amy and her husband, Jared.

Next to Belinda sat a young Amish woman with auburn hair. She held a small boy in her lap, and a little girl sat beside her. Virginia had not seen this woman before, and wondered if she too might be related to the King family. From what Virginia had heard, the Amish liked big families, so there was no telling how many people in this barn were related to either the bride or groom.

Virginia nudged Earl when some chant-like singing began, but she didn't understand any of the words, since they were sung in a foreign language. She had heard this type of singing with no musical instruments, before, when the Kings had church at their place and during Amy's wedding. But she'd never been seated in the midst of it all.

Earl nudged Virginia right back and leaned close to her ear. "This is sure different than any wedding I've ever been to. I wonder what's next." He kept his voice down, and with the singing going on, Virginia felt sure no one had heard him.

She yawned and glanced at her watch. *Wish I'd thought to bring a pen and tablet with me. I could have taken notes so I could remember all the details of this unusual wedding to tell Stella about.*

As Belinda listened to the bishop preach, her thoughts went to Herschel. In another two months they would be sitting in this barn again, only this time the preacher's message would be meant for them.

The thought of marrying Herschel brought a smile to Belinda's lips. She still could not believe that he'd agreed to move to Strasburg and help her run the greenhouse once they were married.

Two things still bothered Belinda. One was concern over whether more vandalism or threats would occur. The other was Henry's attitude toward Herschel. If she went through with her plans to marry Herschel, how would it affect her relationship with her son? Henry had never come to grips with the loss of his father and brother, and he'd made it adamantly clear that he would not accept Herschel as his stepfather. Surely that would all change once she and Herschel were married. Belinda's new husband would prove to her son that he not only cared about her welfare but Henry's as well.

Belinda's thoughts changed direction as she looked down at the precious grandchild she held, noting his slow, even breathing. The sleeping baby was so sweet and innocent, with not a care in the world. *If only such innocence could last forever. It's a shame every baby that's born must grow up and endure life's hurdles.*

Belinda reflected on a verse of scripture she'd read during her devotional time the other day. *"I will say of the Lord, He is my refuge and my fortress: my God; in him will I trust."* Indeed that was what everyone who followed Christ needed to do. *We need to trust.*

She touched the infant's tiny hand and stroked it gently. *I wonder what lies ahead for this special child. Will Amy and Jared be blessed with more children? I'm sure they will be good parents to this little one and any brothers or sisters he may have.*

Sylvia sat across from her groom, listening to the preacher's message and preparing to stand before the bishop and recite her vows to Dennis. She remembered the day she and Toby had said the same vows. In some ways it seemed like only yesterday, but in other ways it felt like a long time ago. Although Sylvia would never forget what she and Toby once had, she felt ready to marry Dennis and be the best wife she could.

Sylvia thought about her children. They'd both been so young when their daddy died. Although it was possible for Allen to have some vague memories of Toby, Rachel was only a baby when her father had been taken from her, and she would have no memory of him whatsoever. The only father her children would ever really know was Dennis. Sylvia felt certain her new husband would be a good daddy to Rachel, Allen, and any future children they may have.

Although she was supposed to concentrate on the bishop's message, Sylvia's thoughts continued on—this time to her mother. She was glad Mom had found a man she loved and hoped that she and Herschel would have many good years together. Sylvia was also pleased that Herschel would be moving to Mom's home after they were married and was willing to help out in the greenhouse. It would be hard for her mother to sell her home and the greenhouse and have to move to another Amish community, even if it was within commuting distance. With a grown man living in Mom's home, perhaps the person responsible for the vandalism, threatening notes, and phone calls, would give up and leave them alone. If the things had been done by the man who owned the greenhouse on the other side of town, surely he was smart enough to realize that Mom's business was no threat to him. From what Sylvia had heard, the new greenhouse was doing a good business, so there really was no competition.

Sylvia glanced at Henry, sitting beside Dennis. Her brother looked so grown-up today, dressed in his church clothes and sitting so straight and tall. She was glad Dennis had asked Henry to be one of his witnesses. He and Henry had become close and had a lot in common, with their interest in birds as well as their dogs. She hoped someday in the future Henry would find the happiness in life that he deserved. It had been hard on him, losing both Dad and Abe, and then taking on so many extra duties and chores that he didn't enjoy. Perhaps once Herschel began helping Mom in the greenhouse and doing other chores around the place, Henry would have more freedom to enjoy life. And some day, a few years down the road, her younger brother would settle down, find a wife, and start a family of his own.

Sylvia pushed her thoughts aside when the bishop called her and Dennis to stand before him. It was finally time to say their vows.

Herschel gave his full attention to the bride and groom as they rose from their seats and took their place in front of the bishop. Dennis and Sylvia were still in the prime of life and Lord willing would have many years together. With Herschel and Belinda being an older couple, their time as husband and wife would likely be shorter. But it didn't matter. Herschel would live each day to its fullest and try to never take his spouse for granted. With God's help and guidance he would do his best to be a good husband. Herschel hoped he could form a lasting bond with all of Belinda's family—especially Henry, who still seemed aloof whenever Herschel was around.

Seated on the men's side of the room, Herschel could only see the back of Henry's head as he sat straight and tall. Like the others here today, he was about to witness his sister and Dennis respond to the bishop's questions and state their vows.

Herschel rested his hands in his lap and listened.

The bishop looked at Dennis. "Can you confess, brother, that you accept this, our sister, as your wife, and that you will not leave her until death separates you? And do you believe that this is from the Lord and that you have come thus far by your faith and prayers?"

Dennis answered, "Yes."

Then it was Sylvia's turn to respond after the bishop asked her a similar question. She too answered, "Yes."

The minister continued by asking the bride and groom another pertinent question. Once they'd both replied affirmatively, he took Sylvia's right hand and placed it in Dennis's right hand, putting his own hands above and beneath their hands. He then continued with a blessing. Following that, all three of them bent their knees in a partial bow.

"Go forth in the name of the Lord," the minister directed. "You are now man and wife."

Sylvia and Dennis seemed to radiate a blissful glow as they returned to their seats.

Herschel felt a thickening form in his throat. He was eager to answer those same questions when he and Belinda stood before their bishop in December.

Virginia couldn't believe she had made it through the entire wedding service without falling asleep or getting out of her chair. Although it had been uncomfortable to sit for three hours and listen to the singing and preaching in another language, she'd been fascinated with the whole procedure. She had waited for the preacher to pronounce the bride and groom as man and wife, followed by them sealing it with a kiss, but that moment never came. No walking up or down an aisle, as in a traditional English wedding; no musical instruments; and no hand-holding or kiss. Strange but interesting nonetheless.

After everyone left the barn, most of the people gathered in groups to visit while they waited for the first meal of the day that would be served inside the white tents that had been erected in the yard.

Virginia and Earl stood off by themselves until Jared and Amy came up to them.

"I'm glad you could be at my sister's wedding." Amy smiled. "It was too bad you weren't able to make it to ours."

"What are you talking about?" Virginia's brows squished together. "We didn't come because we never got an invitation to your wedding."

"I'm so sorry. You were on our list, and I thought your invitation had been sent." Amy placed her hand on Virginia's arm. "Please accept my apologies. It certainly wasn't intentional."

"It's all right," Earl spoke up. "Mail gets lost sometimes, and at least we got to be here for your sister's wedding."

Jared and Amy both nodded.

"Your mother told me that you had a baby recently." Virginia's comment was directed at Amy. "Was that the infant she held during the wedding?"

"Yes. Jared and I are pleased that God gave us a healthy little boy."

Virginia wasn't surprised to hear a mention of God, since the Amish were quite religious. She, however, had no interest in God, because He had done nothing for her. Most of Virginia's life had been a struggle, and as far as she knew, no prayer she'd ever uttered had been answered—at least not in the way she wanted.

"Where is your baby?" Virginia questioned. "Does your mom still have him?"

Amy shook her head. "Jared's mother is holding him now, and no doubt, he'll be passed to other family members as the day goes on." She laughed. "The only time I'll probably get to hold Dewayne is when he wants to be fed or is in need of a diaper change." She looked to her right. "And speaking of relatives, here comes Mom with my oldest brother and his family."

Virginia watched as Belinda approached. A tall, bearded man walked with her, along with an auburn-haired Amish woman and two children. The young girl was next to her mother, but the Amish man held the little boy in his arms.

"Virginia and Earl, I'd like you to meet my son Ezekiel. He's the one I told you lives in New York." Belinda gestured to the young woman beside him. "This is his wife, Michelle, and their children, Angela Mary and Vernon."

Ezekiel reached out and shook Earl's hand. "Nice to meet you."

Earl responded, "Same here."

It dawned on Virginia that Ezekiel's wife must be the daughter-in-law Belinda had told her used to be English. There was something familiar about the woman's pretty blue eyes, auburn hair, and creamy complexion. Virginia wondered if she may have seen her somewhere—perhaps on some occasion when Ezekiel's family had been visiting their family here and gone out shopping.

Virginia extended her hand to the woman. "Michelle is a pretty name. I knew a little girl by that name once. In fact, she was—"

Michelle's face paled, and she blinked multiple times. "Ma...mama?" She swayed slightly, as though she might faint. "No, it can't be. I'm just feeling *verhuddelt*."

Chapter 41

"What's going on, Michelle? Why are you confused?" Ezekiel put his hand on the small of his wife's back.

With a shaky hand, Michelle pointed at Virginia. "Is–is your name Ginny Taylor?"

Virginia bit down on her lower lip until she tasted blood. "It used to be."

"I knew it!" Michelle looked up at Ezekiel, then back at Virginia. "This woman is my mother. I haven't seen her since I was a young girl, and she's older-looking now, but I'd recognize her face and that bright red hair anywhere."

Virginia's eyes widened and she grabbed Earl's arm for support. "Oh, my word. . . Can this really be true?"

"I don't know how, but I believe it is." Michelle drew in a breath and blew it out quickly. "How'd you know I was here? Have you been tracking me somehow?"

Virginia shook her head. "How could I have known? When Child Protective Services took you and your brothers, I thought I'd never see you again."

Everyone began talking at once until Belinda held up her hand. "We won't start eating for another half hour or so. Why don't we all go into the house so we can talk privately and figure out what's going on?"

Michelle shook her head vigorously. "I don't want to talk to this woman. She's a child abuser, and I don't want her anywhere near our children." She stood in front of the little girl as though the child needed protection.

"I'm so sorry. I never meant to hurt you." Virginia reached out her hand toward Michelle, but the wide-eyed young woman took another step back. *Michelle doesn't want to talk to me. She must be harboring anger for the way I treated her as a child. I can't blame her for hating me. Oh my—I can't believe I'm standing here talking to my very own daughter who I never thought I would see again.*

"Let's do as Mom suggested and go inside." Ezekiel guided Michelle toward the house but paused when she stopped walking.

Michelle looked over at Amy. "Would you and Jared please take the kinner for a while? I don't want to upset them."

"Of course." Jared took the baby from him, and Amy said something in Pennsylvania Dutch before motioning for the little girl to come with her.

When Ezekiel, Michelle, Earl, and Virginia entered the house behind Belinda, she asked them to all take a seat in the living room.

Virginia's mouth felt so dry she could barely swallow, and her leg had begun to throb, so it was a relief to sit on the couch.

Belinda sat next to Virginia, with Earl on the other side of her, while Michelle and Ezekiel seated themselves in two chairs facing them.

Michelle massaged her forehead as she stared at Virginia with her head cocked to one side. "Where's my dad? Did you finally get fed up with him and file for divorce?"

"No, I remained faithful to him until he passed away several years ago." She reached over and took Earl's hand. The warmth of it and the gentle squeeze he gave her fingers helped Virginia find the courage to say more. "Earl's my husband now, and he's a good man. It's because of a job change for him that we ended up moving here," she added.

"I see." Michelle's voice was barely above a whisper, and she kept glancing at Belinda, as if needing encouragement or reassurance.

Virginia studied her daughter's face. Michelle had grown into a beautiful woman, even without makeup and fancy clothes. It didn't seem possible that she had become Amish. And what were the odds that Michelle would be related to Virginia and Earl's neighbor? It all seemed like a dream, or maybe it was a miracle. After all these years of wondering where her children could be, did God have a hand in bringing Virginia and Michelle together? Would they be able to work things out and have some sort of relationship?

Pausing to answer questions, Michelle gave her mother a brief explanation of where all she had been from the time she and her brothers were taken from home and what had lead up to her joining the Amish church and marrying Ezekiel.

"That's incredible." Virginia looked at her husband. "Don't you think so, Earl?"

"Yep. Never heard a story quite like that one. It almost seems impossible."

"It's all true," Michelle assured him. "I faced some dark, depressing days until I met Ezekiel and his family. I'm ever so thankful God led me to them."

Virginia tilted her body toward Michelle. "Do you know where your brothers are?"

"Yes, I do, but I'm not sure they would want to see you. It was hard for Ernie and Jack to be separated from me, and we've only been reunited for a few years."

"So they're both doing all right?"

Yes, but no thanks to you. Michelle managed to nod as she struggled with her pent-up emotions.

"Maybe you could call Jack and Ernie," Ezekiel suggested, looking at Michelle. "At least let them know you and your mother have been reunited, and see if they'd be willing to talk with her."

Michelle looked down at her hands, now folded in her lap. "I don't know."

"You did try to contact your parents once, remember?" Ezekiel responded.

"Yes," she admitted quietly. After accepting Christ as her Savior, Michelle had wanted to let her mom and dad know that she'd forgiven them for their ill treatment toward herself, Ernie, and Jack. But now, with her mother sitting a few feet away, Michelle found it difficult not to let bitterness and resentment resurface. It wasn't the Amish way to refuse to forgive someone who had hurt them, and it certainly wasn't what God expected of her either.

The words of Matthew 6:14 popped into Michelle's head: *"For if ye forgive men their trespasses, your heavenly Father will also forgive you."*

I forgave my mom once, but she didn't know it, so now I need to do it again and mean it.

Michelle got up and asked her mother-in-law if she could take her place on the couch. When Belinda stood, Michelle sat next to Virginia. Feeling a sense of peace that had suddenly come over her, she turned to the woman who had given birth to her, and said, "I forgive you, Mama, and I promise to let Jack and Ernie know that we have been reunited." Gulping back a sob, Michelle hugged her mother.

🐦

"Are you as hallich as I am right now?" Dennis asked, leaning close to Sylvia as they sat at their corner table during the wedding meal.

"Jah, I'm very happy. Everyone else seems to be having a good time. Just look at the smiles on their faces."

He chuckled. "It must be all the good food they've helped themselves to as the bowls and platters have been brought to the table and passed around."

Sylvia motioned with her head toward the table where Ezekiel sat with his family. Virginia and Earl sat across from them, and there seemed to be quite a conversation going on. "Looks like my bruder and Michelle are getting acquainted with our neighbors from across the street."

"Have they met them before, or is this the first time?"

"I don't believe Virginia or her husband have been over here when Ezekiel and Michelle have come for a visit."

"They certainly seem to be getting along well, and that Earl's eating enough food for three people."

Sylvia gave Dennis's arm a poke. "Now don't be critical. This is only our first meal of the day. By the time it's all been said and done, you and I will probably need wheelbarrows to carry us out of the tent."

Dennis leaned closer. "You're so cute when you tease. Do you know how hard it is for me to keep from kissing you right now?"

Sylvia's cheeks warmed. "That will have to wait until later, when there aren't so many people watching us."

"I bet most folks aren't paying any attention to us. They're too busy eating and talking with the people around them."

"That could be." Sylvia took a sip from her glass of fruit punch, while she thought about the nice card and note she'd received from Toby's parents earlier this week. In addition to congratulating Sylvia on her upcoming marriage, the Beilers had given her their blessing. The note stated that they were happy Sylvia had found love again, and they felt sure their son would want her to be happy. It meant a lot to Sylvia to have received her previous in-laws' approval.

She looked over at the table where Dennis's mother; his brother, Gerald; and his three older sisters, Marla, Dorcas, and Hannah sat with their families. How nice it was that they could all come down from Dauphin County for the wedding. She hadn't always felt this way, but from the warm greeting she'd received from them when they'd arrived last evening, she felt sure that they too approved of her marrying Dennis.

Next Sylvia's gaze came to rest on the table where her mother sat beside Herschel. She smiled. *Only two months to go, and then it'll be Mr. and Mrs. Herschel Fisher sharing a meal with their wedding guests.*

That evening after all the visitors had gone home, Belinda sat on the porch swing beside Herschel.

"It was a good day, jah?" Herschel took hold of her hand.

"Yes, a very good day—for Sylvia and Dennis as well as for Michelle and Virginia." A few minutes ago, Belinda had filled Herschel in on what had transpired before the first wedding meal of the day.

"Sure amazes me sometimes how God works things out in a person's life—often in ways least expected."

"You're right about that." Belinda leaned her head against his shoulder. "I never would have dreamed I could fall in love again or find a man as kind and gentle as you."

Virginia took off her bedroom slippers and curled up on the couch with Goldie. Earl had one of his favorite TV shows on and seemed totally absorbed in watching it.

When the movie paused and an advertisement came on, she asked if he wanted something to eat or drink.

Earl angled his body so he was looking at her. "I'm still full from all that food we had after the wedding today, but a glass of cold cider would sure hit the spot."

"Okay."

Virginia got off the couch and headed to the kitchen. When she returned a few minutes later, Earl's eyes were closed, so she figured he may have fallen asleep.

She set the glass of cider on the small table beside his chair and was about to head back to the couch, when Earl called out to her. "Hey, where are ya going? Why don't you sit in the other recliner and we can watch the rest of the show together."

Virginia had no desire to watch a movie that was half over, but she did as he asked.

"Today was certainly full of surprises, wasn't it?"

"Yep."

"I never thought I'd reconnect with my daughter, let alone that she'd be related to those Plain folks across the street."

"Does that mean you're gonna change your attitude about them?" He took another drink from his glass.

"I don't know, Earl. It does put a different light on things." Virginia hit the lever on the recliner and leaned back for a more comfortable position. "Michelle wants to visit with me again tomorrow. We have a lot of catching up to do."

"Won't she and her family be going back to their home in New York?"

"Not for a few more days." Virginia gave a deep, gratifying sigh. "I still can't believe she was willing to forgive me for all the years of abuse I put her through."

Earl frowned. "I never knew till today that you had mistreated your children. I can't even picture it in my head."

"I never meant to be a bad mother, and I wasn't at first. But when Herb began beating on me, I became so angry I ended up taking it out on the children." Her eyes grew hot with the need to cry, and her throat ached when she swallowed. "After the kids were taken from us, Herb continued to abuse me." She lifted her bum leg. "He did this to me when he got drunk one night and was in a rage."

"Why didn't you leave him? You had every right to."

"I tried several times, but he always came after me, promising never to do it again." She sniffed as tears sprang to her eyes. "I wanted to get the kids back, but I didn't have a job and couldn't have provided for them if I'd struck out on my own."

"You shoulda got away from him. You shoulda got some help."

"I know that now, but it's too late to go back and do things over." Virginia paused to collect herself. "You know what?"

"What?"

"This is the happiest I've been in years. I not only found my daughter today, but I discovered two grandchildren I didn't know about. And with any luck, I may get to see my boys soon too."

Chapter 42

Clymer

Excitement combined with nervousness welled in Virginia's chest as they followed Earl's GPS to Ezekiel and Michelle's house. They'd been invited for Thanksgiving dinner, and Jack and Ernie would be there too. *My sons must want to see me,* Virginia told herself. *Otherwise, they wouldn't have agreed for us to meet at Michelle and Ezekiel's house.*

She fiddled with her dangly earrings and blew out a quick breath. *I hope I don't say or do anything wrong while we're there. I don't want to mess up our reunion and lose contact with my sons yet again.*

"Stop fidgeting and try to relax." Earl bumped Virginia's arm with his elbow. "We're almost there."

"I can't help it. The closer we get, the more nervous I become."

"If you're that nervous, then maybe we should have stayed home."

She shook her head. "No way! I've spent too many years wishing I could see my children again, and I won't miss this opportunity no matter how it turns out."

"Which I'm sure will be fine. Look how nice your daughter was about accepting you back into her life."

Virginia pulled a tissue out of her purse and blew her nose. "True, and she even said she's forgiven me for the way I treated her in the past."

"So there you go. . . If she forgave you, then her brothers probably will too. That's how it is with those Amish folks."

"But Ernie and Jack are not Amish. They may not even be religious."

"Then you oughta get along with them just fine, since you're not religious either."

Virginia clasped her hands together in her lap. When she and Michelle had gotten together the day after Sylvia's wedding, they'd spent part of the time talking about God and what a difference it had made in Michelle's life when she'd become a Christian. Michelle had shared several scriptures with Virginia, and even written them down. The following week, Virginia went out and purchased a Bible. Ever since then she'd read a few passages from God's Word each day.

I wonder what Earl would say if he knew that. He had told Virginia several times since they got married that he had no need of a religious crutch and thought people who needed it were weak.

Virginia picked at a hangnail on her thumb. *Guess that makes me weak, because I've come to the conclusion that I need a personal relationship with Christ, and I'm hoping Michelle can tell me what I need to do.*

Strasburg

As Belinda and her daughters prepared their Thanksgiving meal, which they would be sharing with Herschel and his parents, she decided to ask them a question that had been weighing on her mind the past two weeks.

She joined them at the counter where they were peeling potatoes. "I'm concerned about something, and I need your opinions."

Amy's brows furrowed. "You look so serious. What is it, Mom?"

"Henry has still not accepted the idea of me marrying Herschel, and I'm wondering if it would be best if I called off the wedding."

Sylvia shook her head vigorously. "No, that would not be best—for you, for Herschel, or even for Henry."

"Why do you say that?" Belinda felt a tightening in her chest. "Don't your brother's feelings count for anything?"

"Of course they do," Amy interjected, "but Henry is being selfish and unreasonable about your relationship with Herschel."

"That's right," Sylvia agreed. "If he cared about anyone other than himself, he would quit moping around and be as happy for you as we both are."

"I've known for some time that you and Herschel were meant for each other." Amy put the potato peeler down and placed one hand on the small of Belinda's back. "Herschel is a wonderful man, and he loves you very much. If you don't marry him, I'm afraid you'll regret it for the rest of your life."

"I agree with my sister." Sylvia touched Belinda's arm and gave it a few pats. "And remember this—Henry will not be living at home with your forever. Eventually he'll be old enough to move out and start a life of his own—maybe even with a wife."

Belinda breathed in and out, lightly clasping her hands together as she reflected on all that her daughters had said. The words they'd spoken made sense, but she would need to do some serious praying before reaching a final decision.

Clymer

"This meal you fixed for all of us is sure good, Michelle. Thanks for inviting Earl and me to join you and your family today." Virginia looked over at her two grandchildren. They were both so sweet and well-behaved.

Michelle smiled. "You're welcome. I'm glad you could come, Mama. And you too, Earl."

He smiled and helped himself to another piece of turkey.

Virginia looked across the table to where Ernie and Jack sat with their wives. "And thank you for agreeing to see me, and for listening to my apology for not being the kind of mother you needed and deserved."

Jack looked straight at her. "It's in the past, so there'd be no point in me holding a grudge. Besides, Ernie and I had foster parents who treated us well."

Ernie nodded but made no comment. Virginia wasn't sure if he'd forgiven her, but at least he had been cordial since she and Earl had arrived. No doubt it would take some time for Virginia to gain her children's trust, and she would do everything in her power to make it happen. How good it was to know that Michelle, Jack, and Ernie were doing well and had moved on with their lives, in spite of their terrible childhood. Things could have turned out much differently for them if they'd stayed with Virginia and Herb.

Virginia felt a dull pain throughout her body and struggled to keep her tears from falling. *I was a horrible mother and I have a lot to make up for, but I don't see how God could forgive me.* She looked over at Michelle. "After dinner, I'll help you with the dishes and clean up the kitchen. It'll give us some time to talk, because I have some questions about the Bible I'd like to ask you about."

Michelle smiled. "Of course, Mama. I'd be happy to answer any of your questions. And since Ezekiel is a minister in our church district here, I'm sure he would too."

Ezekiel agreed.

Although Virginia still didn't understand why Michelle had decided to give up modern things for the Plain life, she had obviously chosen well when she married Ezekiel. In the short time Virginia had known him, she'd become certain that he loved her daughter and would always treat her and their children well.

Strasburg

After their meal, Henry excused himself, saying he wanted to go out to the barn to check on the animals. Herschel had a feeling that Belinda's son just wanted to be alone and perhaps away from him.

The women began clearing the table, suggesting that the men go to the living room to visit. Herschel waited about fifteen minutes and then he told his dad, along with Jared and Dennis, that he was going outside for some fresh air.

"Sure, go ahead," Jared said. "When you come back in, maybe we can get a board game going."

"Okay." Herschel put his jacket and hat on, then left the house and headed straight for the barn. He figured it was about time he and Henry had a serious talk.

Upon entering the barn and seeing no sign of the young man, Herschel climbed the ladder up to the loft. Sure enough, Henry sat crossed-legged in front of the large open window, staring out at the yard.

"What are ya up to?" Herschel asked, taking a seat beside him.

"Just doin' some thinking and watchin' for birds." Henry sat quietly for several minutes, and then he turned to face Herschel. "You may as well know this right now—you ain't never gonna be my daed."

Herschel put his hand on Henry's shoulder. "I don't expect to be your dad, but I would like to be your friend. For your mother's sake, if nothing else, are you willing to give me a chance?"

Henry shrugged. "We'll see."

"All right. For now at least, that's good enough." Herschel wished there was something he could say or do to win Henry's favor, but he couldn't think of a thing other than to continue praying about it. The problem was, he and Belinda would be getting married in two weeks. If Henry didn't show some acceptance of him soon, Herschel might feel compelled to call off the wedding. As much as he loved Belinda and wanted to be her husband, he didn't see how they could make it work if her son kept his negative attitude and did not accept him.

"What kind of birds are you watching for?"

"Nothin' in particular. Just whatever birds come to the feeders in our yard." Henry glanced at Herschel and then looked away. "I keep a journal of all the birds I see, and sometimes if one of them is kinda rare or a bird not seen too often around here, I call the birding hotline and leave a message. That way, others, who are also bird-watchers, can keep an eye out for that particular bird."

"Sounds like an interesting hobby."

"Yeah. It helps to take my mind off all the problems we've had around here since my daed, brother, and brother-in-law died."

"I understand about that. I hurt really bad when my wife passed away, and it was hard for me not to dwell on it." Herschel laid a hand against his breastbone. "For the longest while I visited Mattie's grave almost every day. Even put flowers on the plot of dirt where she was buried, even though it wasn't something our church leaders approved of."

"Guess we all do some things others don't like." Henry groaned. "I've been trying to figure out who's done all the vandalism to our place, but Mom and my sisters think I'm wasting my time." His shoulders slumped. "I've been the only man in this family since Dad died, and I haven't done a good job of protecting Mom or my sisters."

"No one's been physically hurt though, right?"

"Nope, but every act of vandalism and threatening note has left them—and me—nervous and wondering when the next nasty thing will be done." Henry rubbed his forehead. "I have several suspects in mind, but so far, I've found no proof that any of them are guilty."

"Maybe the two of us can put our thinking caps on and come up with some answers together," Herschel offered. "Would that be okay with you?"

Henry hesitated but finally answered, "I guess so."

Herschel gave Henry's shoulder a light squeeze. "Remember the old saying. Two heads are better than one."

As they approached their own home late that night, Virginia felt the need to tell her husband what had transpired when she was in the kitchen with Michelle after their meal.

"You know something, Earl?"

"What's that?"

"As glad as I am about having found my three children, I'm even happier now, because I found Jesus today."

"Is that so? I didn't know He was missing."

"That's not funny, Earl. What I meant was, I accepted Jesus as my Savior and asked Him to forgive my sins. Michelle helped me recite the sinner's prayer."

Earl gave a piglike snort but said nothing.

Virginia couldn't help but wonder what he was thinking. Did Earl believe she'd become a religious fanatic, or might he too be interested in learning about Jesus? *I wonder how he would respond if I shared a few Bible verses with him.* She pursed her lips. *I may as well try, so here goes...*

"Two of those passages of scripture Michelle read to me are found in John 3:16 and 17. Would like to hear them?"

"Not particularly."

Ignoring his response, Virginia reached into her purse and pulled out a slip of paper, along with the small flashlight she kept in there. "Here's what verse 16 says, Earl: 'For God so loved the world, that he gave his only begotten Son, that whosoever believeth in him should not perish, but have everlasting life.'"

Virginia paused to see if Earl would comment, but when he said nothing, she continued. "Verse 17 of that same chapter says: 'For God sent not his Son into the world to condemn the world; but that the world though him might be saved.'"

"Super."

Virginia tried to ignore her husband's sarcastic tone and read him another verse she had written down today. "And 1 John 1:9 says: 'If we confess our sins, [God] is faithful and just to forgive us our sins, and to cleanse us from all unrighteousness.'"

"I don't need a sermon, Virginia. And if you don't mind, I'd like to change the subject. Better yet, let's listen to some music." Earl turned on the radio and upped the volume.

Virginia leaned heavily against the seat and closed her eyes. *Guess I shouldn't have said anything to him right now. Maybe some other time if I bring up the topic he'll be more receptive. If I become the person God wants me to be, Earl might realize that he needs the Lord too.*

Chapter 43

With just a week before the wedding, Belinda knew she had to make a decision. She'd prayed about it, talked it over with her girls, and asked herself many times if marrying Herschel was the right thing to do.

I need to speak with Henry again, Belinda told herself as she looked out the kitchen window and saw him walking toward the house.

She went to the back door and opened it for him, since his hands were holding a box.

"We won't be going to the greenhouse this morning," Henry announced when he stepped inside. "Someone broke in, and the place is a mess. I brought in the few jars of honey that hadn't been broken."

Belinda's thoughts went blank, as if her brain had stopped working. She stood staring at the box he held.

"Mom, did ya hear what I said? The place is trashed. Gift items we were hoping people would buy for Christmas gifts are ruined; all the Christmas cactus and poinsettias were knocked on the floor, and it looks like someone trampled on 'em." Henry shook his head. "There ain't much left that we can salvage."

Belinda's brain started working again, and her spine stiffened. "Whoever left that last threatening message on our answering machine has finally made good on their promise because I haven't sold our home or the greenhouse." She paused long enough to rub her forehead and instructed Henry to put the box on the kitchen table. "What are we going to do, Son? If the person responsible for this attack can do something so mean and destructive, there's no telling what else he or she might do if we don't sell our place and move." Belinda sucked in some air. "I think it's time to call the sheriff."

"Not yet, Mom. Whoever did this dropped something, and I believe I know who it belongs to." Henry set the box on the table, reached into his pocket, and pulled out a small knife. "I found this outside the greenhouse by the door that was broken into."

Belinda twisted her head-covering ties around her fingers. "Then we need to call the sheriff and tell him you think you know who's behind all the vandalism."

"If it's who I think it is, I wanna take care of it by myself."

"You believe it's Monroe, don't you, Son?"

"I can't say for sure till I've confronted the person, and I'm gonna do that right now." He turned toward the door.

Belinda's pulse quickened as she reached out and clasped her son's arm. "Wait, Henry. You can't go alone. What if the person you accuse is innocent? Or worse yet, what if they're guilty and see your accusation as a threat." She gripped his arm tighter. "They could become angry and your life might be in danger."

Henry shook his head with a determined expression. "I don't care. I wanna look this person in the face and ask why they would do such horrible things to us. After they admit their guilt, then you can call the sheriff." Henry pulled away and dashed out the door.

Belinda was right behind him. "Henry, wait!"

He'd only made it halfway across the lawn when a horse and buggy came into the yard. When it pulled up to the hitching rail and Herschel got out, Belinda breathed a sigh of relief.

Rubbing her arms against the cold, she ran out to meet him. "Someone broke into the greenhouse during the night, and they ruined all the plants, flowers, and gift items." She paused to draw a quick breath. "Henry thinks he knows who did it, and he wants to go after the person by himself."

Herschel's brows knit together, and he pulled Belinda into his arms. "It's cold out here, and you're shaking. You need to go inside and put a jacket on."

Despite holding her arms across her chest, Belinda continued to tremble. "Didn't you hear what I said? My son is about to put himself in what could be a dangerous situation."

"Yes, I understand, and I'll go with him. Just please, go into the house."

Belinda wasn't sure whether to do as he said or insist on going along. But her teeth had begun to chatter, and she felt as though she might pass out from the cold.

She touched her forehead. *Or maybe it's fear that's making me feel lightheaded. Fear for the safety of my son and the man I've come to love.*

After Belinda went inside, Herschel walked over to Henry, who was taking his dog out of the pen. "Your mamm told me what happened in the greenhouse last night. I'm sure sorry to hear it."

Henry's fist tightened around Blackie's collar as he turned to face Herschel. "Yeah, and I think I know who did it." He clipped a leash onto the dog's collar. "I'm goin' to confront the person, and I'm takin' my hund along in case there's trouble."

"I'm sure your dog would offer protection, but it might be a good idea if I go with you."

Henry angled his head toward Herschel. "You'd do that for me?"

"Of course. I not only care about your mother's welfare, but yours as well."

"Really?" Henry spoke in a disbelieving tone.

"Definitely."

Belinda's son gave Herschel a hint of a smile before reaching into his jacket pocket and pulling out a pocketknife. "See this?"

"Yes."

"I think it belongs to the person who broke into the greenhouse and trashed the place." He held it up higher. "Have you ever seen it before?"

Herschel shook his head. "I don't believe so."

"Well, I have, so it's to that person's house I think we oughta go."

"All right. Should we take my horse and buggy?"

"No need for that. He's headed this way right now."

When Henry pointed at the man walking up the driveway, Herschel's mouth dropped open. "Henry, are you sure about that? We shouldn't make any accusations until we have some proof."

Henry held out the knife in his hand. "Here's the proof."

Walking beside Henry and his dog, Herschel made his way down the driveway, meeting the man coming toward them halfway.

"Good morning, Henry," Earl said. "I came over to talk to your mother."

"She's in the house, but I'd like to talk to you."

Henry spoke with an assurance that surprised Herschel. He figured the boy might be shaking in his boots. Herschel wanted to ask Belinda's neighbor a few questions himself, but figured he'd let Henry speak first.

"I don't have time for your questions." Earl moved past Henry and Herschel, and made his way up the driveway at a fast pace.

Herschel looked at Henry, noticing the determined set of his jaw. "We'd better go in with him. You can ask your questions when we're in the house."

Belinda was surprised when she heard a knock on the door—actually, it sounded more like pounding. Thinking it might be Herschel coming to check on her before he left with Henry, she quickly opened the door. She was equally surprised when she saw Earl on the porch, with Henry, Herschel, and Blackie coming up behind him.

"What's going on?" Her gaze traveled from Earl, to Herschel, and then to her son.

"Herschel and I saw Earl coming up our driveway, and when I said there were some questions I wanted to ask him, he said he needed to talk to you."

"Come inside, all of you, and warm yourselves." When they entered the house and followed Belinda to the living room, she gestured to the fire crackling in the fireplace.

Earl hesitated at first, but then took the chair closest to the fire.

Henry wasted no time in stepping in front of him. "Is this yours?" He held the knife out to Earl.

"Yes, it is. Guess I must have dropped it when—" A red blotch erupted on Earl's cheeks as he looked over at Belinda. "I came here this morning to apologize, because I have a confession to make."

"What kind of confession?"

"I'm the person responsible for all of the nasty things that have been done to your place."

Henry snapped his fingers. "I knew it! As soon as I found that pocketknife, which I saw you fiddling with before we all sat down to eat after Sylvia and Dennis's wedding, I realized it must have been you who'd done all the vandalism." Henry's eyes narrowed. "How could you do all those things? Haven't we been good neighbors?"

When Belinda saw her son's nostrils flare, she felt it was time to take over. "Yes, Earl, please explain why you would want to hurt us."

Earl's chin practically dropped to his chest as his posture slumped. "I did it for my wife."

"What?" Belinda's voice cracked. "Are you saying that Virginia asked you to do all those things?"

He looked up and shook his head.

"Then please explain," Herschel interjected.

Earl moaned. "From the time we first moved here, all Virginia did was complain about the noise from the traffic and the smell from the horses on the road that separates our homes. She blamed it on the fact that your place of business brought in so many people who might otherwise not have traveled our road. I figured if I scared you bad enough, you'd sell out and move, and then there'd finally be some peace in my home."

Belinda lowered herself into the rocking chair at the shock of what he'd said. At one time she'd felt Virginia didn't care for her, but lately, the woman had seemed more friendly—especially after learning that her long-lost daughter was married to Belinda's son. "Did your wife know you were doing all those things to us?" she asked.

"Virginia had no idea." Earl dropped his gaze again. "After she was reunited with Michelle, Virginia stopped complaining about the traffic, noise, and smell. But then something I never expected happened."

"What was it?" Henry and his dog had taken a seat on the floor, but he never stopped looking at Earl.

"She got religious."

Herschel took the chair beside Belinda and placed his hand on her arm. "Is that a bad thing, Earl?"

"It was to me. She kept quoting Bible verses, and I began to panic."

"How come?" Belinda spoke in a gentle tone. In spite of all that he'd done to them, she felt compassion for this poor, confused man.

"I panicked because I didn't want to acknowledge that I'm a sinner. Last night, after Virginia went to bed, I snuck out of the house, came over here, and broke into your greenhouse. In a rage, I shouted at God for turning Virginia into a different person and trying to change me. I went ballistic and wrecked nearly everything in the building."

Belinda sat quietly, unsure of what to say, but Earl continued before she was able to formulate a response.

"This morning, after getting little or no sleep last night, I got up before Virginia did and went out to the living room, where I picked up her Bible. I found John 3:16–17, which were two of the verses she had quoted to me on our ride home from Clymer on Thanksgiving." Earl put both hands against his red cheeks. "I sat there with tears running down my face and acknowledged Jesus as the Son of God, and I asked Him to forgive me of all my sins." He folded his hands, sighing deeply. "I'm ashamed of what I did, and I came here to confess and ask your forgiveness, which I clearly don't deserve." Tears welled in the man's eyes. "I'll do anything in my power to make it up to you."

Belinda got up from her chair and walked over to stand beside him. Reaching out to touch Earl's arm, she said: "Your apology is accepted. I forgive you."

"Thank you for being so gracious." Earl reached into his pocket and pulled out a hanky, which he used to dry his damp cheeks. "I'm supposed to be at work in half an hour, but when I get home this evening, I'll be over to clean up the mess I made. I will also pay for the damage I've caused since that first act of vandalism, even if I have to use all of my savings." He rose from his chair. "Thank you for listening to me this morning and for your forgiving spirit. I'll see you later in the day." Earl said goodbye and hurried out the door.

"Wow, that was sure somethin' I never expected." Henry pushed his bangs out of his face. "Do you believe him, Mom? Do you think Earl will be over after work to clean up the mess he made?"

"I have no reason not to believe him. He seemed sincere in his apology, Son."

"Speaking of apologies, I owe you and Herschel one."

Belinda angled her body toward Henry. "Oh?"

"I'm sorry for not accepting your decision to get married. It's obvious that you both love each other, and I was wrong for trying to come between you." Henry looked over at Herschel. "I appreciate you wanting to go with me when I said I was going to confront the person who had done the vandalism. It proved how much you care about all of us."

Herschel moved his head slowly up and down. "I care very much, Henry. And I promise to be your friend and not act like a daed, because no one can replace your father."

"Thank you." Henry moved toward the door with Blackie. "Guess I'd better feed this fellow before I put him back in his pen. I'll leave you two alone now to talk about your wedding, 'cause it'll be taking place soon."

When Henry went out the door, Herschel pulled Belinda gently to her feet and wrapped his arms around her. "Any doubts about marrying me?" he whispered against her ear.

"Absolutely none." Belinda smiled up at him. "Next week at this time, I'll become Mrs. Herschel Fisher."

Epilogue

Four months later

With a cup of coffee in her hand, Belinda stepped out the front door and handed it to her husband.

"Danki." Herschel smiled as she took a seat on the porch swing beside him. It was a pleasant morning, and she savored these moments before it was time to open the greenhouse.

"Would you look at all the robins out there on the lawn, searching for worms." Herschel pointed.

She smiled. "It's that time of the year again."

He grinned back at her. "Henry gave me a lesson the other day on those red-breasted birds."

"Oh did he now? Are you ready to join him in his bird-watching endeavors?"

"I doubt I'll ever be as serious about it as your son is, but he can still teach me a lot."

Belinda leaned her head against his shoulder. "I'm glad you and Henry have been getting along so well since our marriage."

"Same here. Although I know he'll never think of me as his father, Henry is the son I never had."

"He sees you as a friend he can look up to and learn from. That should count for something."

"It does." Herschel laughed when Blackie ran across the lawn near the porch, in pursuit of the stick Henry had thrown for him. "Living here with you and Henry and being involved in your greenhouse business makes me happy. I don't miss working at the bulk-food store one bit."

She clasped his hand. "I'm happy and contented having you here too.

I can't imagine my life without you."

"That goes double for me." Herschel lifted Belinda's hand and kissed her fingers.

Belinda spotted her neighbor walk across the road to get her mail and waved. Virginia waved back. Since Virginia and Earl had become Christians, they'd started going to church every Sunday. Virginia had told Belinda the other day that she and Earl were studying the Bible together.

Last night as Belinda and Herschel had held their devotions together before going to bed, they'd read the second verse in Psalm 91, and it spoke to her heart. *I will say of the Lord, He is my refuge and my fortress: my God; in him will I trust."*

Belinda thought about Monroe. He'd moved to the Amish settlement near Harrisburg three months ago to run his new business. Last week she'd received a letter from him, wishing her and Herschel well and giving them an update on how things were going for him. Recently Monroe had begun courting a woman in her late forties who had never been married. They got along well, and Monroe felt in time there could be talk of marriage. Belinda wished him well.

Smiling, her gaze went to the greenhouse, and the second building they had added last month. Their business was doing well, and Belinda no longer had to worry about anyone vandalizing their place or trying to get them to move. Her grown children were happy, and their marriages were strong. The grandchildren were growing, and soon another little one would come along, as Sylvia and Dennis were expecting their first child together this fall. Michelle and Ezekiel came to visit often, and they spent part of their time with Virginia and Earl.

What more could I ask for? Belinda closed her eyes and lifted a silent prayer. *Heavenly Father, I thank You for Your goodness to us and for Your watchful eye. I have sensed Your presence through the good times as well as the bad. My greatest desire is to bless others the way You have blessed me.*

Belinda opened her eyes and smiled when she saw Maude at the mailbox, talking to Virginia. Although the elderly woman had a nice cozy cabin to live in year round, Belinda had continued to give her things in order to help out.

Belinda leaned closer to her husband and released a contented sigh.

Even though it had been a difficult couple of years following the death of three special people in their family, God had always been at their side, helping them through each trial. This spring and, Lord willing, for a good many more years together, Belinda and Herschel could relax and enjoy the cheerful sound of the robin's greeting.

Belinda's Savory Baked Beans

1 pound dry navy beans

2 bay leaves

¾ cup ketchup

½ cup brown sugar

¼ cup molasses

1 tablespoon dry mustard

1 medium onion, chopped

1½ cups cut-up cooked ham
or ham lunch meat

Combine navy beans and bay leaves in large bowl. Cover with water and let soak overnight. Drain and place in large kettle, cover with water, and boil. Cook 45 minutes or until tender. Drain beans, reserving liquid. In a bowl combine ketchup, brown sugar, molasses, dry mustard, onion, and ham. Place beans in uncovered roasting pan, stir ketchup mix in and add reserved liquid. Bake at 350 degrees for 3 hours. Add more liquid if contents in roasting pan become too dry.

Discussion Questions

1. Virginia felt uncomfortable around her Amish neighbors because their way of living was different from hers. Is it possible to have a friendship with someone whose lifestyle is not the same as yours? How should we treat our neighbors?

2. After Belinda's husband died, she never expected to fall in love again or to be courted by two very different men. Do you think it was right for her to see both men socially? How did it help her decide which one to choose?

3. Belinda's son Henry was determined to find out who was behind the vandalism and threatening messages his family had received since his father, brother, and brother-in-law died. Do you think his motive for wanting to do this was only because he was concerned for the safety of his family? Or did Henry believe that if he could learn the person's identity, it would prove to his mother and siblings that, although still a teenager, he could behave as a responsible adult?

4. Amy tried her hand at matchmaking because she was convinced that Herschel was the best man for her mother. Have you ever become a matchmaker? If so, how did it turn out?

5. Sylvia postponed her wedding to Dennis for a few months in order to help her mother in the greenhouse. Do you think it was necessary for her to do that, or should Belinda have insisted that her daughter keep her original plans? Have you ever set an important plan or event aside to help someone else? If so, how did it make you feel?

6. Monroe had been interested in Belinda since they were teenagers and was disappointed when she married someone else. When Belinda became a widow, Monroe felt he was given a second chance. Do you think Monroe did the right thing by pressuring Belinda to marry him? Have you ever been in a similar situation? If so, what did you do about it?

7. Herschel had been a widower for some time and spent many years pining for his wife. Until he met Belinda, he never thought he would fall in love again. But Herschel felt inferior to Belinda's other suitor because he was less successful than Monroe in material things. Should a person ever let their lack of success keep them from establishing a relationship with someone they love? How can we rise beyond our insecurities when others are more successful?

8. Belinda was kindhearted and giving, even to an elderly woman who had stolen things from her. What verses in the Bible teach us how we should respond to people who have been unkind or used us? How are we supposed to treat widows and those who are poor?

9. Virginia had kept her past hidden from others because she felt ashamed of how she had treated her children. Is there something in your past that you have shared with only a few people, or perhaps no one, because you were afraid of people's reactions? Is it important to share past mistakes with others, or would it be better to keep quiet about our mistakes, even if someone could benefit from knowing?

10. When Michelle met her mother for the first time after many years, did she respond the way most people would? Was Michelle's willingness to forgive her mother something she had to force herself to do, or did it come naturally because of her faith in God? What does the Bible say about forgiveness?

11. When the truth was revealed about who had been doing the vandalism to the Kings' property, how did you feel about the way Belinda reacted? Should she have let the sheriff know, even though the one who'd done it apologized? How would you have dealt with such a situation?

12. How did forgiveness play into this story? Does forgiveness mean we don't have to hold people accountable for their actions?

13. Why are some people able to forgive someone who has wronged them, while others harbor anger and resentment toward those who have hurt them or their loved ones? How can we learn from Christ's example to forgive others?

14. Henry loved his father very much and became upset when his mother decided to marry another man. He was worried that her new husband might try to act as though he was his father. Were Henry's fears legitimate? Did the man Belinda planned to marry handle things well with Henry? Have you or someone you know faced a similar situation—either as a child whose parent decided to remarry, or as the parent who felt concerned about the children when he or she decided to marry again? What can a parent say to a child who feels anxious about a new person coming into their lives?

15. By reading this book, did you learn anything about the Amish way of life that you didn't already know? Did it help you understand why the Plain people adhere to their traditions?

16. Were there any scriptures mentioned in this book that spoke to your heart or helped you in some way?

About the Author

New York Times bestselling and award-winning author **Wanda E. Brunstetter** is one of the founders of the Amish fiction genre. She has written more than 100 books translated into four languages. With over 12 million copies sold, Wanda's stories consistently earn spots on the nation's most prestigious bestseller lists and have received numerous awards.

Wanda's ancestors were part of the Anabaptist faith, and her novels are based on personal research intended to accurately portray the Amish way of life. Her books are well-read and trusted by many Amish, who credit her for giving readers a deeper understanding of the people and their customs.

When Wanda visits her Amish friends, she finds herself drawn to their peaceful lifestyle, sincerity, and close family ties. Wanda enjoys photography, ventriloquism, gardening, bird-watching, beachcombing, and spending time with her family. She and her husband, Richard, have been blessed with two grown children, six grandchildren, and two great-grandchildren.

Check out Wanda's website at www.wandabrunstetter.com.